THE GEOHEX
OF
WRAITH COUNTY

FOUR WINDS - ONE STORM

THE GEOHEX
OF
WRAITH COUNTY
BOOK II

BY
AARON
HOLLINGSWORTH

Copyedited by
Bryan Thomas Schmidt

Eightfold Wrath Books
Kansas City

Four Winds – One Storm: The Geohex of Wraith County
Copyright © 2014 Aaron Hollingsworth
Registration Number TXu 1-889-681
All Rights Reserved.
ISBN 9-781495-242731

This book is a work of fiction. All characters in this novel are fictitious. Any resemblance to actual events or locales or persons, living or dead, is entirely coincidental.

Cover Art by Stephanie Hollingsworth
Cover Photography by Heather Lewis
Cover Model: Julie Maulding

Beta Readers: David "Dax" Bauer, Thomas Sidman, Julie Maulding, Stephanie Johnston, Jennifer Bauman, and Lisi Chance.

For Harold Ramus, Maker and Breaker of Geohexes
and
Bob Anderson, Kensai of the Western Screen

Introduction

When I was a kid I enjoyed playing with two things: action figures and dead animals. The former were expensive and could only be acquired on birthdays and Christmas. The latter was free, but not always easy to come by. Whenever I found a carcass I'd bury it, wait a year, exhume the bones and BAM; new toys! Countless hours were spent as good guy fought bad guy, the clash of plastic muscle and plastic steel amidst the varmint bones strewn o'er the shag carpet. When comics caught my interest my death fixation remained. I sought out titles featuring undead, ghosts, angels, and demons. The occult and macabre gave me more thrills than chills. Gothic style, horror films, ghost legends...they all oozed beauty and coolness. In my twenties I discovered role-playing games. Through them I rediscovered the joy of participating in fantastic conflicts that action figures once provided. I was able to create heroes and send them to face the challenges of the Game Master. Most of my heroes died very unheroic deaths in those days...

It seemed that in ghost/horror stories the main characters were just ordinary folk. And often, even if they tried to be heroes, the dark supernatural forces would almost always conquer them. But what if "real" heroes had to deal with haunted horrors? What if Spiderman's arch enemy was the vengeful spirit of his Uncle Ben? What if Xavier's School for Gifted Youngsters had been built atop an Indian graveyard? What if Jason Voorhees desired the One Ring and started taking out members of the Fellowship one by one? Cross-fandom fun aside, what if extraordinary heroes took on the minions of death? Well, read on and you'll soon find out.

A running theme in speculative fiction is dealing with death. This can mean many things, from coping with the loss of a loved one to literally bargaining with the Reaper for another year of life. Death represents the unknown and is therefore a scary thing. Even if one is certain of what comes next, the act of dying is unsavory and daunting. As one studies and familiarizes one's self with death it may lose its edge of fright. Is this the moral of my story? One of a few, probably. The point is a fear can become a thrill, a weakness a strength.

Then I remember my action figures and think, *"Nah, who am I kidding? The point is good guys need to beat bad guys. And when they do it, it must be done in the coolest way possible. NO, I TAKE THAT BACK! They must do it in cool, IMPOSSIBLE ways!"*

-Aaron Hollingsworth   Winter 2014

Acknowledgments

Special thanks on this book goes to Jonathan Homan for his scientific expertise, Linda Reed for solving a problem, the Teachers and Staff of Raytown South High School for putting up with my random questions, Robert Davidson and Chris Davidson for brainstorming with me, The Kansas City Science Fiction and Fantasy Society, Stephanie Hull for sharing her holy wisdom on a certain subject, Dan Handley for his advice, Cassandra Hollingsworth for her feedback, James Murphy and Ken Keller for their generous sharing of technical and stylistic advice and experience, and everyone else I thanked in the previous book.

Pyrotheurgy begins with the acknowledgment that heat is the most important force. Like most methods of redefining reality, Pyrotheurgy is based on the three facets of the mind; the Objective, the Subjective, and the Receptive.

The **Objective Thought** is the scientific understanding that Friction becomes Heat becomes Flame becomes Light. It is the academic aspect of the philocreed.

The **Subjective Thought** is the exploration and perception of heat and coming to a conclusion on what it means, how it matters for the individual. One's personal morality is often derived this way. This is the aesthetic aspect of the philocreed.

The **Receptive Thought** is knowing how the fire perceives the world around it. It is reading the pyroglyphics in a roaring blaze. It is reading the thoughts of heat through pyropathy. It is knowing what the fire knows. This is the communal aspect of the philocreed.

When these three facets become active in the mind, the maxims of the Sacred Flame Philocreed will be fully understood. Adhere to the wisdom these maxims provide and their mystic power shall be yours.

-an excerpt from the Book of the Sacred Flame

xi

Chapter 1

The Phantasm Road

Hindin raised his hand over the unlit candle and focused his emerald stare at the frayed wick. "*A burnt child fears the fire,*" he told the wick.

Nothing happened.

"*A burnt child fears the fire,*" he repeated. The wick ignored him, and a seven foot tall man made of stone and steel wasn't easy to ignore.

He dropped his hand in his lap and sighed.

"*Why will it not light?*" he thought. "*According to The Book of the Sacred Flame, this is the simplest maxim to comprehend and cast.*" He wanted to blame his surroundings for distracting him. The wobbling interior of a covered freight wagon was not the best place to practice maxims.

Will called back at him from the shotgun seat. "Any luck, Rev?"

Hindin Revetz stared down at the candle. "None."

"It's prob'ly fer the best. We don't want you burnin' our new wagon down. Ain't that right, Polly?"

Hindin turned his head to see Polly huddled in a blanket in the rear of the wagon. A lavender-skinned drakeri with short hair that shined like silk, her ears rose up in double points. Strewn across her solid black eyes were three golden irises without pupils. The teenage girl offered nothing but a disinterested glance in response to Will's question, as if she were thinking of something else.

Hindin turned his attention back to the wick. Raising his large steel hand above the wobbling candle, he said again, "*A burnt child fears the fire!*" Still nothing happened.

"Not so much as a spark," Hindin grumbled.

1

Will scoffed and shook his head. A young tendikeye man, handsome and tanned skinned, sandy blonde quills grew atop his head and his ears like that of an echidna or porcupine. His hands and feet were twice the size of a human's. Will Foundling had no love for theurgy or anything else he could not understand. But he was a tried friend and true, and Hindin owed him his life.

Will turned his cocky grin to the driver sitting next to him. "Draw rein, Rög. We're almost on the outskirts of the city. It's 'bout time I lay down the road rules."

The driver was a burly human who preferred to be called Sir Röger Yamus. He reined up the four beasts pulling them, bringing the wagon to a slow stop. "Rules?" he said. "I followed a rule once. It led me astray." His brown eyes twinkled with mischief from inside his ornate silver helm.

Hindin scooted to make room as Will and Röger entered the wagon's interior. Will hunkered down. Röger took a knee.

"We'll make our camps on the roadside," Will started. "Each of us needs to unhitch an' groom their own bileer each an' every night. These're fine animals we got, an' we wanna keep on their good sides."

Röger scoffed. "I don't see why we can't just stay at roadside inns and pay for stable care."

"The fact we have money does not mean we need to spend it," Hindin said, his voice a smooth baritone. "I agree with Will. We should save our resources at least until we reach this haunted county you spoke of. Additionally, this wagon can protect the four of us from the elements while we sleep."

Röger groaned and looked to the girl sitting beside his two opponents. "Well, what do *you* think, Polly? Do you think sharing a musky wagon with three men for the next week is a good idea? Wouldn't you rather sleep in a cozy bed in your own room and be able to bathe in private?"

Polly pulled her knees in and hugged them, regarding the human with a mix of annoyance and disgust.

"Well?" Röger asked.

"I'm tinking," she said. She glanced down at the septagram tattoo on her forearm. Her bottom lip pouted out. "I side wit' Will and Hindin. For my own reasons."

Röger frowned and shook his head. "And would you care to

2

share those reasons, oh great and mysterious theurgess?"

Polly bared her teeth. "I'd be leaving a trail for my mother. If any innkeeper sees my face, it would be a clue for her. I intend to remain unseen until we reach de county. And as long I keep using my alias and keep my theurgy secret, she won't find me."

Will looked at her, arching a quilled eyebrow. "You sure 'bout that, Pol?"

She ground her teeth. "It is de only ting about dis journey I am sure of. Why must we investigate an entire county haunted by ghosts?"

Röger stood, placing his hands on his waist. "Polly. You are being very uncute right now. Stop it."

She glared up at him as if he were a new species of worm. "I'm not trying to be cute, Röger."

"I know. And usually you don't have to try. That tells me that something is seriously wrong."

Polly's mouth opened, but Röger cut her off. "You see, Polly-pop. You're cute when you're cheerful and when you're mad. But right now you're---"

"Disagreeable?" she asked, her eyes narrowing.

"Indifferent," Röger corrected. "You don't care about hunting ghosts in an impoverished county that you've never been to."

"No. And I why should I?"

Röger raised his chin, causing the gleam of his helm to shift. "Because *Blood must flow.* Isn't that what you blood theurges say? You must always be on the move, like blood. You must be the blood that flows into a dying limb to save it. This county is such a limb. It needs saving. So, be a good girl, go with the *flow,* and be cute, got it?"

Polly fumed and scowled up at him. For an instant, her gold irises flashed red.

Röger only laughed and clapped his hands together. "That's better!"

Hindin, wishing to diffuse the situation, addressed Polly with his own reasoning. "Polly, there would be much to learn. I have always been curious as to how my chimancy would react with necrotheurgy of that nature and scale. And with my new found pyrotheurgic powers I feel that, academically, this venture would

3

prove fruitful for personal growth. You should be just as curious as to how your blood theurgy could relate. Furthermore, I have heard that this county is poor due to the negative energies that plague its crops. Perhaps we can unearth some solutions to improve conditions there."

Röger nodded in approval. "Education! What could be more important?" He turned to Will. "What do you think?"

Will gave a lazy shrug, smiling at Polly as if she were a child. "Pol, you gotta relative yer hidin' from. I gotta relative I need to find. You got a fake name you go by. I gotta name I need to *make*. My uncle Brem is hidin' out somewhere in this sense-fersaken country, an' the only way I can fish him out is by gettin' famous. Only way I can do that is by findin' place where my guns an' blades can be put to good use."

Polly returned his smile, and it was twice as condescending. "Blades an' guns are useless against ghosts, you halfwit." Her eyes gleamed with icy satisfaction.

Will's jaw clenched.

Röger let out a snort and punched his arm. "I never believed drakeri were descended from dragons until now!" he said with a laugh. "Because what came out of her mouth just burned you, Will!"

Hindin thought he saw Polly start to smile at the joke. But the expression soon died as she turned her gaze to Röger.

"And what of you, Sir Röger? I understand dat your curse keeps you from staying in one place for too long. But why did you suggest Wraith County? What is dere dat *you* want?"

Röger shrugged. "I need a new axe."

"A new axe?"

"Well, not new. It's ancient, really. But it's one of the few weapons I know of that can stand up to my swings. It has a blade that never rusts or dulls and shines like a mirror." He let out a dark laugh. "I need that axe. Or else I'll have to rely on my claws." He held up his dark skinned hands. The nails were trimmed and blunt, but that was only because Röger was in a good mood.

Hindin frowned. "Sir Röger, I take it this axe is theurgically enhanced. How do you propose to pay for such a weapon?"

"It's free," Röger said, scratching a thick arm sleeved with tattoos. "All we need to do is get rid of the ghost that's possessing it."

4

Hindin put his candle away. "And how does one get rid of a ghost, Sir Röger?"

Röger spread his hands. "The same way you skin a cat."

Hindin's steel brow furrowed at this. "What...?"

Will translated the answer. "There's more'n one way, Rev."

❖

They traveled for ten days. On their map the road was simply labelled Coach Rd P. Locals called it 'the Phantasm Road' because of the cursed land to which it led.

As the inns, way stations, and houses grew further and further apart, Will Foundling grew more at ease. Far behind him was the crowded city where he and his companions had met. Before him lay forests, muddy creeks, farmland, winding dirt roads, and rolling hills covered in rocks and trees. He felt at home, though still far from it physically.

He sat in the wagon's shotgun seat, cradling a long barreled rifle, not a scatter gun. Whenever a wheel hit a dip or rock, he wondered whether it would be wise to shoot from it. Not that he ever had to. No one or nothing ever came their way from the land called Wraith County, least of all highwaymen.

Röger, who had been talkative for most of the trip, was presently silent as they approached an old oakwood sign that had once read *Now Entering Apple County*. The word *Wraith* was painted over *Apple* in crude letters.

"*A haunted county*," Will thought. A cool, autumn breeze brushed over him and through his quills. Coming from a warmer huncell, Will never much cared for cold weather. Though there was something queerly soothing about it. The air was easier to breathe. The chill breezes seemed to sharpen his senses.

"Keep an eye on the bileers," Röger said, his voice booming from within his helm. "See how they react when we pass the sign."

Will shifted his eyes from the big man at the reins to the four beasts pulling their wagon. Bileers were a domesticated form of elk, brawny with auburn coats, thick hooves, and regal horn-like antlers arching from their wide brows curving down beside their strong

5

shoulders.

"What should I be watchin' for?" Will asked, eying each animal in turn.

Röger nodded toward the sign. "Watch for them to buck and stall. A necrotheurgess once told me that bileers can sense ghosts through their antlers."

Will squinted. "How's that?"

"The antlers are made of dead cells. They're basically just lifeless bones. They function like antennae and catch the weird vibes ghosts put out. The signal goes straight to their brains, and they freak out."

Will smiled and shook his head. "Yer pullin' my leg."

The brawny human grunted a laugh. "If I was you'd be minus a leg."

Will sat back and regarded the man. "Rög, my momma may've raised a fool, but not a total fool. I know everythin' about bileers and they can't do that."

Röger leaned on him, his massive tattooed shoulder nearly knocking Will from his seat. "But..." he began, "do you know everything about ghosts?" He sat back up straight again, letting Will do the same.

Will, having no answer worth admitting, frowned and turned his sights back to the road. When they had passed the sign and nothing happened, he turned back to Röger with a cocky grin. "Told you so."

Röger only shrugged again. "That just means there were no ghosts at that spot."

Will hung his head. "Brown Gut Snake," he cursed at the seeming absurdity of it all.

The road slithered into a forest, becoming an arching tunnel of trees that wound its way through a labyrinth of timbered ridges. The road hugged the rocky bases with a shallow creek to one side. Once inside the confining growth, the day was swallowed by a false night and the branches whispered secrets to each other.

Will did not trust his eyes in such a place. And so, closing them, he opened his ears and harked the surrounding wood. Harking was to listening as observing was to looking. It was a craft taught to few tendikeye and Will was one such. All tendikeye ears were sensitive, but only a Harker's were keen enough to surgically

6

separate one sound from another.

Will heard the slow flow of the muddy creek, the irate flutter of a jayhawk's wings. He heard the occasional fall of a dead leaf, and could tell its type by the sound it made cutting through the air. He heard a ribbon snake slither up a rocky incline. For several miles, he viewed every angle of the tunnel of trees through his quill-adorned ears. Then, to his left, he heard the forest abruptly end, its sounds replaced by the soft hisses of countless blades of tall grass. He opened his eyes and looked.

Will pulled out a cigarette as he surveyed the changed scenery. To his left was a rolling sea of grass swaying in the gentle wind. A tall, stone grain silo stood near the road's edge. Here and there slouching scarecrows could be seen minding their own business. To the right was an orchard of short, gnarled apple trees. It was nearing the time of harvest, but not a single apple hung on branch or bough. Tiny gray-petaled wildflowers grew like specks of dust all over the landscape. Will did not like the look or smell of those flowers one bit. "*Necropoppies...filthy weeds...*"

As the wagon rolled on, an old farm house came into view. It was gray with age, as was the barn next to it. A tree limb had grown out of a broken glass window of the dilapidated house. Boards were bowing loose off the sides. Not a single fleck of paint remained. The property's barbed-wire fence was so rusted it would have crumbled in a grasping hand.

For Will, the sight of an abandoned farm was as unheard of as an abandoned cradle. "No one lives there," he whispered to Röger.

Röger regarded the homestead. "Yeah, but that doesn't mean it's deserted."

Will furrowed his brow, not catching his friend's meaning. "How's that, Rög?"

Röger gave a cautious chuckle. "Of course no one *lives* there. But something that used to live, but doesn't anymore, might still be there."

Will shifted his eyes from the house to his companion. "Like a dead cat'r sumthin'?"

From inside the wagon came Polly's high, raspy voice. "He means dere might be ghosts, you thick-skulled, under educated rancher!"

7

The words stung Will's ears, as well as his pride. "I ain't no dang rancher!" he hollered back. "I'm a farmer. A rancher ain't nuthin' but a shepherd with a fence. Idiot range rapin' traitors, the whole lot of 'em! Real tendikeye don't keep animals fer food. We hunt, an' don't you ferget it!"

"I already have!" answered Polly.

A gust of cold wind blew across the field of gray flowers and dying grass into Will's face. He felt an odd tingle in his pronounced nose, but paid it little mind. Looking back at the field, he caught sight of a magpie flying out from between the buttons of a scarecrow's shirt, sending up a puff of straw as it went. He lit his cigarette and turned to Röger. "I've hunted men an' I've hunted beasts. But spook huntin' is new to me an' I hate new things."

"Having second thoughts, Mr. Foundling?" Röger asked.

The tendikeye shook his head. "Naw, 'cause I didn't think it through the first time."

"Dats'a surprise!" laughed Polly in the wagon.

Will's eye twitched. He'd had enough. He set his rifle on his seat and did a backwards somersault into the wagon. Tumbling past a meditating Hindin, who sat in ponderous silence, he stopped just short of where Polly sat wrapped in a thick wool blanket. Her double-pointed ears rose to alertness as the tendikeye's face stopped just inches from hers. For a moment they shared breath.

"Back off," she warned him. "You know what I am capable of."

Will nodded, his face stern and hard despite his youth. "Snide remarks. It's unladylike, Polly. You wanna ride shotgun fer awhile?"

"Can I use your shotgun?" she asked.

"It's a rifle, an' no. No one handles *Falcona* but me. But it's gettin' spooky out there. You might cotton to it."

"I'll pass, kind sir," she said.

He kept his disapproving eyes locked with hers as the rattling wagon slowed to a halt.

Will turned his head. "Hey, Rög. Why've we stopped?" he called to the driver.

"To camp," the big man called back. "I see a well near the barn. The creek is miles behind us now. Who knows when we'll see another one?"

8

"Yeah, but..." the tendikeye started as he walked back to the wagon's front. "But didn't you hint that that homestead might be haunted?"

"Yeah, so? Are you scared?" Röger's brown eyes teased through his helm.

Will feigned a laugh. "Reverse psychiatrics don't work on me. It's jus' that we still got daylight to burn."

Will did not have to see Röger's mouth to tell that the human was about to debate him. He found himself in no mood to argue. "Okay, okay." Will poked his head back into the wagon. "Alright, you two, we're stoppin' fer the...Hey! Where'd Polly go?"

The pretty girl had gone, leaving her blanket. Will looked to Hindin for answer.

The meditating man of stone and steel opened his eyes, two finely cut emeralds that shifted to Will. "I believe she exited out the back," he said, looking dazed and groggy.

"You feelin' okay there, Rev?" Will asked him. "You gettin' coach-sick?"

"It is nothing," Hindin Revetz replied. "I was attempting another inner divination to better understand my pyrotheurgy. It appears to be a lost cause, however. Chi works differently than fire, I think. Perhaps I am going about it improperly. What do you think?"

Will raised his quill eyebrows. "I think yer crazy. An' I think our blood mystic is missin'."

Hindin got the message. "In that case, I will assist you in finding Polly."

The three men left the wagon in search of their theurgess. She had a knack for disappearing, though it had nothing to do with mysticism. Solitude had become a rare commodity for her while sharing a wagon with her three companions.

The young woman stood atop one of the old fence posts, a vision of scarlet and violet. She wore a blood red quellinne, a garment consisting of a short cape and a single wide sleeve covering her right arm. The garment was fastened to her shirt by a ruby crested brooch. She stared at the house, oblivious to the chilling fingers of the wind.

"Hey, Pol!" Will called, but the wind's howl covered his words. He looked up to see gray clouds turning black.

9

"We gotta dive for timber," Röger ordered. "The barn looks safe enough to store the wagon. I'd bet the bileers wouldn't mind either. I'm sure they're sick of being tied to trees during storms. Maybe we could crash in the house."

Will returned his stare to Polly. He left his two comrades by the wagon. With a tremendous leap, he brought himself closer to her. He looked at the house again, not cottoning to its unwelcoming eeriness.

"Do ya...sense anythin' not right?" he asked her, not sure how to word the question.

The petite young woman closed her eyes in frustration. "When do I not, Will? But, of course, intuition is different dan sensing blood lust. I sense a few tiny hearts thumping inside de house. Likely nothing more dan a squirrel or rodent. Yet my own heart warns me of great harm."

Will flicked ash off his cigarette. "Rög thinks we oughta lodge in it fer the night. 'Less yer afraid o' mice, that is."

She ignored the joke. "I welcome de change," she replied with a faint smirk. "You and dat human are making de wagon stink."

"What about yer weird-feelin'?" he asked, dropping his spent cigarette and stepping on it with a large boot.

She smiled. "I trust it less dan I trust you. You will keep me safe. You are good for dat at least." She hopped off the fence post and ran to the gate nearest the house.

Will reached into the inner pocket of his snakeskin dust coat for another cigarette. As he cupped one of his large hands around his lighter's flame, he thought about what Polly had said. Deciding not to entertain his sudden confusion, he exhaled the smoke like an unwelcomed ghost. He felt his nose tingle again. "A ghost-huntin' we will go," he muttered.

Röger and Hindin had little difficulty pulling the barn doors open, thanks to the two men's size. The old rusty hinges popped loose, producing faint puffs of reddish brown. To Hindin, the high

10

ceilinged structure appeared to be a cavernous mouth composed of roughly cut tree carcasses, an imposing hall of despair. Ancient stables were lined like benches at a philocreed temple. Poorly tended webs hung from the rafters like tattered curtains in an old stage house.

Röger saw Will smile in admiration. "Jus' look at that! These drakeri sure know how to build a barn that lasts. If all the hay wudn't eaten up by time, I'd just as soon sleep in here. Heck, I bet the roof don't even leak that bad. Whatchu think, Rev?"

Hindin Revetz nodded. "Building a structure with scraps of dead vegetation is rather base for lasting architecture. But in a land without a decent quarry, who is to blame?" The tall, steel-skinned man took a few steps inside, leaving deep imprints of his iron sandals in the dirt floor. "I think it best that I remain here. The farmhouse no doubt has a cellar, basement, or some structural equivalent. Although I am light for my race, I fear I still may compromise the integrity of its main floor."

"Then we might as well all stay," Will said, crossing his arms.

Röger let out a thick chuckle. "You capon."

Polly could not help but smile. "I want to explore de house, too."

Will turned to Röger and Polly both and defended his reluctance. "Now, I didn't say we couldn't take a look-see. It's jus' that stayin' here might be our best option. 'Sides, if that house still has beds, they're prob'ly rotted to hell. If the chimney ain't choked with weeds, its stones are fit to collapse."

It was decided that Röger, Will, and Polly would explore the farmhouse while Hindin tended the wagon and bileers. The first icy drops of rain pattered down Röger's helm. Their lanterns enclosed half-melted candles. The spindly trees in the area rocked in the wind like traumatized victims of some malign deed.

As the three investigators approached the front porch, Will pinched his lighter from his pocket. After lighting his lantern, he passed it to the others who in turn lit their own. Röger was the first to try the door. The cracked porcelain knob spun with no sound of a bolt unfastening. The human pulled it, and the knob came out loose in his hand. With a shrug he tossed it aside. "Should I punch it in?" he asked himself aloud. He gave the door a slight push. The door did

11

not give. "The wood looks warped. It's probably wedged in the frame." He cocked his fist back.

"Wait," Polly said. She raised her arm and gently rapped on the door with her fist. As it slowly opened before them, the two men backed away and the girl's eyes widened. Raising her other arm, she cast the light of her lantern into the house. She saw only a room with dim doorways to other rooms and a narrow stairway going up. "Hello," she called out shyly. "May we come in?"

"They opened the door for us, didn't they?" Röger whispered into her ear.

Before she could respond, Röger heard a shuddering panting behind him. He turned to see Will, pale and shivering, his eyes fixed on the doorway. Röger turned his head to see what his friend beheld, but saw nothing. Will drew his Mark Twain pistol in a flash, aiming the two barrels at the open entrance. "Get back!" he yelled.

Assuming he was addressing them, Röger and Polly leapt off the porch.

"Will, what is it?" Polly asked.

The tendikeye answered with a scream that was quickly swallowed by the raging wind. He fired two shots into the mouth of the terrible house. Then, as if gravity had shifted its greedy pull, Will Foundling *fell* into the house. The door slammed shut, cutting off his cry. The porcelain doorknob flew up from where it had landed and promptly stabbed itself back into its hole.

Once, when Will was just a boy, he'd heard that a house in a nearby town was haunted. The house belonged to an old shut-in who had murdered his wife when they were both still young. For forty years, he'd kept her body hidden in the attic as her fractured spirit drove him into a secluded madness.

When the truth was discovered, a posse was organized by the two town Bonewardens. The shut-in refused to leave without a fight. After a stalemate of gunfire, the Bonewardens ordered the house to be burned with the man still in it.

After the blaze, all the leftover metal, from the old stove to the nails, was gathered and given to the local blacksmith for scrap. The blacksmith made hundreds of railroad spikes which he sold at cost to a railroad company in a neighboring state. The site where the house had been was plowed over and planted with millet. A year later the millet was inspected and found to be of reasonable quality. The cursed area was officially clean.

Later, folk would say that the house probably hadn't been haunted at all, and that the hermit was only mad from 'shot nerves for keepin' such a furtive secret'. It was common truth that ghosts could not be seen, but their actions could. Only necrotheurges, animists, and post-morts could see the fractured husks of the soul that still held grudges.

So, imagine Will's surprise when he *saw* a semi-transparent apparition reaching for Polly's face as she asked if they could come in.

"Get back!" he told it, whipping out his gun.

For a fleeting instant, the spook paused as Polly jumped off the porch. With baleful disappointment, the spook fixed its gaze on Will. Any mountain of courage the tendikeye had was blasted away as the ghost grasped his wrist.

Will fired his two shots into its empty eye sockets to no effect. A weightless feeling overtook him. With ease the ghastly thing yanked him inside. The door slammed shut behind him. He tried to move but was frozen in fright.

Normally, he would leave little time for fear. He loathed the tension that built before a fight. Often, he would end one before it began. No time to be afraid. No time until now, that is.

For alas, he was tendikeye. The fear produced by a ghost was mystical in nature, or against nature, according to some. The long progression of the quilled race had rendered them theurgically inept and substantially sensitive to the supernatural. This all meant that Will Foundling was up Waste Creek with no paddle. And his canoe just capsized.

The pale green ghost looked to be formed from watery jelly, yet it moved like smoke. Will could not tell what race it had been, much less its sex. It had no expression, yet he could tell it was angry.

"Please, let them go!" the ghost yelled in a quavering voice. "Please, Please! I'll do it if you just let them go!"

13

Will shook his head, not wanting to hear or see anymore. He dropped his lantern. The candle went out as it bounced and rolled on the hardwood floor. The ghost still had a hold of his wrist. Will knew countless ways to get out of a wrist grapple, but none of them came to mind. Instead, he drew his machete with his free hand, slashing through the waist of his captor.

For a brief instant, he felt the cold grip of the ghost loosen on his gun hand. He yanked it free and took a step back. Now, with his blade and gun in his trained hands, his confidence started to stir.

"I'm sorry about your family! But, please, spare mine!" the ghost cried.

The tendikeye knew not what the spook meant, nor did he care. His bullets and blade had no effect on it. That was enough reason to skedaddle. He turned for the front door that had closed behind him. With legs that could launch him onto the roof of a one story house, he prepared to kick the door.

Instead, the door struck him!

"We're coming, Will!" came a familiar voice from behind the heavy wooden rectangle.

The door, propelled by a charging, well-intentioned Röger, flew at Will with such speed and force, that it knocked him flat on his back and shattered to pieces.

"Oh, waste! Sorry!" the human gasped, looking down to see what he had done.

"You should have let me pick de door lock instead of arguing wit' me!" Polly hissed, running in after him. She knelt down by Will, who was brushing off the wooden debris. "Tell me what happened!" she demanded without a shred of sympathy.

Still shaken, Will turned back to see where the ghost had been. It was gone.

"Where'd it go?" he whispered. "There was a...a ghost. There really *is* a spook in this dad-gum place!"

"You *saw* it?" she asked. "You?"

"Heard it, too." He was beginning to calm down. There was no sense in letting her see him so afraid.

Polly looked up from him and stood. Up and down she scanned with cold eyes. "Was it because he was de weakest target?" she questioned. She took a deep breath through her nose and her

14

eyes widened. "De kitchen," she whispered with a hiss in her throat. She then started for one of the doorways.

"Wait, Polly," Röger blurted. "What should we do?" He helped Will to his feet.

"How should I know?" she answered with a shrug.

The two men followed her. Will still had his gun and machete out.

"Put dose away," Polly groused. "It's like watching a scared little boy holding on to his pee pee."

"Don't deny a man his comforts," Röger returned in Will's defense. He gave the sour-faced tendikeye a hard pat on the back.

The two men followed her into the room that had once served as the kitchen. It was a decrepit space covered with ceramic tile, cracked and ruined with age. A tree had sprouted from the floor and made a hole through the ceiling. There was no trace of dishes or cups or a single wooden spoon. The cupboards were bare, with the exception of spider webs.

Polly sniffed at the air. Her nose led her by the old pump sink. She reached into her roomy sleeve and pulled out a white handled dagger. She climbed up onto the sink. Stabbing the old wood ceiling, she pried out a tiny chuck of the aged timber. After she got down, she popped the piece of wood into her mouth.

"What are you..?" Will began to ask with a disgusted look.

She raised a finger as she chewed. It pointed to the spot where she had stabbed. After swallowing, she answered. "See how dat part of de ceiling is darker dan de rest? It's blood, old blood. Just enough to give me de last memory of who it belonged to."

The two men stood in silent discomfort as she closed her eyes and whispered incoherently. Blood was the power of her theurgy, and with it came a philocreed of violence and malice. This girl was more than just moody. She walked a path some said was darker than death mysticism.

"Suicide," she said as her eyes snapped open. "A man. Dere was a desperation in de flavor. Strong despair. But it was tempered wit' hope, if dat makes sense. He shot his brains out onto de ceiling. Luckily, it stained well enough for me to find out."

"How long ago?" Röger asked.

"I don't know. At least a lifetime. Maybe two or three."

"My lifetime or yers?" Will asked.

15

"Mine," she replied. "Twelve hundred years or so. Dis house is even older dan it seems. De dark energies are preserving it somehow."

"Hello?" came a voice suddenly from behind them. All three jumped, but the fear left as soon as it came. It was only Hindin at the front entrance. "I heard Will's gun," he called.

"We're in here, Rev!" Will called, annoyed by being made so jumpy. "We'll be right out."

The four retreated from the house, through the cold rain, and back into the barn. Hindin was the first one in.

"I need my towel." Hindin said, stepping into the wagon. "What happened in there?"

As the malruka dried off his steel skin, the three described their brief ordeal to him.

"Ah!" the malruka exclaimed, pointing a finger at them. "It is obvious. The ghost that Will beheld was the man who killed himself. But why? He mentioned money, payment of some kind. No doubt he was the owner of this orchard. And when his trees refused to yield, he became desperate. It is probable that he was unable to pay his yearly taxes. And so, in a fit of despair, he took his own life. It makes sense. When someone dies with a deep sense of regret, their spirits have trouble dissipating." He paced around them. "This is but one mystery in a county consisting of small towns, rural villages, deserted hamlets, and remote thorpes, each with their own ghost legend. And you say, Sir Röger, that the entire county is under a Geohex?"

"Geohex?" Will asked.

"It means *land curse*," Röger answered. "And yeah, the whole county is infected from border to border. I passed through here about a hundred-and-twenty years ago. I didn't stay long. After watching two skeletons shoot each other with rusted pistols in a duel they both lost centuries ago, that was enough for me. Even when the locals told me that it was a nightly thing, and that they never hurt anyone but each other, it still creeped me out."

"Creeped *you* out?" Will asked with a wry smile. "A were-bit Black Vest got scared off by a couple o' bonewalkers? Me an' Rev encountered them a time 'r two. Ain't nuthin' a wedge axe won't fix."

The brawny man hung his head and laughed. "Will, I've

16

fought every kind of post-mort you can think of. From the brittlest skeleton to the rankest Bregenite to the oldest of Hemogoblins. But the reason I got scared back then was the same reason you nearly crapped your pants in that house just now: *Necrofear*. The fear of impending death that exudes from those cursed to exist long after they should have stopped existing. This ain't no army of slow corpses puppeted by some deadhead necrotheurge. This is getting to know the not-so-dearly-departed on a psychological level." Röger smiled in his helmet, for he could see the effect it was having on Will.

The tendikeye made a sour face and crossed his arms. "Well, they wouldn't have this problem if they'd just burn their dead. Buryin' bodies in graves!" He spat at the ground. "Waste o' good soil!"

◈

That night, ignoring the crashing downpour, they each enjoyed the privacy afforded by the stables.

Polly slept the soundest, but not out of any sense of comfort. She had spent too many nights in her life paranoid and unsure, only to be left fatigued the next day. Now she had friends to help keep watch, for which she was silently grateful.

Hindin performed his moving meditation, as he called it. It was a fighting form as slow as it was fluid. Shifting from one posture to the next, he showed no pause in the transitions. He was slender and lean, with an ideal body that made hardly a sound as it reminded itself how to maim and subdue. When he was finished, he took the one-legged pose of a Great Cobalt Heron, and slept.

Will barely slept at all. He was too laden with thought. How was he able to see ghosts? Beneath that thought were memories all unpleasant, the most unwanted of images that come on the cusp of sleep and consciousness. Two assassins trying to kill the four of them on a rainy city street, and nearly succeeding. A cobalt blade slashing his wrist deep enough split the skin. No other blade had ever bit him so deep. For as long as he could remember Will was tougher than any tendikeye had a right to be. It was a supernatural

17

"curse" that got him banished from his homeland. Was it much more than just a curse? He had no clue until that night. Cobalt was the only metal that could pierce the hide of Lemuertians, the immortal enemies of the tendikeye. *"Does this mean I'm a halfbreed?"* Will thought in the dark enclosure. This question he would have asked with Hindin, for they had been friends these last few months. Now that they traveled with two newer companions, he was less inclined to bring it up.

And as for Sir Röger Yamus, he had gone without taking advantage of a woman for a whole week. So, when he was sure everyone was asleep, he promptly took advantage of himself.

Chapter 2
Drowsy Nook

Part 1

◈

As the morning hour took its turn, the Huncell dome enclosing the land and seas illuminated them with its gentle glow. The storm had passed, leaving the ground soggy and a nearby orchard sparkling with wet leaves. One of the barn doors creaked opened, with Will walking out stiff and shirtless. The mud was caking onto the bottoms of his big bare feet. He didn't mind that as much as the three men on bileers pointing shotguns at him. He looked up long enough to see their matching dark orange uniforms.

"*Law men*," he thought, turning his attention to a small cedar tree. "*They can wait.*"

The three men remained silent, ever keeping him in their sights. Like most of the natives of country of Doflend they were purple-skinned Drakeri like Polly.

"Mornin', fellas," he called out. His back was turned to them as he let nature take its course against the sapling.

"Good morning," one of them answered. "Did you know that there's a town three miles up the road? Drowsy Nook, it's called. We have an inn there, very affordable. Privies, as well."

"Wish I'da known that before the storm," the tendikeye replied, turning around and buttoning up. "Only road sign we saw was the county limit marker."

"Blame Embrenil County for that," the oldest man returned. "Welcome to the place the government forgot. Welcome to Apple County, stranger."

Will studied their guns and uniforms. "I sure don't feel welcome, deputy."

"Why are you here?" the law man asked.

Röger and Hindin stepped out out of the barn. The tall malruka was all too glad to answer the question.

"We are here to rid your county of its Geohex, and thereby justify our being welcome here, albeit in a retroactive sense."

"Huh?" a younger deputy let out.

"We wanna rid this land of its curse," Will translated. He gave a stern look to Hindin. "Rev, I swear. Sometimes I think you aim too high."

"Would you quit with the guns, already?" Röger pleaded. "We came here to do you people a favor. Sorry for trespassing. Are you planning on hauling us in and fining us? If so, we'll withdraw our apologies and leave you cursed. But I gotta tell you, the four of us are big spenders, and it might do your economy some good to let us in peacefully."

"Rög, buckle yer lip!" Will yelled, suddenly feeling his cool slipping away.

But the human continued, undeterred. "Now, you three look like honest deputies to me. I've run into cops that would have shot us in our sleep, buggered our limp corpses, took our money, and buried us somewhere remote. But you guys didn't do that. Why? Because you're honest. And as honest cops, you can understand an honest mistake. We were a bit clueless on how far the nearest town was. It was about to rain, and we had a wagon with bileers to worry about."

"You look familiar," the old one responded. "I've seen a helmet like that before. What's your name?"

"Sir Röger Yamus!" Röger said, puffed with pride. "Great, great grandson of the legendary man whose name I share. In fact, this helmet belonged to him." Will rolled his eyes at the lie.

The old deputy holstered his rifle and squint his eyes. He urged his steed closer. "I wouldn't call Röger Yamus legendary. He was arrested here a century ago for being unruly. Kindly remove your helmet." The old man's eyes widened as the human obeyed. "You look just like him, boy!"

"Strong blood!" Röger replied, flexing a thick bicep. "You could almost say it's a curse."

After a moment of what looked like careful thought, the deputy spoke. "You three aren't the first Excursionists to wander here, claiming you'll bring an end to the Geohex. And I doubt you'll

20

be the last. As for the matter of trespassing, that is for the sheriff to settle on. Ready your wagon and come with us."

The travelers complied with haste. When Polly became visible to the officers, they asked her for her age and where her parents were.

"Eighteen," she answered. "And I have no parents to speak of."

They responded with suspicious looks, but asked no more.

Forced to skip breakfast, the travelers readied their wagon and followed the officers to town. It was a valley town wedged between two forest-covered hills. It seemed to cut into the east hill, giving it a closed-in air. The day was new yet, and Drowsy Nook looked far from drowsy. The people there were mostly Drakeri, with the occasional human family standing out. All the men wore black denim breeches, while most of the women wore matching skirts cut off at mid-shin.

This apparent submission to conformity urged Hindin to ask "Officers? What is the dominate philocreed here?"

"United Algebraist," one answered. "We adhere to the truths of Algebraic Law. The recognition of these truths sets our town apart from neighboring towns."

"Most intriguing," Hindin replied. Will watched as the malruka pulled a book from his duffel bag and flipped through it.

They soon entered the town square where no eye could miss its massive centerpiece—a grand petrified stump of an ancient redwood tree. It rose up like a great circular platform with steps carved into its sides. In its center was a stone block of wood that had been left behind when the great tree was felled. Embedded in that old block was an obscenely large axe, the blade as wide as a man's torso, with a dark spotless sheen. The handle was as long as a rake handle, but much thicker.   Röger asked to halt for a moment. "I want to see if I can succeed where my, uh, great granddad failed."

The old deputy smiled. "You know our legend, then? Go ahead! Have a try. If you can yank it free, it's yours. And good luck to you, sir."

The human brute jumped from the wagon to the stump's level platform. The few people who saw the great leap stopped to watch. Others looked on out of meager curiosity.

Röger circled around the axe like it was an old enemy. His

21

eyes blazed with desire and hate, meshing into a grim determination. He charged the handle, grasping it from underneath and ramming with his shoulder. A grunting growl rumbled from within his being. Every muscle in his body tensed to nearly twice their normal size. And as he strained against the immovable object, it seemed as if he was starting to grow larger.

"*Aw, Gut Snake!*" Will thought. "*He'd better not change here an' now!*"

But after a tense moment of struggling, Röger Yamus gave up. He then muttered something only Will could hear. "After all this time, I still can't budge it!"

"Okay, that's enough," a deputy called. "It's time to see the sheriff."

A feeling of dread crept into the big human. "*Old Sheriff Farnuff. I hope that he doesn't recognize me.*"

All the townsfolk who had been watching, shrugged their shoulders and went about their business.

The Station House had the look of a quaint old mansion modified for public use. They were taken to a side stairway that led down to the basement level.

"Down here, please," a deputy ordered.

"You ain't gonna take our weapons?" Will asked.

"You haven't given us reason to yet," a younger one answered. "Besides, if you can hurt *our* Sheriff, we'll be very impressed." He smiled at the tendikeye with a sly prideful grin.

Will did not like it. And when the deputy turned his smile to Polly, she looked down, fighting the urge to blush. Will liked that even less.

The stairs led to the door to the sheriff's office. Once inside, Hindin was the first to speak as they beheld the sheriff of Drowsy Nook. "Slate be praised!" the Hindin exclaimed by order of greeting.

"Slate be praised," the sheriff responded. He was another Malruka, a man of stone and metal. But unlike Hindin, he was full-sized. He resembled a ten foot tall, hulking statue of mottled marble. Ornate plates of armor were affixed to his shoulders, upper back, forearms and shins, giving him a knightly appearance. His stern eyes were two dark garnets set in carved sockets. Around his neck was a thick scarf of chain mail. There was a sign on his granite desk that read *Sheriff Edifice Teige.*

22

"You're the Sheriff?" Röger asked, possibly not seeing the sign.

"Yes," the stone man answered, mildly offended. He looked to his deputies. "These are the trespassers?"

The three officers nodded.

He turned his eyes to the group. "This town takes no chances with sneakabouts. Not in these last fifty years. That isn't to say that new people aren't welcome. So, if you please, tell us who you are and why you've come here."

Hindin stepped forward, bowing formal. "We are the Excursionist group known as *Four Winds-One Storm.*" He took a wooden tube from the pocket of his white canvas pants. Opening the tube, he pulled out a rolled up document. "This certificate grants us full rights to investigate any crime or nuisance throughout the seven cities of Doflend. We are here for such a purpose."

"What crime would that be?" the Sheriff asked, taking the permit and examining it.

"No crime in particular, sheriff. We are here to cleanse this land of its Geohex."

The sheriff looked up. "Is that so? Why? What is it to you, little brother? Not that I wouldn't mind having the specters of this town exorcised. But, as Excursionists, you must have some agenda. So, which "F" is it?"

"Which 'eff'?" Polly asked.

"Fortune, fame, or freedom, he means," Will answered. "Freedom meanin' either fightin' fer the freedom of others or enjoyin' yer own, y'know, fightin' fer the thrill of it an' wut not." He turned his tanned face to the Sheriff. "I'm Will Foundling, Sheriff, an' I'm in it fer the fame. Not fer the sake o' vanity mind you."

The sheriff grinned, showing steel teeth. "But to prove to the world that not all tendikeye are blood thirsty savages?"

Will let out a chuckle. "Naw, nuthin' that noble. Glory's just the dump that justice takes when it's settled. I'm lookin' fer a tendikeye man called Brem Hoffin. Ye seen 'im?"

"If I have, I wouldn't have known it, for it is a name I've never heard before. Is he someone you intend to kill? A bounty perhaps?"

"Naw, just an old friend. He's a wingless Bukk, like me, only older an' not as purdy. I'm jus' tryin' to cultivate a reputation as a

23

means to get his attention. An' if that means spook-huntin' in yer neck o' the woods, so be it."

"Right," the Sheriff returned, looking confused and annoyed. "And you, little brother?" he asked Hindin. "Why do you live this life as vagrant hero?"

"Hindin Revetz is my name. I do this because I am able. Because, like you, I had the blessing of being born a Malruka. I simply intend to combat the various ills of the Cluster before my two centuries are up."

"Ills such as the ghosts haunting my county?"

"Yes, your honor, for the time being. My primary goal is to amass enough knowledge to someday establish an academy for innovative, progressive learning. But seeing as how I am only twenty-eight, I still have a long way to go."

"I see," replied the Sheriff with a nod. "And you, young lady?" he inquired of Polly. His garnet eyes seemed to shift color as he looked full upon her. "Why, you still have the trace looks of a child. Why do you walk this hazardous path?"

Polly hated being put on the spot, and especially being made to talk in front of men she did not know. "I...am Polly Gone of de wild forests of Chume. I...I...honestly cannot tell why I am an Excursionist. Dere seems to be no better place for me, really. But, compared to life in Chume, it is...good...a good ting, I mean."

Sheriff Edifice smiled. "Well. That's nice to hear." Sarcasm dripped from his every word. He shifted his gaze to Röger. "And you?"

Röger puffed out his chest. "I, good sir, am none other than Sir Röger Yamus the Second. Great, great grandson of the first Sir Röger Yamus the Black Vest, a man who spent the night in this very jail many years ago. I have heard the legend of the Headsman's Axe in bedtime stories as a child. My ancestor failed to pull the axe or end this town's paranormal affliction. So I have returned, I mean *come* to succeed where my granddad had failed. Family honor and all that!"

The marble brute behind the desk let out a condescending laugh. "Well! The honor is mine to have you here, all of you! We'll let the charges slide."

"We ain't in trouble?" Will asked.

"Of course not. Why, I, too, was an Excursionist before I

came here and settled down. Tell me: What are your qualifications?" He observed the four of them. "I see Mr. Foundling has a rather fancy sword and pistol on his belt. Ms. Gone no doubt has something up her sleeve, either literally or figuratively or both. And Mr. Yamus and Mr. Revetz are completely unarmed."

"I'll be armed soon," Röger said.

"Bullets and blades don't kill ghosts," retorted the Sheriff. "Theurgy is needed to fight them. Strong theurgy, and the right kind at that. Are any of you Animist theurges, or if chance allows, good necrotheurges?"

"No, your honor," Hindin replied.

"Then consider yourselves lucky. Every Animist Shaman that comes through here goes insane."

"Maybe we don't need theurgy," Will proposed. "I hear tell most ghosts stick around on account o' unfinished business. Maybe all we hafta do is finish it for 'em."

The stern eyed stone man grinned down at the wild-eyed tendikeye. "Do you know our town's legend?" He reached into the hollow of his desk and flipped something shiny at Will. The tendikeye's arm turned into a blur of motion as his large hand enveloped the object.

Will saw that is was a twenty grotz piece.

The sheriff gloated openly. "Go to the Cudgel Law Saloon across the street. Buy the old men there a round of wheat beer. Then ask them to recite the poem of old Jole Sarai. Now, if you'll all excuse me, I have paper work to do."

"We are free to investigate, then?" Hindin asked.

"Why not?" the sheriff said with a shrug. "You all seem like decent folks. You have documentation. But if you do bad things, you'd better hope that I get to you before our local ghost does."

⌖

Will Foundling squeezed the coin in his hand as if trying to squish a cricket. He did not dare place it in his pocket. That would mean he accepted it as his own property. He would accept no man's charity, stone or otherwise. He would place it directly on the saloon

25

bar and listen to the old men's nursery rhyme. He thanked the sheriff for his time and insisted to his teammates that he go alone.

"That is fine," Hindin replied, dropping a heavy hand on Röger's shoulder. "Sir Röger and I have things to discuss."

The human looked up at him with smiling eyes that hid a flash of pain. "Happy to, big guy...er...I mean, Master Hindin!"

"Where's my coin pouch?" Polly cried. She was patting herself down, searching her person. "I fastened it wit' a bosun's knot to my belt."

"Did you have it when you entered town?" the younger deputy asked, stepping in front of her.

"I am sure of it," the girl replied in a hissing whisper.

"Well," he started with a nervous laugh "I think I might know where it is." He turned to the Sheriff. "Is it alright if I take her to the Pilfer House?"

"Yes, of course," said the Sheriff Teige, dismissing them with a wave. "Now, all of you please clear out of my office. I have an important letter to write."

Once outside, the kindly faced deputy escorted Polly in one direction. Hindin and Röger went another.

Will made his way across the dirt street, leaping over an ox-drawn cart in the process. Before placing a single boot on the saloon steps, his eyes fixed on a sign nailed to an awning post.

NOTICE
YOU ARE ABOUT TO ENTER AN ESTABLISHMENT WHERE CERTAIN RULES APPLY. IF YOU BE GETTING THE URGE TO DO A FELLOW CUSTOMER SERIOUS HARM, USE NOTHING MORE THAN A FASHIONED PIECE OF TIMBER TO SETTLE YOUR DISPUTES. NO FIST, NOR GUN, NOR BLADE IS TO BE DRAWN, SHOULD A BRAWL OCCUR. BREAKERS OF THE CUDGEL LAW SALOON WILL WISH THEY HADN'T.

The tendikeye smiled at this apparent nonsense, and went in. It was an old yet well-kept saloon, littered with a half dozen elderly Drakeri men. Most were thin, and their indigo complexions were fading into a pale lavender. He walked straight for the bar, which was tended by an old drakeri woman. With a hardy smack, he set the twenty grotz piece on the smooth oak surface.

"Wheat beer fer everyone, please," he said loud enough for all to hear.

The woman took the money and readied six glasses. Taking her time, she filled each glass from a wooden barrel mounted on a shelf. Two of the darkened glasses she passed to two men at the bar. The others she carried nimbly to the ones at the tables.

To Will's trepidation, not a single man acknowledged what was set before him. He waited two whole minutes before one man finished the glass he already had. To the young tendikeye's surprise, the old geezer ordered another glass of wheat beer, seemingly oblivious to the full glass in front of him.

"Hey now!" Will started, raising a pointed finger in the air.

All at once, the two men at the bar were off their stools and on their feet. In their wrinkled hands were knotted canes.

"Whooyah think y'are?" one of them grumbled.

"I don't think, ol' timer. I know. Will Foundling's my name." His hands had already fallen to his sword and pistol.

"Yah bring a gun an' a chopper to a stick fight, new timer?" the other barked, baring his toothless gums in a snarl.

"No, sir," Will replied. He raised his hands slowly. "I jus' came to hear 'bout yer town spook."

The other men stood up from their tables, scooting chairs as their legs straightened. Like the two men before, they seemed to pull sticks out from nowhere.

"He wants to know aboot the Headsman!" one of them exclaimed, as if insulted. "Tell us, boy, have yah ever killed a man unjustly?"

Will raised a quill eyebrow. "Depends on what you view as unjust, sir. If it's any o' yer DAD-GUM business!"

"The Headsman will know if yah deserve punishment, boy. And if yah want clarification on how he deals his justice, you'll either take your lumps or give them!"

Will relaxed his knees and shoulders. "But I bought you all a beer! What gives?"

"Oh, yer prickly head's gonna give if you don't man up right soon! A challenge is a challenge!"

It was the last warning they gave him. All at once, they came

27

at him with their cudgel-canes, each striking strategically at a different spot. They had no doubt done this before. Will could make out the many scars on their ancient faces. These old men belonged to some kind of gang, and this was their club house. No sweet grandfathers here, just seasoned head-busters. But more than he underestimated them, they underestimated him.

Three hits he took, two he evaded, and one he disarmed with a catch-twist-and yank. He leapt out of the circle of fury, knocking one man on the back as he landed. The weapon he had snatched was long and L-shaped. With it he attacked their canes first, knocking away their chance to defend. This way and that, he walloped their wrists and knees, disarming and slowing them down.

When only two were left, he understood who the top-dogs were. They were the same two who sat at the bar. They came at him hard, one swinging low and to the left, the other attacking high and to the right. Will immediately dropped his weapon and caught them both in his thick padded hands.

"You old coots specialize in attackin' at the same time. That means when I see one o' you swing; I know the other is, too."

"SO?" one of them yelled, tugging on his captured cane.

"So..." Will started as he jumped and twisted in the air, pulling loose the two cudgel-canes. With a momentum-building flip, he came down on their shoulders, breaking their own weapons against them. The two old men fell writhing and hollering.

Will bared his teeth. "So, you got too comfortable in yer routine! Now, tell me about the Headsman."

"Alright, alright, yah spiky-haired papoose!" came a voice from behind. It was an old man he had disarmed. "Cudgel Law dictates that winners get requests granted." He went over to his table, rubbing his sore wrist. He picked up the glass that was brought to him and asked "What name are we drinking to, new timer? 'Will Foundling' is it?"

"Yessir."

"Well then, here's to your health...and mine." The old drakeri downed the draught in six steady gulps. And as he drank, he rotated his broken wrist. An eerie blue light emanated from the joint. And as Will watched, the other men did the same: raising their glasses to him and having light glow from their injuries.

Will peered at them all with suspicion. "What's the deal here,

28

boys? What kinda saloon is this?"

"A mystic one," the old lady behind the counter answered. "My grandfather founded this saloon before the Omni-War over three thousand years ago. Oh, sure, it's been rebuilt dozens of times, but his wheat beer recipe never changes."

"I'd still trade my wife and kids for that formula, Dori," jested one of the men.

The woman continued. "The beer heals any wound that is dealt by a wooden object so long as the wound was dealt in *this* establishment. It won't heal knife wounds, or the like. So, this is a far cry from a Healer's Temple. But the second you laid that coin down, you challenged every man here. That's just the way it works I'm afraid."

"That Sheriff is dead!" Will thought. "Are you a mystic then?" he asked the woman.

"Me? No. My grandfather was the theurge of the family. I just follow his recipe. Care for a glass to tend your hurts?"

"I'm a tendikeye, ma'am. Of course not."

"Oh, well I've known a few who weren't shy to *The Paths.*"

Will sneered "Me, too. They're called traitors. The Philocreeds are nuthin' more'n foolish notions set to faith. Now, would one of you be so kind to tell me about yer Headsman ghost?"

The six old men stood up straight, placing their hats over their hearts. One by one, they took turns reciting verses of an ancient yarn. And with each passing line, Will Foundling became more and more unsettled.

There's an axe embedded in a weathered stump,
In the middle of Drowsy Square,
Where many a man had lost his hand,
Or all their necks could spare,
The headsman's name was Jole Sarai,
A widowed father of one,
A mask he wore to secure his secret,
To live quietly with his son,
The townsfolk presumed his wife had left,
Enough money to never go broke,
But the judge and mayor would pay for his favors,
At one thousand grotz per stroke,

29

One day his secret leaked out,
And the townsfolk shunned and sneered,
For there was no family yet untouched,
By his axe that brought such fear,
Dismissed from his duties, Jole soon became broke,
So he sold his possessions and bileer,
But a faithful steed he soon would need,
When he felt a father's greatest fear,
One night his son had taken ill,
And the doctor was leagues away,
And none would lend a bileer to ride,
To speed him on his way,
And so he ran all night and day,
With the medicine in hand,
The worry for his sickly son,
following as he ran,
His lungs did burn, His heart did pound,
His thoughts stormed in his brain,
In an exhausted state, he arrived too late,
His child was by sickness slain.
His heart gave out from grief and strain,
But his tortured soul endured,
With help denied, he swore as he died,
His vengeance would be secured,
And all who denied him would end up dead,
Some lost both hands and some lost their heads,
The headsman is dead but his work continues,
When his axe floats, it seeks bone and sinew,
The guilty he finds before law condemns,
Never shows mercy – allows no amends,
Old Jole Sarai the unseen keeper of order,
In Drowsy Nook past the Wraith County border.

Taking off his kepi hat and smiling, the young deputy introduced himself. "Deputy Drume Arteen, at your service, miss."

30

"Polly Gone, willing to make use of it," the young woman answered flatly. She could not help but notice the look on his face: warm, caring, and curious. She did not like the effect it was having on her. She wondered how cold she had to be to make him change it. "What is dis Pilfer House you are taking me to? Is dat where you take advantage of defenseless women?"

"I assure you, Miss Gone: the advantage is all yours." There was no change. "Please, this way." He made a gentlemanly gesture, showing her where to go.

After ten or so steps, Polly demanded, "My question, officer, will you answer it? Or are you tinking of someting clever to say?"

The man smiled, revealing a row of perfect teeth that drew her eyes. "Ah, yes, the Pilfer House. It's a minor legend around here. Nothing compared to the Headsman, although it is related." He went on to tell the story.

"Long ago, there was a pick pocket in town named Jerf Bendre. He was a lowdown, good for nothing, socially back-stabbing, gutless, friendless thief, or so the legend goes. Anyway, he got caught stealing someone's diary, or some say it was a book of hand written poems. He was judged and sentenced according to the Law of Division which states: *If you divide a negative deed by another negative deed, then you have done a positive deed.* He got his hand chopped off, and thus, the judicial equation was complete. He then ran off and faded away into obscurity. But here's the kicker. The ghost of his severed hand stayed in Drowsy Nook!" The deputy made a comical gesture as if his own hand had a mind of its own.

Polly took note that it was a good hand for a man to have, strong and wide.

The deputy continued. "Ever since, it has been recommended that too many coins should never be gathered in one place. Because whenever they turn up missing, the money usually ends up in the house that Jerf Bendre once lived in."

"De Pilfer House," she said with a slight nod.

The man touched the tip of his nose with his finger. She could not help but laugh a little. His face grew warmer. "I'm sorry to see you so inconvenienced," he spoke softly.

"*No, you are not,*" she thought as she smiled.

Four small town blocks passed in silence, but it was a

31

comfortable silence nonetheless. She took in the sights of what seemed like pleasant, simple, small town life.

The young deputy exchanged passing greetings with several folk going about their daily errands. Polly then remembered that the deputy had ridden a bileer.

"Why aren't we riding your steed?" she asked with playful suspicion. "Would it not have been faster?"

"Certainly. And also inappropriate," he looked to be fighting the urge to grin. "You see, in this area, there are rules to sharing your bileer with a woman. If she is your wife, she sits in front of you. If you are on a date, she sits behind you. If she is under arrest, she is to be placed before the rider on her stomach over the steed and ruthlessly spanked every tenth gallop. And since you are neither of these, we are walking."

She raised an eyebrow. "Do you expect me to believe dat last one?"

"How about you do something illegal and find out? Unless, of course, you are *with* one of those gentlemen you entered town with."

Her head jerked back in surprise. "Wit' one of...? Oh no! None of dem are my thralls--. Um, none of dem are wit' me, as you say."

The man stopped walking, looking at her with blatant adoration. "We're here," he declared, pointing with his thumb to a small old house. "I'll go inside and retrieve your money."

"I will go wit' you den," she offered.

"Not afraid of ghosts?"

"We encountered one in dat farm house yesternight before de storm. Do you know about dat one, as well?"

"Old man Erkett," he said, his mouth tightening. "He blew his brains out when his farm stopped growing apples. You'll find a lot of that in this county, ghosts of apple barons. Their hearts were tied to the land, and the land got cursed." He smiled a sad smile as he opened the front door. "After you."

She had to follow quickly, for the long-legged man had probably been in there thousands of times. The house was void of furniture and the walls were bare. They came to what looked like a den with a brick tile floor. In the corner of the room was an old crowbar which the deputy took to pry up a large loose brick. Under the brick was a shadowy hole. He got down on his belly and reached in all the way to his shoulder.

"Got it," he announced. And up with his hand he pulled out a red leather coin pouch.

"Dat's it!" she said, astonished. Her eyes narrowed in suspicion. "Wait. How do I know dat you did not take it from me and hide it up your sleeve de whole time?"

The deputy laughed, rubbing the back of his neck as he handed her the pouch. "I'm slick, but not *that* slick! Gee, you are a chary one!"

"Cherry?!" she asked, suddenly offended and blushing. "Wh-What do you-?!"

"No, C-H-A-R-Y. Chary. It means cautious and careful." His smile widened.

"Oh," she said, understanding.

"But I guess that's a good thing if you're going investigate the hauntings. If you ask me, there is no mystery to solve. The state of this land is its true equation. The *product of a positive number and a negative number will always be a negative number.* Too many bad things happened here, that's all. But I do know of at least one good thing."

"What is dat?" she asked.

"The annual county fair held every Autumn. There's music to lighten your feet, good food fresh from the harvest, and contests of skill for bragging rights and kittens. It's in two weeks as a matter of fact. And, well, I should be very pleased if you were to ride there with me on the back of my saddle."

Polly felt her jaw loosen. It was the first time a man had dared ask her out on a formal date. Her mouth opened and closed, but no words came out. Then she snapped out of her daze. "Tank you, but I don't tink I can."

Deputy Arteen raised his hands and shrugged. "Well, if you plan on ridding the entire county of ghosts, I doubt that you and your friends will do it overnight. And if *the equation* keeps you here that long, then why not?"

The weight of flattery she felt almost made her give in, but too many other thoughts were in the way. "*I cannot risk being discovered. But I could lie low in dis place a while. A month is not so long. But I hate parties and social gatherings. A fair full of*

33

yokels would be just too much. But he does have a nice face, dopey, but nice. And that uniform...NO! I can't! I just can't!"

"I must regretfully refuse," she said. "I am sorry. I can make no promises on whether I will be in one place or de next."

"Understood," he replied, readjusting his posture to that of a deputy on duty. "However, in the unlikely equation that I see you there, would you be my date?"

"*If* you see me dere," she answered with a nod, knowing deep down that she would make no attempt to go. "Tanks again, Deputy Drume Arteen, for retrieving my pouch."

◇

Shortly after parting ways with Will and Polly, Röger Yamus found out just how strong *and* fast Hindin Revetz was. Before he knew it, his boots were swept off the ground, his helmet was turned around backwards, his arms were pinned by what felt like a steel constrictor snake, and he was being carried off at great speed. Before he had the slightest notion of reacting, he felt himself being placed down and having his helm spun forward.

He saw that he was now behind the station house with no one nearby but his stern-faced companion. "Sir Röger," Hindin started, "why were we not made aware that you had a history of running amok in this settlement?"

"Hey, I told you I came through here," the human defended.

"You were jailed here!"

"It wasn't my fault. I went into this bar and mistakenly hit on this guy's granddaughter. Before I knew it, I was being attacked by a bunch of old men with sticks. So, after giving them an honest pounding, the sheriff, and it was a different sheriff back then, arrested me for not fighting on their terms. I tell ya, big guy, these Algebraists out here got strange customs. Besides, that was like a hundred years ago."

"Which is not that long for a Drakeri," Hindin said, glaring. "Posing as your own descendant is dubious ruse that I am not comfortable taking part in. It is dishonest, unlawful, and—"

"Necessary," Röger added, his voice lowering. "I spent two

34

months in this town, trying to undo the curse of that axe. I made a few friends and enemies, but the former sheriff eventually ran me out. I waited a long time before I thought it was safe to come back. And even though I'm stronger now, I still couldn't pull that shunting thing out!"

"The axe in the square," Hindin said, his eyes shifting direction. "What is its story?"

The burly human sighed and hung his head for a moment. "That petrified stump out there. Legend says that it was a tree planted by the Myth Render himself when the Draybair Cluster was young, before the Huncells were connected, even. This was once a holy place. But after a few dozen eons of war, strife, and corporations, the place went the way of all great things: to waste. The tree was cut down, but some say it just died and fell. Either way, sometime shortly after the Omni-war about two-thousand years ago, the people made it a chopping block for the condemned.

The executioner had to keep his identity a secret, because he was a local. Somebody might have taken it personal whenever he cut off a friend or relative's head or hand. And wouldn't you know it, when his secret got out, the whole town turned their backs to him. Even when his only son was sick and dying, no one would lend him a steed to ride and get medicine. He died, too, of exhaustion from running to get help.

"And get this, since that happened, there hasn't been a single trial for murder or theft in this town. The ghost of the executioner carries out the sentence before the guilty even get caught. It knows when someone did something wrong here. But sometimes, people are found dead in their beds, chopped by that axe, and no one ever knows what they did to deserve it. It's even gotten to the point where the people just assume that a person was guilty of *something,* and that the ghost probably had a good reason for doing it.

"But that's just passive bullturd. The people of this town know in their hearts that they live in fear. It's not up to the dead to judge the living. So, yeah: I think it's up to people like us to knock this spook out of commission. In fact, I was on my way down here when I met you and the others in Embrenil."

"But why did you not tell us of your past exploits on the journey?" the malruka asked, crossing his arms.

35

"I didn't want any of you to get discouraged and think: if Sir Röger couldn't get anything done down here, what chance do we have?"

Hindin showed no recognition of humor from the human's joke.

"Okay," Röger continued, "the truth. I wanted to tell you all as soon as we got here. I'm bad at telling tales, and I wanted to use the town as a real-life visual aid, you know? And I would've if the cops hadn't've hauled us in. Shuntin' pigs! Can you believe those maggots?"

Hindin sighed and rested his hands upon his narrow hips. "No, Sir Röger, but I can believe you. Come. Let us have another look at that axe."

With the matter settled, the two men strolled around the building toward the square. As they did, the hulking Sheriff Edifice Teige emerged from his stairway.

"Still here?" he asked them.

"I wish to inquire about that axe," Hindin said. "My companion, Sir Röger, tried to loosen it earlier. Am I to understand that whoever can pull it may keep it?"

"That's right," the Sheriff replied with a grim frown. "An Animist Shaman once prophesied that whoever could steal it from the ghost and take it past the town border would end its bloody reign. But believe me, I've tried myself to yank it free. And even over the centuries, others have tried various ways of getting rid of it. Dynamite, theurgy, brute strength—none of it works. Neither the axe nor the stump can be destroyed. But if you and your friend can get it, I would be truly overjoyed, fact be known. The four of you must be very powerful to have earned that document."

There was something arrogant and condescending in the Sheriff's voice that Hindin did not like. But all the same, he bowed respectfully and made his way to the stump-platform. The Sheriff smiled brightly as he went about his business. But the smile melted to confusion when Hindin leapt onto the platform without so much as running start and landed as lightly as a butterfly.

Both Röger and the Sheriff inched up to the massive stump.

Firstl, Hindin examined the blade. Malruka pride themselves in their knowledge of metals and stone. No sooner had he knelt down and touched the side of the blade than his face

36

revealed a puzzled curiosity. He tapped the metal several times and let out an astonished "Hmm! This...this axe is made of hematite, or *blood iron* as some call it. It is quite common in all the huncells save Cloiherune. And here in Doflend it is most rare. This is all quite unnerving because, while it is a hard metal it is known for being extremely brittle. The fact that this blade has not shattered like a window yet is nothing short of miraculous."

He observed the angle in which the blade was embedded. He had earlier witnessed Röger trying to use upward leverage. Placing his hand on the end of the long handle, Hindin started to apply pressure with his palm. Pushing this way and that, he tried to sense a weakness, but found none. The long wooden haft showed no sign of bending. He then went over to study the axe head again. His face shown almost perfectly in its reflective sheen. The reflection seemed to convey a look of dread even though he himself felt none.

"Are you trying to scare me by making me think I'm afraid?" Hindin asked the axe in a soft whisper. The reflection's expression then changed to a gloating one. Hindin knew that he wasn't the one changing it.

"What other tricks do you know?" he asked the blade, daring it. The reflection became normal. Hindin then turned to face the Sheriff and Röger. "Gentlemen, I will stay with it."

"Stay with it? What do you mean?" Röger asked.

"I will stay and keep the axe under guard while Sir Röger, Will, and Polly gather information."

"Good luck with all that," snarked the Sheriff before walking away. "I have a letter to deliver. Good day to you all." He walked with a mindful gait, as he was nearly twice as tall and thrice as wide as everyone else. The thick chain-mail scarf he wore swayed as he walked. Strapped to his back was a gun the size of a small cannon.

Will stepped out of the saloon, pale and bothered, letting each boot drop lethargically onto the wooden steps. His eyes caught the departing Sheriff. He swallowed hard with a dry throat. On a happier day, he would chew the lawman's stony hide for sending him to get beaten up. But not after getting his nerves shot by a farmer's ghost and hearing a tale more chilling than any campfire yarn. His blue-gray eyes shifted to the stump platform. Lighting a cigarette, he slowly ambled over to it.

He did not notice Hindin and Röger looking at him as he surveyed the stump. After two dozen or so steps he had made a complete lap around it. As he examined the stump's giant roots, he grew more relaxed.

"Redwood," he declared, exhaling smoke. "Had to've been planted. Ain't no Redwoods in this Huncell. Ground ain't suitable to grow it either." He shambled up the steps, meeting eyes with Hindin. "Rev ol' buddy, I think we've met our match."

"I disagree," replied the malruka before turning to Röger. "Would you please fetch my duffel bag of books?"

"Yeah, yeah," the human answered, annoyed by the request. He turned and left the two of them.

Will was counting the rings on the massive platform. "This tree grew to be three thousand years 'r more. I hear tell it takes tens o' thousands to turn 'em into rock after they've died."

Hindin tapped his iron sandal on the stone surface. "Sir Röger said that it was planted by Myth Render, The Father of Fables."

"The Lord o' Legends, eh? Z'at so?" Will looked down again. "Well, maybe. This tree's been here longer than before the Huncells were brought together. An' it's said Myth Render could travel freely between 'em before that. That's all fine an' good. I could see how he could've taken a seed from my Huncell an' planted it here. Sure as death don't see *why*, though. What's yer take on it, Rev?"

"I do not know. I could formulate a dozen theories at this point. And that is too many to move forward with."

The tendikeye raised his eyebrows and chuckled. "Then we oughta narrow 'em down by talkin' to folk about this headsman spook."

"I will leave that to you, Polly, and Sir Röger. I have resolved to stay and watch over this haunted axe, for days if I must."

"You sure? Looks like an' awful mean-lookin' hacker. I'd bet it could do even a Malruka in with enough solid hits. Be careful. The old men in that saloon tol' me 'bout it. Executioners don't mess around."

38

Just then, Polly ambled over with Deputy Arteen by her side.

"You get yer money back?" Will asked her.

"Yes," she answered. "And dis deputy told me de Executioner legend on de way back." She looked up at the officer. "Are you *sure* dat de Headsman only kills murderers who have killed in dis town?"

"I'm pretty sure," the deputy replied, his eyes narrowing.

"Tank you den. You can go now." She waved him off like a queen would a handmaiden.

The man smiled and bowed, then took his leave.

She looked back to Will and Hindin. "Is dere any blood left on the axe head?" she asked, stepping forward.

"None that I can see," said Hindin.

She went up the steps, taking a deep breath. "Hmm. Maybe some..." She walked over to the half-embedded blade, knelt down, and gave it a slow lick with her tongue.

Will was struck by the strangeness of seeing Polly and her reflection licking each other.

Polly let the taste of the blade linger for a moment before saying "Not enough. De blade's surface is too polished to hold any blood."

Just then, Röger came running up, carrying Hindin's bag and a couple of long objects wrapped up in blankets. "Here you go, Hindin!" he called out, tossing the duffel bags of books as if it were a pillow up to Hindin.

"Thank you, kind sir," Hindin replied, catching it in his arms. Shifting his emerald gaze to all of them, he spoke "As I stated before, I will stay both day and night to watch over the haunted weapon. The three of you should seek answers that will nullify this mystery. Feel free to come to me and discuss any and every detail. I wish you all luck, and suggest that you stick together."

"You heard 'im!" Will proclaimed. But just he hopped off the old stump, his eye caught the sight of something by the axe, something not right. But when he turned and looked, nothing was there. His heart jumped to his throat, pounding like a kettledrum.

"Where do we go first?" Polly asked.

"Blacksmith," Röger answered. He looked at Will. "You okay, man?"

"Fine," the tendikeye replied, lying. "Let's git. But first, let me button my duster. It's colder'n a witch's teat out here. No offense, Miss Polly."

"None taken," she said, crossing her arms. "*It does not feel cold to me,*" she thought with a shrug.

Part 2

The three Excursionists rode up in their wagon to a building resembling a gray, two story tool shed. The sign out front read in big red letters: *Jimmy-Dan's Blacksmithee and Wagon Repair.*

"Might as well let 'im inspect our vehicle, too," Will suggested. "If we're gonna ride from town to town, we oughta make sure it's maintained."

"You got to be kidding!" Röger said. "This baby's still new! If anything, we need to find a stable to keep the bileers for the night. But first thing's first." He hopped out of the driver's seat and onto the gravel road. "One of you needs to stay with the wagon," he told Will and Polly.

"I will" said Polly, climbing up to replace Röger in the driver's seat.

"You sure?" Will asked her, trying to sound polite.

"Go," she said.

The tendikeye and human entered the smithee to see almost a dozen drakeri men sawing wood, hammering hot steel, measuring lumber, and a few standing around looking important.

One of the important-looking men came up to greet them. He was a stocky, middle-aged drakeri with chubby, pointed ears. "Cannah help yez?" he asked in a fat-cheeked voice.

"Yeah," Röger replied. "I need a sword made, a *billblade.*"

The stocky man grimaced. "This is a wagon shop, kid."

"I realize that, sir. That's why it should be no problem for you. Wagons are more complex than swords. I can give you a simple design to go by."

40

"It's not something we normally do," said the man. "A custom project with us isn't cheap."

"It will be cheap to *me,* old timer," Röger replied. He reached into his coin pouch, pulled three coins out, and dropped them on the table. They were shiny, new hundred grotz pieces. "There's just to get you started."

"It may take a week or so to get it done," the man warned as he picked up the coins.

"That's fine," Röger said with a shrug. "In the meantime, I'll work on getting a new axe. I got my eye on that one in the square, you know." He made sure he said it loud enough for the whole shop to hear.

And hear it they did. The work around them stopped. And Will and Röger felt their doubtful stares.

The hard-blinking, beady-eyed stare of the short, old one bothered them the most. "Yeah, we heard tell about you trying to pull it out," he chuckled.

Another man approached, looking younger. "The people of this town must bear the weight of their ancestors' sin. The headsman Jole Sarai only did his appointed duty. And for that, his neighbors let his little boy die. All he needed was a steed to carry him. But the relatives of those he had punished closed their doors on his face. Who are any of us to judge him now?"

"Fer a blacksmith, you speak an awful lot like a politician," Will told the man.

The man straightened his posture. "I'm the assistant supervisor," the man barked. "Ebwin Merquintech is my name. Who may I ask are you?"

"Will Foundling," the tendikeye replied with sarcastic joy. "Nice to meetcha!" Will paused a second to take in the man's growing contempt. "You see, you folks're in luck. We, that is, me an' my buddy here, are one halfa Four Winds-One Storm. We jus' got back from Embrenil, ye see. An' we had us an ol' fashioned witch hunt, saved the whole city, near as I can tell. So, savin' yer town seems a bit easy to us."

"Hey! I remember reading about that in the paper!" a man in the back called out. Slowly but surely, the other working men nodded while searching their memories.

"That's right," Will told them. "An' now we're here to free

41

ya'll of yer..." He paused and looked to Röger. "What's that cursed land word again?"

"Geohex," Röger whispered.

"GEOHEX!" Will proclaimed. "Ya see, You folks got a problem an' we're the solution."

"Are you wanting to perform an *inverse operation?*" the assistant supervisor asked, crossing his arms.

"A wut?" Will blurted. "Um, sure, I guess. If that means rid you of yer spook."

"It does."

"Well then, spread the word, Mr. Mertchinek."

"That's Merquintech, bukk."

A dark grin widened on Will's face. "Aw, now you can call me Will. I don't mind a bit."

The assistant supervisor was not used to being treated like an ass in front of his workers. "We get along just fine with the Headman's spirit watching over us. Our town doesn't need saving."

Will looked over at the laborers. "You agree with this guy?" The men responded by hanging their heads and remaining silent. That was answer enough for him. He shot his cold blue gaze back at the assistant supervisor. "By the time you fix up my buddy's weapon, we'll have yer ghost outta here. You can bet on that."

Merquintech scowled. "Well, we aren't going to fix anything. Take your money and go!" the man ordered, pointing at the entrance.

"Wait now, Ebwin," the stocky older man said. "Their money's good here." As he spoke his soft eyes hardened, and it was clear who was really in charge.

The younger man sneered and looked away. "Get back to work! All of you!"

The stocky man shook his head before looking at Röger. "So, a billblade is what you want, is it? Basically, a claymore with a hook on the end, right?"

Röger steepled his fingers. "Kind of. But it still needs a thrusting point. If you could give me a pencil and paper..."

The man showed Röger to a drafting table.

Will watched with interest as the human mapped out a complex diagram of the weapon. It included several sketches of all the parts in different angles, as well as specific instructions on how

42

to forge the blade itself. Everything was mapped out to the smallest detail.

The stocky drakeri man looked over the plans and nodded. "This'll help. You seem to know a lot about weapon smithing, sir."

Röger shrugged. "Naw, just *this* weapon in particular. I've had it lost or broken tons of times...just like my heart."

The stocky man chuckled. "You go through a lot of weapons, then?"

Röger grinned. "It's better than a lot of weapons going through *me*."

The stocky man's chuckle turned into a laugh. Will could not help but join in.

"I'll tell you what," offered the man in charge. "I can have it done in one week's time for seven hundred fifty. That will include your deposit."

"Deal!"

On the way out Röger chuckled nervously. "Will, I don't think that assistant supervisor liked you. I honestly think you rub some people the wrong way."

"Nonsense," the tendikeye replied, pulling out a cigarette. "Pissin' off someone who's in charge is the best way to make yerself known. I reckoned you knew that."

"No," the Röger replied. "I just do it for fun."

Thousands of feet above and around in all directions the half stone/half fleshy membrane huncell walls that encapsulated the realm darkened. Hundreds of hunveins loomed above in the geogranic ceiling of the huncell, like frozen streaks of lightning in the atmosphere. Directly above Wraith County was a particular hunvein known as *Crow's Foot* for its talon-like appearance. Although it was considered a poor hunvein to be born under, it shown bright enough to cast a helpful glow on haunted nights.

Will, Polly, and Röger had taken shelter at the local inn.

It was close to midnight as Hindin Revetz read his book entitled *Numerologyst Philocreeds*. Nearly every light was out in the surrounding town. The gusts of Autumn swept over his steel skin, chilling it colder than an assassin's blade. Even if he were flesh and blood, the icy breath of the changing season would not pester him. No minor discomfort could undermine the elation of learning something new. To Hindin, Algebraic Law held an appealing, if not curious view on life. He considered and meditated on this *tao of missing numbers replaced by letters* as the night worn on. And from his book he gleaned many things about Algebraists and their ways.

10=The Individual You
X=What is Missing from Your Life or What Should Not be in It
5=The Resulting Equation
10+X=5
X=-5

The moral is thus: Who you are and why you are where you are at in life can be measured by what you have not yet accomplished.

Feeling more entertained than enlightened, Hindin read through several of these numerical parables before finally acquiring a satisfactory epiphany. He looked up at the mighty axe embedded in the prehistoric stump and said, "Your 'missing number' was the respect of your fellow townsfolk, was it not? It was also the steed that they would not lend you. Why do you go on with the duty of which you were relieved? Why not surrender your fractured soul to the world and be reborn as a thousand different things? Are you as happy being a haunting avenger as you were a loving father? If not, Headsman, give up you horrific existence and let your death be concluded."

The axe made no sign of reply. Yet Hindin could feel an energy stirring.

"If you do not give up your duty, ghost. Then be informed that I will sit and wait to *obstruct* any and all justice you intend to deal out. Be it theft, murder, or high treason; I will never let you carry out your aberrant agenda."

The axe flickered, rising up and dropped down in the blink of an eye, a flash of malicious steel. Hindin, who had been sitting cross-legged while reading, quickly moved to one knee with his arm

44

extended upward. The thick book he had been reading had been clapped shut by his hand, catching the massive blade betwixt its pages before the axe gained sufficient momentum.

"I have you now," Hindin half-whispered.

He could feel the axehead trying to pull itself free. But his grip was secure. With his free hand, he grasped the handle. It did not feel like the axe had a mind of its own. It felt like someone was holding it. The malruka threw a fast kick down the length of the axe's haft. But to his dismay, his foot met with nothing but chilled air.

"So, it is a ghost," he thought. *"Not just an invisible person."*

He felt the various angles in which the weapon was being yanked and pulled. The entity holding the other end held fast. Hindin attempted many a twist and turn in an attempt to disarm the wielder. But it was not weight, strength, nor gravity that gripped the axe; it was a malevolent will.

The will tried to attack its steel-skinned captor, but Hindin could feel what it was attempting and ruined every try.

"You are a mere executioner," Hindin stated with a touch of sympathy. "You are accustomed to attacking the helpless and unready."

Now feeling assured of his hold on the weapon, Hindin attempted to run away with it ghost and all. He would try to run out from the town border, thus breaking the curse. But alas, the axe would not be pulled from the platform. Hindin could wrestle it with some effort, but it was clear he needed assistance.

"Help!" he called. "Help me! I have the axe!"

A long, exhausting minute passed before a small crowd emerged, many of them men still wearing their pajamas and carrying large sharp farm tools. Some had brought flintlock rifles, but soon saw the folly in bringing them. In little time, Sheriff Edifice had also arrived. The tall brute stood in awe and disbelief of what he saw.

"Help me, Sheriff!" Hindin shouted as the axe wriggled about wild and jerking.

For a grouping of seconds, the marble Sheriff hesitated. Then a blur of motion bounced off of his bulky shoulder. It was Will Foundling wearing nothing but his big boots and a pair of boxers. In

45

his hands he carried a length of thick rope. As the tendikeye landed on the platform, he lashed the rope around axe's long handle.

"That will not work!" Hindin told him.

"You don't even know what I'm gonna try!" Will shot back. He secured the knot tightly near the axehead.

"Toss it to me, Will!" shouted a voice from the crowd. It was Röger reaching out with his hands.

"'Kay!" Will answered, ready to throw the loose end to the Black Vest. But just as Will was about to throw the rope, he caught a glimpse of something out of the corner of his eye, something oddly not right. Slowly, he turned his gaze toward the axe's handle, ignoring Röger's pleas to throw the line. His blue-gray eyes blinked hard and his chest started to rise. A blood curdling scream erupted from his horrified face.

"Will! What is wrong?!" Hindin yelled as the axe broke free from his grapple.

Will kept screaming until his breath ran out. His throat tightened as the axe reared back to chop him down. But just before the swing finished it arc, Hindin tackled him. Both men rolled off the platform stump.

The axe floated toward them. Sheriff Edifice, seeing the opportunity, climbed onto the platform, trying to sneak up on the axe. But the sound of marble feet scraping petrified wood alerted the ghost's attention. The axe swung back around in a fast half circle, chopping hard into the thick mesh of the malruka's chain mail scarf.

"Ow! You piece of scrap!" he exclaimed, trying to grasp at the handle.

But then the axe spun at a dizzying speed. The Sheriff took a few cautious steps back. Then with an ear-piercing clang, the axe embedded itself into the chopping block once more.

Before the gathered crowd, the Sheriff roared in anger at the axe. "I hate you! *I Hate Yooou*!!!" He punched and slammed it with his boulder-sized fists. But the weapon showed no signs of budging or breaking.

Will still screamed like a madman, trying to slip free of Hindin's hold.

"Calm down, Will! Please, calm down!" his friend pleaded.

Polly, wearing nothing but a long red nightgown, wedged her way through the crowd. Kneeling beside Hindin and the wailing

46

tendikeye, she placed her fingertips on Will's neck. For a moment her eyes glowed red, then the tendikeye stopped screaming.

Just before Will passed out, he mumbled softly, "It was a little boy..."

It was the next morning after breakfast. The four comrades walked in silence through a nearby grove, waiting for Will to speak. At last, he stopped in a small clearing and addressed them. He looked as if he had not slept.

"It all started when that post-mort assassin cut me back in the city." He pulled up the sleeve of his snake-scale dust coat, revealing a faint scar on his wrist. "This is the only scar a blade ever left on me. I've been hit a time or two by swords that'll cleave a cow in half, and it never left more'n a scratch an' nasty bruise. The blade that did this was barely big enough to spread butter on account of some curse or charm laid on me before my parents found me on their doorstep. Fer years I never had a clue what kind o' theurgy it was that made me tough as a malruka, not until that assassin's blade cut me. The blade was metallic blue, *Vaughn,* also called charm-cutter steel or cobalt. It's the one thing that can lay open the hides of Lemuertians like nothin' else."

"I was hoping you'd let this go, Will," Röger said with a sigh. "I've met a few Lemuertian halfbreeds, and you don't fit the bill."

"Then why is it I can see ghosts, Rög?" Will paced about, crushing fallen leaves. "It's a fact that most Lemuertians are...What's that word, Rev?"

"Necro-Receptive," Hindin answered with sloping shoulders.

"Necro-Receptive!" Will parroted. "Bein' able to see the dead an' use necrotheurgy. How else could a tendikeye be able to use theurgy unless he was mishmashed?" He waited for a response from his friends. They all looked worried for him. "I ain't crazy," he said sighing.

"I think you jump to conclusions," Polly spoke. "I have tasted your blood, Will. You are all tendikeye."

47

"How you know that fer sure? You drink a lot a tendikeye blood in yer time?" Will asked, his eyes narrowing.

She crossed her arms in half-hidden shame. "I do not wish to say."

Will nodded and made a wicked grin. "Okay then." He looked back up at Hindin. "Rev, ain't you always tellin' me I enjoy killin' too much? Dudn't that sound like how a Lemuertian's mind works?"

Hindin shook his head, saying "Bullturd."

Everyone gaped in shock, for Hindin Revetz was not one to use profanity.

He continued: "You take too much pride in your ability to dispatch foes, but you are no sadist, dear friend. This excursion into this county has shattered your nerves and now your mind seeks reason when there is none to be found."

"I didn't get trained fer this, Rev!" Will blasted back. "I was cut out to hunt down bandits an' highwaymen! To track enemies through wild terrain! I was trained to be a Dasaru Bushwhacker, not some dang spook detective."

"What did the little boy look like?" Röger asked, his deep voice calm.

"*What*?!" the other three collectively blurted.

The silver helmed human looked at them all with a disciplining stare, ending with Will. "You said yesternight that the wielder of the axe, the *ghost* in the square, was a little boy. What did he look like?"

The tendikeye frowned as he rubbed his brow. "Drakeri. About nine, ten years old. Brown sweater, matchin' short pants. Loafer shoes."

"Did he look more than just dead, sick maybe?"

"Yeah."

Röger slapped his hands together so fast and loud, it startled everyone. "I knew it! It was the kid the whole time! Don't you all see? Jole Sarai died from grief and exhaustion. But it was his kid who died first. Just imagine. Your dad is the town executioner, then when he gets found out the whole town turns their back on you both. The kid probably felt excluded, but maybe he was also proud of his dad in some sick way. Knowing that his dad was the town death-dealer could have warped his mind. Then when he got a fever

48

and was dying, he was left alone, hoping that his dad would get home in time. Maybe, just maybe, the fever caused his mind to snap the rest of the way, right before he died! Think about it: betrayal, bloodshed, madness, and confusion. What more does it take to make a ghost?"

❖

A short time later in the Sheriff's basement office, Röger asked the Sheriff. "You believe us?"

"Of course I do," said Sheriff Teige as he rose from his desk. "It's the first report I've heard that makes any sense! But how can knowing it is the son and not the father help you, me, or the town, for that matter? Furthermore, how is it the tendikeye is able to see it?"

"We do not know, your honor," Hindin answered. "But the present import is cleansing this town. The ghost attacked me yesternight because I said I would obstruct it from its duty. Tell me, in the olden days, was it grounds for execution to keep an executioner from performing his task?"

"I believe so. Probably," answered the Sheriff, shrugging his huge shoulders. "I've only had the badge these last fifty-two years."

"How did that happen?" Röger asked. He had been secretly itching to know since they arrived. A hundred years ago, it had been a different sheriff he'd dealt with.

The immense marble man sat back down on his stone slab of a chair and frowned in thought. He crossed his arms, then uncrossed them. Then he finally spoke. "There is a large gang of miscreants in this county known as the Trotting Swans. Don't let the name fool you. These Drakeri are vicious. Purple is their color, not just their skin, mind you. It's what they wear, too. They ride around on velocipedes, most of the time to show off or look tough. They aren't hell raisers so much as organized criminals.

"One day, a group of three tried to come through this town hauling an entire wagon load of *gray dust* flowers bound for Embrenil. The sheriff at the time, a man called Farnuff, had known for years that they smuggled the drug. However, when they tried to

49

come through with so much, he'd had enough.

"He arrested the three men and destroyed the shipment in a bonfire, wagon and all. Then things turned for worse. Nine more Swans rode in with guns drawn. They killed the sheriff, freed their friends, and took the whole town hostage for two days. On top of that, seven more townsfolk, would-be heroes all, lost their lives.

"I was an Excursionist like you all back then, only a bit more down on my luck. I wandered here in the early morn, snuck around, and saw what was going on. Throughout the day I kept a safe distance, observing the positions of each of them. By nightfall, I made my move. I can't say I'm proud of sneaking up on and flattening a dozen men in cold blood. But it was the only way to save this town from more grief. The people here offered me the position of sheriff, and I, lacking a home and purpose, accepted.

"There are still plenty of Trotting Swans in this county. But they avoid this town. Their official statement was that the band that came here ceased to be members the second they butchered the sheriff. But that's a lie. They're in league with Count Slanidrac as 'reserve militia in times of war' and 'monster abatement brigade'. Lies, I tell you. Lies!"

Will scratched his chin. "How were *you* able to ambush that many outlaws? No offense, but you ain't built fer skulkin'."

The sheriff grinned, his garnet eyes twinkling. "It was stormy out. Whenever lightning flashed, I waited for thunder. That's when I would run and crush a man or two. I'm quite fast when I wish to be."

"What was the Count's reaction to you killing them and taking over the post?" Hindin asked.

The sheriff laughed in answer. "He said *Good Job*. I'm one of his favorite Sheriffs, or so he says. The Count is a hard guy to get to know."

"Is he a theurge of some kind?" asked Röger.

"Nope. Makes lying a whole lot easier since he has no theurgic philocreed to swear by."

"What about de axe?" Polly asked, turning everyone's head. "De axe kills anyone who commits murder in dis town. Why did it not slay de bandits?"

"That's...a very good question, Miss Gone. Heh...funny name you got...no offense intended, of course."

50

Polly relaxed every muscle in her pretty face, waiting for the marble man's answer.

"I honestly don't know," he said, wondering what she was thinking.

"And de axe has never attacked you?" she asked. "For killing all dose men in *cold blood* as you say."

"Not since yesternight," he answered, rubbing the end of his steel scarf between his fingers. "And it only attacked me because he provoked it." He made a gesture toward Hindin. "Not that I'm complaining about it. No one has ever pissed off the ghost enough to make it fight. I was impressed."

"Thank you," Hindin replied, with a courteous nod. "But I doubt I am able to repeat the result. The ghost needs some other form of coaxing." The steel-skinned man turned his head to Will.

"What?" grunted the tendikeye. "If yer thinkin' what I know yer thinkin' then you best be thinkin' somethin' else!"

Hindin smiled with mock sympathy down at his dear friend.

"Don't you give me that look, Rev! I *know* that look! That's the 'Sorry-Will-but-I-gotta-make-you-do-it' look! Well, go munch onna donkey chip, alla y'all! That's one round o' fresh donkey chips fer everybody...on me! I ain't dealin' with no more spooks!"

It was late evening. The team gathered to stand on the ancient stump. Everyone in town was there—man, woman, and child. A committee of protestors had also assembled to express their disapproval of the heroes and whatever they were up to. Others who were less zealous were there just to witness what might happen.

"Leave it alone!" a man yelled.

"You are only causing trouble!" a distraught woman cried.

"It's a part of our heritage!" another man shouted. Will recognized him as Ebwin Mertchinek, that assistant supervisor.

The committee was passing around petitions, urging everyone to sign an agreement to ban the team.

The Sheriff was wading through the crowd, expressing his disapproval. "The law doesn't work like this, everyone! They have a

51

right to research any case in the country. Stop passing around those papers!"

"What is your plan, deary?" an elderly woman asked Polly from below the platform.

The red clad girl replied only with a look of doubt.

The four heroes exchanged glances followed by nods. With a few fluid steps, Hindin leapt atop the handle of the cursed axe, perching like a long limbed bird. He needed only to raise a hand to silence the impressed crowd.

"Thank you," he began. "Sum Total of Drowsy Nook, for a disproportionate excess of years, you have allowed your fates to be calculated by an integer that has fallen on the left side of Zero. Your ghost is a negative number used to resolve your most critical equations."

"Who are you to interpret Algebraic Law?" an old man challenged.

"I am Hindin Angledar Revetz, Chimancer and Hatchling of the Sacred Flame. Master of my own fate and of those I name Enemy! I and my companions are here to perform the inverse operation of bringing the ghost to Zero, thus allowing its soul to shatter and dissipate naturally. To do this, we must–"

"Add a positive number to it?" the assistant supervisor said. "We already do that, Mr. Revetz. Every year, on the anniversary of his death, we sacrifice a living bileer on that very platform to appease the headsman's spirit in recompense for the steed he was denied in life!"

"I hate to break this to y'all," Will started, "but the ghost ain't the headsman. It was his son! The one who died of a fever!"

The people gasped at the tendikeye's words. Some of them looked angry and offended and called him a liar.

One man who seemed to believe the tendikeye raised his hand to make a suggestion. "If it's the boy, then maybe we should pour medicine on the stump instead of bileer blood!"

He was answered by many removed hats being slapped against his head.

"Enough!" Sheriff Edifice shouted like a temple bell. "Everyone is to return to their homes where they can be safe. The Excursionists and I have made a deal. If the axe is not removed by tomorrow morning, they will leave and never return."

"It won't work, whatever your plan is!" the assistant supervisor yelled before taking his leave.

"We wish you all the best o' luck, sonny!" cheered an old man carrying a gnarled walking stick. Will recognized him as one of the geezers from the Cudgel Law Saloon.

Will gave him a casual salute. "Thank you, sir. Tell the boys at the saloon I said howdy."

Polly was startled by a tapping on her ankle. She looked down to see the adoring face of Deputy Arteen.

"Me and the other officers are going to stick around. You know, in case things get difficult."

His smile made her smile. "Tank you, Officer," she said. "We may have need of you."

Röger knelt, trying to get the attention of a big busted Drakeri woman. "Hey, can I get a kiss for good luck?" He was ignored.

The older deputy who had escorted the team in to town, a man whose name was Kellyr, rode up to Hindin on his bileer. "Nice speech, son. It was almost convincing. But even if the ghost truly is a negative integer, how could you possibly determine what the positive number could be to neutralize the equation?"

"Addition was never my plan, sir," the malruka replied, hoping off the axe's handle. "I intend to solve this through multiplicational means. Does not your philocreed state that *The product of two negative numbers will always be a positive number?*"

The older deputy gaped slightly in confusion.

"Two birds. One stone," the malruka translated.

Before Hindin divulged the plan to the Sheriff and his three officers, he first made it a point to acknowledge with much gratitude Polly's contribution to the plan, which made her blush from embarrassment. He revealed his strategy to them behind the police station building, out of view from the stump.

"This is crazy," Deputy Spane said, keeping his voice low.

"So was considered every new idea before it was tried," Hindin returned. "Now everyone, give me your money pouches."

They did so, some with a few remarks of suspicion.

Hindin looked at the eight coin bags and then at Deputy Arteen. "Are you certain that this will suffice?"

"Should," the man replied. "This much money gathered together..."

"Good," Hindin replied. "Sir Röger, is the wagon ready?"

"Should be by the time I get there."

"Are you sure it is in the right place?" Hindin asked, already annoyed by the human's lax attitude.

Röger hesitated, displaying his uncertainty for all to see.

Hindin sighed in frustration. "Polly, go with him. Please, make sure."

The human brute and the girl in red took off on foot down the dark street.

Hindin looked at Will, who was growing pale. "Are you ready?"

"No," Will replied. "You don't know what it's like to look a ghost in the eye."

Hindin placed a cold friendly hand on the tendikeye's shoulder. "Enlighten me after this is over."

Will let out a nervous laugh and spat into the dirt. "My quills're gonna turn white after this." Without hesitation, he climbed the backside of the building. His large hands were accustomed to scaling steep, rocky hills or any variety of tree. But this cubic atrocity of hewn stone bricks forced him to make a more repetitive and less natural climbing procedure.

By the time he was atop the highest spire, clad in night and snake hide, he whistled with flawless pitch that he was ready. Seeing the stump-platform below, he focused his sharp eyes on the shape of the headsman's axe. It reminded him of an abandoned plow sticking out of parched soil. His heart pulsed in his quill-tipped ears.

He saw a tall, dark figure approach the axe. He knew it was only Hindin tying the eight money pouches to the axe in some clever tangle of a knot, yet the sight still tested his nerves. Tip-toeing away like a child laying a prankish trap, Hindin was soon out of sight.

Now it was time to wait. That was one thing Will was sure he

54

could excel in. He remembered how his old teacher used to make him sit and watch incense burn out, viewing the orange cherry of heat slowly make its way down the stick, not uttering a word to pass the time. Patience is not a virtue for the Dasaru Bushwhacker, it is a necessity. He slowly drew his two barreled, U-shaped pistol from the holster on his hip, his Mark Twain Special. He could feel the farewell caress of the leather through the polished steel barrels. Calm fell over him like a familiar blanket. And he waited, silent and still as the shingles he sat upon.

Time passed like a wide lazy river. There was no hurry, no sign of flow or passage. There was only a singular moment stretched as far as it needed to go. Patience was about to pay off big.

It flew down upon the small bags of coins like a small, dark hunting bird. In tenacious haste it pulled and yanked at the pouches, until in a flash of desperation, it wrapped itself around the handle of the cursed axe! Will's eyes widened, half in fear, half in hope. Then with a sudden tug, the tiny apparition broke the axe blade's hold from the long-dead tree stump. In no time, it started to carry the massive weapon down the street.

Will raised his gun and fired a shot in the air. With terror, he watched the ghost of a disembodied hand floating, carrying away the axe and money.

That terror doubled when he saw another ghost rise up out of the stump. It was the boy, just as Will remembered him. The child walked in a sickly gait toward the ghost hand, his face twisted in a furious scream, a silent scream that Will could only hear in his own heart. The hand floated away faster with its prize, leading the slow boy in a chase down the street.

"Come on, boys!" Will cried to the men below. His green-scaled duster flapped wildly as he jumped to the ground.

"The axe came loose and floated away!" Hindin shouted. "Was it the ghost hand?"

"Yep. But the kid's on its tail! We gotta beat it to the punch! Git a move on!" Will ran with the speed of a caffeinated squirrel.

The three mounted officers followed him at full dash. Hindin and the Sheriff trailed behind, not realizing that the ghost of the headsman's son was running alongside them.

Will ran, propelled by fear and well-honed vigor, his footfalls making no sound and the dust under his boots barely disturbed. The floating axe and the smoke-like hand that carried it came into his view. A few breaths later, so too did the team's wagon. He could see Röger's helmed head peeking from around the front.

"It's about time!" called out Röger. "We've been waiting over an hour!" The brute jumped out of the coachman's seat and dashed toward the floating axe.

The spectral hand, with its cunning limited to pilfering, sensed the two men coming at it from both sides. It was the hand of a cowardly thief, not a warrior. Dropping the money laden axe to the ground, it fled into the nearby house it recognized as its home.

Will was the first to get to the prone weapon. He scooped it up as he ran to the wagon. He glanced back, seeing the officers close behind. Behind them was the cursed spirit of the child, its face blazing with desperate rage.

Hindin and the Sheriff's heavy stamping treads could be heard but not seen in the blackness of night.

"Rög!" the tendikeye called. "Get that wagon movin'!"

Röger turned to dash back to the wagon, but Polly had also heard Will's order, seated in the shotgun seat waiting. Snatching the reins and whipping them, she let out a banshee cry "YAH!" spooking the team of bileers to move. They took off, pulling the wagon like it was a bullet from a gun.

Röger sprinted to catch up and leapt into the back. He turned, looking back at Will. Holding his hands out, he yelled "Toss me the axe!"

The tendikeye was worried that the weight of the money pouches would ruin his aim. Quickly unsheathing his machete, he sliced through the tangle of straps. The pouches fell free to the dirt, jingling and spilling with square grotz coins. In a blink he sheathed his blade, still running like a madman. Gripping the axe handle with both hands, Will began to run sideways. Swinging the axe like it was an oversized golf club, he let it loose to flip and fall safely into Röger's hands.

"Got it!" Röger yelled in triumph.

The mounted officers then caught up to the dashing wagon.

"How far is the border?" Röger yelled to them.

"About a half mile!" old Deputy Kellyr answered, looking terrified and thrilled all at once.

Will was beginning to wear down. He was so scared of being

56

chased by and chasing after ghosts that he had forgotten to breathe. He felt an icy presence behind him. He knew what it was, and refused to look back. A surge of adrenaline raised his waning pace.

"*Nevah look back when eluding the enemy!*" his teacher's voice echoed in his mind. "*No mattah what hits your back--be it blade, bullet, or spell! Only a fool acknowledges despair while he yet draws breath!*"

Will hated that a child had sown such fear in him. He hated this new flavor of terror, this *necrofear* that his race was so weak against. He hated feeling helpless. He had trained that feeling away, he had thought. He found no answer as his legs and lungs started to burn.

Still, he ran. He could see the wagon fading far into the night. Still, he ran. His mind flashed with blank light as the ghost of the boy ran through him. Still, he ran.

He could see the boy leaving him far behind and gaining on the wagon. Dizziness started to overtake him. He stumbled and slowed, ready to fall and surrender to unconsciousness. Then he felt a lithe, cold arm wrap around his waist and lift him off his weary legs.

"I have you, my friend." Hindin told him. He and the Sheriff were still treading at their same pace.

"Where is it?" the Sheriff asked. "Do you still see the ghost?"

Will pointed up the road. "It's still...chasin' 'em." His head pounded. His stomach churned.

The Sheriff looked forward as he ran, his garnet eyes blazing with wild hope. "They're gonna make it!" he cried. "We're gonna break the curse!" In his bounding excitement, he did not notice that his chainmail scarf had fallen off.

Röger ran to the front of the wagon. Polly was whipping the reins in fury.

"Okay", he told her. "I got the axe! Now let me drive."

"Never!" she shouted. The thrill of running from something invisible excited the young lass beyond her own reckoning.

But lurking in the back of the wagon was a new passenger. The obsessed spirit of the executioner's son was now on board. Propelled by hatred, vengeance, and a twisted sense of duty, he crept up to the human who sat in the shotgun seat.

Röger felt a pair of cold chills pierce through his torso. Something tried to grasp at the axe he held.

"Oh, waste!" he squealed. "It's here!" He caught a glimpse of Deputy Arteen riding alongside them."Catch!" Röger yelled.

"What?" the deputy yelled back as the brute tossed the giant hacking tool at him. Arteen made a sudden grimace of shock and panic as the axe flew at him. He tried to catch it with a free hand, but the angle was wrong, and it landed in the dirt.

"Stop!" Röger told Polly.

And she did.

They were now on the outskirts of town, surrounded by dark fields and crooked trees. The ghost, not governed by the laws of momentum, leapt off the wagon easily and ran to its prized possession.

Deputy Spane was also headed for it. He hopped off his steed and made a mad dash, unaware of the ghost.

"The ghost is gonna git it first!" Will yelled.

The deputy's hands were a few feet away from the axe. The ghost's were mere inches away.

Then came the loud report of a cannon. The axe was blasted into the air in an explosion of dirt and rock. Both the deputy and the ghost turned see the Sheriff not ninety feet away, his oversized pistol smoking in his boulder-sized hand.

"Good shot, brother!" Hindin told the sheriff, running alongside.

"I'm impressed," Will agreed as he was still being carried under Hindin's arm.

The axe landed with its blade sinking into a nearby elm tree. The ghost tried to make for it, but old Deputy Kellyr rode by, snatching it out. The ghost ran at him.

"Toss it!" Will yelled. "I see him comin' at ya!"

The old man obeyed, tossing it to Deputy Spane. By the time the ghost could get to him, Will, Hindin, and the Sheriff had arrived.

"Toss ME the axe!" Hindin called, dropping Will on his face.

58

The deputy complied and threw the heavy axe as hard as he could.

Hindin had to make a diving attempt, but he caught it.

"Now, it's comin' fer you, Rev!" Will called, keeping his eye on the frustrated specter.

"The town border is just at the end of this road!" Sheriff Edifice cried.

"Can you do the honors, Sheriff?" Hindin asked, tossing him the axe.

The hulking brute grinned wickedly as he caught it by the handle. In his enormous hand it looked like a mere hatchet. With all his might, he swung his mighty arm and let the cursed weapon fly. Will watched in heartbreaking terror as the boy leapt in vain to retrieve his instrument of death. As the axe spun through the air and out of sight, the boy fell to his knees and covered his face, defeated and ashamed. *"Like a mean game o' keep-away,"* Will thought.

Röger and Polly had leapt off the wagon and joined them. "Did it work?" the human asked.

Everyone looked to Will, who lay still on his belly watching what everyone else could not see. He saw boy now weeping, bawling and sobbing in haunting silence. Will now felt a different form of helplessness. He suddenly wanted to comfort the child, but didn't know how.

"Will?" Hindin asked. "What it is it? What do you see?"

He told them, and the Sheriff laughed. "He's a sore loser!" The huge malruka looked where the tendikeye was looking. "That's right, brat! Your reign is over! I'm in charge now! I am justice!"

Will saw the boy stop crying. The ghost stood and looked at the Sheriff with contempt in its dead eyes. It then looked over at Will and pointed at the marble lawman. The boy's pale lips mouthed a word over and over again. Will's eyes were trained to read lips. It was part of being a good bushwhacker.

"Guilty?" the tendikeye asked as he got up off the ground. "What's he guilty of?"

The ghost glowed in response to the spoken word. Through some miraculous manifestation everyone there could see him now and the light he shown.

The three officers were the first to notice what the boy was

59

pointing at. It did not take long for the others to notice, either. Upon the Sheriff's thick marble neck was a notch nearly two inches thick and six inches deep. Such a notch could only have been made by a large, thick blade.

Deputy Arteen looked to his sheriff of half a century. "You started wearing that scarf shortly after becoming Sheriff. Have you been hiding that notch all this time? Why?"

"It attacked you as you slept, didn't it?" Deputy Kellyr said, his eyes narrowing.

The Sheriff covered his neck and backed away. "Wait," he said. "You seen the axe attack these excursionists yesternight. They never murdered anyone here. And neither did I. The only men I ever killed were those Trotting Swans! That *has* to be why the boy chopped me as I slept!"

"But you kept that wound secret for fifty years, Edifice!" Deputy Spane said. "Why?"

"I killed a highwayman two years ago," Deputy Arteen said. "The ghost didn't kill me for that. It only slew the guilty."

Röger stepped up. "You must admit, Sheriff Ed; you coming here just in time to be a big hero...?" He let the question hang.

"How did you know dey would be dere dat day?" Polly asked, her cold stare discerning.

The Sheriff, dumbfounded, looked to Hindin for support. The shorter malruka peered up at him. "What part did you play before this, Edifice? I pray that one of *our* number has not gone against the sacred teachings. Explain yourself."

The Sheriff dropped his one-shot pistol to the ground. "The truth," he started, his voice low and grave. "I have nothing to gain by telling it." He looked at the men he had been commanding for five decades. "I just wanted a place to settle down, you know? What better way to gain the respect of a town than enter as a hero? It was time for a change. A rook had to replace a knight. Old Sheriff Farnuff had to die."

He looked at Hindin with mad desperation. "You can understand, right, little brother? You understand why I would let it happen for two more days? The worse things got, the better I could make them. Besides, these fleshlings needed a stronger leader. The old sheriff just wasn't cutting it. He had to be sacrificed. None of this was my plan. That's all the truth you're gonna get, little

60

brother."

Hindin Revetz adjusted his stance. "You are no brother of mine, Edifice."

Now everyone, including the Sheriff, stood ready for anything.

Deputy Spane was the first to draw his shot gun. "You're under arrest!" he shouted, the words furious and bitter.

The two other officers drew their weapons, as well.

"Surrender, Edifice." Deputy Kellyr ordered. "Tell us everything. Confess and explain this whole ruse, and your punishment will be less severe."

"You heard him, dirt-baby!" Will yelled, backing away a safer distance while drawing his pistol and blade. "Fess up an' come clean! What else are ya hidin'?"

Edifice scowled at them all. "You think your guns are a threat to me? Me?" His dark red eyes sparkled with malice as they shifted to each man aiming a gun at him. At first, his huge shoulders drooped as if relaxed and submissive. Every gunman, including Will, relaxed their trigger fingers in turn. Then in a burst of explosive rage, the man-shaped mountain of marble charged at them all. Edifice managed to advance two whole strides before a small white handled dagger flew into his left eye, wedging itself between the garnet gem and the marble socket. The stone behemoth hissed in pain and anger.

Everyone looked where the dagger had come from. Polly stood the furthest away. In her eyes was a cold serenity. In her hand was a stone from the road. She was smiling. "I tink dis road could use some marble gravel, don't you, boys?"

Edifice wailed in hate and charged into their midst. Three shotgun blasts sprayed dozens of lead pellets, blasting away at his surface.

Will fired several ten millimeter rounds into his legs. Hindin struck him with a series of undulating palm strikes. The hulking malruka ignored the shower of lead and slammed his fist into the torso of Deputy Spane. The Drakeri was killed instantly and flew limp and lifeless into a nearby field. Hindin threw a high kick at the Sheriff's chest, but it was blocked by an armored forearm. Edifice's

61

head turned to face Hindin. Polly seized her opportunity, and threw the stone she had been holding. The stone struck the handle of the blade she had thrown into his eye socket, popping both the knife and the garnet eye out.

Edifice roared like a madman. "You little fleshling bitch! I'll kill you!" He knocked Hindin to the ground, then grabbed Will by the leg.

Will quickly felt his head and arm being grasped by the malruka's other stony hand. He was about to be pulled apart. Then he heard a loud thud followed by an ear-splitting crack. The hand that clutched his arm and head fell to pieces before his eyes. For a split second, he saw Röger holding his own fist. All four knuckles were bleeding. Then Will felt himself being flung like a rag doll into a nearby tree stump. His head bounced against it so hard, that when he fell to the ground unconscious, nearly every autumn leaf fell loose upon him.

The two mounted officers kept a safe distance. Arteen road up to Polly, offering his hand. "Hop on!" he offered.

"No. My place is wit' my team."

Röger felt that all the bones in his hand were broken. But the pain of feeling them heal and reset themselves was bad enough. He felt a familiar feeling buzzing in the back of his skull. He was about to transform! Then a sudden uppercut from the Sheriff's rocky stump sent him flying high into the night. There was a loud crash in the nearby wagon. The axles snapped like twigs. The canvas cover had caved in. Röger lay motionless upon the broken heap.

The raging powerhouse swung his mighty limbs at Hindin, laughing with pain and madness. "You think you'll be a better hero if you kill me? Is that it? Ha! Who will lead them after you're done? You think they are wise enough to govern themselves? They've let a shunting ghost deal justice to them for three thousand years! Their moral values are based on numerical equations! This whole county-!"

Edifices words were cut short. Hindin had spent enough time defending to analyze the Sheriff's attack pattern. The Chimancer's arms turned into a blur of complex parries and chops. Edifice tried to block with his armored forearms, but Hindin grasped them, swinging himself under the massive appendages, and shot his steel heels into the powerhouse's legs. The thick marble thighs and knees had already been fractured by Will's bullets. Hindin's explosive kicks sundered them to pieces. The hulking villain fell down onto his foe. Hindin was pinned beneath him.

"You squirmy little bastard!" Edifice yelled, gripping Hindin's throat with the only hand he had left. "Die!" he yelled. Then the corrupt lawman felt something long and hard get wedged into the deep notch in his neck.

Polly had picked up Deputy Spane's shotgun, her hands held it like a great lever sticking out of the malruka's old wound. Edifice looked up at her with his one good eye. Then with all her might Polly pushed against her makeshift tool. The Sheriff's mouth opened to say something, but no words came out. A thin crack had traveled the rest of the way through his neck. His heavy, iron plated head fell off his shoulders. His face, frozen in a state of fear and surprise, landed in the dirt of the old road.

Hindin came out from beneath the torso of the broken corpse. He, Polly, and the two remaining officers saw the ghost of the boy once more. The child's face was tranquil now, still sad, but at peace. He waved at them in that shy way little boy's wave. Hindin nodded back.

Polly looked at him with confused sympathy. The two deputies removed their kepi hats. The image shattered into a thousand glittering shards that blew away in a thousand different directions.

Will and Röger awoke from their battered states to see that the victory was won. Thus ended the Legend of the Steedless Headsman of Drowsy Nook.

The rest of the night and the day after brought uneasy minds and heavy hearts. The curse of the town had been lifted, but at an unfathomable cost. A deputy had been slain, leaving behind a throng of family and friends. The venerated Sheriff had been exposed as a fraud, and was now dead, unable to answer a town full of questions. For some of the locals it was all too much, and they refused to believe anything Deputy Kellyr and Arteen had to say.

The new heroes in town were not celebrated or rewarded. The town was simply too distraught to express gratitude. For the most part, the locals treated the heroes with modest respect. Many stood in awe and wariness of the large human that now carried the Headsman's axe on his shoulder. That was reward enough as far as Röger was concerned.

Hindin took it upon himself to bury the remains of Edifice Teige. He kept a large piece of the torso, however, to be fashioned into a heroic monument for Deputy Spane. Polly kept the garnet eyes, claim their deep red color gave them theurgical value.

Polly and Drume Arteen stood under a tall pine where no one could see them.

"Congratulations for becoming de new sheriff," she said, tucking a short lock of hair behind her ear.

"I only got it because Kellyr didn't want the job," the handsome deputy said with a sad laugh. He looked on past a field of dead grass at the town he was now responsible for. "Change hurts," he said with a sigh. "Even when it's a change for the better. We are going to have to elect a judge now. For so long, we didn't need one. Lawyers are going to come here, too. One form of corruption has been destroyed making room for a different one."

"Only if you let it," the young woman assured.

Sheriff Arteen kissed her as if it were as natural as breathing. It was a momentary embrace of lips, dry but sweet, brief but welcoming. "Say you'll meet me at the county fair," he told her. "Would you give me that promise?"

"If you see me dere," she answered with tender eyes. She took his hand, squeezed it, and then left him there beneath the boughs of evergreen.

◇

The wagon was in the wagon shop being repaired. It would be a while before it was again ready for travel.

The Four Winds met at the edge of town. All sat upon their bileers save Hindin and Will, who had paid a stableman to watch over the other two beasts.

Polly regarded Sir Röger, who sat tall and proud atop his steed. The gleaming axe of the deceased executioner was strapped to his back.

"So," she started, "you got what you always wanted, Sir Röger. You managed to convince us to aid you in your unfinished business. Wit' out even filling us in first on your past attempt, no less. After a near century, your noble quest is over."

The big man shrugged. "Noble quests are for fat heads with something to prove. This just needed to be taken care of."

Her wry smile shifted into a mild sneer. "Why did you not tell us you had been here before and failed? You have no personal stake here. None of us do. I will admit dat dere is some personal satisfaction in helping people and denying corrupt men deir tomorrows. But how is dis whole county being haunted any of our business?"

Röger's eyes smiled through his helm, then shifted to Will and Hindin. "She makes an interesting point, fellas. None of us have family here. None of us were born or raised here. And even if we could manage to break the Geohex, I doubt any of us would want to settle here."

"Same as everywhere else," Will said. He pressed a nostril shut and blew snot out onto the ground. "Ain't like any of us got a home or family to worry about. 'Least fer the moment, anyway."

Hindin spoke. "Polly, please, bear in mind: While your company is welcome, know that you are not obligated to put yourself in harm's way. I understand that you are only with us to better escape your mother's grasp. I also understand that your *philocreed* does not dictate the performance of good deeds to your fellow sentient beings. You have the soul of an assassin. It is who you are and what you do. But, at this point in time, your path is empty. There is no one to kill, no blood to shed. You are young and without purpose. That is why you are so frustrated."

Will raised his chin. "An' believe me, Pol. I know the feelin'. Bein' an Excursionist ain't muchuva picnic, but it's really all folks like us got. We got no home or family to protect. But we can protect the homes an' families of others 'til we find a purpose all our own."

"Yeah, Polly-pop," Röger rumbled. "I've tried to settle down and keep my blades clean. My curse won't let me do that. So, when I

65

see that an entire county is cursed, I think, maybe I should do something about that."

Will nodded. "Makes sense to me."

"And me," Hindin added. He watched Polly's face still struggling with doubt. "It is not a simple fact that we have nothing better to do. Boredom is not our motivation."

"Den what *is* my motivation?" she asked.

The tall steel man spread his hands. "I have no idea. However, inaction will never lead you to the answer."

She smiled. "Even if I sit and meditate for hours like you? Is dat not inaction?"

Hindin returned the smile. "You have little to meditate *on,* young one. Through action comes experience which will provide memories by which you may base all future speculations. And as you speculate on why your life has gone the way it has, your own tao will become clearer to you."

"So, quit yer bitchin' an' let's high-tail it!" Will added.

Polly turned her head and tried to glare at the tendikeye. But the face he was making was too comical. Instead she laughed. "Fine den. We meet back here in ten days?"

"That's the plan." Röger replied. "We have a lot of ground to cover and information to collect. The wagon should be repaired by then. Investigating towns separately will also draw less attention." He took a deep breath. "Plus, I'm sure we all could use some alone-time after being cooped up in that wagon for so long."

"Here here!" Will agreed, anticipation flickering in his eyes. "We each get our own town to turn stones in fer a whole week."

"It will be a good opportunity to learn more about ghosts," said Hindin. "This town only had two. Many townsfolk informed me that the other towns have more. Be careful, everyone. We do not want to add more ghosts here than when we arrived." The malruka smiled and glanced about them all.

For the space of a few seconds, no one responded.

Hindin frowned and added "By adding more ghosts, I mean us getting killed here."

Will rolled his eyes. "Yeah, we got it the first time, Rev."

Chapter 3
The Slayer Who Ran

Part 1

The town of Barnhart was made up mostly of narrow, winding back roads sparsely strewn with small ordinary houses. Its main road showcased a junk swapper's marketplace and a town crypt built into a rocky hillside. It, like the last town, seemed as if it were sleeping. Or more like sleepwalking.

Polly rode most of the day, steering the steed's antlers this way and that, looking for an inn to stay at. She instead came upon a small milk and coffee stand at the edge of the marketplace. There, a mother and her two young boys were being served by a kind-faced old man.

The two boys, seeing the great steed that Polly rode, immediately tried to run up and pet it.

"Look at the bileer, momma!"

"Can we pet it?" the younger child asked its mother.

The mother pinched the boy's jackets, holding them back. "Not so close," she told them. "Let the young lady dismount and then ask her nicely."

Polly had hated her own childhood and thus despised children. She hid it well, though as she slid off the side of her steed.

"Can we pet your bileer, please?" the older boy asked.

Polly nodded in response as she hitched the animal to a post. "His name is Waltre."

"What breed is it?" the mother asked, smiling.

The young girl cleared her throat as she approached the stand. "Tremiun Auburn, I am told. But I sense that de dealer lied or was unsure. Dere may be a hint of Paldife in its bloodline."

Behind a counter full of pitchers and cups the man smiled at

Polly. "What'll it be?"

Polly raised her chin. "Tea, if you have it."

"We have coffee and we have milk."

"Both, den. Wit' cane sugar, please."

"You seem to know a lot about bileers," the mother said, eying the animal. "Are you from Chume?"

"Raised dere," Polly answered, trying to avoid eye contact.

The mother smiled with a huge-toothed grin. "I could tell by your accent. My brother goes there on business every ten years or so."

"Oh?" Polly asked, taking the steaming clay mug being served to her.

"Mmm hmm," the mother continued, shifting her attention to her boys. "He's a spice merchant. He's the one who keeps the town spiced up, you could say."

Polly turned to look at the commuting passersby. They were all dreary folk pushing prams about on dusty gray gravel. Nothing about them looked remotely spicy to her. She winced at the taste of the coffee. "You should have your brother pick up some tea de next time he journs."

"That'll be two grotz for the drink, miss," the operator told her, his face now not so kind. "If you want tea, you should go to her brother's dry goods store over on Cash Street. He also gets tea from Chume, I think."

"Actually," Polly started. "My business here extends beyond tea or coffee. I am in need of an inn."

"The inn closed for good years ago," replied the operator. "Ever since the coal mine closed down. There's a...place...you could stay, though. It's between here and Pevulaneum."

"Are you suggesting that whorehouse, Willy?" the mother said, her voice edged and scathing. "Tricks and Treats? How dare you suggest that place to this young lady."

The man shrugged his narrow shoulders. "It's the only place that charges by the night, or the hour."

"Nonsense!" the woman exclaimed, shaking her finger at the old man as if she were his mother. "I'm disappointed in you, Willy!" She then turned to Polly, extending her hand. "My name is Fritz Gladish. My husband's the local leather smith."

"Polly Gone," Polly replied awkwardly, taking the woman's

68

hand. "I am an Excursionist investigating de hauntings in dis county."

The woman's smiling face shifted to an expression of concern. "How old are you, dear?"

"Eighteen."

"My, but you are still so young. I see no weapons on you. Are you a theurge?"

Polly took a slow deep breath. Reaching up the one long sleeve of her garment, she produced a small, white-handled dagger. "I am skilled in ways dat make me safe." She then slid the dagger back.

The woman showed no certainty that she knew what the girl meant by her words or gesture. Still, Fritz Gladish gave Polly the impression that she either wanted to help, or at the very least, keep an eye on this new girl in town. "My husband and I own an old stable house. It has a room packed full of old junk. I can have him and my boys clear it out."

"Dere is no need-" Polly started, trying to sound modest.

"Yes, there is," Fritz said, her tone firm. "I've been looking for an excuse to get them to do it."

The woman's house was only a few minutes away.

Polly soon found that Fritz Gladish wore the pants in the family. Her husband, Fulton, came off as dangerous, yet quiet man. He was very tall and thick-limbed compared to his pear-shaped wife. He barely looked at Polly as Fritz explained to him that the girl would be staying a few days.

"I have money," Polly told them. "I can compensate you." She was about to reach into her pouch when Fritz stopped her.

"Don't worry about it," the woman told her. She then turned to her husband. "Think you and the boys can have it cleaned by supper?"

The man nodded. "Boys!" he yelled sudden and loud. "You got work to do!"

The two children came when called with looks of mild

resentment.

As the three males worked outside, the two women remained in the kitchen, fixing supper. Polly was given vegetables to chop as Fritz tended the stove.

"They're going be hungry, Miss Gone," the woman said, urging her to work faster.

Polly's knife work became a blur as she diced an onion into hundreds of pieces. "I am told dat dere is a ghost story in every town in Wraith County. What is de story here?"

"After supper," Fritz replied.

The father and his sons came in long after the meal was prepared. After washing up and eating, the boys were sent to bed. Fulton and Fritz talked as she cleared off the table.

"All clean then, is it?" Fritz asked her husband.

He nodded as he lit his pipe. "Clean enough. Added most of it to the brush pile. Should burn just fine."

"You didn't throw my mother's old papasan to the pile, did you?" she asked, pausing from her work.

The man exhaled slow and hard. "Did we need it?" he asked. "It was too big for the living room."

Fritz frowned. "What else is the poor girl going to sleep on, you idiot?"

The man chuckled out a cloud of smoke. "Yes, dear, I left it in there." He looked over at Polly. "I also stabled your steed. Fine animal you have there, miss."

"Tank you," said Polly as she pinched a hidden tattoo on her forearm under the table. The man made her nervous.

When the table had been cleared, Fritz at last sat down. "Now," she said with a sigh. "why are you so concerned about the ghosts here?"

At first, Polly wanted to say *because my friends are.* But that was not true. She was, in fact, growing very curious about it. "I am part of a band of Excursionists called Four Winds-One Storm. We have decided to investigate de entire county in hopes of breaking de Geohex. So far, we have already expelled de Headsman ghost in Drowsy Nook. My teammate, Röger Yamus, now carries the Headsman's axe as a trophy. So we are scouting de towns in search of other hauntings."

The man and wife looked at each other for a moment. Then

70

Fritz addressed their guest. "My husband is a member of the Trotting Swans. Have you heard of them?"

Polly's eyes widened. "Yes. De Sheriff of Drowsy Nook told us of his...encounter wit' dem."

"Those were ex-members," Fulton said, pointing at her with a big finger..

"Of course," Polly returned, growing more nervous and trying to hide it.

"Don't believe everything that malruka tells you," Fulton said. "We Swans are a brotherhood dedicated to preserving the welfare of this county. We all have families to protect and oaths to keep. We alone are responsible for monster abatement between the town borders. We even have a Lemuertian head mounted in a member's house. Excursionists are not needed here."

"What about de ghosts?" Polly asked.

"What about them?" he replied with a shrug. "Every necrotheurge who has tried to control them and every Animist Shaman who has tried to exorcise them has gone mad or died."

"Well, I am neither," Polly told him, her expression darkening. "No one on my team is a spirit theurge. But three days after our arrival, we were able to solve the mystery and expel de ghost."

"Is that so?" the man said with a laugh. "And how did the good Sheriff Edifice take to that?"

His words aside, there was something in Fulton's voice that irritated Polly, something she could not quite comprehend. "He was overjoyed," she said.

"Oh, I bet he was!" The man lipped his pipe, grinning like a maniac. "Now he can deal what *he* calls justice in his town without that axe bothering him." He cackled bitter while shaking his head.

Polly decided to reveal no more. Instead, she smiled along with him. "*He can find out I killed Edifice Teige on his own,*" she thought. "*I'll bet de news will get here by tomorrow. By den, I'll be somewhere else.*" She could not help but smile.

Just then, five hard knocks sounded from the front door.

"It's for me," Fulton said as he rose up. He walked briskly out of the room.

Polly could hear him opening the front door.

"Hey, boys.," Fulton's voice greeted.

"You're not gonna believe this waste," another man's voice told him.

Then Polly heard the door close.

Polly looked across the table at Fritz. She had a good idea of what was being talked about outside. Both of them did, Polly could tell.

After a few tense moments, the front door opened again. In came Fulton and two other rough-looking men who wore purple scarves and jeans. They looked at the visiting girl with curiosity.

"Honey," Fulton started, addressing his wife. "Me and my friend are going for a ride." He paused, glancing at Polly. "I think I've earned it for cleaning out a space for our guest."

"I don't care," Fritz answered with a shrug.

Fulton smiled at his wife, then at Polly. Touching his right ear with his left hand, he bowed to her. The two men behind him did the same. It was an odd, yet obvious show of respect.

She nodded back, not knowing what else to do. The men took their leave.

Fritz looked at Polly with growing concern. "About our local ghost legends," she started. "Do you still wish to know about them?"

"Please," Polly returned.

"Well then. Until last week, Barnhart only had two to speak of. Now it has three. The oldest is the dueling skeletons. About two thousand years ago, two young men quarreled over the hand of a young lady. They had a traditional duel using pistols. But both men died. And now, night after night, you can witness their duel reenacted by their bones. It's quite a show the first time you see it. But it gets old if you're local.

"The second haunting concerns the old coal mine. That was how this town got started, you see? Five centuries ago, they used canaries to tell if the air was poisonous or not. The birds are very sensitive to cave fumes. Well, one day, low and behold, the mine was suddenly lit up by the glowing ghosts of thousands of canaries who'd perished over the years. These ghost birds weren't the sweet, delicate pets they were in life, no. These were evil, vengeful spirits that swarmed the miners and frightened them out of the mine. It's been closed ever since."

The woman paused at the sound of velocipede bells and skidding wheels coming from outside. She let out a short laugh that

72

ended in a sigh. "Must be an emergency meeting," she assumed out loud. "He'll probably be gone all night."

"*I hope so,*" Polly thought. "What about de third haunting?" she asked. "De recent one."

"Oh yes, well, you can ask my sister-in-law about that one. She was found last week on Trokday morning, sleeping in the cemetery. She said that she was visiting the grave of Remus Kach, an old family friend who was hanged for murder these ten years past. She was taking one of her little midnight strolls and decided to swing by to pay her respects. Well, wouldn't you know it! Just as she came within sight of the grave, she saw the visage of Remus looking down at his own grave marker! And poor Resula, that's her name by the way, she was so shocked that she passed out from fright. Ever since that encounter, she and my brother Mark are convinced that Remus' spirit has remained intact because he was wrongly convicted."

"What kind of murder was it?" Polly asked.

"The man, well, the victim was stabbed to death. Juniper Beech, I think his name was. It happened over by Town Hall on Main Street. There were only a few witnesses, but all were of honest repute."

Polly nodded, taking it all in. She swallowed. "Dere is someting dat I did not say earlier. The Sheriff, Edifice Teige. He is dead. We discovered dat he somehow knew dat de raid on de Drowsy Nook would happen. He basically admitted dat he waited for de bikers to devastate de town before moving in to save it. He tried to kill us to maintain his secret or at least escape. But…"

"You killed him?" the woman blurted with worry growing in her eyes.

"Yes. But on my philocreed, you have noting to fear. De other deputies were present when he confessed…what little he confessed."

"So, you *are* a mystic." Fritz said, drawling the words. "What is your path? Pyrotheurgy? Geotheurgy?"

Polly shook her head. "De less you know, de better off you will be, Mrs. Gladish."

"The same goes to you, dear." Fritz said, a chill edge in her tone. "Feel free to poke your pretty nose into any ghost business you want. And I'm sure my husband and his friends appreciate you

73

ridding our humble county of that corrupt official. But mind you, the Trotting Swans run things here."

"Dat seems evident, ma'am," the girl replied with a cautious bow. Polly felt she should be acting timid toward this woman, and she was indeed nervous. But deep down Polly felt challenged by her own curiosity. *"Who is dis bitch to tell me what to do?"*

After Fritz showed her where she would be lodging, Polly waited until night grew its darkest. When she was sure everyone in the house was asleep, she crept outside the stable house with her dagger in hand. Dipping the keen point into the center of her palm, a dark pool of crimson welled in her hand. She then whispered words that even if they were heard would not be understood by anyone but a Crimson Theurge.

"Immunoglobulin-anguis. De Red River is de moat dat protects my temple." The little pool of blood took the shape of a tiny snake that looked up at her in docile obedience.

"Go," she ordered it as she knelt down and let it slither into the grass.

The liquid serpent began to trace its way around stable house, leaving a thin trail of red. By the time it had made its way back around, it was the size of a grub worm. The snake all but disappeared when it finally touched the beginning of its trail.

Polly smiled as she went back inside. Two months ago, she would have had to walk around the entire structure and waste a lot more precious blood to make a decent protection circle. Her power was augmenting. But power such as hers could not come without sacrifice. She would have to kill again eventually. Blood would have to spill. Blood must flow. *"And ghosts do not bleed,"* she thought as she climbed into bed. As she tucked herself in, a part of her heart wished that Fulton Gladish would try to step over the red line outside her door.

Polly awoke before dawn and put her boots on. She reached into her rucksack and pulled out a pen, a vial of ink, and parchment. Not wanting to waste too much, she folded and ripped the long

74

rectangular strand from the hempen paper. She kept the note short and sweet.

Mrs. and Mr. Gladish,
I believe you have given me plenty to work with. Thank you for dinner and boarding.

-Polly Gone

She left the note in the center of the bowl-shaped bed she had slept in and walked out the door. The light of dawn grew softly from all around the Huncell. The cool country breeze was sweet and refreshing. She turned to retrieve her steed, but a startling sight caught her eye. The corpse of a red-tailed squirrel lay sprawled across the border of the red circle she had made yesternight. The red line was now nearly gone, cleansed by the morning dew.

"Waste!" she cursed aloud in a tight whisper. The protection circle was created to render trespassers unconscious and alert her when it was disturbed. The squirrel was not big enough trip the theurgical alarm, and the booby trap must have put it into cardiac arrest. The energy must have been too strong for so small a creature.

"Waste!" she exclaimed again. There was a fair amount of guilt, to be sure. But a wave of intense paranoia flooded her mind. *"What if dey tink I killed it on purpose?"* she thought. *"How would dey know? De woman knew I was a mystic. Maybe she'll tink it was a curse."* Then an awful notion came to her mind.

Slowly, she sneaked around the stable house. Her fears were answered. Along that same faint red line, she found a calico cat, a ribbon snake, a rabbit, and a small box turtle. Her bottom lip quivered as she picked them up like a sad little girl picking up her ruined stuffed animals after leaving them outside too long. With shaking hands she crammed them all (including the squirrel) into her rucksack.

She made one more paranoid glance at the Gladish homestead before hopping on her steed and riding off. She kept riding for awhile, not knowing where she was going. She reached a piece of road where she could see no houses. She took off her rucksack and dug through it. The animals were already beginning to go stiff. With disgust, she began to fling them one by one into a

75

wooded area. *"I wonder if dis cat had been a pet of the Gladish's,"* she thought as she tossed it to the thick brush.

When all were tossed, she sighed atop her antlered steed. *"Even though my power is growing, I do not have complete control of it. Mother, as sinister as she is, never killed anyting by accident. It was always for some sick purpose."* Polly could hear her mother's voice laughing inside her head. *"Focus, my petite! Focus from de pit of your lady-pocket!"*

She winced from the memory, and her stomach churned from morning hunger. She gave her steed a kick with her heel, and trotted down the road. She soon came to the old junk market from the day before. After deciding to ride past it this time, she arrived at a rural commercial intersection. The stone street markers on the corners read: Cash and Main.

The police station was nothing more than a drab one story brick building. The post office was a small white shack with two bileers hitched out front. The blacksmith had his shop door open as he banged away on a new shovel head. A sign on a tin roofed building read *Mark's Dry Goods and Feed*. The largest building which was made of large logs had its windows and doors boarded up. The old sign on it read in flaking paint *Barnhart Coalmine Home Office*.

A trail of smoke reached upward from a diner called *The Windmill*. Polly found herself being led there by her nose. The smell of raspberry pancakes and agave syrup was in the air with traces of sizzling swine fat and onion-laced omelets. When she entered the establishment, every wall was decorated with paintings of butterflies. She was seated by a rotund human woman with kind, bloodshot eyes hugged by thick old eyelids.

"Would you like to hear the special, miss?" the woman asked.

"No need," Polly replied. "Just fix me a plate wit' a little bit of everything. Please."

The woman smiled, nodded once, and left. Polly's attention shifted to one of the butterfly paintings, not out of interest for the folk art, but to avoid eye contact with any fellow customers. As she waited, the outside irises in her triple-irised eyes noticed the old men, some human, some Drakeri, chatting away over coffee and lit pipes of rank tobacco. The old Drakeri were telling the old humans how hard it was being a coal miner compared to being a farmer. She listened to their boring conversations for fifteen minutes while staring directly at a painted swarm of monarch butterflies in a field of bright green, a scene not to be found in this cold, rolling land teeming with dark evergreens.

"*It is bad and good dat I am alone now,*" she thought to herself as she pinched the tattoo on her forearm. "*Wit' my friends elsewhere I am now harder to find but easier to catch. 'Elusiveness is our armor,' Mother used to say.*"

When she finally got her food, she looked up at the red-eyed woman. They were unpleasant eyes to look at, as if the woman spent more time crying through them than seeing anything worthwhile. They were the kind of eyes where the whites had been yellowed with/from age and worry. Polly wanted so badly to touch them, and not just to alleviate possible vision problems. She could not stand the sight of them. It bothered her knowing that such eyes existed.

"Tank you," Polly said as the woman set the plate down.

The waitress smiled. "I can tell that you are new to town, dear. You should know that it is our custom to pay *as* you are being served. The charge is eight grotz."

"Certainly," Polly replied, reaching into her coin pouch. She pinched out nine grotz coins, took the waitress' wrist, and dumped the handful of coins into her fat palm.

"*Hebweath Cved Jey Hele,*" *Polly* spoke, her accent thickening as she clenched the woman's hand.

The old woman's eyes began to water and sting. She started rubbing them with her chubby, pale forearm. "What did that mean?" she asked, wincing away the irritation.

"It means *Dat which is beautiful, behold.* It is a blessing where I come from, Chume."

The waitress brought her arm down, revealing clear eyes with white and blue in bold contrast. "Oh, isn't that...nice. Well, enjoy your breakfast."

Polly enjoyed her breakfast with the joy of knowing those ugly eyes would never disturb her again. And as she ate, she decided where to go first once she had finished.

Mark's Dry Goods and Feed store was different than a city grocery store. Instead of finely lacquered shelves stocked with dainty paper packages and small glass jars, there were row upon row of barrels and rough spun sacks, all loaded with various grains, oats, and coffee. She noticed a display of assorted tea and smiled— *swanslobe, hawklash, and toadlip,* they were all teas from Chume, the only things she missed from living there. She decided to purchase a bit of each.

"Excuse me. Excuse me?" she called, looking around for help.

"Yes, miss?" a youth answered, appearing from behind a pyramid of barrels. He wore a white button-up shirt with a black vest and a white apron tied around his narrow waist. He smiled bright, exposing an overbite that displayed slightly more gum than tooth. "Can I help you with something?" he asked in a husky voice bigger than his narrow frame.

"Yes," she replied, pointing at the tea display. "I would like some of dis Chumish tea. One ounce of each."

"Okay," he answered, with a jerking nod. He opened a small box near the barrels of tea leaves and pulled out three sheets of waxed paper. "So, are you from there?" he asked, scooping the tea with a measuring spoon. "Chume, I mean. I-I noticed you had an accent. Are you from there, I mean?"

She raised an eyebrow, wondering if the boy was nervous or just touched in the head. "Yes," she answered, now looking at him directly.

He looked only a tad younger than her. He was a thin, slender-faced Drakeri with dopey bright gold eyes. "We also have feed for your bileer," he told her as he folded the paper into packets for the tea.

"You watched me ride up?" she asked, looking at him with curious accusation.

"W-Well, yeah. I noticed you." He rotated the packets in his hands.

Polly noticed that they were good hands for a shop boy to have. She could hear the poor boy's heart starting to race. She could not help herself. She could see the boy was jittery. Usually she was

78

the one who was uneasy around people, due to her general distrust of anyone. In the few seconds she spent watching him grow more tense and bashful, she relished the secret pride kindled within her. She had power over him.

"Den it shows dat you are very attentive," she declared with a smile that shattered the boy's reason. "You watched me from de moment I arrived, waiting to offer your assistance. Tank you, sir."

The boy looked confused, but somewhat relieved. "Oh, sure. You're welcome." He handed her the packets, holding back a grin. "So, do you want oats? Not for you, I mean. For your animal. Unless you like oats, too."

"I will also have a bag of oats," she replied in a queenly fashion.

She watched with hidden glee as the boy stumbled to a barrel of oats. Using a large tin scoop, he shoveled thousands of light brown flakes into a small burlap sack. When he was done, he tied the sack shut with a piece of twine. "Anything else?" he asked like a happy puppy.

"Dere is one more ting," she sighed in a drowsy, seductive voice.

The boy leaned forward, eagerly awaiting whatever she might say.

"Tell me all dat you know about Remus Kach. And de Spinsers who own dis shop."

The boy's eyes widened. "I'm Izzyk Spinser," he said. "My parents own this place. My dad's not here right now, though." His eyes narrowed. "Why? I mean, why do you want to know about Remus?"

Seeing that he was caught off guard, she chilled her tone and went straight in with more direct questioning. "You use only his first name. Did you know him?" She took a step forward.

"Yeah, when I was little." He took a step back.

"He was close to your family, no? How close?" She took a step forward.

"Him and my dad were best friends...since they were kids." He took step back.

"Do *you* tink he was a murderer? Dat he was rightfully executed?" She took a step forward.

"No." He took a step back.

79

"No dat he did not kill anyone? Or no dat he was rightfully hanged? Dat is how you kill your killers, no? String dem up and make dem dance wit' noting to dance on?" She took three steps forward.

"Why are you asking me this?" he asked, taking four and a half steps back before tripping over a sack of grain. His back slammed loudly against the wooden floor planks. Dazed and looking up, he saw that the strange pretty girl was kneeling beside him.

"Hello, Izzyk. My name is Polly Gone. I am here to study de ghost legends of your town. I am part of an Excursionist group dat is investigating de Geohex."

He gazed up into her lavender face. "Are you...Did you undo the curse of Drowsy Nook?"

"Mmm," she replied with a nod.

"That was you? The other customers have been talking about it all morning."

"Do you need help up?" She offered a hand.

He nodded and took her hand. It was small compared to his, but strong and smooth. But before Izzyk had time to fully enjoy the sensation, he was yanked to his feet.

"Thanks," he replied, wondering what to say next.

"Did you hurt yourself?"

"Uh, no. You sure are pushy, though."

"Sometimes I have to be," Polly laughed.

"Well, not with me. Haven't you ever...I mean...Never mind."

"Ever what?" she asked, prying.

The boy took a deep breath and squared his shoulders. "What, I mean, what do you care about Barnhart? I mean, are any of you from here or near here? Why do you care about the Geohex?"

"I don't, really. I am curious."

"Curiosity killed the cat."

"I found dat out dis morning," she said with a guilty titter.

His dopey eyes grew puzzled. Then he noticed other customers coming in. "I can answer your questions later if you want. My folks can, too. We all think that Remus was innocent. And it doesn't surprise my dad that his spirit isn't at peace. Would you like to come to our house for supper tonight?"

80

"I would and I will."

She was indeed curious, and she could not help but wonder how her friends were fairing. Were they simply gathering info like her? Or were they actually trying to solve cases on their own? She figured Hindin was smart enough to solve a case without help. The tendikeye was stubborn and cunning and lucky enough to try. And even Röger seemed to know more than he let on.

She had a dreadful thought that her three male companions would lift the curses of the towns they were exploring. And they would all feel the need to go to Barnhart and lend a helping hand to the little lady who had merely found a few clues there, saying things like "good job" and "that-a-girl" to congratulate her on being so useful.

"*No shunting way!*" she thought as she left the store. "*If dey tink I need deir help wit' dis, den dey are surely daft!*"

It was a ten day week, and Polly had eight and a half to prove that she was no man's helper.

Polly later found that Izzyk's parents were far less timid than he was. They invited her into their home with sincere courtesy, both taking turns shaking her hand. Mark Spinser was a balding, mustached man of proud bearing. Resula, his wife, was a colorfully dressed woman with her long black hair bound in a loose ponytail who seemed laid back and easygoing. The table and house had a simple country elegance. The dining room had a large window that overlooked an outside garden now littered with fallen leaves. The table was set with hot pots, small baskets of bread, and fine china with real silver cutlery. They warmly invited her to sit and joined her around the table.

Polly was admiring the quality of her plate when Mark Spinser placed a folded newspaper on top of it. The headline read *Excursionists Break the Headsman's Curse and Expose Police Corruption.* The article went into great detail about Polly and her companion's recent exploits in Drowsy Nook. She glanced up at Mark Spinser who had settled into the chair across from her.

81

"Normally," the man started, clearing his throat, "if a young girl such as yourself came here claiming to be a legit investigator, I would find it hard to take you seriously. Morbid curiosity has brought many an excursionist and tourist to this county. They all desire to see ghosts and witness the curses of the Geohex. All have failed or gotten more than they bargained for, until now." He gestured to the newspaper. "You are part of this excursionist band, this Four Winds-One Storm?"

She nodded. The smell of the bread was making her mouth water.

"In that case, I'm relieved to have you join us." The man took a deep breath.

Polly could sense his blood pumping irregularly through his head and neck. "*He is composing his emotions. Sloppily,*" she noticed.

Mark adjusted his glasses. "Remus Kach was like a brother to me. We shared every secret and dream. We both grew up here in Barnhart. Both our fathers worked at the coalmine. He was the kind who was rarely serious, but always reliable. He even helped me build this house when Resula and I became engaged. This house and a grave are all that's left of him now.

"Only ten years ago, nearly to the day, I was stocking my shop late into the night. I heard a commotion outside. A mob had formed. Torches, pitchforks, shotguns, you name it. They were hunting someone. When I asked who, they said they were going to Remus' house, that he killed old Juniper Beech by the town hall. I went with them, if only to calm them down and keep them from hurting my friend. But the house was empty when we arrived."

Resula, his wife, began pouring tea for everyone. Polly thanked her with a smile. The hostess smiled back and turned a sad look at her husband.

The man took a sip from his cup and continued. "He was found the next morning, hiding in the woods. The case never went to trial. He wouldn't say anything at the hearing, nothing. The judge asked if he was guilty or not. No response. The judge asked if he understood the consequences of not defending himself. Remus looked him dead in the eye and nodded once. Just once!" The man fought back tears as his voice cracked.

"*He does not want to cry in front of his son,*" Polly thought.

82

"And dat bread smells really good!"

Mark continued. "That was the most anyone ever got out of him before he was hanged. A lot of people swore they saw shame in his eyes. But I knew better. Remus Kach was as good a man as there ever was."

Polly sipped at her tea, thinking it was the polite thing to do before asking "Do you have any suspicions on why he willingly went to his death?"

"A few. One in particular. I'm not sure you'd want to be involved."

"I made de journey here, did I not?"

The man shrugged. "Okay, then. He may have been involved with the wrong people. Drug-runners. There's a special flower that only grows in these hills. The flower is called the *Gray Dust Poppy*. It is not actually a member of the poppy family. It's just called that for its opiate-like effect. It's how the local biker gang makes their extra pocket money. I should know."

Polly recalled Fulton Gladish, this man's brother-in-law. "How would you know?" she asked, seeming coy.

The man held his tongue at first. His face showed embarrassment and shame. "My sister's husband is a member. He once tried to enlist me. I go to a lot of different places to get my goods for the store. As far as Chume, sometimes. He wanted me to transport the drug in my caravan."

Polly nodded. "Why do you tink your friend was involved?" she asked, not wanting to stay on the subject of Chume for too long.

The man shook his head and sighed. "Remus was a user. It was his only vice. He took the drug to escape his loneliness, I suppose. He never met the right girl, a fact that always bothered him."

Polly took another sip from her cup and set it down fast but gently. She really wanted to tear into the bread before her, but it might seem a tad impolite. "Is it possible dat he was addicted? And dat he owed de bikers money?"

"Maybe. But I would have lent it to him. I'm sure he would have known that."

Polly glanced around the room as the details of the story swam in her head. Then her eyes settled on Resula. "What about you?" she asked the woman.

"Me?" Resula said, startled.

Polly sat up in her chair, making herself look taller. "De story I have heard tells dat you have seen Remus' pnuema, his ghost. Please, tell me about it."

"What do you want to know?"

"Everyting."

The woman furrowed her brow in thought and laced her fingers together, resting her hands on the table. "I like to go for walks sometimes. A lot of people in town know me and like to stop me for conversation. But the reason I walk is to keep in shape, not chat. That's why I walk at night, when everyone's asleep." She let out an embarrassed chuckle. "I bet that if I got to walk as much as an excursionist, I'd have a body more like yours."

Polly smiled at first, but then nodded for the woman to continue.

Resula took a gulp from her cup and let out a sigh. "Something...told me to pay Remus a visit that night, his grave I mean. Mark and I had visited it enough times. So I knew my way around the markers. It was a bright night. The sky was clear so all the hunveins could be seen, not a single cloud." She took her head and shuddered at the memory. "I saw him standing there, what, I'd say twenty yards before I got there. I couldn't believe it. But with every step I took I began to. It was Remus." Her lips began to quiver and tears fell without warning from her eyes. She wiped at them with the heels of her palms. "When he turned to look at me, he was crying. It was definitely him." She sniffed with wet nostrils as her husband reached for her hand. She took it and squeezed. "The next thing I remember, I was surrounded by people and it was morning. I'd passed out and they had found me there. I must have blacked out from the fright, shock ...*necrofear*. I don't know. I have never passed out a day in my life. Just ask my husband."

Without hesitation Polly turned to Mark. "Has she ever passed out before?'

The man began to shake his head, but then stopped himself and smiled. "Only when she drinks."

The couple shared a sweet, short-lived laugh, then fell into a grim silence.

Polly frowned, not knowing what else to ask. She glanced around the room and her eye caught something. She was amazed that she had not seen it before: an upright piano. A tall stack of papers were on the bench. "May I play your piano?" she asked, her eyes growing wide as she studied it.

The husband and wife exchanged a confused look. "Um, sure," Mark said. "Izzyk, take those papers off the bench."

"Yes sir," replied the boy. He went over to the awkward stack of various parchments. He had to bend over and hug them to pick them up. But as he straightened up to lift them, they spilled out of his arms and unto the floor. "S-Sorry!" he stammered. He aimed the apology more at Polly than his parents.

Many different things had spilled onto the floor. Among them was an old gray photograph of an almost handsome Drakeri man. Polly picked it up and looked at the couple. "Dis is him? Remus?" she asked, a smile curving on her lips.

They nodded. Then Mark and Resula Spinser sensed a sudden, subtle change in the girl who was visiting them. She seemed more relaxed, yet more intense; distracted, yet focused. Their hearts quickened, and the air in the room seemed heavier.

Polly sat down on the bench with delicate poise. She set the photograph in the place where sheet music would be and looked at the picture like a mother adoring a sleeping babe as her fingers pressed against the row of keys. A smooth melody chimed from within the large wooden box. With deft maneuvers, her right hand rolled on the notes of a bright, warm tune with a simple but wholesome melody. She stared at the image of Remus Kach as if the music was written upon his face. She played the progression slow and sad, adding subtle variations here and there.

"So, you tink he may have been framed?" she asked the couple as she played.

"I think so," Mark's voice answered from behind.

"And you tink he let himself be framed?"

"Yes. Maybe."

Polly began to rock and sway to the music. "Yet he wasn't at his house when de mob first went to find him." The warm melody grew colder. She still played slow, but struck the keys harder, as if jabbing out of spite. "Funny. Did he avoid de possible death from the mob just to let de law do it instead? Dat is so strange."

"Of course it's strange," Mark said, his voice growing tight. "He never gave an explanation."

85

Polly closed her eyes and lost herself in the music. Something hatched inside her mind like a serpent from an egg. It was a side of her she had kept hidden. Her slender waist shifted about like a snake, her round backside grinding against the surface of the bench. Izzyk's jaw dropped at the sight. Polly's mouth opened into a wide, toothy grin aimed upwards. "Or maybe his conscience reawakened when he was caught. And de only ting dat eased it was to die."

"Then why is he a ghost?" Resula asked with confused frustration.

The volume of the tune shrunk to an ivory whisper. Polly gasped in ecstasy and laughed like a wicked young queen. Her head spun in a quarter turn, casting a one-eyed stare at the startled couple. "Would you two please not sit so close to each other? One of you is not telling me everyting. Your hearts are too close together for me to tell which is which!"

"What?!" Mark replied, straightening in his chair.

Polly's smile turned into a wild grimace. Her fingers pecked out a minor shuffle as she writhed in her seat. "Which is which? Witch is witch! Switch is switch!" she said, cackling. Her eyes illuminated with red light as she laughed at her host and hostess with maniacal glee, her fingers dancing out fiendish rhythms and bold discord all the while.

Resula gripped her husband's hand in terror. He gripped back. Izzyk felt teenage lust mingle with primal fear. Polly could hear their hearts pumping along with the tune she played.

That was when Fritz Gladish, her husband Fulton, and their two sons walked in. "Who is playing that?" the short woman asked as she entered the room. Her eyes stopped on Polly.

The music ended. Polly froze like a cat caught clawing the curtains. Her eyes glanced from the piano to Fritz Gladish to the bread on the table and then back to Fritz.

"You," Fritz droned with sudden apprehension. "Hello, Polly. How are you?" Her eyes softened, but her lips pursed.

Fulton straightened his massive shoulders. His large watery eyes seemed to clear as he looked at her. His face made a studious glower, then raised into a dark grin.

"You know her?" Resula asked Fritz in heavy breath.

Fritz placed her hands on her wide hips. "I gave her a place

86

to stay yesternight. She left without so much as a goodbye."

"I left a note," Polly said in her defense. Her attitude shifted back to passive.

The room grew tense. Everyone glanced at everyone else until Fritz broke the silence.

"Oh, I understand, Polly," the woman said with sudden warmth. She looked at Mark and Relusa. "I told her about you two yesternight. I'm glad she decided to contact you." She looked at Polly again, smiling. "So, what have you found out so far, Miss Gone? Any leads?" There was condescending accusation in her words. As if she thought Polly was no longer trustworthy.

Polly felt like shrinking as she turned around on the bench. All eyes were upon her, pinning her in place. She felt as if *she* was the one being investigated. But as she spoke in answer, her sense of purpose returned. "My methods of inquiry may seem strange," she explained softly, shifting her gaze back to everyone. "But I am not here for social reasons. I am here to find out de cause of de Geohex. Dat's all. And if my teammates and I have to turn over every tombstone to find out why de dead aren't dissipating, we will."

Mark stood up from the table, planting is palm on the surface. "You said something about my wife and I keeping something from you. What did you mean by that?"

Polly took a thoughtful breath before answering. "If I explain my methods, Mr. Spinser, den dere would be no point in using dem. I was studying you and your wife. But we were interrupted." She tilted her head toward Fritz.

"That does not answer my question!" Mark growled impatiently.

Polly raised her chin. "Either you or your wife are not telling me everyting."

Fritz cast a demanding look at her husband. "Agave, take the boys outside."

The big man frowned, but nodded in reply. He placed his hands on the boys' shoulders and ushered them out. As he left, he cast a menacing glace at Polly.

She returned it. "*Try me*," she thought.

Mark Spinser rubbed his face with both hands before asking "What more do you need to know? Do you think we're lying?"

"No. Just excluding. It eases de nerves so much more dan a

lie."

Resula crossed her arms and sneered. "Speaking of *nerve*, you sure have a lot of it."

Polly crossed her arms and legs, mocking the woman. "What about de murder victim your friend was accused of killing, Juniper Beech? Neither of you were inclined to speak about him. Did you know him?"

Mark shook his head. "He came by the shop like everyone else in town. He had a wife and daughter."

"But they moved to Copse dur Crakktun a year after he died," Resula added.

Polly nodded and narrowed her eyes. "And was any reason given why Remus would stab dis man to death?"

They shook their heads.

Polly breathed an uneasy sigh as she looked at the couple. It was clear to her now that she was getting on their bad side. "I'm sorry if I've offended you, any of you. You invited me over for dinner to ask questions, not disturb you."

"You just take your job very seriously, that's all," Izzyk said with a hopeful smile. He looked to his parents. "Mom, Dad, she's just doing her job. I mean, we have nothing to hide. I mean, maybe it's a part of her job to be suspicious of every little thing. Like a detective."

"Or maybe it's just how she naturally is," Fritz added with spiteful sweetness.

Polly smiled up at her and thought "*Now I do hope dat was your cat I killed!*" She stood up with impeccable posture and elegant poise. "I must be off. Would any of you mind directing me to de graveyard? I wish to see dis ghost myself."

Everyone hesitated but Izzyk. "I can take you!" he exclaimed, raising his hand as if in a classroom.

"Absolutely not!" Resula protested. She cast a sour look at Polly. "I don't trust you, young lady. Why did you act so crazy just now at our piano? Are you some kind of Sonic Alchemist?"

"I have often wished to be," Polly said with a shrug of one shoulder. "But, alas, it is not so. I do not trust you, either, Madam Spinser. Nor anyone I've met in dis town. If I did, dat would make me a bad detective, no?"

Resula did not answer. She only scowled.

Polly tilted her head toward Izzyk. "As for your son, I tink he would make a sufficient guide." She then looked at Fritz. "After all, he could keep an eye on me for all of you while I roam your town."

Resula and Fritz frowned at each other. There was begrudged, agreement in their eyes.

"Fine," Resula muttered.

"Yes!" Izzyk said.

Without another word, Polly snatched a dinner roll off the table and walked out.

Izzyk grabbed his coat and followed.

Once outside the front door, the two of them passed Fulton and his sons playing beneath a willow tree.

The large man told his boys to stay and approached Polly on long brisk legs. "Ms. Gone. A word, if you would?" he asked, moving in close enough to grab her.

"I would," she answered, not backing down.

The man's face peered down at her as a tiger studies prey. "Ms. Gone, we of the Trotting Swans are grateful for the valor of you and your crew. Edifice Teige had it coming to him. However, there is a jurisdiction that my fellow brethren have established. In short, this county is our turf. And it is given to none to snoop about without our blessing."

Polly smirked. "You tink I give a waste about your *flower delivery service?*"

Fulton's spine straightened, but his face did not change.

Polly tilted her head as she looked up at the man. "Why should I care if someone willingly dulls deir wits for kicks? I have studied toxins and drugs, Mr. Gladish. De Graydust Poppy is rare in dis huncell, which makes it all de more valuable. I doubt you get much work as a leather smith in dis town, which is why you sell de drug in other counties. Tell me, do you tink I know too much?"

Fulton Gladish frowned. "Yes. My in-law must have a big mouth."

Polly's eyes grew cold as she shrugged. "Dat's fine by me. But I understand *your* motivations more dan you do mine. Who, den, has de advantage over de other?"

The big man shook his head in disapproval. "If I had theurgic power to swear by, as I suspect *you* do, I would assure you that the Swans had nothing to do with Remus' death. Or that of

89

Juniper Beech, for that matter."

Polly narrowed her eyes, regarding the man. She now understood the danger he represented. Not only was he a kin-leader, looking out for his loved ones and protecting his way of life. There was a disciplined intelligence about him. He was no mere thug or bandit. And if the other members of his guild carried themselves as he did, she was in trouble.

"We are here to find ghosts," she said in as plain a fashion as she could manage. "And to break de Geohex on dis land. Dat's all."

Fulton grinned as he considered her words. "There are only four of you and eighty-six of us."

"All de more reason not to be concerned," she answered. She shifted her head and saw Izzyk. He was now several paces away, standing behind a small tree.

Fulton glanced at him, gave Polly an appraising look, and turned back to play with his sons.

"Th-This way, Miss Gone." Izzyk stammered, nodding his head to the road.

Polly followed him, never looking back at her threatener. They reached the edge of the front yard. There, Polly's bileer steed, whom she'd named Waltre, was tied to the wood fence, grunting and stamping in disapproval of its bonds. She gave his ears a soothing caress and untied his reins. "Come, Waltre. Stop being grumpy. You're walking wit' us."

After several nervous moments, Polly got tired of the pounding racket coming from the boy's chest. "Calm down," she said.

"It's kind of hard to," he replied. "Uncle Fulton has a dark side. All the Swans do." He took a few unsteady breaths. "So. Um. *Are* you a mystic? I mean, it's none of my business. But...well...are you?"

"Mmm hmm," she answered with a nod. "But my philocreed has no use for followers or preaching a way of life to de masses. I live it and walk its path. I set my goal and focus my power on it until I succeed. Purpose is de heart of focus."

"Well, what power would that be? What kind of theurgy?"

Polly moved in closer to the boy. She then sensed a new nervousness in him; carnal. "Can you keep a secret?" she asked in a soft whisper.

90

For an instant, he was lost in her eyes. "Yes."

Polly erupted with laughter, startling him. "Izzyk, Izzyk, Izzyk," she teased, shaking her head. "Only a dead man can keep a secret."

The boy frowned. "Well, at least tell me why you acted so weird at the piano."

Polly shrugged. "Oh. Dat. I was listening to deir heart beats. They both beat as one, a sign of genuine love. I played my tune to dat beat. As I began to ask accusatory questions, I detected a slight break in de rhythm. Music gives me a sense a pace. One of dem was not being completely honest wit' me. But dey were sitting so close together dat I could not discern who it was. Den your nosy aunt came in."

The boy laughed. "Yeah. She is kinda nosy. I bet she'll tell the whole town about you now."

Polly hunched and sneered. Then she looked back at the teenager. He looked worried. "What's de matter?"

The boy shrugged and frowned. "If my folks are hiding something, I mean, I hope it's nothing serious."

Polly wanted to say *"Why hide something dat is not serious?"* But decided to keep her mouth shut.

Part 2

The grave of Remus Kach was marked by a crude pile of rocks, leftover bits of rubble made by the local tombstone carver. While nearly every other grave had a stately stone tablet to identify its resident, the grave of a convicted murderer looked like a quarry pile. Thus were such men remembered, as a pile of waste broken off from a more meaningful whole.

Waltre the bileer chewed grass beneath the tree he was tied to. A part of him missed the city. But while his mouth was full, his heart was content.

Chilled wind brushed against Polly and her guide. They stood beside the grave, silent for many moments. The evening gloam seemed more like night due to thick clouds overhead. The weather stirred as if the wind itself was terrified and escaping some unknown horror.

Unlike the boy at her side, Polly did not shiver from anxiety or the cold, for her heart was racing to circulate her blood faster to fight off the chill. She could hear the pattern of Izzyk's heartbeat. He did not want to be here, standing so close to a cursed grave.

"So, dis is him?" she asked.

The boy nodded, folding his arms. Tiny beads of rain appeared on his glasses.

She regarded the rocky mound and made a half-grin. "What was your mother like after she saw him?"

The boy shrugged. "She cried a lot. More than I've ever seen her cry. She also took ill from passing out and laying here all night."

Polly looked at the ground. Dry, dead yellow grass spouting from dry gray dirt. It did not look very comfortable. She knelt down, placing a hand on one of the jagged stones. "Did you see him hang?"

Izzyk did not answer right away. "Yes. I wasn't supposed to. But I snuck out of the house and hid in the crowd."

"So, you watched him die."

"Yes."

Polly lowered her chin slightly. "Was it a drop hanging or did they hoist him by his neck?"

He wiped the droplets from his lenses. "Why do you ask?"

Polly shrugged. "Maybe he's not dead. Perhaps, he could have survived if he'd been hoisted. Maybe your mother actually saw him and not his ghost."

The boy frowned and shook his head. "No. He died. They dropped him from a high scaffold. His neck broke and stretched like the sleeve of a yarn sweater."

Polly regarded the boy and sighed. She knelt and began sorting through the rock pile. With careful eyes, she examined each piece she picked up. After checking a dozen or so, she stood, shaking her head. "Dese rocks have not been disturbed in years. If it

92

was Remus, it had to have been a ghost and not some post mort."

Izzyk shrugged. "The only talk of walking corpses I know of are in Pevulanium, out past Tanglefoot. Rumors mostly." A flash of far off lightning reflected in his spectacles.

Then a crack of thunder sucker punched their ears.

Polly frowned down at the pile of rocks, then beheld the crowded atmosphere above. "I must find shelter soon. Do you tink de authorities would mind if I spent de night in de coalmine?"

"What? Are you crazy?" the boy responded. "That place is haunted! Why there?"

She shook her head. "Dere are no inns in dis town. And I can trust no one, especially your uncle. It would be best if I stayed somewhere where no one knows where I am."

The young man frowned. "Okay. I will take you. But then I need to hurry home."

"Tank you, Izzyk." She rewarded him with a gracious smile and a curtsy. It was enough to make him forget the rain.

"Y-You're welcome, Miss Gone."

Before leaving, Polly looked behind her shoulder, watching the tall grass stir over the rolling cemetery hills. "*I am sorry, Mr. Kach. But you may have to wait.*"

The mine entrance was not what she had expected. Instead of a huge jagged crack in the side of a mountain, the old entrance was like a giant doorway on the side of a tall cliff. It reminded her of the front door of a High Theurge she once fought, only this doorway was bigger, nearly forty feet high and half as wide. The long trunks of many felled trees stood side by side, wedged into the massive portal. Each one was naked of bark and covered with graffiti, placed there to keep people out.

"*Or keep someting else in,*" Polly thought with a shiver.

The rain poured as thunder blared at them in an angry, accusing roar. Waltre yipped in primal disagreement as Polly hitched him to a nearby tree. "It's okay, Waltre. Izzyk will take you somewhere warm and dry tonight. Promise." She gave him a kiss on the nose.

"This way," Izzyk told Polly as he slipped between two trunks that were far enough apart.

Polly followed. Turning sideways, she wriggled between the two trunks carefully, one boob at a time. Once inside she saw only darkness. "Izzyk? Where are you?"

Before he could answer, the lightning flashed from outside. The features of the youth lit up in a stuttering flicker, just inches from her face. Polly squeaked in surprise, and suddenly felt embarrassed.

His voice spoke in the darkness. "I'm sorry. I mean, we should have stopped by my house or the store for a lantern."

"It's fine, Izzyk. I will be alright. Dis is what I requested and you delivered me."

She reached up with her hand where she last saw his head. She felt the cold wire frames of his glasses and the chilly wet curls of his hair. For an instant, her fingers glided through his hair like three vipers racing through tall grass.

"Tank you, young sir. You may go now."

"But...!"

"I said take your leave." A smug grin curled her lips. "You will see me tomorrow. Promise."

"O-Okay, but the cave..."

"I will be fine. Now go. I am cold and wet and tired."

There was a pause in the darkness. "Okay, Miss Gone. I-I gotta open the shop tomorrow, so I can't be here in the morning to check on you. I'll have your bileer there waiting for you out front."

She heard his clumsy footsteps and his clothing scuff against the two poles as he slipped through them.

"Good luck," he called from outside. And then he was gone.

"*Finally,*" she thought.

She turned and regarded the utter blackness of the cave. Now was the perfect time to try out a new power. Her bloody wisdom had augmented after her visit to the city of Embrenil. Her faith had grown and evolved into a more clarified sense of confidence. She smiled at the darkness with a cold, gloating grin. The secrets it contained would become hers soon enough. Her heart pulsed like a harsh whip cracking against a large drum. Heat washed through her in waves, quelling the chill from her hands and

94

feet. She looked down at her hands, her blue veins and red blood vessels glowed from beneath her skin. All around her, the rough-hewn walls of the cave were covered in red light. To her surprise, the floor was made of smooth concrete as vast as a ballroom. She could make out various tunnel openings throughout the room and a large sign posted high on the wall, but it was still too dark to read it.

"No problem," she thought. *"I'll just shed more light."*

Of course, shedding more light meant shedding more clothing, which was why she'd sent Izzyk away in the first place. She removed the wet clothes that clung to her body, everything but her boots, the knife strapped to her forearm, and matching red bra and panties. The blood beneath her damp smooth skin shown with the brilliance of thousands of red and blue lightning bolts weaving together. The soft red light illuminated the entire cavern, as if dusk or dawn had infiltrated the enclosure. The large old sign spelled out the words *Spirling Wheels Roller Rink*.

"So," she mused. "Dey tried to convert dis old coalmine into a skating rink. Looks like it went under." She walked around and noticed a rickety old booth beside several wooden shelves. Everything was blanketed with cobwebs. Inching closer to it, she saw that the webs were covered in fine dust ages old. Any spiders that may have been there would be long dead. She walked around the booth, cleared away some webs with the dagger, and found three drawers with stained brass handles.

She pulled the middle drawer first. It was empty.

Then she pulled the one on the left. Nothing.

Then she pulled the one on the right. The handle broke off in her hand. An annoyed hiss escaped her teeth. Still holding the dagger, she gripped the drawer with her fingernails and pulled. Inside was a skittering spider as long as her forearm. Before she could even pull her hand away, the spider leapt to her face, covering her mouth like the hand of a kidnapper. She let out a scream and slapped at her face with her free hand. As she did so, the large arachnid rammed its multifaceted face into her left nostril. She could feel its tiny mandibles buzzing behind the corner of her eye. *"It's trying to get inside my face!"*

She gripped it by its bulbous body and slammed it onto the counter. Without thinking, she reversed the grip of her knife and stabbed at the bug as a jilted housewife stabs her cheating husband. Her mark was prone and her aim was true. The white-handled dagger pinned the little bastard in place, buried to the hilt. She backed off so fast that she slammed her back against the wall. She could not believe her eyes. The thing was still moving. Its legs showed no sign of curling, twitching, or slowing down. They simply kept moving as if the bug was not hurt.

Polly inched closer and slowly raised her hand. She focused her senses to get a lock on the creature's blood. If she could command it to bleed faster, she could get her dagger back with little worry or wait. She closed her eyes and whispered something secret and forbidden. Nothing happened. She could sense no blood. She opened her eyes to see the critter. It kept wriggling defiantly.

"It's already dead!" she gasped in realization. It was the exoskeletal remains of a large arachnid animated no doubt by the dark forces of the Geohex. "*Great*," she thought with a disgusted look.

She climbed atop the counter, looked down at the creepy crawler and swallowed hard. Taking two quick steps, she stamped her booted feet on both sides of her weapon, crushing the bug beneath her. Without hesitating, she bent over, yanked her dagger free, and twisted her body this way and that, grinding her boots into the post mort pest. "Dat's what you get for trying to bite my brain!"

She then hopped off the counter and admired her work. The spider was now nothing more than ground dust. She rubbed her nose and scowled as a spike of revulsion careened with her spine. She knew right then and there that she would not get any sleep tonight. "*Might as well see how many other ways I can get killed.*"

Readying her knife in a defensive grip, she approached the web-covered shelves. She stood a good five paces from them and raised her arms. Luminous blue veins slithered out of her skin from her wrists. They were long and spindly and covered with small barbs. She commanded them to tear way the curtain of webbing to reveal what threats or treasures the old shelves contained.

Polly arched an eyebrow and rolled her eyes. "Roller skates," she said flatly. "Of course. What else would dere be?" She wondered to herself why the skates were not taken when the business closed down. Then she shrugged in apathy and drew her veins back into her arms.

96

She approached the shelves with searching eyes. "Let's see. Size eight...size eight...Ah! Here!" She knelt down and picked up what looked like an old pair of shoes with metal soles and little wooden wheels. She spun each wheel, inspecting them. The leather and laces were stiff with rot and fell apart in her hands. But that was fine. She had an idea.

She set the skates down and used her knife to cut away most of the leather. She then removed her boots and socks. Her feet felt relieved to feel the cool air of the cave. She placed one foot upon a shoeless skate. Two more glowing blue veins slithered out the sides of her ankles and weaved tightly around the skate like the cords of a sandal. She repeated the process with the other foot, and before too long, Polly was skating freely around the abandoned rink like a carefree purple pixie. Although she was actually quite far from carefree. The light from her body let her see where she was going. But that did not mean that she *knew* where she was going.

She went into a tunnel entrance. The floor was smooth with flat cement. Not thirty feet into the tunnel, her eye caught something shiny. Embedded in the wall, not six feet off the ground, was a large mining pick. The pointed side was sticking deep into the rock wall while the flat side faced outward. The metal pick head was as polished as a silver tea set. The wooden handle was sanded smooth and stained an elegant dark brown. Below the handsome tool was a brass plaque that read:

IN MEMORY OF THE EIGHTEEN MEN WHO LOST THEIR LIVES IN THE SERVICE OF THEIR EMPLOYERS AND THEIR FAMILIES. GONE BUT NOT FORGOTTEN.

"*Not completely gone,*" Polly guessed.

She investigated the other tunnel entrances, and found that they too were smoothed out with cement. It became apparent that many of the tunnels interconnected, that the entire place was a labyrinth of weaving twists and turns. "*A skate maze,*" she thought. "*What an odd idea. I'm sure a few couples had fun losing and finding each other in dis.*"

She went back to the main rink area, took her dagger out,

and sliced the palm of her right hand open. Bright red blood pooled in her hand, yet it would not drip until she told it to. She then reentered the skate-maze. Every so often, she would let a few drops fall to the floor as a glowing reminder of her passing by.

"Skating," she mused. It was one of many pleasures that her mother indulged her with. Other than never letting her save the people her mother tortured and murdered, Polly's childhood was far from restrictive. Anything she wanted to do or try: piano lessons, bileer riding, skating. Her mother, Veluora the Red Witch of Chume, was the epitome of encouragement. All her daughter had to do was maintain her studies as a Crimson Theurgess and occasionally aid her mother in psycho-spiritual sacrifices. Her mother. Her loving mother, who always wiped away her daughters tears of horror and regret. The supportive nurturer who would tell her that killing people was all part of growing up and becoming a woman. The very woman who'd taught her that nothing was more important than blood. Blood was the source of all bonds. And sometimes those bonds needed to be cut.

Polly made a sour face as she remembered. *"Well, I certainly cut dose bonds when I ran away. Didn't I, you evil bitch?"*

"Liddy!" a man's voice shouted with anger.

Polly's heart did a somersault as her body froze in sudden fright. She lost her balance and fell hard on her behind.

"Liddy Belnap! I have told you and told you not to visit me at work!"

Polly looked around. The voice was coming from directly in front of her, yet she saw nothing. "Who's dere?" she asked.

"Does your mother know you're here?" the man's voice asked.

Polly gulped and shrugged a shivering shoulder. "I-I hope not."

She heard the voice sigh, as if frustrated. "Liddy, you know you can't be here. It's not safe. You should go home now. If Bossman Beech sees you, daddy could get in big trouble."

"Daddy?" Polly parroted, confused.

"Yes, sweetheart?"

Polly's throat went dry. A ghost was talking to her. A ghost was mistaking her for his daughter. He did not even know he was a ghost. Worse, he was invisible and she glowing in the dark in her bra and panties. Without thinking she covered herself with her hands and arms, accidentally smearing blood on her left breast from her cut hand.

"You're hurt!" the man's voice cried. "Oh, poor baby. Let me get a look at that."

Polly felt two gentle hands grab her wrist. She felt something soft and bristly press against the wound on her palm. Then she saw some of her glowing blood rise from her hand. It was in the shape of a smiling mouth. "There," the mouth said. "All better."

Polly's left cheek twisted into a mad smirk. She began to laugh from utter terror. The floating bloody mouth began to laugh with her in a bubbly strain of gasps and cackles. They laughed until her stomach hurt and her mind was an aimless blur.

Then the glowing bloody ghost mouth stopped laughing. It frowned in disgust and confusion. "Who are you?" it asked.

Polly fought the urge to scream. Her tongue felt heavy as she spoke. "M-My name is Polly, Polly Gone. Please, I know tings...tings don't make sense right now. But you need to tell me who you are and what you remember."

The mouth opened and closed as if considering her words. It stalled for nearly a minute before answering. "All I can do is remember. Memories are...are all I have, and all I am. I know it sounds crazy. Is this a dream or something, Polly?" The man's voice seemed tired and depressed all of a sudden.

Polly considered his words and how he used them. "All I can tell you is dat you are not awake...or asleep. What is your name, sir?"

The mouth stalled with its bottom lip quivering. "My name is Jom Belnap. My wife's name is Julee. We have three kids, Austen, Orson, and Lidia. I work at the Barnhart coal mine. My badge number is 785816913. I'm the assistant foreman in charge of the canaries."

"Canaries?" she asked.

The bloody mouth moved up and down. "Yes. We use caged canaries to alert us of methane leakage. We have to keep pouring water on the rock to keep the coal dust from rising. But the water causes the rock to release methane gas into the air. You can't see it, taste it, or smell it. But it can kill you easily. The canaries are very sensitive to it. My job is to watch them for signs of poisoning. Whenever a canary starts to act funny and drops dead, I know it's time to alert the boys to leave immediately."

"How many canaries have died, do you tink?"

"Oh, thousands. Thousands of little heroes who gave their lives to save us."

Polly smiled. She could tell that the man had taken pride in his work. He did not seem like a tormented spirit. But, of course, she had only just met the guy. She took a deep breath and asked her next question. "Jom, what year is it?"

"2642 A. T. Why?"

Polly frowned. "*206 years,*" she thought. All his children would be grown by now. His wife probably remarried. "Jom, please. I need you to stay calm. Very, very calm."

The mouth looked confused. "Okay,".

Polly's face scrunched with worry. "Jom, I won't lie to you. You are a ghost. You died here, Jom. And I need you to tell me how."

The mouth gaped as if it was yawning. It made a sound as if it were choking to death. "Hhhhh-huh-help us!" it said in a gagging stammer. "Get us out of here! Clear the rocks! Juniper, can you hear me? Go—hhuh—get a crew to move these—hhuh—move these—HHUH!!!" The mouth continued to cough and wheeze while trying to speak. Polly could only watch and listen in helpless despair as the mouth slowly lowered down to the floor like the ghost was laying its head down sideways. Soon the mouth stopped moving, stopped making noise. The glowing blood that illuminated it dripped completely to the floor in a tiny puddle.

That's when Polly heard the canaries coming.

The red light she cast throughout the tunnels became blocked by a massive cloud of shadow. Hundreds of tiny silhouettes flittered and fluttered on the rocky walls. The sound of countless little wings thumped in the air, stirring a chilled wind around her. And even though they were invisible, their presence surrounded her in a grip of solid fear. She fell into a prone fit of panic. Her throat buzzed, yet she could not hear herself scream.

The mind numbing sonic assault of the ghost birds' chirping filled her ears like lava. Tweeting and chirping, chirping and

100

tweeting. Each one singing its own little song of confusion and unyielding terror. The avian chorus of death flooded through her mind, sending earthquakes through her every nerve. Hundreds of tiny fractured souls flew through her own soul, pecking at it here and there. Each and every one of them flew into her mind, clogging it with despair and madness.

Polly was dying from it. She knew it. It was all she knew. Her mind plummeted into a well empty of reason. And as death crept in to fill the voids life was leaving behind, Polly had an epiphany. This was how the birds felt as they died.

Though her mind was drowning in madness, she reached deep into her memories to catch a breath of sanity. She recalled her first sacrifice.

In front of a stately old chateau, surrounded by the wild growth of the Chume forest, Polly faced off against a prisoner. The prisoner was a young man. He was naked from the waist up and covered in cuts and scratches. They were both holding identical daggers. She was thirteen years old.

There was a beautiful woman sitting on the front porch. She slouched forward on a wicker recliner and wore a low cut house dress. She held a glass of the young man's blood and sipped it like Summer tea. "Come on, Polmeeshia!" she cheered with a hungry grin. "I bled dis one plenty for you. He should be nice and slow!"

This was the third such man Polmeeshia faced. The last two had been able to defeat her. She had been too timid, too compassionate. Her mother had promised them that if they could beat her daughter, she would stop torturing them and they would be set free. Of course, that's not what happened. Each time Polly would lose, Veluora would run off the porch to save and heal her. Then Veluora would torture the men until their hearts gave out.

Polmeeshia gripped her knife. The man looked exhausted, scared, and hopeful. He showed little sympathy for the spawn of his captor. He was a prisoner of a mad witch and her witchling daughter. And even if he would not be granted his freedom, he still had the prospect of killing the one thing the witch loved. Polmeeshia relaxed her wrist. His suffering would be soon over.

The young man made a desperate thrust for her throat. He was taller than her and had more reach. But his knees were weak, and he was forced to hunch over. He rushed in, ready to slash if she

101

decided to dodge to either side. The girl's feet remained planted. She spun her knife in her fingers, reversing the grip. In a lightning fast motion, she made a sideways stab at his wrist. The blade stabbed between the bones in his forearm. Her right foot spun behind her in a tight circle as she rotated the knife like a lever. The man's arm twisted around his back, popping and snapping as bone separated from muscle. His own blade fell from his grasp. Polmeeshia caught it with her free hand. The man screamed. She put the caught knife through his neck and slashed outward, cutting off the man's shout. A part of her was glad that she stood behind him. The sight of his opened throat would not have bothered her. But seeing the expression on his face would make her retch in the grass. The prisoner fell face down, twisted, lurched, and fell into a life-draining sleep. A puddle of dark red was forming beneath him.

"Now!" her mother cried from the porch. "Do it now! Say de chant! Not before or after, but *as* de soul shatters!"

Polmeeshia glanced at her and gave a sharp nod. She fell into a crouch and splashed a hand into the blood puddle. She was very careful not to stutter as she uttered a rhythmic riff of odd syllables. The concentration it took to recite the incantation forced her mind open in just the right way. Invisible spheres of energy bloomed within her like a line of multi-hued roses, each one corresponding to a different set of organs. The blooms became loose like wheels on a suspended axle. And as the man laying beside her died, his soul exploded. Thousands of fragments should have flown in every direction, but most of them went through her instead. The shards that had once made up the man's spirit grazed against her loosened blooms, making them spin at tornado-like speeds. The power of the Blood Mystic awoke within her that day. An emotion like love filled her entire heart as if a balloon were filling with light. Her very soul seemed to gain a will of its own and bonded with her in a closer union of spirit and flesh.

Suddenly, the *philocreed* her mother had raised her on made sense. When the bonds of life are pulled taut like a rope, cutting that rope releases the energy needed to influence the world as you deem fit. And as Polly Gone recalled this memory, she saw a way to deal with the swarm of cursed bird spirits that hounded her.

Each and every bird had been a sacrifice. Their deaths had meaning for saving the lives of many men. And given the fact that

102

they were only animals with tiny bird minds, they should not be smart enough to hold a grudge bad enough to become ghosts. Polly was no necrotheurge, but she had studied enough to know that much. These bird ghosts were nothing more than wild soul energy. They were attacking her mentally. Each one flew through the endless caverns of her mind. She would soon trap them there.

For an instant, Polly surrendered her mind to the flock of death. Laying there on the cold floor, she forced her every muscle and nerve to relax. Every solid part of her melted like a wax candle in a bonfire. Her glowing body yielded into a large glimmering puddle of blood. In that state, her mind was not capable of normal thought, since her mind was not hindered by having five senses to confuse it. She had become as still and serene as a little pond. The canaries were trapped inside her calm, crimson little void of a world. Then came the tricky part.

Polly had to will her liquid self into a perfect circle. Simply spreading out could not guarantee that. She had to spin, swirl. She spun and spun, coating the smooth concrete ground as the light of the blood began to dim. Now devoid of all thought, she had only that one feeling to hold her together. It was that feeling like love, truth, a faith so strong that only a truly devoted theurge could understand it. The blood of a sacrifice could steer the soul as it was released. But using her own blood could duplicate it in such a way that she could destroy her own soul to get the same effect. But *her* soul was not the only soul trapped in the blood.

The puddle spun faster and faster until Polly's spirit formed a swirling glowing ring around it. Slow and steady, the ring of light shrank into the middle of the crimson vortex. Hundreds of tiny pinpoints of light that were the canaries' ghosts began to be herded and funneled into the center. Polly's ring-shaped spirit closed in around them, crushing them against each other. One by one, the little pinpoints of spirit disappeared in a series of tiny sparkling pops, until all that was left was a solid circle of blazing red.

An hour passed before she awoke. Polly was naked, cold and stiff. The cave floor had not been the worst thing she had ever slept on, but it came close. Even after she had opened her eyes, there was still utter darkness. The taste of old copper was in the air. Sluggish and dazed, she crawled around in search for her underwear. It was part of the *Philocreed of Hematonomy,* that all bloodcasters must

103

wear red in order to work their theurgy. Which meant that she could not use her powers until she put on her red bra and/or panties. She fumbled around for a few minutes until she found the skimpy underbottoms and bra. They were as cold as ice and soaked. "Dammit."

After a lot more cursing and some reluctance, Polly was able to use her theurgy again. She willed the blood beneath her skin to glow once more, but now it was not as bright. She could only see a few feet around her. After pulling off such a maneuver to defeat the canary swarm, her energy had diminished. Still, a part of her felt proud. If only her mother had been there to see her execute *Treppe de Pnuema, Snare the Soul,* on multiple disembodied spirits. The dangerous, high level endeavor was meant as a booby trap for living beings. And not only had she used it with success, but she had discovered a new use for it.

"Would Mother be proud...or envious?" she pondered with a smug curl of her lips.

She picked up her dagger, but decided to leave the skates. Even summoning her ankle veins would use too much energy. She would have to conserve her power until her next sacrifice. The little puddles of glowing blood she had left as markers had all gone out. She wondered how long she had been asleep. The tunnels went on and on with no familiar signs. She was lost in a pitch black maze with only a little light to keep her from bumping into things. The smug feeling of besting a swarm of dead birds went away. Uncertainty grew with every step she took. She soon felt herself walking in a downward incline. The smooth cement beneath her feet ended, replaced by a rough rock floor.

"Dis is defiantly not de way I came," she told herself. A sound made her ear twitch. There was a faint, far off sound of people screaming. Terrible, terrible screaming. It was coming from deep down the tunnel. Even though the sound was faint, Polly froze in frightened hesitation. She clenched her teeth and shook her head. She wanted out of this place. A wave of fear soaked into her.

"No! I can't help you!" she yelled down the tunnel. "I can't! I can't...". Her eyelids began to spill tears. She covered her mouth, then her ears. She hated herself for being so afraid. She could understand why a person would simply try to kill her. The possible motives lead her to understanding the nature of the foe's rancor.

104

But the feeling that ghosts gave off! Knowing that they were nearby, yet unseen. It seemed to enhance her senses in the worst ways, so that every sound, every trick of shadow, and every cold breeze nipped at her soul.

She turned to run. The men making those voices were beyond saving. She was only a Crimson Theurgess who dared to meddle with bloodless poltergeists. She ran a total of four steps before she stopped. A sudden rage grew inside her. It was aimed at her own self. She realized that there would never be another chance like this one, and she had just tried to run from it. Her power was weak, but her body was still strong and able.

The supernatural fear emanating from the tunnel felt like a giant curtain of doubt. And she was hiding behind that curtain. It was then that she realized she had nothing to gain by running from the unknown. But by approaching the unknown and facing it head-on, the rewards could be limitless. The fear that clogged her reason was not her own fear at all, merely the lingering fear of death. She dismissed the fear, as it was of no use to her, and continued her descent.

After several minutes of careful stepping, Polly came to a blockade in the tunnel. It was just like the massive entrance outside the mine, only much smaller. Over a dozen shafts resembling tall fence posts were wedged into the hall, creating a wall of wood. What at first looked like graffiti Polly recognized as theurgical inscriptions partially familiar words and symbols arranged in a diagram with old red barn paint. She could only make out parts of it, but concluded that it was indeed a seal of some kind.

"Necrotheurgic or Animistic?" she wondered aloud. The spirits of the dead almost always differed from spirits of the land. But their rituals both involved diagram seals. Polly arched an eyebrow. "It's both?" she asked, her eyes widening.

There it was in front of her--a mixture of two or three theurgies, two or three *philocreeds* merged into one. The spirits of the land were being suppressed or replaced by spirits of the dead.

105

She suspected that *Geonomy* might be involved, as well. Whoever was responsible for this diagram, Polly suspected the mystic-in-question was extremely powerful and insane. The combination of such oppositional schools of thought were impossible in a healthy, reasoning mind. "Ghosts aren't de cause of the Geohex, but de effect!"

She could still hear the choking moans of dead men behind the wooden blockade. They would haunt her memory for all her remaining days unless she did something soon. She felt bad that she had nothing to draw a copy of the seal on. She would just have to remember what it looked like. She looked down, hoping to find a heavy rock. No luck.

"Okay den," she sighed. She kicked the wall. And kicked it again. And kicked it some more. She used every kind of kick she knew using the sole of her foot. Nothing budged. A sigh of frustration gusted out her nose.

"I'm holding back," she thought. *"If I had my boots, I would not be afraid to kick harder."* After considering another harder round of kicking, she dismissed it. The posts making up the blockade were just too thick. Instead, she examined how they were fixed into the passage way. Each post shaft had been cut to the exact height of the ceiling about eight feet high. The bottoms of the posts were all dented with coaster-sized circles, indicating that a sledgehammer had been used to knock the posts in place. *"Just like de support beams in Mother's basement,"* she thought. *"Sometimes de basement would flood when it rained. It made de bottoms of de beams swell wit' moisture. I wonder..."*

She knelt down before the blockade and bit into her wrist. The blood came, but she stopped when she thought she had enough to work with. Making a dismissive gesture with her hands, she commanded the dark puddle to soak into the bottoms of three posts. It took her several minutes of tedious concentration to get it all into the old dead wood. She then stood and backed away.

The choking moans of the dead men left her mind as she focused on what needed to be done. She lifted her hand with the wounded wrist, all doubts in her mind quelled and buried. With all her mind, heart, and soul, she commanded her blood to return to her. The three posts popped out bottoms-first and flew at her like falling debris.

106

She shrieked and dived out of harm's way. *"Dat worked too well!"*

Polly arose to see what lay behind the blockade. Rocks. Lots and lots of rocks. They formed a sloped wall slanting upward, indicating that this was indeed the sight of the legendary cave in. The sounds of the ever-dying voices grew louder.

"Juniper! Get us out of here!"

"Help! Help us *Please*!!!"

"Don't let us die down here, you coward!"

"MOOOOOOOOO!"

"Moo?" Polly repeated. "Do dey have a cow in dere wit' dem?" She smacked herself. "Not a cow! It's a work ox! Dey must have used it to transport coal. And it died in dere wit' dem." She could not help but pity the poor animal.

She became aware of a faint glowing, and it was not coming from her. The three posts she had pulled out all seemed to shine like hot orange embers where the red seal had been painted on them. Her eyes shifted to the circular design on the remaining posts. The seal on the wooden wall, now broken by her meddling, flashed like a magnesium camera. For an instant, she was blind, and as her vision returned, speckled with hazy dots, she was shocked by the sudden silence. The screaming pleas of the ghosts had stopped.

"I did it?" she asked herself in a shocked whisper. "Did I break de curse by breaking de seal?"

The answer was no.

Her heart stuttered at the rumble of boulders being moved. Loud cracks and heavy thuds came from the other side of the debris.

Polly backed away. Before she reached her seventh step, something pushed its way through and over the rock heap. It had the skull of a huge ox for a head, with horns jutting out like the lower fangs of a dragon. Its hollow eye sockets blazed with orange light. Two great arms were clearing rocks out of the way. They looked at first like two withered white tree trunks, but a second glance revealed that they were made of the arm bones of dozens of men.

Polly turned and ran, hearing a deafening crash. She could not keep from turning her head to look. The hulking brute had gotten through the rock debris and smashed the post wall to splinters. It was as tall and wide as a full-sized malruka. Its entire

107

body was composed of ox and Drakeri bones, stark white, and covered in spider webs. The bones seemed to be connected through some unnatural force and design. The Bonebrute stood like a man with two legs and two arms. Its massive rib cage contained the chomping and twitching skulls of the dead miners like madmen behind bars. The skulls all looked terrified and confused. But not the ox skull. Its gleaming eyes locked on the blood theurge with an eerie fixation.

Polly screamed as she ran. Never before had she moved so swiftly. Never again would she hit a vocal note so high and clear in her terrified shriek.

The Bonebrute followed, its thousands of pieces sounding like a half-dozen warped wooden xylophones.

She charged back up the tunnel and her skates came into view. The care for conserving her power was long gone now. She stepped onto them and expelled her ankle veins to lash them to her feet. The Bonebrute closed in. She steadied her balance and pushed hard against the floor. The hulking terror reached down to grab her.

Hundreds of boney fingers latched onto Polly's hair and the skin of her back. By instinct, she tried to do a fast cartwheel, twisting out of the monster's painful grasp. But something snagged her up in mid-turn, and she landed hard on her hip.

She wasted no time getting up and skating away. She turned her head again to see the Bonebrute holding something red and flagging.

"My bra!" she cried with shocked anger. "Dat's my favorite bra!"

She skated away as fast as she could in spite of the cold breeze on her bare skin.

The Bonebrute trudged after her, but was soon lost from sight as the passageway curved.

The red light from her body dimmed as her power ebbed. She could only see a few paces around her. The constant stomping of the Bonebrute filled her ears, never slowing down or speeding up, a steady reminder that death was coming. With her legs burning, she skated through the maze tunnels, trying to remember the way she'd come. There was no telling how long each tunnel was with her sight so limited. She turned each corner on a whim.

The steady beat of the monster's steps made her think that it somehow knew exactly where to go, where to follow. She saw no clues to help her escape. She was lost and trapped, tortured by her own desperate hope for survival. There *was* a way out, but she just could not find it.

She stopped to rest a few times, to think things through. But then the loud stamps of the Bonebrute grew louder and closer again. She was faster than it. But it would eventually out last her.

She shivered in cold sweat. All she had now was her belt, knife and sheath, a red pair of panties, a pair of antique roller skates, and a little bit of energy, and blood theurgy was all but useless against a creature without blood. She took a deep breath as she glided over the cement surface through the winding maze. She would have to find a way to fight it. "*But how?*"

She turned a corner and found herself skating close behind the huge monster. Its entire back was made of row after row of spinal columns. She tried not to shriek as she avoided colliding into it. She somehow managed to succeed in both. But all the same, the monster turned and swung its massive arm around at her. She ducked just in time as the limb passed over her and smashed into the stone wall with a rumbling and cracking as stone shards rained down from the fractured wall.

She tucked and rolled between the Bonebrute's legs. But as she completed the lightning quick somersault, the wooden wheels of her skates shattered on the floor. "*No!*"

She was up and running before the Bonebrute could turn again. The muscles in her thighs rippled. Her throat was desert dry from both thirst and terror. The night was taking its toll on her body and mind. She wanted to throw up. She was so tired, her eyes stung. But her ears could still hear the tireless terror stamping closer at that frightful steady pace. She could not out run it for long.

The light of her power grew dimmer. She could feel the dark wings of death embrace her spirit. Her hand fell to her dagger. The thought of being torn apart by that *thing* became too much to bear. It seemed better to take her own life and let her spirit explode throughout eternity. It would be quick and easy.

"*No!*" she shouted in her mind. It was not that she was afraid to kill herself. She was just too stubborn. When the monster would finally caught up and closed in, she would go down fighting.

Then the maze entrance from the skating rink area came

into view. For an instant, the lightning from outside lit up the tunnel and rink. With any luck she could at least make it to the cave entrance where the monster would be too big to fit through.

She turned her head to see how close the Bonebrute was. Her eyes widened in shock. The monster was gone

She shook her head. *"No time to tink!"* She was getting closer to the large rink area.

Then the Bonebrute stepped in front of the tunnel entrance, not more than thirty feet away. Polly stopped and stumbled, trying not to fall and wondered how it could have gotten in front of her. *"It must have known a short cut and waited for me here."*

Her heart sank and her lungs burned. The air she breathed would not go in and out fast enough. She glared in defiance at the hulking horror and cackled like a raspy chipmunk.

"You should know someting first," she said between breaths. "I am going to be de *last* person to die in dis place. Dere are three men, friends of mine, who will come settle de score. Any one of dem could destroy you! You just got lucky tonight, dat's all!"

The orange eye sockets of the great horned monster blazed bright enough to light the tunnel like a grand hallway. It moved forward.

Polly drew her knife and caught her breath. Just then, she noticed that she stood right next to the heavy duty memorial mining pick that was embedded in the wall. "Oh," she cooed with a devious grin. "I can do more damage wit' you!" she told the pick.

She sheathed her blade and grasped at the old tool's handle.

The Bonebrute edged closer.

Polly sneered at it has she hopped to brace both her feet against the wall. She pulled at the pick with all her might. She strained and screamed as the monster closed in. A bolt of primal fear tightened her muscles and the pick came loose from the rock. *"I'm at least going to smash its head to pieces!"* she thought as she readied herself for a swing.

She squared her stance and faced the enemy. The pick felt heavy, but she did not mind. One good hit would be an adequate parting gift from her short life.

The Bonebute paused, stopping just out of range of her weapon, and collapsed into a big pile of bones.

Fear and rage were replaced with confusion. Polly stepped

back with care. She watched as the pile of bones separated into nineteen skeletons. Eighteen Drakeri and one big ox.

"*Is it changing tactics?*" she thought, biting her lip and shivering. "*Are dey going to surround me?*"

One of the Drakeri skeletons stepped forward and raised its arms. "Thank you!" it said in a man's voice.

Polly peed herself a little. "What?"

"You broke the curse, Liddy." the skeleton replied. "Daddy is so proud of you!"

Polly narrowed her stare. "Jom? Jom Belnap? I talked to you earlier, right?"

The skeleton scratched its skull and snapped its finger bones. "Oh yeah! That's right. You aren't my daughter." Then he just seemed to stand and stare.

Polly looked at them all. Even without eyes, she could tell that they were staring at something. She then realized that she was naked except for her panties. She dropped the pick and covered her chest-fruits with her arms. "Perverts!"

The skeletons all shrugged and snickered. The ox mooed.

The bones of Jom Belnap spoke once more. "Sorry. It's been a while for us. Anyway, we are all grateful for your help. We can now move on and become a part of all things new. Goodbye, sweet girl."

Before Polly could yell "Wait," the skeletons fell apart, leaving her alone in the darkness.

Part 3

"And then what happened?" Izzyk asked as he handed Polly a hot cup of *hawklash* tea.

Polly took the cup. "I went back to my clothes, put dem on, took matches from my rucksack, and built a small fire out of de ox's bones. I did not use de men's bones because dey probably still have family here in town. After dat, I slept."

The boy made a face of confused revulsion. "How could you sleep in that place after what you went through?"

111

Polly took a long drink while considering the question. "It's strange. Normally, I would run away. But de moment dat de skeletons fell apart, all de fear and uneasiness went away, like it was lifted off of me. De sudden absence of all dat...negativity...was a relief. I was at peace, and so was de cave." She started coughing.

"Sit back," Izzyk insisted. "Please, drink more tea." He sat up straight in his chair, giving her his full attention.

They were in the storage room in the back of his father's shop. It was mid-afternoon when she had come in, so he'd closed up an hour early. His eyes shifted over to the large, gleaming mining pick resting by her chair. "Why did you take *that* with you? Souvenir?"

Polly finished her cup and cleared her throat. "I have a theory."

Izzyk blinked his eyes. "A theory? Well, what is it?"

Polly shook her head. "It is only an idea right now. And I can't risk putting faith in something dat may be untrue. My theurgy is weak enough as it is."

The boy nodded with unsure eyes. He reached down and gently took Polly's arm. To her own surprise, she let him. He slid up the wide sleeve of her *quellinne*, unfastened the dagger and sheath buckled to her forearm, and revealed the tattoo that was on it. It was a septagram made of seven curving intersecting lines that met in seven points. Three of the lines were black, four were blood red. Something about the design reminded him of a butterfly or moth. "So, it's true. You really are a Blood Mystic." He looked back up at her face.

Polly made no reply. She looked back at him with odd curiosity. This usually nervous boy now seemed more like a man than a teenager. "Izzyk," she said softly. "By my philocreed, I have no intention of murdering anyone who is innocent."

He smirked. "That's funny. What you intend and what you do might not be the same."

She could not help but smile along. "Izzyk..."

He let go of her arm and made a dismissive gesture. "You've already revealed yourself—your secret—in the story you've just told me. You could have left the blood parts out. But you didn't."

"I need your trust," she urged.

"And you almost have it."

112

Polly raised her chin and crossed her arms. "What do you mean *almost?*"

He took a deep breath and straightened his shoulders. "Well, first off, you haven't killed me. And second, I mean, I'm no expert on theurges, but I *do* know that no matter which path you follow, you all keep your word. If, of course, you swear by your philocreed."

Polly nodded. "It is called an *essence oath.* When I swear on my philocreed, I swear on my own soul. If I break my word, I cripple my own spirit and lose my powers."

The young man straightened his glasses. "And I've heard that such oaths can be secured by making a deal of some sort."

She raised her chin as if a sword point had just been put to her throat. "I'm listening. My theurgy can do many tings. Shall I bless your bloodline to prevent the next three generations from still birth? What about a delayed healing maxim? De next time you get cut badly, your wound will close immediately."

Izzyk shook his head. "I don't want to barter for a blessing, Ms. Gone. Nor do I want to extort you for keeping secrets. That's not how I was brought up." He paused.

Polly could tell that he was choosing his words with care.

"The Autumn Festival is coming up soon. Would you care to, I mean, care to attend it with me?"

Polly's lavender face flushed indigo. "You are asking me out?'

He shrugged and nodded.

Polly's mouth opened several seconds before words came out. "Dat's very sweet of you. But I don't tink I'll be available."

"Why not?"

She raised her palms and dropped them in her lap. "I don't know what my travel mates will be doing. I don't know where all dis Geohex business will take me. I don't know when or where I'll be needed."

The young man smiled. "Well, at least you'll know where you'll be wanted."

Polly had to consciously catch herself from saying yes. "Tank you for asking me, Izzyk. But why not ask a local girl?"

He laughed a little and looked at the floor. "I've always been too shy...until now."

"Why now?"

113

He raised his head, adjusted his glasses, and cleared his throat. "Because Ms. Gone, you are the most beautiful girl I've ever seen. And I had this feeling that if I could muster the courage to ask you, then even if you said no, it would be a step forward for me. And just now, it occurred to me: If I had the guts to ask you, a theurge of one of the Cluster's most feared powers, then I would never be shy again."

Polly had no words for reply. She looked down at her tattoo to see if it was glowing at the corners. It was not. She made a half smile and met his eyes again. She opened her mouth to speak, but the young man spoke first.

"The Bierce/White duel is about to start," he said.

"The what?"

"It's a nightly duel between two skeletons. Their cursed spirits reenact the pistol match they had hundreds of years ago. It's not far. I grew up watching it a thousand times. Would you at least like to see it with me?"

Polly raised an eyebrow. "Fritz told me someting about dat. I was planning on going dere anyway." She cracked a smile. "But you may take me dere...if you want."

The young man smirked. "Let's get you fed. Then we can go. There's plenty to eat here. No charge."

Polly stood up and nodded in gratitude. "Tank you. But I only need a few tings to eat on de way." She reached down and picked up the mining tool.

"You're taking that thing with you?" he asked.

"Everywhere I go," she replied. "It's not as heavy as it looks."

"But why? It's not like it's going to float away."

Polly looked away and her smile shifted into a thoughtful frown. "You never know. It just might."

He looked at her curiously for a moment. "Okay then. I'll get a basket and put some eatables in it."

"Izzyk?" she said, turning to him.

"Yes, Ms. Gone?"

"Please, tell no one dat de mine's curse is lifted. Not yet."

"All right. May I ask why?"

"I tink de Geohex was caused by someone, possibly a theurge. I don't want to draw more attention dan I already have."

The young man furrowed his brow. "You really think that? I

114

always thought it was because so many evil things have happened here."

Polly buckled her knife back onto her arm. "Or maybe someone wanted to preserve dat evil." She held up the mining pick she had claimed. The gleaming metal was polished hematite. "Before we go, I need to wrap dis in someting. People in town might recognize it."

Izzyk crossed his arms and pointed at it. "I bet if we tied a sheet cloth around it just right, we could just tell people it's a crossbow. Not too many crossbows have been seen around here."

Polly looked at him, astonished. "Dat would be a clever deceit."

Just a short walk past the Hick's Family pumpkin farm, a large clearing was nestled by a sparse grove of cedar trees. An oval-shaped split-rail fence enclosed a rocky patch of dirt where nothing grew. And there on the clay, exactly ten paces apart, lay the skeletons of two Drakeri men. Polly saw that one skeleton had broken ribs in the front. The other had the top half of its skull missing from the eye sockets up. In their boney right hands were the rusty remnants of pistols.

Other people had come besides Polly and the young shopkeeper. There were clusters of children and teenagers, old couples, groups of farmhands wearing dirt-stained clothes. There were mothers carrying babies in their arms or in their bellies. Young couples held hands as middle-aged couples talked to their friends. Polly spotted Fritz Gladish tending to her sons as her peacefully menacing husband Fulton chatted with his biker buddies. All of those men wore the purple attire of the Trotting Swans, and all were glancing at her as they talked.

"I can't believe it," Izzyk murmured. "Almost the whole town is here!"

"Dis isn't normal?"

The young man shook his head. "People only come here when they're bored. The duel happens nightly, and it's always the

115

same."

Polly glanced around. She could sense it now. Nearly every eye was on her, indirectly or in fleeting glances. "Dey are here because of me, aren't dey?" she whispered.

At first, the young man made no reply. The answer was plain on his face. "They all know about what you did in Drowsy Nook. Rumor is that you might be a powerful shaman or necrotheurge." His eyes swept over the crowd. "Everybody looks like they got ready in a hurry. They must have heard you were heading this way."

Polly felt her stomach churn. She was all too aware of the eyes now. Her gaze dropped to the ground as she yearned to be invisible. Looking up, she met the eyes of Fritz Gladish. The pear-shaped Drakeri woman glared at her with wary contempt before whispering something into her husband's ear. Polly froze as Fulton's cold stare shifted to her.

"Hullo," came a voice from behind, startling her.

She and Izzyk turned to see his parents, Resula and Mark.

"M-Mom? Dad?" Izzyk blurted. "You're here, too?"

"Of course," Mark said. He turned to Polly. "Making progress, Ms. Gone?"

"I am." She felt smaller from all the attention.

"Oh? How?" Mark asked with doubt in his eyes.

"I, um, I..." Polly looked away and took a shallow breath. "I am learning much of de history of your town's curses. I have gathered a few traces dat may help me find answers."

"Traces?" Resula asked. "Like clues?"

"I tink so. Yes. Dat is a better word."

The woman frowned. "Do you have any idea why Remus' ghost appeared to me?" There was an edge to her voice.

Polly raised her shoulders and shook her head. "For now, all I have is theories."

"All you have is what?"

"It's starting!" someone shouted.

Polly felt Izzyk's hands turn her around. "Watch!" he said.

A hush fell over the townsfolk as the bones of the two dead men began to stir.

The skeletons shook upon the ground as if a herd of wild bileers were stampeding nearby. Polly took a deep breath and felt the haunted air chill her lungs. The skeletons rose a piece at a time

116

and stood in rigid opposition to each other. They clutched their rust-caked revolvers and faced off, a wave of almost tangible hatred swirled around the inside of the fence.

"*Blood lust,*" Polly thought. "*Dey are, or were, mutual enemies. Dey hate wit' equal measure! Both share de same desire to kill. Rare is such a balance!*"

She watched a thin vortex of wind kick up a cloud of dust and clay debris.

The skeleton with the shattered ribs opened its jaw. "Give it up, Bierce! The girl is spoken for. Her father has already agreed to the marriage!"

"She doesn't want you, White!" responded the broken skulled skeleton. His voice sounded much younger. "Her father knows this as well as you!"

At this point, every woman and girl in the crowd joined in on the unfolding drama, their voices speaking as one. "Luis! Mathu! Stop this, please!"

The skeleton of Mathu White turned its head to the crowd. "Stay out of this, Genay! This little pest has charmed away your reason. He's trash! And I'm going to take him out!"

"You don't deserve her!" roared the bones of Luis Bierce. "No girl in her right mind would have you until you inherited a share of the coalmine, you gutless patron-to-whores! You blind her destitute family with the promise of security and comfort. But the worm of corruption has long since tainted your core!"

"Fancy words, yarn spinner!" Mathu White replied. "Now let's see how fancy your gunmanship is!"

"So be it!" Bierce replied.

The two skeletons lurched toward each other until they stood within arms' reach. Then, without a word, they turned their backs to each other.

"Please! Don't do this!" the women of the crowd yelled. "I don't want someone to die because of me!"

Polly leaned on Izzyk and asked "Are dey women reciting what de girl said all dose years ago?"

Izzyk made a grunt of approval. "Even after two generations, we still remember the words of Genay Bhowmin, the town beauty."

Polly watched on, mesmerized by the skeletons' duel. "Dese men relive deir deaths every night?"

117

"Just watch," the young man urged.

The skull of Mathu White turned to address his foe. His voice seemed softer now. "Luis, we don't need to do this. I promise you I'll be good to her. But you need to either leave town or die."

Luis Bierce's bones were shaking from fear and rage. "I'd rather die than not be with her. Can you say the same, Mathu?"

Mathu White hung his head. "You're a fool, boy."

"Count us out. On ten, one of us dies. Agreed?"

"Agreed," replied Mathu White's spirit. And as he counted, his pace was steady, without pause or break in rhythm. With each number, the two bone men stepped away.

"*One! Two!*"

"*Luis! Mathu! I beg of you!*" the women of Barnhart wailed with mournful passion.

"*Three! Four! Five!*"

"*You mustn't do this! This isn't what I want!*" the women cried so loud it hurt Polly's ears.

"*Six! Seven! Eight!*"

"*I won't marry either of you!!! Please!*"

"*Nine! Ten!*"

At that moment, every female in the crowd screamed a guttural, wordless sound that almost made Polly scream along.

The two skeletons turned and aimed their weapons. The loud report of a pistol flooded the air and dispersed into oblivion.

Mathu White clutched his broken ribs, looked at his boney hands, and fell exactly where he had risen. He twitched and made gurgling sounds, and then became still.

The still standing remains of Luis Bierce looked to the crowd. "Genay...please don't cry. I beat him. Don't shed a single tear for that bastard. We're free to love each other now."

"Oh, Luis," the women whimpered in soft, sad voices. "We are not free to do such a thing. We will never be free to love each other again. I loved you for your pureness of heart, your kindness. How could I ever love a killer?"

The skull of the gunman shook back and forth as if it did not understand. The shaking continued until it seemed to convey denial and panic. "Genay...don't go..."

And then it pointed the rusty piece of metal beneath its chin. There was another thunder-loud crack in the air, and the bones of

Luis Bierce fell back to where they had lain.

There was a moment's silence in the crowd. Then every eye turned to Polly Gone, awaiting her response.

"Is dere nothing more to it?" she asked Izzyk.

"That's it," he shrugged.

Polly shuddered and regarded the townsfolk. "Hasn't anyone ever tried to bury dem? To give dem a proper funeral? Did dey just stay dere and rot?"

"Many have tried to bury them," a woman's voice replied. Fritz Gladish stepped out of the crowd and stood before Polly, her chin held high. "Ever since the day of the duel, this patch of ground has been haunted. Several people have tried to recover the bodies. Some have even managed to get close enough to touch them. But the *necrofear* always wins out. That's why this fence is up, deary. The aura of death is too strong to interrupt this nightly duel. Besides, this place serves as a reminder of our town's history. It's why we've outlawed fights to the death in this town, unlike those rascals in Pevulaneum. The last person brave enough to hop this fence was a necrotheurge called Mortimur the Daring. He tried to command the spirits of these men to dissipate. The backlash of the *necrofear* drove him mad. He started running around, stripping off his clothes and laughing hysterically. Then he began tearing off his own skin and flesh, tripping on his own guts as he kept laughing and running and screaming *'I'm naked! I'm naked!'* There are still sightings of his skeleton running and raving throughout the county to this very day."

Polly cringed as she felt the last of her power stir inside her. A flash of inspired truth illuminated her mind. She looked at Fritz as if the woman were a mere child telling silly ghost stories. Polly raised her head and addressed the crowd in a loud clear voice. "Tell me. Tell me dat de bloodlines of dese two men did not end wit' dem. Tell me that dere are still dose among you who are kin to dese poor souls!"

Nearly a quarter of the town raised their hands and gave answer. "I need one from each," she told them as she pushed past Fritz. "I require a member from de White family and de Bierce family to aid me in ending dis curse."

There were many curious volunteers who stepped forward. After a minute of questioning them, Polly decided on Alfeus White,

119

the great nephew of the man who lost the duel.

"And who among you are related to Luis Bierce?" Polly asked the crowd.

After a long, uneasy moment, only one man stepped forward and raised his hand: Fulton Gladish. His face was calm, but defiant. "I am," he rumbled. "I am his fourth cousin. What's it to you?"

Polly looked at him without any trace of fear or pride. "I need your blood, Mr. Gladish. Both you and Mr. White here."

The large man did not respond. There was murmuring in the crowd. He looked over to his wife. Fritz was shaking her head at him. He looked back at Polly. "How much do you need?" he asked.

The crowd went quiet.

Polly thought for a moment. "More than Mr. White, I tink. Since de bloodline is thinner wit' you, I will require much more. But not enough to kill you."

The man blinked three times and lowered his gaze. "Earn it then." He stalked toward her.

People got out of his way as fast as they could. In little time, they cleared a path between him and her.

Polly considered using her theurgy, but she had little left and revealing too much of it was risky. Most people did not know much about the true nature of blood casting, and Polly preferred to keep it that way. She then considered her hidden dagger, but she saw that Fulton's hands were empty. Too many eyes were watching for her to fight dirty.

The big man came in with a fast left jab aimed at her face. She ducked beneath his extended arm and landed a solid punch to his ribs. It had no effect. He opened the fist he had just thrown and dropped his palm on her head. Thick fingers took hold of her hair. She punched at his wrist and elbow, trying to break his hold. But her technique got sloppy as he tugged her off balance. His knee smashed into her stomach. Her eyes bulged as the blow sickened her. His right fist came in and punched her cheek, rattling her senses.

Fulton let go of her hair at the moment of impact, sending her crashing to the ground in a nauseous daze.

"You don't belong here, little girl!" he yelled down at her. "We don't need Excursionists coming in, upsetting the balance we maintain!"

120

Polly rolled off her back in a reverse somersault, putting distance between them. *"Left handed,"* she thought. *"If he weren't, dat punch would have knocked me out."* She was on her feet again, ready and steady.

Fulton did not hesitate. He came in like a brawler, merciless and unrelenting. Polly knew better than to stay within reach. She backed away and evaded each strike.

A circle of onlookers formed around them.

She did her best to find a weakness, but was too busy dodging. She could not avoid seeing the look on the large man's face. Angry. Intelligent. And something like a possessive pride that she did not understand.

Then she saw his weakness.

"You fight small women quite well, Fulton! Is dis someting you learned on your own or did your father teach you?"

"You are more than some common little woman," he argued. "It is purely out of respect that I go all out. Enemy or not, I take no chances with a threat!"

"Only a man like you would see a little girl as a threat," she said, cackling.

The man paused and squinted his eyes. "You're planning something. Or holding something back. Why is my blood so necessary? Why is ending the curses necessary? For what? So that apples can grow here again?" As he spoke he spread his hands for a split second.

Polly dived forward, her hands planting firm on the ground. As her head went down, her left heel came up in a fast arch. She felt her calf muscle collide with Fulton's blocking forearms. And in that instance of contact, she could sense exactly where his face would be.

Her other leg rose like the hand of a speeding clock, following the path of the first leg. She felt the heel of her boot smack into something solid. She pushed hard against the ground, springing up as she completed the tumble. The world spun for an instant, then Polly found herself sitting on the chest of her fallen foe.

Fulton's nose was smashed flat against his face. The bridge had split open and his nostrils gushed red. Fulton looked up at the grinning girl sitting on his chest through dazed, tear-flooded eyes.

"Guess who just popped your nose-cherry, Fulton?" She

pointed at her chest with her thumb. "Dis girl!"

Fulton roared in pain and covered his face. Polly got off him and up to her feet. "I can tell when a nose has never been broken," she said, pacing around him. "And de first time it happens, it bleeds and bleeds and bleeds. Nothing can prepare you for it."

She watched calmly as he rolled onto his side, cradling his busted face. The front of his purple shirt was already soaked with dark red.

"Give me your shirt, you bastard. It has what I need."

He did. Then his wife and biker buddies helped him up. All of them looked at her with mixtures of hatred and amazement. "Let's go, agave," Fritz barked at her husband.

"No," Fulton said, wiping at his eyes. "I want to stay and watch her fail at whatever she has planned!"

Polly ignored them. She went up to Alfeus White, bloody shirt in hand. "I will only need a few drops from you, Mr. White, if you please."

The middle-aged farmer looked over at Fulton and chuckled. "Lucky me," he joked.

Polly drew her dagger from up her sleeve. "Your finger, please."

"If it's all the same to you, little miss, could you cut my arm instead? I work with my hands."

"Of course," she said with a sweet smile. "Tank you." She took her knife and made the smallest of nicks on his forearm. The blood came out in thick, almost black droplets. She quickly sheathed her knife and caught the drops on the still dry sleeve of the bloody shirt.

She stepped over to Izzyk.

"Are you okay?" he asked.

"I'm fine," she said, a welt forming under her eye.

He looked at her with doubt and concern. "Polly, how do you know this will work? Have you ever tried anything like this before?"

Her eyes sharpened. "Listen to me now. Theurgy is a science, art, and craft. It is an extension, an expression, of who I am. I am a theurge, Izzyk. I work wonders."

She knelt down and picked up the cleverly wrapped mining pick. Many people gasped in shock as she revealed the gleaming metal of the tool once used as a memorial piece. She ignored the flood of comments and questions buzzing from them. She faced the crowd and held the tool up high. All went quiet.

"Many of you know what dis is. Yesternight I entered your haunted coal mine. I will not tell you what I saw and I will not tell you what I did. But I will tell you dat de mine is now clear of ghosts and de curse is lifted. De bones of de dead dere await retrieval. I have claimed dis pick as a votive offering in exchange for my service, so you need not tank me. I do what I will and take what I wish. And now wit' dis instrument I will break another curse because my heart tells me to do so."

Resting the pick on her shoulder, she stepped up to the fence. The rail fence was nothing more than long planks of timber placed so they would simply lay on each other. She kicked over a section with little trouble, and kept walking.

The townsfolk watched with bated breath as the strange girl walked toward the skeletons. Polly felt the exact same feeling she had felt in the mine cave the night before. It was no different than the punch she had just taken, unpleasant and jolting at first, but she had gone through it enough times to keep going.

The *necrofear* surrounded her as she reached the middle. The hatred and fear that swirled around her seemed so petty compared to the hate she already carried in her heart. She placed the mining pick on the ground. She then took the bloody shirt and held it over the pick head. She sent her will into the cotton fibers of the shirt and began to push out the blood. The dripping drops of crimson turned into a thin stream that poured onto the gleaming metal. Polly moved the shirt back and forth, coating the dark shiny pick head with blood until every last drop had drained out. She tossed the dry shirt aside and took up the pick. Closing her eyes, she began to speak.

"Luis...Mathu...I bid thee awaken from your nightmare. Your families have given deir own blood to see you at peace. Live on in deir memories. Let your souls spread throughout eternity." She then walked over to the bones of Mathu White, raised the pick high above her head, and began to dig him a grave.

After the first few swings, she noticed the skeleton raise its head and look at her. "I'm so sleepy," he said in a soft voice. He then made a weak laugh. "A beautiful woman is making my bed. Isn't

123

she?"

Polly felt a lump grow in her throat. She smiled and kept digging.

"This is how I always wanted to go. Surrounded by family. I wish they would come closer."

Polly turned to the crowd. "White Family! Get over here now!"

At first, the people hesitated. But Alfeus White soon took charge and led his kinfolk inside the broken fence. They felt no supernatural terror surround them, only the love of a relative they never knew. They gathered around the talking bones of Mathu as if he were a dying grandfather, and not some post-mort monster.

As Polly dug into the clay dirt, she overheard the family telling stories to the dying ghost that resided in those old bones. She heard Mathu's laughter as small children went up and talked to him with shy, curious voices. All took turns sitting beside him and holding his boney hand, sharing words of tenderness.

As she dug, Polly bore witness to the bond only family can forge. It was a bond that transcended the power of Death and Time's separation of generations. It was the bond of Blood. When she finished digging a hole about mid-thigh deep, the White Family picked up the remains of their ancestor and lay him gently in the ground.

The skull turned its gaze to Polly. "Now, I think it's time I got tucked in."

Polly nodded as the tears came. She watched as Alfeus, the farmer, picked up a handful of loose dirt and sprinkled it onto the bones. The skeleton went still and said no more.

"We'll finish this from here," Alfeus offered. "You can get started on Luis."

Polly nodded and walked to the other set of bones. As she did, she looked to Fulton and Fritz. The couple only gave her dirty looks and left for home. She wiped sweat from her brow and went to work on the next grave.

"I was so stupid," sighed the bones of Luis Bierce. "I killed a man and myself all because I could not have her. Over the last two thousand years I have seen countless girls watch me reenact this horrible fight. Many of them seemed just as wonderful as her. I could have lived at least another millennia and found love again,

124

eventually."

"Why did it go on for so long?" Polly asked as she broke up the dirt. "What compelled you to keep killing each other night after night?"

"I don't know. I just don't know. But something changed. Yesternight, I think. Even though we went through the motions again just now, something odd was happening. We were stirring in our death-sleep you could say. And then, *you* woke us up. Thank you for that."

"My pleasure, Luis. I am sorry dat your family won't come to see you off."

"Oh, I don't mind. I have you to keep me company. You're pretty to look at. Just as pretty as *she* was, I think."

Polly smiled. "I am honored you tink dat, Luis."

When she finished digging, members of the White Family offered to lay Luis to rest. He politely refused and crawled into the grave on his own. He sat up and made a come hither gesture to Polly. "I need to tell you a secret. Come closer."

Polly knelt down. "Okay."

"Closer," the skeleton beckoned. "So no one else knows."

She leaned down further, close enough for him to whisper in her ear. She felt the teeth of the skull press softly against her cheek and heard to sound of a kiss.

Polly sat back up, shocked and smiling. "You sneaky...!"

The bones of Luis Bierce seemed to grin at her with roguish pride. And then they collapsed into the shallow earth.

Polly's vision clouded over from the tears in her eyes, sweet uninvited tears. She heard a mixture of cheering and weeping from the townsfolk. Even Izzyk looked on with wonder. She felt it coming from all around her: Gratitude. It was an emotion so strange, so foreign to her. It was like sweet honey in a rotten tooth's cavity. They were strangers. They were fools, the townsfolk. They thought she did this for them, and not her own selfish want.

They began closing in from all around, no longer fearing the once haunted clay. Praises came from all sides, words like "Lady Gone!" and "Hail! Polly the Red!"

"Oh, no," she said under her breath. She was not like other theurges. Her *philocreed* was not meant for the masses to live by. They were supposed to *die* by it. And now her theurgy was all but

125

drained. She felt vulnerable. She had just beaten up a local gangster and used his own blood to end a haunting.

"Why did he not want me to end de curse?" she thought as she picked up the shiny mining pick. Darting straight through the thinnest portion of the crowd, she ignored people's requests to stop. She ran fast and hard into the grove of sparse evergreens. She ran for minutes on end, long past the point of any townsperson being able to find her.

She dropped the pick and collapsed beneath a humongous pine tree. The dead orange needles on the ground cushioned her fall like an old familiar bed. The bristly boughs above her blocked out the fading light of evening. This wood was dark. The other towering pines nearby made it so the light of day never shown through. The darkness was comforting in that it gave her a place to hide. But the cold it wrought made her shiver. She was worried, and the shivering only made it worse. As she pondered the brutal motivations of Fulton Gladish, she fell into a deep sleep, still shaking all through the cold night.

Part 4

"Where did you sleep yesternight?" Izzyk asked as Polly shuffled through the front door of his home.

"In de pines," she answered.

"In the pines?" he parroted. "Are you crazy?"

She looked away and giggled uncontrollably. "Maybe. Maybe it's de only way to understand a crazy world!"

The young man arched an eyebrow and glared at her. "You look like the cat dragged you all over town before stopping here."

"Oh?" she chuckled, pulling pine needles out of her hair. "I thought you said I was de most beau-"

He covered her mouth with his hand. "My parents are awake!" he said in a loud whisper. "We were just about to have breakfast." He paused for a moment. "Would you care to join us? They were very impressed with you yesterday. I was, too."

She tenderly removed his hand and smiled. "As hungry as I am, I would not mind eating wit' your aunt Fritz and uncle Fulton."

He looked at her face and frowned. "He gave you quite a shiner. That bruise looks horrible."

Polly shrugged. "Not as bad as his nose, I am sure."

Mark and Resula Spinser kept silent when Polly entered the dining room. The man of the house only rose from his chair to pull out another for her. The lady of the house went to the cupboard to fetch another plate and utensils. Although they did not speak to her, they made it clear through their warm smiles and gestures that she was indeed welcome.

Polly ate her fill. No words were spoken at the table all the while. It seemed as if the Spinser Family were waiting for her to speak first. She washed her food down with a pint of milk.

"Tank you," she said. Breaking the silence did not come easy. "I know dat when I first entered your house, I acted a little strange."

"That was before we knew you were a theurge," Mark said. "It is not for us to understand your ways."

Polly closed her eyes and shook her head. "Don't tink dat way, Mr. Spinser, please. I am not dat kind of theurge. My truth is not de same as yours."

"Are you an Animist Shaman?" Resula asked. "A necrotheurge? People have been speculating since yesterday what your path is." She stared at Polly for a long moment. The woman's face grew worried. "Are you a blood theurge?"

Polly took a deep, uneasy breath and sighed. She looked at Mark Spinser, who also looked more than a little concerned. "You were right, Mr. Spinser. It is not for you to understand me or my ways."

Mark Spinser looked at the blood and earth stained mining pick the girl had brought in. "You acquired that from the coalmine," he said.

Polly nodded. "De curse dere has been lifted as well. What do you know about dis pick, Mr. Spinser?"

The man's jaw dropped, as he regarded the girl. "You broke the mine's curse, too?"

"Yes," Polly said waving the question away. "But I need to know more about dis pick. Who made it? Who commissioned it? Who decided dat it should be used as a monument piece?"

127

Mark and Resula looked at each other. Communicating only as a husband and wife can do, through their eyes.

"Juniper Beech," the woman uttered.

Polly sat back in her chair and caught a burp in her mouth. "De same man dat your friend, Remus Kach, supposedly killed. When I was exploring de coalmines, I heard many ghosts asking him for help or cursing his name."

Mark nodded. "He was the soul survivor of the mining accident that killed all those men. He was devastated. He was their supervisor and blamed himself for their deaths."

"He blamed de right person, den," Polly said with a smirk. "It was *his* idea for de mining pick, yes?"

Mark nodded faster, his eyes growing "Juniper commissioned it and even installed it personally."

"Do you know who fashioned it for him?"

Mark shook his head.

Polly bared her teeth in a grin. "Dat is all I need to know and all I am willing to share. What about your brother-in-law, Fulton? Why did he try to stop me yesterday? Why does he want de land to stay cursed?"

"The Gray Dust Poppy," Resula answered. "They believe that the Geohex causes it to grow. It's how most of the Trotting Swans make money to support their families."

Mark nodded in agreement. "As much as I don't like it, I must admit that it keeps the county's economy afloat."

Polly frowned in thought, "So, as long as I and my travel mates find ways to break curses, de Trotting Swans are our enemies." She bit her lip and combed her fingers through her hair. "Sheriff Edifice Teige was deir enemy, too. He killed several of dem after dey killed de previous sheriff. Teige even admitted dat he only killed dem to be a hero in de people's eyes. Fulton Gladish said dat de Swans Teige killed were ex-members, but he expressed gratitude when he found out my team and I killed Teige. If only I knew why de sheriff before him was killed in de first place, I might make better sense of dis."

"There is a rumor," Mark started softly.

Polly raised her eyes to meet his.

The man leaned in. "Sheriff Farnuff was supposedly killed by the Swans because he denied them passage through Drowsy

128

Nook. The Swans needed a route through the town to get to Embrenil. I can imagine they would make quite a profit selling the flower in a city that size."

Polly's eyes widened. "And Edifice Teige became an even worse obstacle for dem. No wonder Fulton seemed grateful to me at first." It was at that point Polly fell silent. And in that silence she considered many things. Was Fulton worth killing? Were *any* of the Trotting Swans worth killing? They were drug smugglers, responsible for poisoning their neighbors. Her theurgy, her power, was all but spent. She could not even heal the bruise on her face. She had to make a sacrifice soon.

"Who will it be?" she thought. It was then she decided that if Fulton or any other Swan laid a hand on her, she would cut their blood free and shatter their soul.

"We need to talk more about Juniper Beech," Resula insisted. "Maybe there's a connection, I mean, with Remus. If you say that Juniper might have been responsible for killing his own workers and cursing the cave, maybe that had something to do with why he was murdered."

Polly crossed her arms. "You still tink Remus Kach was innocent?"

"I know it," the woman insisted.

Polly closed her eyes and tried to listen to the woman's heart beat. She heard nothing. Her power was dwindling. "I can still try to find out. If dat is your wish."

Resula dropped her eyes and paused. "Yes, it is. I saw his ghost that night. The look on his face has haunted my dreams ever since. I want him to move on. He has to. He has to." She began to weep.

Her husband was quick to move to her side and console her. Polly watched as Resula Spinser, a once seemingly strong woman, broke down into loud sobs. Izzyk went over to his parents and put his arms around them.

The sight was too strange for Polly Gone to bear. She stood up and picked up the mining pick. "I'm going to pay Remus a visit. Dose who want to come, grab your coats."

Resula peeked out from her husband's embrace. "You're not going to dig him up, are you?!"

"If I have to," Polly answered with a tilt to her head. "Dis

129

pick is mine now. In ways dat only my heart can comprehend it has aided me in ending two curses in dis town. I intend to keep it wit' me for a while. If de ghost of Remus Kach truly exists, I will find out." She tilted her head to the other side, her face unchanging. "Or not."

In less than a minute, Polly and the three members of the Spinser family were ready to go. In the late morning daylight, they made their way through town. The curving, winding, wooded roads of Barnhart allowed them to walk without too many townsfolk spotting them. Occasionally, someone would recognize the "Miracle Theurge," who ended the curses of the coalmine and the dueling suitors. But Polly made it clear to them that she did not wish to be bothered.

They were almost to the Graveyard when one last person approached her. The Drakeri woman was neither young, nor middle aged. She wore a simple gray and blue dress with a hat to match. Her manner seemed well composed, despite the screaming toddler she carried on her hip. Yet Polly could sense an intense emotion concealed behind her face. "Are you Polly Gone?" the woman asked.

"I am," Polly answered as she stopped. "Why do you ask? Were you not at de Dueling Grounds yesterday?"

"I was not," the woman replied. "I had a child to tend to. But my husband was. He told me of what happened. I have also heard that you cleaned out the coalmine of its evil air. People who have entered there have now been able to recover the bones of their loved ones."

"Dat's nice to know," Polly muttered. "What more do you want from me?"

"I wish to thank you," the woman replied with a similar edge. "My father died in that mine. And because of you, his spirit is no longer stagnant, but is now dispersed and cleansed in the ocean of souls."

Polly felt an odd twist in her stomach. "What was your father's name?"

"Jom Belnap," the woman replied sternly. "My name is Liddy."

"I see." Polly bit her lip. "I except your tanks wit' de utmost humility, Liddy."

"I beg to differ, Miss Gone, for I have not yet given the thanks I intended to."

"Oh?"

The woman shook her head once and knelt low into a humble curtsy. "I wish to treat you to supper. We haven't much variety in our larder. But I can make the most out of simple ingredients."

Polly glanced at the Spinser Family as if she needed their opinion. She then turned back to the woman and her child. "I will not be staying in Barnhart much longer. When would you have me come?"

"Tonight would be fine. On the sixth hour."

"Why so late?" Polly asked.

The woman gave her wailing, squirming child a gentle shake and a shush. "My husband went all the way to Pevulaneum to pick up my brother, Austen. He will no doubt want thank you, too. Father's death hit him the hardest, and I feel that this might bring him closure."

"I see," Polly sighed. She gave the toddler a quick glance and cringed. She was glad to be young and unmothered. "I will come tonight after I attend to a present matter. Where do you live?"

"We live in the little gray house with blue shutters by the northwest side of the Flea Market. Twelve Jaxon Road. Thank you very much, Miss Gone. I will delay you no further. Good day to you all." Liddy curtsied once more, inclining her head to Polly and the Spinser family.

Her toddler let out a high-pitched shriek. Liddy gave her child another comforting shake as she turned and walked off.

"Good day," Polly returned in a whisper. She stood and watched the woman make her way down the road. The lady was no doubt the daughter of the ghost who talked to her in the mine. She felt an odd kinship with Liddy. She knew what it was like to be fatherless. To have no man in her early life to set the standards of all others. Fathers. Men whose words and deeds alone could have shaped their children's views of the world. Liddy's father existed now only as fragments of soul in the eggs, seeds, and wombs wherever life was beginning. And Polly's father did not even know her, or at least not in the way she would want him to.

"Polly?" Izzyk said, jarring her from her thoughts.

"Hmm? Oh. Yes. De graveyard."

131

The four of them were at the Barnhart Graveyard all day. The Sixth Hour was drawing near. Polly was at a loss for ideas, and her power was all but depleted.

She asked the Spinsers once more if Remus Kach had any blood relatives at all. With their blood she might be able to do what she did with the Dueling Suitors. But, alas, they knew of none.

She listened to Resula repeat the tale of her encounter with the ghost in greater detail. But the story yielded no clues.

Polly tried sensing the slightest hint of *necrofear* around the dead man's grave. All she felt was the cool autumn breeze swishing her hair this way and that.

"I'm sorry," she told them. "De coal mine and de Dueling both seemed so difficult, dat I thought dis would be much easier. I feel I have lead you up here for nothing."

Mark Spinser took her hand and smiled. "Don't let it bother you, Miss Gone. You have already done so much. Because of you the Coalmine will soon reopen and this poor town can get back on its feet again. Men will have jobs again. Families will eat because of your deeds. Besides, there will be other chances for you to help Remus' soul if it does indeed need helping."

Polly smiled and then regarded Resula.

The woman stood at the foot of the grave, her troubled face fixed on the rocky pile. "I'm not crazy. I really did see him that night. He stood right where I'm standing."

"I know, dear." Mark said, placing his hands on her shoulders. He placed a kiss on the back of her head. "I believe you." He turned to his son. "Let's go home. Miss Gone has dinner plans to keep."

"Do you think I could go, too?" Izzyk seemed to ask both Polly and his father at the same time.

Mark looked at her.

"It's fine," Polly said. "I don't mind."

Mark looked at his son and Polly back and forth. His lips curved into a knowing smirk. "Sure. Why not?" He put his arm around his wife and they took their leave of the old graveyard.

132

When the couple were out of sight, Polly looked at Izzyk with playful accusation in her eyes. "Why do you feel the need to go wit' me everywhere?"

The young man arched an eyebrow and adjusted his glasses. There was a new cockiness to him that Polly found more than a little appealing. "As if I need to give an answer!" he bragged with a grin.

⬡

"I did not know there would be two of you coming," Liddy said when she met them at her front door. "I fear I may not have enough food for supper."

"Don't worry about it, Miss Liddy." Izzyk assured her. "Just use up whatever you have. Stop by the shop tomorrow and you can restock whatever you need. No charge."

The woman's face grew stern. "We do not need your charity, young Mr. Spinser."

Izzyk waved his hand. "Oh, don't think of it that way. It's not charity. It's reimbursement. I plan on eating like a pig. Besides, you've always been such a good customer."

Liddy allowed herself a smile. She looked at Polly with a smirk. "Such a gentleman he is. Is he *always* this persuasive?"

Polly crossed her arms and fought a blush. "Not always."

Liddy covered her mouth and laughed. "Both of you, please come in. My husband and brother have not yet arrived. Please, pardon the clutter."

The house was a single story tall. The interior consisted of one large living space that served as the den, dining room, and kitchen. Polly saw a hatch door on the floor that no doubt led down to underground bedrooms. The walls were speckled with small photographs in circular wood frames. Polly could tell by how yellow they were that they were centuries old.

"Dis is de house of your father," Polly said as she skimmed over the portraits.

"Yes," Liddy answered. The woman went over to the wall by her wood stove and pointed out a particular portrait. "This is him," she said, before crossing her arms. "I was ten when he died. Shortly

133

after that, my brother, Austen, applied for a position at the mine. He was over fifty by then, and thought he stood a chance at being hired. But the mine closed shortly after the accident. It was the hauntings, you see. People would enter and go mad with fear. Even I ventured in once. But as soon as I heard the chirps of the canaries, I fled. All manner of Excursionists including theurges of all paths failed to tame that wretched place. Some died. Some ran away. Some went insane and were put in Rarkee Infirmary. Some disappeared entirely.

"About two hundred and thirty years ago, an eccentric shaman came and purchased the mine. He converted it into a skate rink. He claimed that if enough people came and had fun inside the mine, the evil spirits would be driven out. It worked for about five years, before he went missing. When that happened, his mysticism could no longer assist us. And the haunting returned."

"I met your father's ghost," Polly said, not sure if she was interrupting the woman.

Liddy fell silent. Her mouth opened, but no words came.

Polly studied the portrait on the wall. The face of Jom Belnap was not what she'd expected. He had soft eyes that seemed a little too close together. His short beard seemed to make up for a weak chin. And his small button nose did not seem to go with his long face. "He talked to me. He thought I was you, sneaking into the mine while he was working."

Liddy twitched from her stomach as a lump formed in her throat. "I used to pay him surprise visits."

Polly nodded, still eying the photo. "He even kissed my hand when he saw dat I had a cut on it. I could tell dat he loved you very much. And after de curse was lifted, his ghost-possessed bones thanked me for bringing peace to him and his coworkers."

Polly was taken by surprise at how fast Liddy could move. Before she could react, the homemaker already held her in a tight embrace. The woman began to sob and shake.

Polly froze, not knowing what to do. She searched her feelings. To her dismay, she could feel nothing. *Is it because I'm surprised? Do I really care at all? If not, why did I bother coming to visit?*

As these questions flooded her befuddled mind, two men entered the home through the front door. Both looked a bit older

134

than Liddy, probably in their fifth century.

"Mr. Oakin!" Izzyk declared with a wry smile. He approached one of the men with a hearty handshake.

"Izzyk the shop boy!" the man exclaimed with a curious grin. "Will you be joining us for dinner, also?"

"He will," Liddy answered as she composed herself. She took a step away from Polly and cleared her throat. She addressed the two men. "Agave, Austen. This is Ms. Polly Gone, the theurge who saved our town and my father's soul from spiritual stagnation."

Mr. Oakin, who was a bear of a man, approached Polly with a big baby-faced grin. He took her hands in his own and peppered them with kisses. "Lady Gone! That is what some are calling you now, yes? You have no idea how honored we are to have you here. The deeds you performed in this town and Drowsy Nook will never be forgotten!"

The other thinner man approached Liddy. "Tell me, little sister, were our father's bones recovered? Where are they?"

The woman nodded. "All eighteen of men's remains were found. Finally. The undertaker has them now. But no one knows whose bones belong to whom. Most of the families have proposed having one large funeral for all of them."

The man closed his eyes, hung his head, and sighed as if a small burden had been lifted off his shoulders. He wore a hat that hid much of his face. When he did raise his head, his face became visible. He looked at the woman who freed his father's ghost.

Polly froze when his sad eyes met hers.

"Miss Gone," Liddy started. "This is my older brother, Austen."

Polly fought with all her guile and glibness to keep her face still. She had to make her body relax as the man stepped toward her.

Austen Belnap removed his hat. "You succeeded where many have failed, Lady Gone," he said with a warm smile.

"By my blood!" Polly thought. *"He looks almost exactly like Remus Kach did in de picture!"* She could not believe what she was seeing. She glanced at Izzyk, to see if he saw what she did. But the young man showed no sign. She could find no words for the man addressing her. So instead, she put her palm over her heart and bowed.

"Wow," Austen exclaimed, cracking a meager smile. "A

135

theurge in the house I grew up in. Are you sure that my father's spirit no longer suffers in that horrid mine?"

Polly nodded. "On my philocreed, Mr. Belnap."

Austen raised his eyebrows. "Well, then. That's good enough for me." He reached into his coat pocket and pulled out a jingling leather pouch. "I've been adding to this for a long time. Four hundred and fifty-three grotz pieces. One for every year I've waited for this very day." He put the heavy pouch in Polly's hand. "You deserve more than this. But it's all I can give."

Polly bit the inside of her bottom lip and nodded in thanks. "Dis will help me on my travels. Tank you, Mr. Belnap."

When dinner was served, everyone sat at the table. Izzyk kept the conversation going, answering most of the questions aimed at Polly. She sat, barely touching her food, only speaking when she felt she had to. Polly made it a point to sit next to Izzyk. She had to handle this situation just right.

"So, Mr. Belnap," she started with a smile. "You live in a neighboring town?"

Austen Belnap swallowed his food and nodded. "Pevulaneum. It's fifteen miles east of here."

"And how long have you lived dere?"

"About one hundred seventy-six years now." He stabbed a piece of meat with his fork.

"But you still visit from time to time, yes?"

Austen was just about to pop the next bite in his mouth when he paused.

"Not often enough!" Liddy answered for him in a playful scolding tone. "He visited a week or two ago. But it had ten years since his last visit."

"I was busy," Austen replied in his defense. "Besides, you know this town holds nothing but bad memories for me."

"Bad memories or bad blood?" Polly asked, her eyes narrowing.

Austen's eyes flashed with what Polly was searching for: paranoia. "What do you mean, Lady Gone?"

"Did you have any enemies here? Someone who did you wrong?"

Austen squinted his eyes. He looked at her, searching for answers in her stare as she did the same.

Polly saw the muscles in his jaw tighten. Even though she had never seen *his* face before, she still recognized it! That's when she knew. A sly smile curved her lips. "I am a theurge, Austen. Do you tink dis is merely a chance meeting?" She was bluffing, of course. But he did not know that. Polly set her elbows on the table and steepled her fingers.

"What are you getting at?" he asked, fear and frustration dripped from his words.

Polly leaned over to Izzyk and whispered something in his ear. The young man looked confused and worried. But he uttered not a word and got up to leave.

"What is all this about?" Liddy asked, her face wrinkling with concern.

"Don't you know?" Polly asked her as she cast a wicked look at Austen.

"She doesn't know!" Austen exclaimed, standing up from his seat. He shook with unease and panic. He looked to Polly, his eyes pleading. "She does not know. She never did."

Polly stood up and met Austen's worried eyes. "But *I* know," she hissed with all the ire and spite she could muster. She picked up the mining pick and held it up passively. "Dis mining pick was imbedded in de rock walls of de coalmine by Juniper Beech. De same man dat many blame for de deaths of dose eighteen men, including your father. When I removed de pick from de rock, de curse ended! I tink dat Juniper Beech also had someting to do wit' cursing de mine. What a pity it is dat Remus Kach murdered him dese ten years past. Now we may never know for sure."

Austen Belnap grimaced as if a bumble bee had just stung his throat. "You think that yellow, two faced son of a whore turned my dad into a ghost after killing him?"

Polly regarded him coldly. "You want answers? So do I. Let's go for a late night stroll, Mr. Belnap. Just you and me. De witching hour draws near!"

The winds of Barnhart hissed in a loud chorus throughout

branches of the trees. In the distance, the creaking groan of an unlatched barn door sang along. The tall grasses of untended fields rustled, singing tenor to the dirge of the late night wind. Here and there, Austen Belnap could see the lights of homes go out for the night. So too were his own hopes dying within him. One spark at a time. The mysterious young woman who walked beside him said nothing. The lantern he carried lit every corner of her face. Yet he had not the slightest clue what she had planned.

"Where are we going?" he asked.

"Where, why, who, when, how......All dese tings we will know soon enough," Polly told him.

A half dozen heavy questions pushed against the man's lips. But instead of asking them, he tried to reason with her. "You came here to solve the ghost stories, right? I heard about what you did in Drowsy Nook. You're a hero, Lady Gone." The man waited to get a reaction. But her face remained still. "I have nothing to do with this Geohex, I swear. I'm a victim of it."

"I know," Polly said calmly. "Come along, Mr. Belnap. All your worries will soon be over." She began to walk faster. "You'd better keep up. If you try to run, you won't get far. Not dis time, Mr. Belnap. Do you understand me?"

Austen swallowed hard and nodded. He kept up with her brisk steps until they reached the cemetery. Though the wind was loud and strong, the atmosphere was clean of clouds. The *Hunveins* thousands of feet above the realm shined like dozens of lightning bolts frozen against the inside of an upside down bowl. The distant veins of light cast a soft glow upon the rolling hills of the graveyard.

Polly and Austen Belnap came to a pile of stones, the resting place of Remus Kach.

"Stand dere," Polly ordered.

"Stand where?" he asked.

"At de foot of de grave, Mr. Belnap. Stand dere and wait. Utter not a word if you want dis to go smoothly."

The man at first did as commanded. But after a few dozen seconds of wonder and worry, he began to tremble. "You're going to summon this man's ghost, aren't you? Aren't you?!"

Polly looked at him as if he were an idiot. She shook her head, partly to say "No," and partly in disgust. She was just about to lecture him on silence again when she heard the sound of footsteps.

138

She turned to look and frowned. "Dey are here."

"Who?"

"Shut up and take off your hat!" she hissed.

The man did so. He looked in the same direction she did and waited. It was not long before Izzyk, Mark, and Resula Spinser came into view.

Mark and his wife froze in shock when they saw Austen Belnap. The woman nearly fainted and let out a weak, stifled scream. Mark's expression was one of pure shock and terror. "Remus!" he cried in a shaky voice. "Remus, is that you?"

"No. It is not," Polly answered. She locked eyes with Resula. "Mrs. Spinser. Is dis de 'ghost' you saw standing here dat night?"

Resula nodded. Her mouth gaped in confusion. "Yes?"

Polly looked at Austen like a mother who caught a child misbehaving. "Well, I can assure you both dat dis is no ghost! See?" She twisted her body as she finished talking. With a sharp turn of her hips, she sent her leg upward, burying her boot into the man's groin.

As Austen fell to his knees, Polly had already maneuvered behind him. Before he knew it, Polly had drawn her knife and jerked his head back by the hair. She rested the edge of her blade against his throat.

"Here he is!" she declared. "De slayer who ran! De man dat every witness mistook for Remus Kach! De man who let Remus Kach die in his place! De true killer of Juniper Beech: Austen Belnap! Look at his face on dis dark night. Even you two thought it was Remus. And now, we have him!"

"Remus Kach was the man the law convicted!" Austen defended. "He said nothing in his own defense! It wasn't my fault he died!"

Mark held tight to his wife. Their hearts swam with confusion, rage, and grief. "You're a Belnap? Then you had kin that died in the mine."

Austen winced as the razor edge stung his sweating skin. "Juniper Beech killed my father. So, I killed him that night. I never meant for Remus to take the blame. I swear! I s-swear!" He began to weep. "I left town and didn't hear until weeks later that Remus was hanged for it! Oh, no...I never forgave myself! Why didn't he just claim his innocence? Then they could have just hunted me down

139

or...I ....I...Why? Why him and not me?" His weeping turned into sobs. "I came to visit his grave, this dishonorable pile of stones! She saw me and fainted. So, I ran away...again. Oh, please forgive me!"

Mark covered his face and screamed in anguish.

Resula fell to her knees and began to bawl her eyes out.

Izzyk stood by them, not knowing what to do or say. He then looked to the woman holding the knife. "Polly, do you know what you are doing?"

Polly grimaced and glared back down at the man she held at her mercy. "Yes," she answered between gritted teeth.

"Do you have a plan?" the young man asked, his voice growing wary and concerned.

"I plan to *react*, Izzyk. De maker of your parent's pain, de man responsible for deir friend's death. I need only your parent's word, and I will set his blood free upon dis pile of rocks! Den, if de soul of Remus Kach *is* perchance cursed to ghosthood, dis sacrifice will free him!"

Mark Spinser dropped his hands from his face. His eyes were wild and bloodshot. "You would do that, Miss Gone? You would give us justice and keep our hands clean of it?"

"I would," Polly answered.

Mark began to nod in approval. "Yes! Yes, avenge my friend!"

"*Noooo!!!!*" Resula shouted, standing up from her crying. "No, please, don't kill him!"

"Resula?" Mark asked, astonished. "Why not? Remus died because of this man!"

"No!" the woman moaned. "No more death or killing!" She closed her eyes and proclaimed through her quivering lips "Remus died because of *me*. He...he was with me the night of the murder...while you were at the store..." She opened her tear-filled eyes to look at her husband. "We were lovers, Mark. Remus and I. We both regretted it, but we still didn't stop. Not until the night Juniper Beech was murdered. When they arrested him, we both knew that the only way to prove his innocence was to expose our affair. I wanted to save him, but couldn't. He willingly went to the noose instead of letting you find out. You were his best friend, Mark. And he was so sorry for wronging you that he-"

Her words were cut off as Mark slapped her hard against her

140

cheek. "How could you? Both of you!" He slapped her again, so hard she almost fell. He was just about to latch on to her neck when Izzyk tackled him to the grass.

"Stop it!" the young man pleaded, trying to hold his father down.

Mad with grief and drunk on rage, Mark Spinser struggled with his son. He screamed and wailed as he tried to free himself.

Resula backed away several feet, watching her husband as fear mingled with the shame on her face.

Polly watched the heartache unfold. She actually found herself thinking *"Mother would revel in dis, de breaking of three hearts!"* Then she tasted something bitter in her mouth. "Enough!" she yelled. "If anybody dies tonight, it will be me who chooses!"

The family froze at her words.

Polly bared her teeth at them. "Go back home, all of you. De mysteries are solved. De curses are lifted. Now I collect my reward!"

"What reward, Polly?" Izzyk asked.

"His blood," she answered, nodding down at the helpless man. "I have performed what I set out to do. Now, my philocreed demands a sacrifice. I tried to include you all in it. But you all have other worries dat are none of my concern."

Resula looked to her with pleading eyes. "Please, Miss Gone! I don't want to live with the guilt of another man's death. Juniper Beech did have it coming. This man took vengeance when the law could not offer justice! I can't blame him for Remus' death."

Polly cackled at her. "Ha! What a well-intentioned whore you have been! You only wished to spare everyone's feelings, yes? Including your own? The bonds of your loves are cut, Resula Spinser. May your heart bleed dry and wither all de rest of your days!"

The woman fell to her knees. Her mouth opened to scream, yet her throat was too tight with grief for sound to come out. She trembled and shook and pulled at her long beautiful hair. When at last she could scream, it was a wail that almost woke the dead.

"And as for you, Mark Spinser!" Polly bellowed. "You who have done no wrong. Continue to do so! Do not let your heart drag you down de road of revenge like dis man before me. Do not bless me wit' de excuse to slit your throat as well. Continue your wholesome life selling nourishment to your neighbors. Go. And decide de fate of your marriage."

"Polly!" Izzyk cried. "You're not going to really kill him, are you?" She could see his trust in her melting on his face.

For a brief moment the grip on her dagger softened. "Get out of here, Izzyk. Take your parents wit' you. If I am to sustain my power, dis man must die. Just leave and never look back."

The young man's head shook in defiance. His hands trembled as he balled them into fists. "This is all wrong. This man needs to be turned into the Law House. They will do justice upon him."

Polly scoffed. "Justice is merely revenge taken by someone the wrong-doer did not wrong. It is a corruption of de natural order, letting officials kill what is yours to kill. I do not begrudge dis man for slaying his father's murderer. What he did was right, as far as I can see. *And* I understand dat he did not intend for Remus Kach to die in his place. However, he made de choice to *let* Remus be remembered as a killer and be buried under a pile of broken rocks dat people spit on as dey pass by. De three of you can stay and watch for all I care. But bear dis in mind: If either of you tell de Law what I did here tonight, I will expose Resula. I will tell dem of how she let an innocent man go on to his death for de sake of her hollow honor."

The eyes of the guilt-ridden housewife widened in terror. Resula covered her mouth to stifle a scream. Shaking her head, she turned away and ran back the way she'd come. Mark, with a torn expression of anger and confusion, followed after her.

Izzyk watched his parents flee from the cemetery. He looked back at Polly, his face displaying the protest of her action. But as he wondered what more harm his parents might inflict upon each other, he followed after them.

"Alone at last," Polly purred with a sigh of relief. Her upper lip curled into a vicious sneer. Bitterness soaked into her voice. "Speak your last words, Austen Belnap. What you sent around has come around."

Austen slumped, almost in a dazed stupor. He simply sat on his knees, unmoving. All his hope had bled away. Fear beyond fear had numbed his mind. He stared at the pile of stones. Then he smiled, sadly. "Thanks again, Lady Gone. At least I lived to know my father's spirit moved on."

Polly was about to drag the edge across his neck. The man's words stirred up no sympathy in her. Then the image of Liddy Belnap flashed in her mind. Polly had only known the woman a few hours, but there was already a bond between them. A small, but significant bond. Polly never knew her father growing up. She had always dreamed of what it would be like to have him there. Polly had no brothers, or at least a brother she grew up with. *"How would Liddy feel to lose a brother, too? Do I really want her to feel dat?"* She took a deep breath and stuttered out the word, "No."

"Huh?" Austen muttered. He felt her hands slap onto his shoulders and spin him around. He fell backward onto the stone pile that was Remus Kach's grave. He looked up to see her knife's point just inches from his face.

"I'm letting you go!" she yelled with a tight throat. "Go back to your sister's house and confess your sins to her. Tell no one of dis night or what happened here. Swear to me!"

"I swear!" he answered, trembling.

Polly gritted her teeth and flicked her wrist. Her dagger's point split his face open from chin to nose. Austen Belnap squealed and covered the wound with his hands. Blood oozed out from between his fingers.

Polly bent down to look him eye to eye. "Dat is so no one ever mistakes you for someone else again. Now, get out of my sight."

Izzyk was waiting by his homestead gate when she returned with Polly's bileer, Waltre, saddled, ready, and hitched to a post. The inside of the house was still lit. The young man sat hunched upon a large smooth stone, staring at the ground with a somber gaze.

Polly could sense his unease when she approached. "I did not kill him," she said.

His eyes lifted to her, then turned back. He said nothing.

Polly paused and frowned. She took a wary step closer. "Your parents are inside?"

His jaw clenched as he closed his eyes and nodded.

"I-I hope dey can work tings out."

"You don't mean that," he argued. "Not after what you said up there."

"I *do* mean it. But not for deir sakes. For yours."

He stood up and looked at her. "You...You don't belong here, Polly."

His words hit her hard, but in her heart they rang true. "Yes. It's seems I do not belong anywhere. Blood must flow. It cannot stay in any one place for too long."

"Is that part of your *philocreed?*"

"It is."

"Blood must flow...," he considered the words. "That's also why you kill people?"

Polly shook her head. "Do not try to understand me. I have yet to fully do so myself. I only try to kill evil people. I'm sorry your parents are having troubles. If you are lucky, dis will be de worst it will get. Dey really do love each other, you know. Deir hearts beat as one."

The young man grimaced with anger. "What would you know about love? Bloody murderer! You didn't come to this town to make life better for us. You came to test yourself, to see what your power could do." He stomped toward her, stopping just inches away. "Blood flows alright, Polly Gone. But it only flows to the bottom without a *heart* to keep it going. And you don't have one!"

Izzyk had no time to react. She moved too swiftly. Before he knew it, Polly had grabbed the sides of his head and pulled his sneering lips onto hers. His mind whirled. The anger he felt melted into a confused oblivion. Her plump lips. Her teeth. Her tongue. Her breath. Nothing else existed in that moment.

The strange girl pulled away only a few inches and waited for his eyes to open. "You are far, far too good for me, Izzyk."

He stood in utter shock as she stepped away and mounted her steed.

"Take care of yourself, and your family," she told him.

Izzyk watched helplessly as she dashed away into the night. For the rest of his life, that kiss would echo in his memory, appearing now and again in his thoughts. Because of *her*, the coalmine would reopen. Because of *her*, two dueling souls had made peace. Because of *her,* the mystery of why an innocent man let himself be hanged was solved.

And because of *her*, Izzyk Spinser was now more man than boy.

The living room of the Gladish residence was crowded with Trotting Swans. Twelve Drakeri men clad in purple biker gear stood, each one of them doing more talking than listening.

"We should have dragged her off the road and given her a shunt-and-cut! We could have buried that mystic slag in the woods and been done with it!"

"But the Law—"

"Shunt the Law! None of us has been arrested since we took out old Farnuff in Drowsy Nook! Besides, she ain't local."

"None of them are."

"But they crumbled Edifice Teige! Do we really want to mess with a group like that?"

"That's when they were together. They're separated now. So, now's the time to get them!"

"Now is *not* the time!" Fulton Gladish yelled.

Everyone shut up. Both his eyes were blackened and his once proud nose now bent inward. But the injury only served to make him look more menacing.

"We will stick to the plan. We're going to let the ghosts take them out. They're fools enough to get involved with the hauntings in these parts. They'll either be driven mad or taken by a curse."

"That's just what you said about that girl when she entered town!" one man argued.

Fulton gritted his teeth. "She's a theurge. She has an edge. The other three are just road-thugs. We deal with the girl ourselves...in our own way."

"And what way is that?" another man challenged.

Fulton, in truth, had no answer. He was just about to make something up when a series of knocks came from the front door.

"Sweetie! Door!" the tall brute yelled into the kitchen.

145

"Getting it!" Fritz yelled back. She looked annoyed as she came out. Making her way past the dozen men, she promptly answered the door. Her spine straightened in surprise when she saw the figure outside. "P-P-Polly?! I mean, Lady Gone?!" she squeaked in surprise. "What are you doing here?" She took several steps back as the beautiful lady in red stepped inside.

The room grew silent and every head turned to behold the unexpected visitor.

Fulton at first glared at her in bitter hatred. But soon his eyes softened. "You are *not* Polly Gone," he told the strange woman.

"No, sir," the woman answered. Her face, although much like Polly's, was fraught with sadness and grief. And also like Polly, she spoke with a thick Chumish accent. "I am her mother. Veluora is my name. Not long ago, my baby girl ran away because of a misunderstanding. Since den I have heard she is running wit' a band of cut throat Excusionists. Oh, please, kind sirs! I have heard she stayed de night here. Please. I just want my baby girl home, safe and sound!"

Fulton raised an eyebrow. "Did you teach her how to do this?" He pointed at his busted nose.

Veluora shrank like a timid old woman. But her eyes showed a hint of pride. "A girl should know how defend herself, sir. Are you the leader of dese men?"

"I am the town shot-caller of our chapter, yes. And quit playing coy, woman! You act as if your daughter is helpless."

The worried expression on her Veluora's face morphed into a sly, seductive grin. Her passive posture straightened, shoulders back, teats out, back slightly arched. She threw off her red velvet cloak with an elegant toss. It landed perfectly onto a nearby coat rack. Her outfit seemed entirely made of red satin ribbons. The thick strands wrapped around her curvaceous body like a poorly wrapped crimson mummy, cleverly exposing a bit of breast, a hint of hip, and a trace of tummy. Her dark purple hair was long and wild with jagged streaks of bright red. Around her narrow waist was a belt sporting a sheathed dagger. Her smug eyes blinked once and flashed with red light.

Every man in the room felt both an overwhelming lust and fear for her. Even Fulton found himself helpless as the woman's will pierced through his heart.

146

She addressed them all with dignified fervor. "Hear me, Oh Swans dat Trot! De men my daughter ride wit' are formidable foes. I will see to dem personally if dey get in our way. I want my daughter back, you want her gone. I have come to dis cursed county to find her. But I need more eyes dan are in my head. I need your eyes, Oh Swans dat Trot! And your bodies, too!"

"Now wait a minute!" Fritz yelled. "What are you doing to them?" She looked at her slack-jawed husband. "Fulton! Snap out of it!" She looked at the lady in red. "What are you doing to them?"

"Guiding deir hearts." Veluora explained. "We all want de same tings. It is reasonable dat we all follow de same courses of action: Mine!" Veloura made a V with her index and middle fingers and pushed the fingertips into her canines. The sharp teeth pricked the skin of her purple digits until blood came out. "Come to me, Men of Barnhart. Let me anoint your eyes, so dat I may see what *you* see."

The men approached her like children gathering around their mother. One by one, she touched her bloody fingers to their eyes. As each man took his turn, he yelped when the salt in her blood stung them.

Veluora was about to anoint Fulton when Fritz picked up a poker from the fireplace. "Don't you dare touch my man, you theurge slattern!" Fritz stood only a few paces away, gripping the poker like a club.

Veluora laughed. "Oh! Am I not allowed to touch him? Then perhaps *he* should touch *me.*" The Red Witch smirked up at Fulton. "I want you to touch me as you touch her. Now."

Fulton obeyed. His will was a mere vapor compared to the Blood Mistress' thundercloud of domination. He ran his hands along Veluora's hips and thighs. He pressed his mouth against hers. One of his large hands started to cup her breast. All the while, Veluora stared at Fritz with gloating eyes.

The housewife exploded in fury and charged.

In a flash, Veluora's knife was out. Her arm flickered like the wing of a hummingbird, delivering a deft cut across Fritz's wrist. The tendons severed, causing the woman's fingers to open. The poker clanged to the floor.

Fritz paused for a moment to stare at the hair-thin wound. Then blood gushed out, and the housewife screamed, more in

147

horror than agony.

Veluora licked her blade, tasting the memories the blood contained. Her eyes flashed red as the recent events of her daughter's exploits from Fritz's perspective played out in her mind. "My. Weren't you just a thorn in her side!" Veluora laughed.

Fritz hugged her arm and screamed. She backed away, stumbling in utter terror, her nightgown soaked in blood.

Veluora's delighted face shifted into an expression of icy rage. She raised her dagger, pointing it at the bleeding housewife. "Scream again and your babies upstairs will awaken. Dey will get curious and come down to see what is happening. Do you want dat, Fritz Gladish?"

Fritz shut her mouth and shook her head. She burst into tears.

The Blood Mistress bared her teeth, every one flawless. "You all may tink you know what is right, but I *know* de truth of *all* tings. Dat is what separates Theurges from peons like you. My path is clear to me and I walk it wit'out error. My baby girl is in danger of straying from De Red River Path. She is a bud dat must be looked after, if she is ever to bloom as I have. My goal is clear. My time will not be wasted. So, my feisty little hostess. Do you now understand your place? Or should I let you bleed to death? So dat your brats can discover your carcass in de morning?"

Chapter 4
Beneath the Profane

Part 1

There was one reason and one reason only Röger wanted to go to Tanglefoot. It was not the fact that it was easy to find or not because its curse legend did not seem too scary. And it was not that he thought he was best suited to investigate it.

It was because of the whores.

"Whores galores!" an old drunk in Drowsy Nook had told him. The man's words still echoed in his mind. "The place is one big party town. Nearly every building is either a bordello, a tavern, a gambling hall, or all three in one! They got top-notch music, dancing show girls, all kinds of entertainment. Ain't no kids allowed in city limits, too. That's law there! Can you believe it? But I'll divulge you this, sonny. It's easy to lose your money in that town. And if you don't watch out, maybe more than that."

That was all Röger could recall from the conversation, since, he too, had been as drunk as a stink-mink. But that was enough for him. It had been twelve days since he'd bedded a lively lass. He figured that since most of his time should be for investigating, he had little time for wooing and winning a woman over. It was better to just buy one, quick and easy. Besides, his money pouch was full and so were his loins. It seemed apropos to drain both in unison.

It was part of his own curse, fact be known. The same lycanthropic energies that regenerated his blood, bone, and flesh also regenerated his reproductive juices. This combined with a dusty old broken heart had rendered him a rover in the jungles of love. It was a life he had been living for over a century. Other than a life of utter solitude, this kind of life seemed his only option.

And so, whilst riding his auburn steed, Sir Röger Yamus closed in on the town of Tanglefoot. His brown eyes gleamed from

149

within his tarnished silver helm, full of purpose and promise. The hematite blade of his infamous Headsman's Axe shined brilliantly as it was strapped to his back. He had made it a point to enter the town at noon, when the Huncell dome above shown its brightest, so those three features caught the daylight perfectly.

The town had no streets, per se, only clusters of buildings with gravel paths leading to and from the other building complexes. It seemed as if the town itself had been laid out like a miniature county, with gated villas and roads connecting like the web strands of a mentally deficient spider. The land rose and fell like the wrinkles in unmade bed sheets. A single line of railroad track cut through the scenery like a stitched wound on the land. Röger counted at least a half-dozen villas as he rode in. Each appeared to have at one large building surrounded by a dozen smaller ones. The land between the villas was full of orchards of barren apple trees. They looked just like the ones on Coachroad P—gnarled and fruitless, as though they had been tortured to death.

The first villa he came to was surrounded by blank gravestones and sported a tall column of stone bricks. And from it came a much taller column of smoke. It had once been a crop silo, too many years ago. But the smell of the smoke, even from a distance, indicated its current purpose. Röger's taste buds awakened as the inside of his nose poured the aroma onto his tongue. He kicked his bileer to a faster trot until his wild eyes beheld the sign attached to the smoking tower.

PAPA G.D.'S BARBEQUE AND SMOKE HOUSE

"Barbeque!" he exclaimed in a tight whisper. Cooked meat on a fiery grill. It was his favorite food in the whole Draybair Cluster. Of course, the last time he'd had it, it had been still alive and screaming. But that had been a while ago, and he did not care to remember that particular meal.

He hitched his steed to the nearest post and approached the establishment. A large shack-like addition was attached to the side of the silo. It had a rusty tin roof resting on top of a box of long wooden planks held together by rusty iron nails. Its only door was

150

covered with chips of old white paint. He almost unhinged it as he entered the place.

The inside was dark. Years of greasy meat-smoke had long since coated the windows. There were half a dozen humans lounging around on mismatched furniture. Some were reading books. Others were playing simple strategic board games. The humans were of the dark brown variety, as Röger's mother had been. The sight and smell of the place immediately made him feel at home.

None of the men rose to greet him save one, a sweet-faced fellow, short and pleasantly portly. Röger could see the age in the man's face and eyes. The handful of decades of smiling at customers had left thick wrinkles. And over half a century of working in smoke had stained the whites of his eyes blood red.

"Welcome! Welcome! Come on in here, big little brother!" the man greeted Röger with practiced enthusiasm. "You're a hungry man, I can tell."

Röger laughed and shrugged. "Fact be known, sir, I had no idea just how hungry I was until I smelled the place." As he finished talking, everyone stopped to look at him.

The old man cocked his head to the side. "You're from the *Homecell,* aren't you? I can tell by the way you talk. How'd you get past Doflend Immigration? They haven't let too many through since my granddaddy made the journ over. Not since the war-split."

Röger raised his palms and grinned. "Immigration is for those who want to settle. Keeping tabs on an Excursionist ain't so easy."

"Excursionist, oh?" the old man asked. "Which kind are you: Merc or Monster Abater?"

Röger let out a deep, rumbling chuckle. He gave the huge axe on his back a friendly pat. "As of two nights ago, I've been a ghost hunter."

Every native eye in the place widened in shock as they recognized the infamous blade. Each of them at some point in their lives could remember walking past that same axe. They recalled the feeling of dread as their eyes caught its sinister gleam. Either as children or adults, they had only seen it embedded in a petrified stump. Now, it hung on the back of a stranger.

The room erupted with questions. Each man stood,

151

marveling in shock and disbelief. They demanded to know what had transpired in their neighboring town.

Röger merely smiled and rubbed his gut. "I don't mind telling the story... on a full stomach. What do you got cooking back there?"

"Pork ribs," the old man answered. His sweet face became grave. "Amongst other things. I'll give you a whole side on the house if you tell us what happened."

"Deal." Röger put out his hand. "Sir Röger Yamus, Independent Black Vest at your service. I, uh, take it that *you* are Papa G. D.?"

"Yes and no," the man answered, taking the man's hand for a brief shake. "My granddaddy was a necromystic. Papa Grave Digger he called his self. He found his niche in dead meat and passed on his secrets to my daddy and my daddy to me. Papa G. D. is just an unofficial title."

"I...see...," Röger replied with growing caution. "He settled here because of the Geohex, didn't he?"

Papa G.D. smiled and gestured to an empty stool. "Let's hear your story first, big little brother, and I'll get those ribs ready."

Röger ate while he spoke. No one seemed to mind. He was hungry for meat; they were hungry for news. He told them of what had transpired in Drowsy Nook, leaving nothing out. And he made clear to them his group's intentions: to break the curses of the Geohex, one town at a time.

"The curse in this town ain't so bad," one man protested with a wry smile. "If you live on the outskirts like we do here. The town don't technically start 'til another mile down the road."

Röger raised an eyebrow. "Do they *make* you all live on the outskirts?" he asked.

The men laughed. "Nah, it ain't like that. We all have families. No kids allowed in town. This is our villa, these houses and this establishment."

Röger nodded. "I take it that's a law because of all the brothels? A decency ordinance?"

"More'n 'at," Papa G.D. answered as he lit up a dreamweed cigarette. "The women-folk don't get pregnant in Tanglefoot. Ever. There was a time before Lady Victa was scorned that this town had another name. Crystus, it was called. Decent town 'corrdin' to

152

Drakeri lore. Way back in the olden days, three generations for the native-folk, three hundred for us, there was a young lass named Victa Norr the Wake Maker. She was a powerful necromystic who married a local rich boy. After a while it became apparent that she couldn't have children. He divorced her and kicked her out. So she laid a curse on the whole town, makin' it so that no one there could ever have kids. That's why we Fevärians live on the outskirts, see?" He passed the cigarette to Röger, who took it gladly.

The old man continued. "After a century or two without babies, many families moved out. The town was all but abandoned until Djänette MySinn moved in."

"Who's she?" Röger inquired.

Papa G.D.'s face went slack, draining of any good humor. "A voluptuary, what some would call a Lust Theurge. But her *philocreed* goes deeper than just a good shunt. She preaches that physical excess and pleasure as not just good things in life, but the only things worth living for. Sexual healing and all that."

Röger chuckled as he took a drag off the dreamweed joint. "Sounds like a woman after my own heart."

Papa G.D. frowned. "She is, fact be known. All those groups of buildings you saw riding in here? Those villas are owned and operated by town council members. Distinguished fleshbrokers, the lot of them. Djänette is the mayor here, since the Council-folk all answer to her."

"The pimps made her leader?"

"Leader, teacher, and provider," the old man stated as he crossed his thick arms and rested them on his big belly. "The fleshbrokers own and operate the bordellos according to her standards. She uses her theurgy to enhance the experience of visitors such as you. She fulfills your desires and cleans out the dusty corners of your heart, and you return the favor by emptying your coin pouch. But the Temple Bordellos ain't the only game in town. There're plenty of girls and boys that work outside the villas independently if you want to save a few grotz. But if you want a spiritual experience, go to the villa temples."

Röger rubbed the back of his neck and smiled. "Sounds like a fair trade, I guess. But I get the feeling that you don't care too much for this voluptuary mayor woman."

The old man shrugged. "When I was a young man, I went

153

once out of curiosity. Temptation is one thing. But mystical temptation..." He shook his head. "It wasn't natural, I tell you, what they did to me, to my heart. All my pain and sadness. They took it from me, robbed me of it."

Röger squinted his eyes and paused. He glanced around at the other men. "So, why not leave town? Or the whole county for that matter?"

A sly smile curled the old man's thick lips. His eyes flashed with a strange pride that made Röger feel uneasy. "This is the only place I can conduct my business...without being judged too bad."

Röger sat back on his stool, bracing his elbow on the counter. His eyes scanned over the men again before settling on Papa G.D. "You're a necrotheurge, too. Aren't you? All of you guys climb the *Bone Ladder*. Am I right?"

The old man made an odd sign with his hands and said "We humans are short-lived compared to the Doflend natives. We exist for a hundred years if we're lucky. Then we die and cease to exist. This is a hard thing to accept for most people. But we're around dying things every day. Every animal we slaughter serves to remind us of what's coming. The *Bone Ladder* is the most simple and truthful *philocreed path* in all the Cluster. Even more so than what Djänette has going out yonder.

"Now, don't get me wrong. I ain't no full blown theurge. But I deal with death on a daily basis. I take pride in my recipes. You tasted my ribs just now. How were they?"

Röger tilted his head and shrugged. "Best I've had in years."

The old man pointed at him and grinned. "You wanna know the recipe? I don't mind sharing it. Ain't no way you can duplicate it! Two spoons pepper, one red, one black. One spoon salt. One spoon garlic salt. Half spoon cinnamon. After you rub it all in, you baste it with agave nectar. And then..." The old man paused to take back the joint for a long puff. He blew out the smoke and watched it dance in the air. "Then, my big, little brother. You take the *anima husk* of the dead animal. You know what that is?"

Röger nodded gravely. "It's the soul's skin, the only thing left of it after you die."

The old man smiled. "I take that skin and I seal it in the dead meat, right after I slit the pig's throat. Gives it a unique flavor that satisfies not only the tongue and belly, but every part of you."

Röger furrowed his brow. "You just fed me a pig's soul?"

"Only part of it. A part that would have gone to waste anyway. Care for another?"

Röger only stared at the man, blinking in shock. He watched Papa G.D.'s mouth open into a big happy smile. His large broken teeth reminded Röger of an ancient cemetery full of busted tombstones. A part of him wanted to smash out those remaining tombstones with his fist. But another part of him really, really wanted to eat more ribs.

Just then, a large door opened in the back of the room, filling the place with smoke and the smell of cooked meat. After a few seconds, Röger was able to peer through the warm white cloud.

One of the younger men led a cow by a piece of hemp rope. "I got that Ginlertville order ready, Papa," he declared.

The old man turned to him. "Now, you smoked that beef with applewood like I told you, right?"

"Sure thing, Papa!" the man answered. "I even used a hunka trunk to make it extra sweet." He gave the cow a friendly pat.

At that instant, the smoke cleared enough for Röger to realize what he was seeing. The cow being led was dead. Its hide clung to it like a crude leather helmet, stitched back together with cheap twine where it had been cut and peeled off. The eyes were replaced with hollow darkness. Its once fatty stomach area was missing, but the fullness of its musculature remained. It walked with an unnerving smoothness, as if gravity only had a partial effect on it. When it mooed, the sound seemed to surround Röger's heart and leave it feeling dirty. But the cursed thing *smelled* delicious!

"You...You barbequed a whole cow?!" Röger blurted.

"Smoked it," Papa G.D. corrected.

"It...it's...walking!"

"Of course it is! How the shunt else am I supposed to deliver seven hundred pounds of meat to a villa that's two miles away? Cart it out with a team of bileers? Too much trouble, I say!"

"It's mooing, too." Röger's bottom lip quivered inside his helmet.

The old man smiled and shrugged. "Old habits die hard. Even after death sometimes." He passed the joint back to Röger, who again took it.

The big guy took a long puff until the dreamweed joint burnt

155

down to a roach. He held the smoke in his lungs a long while as he considered the situation. Then the dreamweed took effect. A feeling of ease hugged his brain, as if it were wedged between a pair of huge, soft, warm breasts. His jaw dropped, opening his mouth into a gaping, idiot's smile. Usually, when he was high, if he sensed any danger, he would get very paranoid. But he sensed none in this place. That did not mean he was positive that the men there meant him no ill. It just meant he felt no danger. He looked at Papa G.D. and smiled. "You sell cooked walking dead cows to the bordellos around town?"

The old man nodded. "And goats and pigs and turkeys, too. Them good-time girls need to eat a lot of meat to keep their strength up."

Röger burst with laughter. "I bet they do!" The rest of the room joined the laughter. Röger slapped his knee. "You're alright, Papa G.D.! I even don't mind that you tricked me!"

The old man made a coy face. "Now, how did I do that, Mister Yamus?"

Röger held up the smoldering roach. "You knew getting me stoned would also get me hungry again. And now I have to *pay* for another slab of ribs! I tell you what, Necrotheurgic Barbeque ain't half bad!"

Papa G.D. held up his hand in a halting gesture. "I prefer to call it *soul food.*"

Röger chuckled through his teeth and reached for his money pouch. "How much are they?"

"Forty grotz a slab."

The big guy let out a whistle. "Awful pricey. But worth it." He put four silver ten grotz piece coins on the counter. They were square with holes in them. It was the last of his smaller coins. He scribbled a mental note to be mindful of the gold he had left.

Papa G.D. pointed at one of his men. "Jasper, go get this man another slab."

As Röger watched the younger man leave to retrieve the meat, he asked the other men in the room "So, do you all work here?"

"We help Papa out," one man answered. He was tall and broad like Röger, but much thinner and leaner. His head was shaved smooth and his large white eyes seemed to jump out from his dark skin. His voice was deep and jarring like an old bent tuba. "We are a family here, a tribe, a clan. We tend the needs of the dead in the town. Each of us is a specialist in the funerary arts."

"You're all undertakers?" Röger asked. "Why does this town need so many?"

The tall lean man smiled. "Many a varied folk come here to have a good time. Sometimes they party too hard. We clean up the mess if they do. Each of us is a specialist to a certain culture's remains disposal practices." He began to point at the others in the room. "Bën cremates old fashioned Drakeri in a crematorium and fashions their ashes into clay memorial pieces. Ryän has the easy job and just buries the more modern of them. Järred, who just went to fetch your ribs, he burns the tendikeye on brush piles and spreads the ashes in a potato field. Ërnie, he's our malruka man, chisels and carves them up, then sells the pieces for scraps or uses them for grave stones."

"And *you* bury or burn the humans, right?" Röger asked. "What's your name, sir?" he held out his hand for a shake. The gesture was friendly. But he could not hide the wariness in his eyes. This guy seemed strange.

"LëCuk," answered the man with a dubious grin. He took the hand and shook it with an iron grip. His skin was cold and smooth like ice. If Röger himself had not the grip of a bear, he would have winced. "Yes, sir. I tend to the needs of *our* dead. Whenever we get something unusual though, like a Miccan or a Chume Fey, we draw lots and do our best."

Röger arched an eyebrow. "How many funerals do you guys do a year?"

"Dozens each."

"Then you guys must be making some serious coin, with all that business coming in."

LëCuk shrugged. "We do not make much. The Villa Council men pay us a flat rate to dispose of the dead. We add in cultural funeral rites as an act of compassion at no extra charge."

"How kind of you," Röger replied, leaning back against the counter top. "So, in a town without children and families, how many of these deaths occur naturally?"

LëCuk's face went dire. "Naturally...or supernaturally? It is so difficult to tell. Some perish from partying too hard, as I have

157

said. Too much drink or smoke, too much of one kind drug or another. It is not unheard of for an old man to retire here with his life's fortune, only to die beneath the fury of a harlot's hips. Many die in fights, even though there is plenty of fun to go around and nothing to fight for. A few have been killed by *Muerchi*, a fiend that stalks the night." He bared his teeth and pointed at a window. "Tanglefoot is a town of fools that die without reason. We do our best to provide its victims with some dignity after their souls shatter to the winds." He took a step closer to Röger and breathed deeply with his nostrils. And his eyes became black pools as the air came in. "I smell it on you, Sir Röger. The residue of thousands of souls that you shattered, lives that you took!"

Röger pushed the man away. The man flew seven feet and landed ass-first into a chair. The chair then slid another two feet and slammed into the wall. LëCuk looked surprised, but not at all afraid.

Röger held up a shaking finger and pointed it at the man. "So, there *is* a Necrotheurge among you! Then heed my words, LëCuk! What you smell on me is *war*! A war that I fought for you, all of you! For nearly every *philocreed's* survival, including yours!"

For a moment, LëCuk looked confused. Then he raised his hands in a maxim casting gesture.

"*Waste!*" Röger thought. He gripped his axe and squared his stance for a fight. To his confusion, he saw the rib bones he had nibbled clean only minutes before float out from behind him.

They were floating past him toward LëCuk. Röger watched with bated breath as the bones drifted inside an invisible ball held in the necrotheurge's hands. The bones spun and twirled in some wild dance of suspension. The tall, lean man whispered something and clucked his tongue. The wet bones dropped into a pattern that only a skilled Death Theurge could recognize. He stared at the bones a moment or two and looked up at Papa G.D. "Papa. Give the man his forty grotz back."

"Why, son?" the old man asked. "What does your gift tell you?"

The fierce white eyes of the tall lean man ran over with tears of jovial sorrow. "That when he goes to town, he will provide us with much business."

Röger felt his jaw clench. "I don't plan on killing anyone, pal.

158

This county has enough ghosts." He glanced at Papa G.D. and nodded. "Thanks anyway, sir." He then turned to the entrance door, one hand resting on his axe's handle.

The effects of the dreamweed wore off as he breathed the outside air. And as his head cleared, an old memory resurfaced in his mind. Long ago, Röger had been riding his bileer through a war-torn city when he noticed the child in a pile of rubble. The boy's body was crushed under the loosened bricks that had been blasted free by bombs. The lower half of his face was mangled and shredded, yet his weary eyes still moved about. Tortured by the life still intact within him, the boy looked up to greet the granter of his death. Röger remembered caressing the boy's soft hair as he unholstered his gun. He pointed the pistol a few inches from the boy's forehead.

The boy, rendered unable to smile with his mouth, opened his eyes wider, not in fear, but joy and gratitude. Röger pulled the trigger and watched the rest of the child's head disappear. *Gratitude for dying!*

He threw down the firearm in disgust and there vowed to never use one again. He felt the beast buzzing in the back of his skull. After hopping back onto his bileer he rode hard and fast to where most of the fighting was going on. The memory only lasted a few seconds before he shook his head.

He climbed onto his bileer and sighed. "Well, Rufus," he nudged the animal "we have a party to go catch. Several parties, I think. Did you know that because of my dumb ass, a lot of people never got to grow old or grow up? That's right. And isn't it funny that I never will either? But unlike them, I'm not dead. So, you know what I'm gonna do? I'm gonna go to town to have a good time, because all those people can't now. Even if it takes a thousand lifetimes, I'm going to do all the good and have all the fun that they couldn't. What? You think that's still selfish? Well, it's not like I can just settle down with a wife and home. I tried it. Doesn't work. Why? What happened when I tried? You're pretty nosy for a steed."

He grasped the bileer's horns and prodded it into a trot. It was evening now. After a mile or so, he felt an odd tingle in his loins. He had passed the border into Tanglefoot. Before he reached the next villa, he passed a shabby abandoned farm house. Like the haunted farm house on Coach Road P, it gave off a faint air of dread and despair. A rusty wrought iron sign read *Nckoons Orchard*.

159

"I should check that out later," he thought. *"But first thing's first."*

◈

The Galvestri Villa was a gated jumble of a dozen or so mismatched buildings, each one pretty in its own way, but rather tacky as a group. Röger loved it. The fence and gate were made of immaculate, whitewashed iron rods that stuck up like the teeth of an ivory comb.

As he rode in, he marveled at the quaint houses and stores. Each one reminded him of a different place he had seen in his travels. And the people, oh the people, even they were mismatched. They were of nearly every civil race in the Cluster; Drakeri, Tendikeye, Fevärian Humans, Malruka. There was even the occasional Chume Fey strolling about. There were no signs of kinship or community, only grown up individuals going about their own business.

"But no Miccans," he thought. *"Thank the veins above!"*

He sidestepped his steed as an ox-drawn wagon came out the entrance. An elderly humanness wearing a wide brimmed hat sat at the reins.

"Good evening, grand lady!" Röger called to her. "I'm new here. Where can a guy get a drink?"

The old woman barely looked at him. "There's an outhouse up the lane. Plenty to drink in there! But if it's spirits you're after, Frumpy Joe's is right next to it. Good day back to ye!"

"Frumpy Joe's!" he repeated with a nod of gratitude. "Thank you, sweet lady!"

The woman turned at him with a nasty scowl. "And if that place ain't good enough for ye, you can slurp up a puddle of ox piss! Plenty of those around!"

"It's nice to have options!" he returned, waving as he went by. He took a deep breath and let out a soothing sigh. "I like meeting new people. Time for a drink, I think."

The outside of the establishment looked decent enough. The awning and porch rails were polished and well maintained. Not a

160

single window was cracked or broken. There were neatly trimmed holly bushes on either side of the front steps. A large sign hung from the awning displaying simple, bold red letters.

FRUMPY JOE'S

Six bileers were tied to the front hitching rail along with two velocipede bikes. The bikes were of heavy duty manufacture, built identically for speed and durability. *"Town guards,"* he thought. *"Either well paid or over paid."*

The first thing he noticed as he entered was the entire inside had been fight-proofed. Iron bars were mounted on the inside of the windows. The tables were round with six benches nailed together in a hexagram around them. The stool seats at the bar were set on wooden poles fixed into the floor. There was no art on the walls. No chandeliers to swing from. About a dozen or so men and women either sat at tables or played billiards.

Two Drakeri men dressed in purple sat at the bar. Although the cut of their clothing differed, the copper badges they wore marked them as officials of some kind. Both nursed mugs of beer.

"Evening Officers," he told them with a casual salute.

One of them made a dismissive gesture as he gulped a swallow. "Ain't no cops in Galvestri. We're Villa security."

"And we're making sure this beer is safe to drink," the other added with a wry grin.

Röger smiled and gave their badges a second look. They still had the same shield shape to them, but were engraved with the outline of a swan. "So," he started, "is it okay if I hold onto my axe? Or do I have to turn it in somewhere?"

At first, they shrugged as if it did not matter. But then their eyes beheld the gleaming blade hanging on his back.

"Is that...?"

"The Headsman's Axe? The Steedless Headsman of Drowsy Nook?"

Röger scratched the back of his neck. "Yeah, it is, or was. But I don't much care for the name. The 'Headsman's Axe' is a bit too grim for me. I prefer a weapon with a more...a more...a more noble title. You guys got any suggestions?"

The two men stammered with confused amazement, trying

161

to assemble sentences.

Just then, two customers in the bar concluded a game of billiards. The loser's pride had received a crippling blow. And so, brandishing a pool cue, he gave his opponent a blow to match across the side of his head. The cue snapped like a housewife's sanity, and a piece of it flew into a pitcher of beer that just happened to be placed on a table where two couples were seated on a double date. The wooden projectile caused the pitcher to explode, sending glass and beer into their faces.

Loud cussing followed as the seated men stood and launched their glasses at the pool players. Other patrons joined in with mixed intentions. And soon, everyone (except Röger and the two security guards) was pounding, punching, beating, clawing, biting, choking, kicking, slapping, and yelling at each other.

Röger looked at the two guards and the pistols they wore. "Aren't you two gonna do something?"

One took a swig of beer and then answered. "Nobody's died yet. Besides, we're out numbered. It's better to join in *after* everyone's softened each other up."

The other guard nodded in agreement. "They'll tire out in a few minutes. Then we can lighten their pockets and detain them easier."

Röger watched as the tavern melee intensified. Blood flowed and a few bones broke. Three people had already fallen limp onto the floor.

"Someone's going to get killed!" He unslung his axe and placed it across three bar stools. "I'll end this if I have to!"

One of the guards gave him an annoyed look as he finished his beer. "Fine. Fine," he muttered, wiping his mouth on his sleeve. He drew his pistol and fired a lazy shot into the ceiling.

At once the bar fight ended and everyone froze.

"Knock it off, you dumb wastes! It's only three o'clock and you're already brawling!"

"Pay up twenty grotz a piece and clear out, all of you!" the other guard ordered. He went through the pacified crowd collecting their money. "Pool cues don't grow on trees, you know!"

Röger regarded the guard who had fired the shot. "Does this happen a lot?"

The guard scowled. "Cut the dung, round ear. How'd you get

162

that axe?"

Röger narrowed his gaze and picked up the weapon. "By breaking the town curse, of course."

The guard shook his head. "That axe has been giving Drowsy Nook trouble since before I was born and you brought it *here*? A place where everyone's guilty of something?"

Röger raised a passive hand. "Relax, pal. The ghost that wielded it dissipated. Drowsy Nook is curse-free."

"Oh really?" the guard scoffed. "We'll check into that then."

"*We*?" Röger asked.

"I'm a Trotting Swan, a county protector. We *run* Wraith County."

"Uh, yeah. That's very interesting. Really. Say, since you kind of ruined my plans for getting drunk, do you think you could at least tell me where I can get laid?" He ignored the sudden anger growing in the man's face and added, "I've got an itch like you wouldn't believe and only a well-seasoned professional can scratch it."

The guard grit his teeth. "Yes. There's our temple bordello just down the lane. The sacred harlots there will be happy to cure your woes. Provided you have the coin."

Röger grinned and patted the man's shoulder. "Thanks, pal."

"Happy to help," the guard replied, patting the big man's shoulder in return.

The force of the touch took Röger off guard, and he stumbled as if a large bear had just nudged past him. "*Strong little guy!*" he thought as he made his way to the door. "*Or maybe he just caught me off balance?*"

"Mister?" the guard asked.

"Yeah? What?"

"My name is Kode Caizre. May I have the honor of learning yours?"

Röger smirked. "Word will soon spread from Drowsy Nook. By then, you and everyone else will find out."

❖

The Temple Bordello occupied an old, pristine plantation house. An immense flagstone walkway led to a huge front porch where a crowd of people chatted and smoked cigars on the front steps. Röger went through the crowd to the entrance door.

A young human wearing a bowler hat greeted him. "Would you like to purchase a ribbon, sir?" he asked.

"What for?"

"To ensure a pleasant temple experience, of course. A white ribbon means you can stay until nightfall, drink your fill of beer or ale, and have the company of a sacred harlot at your table while you enjoy the stage show. A red ribbon lets you stay all night, drink all the hard liquor you want, and gets you an hour in private with a harlot. And a blue ribbon grants you access to our finest wines and champagnes, and you may stay all night with the company of a harlot in private."

"I see. And how much are they?"

"One hundred grotz for white. Two hundred for red. Three hundred for blue."

Röger nodded. "Uh huh. And do I get my choice of girls?"

"Absolutely, sir. All you need do is approach a harlot and bow. She or he will then curtsy or bow and offer their hand. Tie the ribbon around their wrist in a slipknot, and the deal is made."

Röger chuckled. "Each one sounds like a sweet deal. I'll take them all."

The door man's jaw dropped. "One of each, sir? Uh, Okay. That will be six hundred grotz."

Röger laughed a waved his hand. "Just kidding, bud. I'll take a red one. Say, why tie it in a slipknot? Is that so you can keep reusing them? The ribbons, I mean, not the harlots."

As they made the exchange, the man answered. "The knot represents a temporary agreement. The placards on the wall as you go in explain the agreement in full detail." The man bowed and gestured for Röger to enter. "Enjoy your stay. And be sure to read all the rules on the wall before entering the showroom."

"Thank you, sir." replied Röger as he stepped in.

He noticed the rule boards hanging on the entryway wall. They were brown lacquered, with black painted letters scrawling across their surfaces. The big man's eyes widened as he realized that

164

this was no normal list of rules. It was a piece of philocreed scripture. And once he started reading it, he could not stop.

BLESSING OF THE HOUSE

LET ALL WHO ENTER HERE KNOW THEY ARE WELCOME. FEAR NOT YOUR SEED FINDING PURCHASE IN THE WOMBS OF OUR SACRED HARLOTS, NOR FEAR YOU THE PANGS OF DISEASE, NOR THE CONFUSION OF INFATUATED ATTACHMENT. DO NOT DENY YOURSELF WHAT YOU WANT, UNLESS IT CONFLICTS WITH THE WANTS OF ANOTHER. YOU HAVE PAID THE PRICE FOR THAT WHICH IS PRICELESS, YOUR FANTASIES MADE FLESH. ALL FEELINGS MUST FLOW INTO ONE SINGLE STRAND OF EMOTION CALLED DESIRE, LET ALL YOUR LOVE, YOUR HATE, ALL THAT YOU UNDERSTAND, AND ALL THAT YOU ARE CURIOUS TO KNOW, GUIDE YOU TO FULFILLMENT IN THE MOMENT.

He felt his eyes shift to the second board.

THE TEMPLE RIBBONS REPRESENT THE BINDING AGREEMENT BETWEEN THE ATTENDEE AND THE SACRED HARLOT THEY CHOOSE. THE SLIPKNOT REPRESENTS THE TEMPORARY BOND OF LOVE BETWEEN THE TWO. UNLIKE A KNOT OF MATRIMONY, WHICH A TANGLED MESS OF PROMISES. THE SLIPKNOT IS MADE TO BE UNDONE WITH EASE. THE SPIRIT OF LOVE RESIDES IN ALL OF US. IT IS MEANT TO BE SHARED. KNOW YE, THAT THIS IS NO MERE WHOREHOUSE. THE HARLOTS WITHIN ARE ENTRUSTED WITH THE SACRED DUTY

165

OF AWAKENING YOUR POSITIVE SELF. TREAT THEM
WITH THE UTMOST RESPECT AND THEY WILL NOT
DISAPPOINT.

-*Djänette MySinn, High Theurgess of the Slipknot Pact*
Mayor of Tanglefoot

Röger stood there silently for a moment as the words sank
in. He then realized that his own will had been held in suspension.
He blinked hard several times and jerked his gaze away from the
plaque boards.

"*Compulsion!*" his mind screamed. "*Theurgic mind
manipulation!*"

He took a deep breath and gritted his teeth. He went
through a mental list involving his name, his birthday, place of birth,
the schools he attended, his favorite food, drink, songs, the loves of
his life, and the enemies he had long since buried. By the time he
finished the mental list, he was sure of who he was and that his will
was no longer being tampered with.

"*What the shunt?*" he thought. "*An effect was there just
now. I know it.*"

Another man entered the entryway. He also held a red
ribbon. The man gave Röger an oily grin. "This your first time, too,
pal?" he asked.

"Uh, yeah."

The man laughed. "Yeah, these whores better gimme my
money's worth, I'll tell you that much! And if they don't work me
like a proper whore should, I may have to show them how a real
woman gets shunted!" He laughed again and looked at the plaques
on the wall.

Röger watched as the man's expression slowly shifted from
sleazy to confused and then, finally, serene. The man looked back at
Röger, his mouth opened to speak. "Y'know...on second
thought...I'm sure the girls here know what they're doing. I'll just let
them take the lead and see where it takes me...y'know?"

"Yeah," Röger replied. He let the man pass him by. "*Very
subtle theurgy,*" he thought. "*Some kind of suggestive mind control.
I've got to stay on guard.*"

166

The entryway led him past a life-sized sculpture of a naked female. The base of the statue had been cleverly carved to look like a dress that had fallen down the length of her, covering only her feet. Other than being headless and handless, he found her rather stunning. At first, he it thought was a damaged piece. But further inspection revealed that it had been made that way on purpose.

He frowned in confusion and tilted his head. "I don't get it." He shrugged, and continued down the hall.

At last, the hall ended, opening up into the giant showroom, and what a show it contained! The air was filled with music and the smell of dreamweed and fine tobacco. A concave stage hugged its way halfway around a cluster of a dozen round tables. Dancers, both male and female, stepped and swayed in sensual unison to the beat of heavy drums, ominous strings, and haunting woodwinds. Great wrought iron stands held aloft hundreds of candles blending light and shadow throughout the room. Every table could seat a dozen people, and most of them did. The walls and corners were thronged with paintings and sculpture, many of them depicting erotic activity. Customers of all races and walks of life sat at the tables. They ate, drank and chatted with each other or with a harlot by their side.

The harlots were easy to spot, for they all wore gaudy, festive clothing and decorative cosmetics on their faces. In attire, no two harlots were alike. But all of their bodies appeared to be trim and narrow waisted. To Röger's slight disappointment, there was not a single pudgy girl among them. Nonetheless, a particularly top-heavy harlot caught his eye, and he wasted no time in approaching her.

She was a brunette with ivory skin, and lips like a dark red rose. Her hair was done up in a mass of dangling curls. She was human, mostly. Her eyes alluded to a faint drakeri heritage, with their golden brown color and wide irises. Her dress was shaped like a blue bell that frilled out at her breasts and shoulders. She was gorgeous, but her main appeal was the gentle kindness in her face. Röger approached her and bowed, never taking his eyes off hers. She curtsied deeply, in a surrendering way, and extended her arm. Röger took the ribbon and with thick fingers, carefully tied it around her wrist into a slipknot. And so the pact was made.

"I am Florabella Cottonwood," she said warmly. "I vow by the path of my Lady and myself, that the hungers of your body will

167

be sated, the fantasies of your mind will be played out, and that I will bask you in the power of my love until it is time to part ways."

Röger grew somewhat uncomfortable at the use of the "L" word. "I'm Sir Röger Yamus. Um, look, I..."

The woman shushed him. "Be at ease, traveler. The love of a Sacred Harlot is as real as any other. Believe me when I say that I care for your cares and needs. Why pack your heart away while your body has all the fun? My duty to you is also a duty to myself. You are lonely, incredibly lonely. I sense your sadness, your frustration, even your anger. Please, traveler; let me drown those ills with passion and compassion, with caring and love for my fellow living being. Are you hungry?"

"No, I just ate. Had some ribs before I got here."

She smiled. "Poppa G.D.?"

"Yeah."

"Then you must have come in through the west end of town, through Drowsy Nook. I've never been there, but I've heard much. I hear the Sheriff there is boorish."

Röger only shrugged. "So, where are you from, Florabella?"

She gave a sly grin. "I'll tell you after you remove your helmet."

Röger shook his head.

She took a step and pressed up against him. "Very well, Sir Röger Yamus. If mystery is what you offer, then mystery is what I return. Our pasts are irrelevant, anyway. Tell me, what will please you?"

Röger wrapped an arm around her, and the two began to dance slowly to the fast music. "Mystery is why I'm here, other than a good time. I noticed that all the buildings in this villa are well maintained unlike that old farm house down the road. NcKoons Orchard I think the sign said."

"It's a landmark," she answered. "This whole town was once an apple orchard. That house belongs to the man who ran it centuries ago. I say *belongs* because the ghost of the man still resides there. He blew his brains out when the apples stopped growing."

"And was this before or after Victa the Necrowitch cursed the town with infertility?" he asked.

She looked up at him, looking somewhat startled and

168

offended. "Before, I think. If you are only here to investigate, then maybe you should have chosen a pure blood drakeri girl. They've lived longer and know the local history better."

Röger shook his head. "Ah, but who needs a girl when I already have a woman in my arms?" He gave her a playful squeeze. "While I may be conducting an investigation, my main reason for coming here was to find the finest harlot in the temple, share a drink or four, and then shunt her brains out." His dark eyes glinted with a smile.

She touched his strong arms and lightly dug her nails into them. "Maybe I'll shunt *your* brains out before you can shunt *mine.*"

He laughed. "Depends on who has more brains...or who's the better shunter."

She dragged her nails down the length of his arms. "I can't wait to find out." She took one of his hands and started to kiss his fingertips. "But first, a drink. May I suggest sharing a bottle of *Partager Chair?* If we are both tipsy on the same thing, it will not disrupt the chemistry."

Röger laughed and gave her a pinch. "Sounds good, but you'd better make it three. You have a place we can drink it?"

In the privacy of Florabella Cottonwood's parlor, the floor was covered in empty bottles and empty clothes. The walls, the bed, even the floor and ceiling were covered in blue velvet, as if the parlor were a chamber in a castle made of cloth. A three-stemmed candlestick formed a trident of light by the bedside table, illuminating the bodies of the two temporary lovers.

Röger fumbled at the laces of her short corset, her last piece of clothing. "Here. I'll help you get this off," he whispered.

Her hands covered his own. "I prefer to keep it on, if you please." She took one of his hands and placed it on one of her bare breasts.

He smiled and squeezed the mound. "I don't mind if you're

169

a little pudgy in the middle."

She smiled and kissed his chest. "It's not that. I just prefer to keep it on."

He sighed and rolled his eyes. "Is this just because I won't take off my helmet?"

"Not at all." Her eyes met his. There was stubbornness, but also a strong willingness to please. "Fine, traveler. I'll grant your request. Just let me blow these candles out first."

Röger had no desire to argue any further. Light or no light, he wanted that corset off of her. In the new darkness of the parlor, he assisted in its removal. And though his eyes were deprived of the wonder of Florabella's nakedness, his other senses were amply compensated. He felt that she was trim and thin with a smooth, firm belly.

As he was about to take her, he could not help but wonder. *"What's the deal here? She didn't need that thing. She probably has an embarrassing tattoo. Yeah, that must be it. I've got a few myself."*

She wrapped her arms around him as their closeness became togetherness. Softly, she whispered into the earhole of his helmet. *"Omnia vincit amor."*

As nature took its course, the warmth of the harlot's affections melted away his every care. Throughout the hour of being locked into her, Röger forgot that he was a homeless, rootless, cursed vagabond. He forgot the decades of faces of those he had let down. And he forgot the fact that his future would always be the same as is past: unchanging.

In the arms of Florabella Cottonwood, he felt his victims' emotions churning and diluting as a flood of soothing joy spilled into his heart. His ability to think was lost. He could only perceive that something incredibly wonderful was happening. It was not until he yielded his pleasure did he realize that he had been enchanted.

"You're a theurge," he panted through exhausted breaths.

He heard her voice crack. "Not much of one," she replied. He could hear her starting to cry. "I tried to do it, tried to help you. But it was all too much."

He sat up, slowly. "What are you talking about? Did I hurt you?"

She sighed and sniveled. "No. You were perfectly fine, traveler. It was I who faltered. I tried to cleanse away your sadness and regret and pain and rage, all the poisonous things that vex you so. But your troubles are great, and I am still but a novice. I'm so sorry."

"Don't be, Florabella. I feel great. *It* felt great. I feel...I feel strangely at peace."

He felt her touch his collarbone. "You are kind, traveler. But the feeling will only last for an hour or so. I will see that your donation is returned."

"No. No, that's okay." He shrugged to himself in the dark. "So, are all the sacred harlots here theurges?"

"Of course they are. That is why we are sacred, what we do is sacred. But we all vary in skill and power. I'm still a bit new to it, fact be known. The High Theurgess hand picks us all. She recognizes our potential. She instructs us and teaches us her philocreed, helps us awaken our power. She saved me from becoming an Amazon, working the outskirts of the villas. Here we are safe. Here we are sacred."

Röger furrowed his brow and nodded. "Who are the Amazons?"

"It's what we call the common whores here in Tanglefoot. Women with no power. Women dependent on flesh-broker bodyguards and landlords. Thank the Mistress I did not become one of them when I came here."

There was silence in the darkness before Röger broke it. "Well, Miss Florabella Cottonwood, thank you for a wonderful evening. I gotta go now."

"Are you sure you aren't displeased?" she asked. "We could have another go, if you'd like. I would cherish the chance to make it up to you." Her hand slipped beneath the covers on his lap.

Röger smiled and slowly climbed onto her. "You're just making excuses. You just want to get pleased again yourself."

She did not argue.

◈

After the second time around, Röger felt like his mind would be forever wiped clean. But with each breath, he eventually regained his composure. Before too long, he could hear the sacred harlot snoring loudly.

He carefully got out of the bed and got dressed. As he picked up his axe and walked to the door, a curious thought came to him. He turned, pulled a match from a pocket in his vest, and lit it. Kneeling over the bed, he lifted the satin sheet that covered the nude lady beneath and peeked at what she had sought to keep hidden. Scars were all over her lower back, sides, and abdomen. They all looked the same, like vicious bite marks.

The match went out. And soon after, so did he.

He rode out of the Galvestri Villa and back to the NcKoons Orchard farmstead. With every trot of his hooves, the Röger's bileer grew more and more uneasy. He tied off the steed on the iron sign at the edge of the property, and proceeded on foot. The grass was waist high and dead. The long dirt path leading up to the house was thronged with weeds. The winds chilled his bare arms and whistled in his helm's earholes. There was fear in the air, but none in him. It was an odd feeling, the lingering fullness of the harlot's love. He was strangely at ease and tried not to overthink it. Still, he approached with caution.

The house was run down. The nearby barn had long since collapsed. Every piece of wood was gray, bare, and rotted. Every window was either broken or missing. He pulled the axe off his back, the glow if the hunveins made it flash in the night. He made his way to the front door, and saw that there was no doorknob, just a hole where it once had been. He raised a fist and gently wrapped on the door.

After counting out a minute of silence, he pushed the door open and went in. The house was utterly empty. No furniture. Bare walls. Just more dead wood and rusty nails. He stepped gingerly on the floorboard planks, and to his surprise, not one of them so much as creaked.

172

"*Weird*," he thought.

As he explored, he was amazed by how well he was able to see in the dark. Then he realized his axe was glowing. "What the shunt?" he gasped.

He looked at the huge blade, trying to make sense of it. He saw his own reflection in its polished surface. It reflected his confusion perfectly. It also reflected the image of a man standing behind him, aiming a pistol at his head.

Without thinking, he turned and gave the axe a swing that would cut the man in two. But the man was no longer there.

"What are you doing in my house?" an angry voice demanded. "If you got robbing, raping, or killing in your mind, son, I'll happy to remove it with a bullet!"

"I...I'm not here for either of those, sir," Röger stammered. He shifted his eyes from side to side, still seeing nothing. "As a matter of fact, you have nothing to steal, not even a single live pig to rape, and you yourself are too dead to kill."

There was the sound of a pistol being cocked. "Son, I don't want to kill you. But you'd better cut the dung and give me a straight answer. And what's with that axe? Put it down right now!"

Röger had no clue if a ghost's gun could hurt him. He complied with its demands and set his weapon down on the floor.

"Now, tell me, why are you in my house?"

"I think the real question is why are *you* here, Mr NcKoons?"

"I live here, round-ear!"

"No, you don't."

"What do you mean I don't? Wait! I know what this is about! This is because I won't let you round-ears pick my apples, isn't it? Is that why you came here? To give me grief about it?"

"*Just keep the ghost talking,*" Röger thought. "Uh...yes...that's why I came, Mr. NcKoons."

The ghost laughed sickly. "Thought so. What's the matter, human? Is picking apples all you know? Can't find other work besides that? Well, get out of Apple County then! Go back to Fevär where you belong, with all those other commie short-lifes!"

"Commie?" Röger parroted. "We haven't been communist since the Omni-War."

"The what?" the ghost asked. "Oh, the war, you mean. Yeah,

you round-ears should count yourselves fortunate we don't round you all up for national security. You immigrant pieces of trash may claim to hate the regime. But I know you all too well. You would sell my country out to Yenehc for a piece of it."

"*Yenehc?*" Röger thought. "*I learned about him at the academy.*" He addressed the ghost. "That was nearly three thousand years ago, pal. Yenehc and his regime are long gone. The war has been over just as long. Your county doesn't grow apples anymore. It's cursed with ghosts and fear. The land and, uh, some of the women are infertile. You are a ghost, Mr. NcKoons."

Tenseness filled the air. Röger tried to draw breath, but no air came. Voices began to scream inside his head in a discordant chorus of anguish and hatred. His heart ached and his stomach churned rib meat, expensive wine, and pig's soul. He was about to change. His muscles twitched and spasmed as if they each had wills of their own. He could feel his clothes getting tighter. His eyes shifted to the way he'd entered as he knelt down to grab his axe. His legs could no longer feel his body's weight, and with them he dashed toward the open doorway.

The door slammed shut on its own. It did not stop him. The old door exploded in a cloud of dust and splinters. He landed hard in a patch of grass and felt the cool night air enter his lungs and kiss his skin. He wanted to roar at the night, but stopped himself. Releasing the roar might release the beast. He breathed and relaxed. Breathed and relaxed. Breathed and relaxed. He looked over at his right hand still gripping the haft of his axe. He thought about using it to chop the entire house down.

"*Might get in trouble if I do,*" he thought. "*Gotta calm down and get outta here.*"

He trudged through the grass toward his steed. After several hasty steps, he looked up at where he had hitched it. That was when he saw them.

Eight drakeri men on velocipedes. All of them wore purple. Two of the men were the security guards from the bar. They carried lanterns in their hands and pistols in their belts. Others had rifles and shotguns. They surrounded his animal.

Röger only paused for a moment when he saw them. Then he slowly walked their way. "I really don't need this," he whispered to himself.

174

"Mr. Yamus!" one of them called out. "Mr. Röger Yamus of the Four Winds! That's you, right?" It was the inquisitive guard from the bar.

"I'm *Sir* Röger Yamus," the human corrected. "Independent Black Vest, at your service." He never stopped walking. "What was your name again?"

"Kode Caizre. And you were right about earlier. News of your exploits in Drowsy Nook has reached the ears of me and my brethren. I commend you for the killing of that ruke sheriff. He had it coming. But I must ask that you cease your dealings in Wraith County and move on. We of the Trotting Swans run things here. And Excursionists are not welcome or wanted."

Röger snorted beneath his helmet. "Not welcomed or wanted? The townsfolk of Drowsy Nook say otherwise, Kode. And so far, the people of Tanglefoot have also treated me warmly. Everyone but you, that is. So, what's the deal, man? We're no threat to you, unless you're a ghost or monster."

Kode frowned and bared his teeth. "You're shunting with the balance, round-ear! The ghosts in this county have killed countless people over the centuries. They need not be provoked. We Trotting Swans are the true authority here. Drop the Headsman's Axe and call off your investigation."

Röger stopped and regarded the man on the bike telling him what to do. "You know something, Kode Caizre. I used to be a man who took orders. Merde, I even took orders from lesser men than you. I have heard your concerns and will be sure to pass them on to my teammates. But I will no more drop this axe than cut off my own shame with it. So, be wise and return home. Please, for the sake of everything you care about, leave me alone right now. I'm not in a good mood."

Kode scoffed. "I bet you're not. We heard your footfalls inside that house. I'm surprised the necrofright didn't kill you." He turned his head and spat. Then he drew his pistol and rested it on his handle bar. "Drop the axe, round-ear," he ordered.

Röger took a deep breath and eased it out as he looked over the eight men. He could tell that half of them meant business and the other half seemed unsure what to do. He shook his head and replied "No. I refuse. And I don't want to kill any of you. Good night, fellas." Then he walked calmly past them and began to untie his

175

bileer.

There was a sudden report from Kode Caizre's gun, and a gush of gore and blood erupted from the head of Röger's steed. The animal dropped into a lifeless heap in front of him. The smell of blood and gunsmoke filled the air.

"Drop the axe, round-ear!" Kode ordered again.

Röger did not even look at them. He only saw his animal, Rufus Gut-Stomper, dead in the grass. He latched onto his shock in hopes of it helping him stay calm. He felt his hands tremble, and he quickly balled them into fists. "Okay then," he growled. "I guess I'll have to walk."

He stepped onto the road, hearing only the sound of the gravel beneath his boots. He took six more steps away from them. By the time he took his seventh, he heard once more the sound of Kode's gun. His body jerked forward as the bullet tore through his back and lodged into his right lung. He grimaced in agony for a short moment. And then he roared.

It was a roar that could be heard for miles in all directions. It shook the metal of the men's bikes and stung the drums of their ears. Before they could think to fire more shots, they watched in confused horror as the shape of the man that they thought was human contorted and swelled in size.

Kode Caizre's tri-irised eyes bulged in panic as he screamed at his men. "Shoot! Shoot him!"

The monstrous shape darted at them as they fired their guns. They knew not if their aims were true, for the beast showed no sign of injury or hindrance. It roared again, and the fires of their torches blew out.

In the sudden darkness, the beast tore into their midst. If any of them would survive this night, they would then tell the tale of their encounter with the Werekrilp. They would describe the beast as larger than an ox with the grace of a tiger, and how it closely resembled both. They would explain that this particular beast still had the head of a human encased in a helm of ornate silver. They would tell of the fury and tenacity of the horrible creature that made their minds blank with fear. But no such tale would ever be told by these men.

The Werekrilp wielded the axe in one massive clawed hand as if it were a tomahawk. It hacked down upon the nearest man. The

176

man, still straddling his bike, wailed and was quickly silenced as the blade cleaved through him and the bike's frame. The screaming head of another man was crushed and ripped off by the monster's free claw-hand.

A man who had fired a shotgun had dropped his weapon and tried to pedal away. The Werekrilp snatched up the bike by its back tire, shook the man off of it, and then slammed the bike onto him, crushing the man's every bone and every hope. Another two men died from a fatal swing of the axe, sending out a spray of blood around them.

One man drew a crude-looking sword and jabbed the beast in its side. But the blade's tip was halted by a wall of muscle and fur. The Werekrilp turned and clawed out the man's guts in one vicious swipe. Another man tried to run for the house, but tripped and fell over the dead bileer. The axe split his spine and everything beneath it.

The only man left was Kode Caizre.

"I gave you a chance!" the beast roared. "Why is this axe so important, huh?! Huh?! Why are you willing to kill for it?"

Kode said nothing as he backed away. He leveled his pistol at the beast.

Röger growled and held up the big bloody axe. "Ask yourself this: if something is worth killing for, is it also worth dying for?"

Kode fired his last three shots in vain, yelling "Curse you!" He looked more angry and annoyed than afraid, Röger would later remember.

The beast ignored the pin-prick feeling of the bullets in his chest and replied "I already am cursed!" Then he took a single step and swung the axe at Kode's neck.

Kode ducked the blade, squatting into a crouch. Before the Werekrilp could recover from the swing, Kode closed in past his long reach and landed a high kick to the beast's gut.

Röger's eyes bulged as he felt his lungs deflate, so powerful was the blow! The Swan threw another kick, this time at the Werekrilp's ankle. The large beast's footing was robbed from him as the kick swept his massive foot off the ground.

The Werekrilp crashed harshly onto his giant shoulder and let out a wheezing growl. A third kick, just as fast and strong as the last two, pounded thunderously into the mask of Röger's helmet.

"What is this guy, some kind of Chimancer?!" the Werekrilp thought as he blocked another kick with his forearm. The kicks came faster and harder, making it difficult to concentrate. Desperately, he rolled away in a reverse somersault, stood up, and swung his axe wildly with both mighty arms.

The head of Kode Caizre flew off his shoulders, straight up into the night air. After three breaths, the head fell onto the iron sign reading '*NcKoons Orchard*,' spiking itself on the "*d*".

The beast stared at the axe in his hands. He looked around at the cloven bodies of the biker gang. Röger glanced up at the head on the sign. The face of Kode Caizre leered blankly at nothing. He saw blood dripping past the eye-holes in his helmet. He was drenched in it, and it made the night air seem colder. He looked again at the dead men on the ground, but quickly shut his eyes.

"No. I don't want to know if they're wearing wedding rings. I don't need to know if they had families. They tried to kill me. They got what they tried to give, that's all." He rested his axe on his shoulder and went to his dead bileer.

He knelt down and placed his hand on the beast's shoulder. "You deserved a better death than this, Rufus." He then lifted up the dead steed and put it on his other shoulder. He walked to the road, looking left toward the Galvestri Villa, and then right to the way he entered the town of Tanglefoot. He then looked straight ahead again at the rolling hills and mangled trees lit softly by the clear night. It would be eight more days until he could rendezvous with his friends in Drowsy Nook.

He sighed and shook his head. "I bet they're having better luck than me."

Part 2

{◊}

Röger avoided every road he encountered, except to run across them to the other side. He ran until he happened upon a cow pasture. In the lowest point of the land, there was a grove of trees in the midst of a shallow stream. There he consumed the entire carcass

178

of his steed bite by bloody bite. The strong acids in his beastly stomach dissolved the animal enough for him to alter back to his man shape.

He then spent dozens of minutes washing the half dried blood off his skin, clothes, and axe. He removed his boots and took special care only to get the outsides of them wet. When he was done, he folded up his wet clothes and took a dry shirt and a pair of jeans out of his rucksack.

Once he was dry and dressed, he sat and thought. *"The guy said that there are no police here, that the Trotting Swans run this town. Well, chances are I just took out all the Swans in that particular villa. Too soon to tell though. Biker gangs can be bones to be chewed. There may be dozens more after me before too long. And after the others, too, now that they're our enemies."* He looked at his axe. *"There were eight of them. With guns. They wanted this axe bad enough to gather up, try to kill me, and take it. Hmm. If they claim that they run this county, then they must want to keep the status quo. Part of the status quo is the hauntings. This axe is a part of that. They either know something about these hauntings, or at least they think they do. Or maybe they just don't want big changes."*

He stood up, sought out the tallest tree in the grove, and climbed it. Upon reaching the highest point, he looked about and spotted a small cottage just a few hundred yards away. He checked his pocket watch and saw that it was long past Midnight. After getting dressed, he hid his saddle in the high, shaggy branches of a tall pine tree. When all was ready, he left the grove and made his way to the cottage.

It was a quaint house made of mismatched stones and crude mortar. The walls sparkled here and there from the occasional piece of quartz. The wooden shingles on the roof were beginning to weather and split.

"That's a fire hazard," he thought as he approached the front. He gave the door a series of hard raps in quick succession.

After a moment, a woman's voice answered. "Just a minute!"

It turned out to be a few minutes before she opened the door. A red-haired vixen in her mid-to-late thirties, she wore a pink sleeveless nightgown lit up by the candle she held before her. "Hello, there, sir," she greeted Röger with a smile, her eyes glancing back and forth at his helm and axe. "What can I help you with this late at night?"

"Oh, just a place to stay until daylight."

Her eyes widened as she gave a slow nod. "Is that all you'd like, sir? I can provide you with more than that if you have coin to match your desire. All deals are final before you come in. There will be no changing of minds if you opt for my den sofa."

Röger grinned and shrugged. "Well, I'm not a man to waste an obviously good opportunity. What are my options and your prices for such?"

She orated a list of the various services she provided and the fees they entailed. Since Röger felt a twinge of guilt for rousing her so late, he did not bother her with haggling. He chose a delightful combination of two services and put the money in her hand. The amount she asked for seemed much lower than what she could have charged.

"One more thing, stranger, my body is for *you* to cleave into, not your axe. Leave it outside. You can store it in the shed around back."

After he complied with her demand, she let him in with a friendly caress to his shoulder. She then called into to darkness of her home. "It's okay, Amber! Put your gun away!"

"Okay, Rose! Goodnight!" answered a woman's voice from a back room.

"Who's that?" Röger asked.

"My roommate," the redhead replied with a playful sparkle in her eye. "And before you ask about her joining in, the answer is no. We live together, but we do not work together."

Röger laughed. "No worries. She had a gun ready, eh? The whole time?"

She took his hand in hers and led him into her bedroom. "Women in our profession need to be on our toes as much as our backs or knees. Here, you can set your helmet on my dresser."

"That's okay, Rose, was it? I prefer to keep it on."

She tilted her head and ran her hands up his chest and onto his shoulders. "Rose Quartz is my name, stranger. And this house is not one for shame. You can show me your face without worry."

"Thanks, Rose. But no."

180

She made a disregarding frown and shrugged. "Suit yourself." She slid the straps of her gown off her shoulders and let it fall to her feet.

Röger beheld her lean body in the yellow glow of her candle. Feminine curves melded with toned muscle under a smooth, tight cover of pale skin. Her skin would have been flawless, if not for the occasional scar here and there. There was one particular scar on the side of her left breast, which was considerably smaller than her right one. All the scars looked the same as the ones on Florabella Cottonwood, bite marks.

He looked back at the woman's face. She lifted the candle seductively to her lips, and blew it out. In little time, she replaced the candle with something else.

"*Questions...later...*" Röger thought.

❁

It was almost noon. The bell-like clang of an iron skillet followed by a woman yelling "Oh waste!" woke Röger from his sleep.

He rolled out of the bed, stiff and bleary eyed. He heard the sheets ruffling, and looked up to see Rose Quartz's face looking down at him. "You okay, stranger?" she asked. But before he could form a word she said "Of course you are. You're wearing a helmet."

"Why me?!" shouted the voice of her roommate from the other side of the house.

Rose turned her head and yelled "Did you drop the eggs again, Amber?"

"No!" the roommate groused back. "It was the bacon."

Rose rolled her eyes and got out of bed, naked. "Did you try to use your undergarments instead of the oven mitt again? You know that skillet gets too hot for that."

"But I couldn't FIND the oven mitt!"

Rose sighed and looked back down at Röger. "Fun's over stranger. Thank you for your business. You can show yourself out."

As he watched her leave, he saw more scars on her back, butt, and legs. The smell of cheap incense and swine fat filled the air.

He quickly got off the cold floor, hunting for his scattered clothes. He was dressed and booted in less than a minute.

As he stepped out of the bedroom, he kept an ear open toward the kitchen.

"Well, I'm not going to eat it if it's been on the floor," he heard the roommate protest.

"Just rinse it off," Rose argued.

"You can rinse it off. I'll just cook more for me."

"Are you kidding? I'm not going to eat all this bacon! The last thing I need is to get fat and have that *thing* visit me again!"

"I'll eat it!" Röger called out. He quickly followed his nose to the small kitchen/dining area where he found the two women. Rose was still shamelessly without clothing. The fact that her breasts were of drastically different sizes seemed more apparent than the night before.

Her roommate, Amber, wore a form-fitting nightgown. She had one small perky teat on one side and nothing on the other. "I'll eat the pig strips if nobody wants them. I don't mind. I really worked up an appetite yesternight anyway. Wow! I forgot how much redheads take it out of me!"

Rose arched an eyebrow and shrugged a shoulder. "If you insist, stranger. We don't have any clean forks yet."

Röger waved. "Aw, its bacon. I can use my hands."

"You sure can," Rose answered with a sly grin. She put the bacon on a plate and set it on the table. "Have a seat."

He nodded graciously and took a seat. "Thank you both. In return for your kindness, I'll do your dishes."

The two women looked at each other. "A john who does dishes!" Amber exclaimed. "What's next?"

"A john who asks questions," Röger answered as he stuffed two strips into his mouth. He chewed the meat and peered at his two hostesses. He swallowed and said, "I am Sir Röger Yamus of Four Winds-One Storm, Independent Black Vest and Ghost hunter. I'm here to investigate all that's unnatural in this town."

Rose crossed her arms. "Some of what we did yesternight could be considered unnatural, big man. Would you care to be more specific?"

He rested an elbow on the table and pointed at her scars. "I've bedded two women in this town so far, and they both had scars

182

like that, all the same shape and size. And I bet that you and her aren't the only two. So, what's the deal? Did a fleshbroker give you those as some kind of punishment?"

Rose flared her lips. "Amber and I may be amazons, but we don't need pimps. We're independent like you claim to be."

He nodded. "Is that why you're called amazons in this town, because you get by without men?"

She took two fast steps at him, shamelessly putting her breasts in his face. "This is why!" she confessed with a sharp tongue. "The *Muerchi* does this to all the working girls in Tanglefoot. It bites us as we sleep, then sucks out and devours our fat! That's why you won't find any pudgy young girls here. Only men and older gals are spared. The monster keeps us all trim and skinny. Even those temple bitches become his prey. But he always leaves their teats alone for some reason. Not the same for us, though. The *Muerchi* does this to any young girl who opens their legs outside a temple. And if you ask me, that bitch mayor Djänette MySinn and her fleshbroker council are behind it. They know something! You should go question them instead, stranger."

Röger stared at the scar on her shrunken breast and swallowed. "Yeah. I will. But first, tell me about this *Muerchi*. Has anyone ever—"

Just then there was a frantic knock at the front door. Rose and Amber looked up and left the kitchen to answer it. Röger was able to still see them from the kitchen. They opened the door.

"Oh, hello, Gracie," Rose greeted the person outside. "What's wrong?"

"Did you hear about what happened at the NcKoons house yesternight?"

"You're our only neighbor on this road, Gracie," Amber chided. "We get all our news from you."

"Well, then let me come in, and I'll tell you what I heard from a john this morning."

They let in a plump old woman (also with a shrunken breast, but plump nonetheless, he noticed) and she immediately sat down in a chair in the living room. "Well, the john told me that eight swans were found dead outside Galvestri Villa late yesternight on the edge of the NcKoons property."

"No!" Amber exclaimed in thrilled surprised. "What

183

happened? Someone finally got the drop on *them?*"

"It was a bloody massacre! They were all in pieces strewn about the road and grass. One man's head was even impaled on the old NcKoons farm sign. And the weird thing is; is they all had their guns out, and all the guns had been fired empty! And not one of them had been shot in return. Whoever or whatever killed them must have been bulletproof. Some think that they may have fought with a powerful theurge, or a monster, or maybe even the ghost of Farmer NcKoons himself! It's been known that drunken tourists have died while snooping around that place."

"But they always die of fright," Rose Quartz argued. "Who's investigating this?"

The older woman shrugged. "Since it was only Trotting Swans that died, I would guess that the rest of them will look into it."

"Great," Amber groaned. "More of those bastards are going to come here. You both know what's going to happen, right? They're going to shake everyone down for information, and while they're at it, demand a few freebies from us. They'll make the whole town pay, I just know it!"

Rose sighed, and rested her face in her hands. "Whatever they were up to by that haunt-house, I'm sure it was no good." She paused and then sat straight up, eyes wide. "What if they finally found it? What if they tracked down the *Muerchi* like they said they would, and it killed them? Gracie, you said they all had their guns out. And it's long been speculated that the monster is a *laich* of some kind."

"I seriously doubt it," Röger interrupted, walking into the conversation. "Laiches consume certain parts of the body according to their types. Hemogoblins drink blood and eat hearts, Bregenites eat eyes, brains, and nerve clusters, Thermorooks absorb body heat, Homovores eat the muscle, tendons, and cartilage, and Beingnaws eat bones and drink marrow. Those are the only five types of Laiches."

"It might be a Homovore then," Rose contested.

Röger grimly shook his head. "I've dealt with them, honey. They're gluttonous and would never leave a mark alive. Just eating the fat won't satisfy them."

"Then even if the *Muerchi* isn't a laich, do you think it's still

184

possible that maybe it was the thing that killed those men yesternight?"

Röger did his best to make a neutral face. "I don't have enough information to give you an answer. I would have to ask you more about this *Muerchi.*"

Rose made a half-grin and nodded. "That's fine, I guess. I'll get dressed and tell you on the way to the murder scene."

Röger's spine straightened. "The murder scene with those swan guys? Why would you want to go there?"

"I don't. But I figured that you would since you're investigating the town. It *did* happen on the property of a ghost, after all."

Röger laughed nervously. "Yeah. Alright. Let's go. Sounds like a plan."

❖

It was a long walk from Rose's house to the NcKoons Farm. Other than the occasional house or tacky villa, the scenery was rather bleak. Acre after acre of dead grass and bare orchards left little to chat about. Röger felt a strong uneasiness in his stomach. It might have been guilt or just worry. Or it might have been the remains of Rufus Gut-Stomper "stomping" through his guts. He couldn't tell. He had contemplated not bringing his axe along. But in the end, he decided it was best to have it with him. Just in case.

He did not consider himself a master manipulator. But it was easy for him to have Rose Quartz talk about herself for the whole trip. He did not want to be asked risky questions. After a century of getting countless women into bed, he had mastered the trick of getting a woman to distract herself with her own voice.

He listened to her attentively, not just because her voice distracted him from his uneasiness, but mainly because she seemed to be more in-the-know than anyone else in town. As they walked, Rose told him her story.

"My best friend, Sereh, and I came down from Embrenil when we were both sixteen. We lied about our age to find work. We heard this town was a great place to make money. Our plan was to

185

run away, work here for a year or two, and then return to our mothers with enough money to start a better life. We would lie and say we'd joined a circus or became excursionists or something like that when we'd return."

"We were both far from innocent. But no amount of teenage enthusiasm can prepare you for the life of a whore. You quickly learn that all men, whether they act with courtesy and politeness or crude indignation, all men are animals. Sure, some are easier to handle, but some will give you nothing but trouble. But animals they are nonetheless. So, when you have some slobbering lout grunting and leering while getting his jollies on you, just bear in mind that he's just another stupid animal getting what he craves. Now, that's no offense to you, Sir Röger. You were like a very well behaved bileer. But most are just jackasses or pigs.

"Sereh and I couldn't get work at the villas. We didn't have 'the makings' of a sacred harlot. We couldn't find a decent fleshbroker to represent us, either. It was because we were human and age too quickly. A bad long term investment, they said. So, we had to fend for ourselves. There was never a shortage of work though. But we'd almost always get the low end johns who couldn't afford a temple girl. Some were just poor, lonely, honest men. Most were just cheap louts out for a cheap thrill. But all were just animals, as I said before.

"Our rent was high, so we had to work a lot. I could handle it, but it was wearing on Sereh. She started using *gray dust* to cope with it. The flower it comes from grows wild all around here, so it wasn't very expensive. But she became addicted, and it changed her. She ate less and less. She would talk about the visions it gave her. She said it allowed her to see the ghosts all around us. I've heard that the *gray dust poppy* only grows in this county and in Ses Lemuert, and that it allows the user the sight of a necrotheurge. It drove her mad in less than a year. She started sleepwalking while having nightmares. She said that the ghosts of dead johns would rape her night after night. I tried to get her to quit, but she insisted that it gave her control over the visions if she took enough."

Röger looked over at the woman. She was fighting back tears.

"She found a way to end the visions one night. She took a spoon to her eyes and scooped them out. Then she ate them. She was chewing on her second eye when I found her in her room. I couldn't tell if she was laughing or crying in pain. Then she swallowed her own tongue and choked to death. The only people who attended her funeral were me and a few johns who fancied her. I couldn't return to Embrenil after that. What would I tell her mother? Or my mother? It was my idea to come here in the first place. And so..." Tears escaped Rose's eyes, but her voice never wavered. "And so, I will remain here in Tanglefoot to live out my days as a second-rate prostitute. Anchored by my own shame. Sereh will never return to see her mother again. And nor will I."

Röger contemplated what to say to her. He wanted to give words of comfort like *I don't think you're second rate, Rose,* or *You shouldn't blame yourself for Sereh's death,* or *It may not be too late to go back home.* But as he looked at the poor wretched soul through the crying whore's eyes, he realized that nothing he could say could fix her or her life. "*Who am I to give advice anyway?*" he thought.

Instead, he asked her an investigative question. "Rose, who sold her the *gray dust?*"

The woman roughly wiped the tears off her face. She glared onward down the dusty road and sped up the pace of her steps. "The Trotting Swans," she answered through gritted teeth. "And if we make it in time, I might be able to spit on their worthless corpses!"

They arrived too late. Papa G.D. and his band of grave makers were already on the scene. They had just loaded the last of the bodies into a shabby wagon. Röger saw one of the men climbing down from the NcKoons sign carrying the head of Kode Caizre. The man tossed the head into the back of the wagon and said "That's the last of it, Papa."

A large crowd had gathered, nearly the entire villa of Galvestri and two other neighboring villas. There seemed nearly one hundred people, but none dared set foot on the NcKoons property. Only Papa G.D. and his men were brave enough for that.

Dried blood puddles and broken velocipedes were strewn about the road. And a dozen more living Trotting Swans stood around the bike that had been cut cleanly through its steel frame. They talked gravely to each other in soft, nervous voices.

"No beast or monster did this," one said. "Only a Ferroweaver could make a cut like this. Don't you think?"

187

"If it was a Ferroweaver, he didn't act alone. Peetre had his head bitten off by something with sharp teeth."

"Looked like claw marks to me, like the ones on Mkee and Stronol."

"But what were they doing out here? Why did they gather without the rest of us?"

An older man spoke up, and his voice was strong and clear like the clang of a sledgehammer. "Caizre must have been in a hurry. The rest of us were probably too far to be reached. He was always impatient. Now, the question is what could have caused him to get excited enough to form a hunting party?"

Röger watched the older man's eyes shift throughout the crowd, the blood, the bikes, and ending at the haunted house. "And why here?" the man asked his men.

"Do you think the ghost did it, Lance?" a young swan asked him. "Or maybe the Muerchi?"

The older man grunted in disapproval. "The Meurchi only attacks women. And the ghost only kills by necrofright. Something else did this..."

Röger had heard enough. *"They'll never figure it out,"* he thought. He turned to walk toward the crowd, trying to blend in. But a sudden flash of daylight reflected off his axe and directly into the eyes of the older man.

The older man squinted at the glint of the mirror-like steel. "What the...?" Then his wrinkle-framed eyes widened as he caught sight of what had made the flash. "The Headsman's Axe!" he gasped. "So, it's true what they said about Drowsy Nook." He walked through his men straight for Röger. "You there! Stranger! A word, if you would!"

Röger gritted his teeth for an instant before answering the man. "I would." He approached the older man casually, taking note of what the man wore--a rustic yet elegant wide-brimmed hat complimented by a dark brown leather dust coat covered in tarnished brass studs. On his lapel he wore a six-sided copper star with the motif of a swan on it. "I take it you're the Sheriff?" Röger asked him.

The older man's cold eyes seemed to stare through him as he answered. "Tanglefoot has no law, only security. I oversee that security. My name is Lance Shaug." He offered his hand.

188

Röger took it and gave a friendly shake. "Sir Röger Yamus of Four Winds-One Storm. I and my comrades are investigating the Geohex."

"I've caught wind of you," Lance told him. "A gaggle of drunkards were spouting a tale in my tavern yesternight. I had my doubts that the Headsman's curse was broken. In fact, I still do." He shifted his gaze to the huge weapon on Röger's shoulder. "That axe has a habit of dealing out justice as it sees fit."

"I've gathered the same thing about your organization,' Röger replied.

Lance's face never changed. His eyes shifted back to Röger's. In a soft whisper that came out like a low hiss, he said, "My business and your business just became *our* business, human. That axe, be it cursed or not, is a part of my land and my land's history. Hero or not, you've no right to keep it. I'm sure that my dead friends in that wagon felt the same way. Why don't you come along with me and my men? We can straighten this out in private. Maybe we can work out a deal. Gold for the axe maybe?"

Röger could tell that this man was onto him, or at least thought he was. "Judging by how your friends in the wagon are looking, are you sure you want to get me in private?" He watched as Lance's eyes widened in apprehension and anger before adding, "I came to this town alone, by the way. And it's quite a relief knowing that there is no true law here. It just gets in the way, doesn't it, Lance?"

The older man nodded slowly. "Indeed, it does."

Just then, six white bileers pulling a stately coach arrived on the scene. The coach was also white, with ornate trim painted gold and red. The coachman wore a matching suit of the same three colors. He brought the bileers to a sudden halt and promptly hopped out of his seat, landing nimbly on a patch of blood-stained gravel. With a graceful step and a swing of his arm, he opened the coach door.

"It's the mayor!" someone called out.

A hush fell over the crowd. Röger saw many Sacred Harlots rushing to the front and curtsying deeply with their hands over their hearts. Rose Quartz crossed her arms and made a look of disgust. And in the cold eyes of Lance Shaug, Röger spotted a flash of what looked like uneasiness.

189

The creature who emerged from the coach was ageless, flawless, and overwhelmingly female. She turned her head to one side and then the other, displaying a beauty that crippled the flow of time. Her eyes blinked once against the light of the day, with eyelashes that waved like an eagle's wings. She was human, but it was clear she was a theurge bound to a power that few mortals ever touched upon. She wore a white blouse trimmed with small bits of lace, a tight brown skirt, and dark brown high heeled boots that rose up to mid-shin. On her nose sat a pair of gold rimmed spectacles that augmented her large honey brown eyes. And as her devastating stare overlooked the many patches of blood at her feet, her teeth thoughtfully nibbled at her plump bottom lip.

"*Exquisite*" was the word that came to Röger's mind. And it was a word he'd never had use for until he saw her. He felt music in his heart that no voice or instrument could play. And for the fleeting instant that her gaze passed over him, he felt as if he had been born and died.

"Grave Digger," she called. Her voice was dozy yet alert. "Grave Digger, to me, please."

Papa G.D.'s face went slack and business-like. He put his hands in the pockets of his jacket and walked over to her. His men followed closely behind. "Yes, Madam Mayor. Good morning to you."

"The mourning has only begun," she replied. "These fallen...heroes. Many of them have families throughout the county. When you send out letters to alert their next of kin, tell them that their grief is my grief, and that I will lend my best Harlots to comfort them, if they wish."

Papa G.D. took a deep, nervous breath. "I will, Madam."

She inclined her head and said with a genial face, "I will provide you with temple ribbons to pass out at their funerals. Give them only to the men and women who are the most distraught. They will need the most healing."

"Grief is not a malady," he argued. "Grief is the salve to tragedy, Madam. It wouldn't be right to counter grief with carnal delights."

The Madam frowned. "I've no time to debate you, Grave Digger. But you will do as I bid, because I will be funding their funerals out of my own purse."

190

Papa G.D.'s eyes widened. He opened his mouth to speak again, but the Madam cut him off.

"Good day, Grave Digger."

The old man frowned and bowed slightly to her. Just then, Röger saw the grave digger's son, LëCuk, whisper something in the old man's ear. Then both men turned to look directly at him.

"*They know,*" he thought.

"Madam Djänette," LëCuk began "if you would like to know how these men died, I could ask them for you. I brought my candles."

The Madam bared her teeth. "You may rely on your own theurgy, Grave Digger's Son. But I will rely on mine. Now, get that wagon out of here before it acquires a stench."

As the two men took their leave, Lance Shaug stomped his way toward her. "Madam Mayor! Madam Mayor!" he called out as he approached. He whispered low and soft into her ear. And as he did so, her eyes shifted over to Röger and stayed there. Lance seemed to ask her for permission to do something. But the Madam answered something back that he did not react well to. He tried to argue with her, but she would have none of it.

The Madam stepped away from the Trotting Swan leader and addressed Röger with a cheerful grin. "You there in the silver helm! You are new to my town, yes?"

Röger took a wary breath. "Yes, I am new, lady. At least, that's how the women make me feel."

A few people in the crowd chuckled.

"As they should, pilgrim!" she answered with a laugh. "What parts have you seen thus far?"

"I've seen a few interesting parts. Most of them feminine."

More of the crowd laughed.

The Madam bit her bottom lip and tilted her hips. "Would you care to see more?"

A few men in the crowd hooted and hollered.

Röger tried to act cool and shrugged a shoulder. "I don't know. Perhaps." He glanced over at the sour face of Lance Shaug. "Well, okay."

The Madam smiled slyly. "Then accompany me in my coach. It's a chilly day and I'm cold." She turned on one of her narrow heels and swayed her way back to the coach.

191

Röger looked over at Rose Quartz. The woman looked puzzled, having heard his conversation with the old Trotting Swan. "I don't know how these men died," she said. "But I've heard that killers sometimes return to the scenes of their kills."

"You heard right," he replied. "Thanks for giving me a place to stay yesternight."

She closed her mouth tightly and nodded. As he turned away, she asked, "Will I see you again, traveler?" There was as much desire in her words as fear.

Röger smiled and pinched her cheek. "If you're lucky, doll face. If you're lucky."

As he made his way to the Madam's coach, Lance Shaug grabbed his arm.

"This ain't over yet, round ear," the Swan hissed.

"It is for Kode Caizre," Röger replied in a low voice. "And it will be for you and the rest of your drug-pushing back-shooters if you don't steer clear of me and my business." At once, the muscles in Rögers arm spasmed and expanded to freakish proportions, but only for an instant.

The old Swan jumped back about three feet, a look of shock on his face. "How'd you—?!"

Röger gritted his teeth, still keeping his voice down. "I ask the questions, you wrinkled anus. If any of you swans come at me again, I'll cut you all down like the weeds you are." He then went to the Mayor Madam's coach, and got in with her.

Röger was secretly mortified to be in the Madam Mayor's presence. She was a High Theurge of power and influence who clearly knew something about him. Still, it was better than being near a the crowded scene of a massacre that he had secretly created.

As soon as he got in and sat down, the Madam lifted up one of his great arms and cozied up to him. The action was shameless and natural, and it made him smile. She nuzzled her head against his chest, and he caught the scent of her hair. It was as fresh and sweet as a spring rain. It was nearly a minute after the coach got

192

going again before she spoke.

"So," she purred as she placed a hand on his thigh. "One of my Sacred Harlots informed me of your inquisitive visit from yesternight. She mentioned your interest in the Geohex and that haunted orchard house. Another informant told me about your confrontation with Kode Caizre at Frumpy Joe's saloon. There is little in this town I do not know about, Sir Röger Yamus. The Trotting Swans are not the real security here. I and my Harlots are."

Röger's heart beat faster against her ear. "Peace," she whispered, rubbing his leg. "We are not enemies."

He felt all his paranoia and worry drain away, as if it had been robbed from him. "What do you want from me?" he asked.

"Oh, before too long I'd like a good shunting and a tender snuggle. You are a fine make of a man, and I will not let you go to waste. But for now I would like answers in trade. Why are you and your three friends trying to end the Geohex?"

Röger regarded his weapon and confessed thoughtfully, "Well, at first it was just because I wanted this axe. My old one got ruined and I already knew the legend of this one. So, I talked the others into coming down here with me...to help me get it for myself. But the longer I stay here, and the more I see that this county needs help, the more I feel like helping it. The Trotting Swans use the cursed soil to grow Gray Dust Poppies. It's known throughout the Doflend drug trade that Wraith County is where most of the dust comes from. Ending the Geohex would kill off the poppies and get the apple orchards yielding again, hopefully. So, that's another reason."

"But if the curse ends," she started "then that means all my Sacred Harlots would have to practice the hassle of contraception. It would cripple business for the amazon whores as well. But...it would hurt the Swan's business even more. I tell you in truth that I would not like the change. But I might welcome it, even though this town is my beloved creation. I do not approve of the Swan's blatant thuggery. They are responsible for countless deaths by bullet, blade, and that vile poison they peddle."

Röger raised an eyebrow. "Are you sure you'd be okay with the Geohex ending? It would really hurt business for you, too, you know."

"I know," she sighed. "But money is nothing to me. I was

rich when I came here from Fevär. I knew then as I know now that nothing ever lasts. Change happens and conflict is always its cause. And I've had my fill of conflicts." She looked up, her dark gold eyes just inches from his sparkling brown ones. "Take off your helmet," she implored softly.

"I shouldn't," he replied with obvious regret.

Her eyes fluttered slowly as her breath mixed with his. "Tell me, how were you able to kill all those armed men with only this big ugly axe to aid you?"

"They were really bad shots," he lied.

She laughed at his words. "No matter. Either way, I will convince Lance to leave you alone while you conduct your investigation. He will do whatever I ask him."

"Why? Is the old coot in love with you?"

"Lance is not in love *with* me. He's in love *by* me. Long ago, I discovered he and his swan brethren were conspiring to murder me. So, I granted him a theurgic boon that would give all the blissful confidence of a young man in love for the first time."

"You bribed him," Röger said decidedly.

"Not at all. For this boon has a backlash if he does anything to displease me. If he were to betray or kill me, he would relive the worst heartbreak he had ever endured. You see, Sir Yamus, I have a leash around the old goat's heart. And he knows it."

Röger furrowed his brow, trying to fully understand. "So, he feels love, but doesn't love and isn't loved?"

"Yes and no," she answered. "I instill in him a feeling so intense that no other emotion but love can describe it. And I love him as I love you and all people whose hearts still beat. It is my philocreed to love in such a way. But I will use *tough love* on my enemies. I will break their hearts if they betray me."

Röger leaned back, crossing his thick arms. "So, if you've enslaved him, why do you let him and his men get away with pushing gray dust and killing people? You can't tell me that I'm the first guy to get jumped around here."

Djänette frowned. "Because, I can manipulate only him, and not his men. I use him for the time being to assert some control over his subordinates. But if I forced him to order his underlings to mend their wicked ways, they would simply sack and replace him. The swans hold me in check, and I do the same to them. I must be

194

careful. So, would you be my knight, Sir Röger, to tip the scales?" She slid her hand up his thigh.

His hand slid down her back and cupped one of her firm cheeks. "How?" he asked.

"I want you to start by hunting down the *Muerchi,* and bring me its head." She removed her blouse, exposing those same bite scars around her midriff. "It's been nothing but a pain to the women of this town."

It was the most beautiful torso he had ever laid eyes on. And someone or something had marred it. He took a deep breath, trembling with lust and rage. "From this moment on, the monster is my mark. I will find this...this...chubby-chaser, and kill it. For you, Madam Mayor, and the women of this town."

She removed her bra and straddled him eagerly. "Please. Call me Djänette. Call me whatever you want! *Omnia vincit amor!*"

As she engulfed him then and there, her theurgy went to work. The blessing rite had begun.

Throughout the day and long into the night, Röger's mind became diluted with pure joy. All was new again. Everything was funny and beautiful. No cares or worries plagued him. His thoughts were almost entirely replaced with emotions, all of them good, simple, and intense. It was free love in its purest form, in all its boundless glory. They were two creatures passing each other in the dark, acknowledging each other completely. It was no illusion, no mere dream-trick of the mind. It was reality heightened, too real for a mind to fully comprehend.

Röger awoke the following afternoon in Djänette's bed at her mansion home. The first thing he noticed was a matching pair of green-eyed cats laying on his chest, just staring at him.

"Uh...hello..?" he mumbled to them.

They blinked lazily in response. "

You guys should get off me now," he warned.

They closed their eyes as if ignoring him.

"Okay then!" With a sudden jerk, he rolled over, intending

195

to roll off the bed. To his own surprise, he had to roll three times before he finally fell off.   *"This bed is huge!"* he thought as the thud of his body on the floor woke him up completely. He felt a sharp pain in his chest and looked down.

Both cats were still attached by their claws, their eyes open wide in terror and confusion. He screamed, and they immediately leapt off and dashed away. He had half a mind to chase them down, but he soon found himself laughing his ass off.

As he got up and started to dress, he noticed an odd piece of art on the wall. It was a mangled bundle of rope arranged in a complex network of twists and turns, forming a huge knot ball. But the knot had been perfectly cut in half down the middle.

"Hmm...What's that all about?" he wondered out loud.

"Are you looking at my knot?" Djänette's voice called out from the nearby bathroom.

"Yeah!" he called back. "I didn't know you were still here!"

She came out wearing a bathrobe and a towel on her head. The robe was generously left untied. "It is never wise to leave a lover, even a one night stand, alone before they wake. In fact, it can be quite rude. Unless you leave a note. But leaving them alone without a decent goodbye would be like ending a sentence without punctuation, thoughtless and improper."

Röger smiled and nodded graciously. There was something about a woman that could be extremely refined, yet scandalously trashy. "So, what's the story with this knot on the wall? You don't seem the type who would go for oddball art."

"It is symbolic of my *philocreed.*" She poured a glass of water and handed it to him. "Are you familiar with the story of the Conquering King and Unsolvable Knot?"

He shook his head.

She took the towel off her head, picked up an ornate comb from her vanity, and began to straighten her hair. "Once upon a time, a young warlord king took over an ancient city, making himself the new sovereign there. Many considered him a fair ruler, although he was given to making rash decisions. Curious about his new subjects' culture, he learned about a local temple that housed the chariot of a more ancient king. According to local legend, the ancient king could make a knot on his chariot ropes that only he could tie or untie. And any man that could undo the ancient knot was indeed the rightful king. Now, of course, the young warlord saw this as a challenge to his own authority. So, with the entire city watching, he entered the temple, approached the knot, drew his sword, and promptly cut the knot in half! Thus, the knot was undone."

Röger smirked. "Yeah, but I bet many people called him a cheater."

"Was he?" she asked, arching an eyebrow and smirking back. "Because he did things his way? My dear knight, the story has several morals. The old knot represents the convention of senseless tradition. Much like the knot of lifelong matrimony, it binds forever without the option of freedom. And it cannot be undone without great harm being done first, such as a divorce or death or heartbreak. Such knots choke out one's potential for greatness."

Röger scratched his lower back and blinked several times in thought. "Is this why your theurgic order is the Slipknot? A knot that isn't permanent?"

She threw off her robe and pushed him onto the bed. "Such a clever boy!" She scurried on top of him, pinning him down with strong eye contact. "Life is so, so short for many of us. Why must we limit ourselves to falling in love but once? To meet and join with someone new reveals new things about ourselves. The intimacy of unbridled passion and unconditional caring removes the imprisoning armor of our hearts and minds. Sharing our bodies, hearts, and thoughts with as many different individuals as possible lets us grow and evolve beyond the sociological boundaries we once imagined were there and relevant." She adjusted her hips just right and let out a sigh of ecstasy, a hungry smile on her lips. "After I give you one last bounce, I will give you all the information and resources you need to conduct your investigation."

After a delightfully exhaustive tumble with his hostess, Röger asked her questions that only a trained Black Vest would ask, and got the answers he needed.

In his human form, Röger Yamus had the strength of thirty

men. Almost always there was a spring in his step and lightness in his heel. But that particular evening his legs felt like jelly. Every part of him felt relaxed save his heart and mind. The chilly air was sweet and easy to take in. He could not remember a time feeling so healthy or pleasant. He was happy to be alive.

With his axe on his right shoulder, he carried a briefcase in his left hand. It contained a map of the town, a list of the names of every fleshbroker on the town council, every sacred harlot they facilitated, every amazon in town, and the names and homes of every nearby Trotting Swan. It also contained two dozen blue ribbons, five thousand grotz coins, and a summary report of the *Muerchi's* activities.

It read:

The creature has never been spotted or heard. It has been able to enter residencies with locked doors and windows, leaving no signs of ever breaking through them. All victims remain unconscious as it sucks the fat from their bodies. All bite marks left behind are identical in size and shape. It has only ever fed on females (no preferred race). It has been known to take up to forty pounds of fat from a woman in one night. Plump girls that are new in town are usually thinned out within a year. The plumpest are usually targeted first. Older women who cease their periodic bleed are never victimized by the Muerchi. Rarely do victims die, but when they do it is usually due to blood loss or poor health. There are countless legends and theories about what the Muerchi might be. Many suspect it to be a post-mort laich of some sort. Some think it may be a ghost or even a wraith.

He spat on the long gravel road, one of many throughout the town. "This is either going to take a lot of walking...or some riding. First thing's first then."

◈

Back at Papa G.D.'s Smokehouse, Röger stepped into a room of startled people. Every man there, including Papa G.D. and LëCuk, stopped conversing and jolted when they saw him.

198

"Get out of here!" LëCuk ordered as he drew a crude looking knife. "You are bad for business!"

"I beg to differ, grave maker," Röger argued as he placed one thousand grotz on the nearest table. "I have work for you, gentlemen."

LëCuk sneered and took a few steps toward him. "You already gave us plenty of work with those Swans you cut down."

Röger cocked his head and regarded the knife. "That's a pretty cruddy shank for being a butcher."

LëCuk bared his teeth. "That's because I melted a silver grotz onto it after I talked to a few of those corpses. Some of them still had enough soul in them to remember how they died. They told me *everything*."

Röger's eyes widened.

LëCuk continued. "That's right, Werekrilp. And guess what? We've all got them."

Every man in the room, with the exception of Papa G.D., drew a similar knife.

Röger found himself suddenly surrounded by nervous eyes and shaking blades. He frowned and sighed. Slowly, he put down his axe. "Fellas. I'm just here to commission you all for a job. This money should cover it. Use it to buy new knives to replace the ones you ruined."

"You are a monster," LëCuk spat. "You will bring untimely death to countless people if we don't put an end to you here and now."

Röger sighed again and hung his head. "Okay then. You are forcing me to do something I resent."

"Oh? What's that?"

"Use the law to achieve my goals. I hate having to do it. You're really ruining my day. Making me feel like a cop or something." He paused to watch LëCuk's eyes narrow with curiosity. "I'm on official assignment from the Mayor herself. She has given me her favor both theurgically and financially. She has assigned me to hunt down the Muerchi. If you kill me, all you'll have left to justify your actions is my perfectly human carcass. My curse dies with me, bone reader. My money was good here two nights ago. Why not tonight?"

LëCuk scoffed. "It's not *your* money if you got it from that

199

woman!"

"You're really hunting the Muerchi?" one of the men asked, lowering his knife.

Röger nodded to him.

The man began to blink and get angry. "That...That...That monster snuck in my house and drained the ass off my wife!"

"Mine, too!" another man declared. "*And* my girlfriend's!

"It got my daughter and my niece!" added yet another. Soon, all the men except LëCuk were lending their voices in hate and resentment for the Muerchi.

Röger took advantage. "Well, you know what, fellas? Now you got a monster hunting a monster! It takes one to know one, right?"

The grip on LëCuk's knife tightened. "I've heard enough!"

"No! I've heard enough!" shouted Papa G.D. All eyes shifted to the portly old man. "LëCuk, put away your blade. Take this man's money. If we can help him out, then we will help him out. All of you, blades away!"

"Why?" LëCuk asked, never taking his eyes off Röger. "Because money is money, pop? Is that it? Is that all?"

Papa G.D. took out a rag and wiped sweat from his brow. "The Muerchi killed your mother, boy. She had that blood condition. Wouldn't stop bleeding. She was dead when I woke up next to her."

LëCuk turned his head to make eye contact. "I know all this, dad! What's your point? That we let this guy roam free to possibly slaughter others? A man infected by the Werekrilp's bite has no control over the changes. Regardless of the man's intentions, the beast always wins out. We should turn him in or kill him if he resists."

Before anyone could react, Röger's bare arms sprouted a striped layer of fur, his height increased by a head, and his body thickened with rippling muscle. All save his helmed head had changed. Every man except LëCuk backed away in terror.

The fearless necrotheurge raised his knife for a downward stab into the beastman's chest. But Röger was expecting it and very delicately grasped the man by the wrist, careful not to crush his bones.

LëCuk yelped in pain as the clawed hand seized him. The knife dropped, and as the point of the blade stuck into the floor,

Röger shifted back to normal.

"I *can* control my changes," he said. It was a partial lie. He let go of the man's wrist and looked over at Papa G.D. "If your son here really talked to the corpses of those Swans, did he also mention that they were the ones asking for trouble?"

The old man looked at his son, questioning with his bloodshot eyes. LëCuk looked away and sighed. "It's true, dad. They tried to get the axe from him. They...they even shot him in the back while he was trying to get away."

The old man nodded thoughtfully and looked back at Röger. "My wife, her name was Carlota. I got no chance of avenging her, but you do." The old man wiped sweat off his brow with a rag. "So, what kind of job you have in mind for us, young sir?"

❖

The next day, as Röger rode into the villa known as Gooddirt, the dwellers there reacted with laughter and bemusement at the sight of his new steed.

"Did someone place an order for Papa G.D.'s?" one old man asked the whore on his arm.

"Yeah, the one riding it, looks like," the woman answered.

Carrying the proud and shameless hero was a full grown ox. Its great hooves and horns were charred black. All of its guts and viscera had been removed, leaving only the beef jerky muscle attached to the skeleton. Its hide had been expertly removed, tanned and dried, and then sewn back together to make a leather covering for the post-mort beast. It still walked and mooed like it was alive. And it smelled delicious.

"Excuse me!" Röger called out to the onlookers. "I'm looking for Doctor Felgusion. Could you kindly point the way to his practice?"

One man laughed and cried out, "I don't think you need a doctor, friend. It's too late to save that ox!"

Röger went along with the jokes until he had finally got the directions.

The doctor's establishment was a small dark brown house

201

with glass windows stained yellow. The sign over the door displayed a sewing needle tipped with red, the international sign for a non-theurgic healer. Röger hitched up his new mount and went through the entrance door, jingling an unseen bell on the way in.

A young drakeri man sitting behind a desk stood to greet him. "Hullo, sir. How may we help you?"

"Are you Doctor Felgusion?"

"No, sir. I am Doctor Krondole. Perhaps I can be of service."

"I need questions answered, questions about the body. Anatomy, that kind of thing."

The young doctor shrugged his shoulders and smiled. "Doctor Felgusion is with another patient at the moment. But I'm sure I am more than qualified to answer your queries."

"Okay then. The heart is part of the cardiovascular system, right?"

"Yes," the doctor answered with a nod.

"And skulls are part of the skeletal system, right?"

"Yes."

"And your brain is part of your nervous system, right?"

"Yes, of course." The doctor straightened his glasses and sat back in his chair, feeling rather smug.

"Well then," Röger started. "What system does fat belong to?"

The doctor frowned. "Excuse me? Did you say fat?"

"Yeah. Fat," Röger jiggled his gut with his hand. "Every part of the body is also part of a system in the body, right? Well, what system is fat a part of? Is it part of the muscular system maybe?"

The doctor shook his head. "No, no. Fat is fat, Mr...?"

"Röger Yamus. Sir Röger Yamus, Independent Black Vest, Ghost Hunter, and recently assigned by the Madam Mayor to hunt down the *Muerchi.*"

The doctor nodded slowly. "I see. That explains your interest in the nature of fat cells then. But I am afraid that there is no bodily system that fat is a part of."

"But there must be!"

"How so?" asked the doctor.

Röger glanced around the office. "What do you know about laiches?"

"They are post-mort monsters that feast on people's body

202

parts and blood."

Röger nodded. "And did you know that there are at least five documented types of laiches, each one with powers and appetites that correspond with certain systems in the body?"

The doctor shrugged. "Such knowledge is not my forte, Sir Yamus. Are you suggesting that the *Muerchi* is a laich of some kind?"

"More like one of a kind," the Röger explained. "He...or she...consumes fat, but only the fat of young ovulating women. So, I need to know what system of the body fat belongs to."

"But I've already told you. Fat is not part of any system. It's...it's just fat."

Röger narrowed his gaze. "I want a second opinion, doctor."

The drakeri doctor sighed. "Well, you're going to have to wait for it. Please, take a seat and Dr. Fuglesion will see you next. I'll admit that he has read more books than I have. Would you like some coffee?"

Röger sat down in a nearby waiting chair. "Yes, please. Thank you."

The doctor fixed him a mug of something dark and pleasantly robust. As he handed Röger the steamy beverage he said, "It's not often that Tanglefoot gets Black Vests. Tell me, since you are an expertly trained monster hunter, what *are* the five types of laiches?"

Before Röger could answer, another man's voice spoke from around the corner of a hallway. "Hemogoblins, Beingnaws, Thermorooks, Bregenites, and Homovores."

The owner of the voice came around the corner, a tall human with a clean shaven head and thick piercings in his earlobes. "Respectively, one drinks blood, the next eats only bones, the next steals body heat, the next brains, and lastly, the Homovore eats muscle and sinew. Rather disgusting fiends, if not particular in their diets."

"I am impressed, Dr. Fugelsion!" the younger looking drakeri doctor declared.

Doctor Fugelsion shrugged a shoulder. "A Beingnaw killed one of my father's cousins. It prompted me to take interest in the evil bastards." He regarded Röger. "I managed to overhear most of your conversation with my colleague, Sir Yamus. I'm afraid he is

203

right. Fat cells are not part of any bodily system. So, I highly doubt that the *Muerchi* is a laich."

"But its diet is so particular," Röger argued. "It is also a stealthy mother-shunter. Just like a laich, it leaves no tracks, no evidence other than the bite marks. I think it can even turn to vapor to seep through cracks and key holes."

Dr. Fugelsion shook his head. "But only the most ancient laiches can do that."

Röger spread his hands. "Then he's probably an ancient laich!"

The tall doctor crossed his arms and lowered his eyes. "I have examined countless women who woke up with these bite marks. Most had one thing in common: they were still alive, sir. Laiches always murder their prey after or while feeding."

"Only because they have to," Röger argued. "All typical laiches have to remove a specific and crucial part of the body in order to consume it. Fat isn't that crucial at all, is it? Well, it's crucial to the *Muerchi*. But a person can live without it."

Dr. Fugelsion nodded and gave a light smile. "You make a good point and almost a sound argument, sir. But fat is still not part of a bodily system. It is just fat."

Röger sighed, about to give up. It seemed that his hunch/idea had taken him to a dead end. He felt rusty and old. It had been so long since working as a hunter and not just some brute who chopped things. Then his chaotic mind stumbled outside of the box. "Wait a minute," he said carefully. "Wait. Wait. Hey, okay, if fat is not part of a system, then is it at least related to a system in some way?"

"What do you mean?" asked

"How are fat cells formed? Does a certain system produce them?"

"Uh...well...yes. The Lymphatic System. Wait, no. I think it's the Lymphoid System. I tend to get the two mixed up. Both are subsystems, though. I *do* know that. They are basically the same system though. In a way. It depends on what book you read. It's related to the circulatory system. I *do* know that."

"What does it do? How does it work?" Röger asked.

"It circulates lymph, a clear liquid that redistributes lost cells and hauls away foreign cells, such as diseases and other unwanted stuff. The Lymphatic System is basically your immune system. It keeps you healthy. It takes fatty acids absorbed from food and puts it into our fat cells. But still, fat cells are not a true part of the system, just kind of a byproduct of it."

Röger grinned darkly, as if it was all starting to make sense. "Here's one for you, doctors. Are thoughts just *byproducts* of the brain?"

The two doctors exchanged puzzled glances.

"Thoughts," Röger continued, looking half-crazed by an apparent epiphany. "Thoughts are what smart animals, people like you and me, have. A thought has no tissue or cells, but it is something real. A thought can go into the brain through the ears, swim around inside the mind and then ends up becoming more thoughts." He paused with an excited grin, hoping the doctors might get what he was explaining. They did not. So, he continued. "Thoughts are like fat...kinda. We eat fat and get fat. We hear thoughts and then think thoughts! Get it?"

The two doctors shook their heads and began fearing for their safety.

"That's okay!" He gave both men hard pats on the shoulders. "I'll explain. Hemogoblins drink blood to keep from drying out. Bregenites eat brains so they can feel and keep thinking. Thermorooks steal heat to keep from getting cold. Beingnaws eat bones to keep their own bones strong. Homovores do the same with muscles. And the *Muerchi* eats fat in order to keep from getting too skinny! It must be someone in town who is always fluctuating in weight, fat one day, skinny the next. You two know anyone like that?"

They shrugged and shook their heads in answer.

"To be perfectly honest, Sir Yamus," Dr. Fugulsion began, "We haven't had to deal much with the Lymphatic System at all here in Tanglefoot. The system battles disease and infection, conditions that are unheard of in town limits because of the Fertility Curse. You see, both disease and infection are actually microscopic entities that grow by reproduction, something that is impossible here. That's why my partner and I usually only have to worry about setting bones and stitching wounds most of the time. But if you are still interested in the subject... Hmmm. Please, wait here a moment."

The doctor went into the back of the building. A few minutes later he returned with an old book that he promptly handed to Röger. "Here you are. A complete study on the Lymphatic System. It will give you more answers than we can. We really have no use for it here."

"Thanks. Are you giving it to me as a gift or...?"

"Of course not. I am a doctor after all. That will be thirty grotz, please."

Röger rolled his eyes and nodded. "Of course." He gave the man the money.

He stuffed the book in his back pocket and placed his hands on the two doctors' shoulders again. "Gentlemen, I thank you for your time. One last question before I go, is there a store nearby that sells wood lacquer? I need to keep my new steed from rotting."

◎

Röger spent the next hour buying several jars of lacquer from a local general store, stripping the leather hide off of his post-mort ox, and coating the beast's jerky muscles and bones with layer after layer of lacquer until the beast shone in the daylight.

Many curious folk gathered to watch the helmed madman apply each coat as he whistled a nameless tune. None but one individual dared to talk to him as he worked.

"Looks like you missed a spot," came a raspy voice from behind. There was playful teasing in the words.

Röger grunted out a laugh as he tickled the bristles of his brush beneath the beast's shoulder blades. He did not bother to look behind. "I'll do one more coat after this. It should be enough...in theory."

"Being a detective, I am sure you have an eye for details."

Röger shrugged, still focusing on his lacquering. "*Detective* is a bit too refined a title for me and what I do. I'm more of an urban hunter. My tendikeye friend is the rural hunter. If anyone in my team is detective, I'd say my malruka friend, Hindin, is."

"This town is hardly urban," said the voice. "And you. You are hardly human...freak."

Röger turned around to see the face of Kode Caizre, the man

206

he had decapitated by the NcKoons Orchard, glaring at him from beneath a large hooded cloak. The speed and power of the man's kick took Röger by surprise and sent him flying through the air.

"*An inverted roundhouse?*" Röger thought as he landed shoulder first several feet away. He half sat up and looked at his opponent, his ribs throbbing from the impact. "Fancy kick for a dead man!" he shouted.

The cloaked figure settled into a fighting stance. He held no weapons. "Go ahead. Change!" Caizre spat.

Röger got up and pulled his axe.

The crowd around them stirred with frightful interest. A few people ran from the trouble, but many more were arriving to see it.

"Change!" Caizre's face said again from within his hood's cover. "Let these people *see* you!"

The Black Vest glowered. "No need."

He had no time to wonder how the cloaked man had cheated death. In three thunderous steps Röger closed the distance, readying a swing for the man's waist. The cloaked man bent in the middle as he leapt backward, narrowly avoiding the massive blade. In nearly the same instant he sprang forward and kicked one of Röger's hands off of the axe's handle. For an instant, Röger lost control of his weapon.

In that instant, Caizre moved in with a shooting foot thrust to the big man's leg. Röger's eyes widened as he heard and felt his knee collapse. "Change!" Caizre demanded as Röger fell to the ground.

Röger's mind flashed white from the pain. But his arms reacted. Sitting up, he swung the axe with adrenalized speed. He saw nothing as he attacked, so great was the blinding agony. He heard Caizre scream and drop. Regaining his vision, he saw his enemy sitting in front of him. One of Caizre's legs was cut off from the knee down.

"You bastard!" Caizre yelled, more annoyed than in pain. "No one can keep fighting after a knee break!"

"Shut up and die, Caizre!" Röger dropped his axe and clutched his knee, unable to move from the crippling torment of his sundered joint. He could feel the tendons and cartilage slowly putting itself back together. He could heal much faster if he changed into the beast. He could feel the buzzing in his skull. His body was beginning to shift. *"No!"* he thought. *"Too many people are watching! Got to keep control!"*

Just as his muscles began to spasm and grow, the face of Djänette MySinn flashed in his mind. For that instant he could smell her hair, taste her mouth, and feel her soft skin brush up against his own. The transformation stopped cold and he was left with only the pain in his knee.

Caizre grasped his separated leg and attached it to his stump. His blood soaked the ground beneath him. Letting out a gurgling hiss, he raised his hateful eyes at Röger. "You force me to do this! I hate the taste of men!" he growled. His mouth was full of pointy drool-covered teeth.

Röger had no time to react as Caizre scrambled at him, biting viciously into his stomach. A roar loud enough to be heard for three miles escaped Röger's mouth. The mouth of Caizre attached like a tick to the big man's abdomen.

As Röger gasped for breath he heard wet slurping noises. Using all his might, he pushed down on his attacker's shoulders. There was a peeling, ripping sound as Caizre's head began to tear off right where Röger's axe had previously cut it off. The spine, now visible, remained intact, as did the esophagus.

Röger let out another scream, this one a scream of terror, as he beheld the pulsating throat muscles swallowing what the mouth was sucking out. Caizre was drinking the fat from his own gut!

"Muerchi!!!" Röger yelled in sudden realization. All around him, people were gasping and screaming as they repeated the word.

Caizre's vice like jaw loosened as he rolled off of Röger. His hood was down now, showing the head of a creature that was no longer drakeri. Nearly all the purple had drained from his face. His mouth was a barbed maw of bloody greasy gore. His tri-irised eyes were solid black and reflected no light.

With desperation the creature rose to his feet, growling and hissing and gurgling all at once. The pants leg of his trousers settled soaked and bloody around the ankle of his reattached limb. Like a wounded animal he began to run away, limping and snarling as the crowd dispersed back into the shelter of the buildings.

Röger tried to stand, but his leg and abdomen were weakened. His entire midsection felt numb. *"No!"* he thought as he saw Caizre hobbling away down the road. *"He's getting away!"* He

208

was not thinking clearly.

Picking up his axe again, he summoned the last of his strength to get up onto his good knee. With both arms, he threw his axe and fell face-first into the dirt. He raised his head and watched the huge weapon whirl in a high arch and then descend upon the path of the escaping target. The throw was too hard. The axe landed several feet in front of Caizre. Röger watched as his hope turned to despair.

The *Muerchi* picked up the weapon and turned around. Even from thirty yards away, Röger could see the malice in the creature's eyes, the grin on its gory lips. With each step the monster took, its leg seemed to bother him less and less.

It raised the axe and shouted "I was hoping to merely expose you, Röger Yamus. But now you've given me the opportunity to kill you with ease! Now, let's see how well *you* can heal after being decapita---"

The *Muerchi's* words were cut short by the sudden eruption of gunfire. Several bullets tore through him this way and that.

Röger looked around seeing that several of the townsfolk had reemerged with their guns blazing. Nearly all of them were women. From all around the shots rang out, nearly all of them tearing a bloody path through the vile form of the *Muerchi*. Flintlocks, shotguns, pistols, and carbines filled the air of Gooddirt with lead and gun smoke. All around, the women of the villa roared with mad tongues of vengeance.

The *Muerchi* stumbled to and fro as the bullets riddled his flesh and bones. The dirt at his feet caught nearly all of his blood and flesh until he was little more than a battered skeleton barely covered with patches of gore and cloth. Still, he stood and held tight to the axe. As all the shooters hurried to reload their guns, he opened his fanged mouth and yelled.

"Fools! You cannot kill me! Cut me to pieces! Burn me to ash! I cannot die! I have tasted all of you whores! You are my cattle, and you are lucky I have not killed you yet! Your guns...they mean nothing." He looked down at Röger. "You can do your worst and hope for the best, hero! I have no weaknesses like other laiches. Though these bullets hinder me I will return. I'll make you pay. I'll make you all pay!"

Just as another series of shots rang out, the *Meurchi* and

every piece that had been blown off of him turned into a cloud of mist. The cloud was vaguely humanoid in shape and it stretched up into the air, flying away. It carried the axe of the Headsman with it.

"*He's ancient!*" Röger thought.

Röger lay in the dirt for several minutes. He could feel his leg healing, but not fast enough. If the crowd had not gathered around him after the *Muerchi* disappeared, he could have transformed into the beast and healed quickly enough to chase after the monster. All around him the townsfolk tried to help him, even the two doctors tried to get a look at his leg.

"It's okay. It's okay," Röger told them. "It's only a sprain. I'll be fine."

"But your leg was struck backward at least ninety degrees!" argued Dr. Fugulsion. "I saw from my window."

"You need to get your window cleaned, Doc. I'll be fine in a few minutes. I think."

"That was the *Meurchi!*" a woman exclaimed. She hugged herself, taking in the thought of that monster feeding on her. Many other women followed suit. "Look! He sucked this poor man's fat out!"

Röger looked down at his bloody shirt. Sure enough, all the fat around his midsection had been drained away. It took a solid century of dedicated eating and drinking to build up that gut. And now it was gone. Part of him was glad, but only a small part. It was a violation. He saw the women looking down at him with a mixture of terror and sadness. It was a violation. A part of him had been forcibly taken. A violation, pure and simple.

He felt something square and hard underneath his butt. He reached down to grab it and found it was the Lymphatic System book he had just purchased.

A sacred harlot knelt down beside him, setting her smoking carbine on the ground. She placed a caring hand on his shoulder. "Sir, you've just been through a horrific ordeal. Please, come to the temple with me. It's not far. Let me heal the trauma out of your heart and mind."

Röger smiled and politely patted the woman on her rear end. "Thanks, doll. You are a credit to your teacher. But I can't tonight." He peered at the book in his hand. "I have to study."

Part 3

Röger paid for a bottle of whiskey and a cheap sleeping room at the nearest inn he could find. Though many people came to him with questions and concerns, he turned them all away. After downing the whiskey in one pull, he sat up in the bed and did his best to ignore his throbbing leg. *"Should be done healing in an hour,"* he thought. Closing his eyes, he patiently waited for the numbing warmth of the liquor to work into his system.

After several minutes he let out a sigh of small disappointment. He missed his axe terribly. Losing a fight was fine as long as he lived through it. But to lose such a fine weapon was a greater shame.

He picked up the Lymphatic System book, slowly thumbed open the front cover, and began the rigorous endeavor of reading it. It was as he feared. The text was a dense, dry jumble of bland terms and soulless description.

Almost immediately it started to happen. It was a studying hindrance that he had a hard time explaining to people. He tried, tried with all his will to focus on one word at a time, reading each sentence in order. But it was no use. His eyes meandered over the pages aimlessly, his brain absorbing words at random. Nothing made sense to him even though he was perfectly literate. He closed his eyes again and took several slow breaths.

Again he tried to read the condensed sea of terms and phrases, but to little avail. He flipped around the pages and found illustrations in the middle of the book. It showed parts of the humanoid anatomy that were labeled with words, most of which he did not recognize.

-Thoratic Duct

211

-Nodes
-Spleen
-Tonsils
-Conglobate Glands
-Chyliferous Vessels
-Tributaries
-Deep Cervical Glands
-Submaxilllary Glands

The list went on and on...

The crude illustrations portrayed the Lymphatic System as a jumble of small parts clustered together here and there throughout the body. From what he could tell, no part of the system had a central part.

"What is the Muerchi's weakness? How do you attack and destroy this system?" He turned back to the front of the book. *"The purpose of the system is the key."*

He did his best to skim and not meander over the text. *The doctor said it's our 'immune system'. That it protects us from disease and infection. But laiches are immune to disease. And besides, the fertility curse in this town prevents disease and infection from happening. So..."*

He suddenly sat up straight. "Wait a minute!" he exclaimed. An idea came to him. It lingered in his mind for several minutes as he mulled it over. "Maybe," he said to himself. "Just maybe."

After a while of more reading (or attempting to read, at least), his leg healed and he was hungry. He tugged on a cord that dangled by his bedside. It rang a service bell that alerted the staff downstairs. Upon their answering, he ordered a heaping plate of whatever they were cooking that night.

A woman soon arrived holding a round covered platter.

"I hope you aren't allergic to pumpkin," she said with a polite smile. "There's a big slice of pumpkin pie." She lifted off the cover by the nob at the top. "Along with turnip greens, a baked potato, and a side of salted pork."

Röger nodded at the dish. "Looks good. Thank you."

The woman smiled again and gave a nervous curtsy. "Well, if you need anything else, please ring."

"Thanks. See you around."

212

The woman left, closing the door behind her.

Röger began to scarf down his meal and mumble thoughtlessly as he chewed. "See...you...around...around....round....hmm... round..." His eyes shifted to the dome-shaped platter cover. It was round. "*Round.*" He swallowed the last of his pork and an idea began to form in his mind. "Round," he muttered to himself.

He took the slice of pumpkin pie, sniffed it, then looked at it again. "Hmm. Radius, diameter, and...what was that other one? Hindin would know. He could make better sense of this darn book, too." He ate the pie slice in three bites. "Radius, diameter...and...circumference! That's it! Circumference!"

He rose up and went to his briefcase full of information about the town. He pulled out the map of Tanglefoot, unfolded it, and placed it on the floor.

"Blind Bitch's Bane!" he exclaimed.

The main parts in town, the villas and all the houses of the amazons, they were all enclosed in a perfect, yet very subtle, circle. Papa G.D.'s villa was just outside of it.

"Circumference!"

He took out a dull pencil and chewed it into a crude point. "*I need to go buy a good, sharp knife,*" he thought as he spit out the bits of wood and graphite. Using his dinner plate, he was able to outline the hidden circle to make it visible. There it was--the area of land affected by Vikta Wakemaker's curse.

Using the edge of the Lymphatic System book, he drew several lines through the circle until it resembled a wagon wheel with many spokes. It was not an even or exact rendering, and many of the criss-crossing lines did not intersect in the exact same point. But after drawing several lines he settled on the place he believed to be the center. Röger Yamus was no theurge, but he'd lived long enough to know how theurgy worked. "Ha! Like a ripple on a pond!"

Djänette MySinn was not used to worrying. She sat at her desk reading the letter from one of her sacred harlots. It was a full report on Sir Yamus' activities from the day before.

213

......After the Muerchi flew away and was surely gone I rushed immediately to Sir Yamus' aid. He was badly injured, yet sought no medical treatment even with the local doctors offering to help. I offered to take him into my arms and bed at our temple, but he politely refused. He retired for the day privately at the Huntsan Inn. I heard he checked out early this morning and rode off on his post-mort ox mount. Locals said he was headed for the Imperville Villa.

I fear he may be going there to confront the Trotting Swans at their meeting lodge, since it turns out that one of their number is the Muerchi. I fear for the safety of Sir Yamus and the people of that villa. I also fear for myself and the other residents of Gooddirt Villa. The Muerchi said he would take vengeance on us all for shooting him.

With love and loyalty to the Sacred Slipknot,
Ellinoir Manchainkah

Djänette set down the letter and removed her gold-framed reading glasses. She sighed with worry at what it could all mean.

"My sweet knight, my love, and my champion. Why do you venture to the viper's nest?" She stood up from her chair. "Even if he is not looking for a fight, I fear he will find one unless I am there to prevent it."

The Imperville Villa was the largest villa in Tanglefoot. Although it was not the exact center of Tanglefoot, Röger was sure that is was the center of the local fertility curse. He was not surprised to see Lance Shaug and twenty other Trotting Swans waiting for him at the entrance gate, but he was disappointed all the same. All their velocipedes were parked along the villa's walls. He rode his ox mount in a brisk gallop until he came within speaking distance from the men at the gate.

As they all raised their firearms Röger brought his mount to a halt and thought *"Well, look at this! A twenty-one gun salute!"*

"Word spreads fast!" he called out to Lance Shaug.

"Faster than a whore at gunpoint!" the aging drakeri replied. He cocked the hammer back on his pistol.

Röger took a slow breath and chose his words carefully. He could survive twenty-one bullets at once, but not without transforming into a monster and eating half of the shooters. "I'm unarmed. And I'm not here to fight or question anyone."

Lance Shaug scoffed and spat into the dirt. "If you think that we knew that Caizre was the *Muerchi,* you are dead wrong. Some of us have sweethearts that he fed off of. As soon as we find his sorry ass he's as good as dead. Just like you."

Röger shrugged. "I believe you. In fact I hope that you find him someday if I can't. But I'll tell you this much, Shaug, if you kill me now, you'll never be able to kill the *Muerchi.* No one will. Only I know his weakness."

"Oh? And what might that be?" Shaug asked with visible sarcasm.

"I'll be happy to let you know...after you let me conduct my business in this villa. I promise I will try not to take too long."

The Trotting Swan leader considered the human's words for a long moment, but the thought of his dead men, chopped to pieces by this round-eared outsider, weighed too heavily on his mind. Gritting the few teeth he had left, he yelled with rage "You know what I think? I think that the Headsman's Axe gave you power! That is how you were able kill my fellow Swans that night! The theurgic energies of that cursed blade kept their bullets from harming you! And now...and now you don't have it anymore, do you? It was taken from you and now you are nothing more than a man, a normal man! We have every right to kill you now for killing our brethren."

Röger's head dropped and he let out a sad sigh. "And I should kill you for selling gray dust to people, like the amazons of this town. You've ruined a lot of lives for the sake of profit. But I'm going to show you mercy today. Instead of killing you, I'm going to march into this villa and rid this whole town of its curse and eventually break the Geohex. Then your stupid flower won't grow. This county can be clean and new again, if you just let me pass." Röger stepped off his post-mort ox, stepped in front of it, and waited for a reply.

Lance Shaug was unsure if the man was bluffing or not. He

215

looked at the faces of his men. None looked certain of anything. Doubt crept into the heart of every Trotting Swan there. And when the doubt began to change into fear, Lance Shaug lost all reason.

He leveled his pistol at the human and yelled, "To a hell with it! We'll all fire at once to be sure! On the count of three! One! Two!"

"*NO!*" came a woman's voice from behind them.

The Trotting Swans turned to see Djänette MySinn riding up on a beautiful calico bileer. She had arrived from the other side of the villa. Her hair was down and wild in the wind. Even with a face full of desperation, anger sweat and dust from the road, she had never looked more stunning to them.

Many of the younger men almost dropped their guns in the presence of her passion.

"*No!*" she commanded again, this time meeting Lance Shaug's eyes.

The old drakeri man raised his chin in fear and defiance. "Madam Mayor. Please. Please, do not keep me from my duty as security marshal of this fair town! This man killed several of my brethren. As acting Chief Justice, I condemn him to death!"

"And as the Official Mayor, I grant him pardon!" she fired back.

Lances eyes widened. He looked hurt and confused. "But...Djänette. He will ruin everything we love, everything we've built. The curse of Vikta Wakemaker allows your temples to thrive without making bastards. It allows these flowers to grow and help me and my men feed our families. Do not let this outsider take it all from us!"

Djänette raised an eyebrow then sneered in a way that put a cold nail in Lance's heart. "I was an outsider, too, once. In fact, in all my time here, I seem to be the only human you've treated with an ounce of respect. Do you think I like the term 'round-ear'? Outsider indeed! How much blood is already on your hands?"

"But Djänette!"

"Enough!" the theurgess proclaimed. She urged her steed through the line of men to stand by Röger's side. "You will let him pass. You will command your men to lower their guns, and you will let him pass! Do it, Lance! Follow your heart!"

The old drakeri began to shiver and weep. "Follow the heart

216

that you lead by a string? You can't...keep me from doing this, Djänette! My men! My friends!"

Djänette dismounted and opened her arms. Her expression of outrage shifted to sympathy. "Come, Lance. Come. Embrace me and embrace the change Sir Röger brings to us. I have faith in him, and you also. All can be forgiven. For too long, I have profited off another theurgess' hatred. I mean to bless this land without the aid of the Geohex. It will not be so bad, I promise you. Love is stronger than Death. Choose love. Come to me."

Röger could hardly believe the profound heartache in the old man's face. Likewise, the kindness and understanding coming from the High Theurgess seemed so good and pure that it made him question his own moral strength. *"She's just as beautiful on the inside!"* he thought.

But as impressed as he was by Djänette's power to persuade, he did not like the unsure faces of the other Trotting Swans. Many of them looked far too comfortable pointing their guns at her.

"Wait!" Röger cried out. "I, uh. I surrender!"

Lance sniffled and seemed to snap out of his grief. He frowned in confusion. "Surrender? But...we're going to kill you. There's no jail in Tanglefoot."

Röger shrugged and stepped out from behind Djänette. She did not look pleased. Röger faced the Swans with his hands raised. "I surrender," he said again. "You win, Lance. But you also lose."

"What do you mean?" asked the old man.

"I mean I am ready to take twenty-one bullets for the woman who would stand in front of twenty-one guns for me, a woman who would pardon me for killing, a woman that I love more than you ever could, you weak-hearted idiot! Come on! You want death to reign in this land? So be it! Shoot me, and I'll make sure that you all get a chance to become ghosts yourselves!"

Lance Shaug let out a moaning howl as his heart broke, collapsed by his own rage. He pointed his gun at Röger and addressed his men, "One!"

A single tear fell from the eye of Djänette MySinn. She raised her hand high and made a sign with it. "Sisterlings!" she cried.

"Two!" Lance yelled.

All the barrels of the Swans were trained on Röger.

217

The Black Vest braced himself for the volley of hot lead.

Before Lance Shaug could yell, "Three," several shots rang out. None of them belonged to the guns of the Trotting Swans. The shots all came from behind them.

Röger watched in disbelief as all twenty-one Trotting Swans fell dead to the ground. None of them, not even Lance Shaug, knew what hit them. But it soon became apparent to Röger what had.

Hidden behind the gates of the Imperiville Villa, behind trees bushes, behind building walls, and even behind a sign reading *Welcome to Imperiville Villa*, stood sacred harlots holding smoking guns.

Dumbfounded, he turned to look at Djänette. Her face was turned away from the sight of the corpses draining red in the dirt. Her fists shook at her sides. With closed eyes and a trembling voice, she addressed Röger, "Not since...Not since the war have I beheld such ugliness. I tried to avoid this. And now I am trying very hard not to blame you for making me do this, Röger Yamus."

Röger stepped to her. "What does your heart tell you, Djänette?"

She burst into tears and buried her face in his chest.

He held her close for a long moment. In their embrace, they found the understanding they needed. Words were of no use.

The sacred harlots, nearly thirty in number, came out from their hiding spots. Upon seeing the sad eyes of their mistress and teacher, a chain reaction of weeping began amongst them. Some cried because they had never killed before. Some cried because they had been intimate with some of the men dead on the ground. But they all cried because they knew it was the end.

"The rest of the Swans will not forgive this, Mistress," a harlot said with quivering lips. "From all corners of the county, they will rally and they will ride here to take revenge on us. What are we to do, Mistress? We are armed for defense, but we are not fighters as they are."

Djänette composed herself and addressed her pupils. "Hear me, Sisterlings and do not despair. My knight will soon end the Geohex. This he has promised. Do not forget the lessons of the Sacred Slipknot. Do not ever forget how to love. Our time in Wraith County is over. Leave and spread our message of love and freedom throughout this Huncell, throughout the very Cluster if you feel able.

218

Start your own temples and never let anyone disrespect you. I am so sorry that it must end this way. I am so proud of you all!"

The chain reaction of tears began again as all the women wept and wailed. Hugs were exchanged between them all, as well as words of sentiments and kisses both sisterly and erotically romantic.

"Shame they don't have more time to say goodbye," Röger thought as he watched the massive display of passionate affection.

When all the farewells were said, the sacred harlots took up their guns, as well as the guns of the Trotting Swans and their velocipedes and rode off.

"Remember to stay in groups and to warn our fellow sisters in the other villas!" Djänette cried. It was her last command to them. She thought of the one-hundred-and-forty-three sacred harlots she had trained personally, and how they were all leaving her forever. One hundred souls with whom she had shared the power of her love. All gone. Her family, all spreading like bees to start their own hives. Some would succeed, others would fail. Their fates were out of her hands now.

In that moment, she felt lost, empty, and more alone than ever before. Then she felt the warm, strong arms of her knight wrap around her from behind. It was all the comfort she needed. And as she sensed the intense vibration of his heartbeat meld with the soft beats of her own, she knew peace and felt lost in every good way.

"I expect a more...involved form of comforting later on, my knight."

"And so you shall have it, my lady."

❁

They walked into the villa side by side. All around people were slowly coming out of the buildings and into the street.

"Should we expect more trouble?" Röger asked Djänette.

"It is doubtful. All the Swans' kin live in neighboring towns. Tanglefoot is a place where each person is for themselves."

An old man wearing a fancy denim suit and a matching wide-brimmed hat stepped forward. His beard was trimmed to perfection and he did not look happy. "What have you done, Djänette?" he asked with restrained contempt.

"You will address me as Madam Mayor or High Theugress, Fleshbroker Sal. As broker of this villa, you have a responsibility to be professional at all times."

"Professional?" he asked as his two white eyebrows met in a fierce glare. "You've just robbed me of my profession! All my harlots are gone! Do you really expect me to make due with common whores?"

Djänette raised her chin and responded with gleeful elegance. "The Sacred harlots were never yours, Fleshbroker. They were all free women. And whatever you do from now on is your business."

The fleshbroker's face grew dark with rage. He pointed at the town entrance and shouted. "There are nearly two dozen dead Swans out there! What am I going to do when the rest of them come to loot and burn my villa? They'll string me up for letting you rally your harlots to back-shoot their men!"

Djänette nodded, showing a face of sympathy and understanding. "Sal, when you came to Tanglefoot you were a washed up rancher from Cloak Gerardo. You had nothing but good management skills and the rags on your back. I gave you your start here, and this is how you repay me?" Without warning, she placed her palm on his chest and said, *"Do not be upset that it ended, but be glad that it happened."*

The power of the theurgess' maxim took root in the old man's heart and soul. He stepped back and felt the wisdom echo inside him. "They'll come for you, too, Djänette. Our operation is done."

"No, Sal. It has expanded and changed. The harlots are leaving to spread the word. You can do the same."

Sal let out an uneasy sigh. "I just irks me to not have much of a choice in the matter. Very well, Djänette. Good luck to you." He turned and addressed the gathering crowd. "Well, everyone, I can't believe I'm saying this. But...The party's over! I'm scooting on out of Tanglefoot and moving to Embrenil."

"The city?" a man asked. "But I heard the streets there are more dangerous than here!"

Röger added his voice. "I've heard that it's really mellowed

220

out recently. I just came from there. Nice place. Pretty buildings."
He shrugged and smiled.

Within a matter of minutes, most of the residents of the Imperial Villa decided to pack up their belongings and leave. Since Tanglefoot was not a hometown to anyone, the majority of the excavators had been drifters at some point and were content to drift somewhere else. The ones who stayed were either too old to travel or too attached to their homes to leave.

Djänette looked to her knightly companion and said "Sir Röger, I have faith you know the method to the curse's undoing. All the same, I would like to know *how* you know."

Röger pulled the map of Tanglefoot out of his briefcase and showed it to her. He pointed at the crude circle graph he'd drawn over the townscape. "Theurgy mimics natural effects."

"But it *is* natural," she argued.

He nodded. "As I said, theurgic energy works like a natural movement of energy. When it's raw, regardless of the *philocreed* behind it, it moves in a circle, either in a vortex, radiating beams, or in this case, rippling waves. And the source is somewhere in this villa."

"How are you sure it's rippling waves?" she asked, already knowing the answer.

Röger smirked and raised his chin. "Because the curse is made from hate. Vikta Wakemaker was a woman scorned when she laid this curse. Her heart was broken. Her pride was destroyed. She was a necrotheurge with a very clear agenda: to punish this place with her own pain. I can sympathize with that."

"I can't," Djänette said flatly. "The concept is alien to me." She took the map from him and pursed her lips as she looked at it. "Mmmm. Not all the lines you've made intersect in the same place. The source could be anywhere."

Röger put his hands on his waist. "Yeah, well, I didn't have access to a drafting table. Where is the center of the villa itself?"

Djänette touched a finger to her bottom lip and looked

221

around, almost dancing and spinning as she did. "The water well, I presume. But necrotheurges lose power around wells--all that running water which is a strong hydrological source of life. It would have disrupted the ripple of her death power. No, Vikta would have chosen a place more stagnant, more still, more dead. Hmmm. The curse renders wombs infertile. So, the source would be underground nonetheless."

"Why?" asked Röger. "Why not above?"

"Because the soil represents female fertility. Vikta could not bear her husband a child, and so she shared her condition with all women here."

Röger considered the words for several minutes as they meandered aimlessly throughout the villa. Then his thoughts wandered outside the box. "Wait! What if *she* wasn't the problem?"

Djänette looked at him, puzzled.

Röger's brown eyes grew wide in his helmet. "What if Vikta Wakemaker wasn't the infertile one? What if her husband had plenty of gunpowder, but no bullets?"

Djänette began to nod slowly. "It makes sense that the woman would be blamed instead of the man. And all the greater her scorn if she was seated with the blame. To think...To think... That at all this time it might be that the curse is rendering the men here infertile instead of the women!"

Röger clapped his hands loudly. "If that's how it works, then we look above ground, right? What do we look for?"

Djänette crossed her arms and grew astonished by how simple the answer seemed to be. "A symbol of the male's sexual power."

"Like a tree or a big rock?" They began to walk down a gravel-strewn street.

"No, no. It must be something fashioned, man-made. An intentional symbol, like an obelisk or freestanding column." She raised her hands high into the air. "A big, huge phallus!"

Röger snickered. He couldn't help it.

Djänette rolled her eyes and scoffed, dropping her arms. "But all the same, my love, it is still only a theory. I know of no such structures in Tanglefoot. I would not allow them to stand if I did. There are rival *philocreed paths* of passion which use tall phallic structures as symbols of dominance and oppression. Such

222

wickedness is not welcomed by me."

Something caught Röger's eye. He stopped. He turned his head, crossed his arms, and let out an amused, "Huh." He put an arm around Djänette's waist and drew her close, pointing in the direction of a tiny old house made of roughly hewn bricks. "What if it's been hiding in plain sight all this time?"

Behind the house was a tall wooden pole about one foot thick and almost twenty feet high. They walked around to the backyard to find a tiny old tendikeye woman hanging up clothes to dry. Her clothesline was tied to it about five feet up the pole and the other end was attached to the rail of her front porch steps.

"Afternoon, Madam Mayor," the old lady said as she pinned up a large bra with one small cup.

Djänette inclined her head and curtsied. "Ms. Glattis, how are you? I see that you aren't vacating like the others."

The old woman laughed. "If them Trottin' Swans give me trouble I'll bake them a buckshot pie! I may be a broken down old amazon, but I can still load and fire a shotgun right proper. What can I do fer you and yer man-toy?"

Röger walked over to the wooden pole. "What can you tell us about this pole?"

Ms. Glattis shrugged her gray wings and her collarbones made a cracking noise. "It was here when I moved in. I figure it's a kind of *tellfone pole* from before the Omni-War."

Röger shook his head. "No. This...this is a *maiapole*." He put his hand on it and found that it had long been petrified into cold hard stone.

"That sounds familiar," Djänette said. "What exactly is a *maiapole?*"

Röger smiled as he recalled a memory long forgotten. "You're from Fevär like me, Djänette. Tell me you never went to a Spring Festival."

She smiled. "I always attended them. My first kiss was at a Spring Festival, as well as my first...well... Never mind. Go on." She exchanged a knowing grin with the old woman.

Röger pointed at the top of the stone pole. "Remember those wooden poles that people would tie these long streamer ribbons to and dance around?"

The Mayor's eyes lit with nostalgic realization. "Oh! Yes!

223

Maiapoles! I used to dance around them when I was very little. Our dances would create the most intricate braids around the pole. It was fun until I discovered boys. Tell me, love, do you think that's what this is?"

"I'm sure it is," he replied. "Back in ancient times before the Omni-War, we Fevarian humans spread our culture all throughout the Cluster. Finding one here is not that surprising. We were the first to tunnel from one Huncell to another using an Iron Tornado Train. We may be outcasts now in most places, but evidence of our influence still remains."

He began to pace around the pole, looking it up and down. "When I worked as a Black Vest, we were assigned as security every year at the Spring Festival in Lasankav. There was a pretty girl there who I met with every year. Anyanna was her name. She told me all about the maiapole, its history. Even then, when I was... younger... the maiapole dance was just a fun festivity for the fair goers to participate in. But back before the Hunells were connected, even before guns and trains were invented, the Maiapole Dance was a formal theurgic rite of Spring. The Mystics of that time believed that in order to have plentiful crops and healthy babies, the two had to be linked in a theurgic fertility ceremony. All the young men and women had to dance around the pole which represented the male atmosphere penetrating and fertilizing the female soil. And then after the dance they would all partner-up and mate out in the fields. Legend has it that their carnal juices made the crops grow huge, and that in turn, the crops they ate would empower their carnal juices for healthy babies. It was a spiritually symbiotic relationship between the people and their land."

Glattis the tendikeye made a sour face. "That's disgustin'! The only reason to do it in the field is because it's fun an' ya might get caught! Them people musta been lousy farmers to rely on theurgy in such a gross way!"

Djänette had started looking at the ground sometime while Röger was talking. He noticed that something he'd said had bothered her, but he did not ask what. She raised her eyes and regarded the old tendikeye woman. "Ms. Glattis, my companion and I believe that this maiapole may very well be the center-point of Vikta Kemakers fertility curse. Should it come to it, may I have your permission to have it torn down?"

The old woman glanced up at the pole. "Curse? Be my guest! Had I known sooner I'da had it ripped out years ago."

"I don't think it will come to that," Röger said. He was examining it closely, looking for markings or strange patterns. He climbed the pole with the ease of a black bear, but found nothing. *"Wait a minute!"* he thought.

He slid down and hunkered into a squat. There was a tall, uncut patch of grass around the base of the pole. He cleared it away. "Found it!" he exclaimed with wry grin.

Djänette and Ms. Glattis knelt down to gander at what he had uncovered. They both had to squint.

Just above the ground, a needle-thin band of a shining gray metal encircled the base of the pole. It was like gleaming wire, only stiffer and perfectly round.

"That," Röger said, pointing at the thin band. "That's the cause. And all I have to do is cut it off." He reached into the inside of his black vest and pulled out a large hunting knife.

"You told the Swans that you were unarmed," Djänette said.

"Yeah. So? I'm no theurge with a *philocreed* to swear by." He focused his attention on the band around the base of the pole. Using the knife's point, he tried to break the band or at least pry it loose. After nearly a minute of poking, prodding, cussing, and hacking, it became apparent that the knife could not damage or budge it loose, even with Röger's strength behind it. "It's really on there," he groused.

Djänette tilted her head as she studied the band. "Whatever it is, it is choking off the male power the pole represents at the base. How spiteful! Here, my love. Let me try."

Röger laughed and got up. "Sure thing, doll. But I doubt you're stronger than me."

Röger got up and stepped back as Djänette knelt down. Using both of her dainty hands, she grasped the band as if it were the edge of a bowl or large chalice. Djänette closed her eyes and whispered *"I understand now. Omnia vincit amor!"* She stood up, still keeping hold of the band. It slid up the pole with ease as she did so. She looked up the high pole. "If only I could get up there, I could slide this thing off. My love, your assistance, please?"

Röger stepped behind her and placed his hands around her waist just as she was holding the band around the pole. "Are you

225

ready, Djänette?"

She nodded, and Röger tossed her straight up high into the air. She maintained her hold on the cursed metal band, and as she reached the top of the pole it came loose in her hands! Djänette MySinn fell safely into the great strong arms of her lover, just as she trusted she would.

He set her down on her feet and saw that the band had shrunk down in her hands when it came off. He began to ask "Is that a...?"

"A wedding ring," she said, holding up the gleaming band between her thumb and forefinger. It was a hematite ring. "This was *her* wedding ring. She used her hate to wrap it around the maiapole. And it was the power of the love I hold dear that removed it."

Röger brushed a lock of hair from her face. "Well done, my lady. Looks like you got a pretty souvenir."

She looked at the ring and made a face of mild disgust. "No. I loathe wedding rings. They represent an unbreakable contract of love, everything I stand against. Here, my love. Take it and remember me forever." She offered him the ring and he took it gladly.

"I will, Djänette."

Something hard and mean flashed in Djänette's eyes. "Oh, I've no doubt that you will, Border Beast."

As she said the words, the bottom fell out of Röger's stomach and his heart burned and cracked. He felt the pours of his skin open to release a cold bitter sweat. "What did you just say?" His voice shook as his throat tightened.

Djänette only stared at him for a moment before addressing the old woman. "Ms. Glattis, thank you for your time." She reached into her pocket and placed a handful of gold grotz into the tendikeye's hand before embracing her and walking back to the gravel road.

Röger followed Djänette cautiously. He waited until they were a safe distance from anyone before addressing her. "How? How did you know?"

Djänette turned, grinding gravel beneath her heels. Her face, her entire heart and soul emanated raw feelings of outrage, sorrow, and love. "You said you were at the Spring Festival in *Lazankav*. That city was renamed Nosivad after the civil war. No Fevärian calls

226

it Lazankav anymore! Only those who've been alive for over a century still call it that." She crossed her arms, holding her stomach and let out a heavy shuddering sigh. "I had my suspicions from the beginning. Your speech, your old time mannerisms, that helmet you wear, the way those Trotting Swans were torn apart! Did you think what happened at Nailthorn would be forgotten?"

Röger was at a loss for words. He could feel everything she felt.

Tears flooded down Djänette's cheeks. "I remember. I was not there. But by love I remember comforting some of the few survivors of that bloodbath. It was a battle in the middle of the city, the largest ever between the rebels and the regime. In the midst of the fighting, a dragoon riding a black bileer and wearing a silver helmet rode in. He was tall, dark of skin, and strongly built. At first, no one knew what side he was on. Then he changed into a Werekrilp, a Werekrilp with a man's head! You killed over one thousand soldiers that day on both sides!"

Röger bared his teeth inside his helm. "That battle had lasted for over a month! With the eagle egg bombs they were using more civilians were getting killed than fighters. Kids, Djänette! Kids were dying because of their sloppy urban guerrilla combat! The causes were lost on both sides!"

"So, you took matters into your own claws then? You, the Border Beast, appeared twice more in Stoutglenn and Srufidj. Thousands more were butchered!"

"It ended the border battles, Djänette! Both sides had already established their territories. There was no need for them to keep fighting over small bits of land. What I did ended the war."

"Do you think that justifies your actions?"

"No," he replied. "And I was more than just a monster in looks. I knew exactly what I was doing. What I did was evil and *necessary* but I accept it as something I can't go back on. But I *can* move on from it. I can and I am! It's why I avoid wars, no matter what the cause may be. Because causes get lost or worse used just to make more misery. I am no longer that man because I am no longer in that place, that time. I am here, now, with you, and I have a *Muerchi* to kill!"

Djänette wiped her eyes and sniffled as she considered his words. Her hardened features slowly softened back to her exquisite

227

beauty. "I know, my love. I know. Pardon me for condemning you without understanding."

"Thank you for understanding," he said softly, stepping nearer to her.

"I still don't," she replied, stepping nearer to him. "I can feel your loneliness, your pain. You've a good heart that pumps evil blood. If only my love could remove *your* curse as well."

He took her in his arms and held her tight. "I think it has. Not completely. But yesterday when I almost changed, you appeared in my mind, and I was able to calm down."

Djänette let out a crying laugh. "Really? It gives me comfort knowing my gift has aided you."

He brushed his hand down her back, forgetting he was still holding the hematite ring. They both heard it clink onto the gravel road.

"Oh shunt, the ring," Röger said.

As they turned to see it on the ground, they were both startled by what they saw. The ring was slowly rolling and flip-flopping over the gravel away from them, as if some unseen force was pulling it.

After taking a few steps to catch up with the tumbling circle, Röger knelt down to pick it up. He could still feel a small pull on the ring, nothing strong but still noticeable.

He examined it closer. It shined just like the metal of his stolen axe, like a dark mirror. He recalled the petrified tree stump in Drowsy Nook, and then thought about the *maiapole*. He turned to Djänette and said, "Like nails in a coffin lid."

Djänette frowned, not understanding the meaning.

Röger made a fist around the ring. "The Headsman's Axe was attached to a petrified stump in Drowsy Nook. Once my friends and I got it out of the town's border, it broke that curse. The axe is made of Hematite like this ring. Only it isn't normal Hematite. This stuff isn't brittle, and it can even be stretched over a thick pole. It's been theurgically modified."

"Necrotheurgy?" she asked.

Röger nodded gravely. "And here's another thing about Hematite, it's slightly magnetic. But this ring and my axe are even more so. The axe and ring acted as stabilizers, pins, nails. They hold down the Geohex into the land. There has to be others; other objects

228

throughout the county. Each object is from a different curse, through some weird form of, what's the word...Necromagnetism, these objects all connect the curses together. Blind Bitch's Bane! The theurge who devised all this could be a master in Necro and Geotheurgy!"

"Vikta Wakemaker?"

Röger shook his head. "Something tells me she was just a pawn in a greater scheme. I think it could have been a higher ranking necrotheurge, perhaps Oroga himself. Hrmph!" He put the ring on his middle finger and held out his hand in the direction in which it had rolled. "I can feel the pull this way. I'm going to go follow it now. Alone."

Djänette eyed the ring. "Where do you think it will take you, my love?"

Röger grinned darkly. "Straight to my axe. And I'm gonna get it back!" He looked at his lady and removed his helm, showing her his ruggedly handsome face for the first and last time. He kissed her passionately and asked her, "Where is the nearest outhouse in this villa?"

❁

Not more than a fifteen minute walk from where the *maiapole* stood, the *Meurchi* was resting in his ancient lair, a great, massive stone and mortar chimney which had once been part of a mansion that had existed thousands of years ago. Now, it was surrounded by a grove of oaks and maples and covered in gnarled vines and countless generations of moss. On the outside, it was a ruin in every sense of the word. But on the inside, the *Muerchi* kept everything neat and tidy.

He had long since plugged up the bottom and top, having no use for light or ventilation. The only way in or out of the chimney were a few loose stone bricks that the Meurchi would remove and replace as he entered or left. The entrance was high off the ground, and the monster would never walk or climb to his home, but turn to mist and fly there to avoid leaving a trail. In the dry interior of the chimney, he had built several shelves all connected by a ladder. One

229

shelf held his bed, another held his books, another shelf held his clothes chests and several pairs of boots. Yet another held jewelry, money, and other wealth he had stolen over the centuries. And on the last shelf, he kept the great axe that had once belonged to the legendary Headsman of Drowsy Nook. The *Muerchi* had no cause to believe that he would ever be discovered. He was a laich made clever by age and experience.

He had spent the last day healing from all the bullets he'd taken the day before. He sat up in his shelf-bed. "Tonight," he muttered to himself. "Tonight, I will prey. Find a couple of plump whores to suck on. Then when I am fed and back up to speed, I'm going to find that Werekrilp round-ear and cut off his head. Yes! I'll show that amateur how to properly wield a weapon. And then I will return to Gooddirt and make all those slags pay for shooting me. I'll hold them down and eat their spleens as they scream! Then I'll drain their teats flat!" He laughed bitterly.

"Hey, Caizre!" called a deep voice from outside. "I want my axe back, you back-shooting chubby chaser!"

The *Muerchi* went still. He could not believe his ears. "No! How?" He scrambled up his ladder and grabbed the axe.

He heard Röger Yamus call out again. "An old chimney instead of a coffin? I give you credit, man! This is a great hiding spot! I bet you got it real cheap!"

The *Muerchi* kicked the loose bricks of his entrance out and leapt far down below to the grassy grove floor. He landed nimbly on his feet, holding the massive axe in one clawed hand. Shirtless, bootless, and still covered with half-healed bullet holes, he did not look happy to be disturbed. "How the SHUNT did you find me?!" the monster demanded. He was not afraid, but very astonished and angry.

Sir Röger Yamus stood not twenty feet from him, holding only his large hunting knife. He could feel the pull of the hematite ring to the axe growing stronger. "It's not important how I found this place, Caizre," the human said with a shrug of his broad shoulders. He pointed the knife at his foe. "What *is* important is what I'm going to *do* here, and that is end you forever."

The *Meurchi* scoffed and rolled his coal black eyes. "I have no weaknesses, you fool! Did you not listen? I may heal slower than other laiches, but I can recover from *anything*!" He spread his arms

230

in arrogant defiance.

Röger wasted no time and took the opportunity. He threw the knife with awesome speed and power. The blade sank deep into the *Muerchi's* gut with a loud thump. The Black Vest squinted his eyes and placed both hands ponderously on his waist. "Oookay. I'm pretty sure I got it." he said, tilting his head. "Yeah, I did. I win."

The *Muerchi* only frowned in confusion. He looked down at the knife in his belly and shrugged. "You got nothing, you idiot. It doesn't even hurt." He pulled out the blade with his free hand. "I have no weaknesses! None!"

Röger peered at him grimly. "Wrong. I just hit you in the *thoratic duct,* a major part of the Lymphatic System, a system that protects us from infection. That is your weakness, Caizre! Infection! And guess what. I dipped that blade in an outhouse hole before I came here!"

The *Meurchi* gave a curious grin. "My, but aren't you the clever detective! But you forget that Vikta Wakemaker's curse prevents infections from happening here in Tanglefoot! Why else would I make my home in this area for so long? Because the curse cancels out my only weakness!"

Röger held up his hand that had Vikta Wakemaker's ring on it. "You mean the curse that me and Djänette MySinn broke fifteen minutes ago?"

The *Muerchi* stopped grinning. A throbbing headache invaded the ancient his brain. His throat became dry, and it hurt to swallow. His pale, purple skin began to sweat as he experienced hot flashes and cold chills. The wound in his stomach began to swell and leak yellow puss.

"No!" he cried. His aching limbs felt tired and sore. His strength left him. The axe dropped out of his hand, and he soon dropped to his knees. "No! How?"

Röger walked over to him, casually. "It's a long story, one that you don't have time for."

As the reality and agony of defeat mingled with the misery of infection sickness, the *Meurchi* tried in vain to growl hatefully at Röger. Instead, he vomited. Other orifices erupted as well, creating putrid pile-puddles of humanoid lard in the grass beneath him.

Röger reached to pick up his axe, and to his surprise and joy, the weapon itself rose up off the ground and flew into his hand. He

231

felt the hematite ring bond with the axe in some strange, yet fitting reaction of necromagnetism. He then looked down at his suffering enemy and said with a satisfied laugh. "Okay, buttpit. Let's try this again!"

He swung the massive blade, cutting through the *Muerchi's* neck and sending his head flying high into the air. It hit the underside of a large oak branch and exploded. The body melted, bone and all, into a bubbling puddle of rotting fatcells.

Röger caressed his axe and admired it like a lover in his arms. "From this day forward I will call you...Headlauncher!"

❖

Sir Röger Yamus mounted his post-mort ox and returned to the mayoral mansion of Djänette MySinn. It was the last night either of them would sleep there. In the morning, Djänette packed her bags and took her leave of Tanglefoot.

Röger watched as her coach rode away en route to the nearest train station. "She'll be fine," he told himself. His throat was tight and his vision almost grew foggy from sadness. Almost.

He rode his post-mort ox to the NcKoons orchard house before he left. The once stately iron sign and fence had rusted away to tiny bits. The house had collapsed in on itself and the wood turned to dust as soon as he touched it. All over Tanglefoot, the wild gray dust flowers looked as though they were wilting.

The town dissolved almost overnight. Ironically, it was the loss of the curse that scared so many people away. But many more stayed behind. Fate permitting, the town would grow to welcome more families than pleasure seekers, although the prostitution there still remained top notch.

Papa G. D. remained in business as an undertaker and smokehouse master chef. But although his meat was still the best in the county, it never quite tasted the same after the curse broke.

Rose Quartz stayed at first, and tried to sustain the life of an independent whore. But she eventually ended up pregnant and had a change of heart. She returned to Embrenil where her mother took her back with open arms. All was forgiven and life got better.

232

Although she was sure that her most memorable customer did not father her child, she still named her baby boy Röger.

And as for the Sacred Harlots of Tanglefoot. They brought the *philocreed* of the Sacred Slipknot to thousands of lonely hearts, teaching that all unions of love, no matter how long or short, were equally sacred in the fleeting existence of life. They taught that love was an eternal power extending infinitely into the past and future, and that all mortals are welcome to share in its warmth. And that beneath the seemingly profane exterior of lust existed a pure truth about caring for another and for oneself.

Somewhere between Tanglefoot and Drowsy Nook, miles away from any house or settlement, Röger Yamus rode atop his post-mort ox, a sad smile on his lips. He felt relaxed and satisfied from his adventure, but was somewhat sorry it was over. The autumn air was cool and comfortable. The weight of his axe hanging on his back in its leather harness gave him an accomplished feeling. But in the deepest pit of his stomach, he was worried for his friends.

He wondered how they were fairing in a county full of ghosts, evil biker gangs, and monsters. He surmised that, if it came down to it, he could beat any one of his teammates in a fight. And if that were so, what chance had they alone against threats similar to the ones he had just faced and barely survived? He shook his head. "No use worrying about them, Röger," he told himself with a sigh.

"Indeed," came a female voice off to the left side of the road.

Röger's attention snapped to his left.

There walking beside him, keeping a relaxed pace with the tireless ox was a ravishing Drakeri woman dressed in a sultry red dress which showed off far more than what was proper for a fall day. The startled man's roving eyes passed over her enticing figure and wild hair before finally settling on her face. Her face was almost exactly like Polly's.

"Dat was quite impressive, how you slew dat laich," she said with a smug sexy grin. Her accent was Chumish, just like Polly's. She did not face him directly, but Röger saw that the corner pupil of

233

her right eye was fixed on him. "I arrived in Tanglefoot de day after you slew all dose men on deir velocipedes. So much bloodshed attracted my attention from miles away. I had hopes dat it was my little baby girl. But it turned out to only be you."

Röger calmly, coolly reached for the handle of his axe. "I'm sorry to disappoint. I take it you are her mother and teacher? Veluora, right?"

"You could say dat," the woman answered.

Röger checked her hands. No weapons. It still didn't mean she wasn't dangerous. Polly told him and the others that her mother was a master Blood Theurge, deadly and wicked to the core. Fear coiled tightly around his heart.

Röger forced himself to face forward. "You taught her well," he said with a relaxed-looking shrug.

The woman opened her mouth, letting out a raspy cackle that chilled Röger's spine. "Ah, but I still have so much more to teach her! So much more!" She turned her head, displaying her gorgeous face. "Like history, for instance. Do you know de true origin of Werekrilps, Mr. Yamus? I can tell it to you."

Röger scoffed. "I've heard and read about dozens of theories and stories on the subject, milady. I *am* an expert monster slayer, after all."

Veluora waved her hand dismissively. "Lies! All are lies, I assure you." Her eyes flashed red as she said "I swear on my *philocreed* dat what I am about to tell is de truth."

Röger, to his own astonishment, relaxed his grip on the axe and listened to the story the woman told.

"Once upon a time, when de huncell of Gurtangorr was newly discovered by de ancient Fevärians, dey found dat de land was full of two tings: Krilp tribes and Silver. Now, de Krilps were a savage and primal race, barely sentient and wit' no potentiality to become domesticated or civilized. De Fevärians had no use for de dumb brutes. But de Silver..." She let out a cruel giggle. "De Silver interested de Fevärians very much! In no other Huncell in all of de Draybair Cluster can de metal be found and mined!

It was a good time for you round-eared short-lives. You expanded your influence through technological innovation and treachery. Your ancestors considered making war wit' de Krilps, but building and sending de *Iron Tornado* train to get to de new huncell

234

had already hurt deir economy. So dey decided to divide and conquer, play de tribes against each other instead. Dey hired *Hematheurges,* also called hematonomists or simply Blood Theurges. An entire *Cardiette* was hired, in fact."

"*Cardiette*?" Röger asked.

"It is our word for coven or cabal," she replied with a smile that suggested that she knew he would ask. "It consists of eighteen theurges, each one representing a major part of de cardiovascular system. Men are arteries and aortas, women are cavas and veins. My grandmother held de rank of Greater Saphenous. Dis is how I know about what really went on.

"Anyway, de strategy was simple. De *Hematheurges* would capture a krilp from one tribe, kill it and drink its blood to take on de shape of a krilp. In krilp form de *Hematheurges* would attack krilp tribes, making dem tink dat another krilp tribe was starting a war wit' dem. Great distrust, hatred and confusion was sewn, and soon dere was all-out civil war between every tribe." Veluora paused for a moment and added. "It was so beautiful, all that strife and bloodshed!"

Röger let out a bothered grunt. "You speak like you saw it yourself."

Veluora grinned. "Grandmother passed all her memories to my mother before she died. My mother did de same wit' me. And someday I will do the same wit' my daughter. Dis form carries many generations of *Hematheurge* in it. Dis way, every person in our bloodline lives forever. Isn't dat lovely?"

Röger paused and thought *"No wonder Polly ran away, you mad slag!"* "Quite," he answered. "Please, go on with your story."

"Ah, but it is also *your* story, Werekrilp!" she let out a raspy cackle. "De operation was a success. Unity was broken amongst de tribes. De Fevärians moved in with deir fancy machine weapons and made de Krilps scatter. Silver mines were established all over and de *Hematheurges* were paid handsomely in de lustrous metal. After dat, de *Cardiette* disbanded. But five of dem stayed and dared to build mansion homes in de conquered huncell. Dese five *Hematheurges* were human Fevärians. And it is safe to assume dat dey wished to live out de rest of deir short lives in luxury as more and more Fevärians were moving in to settle. De fools should have taken deir money and run just as my grandmother did.

"For among the displaced krilp tribes, deir was a powerful theurge called Nibrud. Nibrud was a *zoonomist,* a theurge attuned to animals. He saw all animals as a chain or web of life and death." Veluora grinned. "And he saw the Fevärians as breakers of dat web. Somehow, he learned of the *Hematheurges* involvement, and swore revenge on all of Fevär by turning its weapons against it. One by one, he challenged de *Hematheurges.* His power, or at least his cause, must have been great for he defeated all five dat remained in Gurtangorr. Now, he did not kill dem, he viewed dem as weapons. He cursed dem. He changed dem all into mad, mindless krilps and sent dem to Fevär to slaughter every human dey could find! And dose humans dat survived deir bite would become human-hunting monsters demselves! Over de next ten years over two million humans were killed or infected by werekrilps. Nibrud had achieved, and is still achieving, his revenge. And de only ting in dis Cluster dat can kill or restrain one of his theurgic monsters is de very Silver dat was stolen from his homecell."

Röger's head hung low. "I've read numerous legends on the subject, both before and after I was bitten. I've never heard that one."

"Lies are all dat you've read. Lies begotten by de same governing forces to cover up deir shameful deeds. Rumors were widely publicized to hide de truth I just told you."

Röger's eyes narrowed in his helmet. "But studies have shown that it' a virus. Like an allergic reaction or plague from when we first encountered the krilps. I've seen the data under a microscope."

Veluora arched an eyebrow. Her tongue stuck out of her mouth like a cat stretching after a nap. She then cleared her throat and explained.

"Dat is only part right. De curse and virus are one in de same. It is a mutating theurgic strain of cells dat effect de bio-chemical make up of de host, you. A werekrilp's blood is laced wit' an element called Selenium. De virus attaches to de Selenium to maintain its consistency. When de host becomes stressed or excited, de endorphins released into de bloodstream cause de virus to detach from de Selenium and mutate rapidly, inducing a change in de host's biological and mental state. You become a murderous

236

beast. When de endorphins run out de virus reattaches to de Selenium and again becomes dormant. However, if Silver is introduced into de body of de host, de lustrous metal bonds wit' de Selenium and destroys de virus it was attached to. A blunt Silver object can hurt a werekrilp quite bad, but it's rarely fatal. But stabs with Silver blades are almost always a sure killer. De intrusion of Silver into de blood allows de Selenium to bond wit' de Silver, forming a new compound dat ruins de lycanthrope's ability to regenerate cells, thus causing death. Dis is de natural, scientific side of de curse dat makes de supernatural theurgy possible. Reality adjusts itself if dere is a will strong enough to make a way." She paused with a smug grin. "Reality is subject to a theurge's interpretation of it."

Röger nodded and twisted his back until he heard it pop. He let out a tired sigh. "You just swore on your philocreed to tell me the truth, not what you've heard, but what really happened."

"Yes. And I have. I have even explained de cause of de effect."

"Why? What do you want from me?"

"I want my daughter back."

Röger scoffed. "She's not mine to give, hotlips."

Veluora tilted her head and smiled. "Do you tink dat all I've told you about werekrilps is all I know about dem?"

As Röger considered the question his axe silently came loose from its harness. "Keep talking," he told her.

Veluora's smile disappeared. "I can treat your condition if you let me reclaim my daughter. De curse is too strong for even I to lift. Nibrud's hatred for humans outweighs my love for dem by a huge margin. But I *can treat* you."

Röger's eyes narrowed in suspicion. "How?" he asked.

"Theurgic blood transfusion. I take your Selenium-laced blood out and put untainted healthy blood in. It will keep the beast from emerging for years on end, and you will retain your immortality. De process would need to be repeated whenever de Selenium builds back up."

"And where would we get the fresh blood from?" he asked.

Veluora shrugged and spread her hands out. "De Cluster is full of it! Blood is de ultimate power of life and death! Securing a person to harvest it from would be simp---"

237

Röger swung his axe and Veluora's head went airborne. High into the air it reached, its wild mass of hair flapping like the tail of a kite. The statuesque body of the Crimson Theurgess fell forward, transforming into a splashing puddle of blood as it hit the rocky ground.

"YAH!!!" Röger shouted to his dead steed, urging it to run. He never looked back. He didn't want to see that head ever again, living or dead. The loud thuds of the ox's hooves drowned out the loud thump of the severed head hitting the road. He would not look back. He couldn't. Sir Röger Yamus was terrified.

And far, far behind the frightened hero, the disembodied head of Veluora turned into a small puddle of blood. Slowly, the smaller puddle joined up with the bigger puddle in the road. After a few seconds of swirling and churning, the red liquid took the form of the woman it had been.

Veloura sat up, naked on the cold gravel, a dissatisfied pout on her lips. "Fool," she muttered. Then her curvaceous form turned back into blood and sank into the ground as if the soil itself sucked her in. Veluora left no trace of her behind. Gone.

Chapter 5
Tears of the Caven Tree

Part 1

Once Will had cleared the spotting distance from Drowsy Nook, he stepped off the gravel road. He counted one thousand paces, always making sure the road stayed within sight. He then restarted his trek, now walking parallel to the road. Through abandoned farmland, thick patches of woods, and muddy water paths, he kept nearly every footfall silent. This was not for fear that anyone would hear him sneaking around. He just did not want a single sound distracting his own ears from the yonder road. Only once did he have to hunker down in the tall grass to avoid detection. As soon as he heard the sound of velocipedes coming down the road, he took off his long rawhide pack and laid it down in the dead grass.

"Hey sweetie," he whispered to the pack, shaking it gently. "Time to wake up. I made breakfast an' the kids 're still asleep." He smiled as he undid the elk horn buttons on the leather case as if they were the buttons on a lover's dress. With focused excitement, he drew out *Falcona,* his prized rifle.

She was a ten millimeter bolt action work of art, practical in design and elegant in her simplicity. Beneath her barrel was a fold-out scythe-shaped bayonet that pointed down instead of out. But Will would not need that part of her. Not today.

Kneeling down, he aimed the gun at the road and looked through her scope. "Okay, Falcona. Let's have us a look-see."

Two drakeri men wearing purple jackets pedaled their velocipedes from the opposite direction. Neither of them looked happy. Will traced over their bodies, looking for weapons. Both men carried four-shooter revolvers. One man sported a boot knife nearly as wide as his leg.

"Lookit that, sweetheart. Them two must be Trottin' Swans like the deputies told us about. They musta caught word that Sheriff Edifice got hisself crumbled. Probably jus' goin' to town to check things out. Scout a bit." He grinned. "Of course, the Swans *do* have a bad history with that town, seein' as how they killed a Sheriff. Then Edifice came an' killed a bunch of 'em to earn hisself the badge. There's bad blood, darlin'. An' I highly doubt the newly christened Sheriff Arteen would welcome these men. So, howsabout we do the good folks o' Drowsy Nook a favor? Naw, Rev an' the others ain't here to stop us. We can have us a little fun before we get to Pevulaneum. I jus' know yer trigger's itchin' as bad as my finger is..."

He took careful aim and paused in thought. *"Rev wouldn't let me do this. He wouldn't understand. Rög or Polly might, but not Rev. I don't believe fer a minute these two are plannin' a pleasant visit. Jus' the sight of' 'em will bring unrest. Their friends murdered the old sheriff, a man sworn to protect his town. I swore to protect Tresaville jus' the same, way back when. I vowed to keep the bad out. But it was beside me the whole time."* He blinked once, pushing the memory from his mind. *"Rev would call this stirrin' the pot. I call it addin' pepper."*

He took a breath and let it out as he squeezed *Falcona's* trigger. The shot rang out like sharp thunder and echoed like a drum in a cave. The front wheel of one of the Swan's bikes erupted in a spiraling shower of sparks before falling off into the rocky dirt. The bike stopped. The biker kept going. The man's face hit the road and slid several feet before his body landed along with it.

The other biker put on his brakes, turning his velocipede sideways into a skidding arc. The man drew his pistol, and looked around for the shooter.

But Will and Falcona were long gone by then.

⬦

Tendikeye were born to jump and run. For them, walking felt as unnecessary as crawling. Their legs were meant for springing

240

and dashing, hopping and scampering. Their lean bodies were reinforced with tendons five times thicker and stronger than a human's. They were fast and wiry, and Will Foundling was no exception. Although he lacked quill-adorned wings that allowed others of his race to glide and change direction in mid-jump, he was faster than most. Moving through the darkened woodlands with uncanny speed and grace, even the few beasts of the forest did not notice him until he passed by within paw's reach and tagged them with a playful pat.

When the woods grew too thick, he took to the trees, climbing and leaping through them like a squirrel. He ran until nightfall, ever keeping the distant road within sight. As the darkened autumn air cooled his sweaty face, he climbed the highest oak and looked to the west.

Not so far away, he beheld the huddled town lights of Pevulaneum. He hopped down to a lower branch that was as thick as his own body, and removed his duster. Pulling hidden straps and buckles from within the duster's sleeves and bottom hem, he rigged up a hammock that hung from the branch. He sat on the high limb and drained his canteen, ate a handful of nuts and dried apricots, rolled and smoked three cigarettes, and listened to the forest until his eyelids felt heavy. Then he climbed into his hammock and went to sleep.

❖

The hands on his ten-hour pocket watch hit 7:50. It was midnight, the Witching Hour. Will awoke drenched in cold sweat. His heart pounded like a madman's hammer. Necrofright was thick in the air, paralyzing him.

The scream of a woman and several angry men stabbed into his ears like hot knives. The women wailed again until something muffled the sound.

"Let her go!" a young man yelled.

Will reacted without thinking. In little more than three seconds, he climbed out of his hammock and strapped on his pistol and machete belt. The sound of the woman's muffled sobs led him to a small clearing. Standing on the branches of another high oak, he peered down at what was happening.

Five drakeri men, all carrying guns, had a man and a woman surrounded. The man was human, young and handsome. The woman was drakeri, young, pretty, and pregnant. The gang of men stood the couple back to back with their wrists bound. One of the men threw a noose-ended rope into the air. It seemed to go over some invisible tree limb before falling back down in a straight line. Another man grasped the noose and pulled it wide over the heads of the two lovers.

Will grimaced and pulled his gun. Six bullets rained down from his Mark Twain Special, piercing through each member of the gang's necks or heads. Nothing happened. None of them even took notice.

Will froze. "*I know I didn't miss!*" he thought.

The hangman tightened the noose around both the lover's necks and glared at the woman. "You're a sick woman, Maise, for mingling blood with this round ear! You think it's decent to bring children into the world, knowing full well that you are going to *out-live them*?" He slapped her across the face. "Human blood is a disease, Maise. You know that. You know that and you didn't even care. You don't deserve to be a mother!" He looked to his friends, ignoring the woman's cries. "Let's get this over with!"

The five men took the other end of the rope. They worked in unison, slowly hoisting the couple into the air. The lovers kicked wildly as their feet left the leaf-covered ground.

Will leapt to the forest floor, throwing his yashinin machete at the rope. The blade did not miss. Nor did it cut. It merely passed through. Will turned to the men and fired his pistol's six remaining rounds at them. *Ka-Krack! Ka-Krack! Ka-Krack!* Nothing.

It then dawned on him what he was witnessing. It was something that had happened a long, long time ago. The people he saw were ghosts, and he was left with no choice but to stand and watch in horror and helplessness how they died.

The men pulled the couple higher and higher as they kicked and stiffened and jerked at the end of the rope. The lovers' eyes bulged and their mouths gaped in silent screams. Will trembled as a cold wind swept through the clearing. His heart drowned in remorse and shame that he could not stop it all from happening.

The men tied the rope off on an invisible tree. Sometime after that, the men disappeared.

Will stood beneath the dead suspended ghosts, watching them for several minutes. His throat was tight and his stomach churned. Just as he started to think about turning away, he saw the woman's dead eyes looking at him. His heart nearly stopped.

The woman's lips moved, yet no words could be heard, even by his ears.

"What...? What is it?" he asked her. "What can I do to help ya, miss?"

Her lips kept moving. Still, no sound came from her or even the forest itself. Then Will heard the creeping sound of a *bow saw* playing *Blood in the Mud*. It was a tendikeye instrument playing an ancient tendikeye battle tune. His eyes glanced around through the trees before returning to the ghosts. They were gone, rope and all.

He retrieved his machete and returned to his camp site in the high oak tree to grab his things, and followed the trail of notes left behind by the song. There, he made sure to reload his gun.

The ominous oaks created a thick canopy overhead. The light of night could only be seen on the uppermost branches. Will ran just below, clad in shadow. As he followed the tune, he took great care to not let his boots hit the branches too hard. After passing through dozens of dozens of trees, he located the source of the haunting melody.

The old tendikeye man sat on the front porch of a large treehouse called a *frezje*. It was a rounded structure completely encircled by a plank platform. Many thick support poles wedged between the house and the many branches held it up. The quills on the old man's head and wings were gray and white. He sat passively, playing a flashing, polished *bow saw*. It was a *tuntrum* instrument; an object meant for war or a peaceful occupation.

Will heard a *click* nearby, followed by a female voice saying, "Don't move, mister. Yer mate is checked, ya hear?"

"Loud an' clear," Will answered, sighing. He sensed that the woman was at least forty feet behind him. "So, tell me, ma'am...or miss...didja hear me comin'?"

"Nossir," she answered. "Yer steps made the leaves shake. Found ya that way."

Will winced in disappointment. "I really made the leaves

243

shake?"

"A bit, mister. But not much. That's some fancy treadin' you do."

Will hung his head and raised his empty hands. "That's what I get fer spendin' a week in the city. Already outta practice!"

The old man on the porch stopped playing and looked up at him. He tilted his head one way, and then the other. "Howdy there, young man," he said.

"Howdy, sir. My name's Will Foundling. As you can see, I'm tendikeye jus' like you. Ain't no need fer pointin' barrels."

The old man nodded. "Well, in that case, kid, ye might as well lay yers down first. I heard yer Mark Twain Special in the woods. No mistakin' that report. An' seein' as how ye got mute feet, an' could hear my bow saw from that far away, I'd wager yer a Dasaru Harker if'n you weren't so young."

"I am, sir."

"Stead-plop!" the old man spat. "Harker's serve a minimum of ten years. Ye can't be more than twenty-five. If ye were a Harker, ye must be a deserter or dismissed. In either case, ye are not wanted here!"

Will's eyes widened as his face contorted into a scowl. "Brem Hoffin, one of the greatest Harker's alive trained me. He gave me this pistol an' blade. An' judgin' by the sound of the gun behind me, it's a muzzle loaded shotgun from forty feet away. It *may* kill me if I'm dead center in the spread. But it'll only be one shot, an' my pistol holds twelve man-killers. Not meanin' to sound smug."

The old man frowned. "How ye know that shotgun ain't loaded with a slug that'll knock yer spine through yer belly?"

Will smirked. "I don't know fer sure. But this forest is bearless an' wolfless. An' puma are easily scared off. This is a tamed wood. Anyone who lives an' hunts in it is more likely to carry scattershot than slugs."

He unbuckled his weapons belt, unslung his rifle, and laid them both on the branch. He then leapt down to a lower branch, never breaking eye contact with the old man. "My apologies, old timer. It's just been a while since I seen an actual *frezje*. An' to run into such distrust from my own kind is hurtful."

He heard the gunwoman land on the branch above him and pick up his weapons.

The old man stood. "This idn't Cloiherune, young timer. Outlaws come in all shapes an' sizes out here. Ye hungry?"

Will nodded. "I can eat."

"Well, ye'll hafta wait til breakfast, I'm afraid. Come on in. I'll break out the guest cot. We'll worry about introductions in the morn'." The old man turned to go back inside.

Will nodded in thanks. "Much obliged, sir. You wouldn't believe what I just saw."

The old man stopped. "Saw? With yer eyes, ye mean?"

"Uh...yeah..."

The old man turned and gave him a mixed look of annoyance and curiosity. "It's late. Let's get on in."

Will followed the old man. As he passed through the doorway, he felt an odd tingle in his brain. He would have no recollection of what happened after that.

✧

Will woke to the sound and smell of venison steaks and eggs sizzling in an iron skillet. The soft glow of morning lit the well-kept house. It was a typical tendikeye living room: rustic, clean, neat. There were one-legged stools instead of chairs and an indoor swinging seat big enough for three people. A warped old *ruan* with a missing string hung on the wall as decoration. The window had a pull-cord so it could open and close like the blade of a guillotine.

"Ye up, mute foot?" came the old man's voice from the next room. "Ye better come get it whilst ye can."

Will sat up and winced. He had to pee really bad. "Uh, sir?" he called back. "I'll need to be excused fer a moment."

Barefoot, Will walked into the next room, which was the kitchen and dining area. There sat the old tendikeye and a woman Will assumed was his daughter. She looked to be in her late twenties and had the same nose and eyes as the old man, only softer and prettier.

She shoveled a piece of egg into her mouth and pointed out the front door. "Ploptree's that way. Three trees to your right."

Will nodded. 'Thanks, miss."

245

He stepped out the door and leapt through the branches, passing three trunks until he reached the hollow dead elm that was used as a toilet. After emptying his bladder into a rotten hole, he turned back.

When he returned, he found an empty stool and a full plate at the table. Before sitting down, he swallowed and regarded his two hosts. "My name is Will Foundling, from Tresiville, Meramac."

"Daiv Tchanly, this is my daughter Ivy. Have a seat Mr. Foundling and dig in."

Will did as he was told. He started on the wild carrots. They were raw and freshly washed. Then he made his way clockwise to the fried mushrooms. Then the poached eggs. Finally, all that was left was the venison steak. He stared at it for a moment.

"Been awhile since you had meat?" Daiv asked.

"A few weeks," Will answered, never taking his eyes off the morsel. He wanted to ask the old man if he had hunted himself in this forest, but feared such a thing might be rude.

"It's okay, mute foot. Ivy shot it three days ago."

"Gave a helluva chase, too," the woman added.

Will tried to eat the steak slowly, but it was too good. In less than four bites, it was gone. He watched the old man pack a pipe and smiled. Will rolled a cigarette.

As both men lit up and blew smoke into the air, the old man regarded his guest and asked a simple question. "Did you try to rescue the lovers from being hanged?"

Will felt sick as his mind vomited up the memory of what he had witnessed the night before. He nodded gravely.

The old man's quilled eyebrows raised. "Did *she* try to talk to you?"

Will swallowed hard and nodded twice.

Daiv took a puff on his pipe. As he spoke, smoke floated out of his mouth and nose. "She only does that when people honestly wish to help them. Of course, they can't be helped, but perhaps they can be freed."

Will took a drag off his cigarette and asked, "Who is she....or...who were they?"

Daiv shrugged his old gray wings. "Maise Linium and her beloved, Allie Baitmenn. Humans hadn't flooded into Doflend as much back in those olden times as they did last century. Because of

246

that, tolerance was quite the commodity. Whenever a round ear came along and charmed one of the natives, it would set the hearts of other natives ablaze. Them two lovers shared and still share the same ill fate. Now, what sets them two apart from other lovers that died in such away is that their shades have yet to erode."

"On account of the Geohex," Will said. It wasn't a question.

The old man touched his pipe to his nose and smiled. "I've been trying to help that couple out for years. Not only do I feel bad for 'em, but they shortened my trees."

"What trees?"

"My caven trees. They're growin' all over this forest, which is legally mine, I'll have ye know."

Will cocked a quilled eyebrow. "I ain't seen no caven trees 'round here."

"That's 'cause ye were too high up."

Will opened his mouth to speak as he narrowed his gaze, "But caven trees are taller than oaks."

Daiv smirked and said "Follow me." He got up from the table and went out the front door. Pushing his feet off the side of his walkway, he spread his wings and glided to the forest floor. Will followed by landing on a nearby tree limb and descending from limb to limb until he caught up with his host. The old man was spry, but Will matched his steps easily.

Will realized something was amiss in this particular neck of the woods. The dark of yesternight had hidden from him a most peculiar sight.

The old man pointed at one of his caven trees. It was as tall as they were, yet it did not have the look of a sapling.

Will approached it and studied its bark, its limbs, and its very leaves. His jaw began to quiver and soon his hands did, too. Will looked at the old tendikeye. "Daiv.....this caven tree looks full grown. Only it should be taller than every other tree here!"

Daiv took a long drag off his pipe and used it to point all around them. The forest was full of caven trees no taller than the two men. "Each one is full grown. Each one has been here before my grandfather's grandfather's grandfather." He picked a tiny nut off a tree and showed it to Will. "There was a time when this nut would have been as big as a rugby ball and more savory than a pecan. But look at it now. No bigger than a rotten grape. And twice as bitter,

247

too. This forest used to supply the town of Pevulaneum with enough full sized caven nuts to feed every man, woman, and child. Not only that, they exported them to Embrenil. It was the town's main economic resource. But I'll tell ye just what happened. A posse 'o Drakeri bigots strung up them lovers ye saw yesternight from the limbs of a caven tree. After that, folks say that the trees themselves were so reviled by such a horrific act that the trees themselves made a pact to shrink down enough so that no one could never ever use their limbs fer hangin' again. And in doing so, they punished the people of Pevulaneum with tiny bitter nuts. And if ye ask me, the people there are just as bitter now." He handed Will the nut.

Will accepted it and reluctantly put it in his mouth. After three chews, the flavor that was let loose on his tongue was too much to bear. He spat it out.

Daiv laughed. "That's how I was able to get this land so cheap. They don't want it no more. No use for it, they say. But I know better. I've spent my youth an' prime workin' the goober fields of Patosi. I pick each and every nut and grind 'em and refine 'em into a butter spread fit fer an emperor. Each tree can yield a jar's worth every year. Me an' Ivy make the trip to Embrenil every Summer an' sell 'em to all the tendikeye restaurants."

Will frowned slightly. "Is that how you make it by out here? Sellin' nut butter? Moneywise, I mean."

Daiv shrugged his wings. "I'm a retired field surgeon. I still got enough severance to keep me fed an' clothed. The land tax here is dirt-cheap. We manage."

Will smiled halfheartedly and looked around. "Still not as nice as home. What made you wanna yank yer roots an' leave?"

Daiv began to walk and gave Will a come along look. "It was before yer time, mute foot. That tune I played yesternight..."

"Blood in the Mud?" Will asked.

The old man nodded. "That was my life. In times of peace, I was a goober farmer an' the best saw player in the county. But in times of war an' rebellion, which seemed to be more often, I was an offensive surgeon called a Sawboy. They teach you what that was at'cher schoolhouse?"

Will shook his head.

The old man bared his yellow teeth. "Figured. My job was simple. On the eve of each battle or skirmish, I'd hide from sight an'

248

play that tune on my saw to let the enemy know that as soon as the battle was over, I'd come at their wounded with my saw an' take off a limb or two. Didn't matter if a wounded arm, leg, or wing could heal in time, I was gonna take it off and patch 'em up just good enough so that they'd be crippled fer the rest o' their lives. That way they would forever be recognized as failed rebels with lost causes and lost limbs. As brutal as it sounds, it was a great tactic. Often, rebels would hear that song an' get so scared that they'd surrender with little fuss. It was a dang good system, too. It would be grantin' mercy an' punishment to the rebels in one action. They'd lose their cause, their will to fight, an' they could then go on back home an' try to make themselves useful in more peaceful ways." He hung his head and kicked a weed. "Then Necluke took the imperial seat. He put an end to all that. He said that all rebels were traitors, even the ones who protested peacefully. Accordin' to him, they didn't deserve a punishment you could live through. He forced all the Sawboys to either retrain as simple medics or retire. I was too dang old to learn new tricks like removin' bullets or treatin' burns. Takin' limbs off cleanly was almost all I knew. So, I said shunt it! I wasn't gonna stick around to see what else Necluke would change. So, I took my wife an' left."

"Where's yer wife now?" Will asked.

Daiv frowned. "She went to the brush pile shortly after Ivy was born. Her blood got infected. It was hard to find work out here in Doflend. These Drakeri live so dang long. A tendikeye's life is too short to be considered for long term employment. What's ten years o' hard work to them? One year for us? Why bother investin' in someone who'd be dead soon?"

Will felt compelled to argue. "Aw, it ain't like that all over, now. I've found plenty o' temporary work as a farmhand in between excursion jobs."

Daiv huffed. "But it was always just temporary, wudn't it? Well, I suppose it wouldn't've been so bad if I was an unattached foundling like ye. Migratory work might have been fun. But I had a baby girl to care fer. So, I asked around an' found out where the cheapest land in Doflend was: Apple County."

"Didja know it was haunted when you bought it?" Will asked.

"Not a clue," Daiv laughed. "All the deeds agent told me was

249

it was four hundred acres o' temperate forest just outside of a small town. The land was mine for two thousand grotz as long as I paid the yearly land tax fer at least ten years. That was twenty-three...twenty-four years ago."

"An' you ain't never had ghost problems?"

"Nuthin' I couldn't handle."

Will blinked in confusion. "How? How do you deal with the necrofright? The ghosts an' black theurgy in the land itself?"

The old man leapt to a high tree limb and perched on it. He studied Will with stern eyes. "I don't know enough about ye yet, mute foot. You say yer a Harker Excursionist. Yer pistol is one of the finest I've seen. Are ye here fer Daddy Long Legs or because o' the Geohex?"

"The Geohex. My friends an' I intend to break it. Who is Daddy Long Legs, pray tell?"

Daiv grunted. "No one you need concern yerself with. Come along." He continued on in the same direction. As Will followed he realized that he was being led to the clearing of the hanged couple.

"Why did you take me here?" Will asked, feeling naked without his weapons.

Daiv folded his arms and leaned on a tree. "Ye said yesternight that ye *saw* somethin'. The hanged couple?"

Will nodded and shrugged. A feeling of worry slithered up his spine. "Yeah. I *saw* them. I saw ghosts with my own two eyes."

The old man's stern stare narrowed. "An' why do ye think that is? Tendikeye can't use theurgy. Ye got any idea why ye can see spirits, mute foot?"

Will bared his teeth. "I got a few ideas why. None o' which are any o' yer business!"

Daiv scoffed. "Brown Gut Snake! Ye were on my property yesternight crackin' shells. When ye got to my home, ye were white as a sheet. I gave ye shelter an' food. By rule o' the abode, I expect answers."

"Answers, eh?" It was Will's turn to scoff. "If I give you answers, what can I expect in return?"

Daiv's eyes softened. He rolled up his sleeve and exposed a tattoo of a rat. "You give me answers, I'll give you answers," the old man offered.

Will's eyes widened at the sight of the tattoo. "Yer a Charm

250

Breaker, too? An actual theurge hunter?"

Daiv smiled and rolled his sleeve back. "Only a novice initiate. I never had the chance fer formal study at no academy. I was self-taught, but certified an' bona fide. I was never keen enough to use it against a maxim spoutin' witch. But I can identify an' treat some theurgic effects. Inquistin', diagnosin'. That kinda thing. So, what say ye? Ye wanna know why ye can see ghosts?"

Will could not hide his worry. "Yes, please. Tell me if you know."

The old man knelt down, picked a gray dust poppy and showed it to Will. "Allergies," he said.

Will's jaw dropped. "Huh?"

"Yep. Yer allergic to the pollen o' gray dust poppies. They grow wild all over the county. A symptom is necrosight an' acute sensitivity to necrofear. I've seen it many times before with others of our kind who've been here, few as they've been." He tossed the flower behind his shoulder.

Will stamped his foot. "Allergies? Are you sure that's all it is?"

Daiv nodded. "An' let me guess, you've also been less bothered by the cold, too. Am I right?"

Will began to laugh. "Yeah! Well, plop in my pocket! That's all it is? An' here I was thinkin' that...thinkin' that..."

"Thinkin' what?"

"I don't know. That it may mean I might be a Lemuertian halfbreed. Ain't that sumthin'?" Will kept chuckling.

Daiv cocked his head to the side. "Well, we ain't exactly ruled *that* out yet."

Will stopped chuckling. He looked at the old man, waiting, watching.

The elderly tendikeye reached into the front pocket of his button up shirt and pulled out a small wooden cigarette box. He opened it and pulled out a deck of cards. "This is a *trump deck*. In it, there's a card designed to combat every major, well-known form of theurgy. I have my home warded in hidden places throughout the *frezje*. The second ye stepped into my home, you fell unconscious onto the floor. Ivy and I had to lift yer heavy ass onto the cot. As you slept, I used every card in this deck to identify what kind of theurgy was on ye."

Will felt his heart speeding up. "Wudya find out?" he asked, trying to stay calm.

Daiv shrugged his wings. "Well, out of all the cards in this deck, only one of them matches up with the energy on ye. And it ain't the Death Path, which may rule ye out as a Lemuertian halfbreed."

Will took two steps forward. He drew up his sleeve to reveal a pink scar on his wrist. "I got this in Embrenil. A post-mort assassin cut me with a blade made of *vaughn*. It was shiny blue. No mistakin' it. Every tendikeye worth his salt knows *that* metal is the only thing to go through Lemuertian hide like butter. Fer as long as I can remember, I've been tough as railroad nails. Swords only scratch. Bullets only bruise or crack bones. If I ain't a halfbreed, what am I?"

"Protected," Daiv answered. "Reinforced is a better word."

"Protection Theurgy?" Will scoffed. "That's what my buddy reckoned at first. I've had quite a few Protection Theurges look at me. They say it ain't it. What makes them wrong an' you right, old man?"

Daiv smiled at the question. "None of them could recognize it because none of them knew the particular maxim that caused this...condition you have. But my cards never lie to me." He drew a card from his deck, and started pacing toward Will. He stopped only a few feet away, held up the card, and then let go of it.

In an instant, it flew on its own and attached itself to Will's chest like a bug landing.

Startled, Will tried to brush off the card. It stuck to his hand. He tried to pinch it off. It stuck to his fingertips. He heard Daiv chuckling, and looked up.

"The cards work like magnets," the old man explained. "Each card is made using different woods an' extracts that react to certain theurgic energies. Only a handful of tendikeye even know how to make 'em. They weren't cheap either. Broke my back fer three summers to buy 'em." He reached and plucked the card off Will's fingers. "As fer the *vaughn* bein' able to cut ye, I got a simple answer. The caster of the maxim was a Lemuertian. Their theurgies are weak against it, too."

Will furrowed his brow and scratched his head. "Why would a creature who lives only fer death an' misery do somethin' like that

252

to me?"

"Why indeed. But I guess that's none o' my concern. That's between you an' it."

❖

Noon arrived with the smell of coffee and potato salad. Will sat at the family's small table, telling the news of Drowsy Nook as he shoveled food into his mouth.

For tendikeye, it was not considered rude to eat while talking. In fact, they recognized the merit in doing two things at once. Daiv and Ivy ate and listened in silence. As Will finished his tale, Daiv went to a cabinet and pulled out a bottle of a greenish yellow liquid.

"Pepperwine?" Will asked.

Daiv grunted in the affirmative as he set the bottle on the table. "It ain't quite Naga Venom. But it'll do the trick." He studied Will under his old brow quills. "I can make a remedy fer yer gray dust allergy. If I give it to you, it will not only take away yer necrosight, but yer necrofright, too. Seein' and feelin' ghosts can't be pleasant. But in truth, I myself have often wished fer the condition. On some nights, when I'm between sleep an' awake, I can hear that yonder woman screamin' fer her life...an' the life o' her unborn. Ghosts get caught up in the injustice they suffered. As they shed their body an' mind, their soul gets imprisoned by the memory. Can you imagine that, mute foot? Bein' forced to dwell on the same bad thing that was done to you and yours fer always an' always?" He poured Will the first glass.

As Will raised the glass to his lips, he pondered the old man's words. "I don't need to imagine such a thing, sir." He downed the entire glass, letting the sweet burn of the spiced liquor clear out his nose, throat, and ears. With a low, slow huff, Will answered "Good stuff. I think I'll hold off on that remedy you got. Thanks all the same. But I'm gonna make the best o' this allergy an' help them souls out."

Daiv arched an eyebrow. "Back in the homecell. One might accuse you of utilizing the supernatural to get yer work done."

253

Will smirked. "Naw. I'm just doin' what Harkers do best, turnin' an obstacle into an advantage."

Ivy rolled her green eyes as she scraped the last of the food off her plate. "Now, Pa. You know if you don't give him that remedy, he'll end up nuttier'n your caven butter. 'Member what they said happened to that Maikul Heuzer fella 'bout three hun'erd years ago? He might've had the same dang condition. Lost all his marbles includin' the shooter when he saw the Drageist in its cave. He crawled down from there shiverin' and whimperin' and chewin' his hands off bit by bit." She looked at Will. "'Least that's what I heard told. He died soon after. Blood loss, Doc Ampa said."

"What's a Drageist?" Will asked.

She sighed and shook her head. "Curiosity kills cats in mysterious ways, Mr. Foundling. You've been warned. The Drageist is a dragon spirit that resides in a hill on the other side of town."

Will's eyes grew wide. "I never saw a dragon spirit before."

Ivy frowned. "I bet that's what Maikul Heuzer said before he went up that hill and went bonkers. It don't like to be bothered. People've gone up there hopin' to get a look at it or outta greed fer the prospect of treasure. The few that come back, return as broken, raving loons. You'd better keep clear of that place, if you prefer livin'."

Will considered the woman's words. Dragons and ghosts were scary. Ghosts were scary. Combining the two was positively frightening. He had no training whatsoever in combating either. Perhaps this was a situation better approached by his entire team. After all, he was only there to collect information. There was no need to rush things.

Then an idea came to him. His brain had accidentally stumbled off its usually narrow path. It was not often that Will's mind developed an abstract thought. And whenever he had one, it nagged at him and filled his being with an almost preternatural motivation.

He looked at Ivy and grinned. "Take me to the cave, Miss Ivy. I just might be hatchin' a plan."

"You sure you wanna take all them weapons with ya?" Ivy asked as they dashed through the woods.

"Yep," Will answered. "You never know, ya know?"

She smiled and gripped the handle of a curved dagger on her belt. "That's why I always have my birthblade on me."

Will's face grew cold. "Must be nice to have one, I guess."

Ivy winced in sudden realization. "Oh, I'm sorry. I didn't think. Pardon my rudeness. I forgot that Foundling's don't have them."

Will heard the sincerity in her voice and glanced at her. She, like most females, looked quite pretty when expressing remorse. "Ain't nothin', Miss Ivy. In truth, I shouldn't be so dang sensitive about it."

"But you are," she returned. "An' I see no fault in it."

Will laughed. "I got plenty o' faults, believe you me."

She smiled, showing almost perfect teeth. A single canine jutted out of place. "The only fault I see in you, Mr. Foundling, is a willingness to get yerself killed." She paused before adding "By the way, keep yer steel holstered and sheathed when we cut through town. Pevulaneum's crawlin' with Swans. Daddy Long Legs is their leader here. We need to avoid him if we can."

"Are *all* the Trottin' Swans trouble?" he asked as he sprung off a branch.

She matched his step and answered him as they soared through the air. "Some more'n others," she said before skipping off the next branch. "They run drugs to feed their families. Some might call that desperation."

"What do you call it?" he asked.

She frowned thinly. "Laziness. And misuse of the land, Pa says, growin' them flowers. I hear that their grandkin were farmers thousands of years ago. All that changed. If it weren't fer all the old barns and silos, I'd've never believed any major farming ever got done here. Them Swans, they've been known to rough folks up. I heard this one woman use to live in town. Ava, I think her name was. She used to date a Swan. Well, when she had enough of the turd and jilted him, he and his friends broke into her house and took turns on her."

"What'd the law do?" Will asked.

255

Ivy shrugged. "Sheriff Poge and her deputies lent a hand in helping her move after she recovered. Yep. All they did was help her relocate to another county far away. No man was punished. Y'see, the Swan's're official militia in times of war an' disaster. If the law even tried to move against them all, it'd be high treason. You can thank the Count fer that. And if you mess with one Swan, you mess with'em all. The ones that wouldn't get arrested would go after the Sheriff an' deputy's families."

Will thought of Edifice Teige. *"That must be why he wudn't afraid of 'em. He had no family."*

The two tendikeye leapt into an open meadow. On the other end of the meadow lay a cluster of houses and buildings. The town of Pevulanium stood waiting for them.

The land was littered with old boxes of rotten wood that were being used as houses. Most of them were shacks, some nicer than others. The streets were made of dusty dirt swallowing old gravel. Small children ran around unwatched, wearing more dirt than clothing. A train track cut though the still herd of shacks, but there was no train station, just a rotted old platform.

The most prominent feature of the town, the water tower, was so ancient, all that remained were three of the four steel posts that once held up the humongous tank. They were like three rust covered giants huddling to conspire some foul deed.

"Welcome to Pevulaneum," Ivy said, catching her breath. "Or what's left of it. The train stops here just once a month. That's how most folk keep track of the dates."

"How do these people get by?" Will asked her.

"Some garden. 'Tatoes, carrots--easy root foods like that. Fruits are dang near impossible to grow here 'cept for berries. Straw, black, or maul grow best. Sheep keepers do well if they can keep their herds out of gray dust patches. Sheep eat it and get ulcers real bad. Everybody wears wool here, even during Summer. Cotton's almost as commodital as silk around here. It don't grow too well, is why." She attempted to smile. "Same with the people. There used to be a lead refinery down by the river. It operated fer over a thousand years. Now the poisonous metal's laced in the dirt an' water."

Will looked around at all the drakeri town folk. They were

poor. But not just moneywise. An elderly couple sat in chairs on their front porch. They looked like they had not smiled in centuries. Here and there, facial expressions were detached, eyes dull.

As Will and Ivy trekked through town Will received odd stares from the townsfolk. But they were not the usual odd stares at his tendikeye features. They were looking at is guns, particularly the one on his waist. Will noticed a rough man wearing purple who glanced at his gun and then his face. The man grinned darkly before running off.

"Hey, Ivy!" a woman called out. "Who's that with ya? Did you finally get a trailblazer?"

Ivy turned and smirked at the thick-waisted drakeri woman with a toddler on her hip. "Retah, you know my trail's been blazed fer years now! This here is Will, a visitor and nothing more."

Will blushed a little. He gave the young mother a friendly nod. "Well met, miss. Will Foundling's the name."

"Nice to meet you," Retah smirked, extending her free hand.

Will hesitated and looked at the hand. In his culture, people only shook hands with family.

"Is he shy?" Retah asked Ivy.

"No," Will quickly answered, breaking tradition with a firm handshake.

Ivy made a dismissive gesture with her wing. "He's not used to our customs is all. He's from Cloiherune."

"Oh, so he still needs to be domesticated!" Retah laughed in a loud high giggle that made Will's ears itch.

Will tilted his head as he looked down at the short woman. "Whatchu know about the Dragon Cave? Me an' her are headed up there. Anythin' I should know?"

Retah made a sour face. "Yeah, don't go! You'll die of fright or go mad. Or worse yet, go missing."

Will shrugged and tried not to show that he cared. "If it gets too scary, I'll high tail it. Say, is there an outhouse around here I could use?" He looked to Ivy. "Yer pa's pepperwine's doin' a number on my guts."

"Sure," Retah replied. She pointed at her nearby home. "You can use mine."

Ivy put her hand on Will's shoulder. "We're in a hurry."

"We are?" Will asked.

257

Ivy's eyes grew serious. "Uh, yeah. You don't mind usin' the woods on the other side of town, do you? You're a Harker. You do it all the time, right?" She smiled, trying to cover her concern.

"Don't worry, Ivy," Retah told her friend. "I don't think D.L.L. is out today."

"Who's D.L.L?" Will asked.

Ivy frowned and swallowed. "Daddy Long Legs. I told you he's the top Swan in town. You don't want to meet him."

Will raised a quilled eyebrow and grinned. "Maybe I do."

Ivy grasped his collar. "You'd have better luck with the Drageist."

Will sighed and nodded in compliance. "Fair enough. But I really can't wait."

Ivy glanced around. "All right then. Just make it quick!"

Retah showed Will to her outhouse. It was a rotted shack that stunk to the high atmosphere.

He thanked the young mother with a nod and went in. His stomach churned with every breath of the boggy air. He tried to be as quick as he could, but a nervousness due to unfamiliar surroundings took him. He grunted and sighed as he tried to expel the misshapen clump of waste from his bowels. *"Shoulda drank more water!"* he thought through his struggle.

At that moment, his ears caught the sounds of doors closing. All around were the faint clicks of latches, bolts, and scraping wood. He peered through a crack between two boards. People were rushing into their houses. Mothers were scooping up their children. He even saw a dog run behind a tree.

He heard Retah whisper to Ivy. "Oh, I'm so sorry! He's coming!"

"Just go. We'll be fine," Ivy answered.

Just as the clumsy tread of Retah's feet died off, the sound of three sets of boots grew louder.

"Where is he?" a man's voice demanded.

"Taking a dump," Ivy answered. "He won't be interested, Daddy. He's not the type."

"We'll just see about that," the man's voice answered.

Will finished up, opened the door, and stepped outside.

Three drakeri men, all dressed in purple, stood within arms length in front of Ivy. The one man to stick out the most was a very

258

tall, sickly thin drakeri wearing a black hat with purple satin trim. Strapped to his was a long-barreled pistol that appeared to be made entirely of blue *vaughn* steel. The man smiled with wicked delight has he glanced at Will's gun before meeting the tendikeye's eyes.

Will recognized the look the man gave him. He had seen it before. This man was an experienced killer who had long forgotten the meaning of fear. The gun and holster he wore had been custom made for a speedy draw. This man was not just any tough with a gun. This was a Lead Dealer.

There seemed to be nothing quite so special about the two men with him, except that one of them had a horrifically wounded face, a face that looked like it had been dragged on a rocky road. Will recognized the man as the one whose bike wheel he had shot out on his way from Drowsy Nook. He tried not to grin.

The tall man took a single step toward him, covering well over a yard in that one stride. He looked down at the tendikeye and tipped his hat.

Will nodded in return.

The man took a deep breath and exhaled in a soft rumble "They call me Daddy Long Legs. But you can call me Daddy for short."

Will grinned and put his hands in his coat pockets, a sign of peace. "Ain't nothin' short about you, Daddy."

The tall man bared his teeth with a smile. "Just my temper, little seed. Just my temper."

Will continued smiling. Forcing his fake grin made his cheeks sting. "And how may I be of service on this fine day?"

"I'd like to see your pistol. I've never held a Mark Twain Special before. A few imitations now and again, but never the real thing." He paused and added. "If that *is* the real thing." He took out his own gun, and offered it handle first.

The tendikeye pulled out his Mark Twain Special, emptied all its chambers, and traded guns with the tall man. The Lead Dealer's weapon was superb, well balanced, well oiled, and pleasing to the eye. It was also big enough to fit Will's large hand. Will looked at the tall man admiring his own weapon, and was amazed. Daddy Long Legs was the only drakeri to ever have fingers long enough to reach both triggers.

"This is a work of art," Daddy said with restrained awe. "I

259

want it for my collection."

"Not fer sale or trade," Will told him.

Daddy regarded him. "Would you like to have the gun you're holding?" he asked.

Will shrugged and nodded. "I like to travel light. But this would be a burden worth barin'. Still, I like mine better. Thanks all the same." He gave pistol back.

Daddy smiled thinly as they traded back their weapons. "I'd like to make you an offer then."

"Not for sale or trade," Will repeated, holstering his gun.

"I propose neither. A gun duel, to the death. The winner takes all the loser's possessions."

Will scoffed. "You got nothin' I want, Daddy."

"You haven't seen all I got, little seed," Daddy replied sharply. "I own 2,650 acres between here and Victor's Grove. I also own several pistols, all well made and well maintained. I am married to the prettiest woman in the county. She'll become your willing whore the rest of your days if you win. You will also win my beloved garden. Would you like to see it?"

"No, he doesn't, Daddy," Ivy said, stepping in.

Daddy's arm flickered in a blur. He held his hand and fingers out like it was a gun. "What's the matter, Ivy? Afraid you'll lose another husband?"

Will was shocked by how fast the man had moved, but did not show it. "Mister, I ain't interested. I ain't no lead dealer. Good day to ya."

Daddy frowned and peered over Will's shoulder. "Is that a long range rifle in your carrying case?"

Will did not answer.

Daddy looked over at his friend with the smashed face. "Jarami, do you suppose this is the shunting coward who shot out your wheel yestermorn? He sure does act a coward."

Jarami attempted to squint with his swollen, bruised eyes. When he opened his mouth to speak, most of his teeth were broken or missing. "Where did you come in from, prick?"

Will smiled with wild eyes. "Drowsy Nook."

Jarami carried a pistol of his own, a four shot revolver. In a fit of sudden rage, he pulled his weapon. Will was already prepared to twist the pistol from the man's grip and put him on the ground.

But Daddy Long Legs was ready, too. Before Jarami could fully draw his piece, Daddy bashed his companion's face with an explosive backfist.

"He's mine!" Daddy yelled as Jarami fell limp onto the dirt. Without missing a beat, the tall drakeri lurched over, meeting Will face to face. "I challenge you, coward! You have done a great offense to my Swan brethren!"

Will glanced down at Jarami. The rest of the man's teeth were now gone. He looked back at the tall man. "I don't duel, Daddy. Ain't my style. Now, if you'll kindly go shunt yerself, the lady and I got a meeting with the Drageist."

Daddy Long Legs tilted his head. "What business do you have with it, or with this town for that matter? The news of you and your comrades killing Edifice Teige has spread like wildfire all throughout the county. You broke the headsman's curse. You've claimed out loud that you want to end the Geohex. Why?"

Will shrugged. "I guess I'm just a trouble maker fer trouble makers."

The other man stepped out from around Daddy. "You want trouble, you got it!"

Daddy Long Legs put his hand on the man's shoulder. "No need, Idgur. He's just a coward, an honorless dog who shoots from a distance. A bushwhacking sissy. Let him go to the Drageist and die of fright." He stood up straight again so to look down at the tendikeye. "I am no backshooter. I am an honorable man. But if you do one more thing to hurt my friends, I'll blow a hole through your spiky head, thread a rope through that hole, hitch it to my bileer, and drag you around this town seven times. Are we clear?"

Will stood on his tiptoes. His large feet making him almost as tall as Daddy. "You really need to work on yer insults, stick boy."

There was a long tense moment while the two men glared at each other. Then, in the exact same instant, they both turned away and walked in different directions.

After several dozen steps, Ivy grabbed Will's arm and whispered "Please, don't duel him, whatever you do. He's killed ninety-nine gunfighters so far. He's been itching to make it one hundred for a while now!"

Will looked at her. "Did he kill yer husband, Ivy? Did I hear him right?"

261

The tendikeye woman scoffed and shook her head in shame. "No. He just scared him outta town is all. Meril was his name. Daddy challenged him, and the chicken turd skipped town without even saying goodbye. Good riddance, I say." She shrugged her wings. "He was only my practice husband anyway."

Part 2

At the bottom of a steep tree-covered hill, an old sign read in bold letters:

DO NOT PASS THIS POINT. HAUNTED CAVE. ANY PERSONS WHO DARE WANDER PAST, NO MATTER THEIR AGE OR IMPORTANCE, WILL NOT BE RESCUED. -PEVULANIUM CIVIC GUARD DEPARTMENT

"No matter their age or importance?" Will questioned as he read the sign aloud.

"Children have been known to go up there," Ivy explained. "As I understand it, the son of the owner of the old lead refinery went up there. You know how boys are curious. First, they sent up a search party, then a posse of civic guards and Excursionists. None of them ever made it back down."

"Sounds promisin'," Will replied as he loaded his pistol.

Ivy looked puzzled as she watched him. "You don't even look nervous, much less terrified."

Will popped a cigarette in his lips. "Should I be?" he asked as he lit up. "If it gets too weird up there, I'll just run out an' back down the hill. Simple as that."

Ivy crossed her arms, impressed by his coolheadedness. "Dasaru," she nicknamed him. "I can't tell if you're being brave or

262

just stupid."

Will smirked and gave her a wink. "Neither. I'm bein' ignorant. See ya in a few. There a good restaurant in town?"

"No," she answered. "But there's a diner by the schoolhouse. It's called *The Country Kitchen*. Simple name, simple food. Are you buying, Dasaru?"

He took a few strides past the warning sign before calling back. "Only if yer willin' to keep me comp'ny!"

Ivy smiled as he made his way through shadows and trees. In a soft whisper, she said, "You come back down alive, Dasaru, and I might give you more than just company."

Not that Will knew it, but he was too proud and insecure to show fear to a person he did not know. Daddy Long Legs had scared him. Walking past that sign had scared him. He hid his fear by ignoring it altogether. He had no real idea what he was getting himself into, barging in on the den of a dragon's ghost. He remembered being a toddler and touching a lit candle for the first time. The pretty little flame had made him gasp and jump back. But no more than a few seconds later, he'd reached out to touch it again. He'd watched for a moment as the fire rose up around his finger. Then in a confused panic, he'd let out a sobbing scream.

And now, as the cave opening came into view, once again fear surrounded him. As regret began to pry open his quickening heart, the necrofright stabbed its way into his chest. His pulse pounded in his ears. He took long, deep, difficult breaths as he inched his way nearer.

"*Stay curious.*" he thought. "Stay curious." he said aloud. "*Seek to understand, jus' like Rev said.*"

Without a shred of hesitation, he shoved his head into the dark opening and made his presence known.

"Hey! Dragon! My name is Will Foundling. I'm here to figure out what's goin' on with you. Maybe we can come to an agreement and help each other out."

In immediate reply, a low, loud growl reverberated from the cave. Will froze as the gut-wrenching sound formed words.

"ARE YOU A NEGOTIATOR?" the growl asked.

"Uh..." Will blurted. "Uh...Yeah! Yes, I am. I came here to humbly request yer assistance."

Will could hear something stirring within the rocky hole.

263

There was a long pause before the growl answered. "I CAN TELL THAT THE CONFEDERAL RESERVE HAS SENT A CRAFTY ONE. TELL ME; DOES YOUR IDEA OF *ASSISTANCE* INVOLVE ME GIVING YOU THE PLATES I'VE STOLEN?"

Will sensed a strange uneasiness from the presence within. "No," he answered, confused by the question. "I'll get down to the point if that's okay with you. There's this couple out in the woods across town. Couple as in mated pair, ya know? Well, they were unjustly hanged by a gang of bigoted nitwits. The couple is just a pair of ghosts now held up by this...this ghostish...ghostly rope. Now, I gotta hunch that if I find a way to cut that rope, it'll end their curse and allow them to move on. That's why I'm here to see you, dragon. I need yer spook-fire to burn through that rope. I figure since you yerself are a ghost, you might be up to the task." He waited a moment before adding, "So, ya up fer it?"

The loud growl died down to a soft rumble, Will felt the sweet ease of relief. Then his keen ears stung with the sudden hiss of a large constricted throat. The darkness lit up as ten thousand blue tongues of flame burst from the cave, engulfing the tendikeye completely, even his screams.

The fire was ice cold, and it froze the spit in his mouth and tears beneath his eyelids. He slapped his hands to his face and screamed in pain. He rubbed and rubbed his eyes until they could see through the frosty haze. And then, there before him, glaring with discerning intensity was the head of the Drageist.

It was like the head of a viper. Smooth, triangular, cold in expression. It had no horns, frills, or jutting spines like dragons he had seen in picture books. Its most distinguishing feature was a flat plate of curved bone protruding from its snout.

"*Jus' like a bottle-nosed turtle,*" Will thought as he flooded his right boot with piss.

The Drageist's eyes glared directly into Will's soul, trying to tear his spirit apart. But the soul residing within the tendikeye did not crumble beneath the weight of its terrible gaze. And so with confused resentment, the beast muttered "YOU...ARE...NOT...LYING."

Will swallowed what felt like a dry potato in his throat. "Why would I lie?" he asked the massive head looming above him.

264

Its long neck reached far into the shadows of the cave.

The creature's beady yellow eyes narrowed in thought. "IF YOU WERE LYING ABOUT ME BEING A GHOST, MY BREATH WOULD HAVE FROZEN YOU SOLID."

"That was *winterfire*?!" Will asked.

The terrible head tilted to the left. "YES. IT IS ALSO CALLED *FROSTFLAME* IN SOME MORTAL CULTURES. HOW DO YOU KNOW OF IT, TENDIKEYE?"

"*Just keep it talkin!*" Will thought. "I met a frigorifist, a frost theurge, awhile back. How are you able to breathe winterfire?"

The Drageist growled and roared "DO NOT DIG FOR THE SPRING OF KNOWLEDGE, IF YOU HAVE NO SHOVEL TO DIG WITH OR BUCKET TO CARRY!"

"Fair enough!" Will cried, having no idea what the creature meant. "Let's keep it simple. I'm tryin' to find a way to end the Geohex in this county. Me an' my compatriots are tryin' to solve an' resolve all the ghost's problems, yerself included."

"GEOHEX, YOU SAY!" the Drageist exclaimed. Its eyes wide in realization. Its jaw dropped as it pondered, exposing a mouth full of razor sharp teeth. Even the bottom and roof of its mouth had teeth.

"THIS EXPLAINS MUCH," the monster muttered. "I HAVE NOT BEEN ABLE TO LEAVE THIS CAVE FOR COUNTLESS SEASONS. OFTEN, I WOULD EVEN REALIZE AND REMEMBER THAT I WAS DEAD. BUT I, THIS SPIRIT, HAVE BEEN TRAPPED IN A PRISON OF CURSED EARTH AND DELUSION. PLEASE, TENDIKEYE! DO NOT LET ME FORGET AGAIN!"

"Okay, okay!" Will answered. "What do I need to do?"

"YOU MUST FIRST HELP ME REMEMBER HOW I DIED. NO DEATH, NO MATTER HOW HEINOUS, CAN CAUSE A DRAGON TO BECOME A GHOST. WE DO NOT HOLD CONFUSED GRUDGES LIKE YOU MORTALS. SOMETHING MUST BE KEEPING ME FROM MOVING ON."

"Okay then," Will answered, trying to calm down and focus. "Maybe if you told me more about yerself it'll help me out. Like, uh, what's yer name? Where you from?"

265

The Drageist frowned and furrowed its brow. "THOSE QUESTIONS HAVE MANY ANSWERS, MORTAL. I WILL TELL YOU MY LAST NAME, *LAST* AS IN *FINAL*. THE DRAKERI NEWSPAPERS CALLED ME THE GREED WYRM, ALTHOUGH GREED WAS NEVER MY PURPOSE. IT WAS A DIFFERENT TIME AND MONEY WAS TREATED WITH LITTLE RESPECT. WEALTH, LIKE ENERGY, CANNOT BE CREATED OR DESTROYED. IT SIMPLY IS. GOLD, SILVER, PRECIOUS STONES--THEY ARE ALL RARE FOR A REASON: TO OFFER TESTAMENT OF AN INDIVIDUAL'S WORTH AND USEFULNESS. THE GROTZ COINS YOU CARRY IN YOUR POCKET, THEY ARE MIXED WITH VARYING MEASURES OF SILVER AND GOLD. WHEN YOU EARNED THEM, YOU POSSESS THEM. WHEN SOMEONE EARNS THEM FROM YOU, YOU GIVE THEM TO THAT PERSON. SUCH WAS NOT THE WAY WHEN LAST I DREW BREATH.

"IT WAS SOMETIME AFTER THE OMNI-WAR. THE DRAKERI MORTALS WERE BEGINNING TO HORDE GOLD AGAIN, AND PRINT FANCY DOCUMENTS TO SHOW PROOF OF OWNERSHIP OF CERTAIN SUMS. BUT AS ALWAYS, SOME INCARNATION OF GOVERNMENT MISSPENT THE NOTES. AND TO COVER THEIR MISTAKES, THEY SIMPLY PRINTED MORE.

"YOU SEE, WHEN AN INDIVIDUAL DOES SUCH A THING, IT IS CALLED FORGERY OR COUNTERFEIT. BUT WHEN A GOVERNMENT DOES IT, THEY CALL IT INFLATION. SO, BY MISSPENDING THEIR OWN MONEY, THEY MADE A CITIZEN'S MONEY WORTH LESS THAN WHAT IT HAD BEEN. INFLATION, YOUNG TENDIKEYE, IS ROBBERY IN ITS PUREST, MOST MONSTROUS FORM.

"SO, I MADE IT MY AIM TO TAKE AS MANY OF THOSE CURSED NOTES AS I COULD. THE MORE THEY PRINTED, THE MORE I STOLE AND DESTROYED! NO BANK COULD KEEP ME OUT. NO BULLET OR BLADE COULD INJURE ME SERIOUSLY ENOUGH TO STOP ME! BUT THE MORE I TOOK, THE MORE THEY PRINTED! AND SO, I DID WHAT HAD TO BE DONE. I BROKE INTO THEIR FORTRESS FACTORY, KILLING HUNDREDS AND TAKING

266

THE PRINTING PLATES THAT CREATED THE CASH NOTES. YES, IT WAS I WHO TOOK THEM AND HID THEM HERE IN THIS VERY CAVE!"

The Drageist's head made a 'follow me' gesture as it slithered back into the hole on the hill's face.

Will was hesitant to enter, but he lit up his flip top lighter and went in. The cave was as cold as winter, with a fat layer of smooth ice under his feet and countless stalactite-sized icicles on the ceiling. He came to a huge cavern with a giant frozen waterfall.

Beside it was the Drageist, a mountain of white writhing coils.

"PUT OUT THAT FOUL FLAME," the beast commanded. "I SHALL ILLUMINATE OUR PALAVER."

Will flipped out the small fire and watched in amazement as the cavern ice lit up in a soft blue-white glow. His heart stuttered as he recognized numerous shapes encased in the ice. They were people--men, women, and children--perfectly preserved in prisons of petrified water.

"Are these the people who...tried to get a look at you?"

The Drageist looked around at the still forms, casually. "INTERLOPERS, YES. NOT GUESTS LIKE YOU. THEY CAME IN WITHOUT ASKING, LED TO THEIR DOOM BY THEIR MORTAL CURIOSITY. BUT WORRY NOT, TENDIKEYE. THEY ARE NOT DEAD, MERELY PRESERVED BY MY OWN CURSE. SAVE ME AND YOU SAVE THEM."

Will gazed about through the clear ice. Faces were contorted in various measures of agony and despair. Every story about dragons he'd ever heard about dragons denounced the creatures as untrustworthy deal makers. He looked at the Drageist, now no longer in fear, but in a clear focused contempt. "On with yer story, monster," he told it. He lit a cigarette with defiant eyes, thinking it might be his last.

The Drageist growled at the word that was used to address him and glared at the woken flame in Will's hand. "GOLD AND SILVER AND PRECIOUS GEMS," it said somberly. "THESE THINGS WHICH YOU MORTALS MINE FROM THE EARTH AND FORGE INTO TRINKETS." It let out a bitter laugh. "YOU ASSUME THAT

267

GREED OR THE LOVE OF SHINY THINGS COMPELS WE DRAGONS TO TAKE IT AND HORDE IT AWAY. GREED! WHAT USE HAVE I FOR SUCH A SIN? AM I NOT STRONGER THAN A BULL ELEPHANT? SWIFTER THAN A SPARROW? AM I NOT WISER THAN ANY HERMIT SAGE WHO SEEKS ENLIGHTENMENT? WHAT DO I NEED MONEY FOR?

"THE ANSWER, YOUNG TENDIKEYE, IS THAT IT IS BETTER OFF WITH ME THAN WITH YOU! THOSE GROTZ COINS IN YOUR POCKET WILL ONLY CAUSE GRIEF. EVEN IF YOU DONATED THEM TO A TEMPLE OF GOOD WILL, THE TEMPLE MANAGER WILL GIVE IT TO A STARVING WIDOW WHO WILL USE IT TO BUY A LOAF OF BREAD FROM A BAKER, WHO WILL USE IT TO PAY TAXES TO FUND A TYRANT'S WAR OF ACQUISITION! I AM A DRAGON, AN EMBODIMENT OF THE DIRT AND STONE BENEATH YOUR FEET. WE ARE NATURE'S REACTION TO YOUR THEFT OF RARE METALS AND GEMS.

"I WAS BORN EONS AGO WHEN THE FIRST MINERS RAPED ENTIRE HILLSIDES FOR MERE GOLD DUST TO MAKE JEWELRY. WHEN A DRAGON KILLS THOUSANDS OF YOU SHORT-LIVED MORTALS FOR THE GOLD IN YOUR POCKETS, WE ARE ONLY RECLAIMING WHAT YOUR ANCESTORS HAVE TAKEN. AND TO HIDE IT FROM US, AND THEN MAKE FANCY DOCUMENTS AND CASH NOTES IN ITS PLACE…!" The Drageist raised its head in revulsion. "SUCH A THING…WAS A CHALLENGE TO MY NATURAL AUTHORITY."

Will looked up at the beast and took three steps forward. "Uh huh. So anyway, how'd you die?"

."I DO NOT RECALL," the Drageist grumbled, lowering its head

"Do not or *cannot?*" Will asked, shivering. "You seem to hold yerself in pretty high regard, what with yer twisted monster logic about monetary theory. I got a buddy I run with that'd love to chat with you about such brown gut snake. But I'm a simple man with a simple plan lookin' fer a simple solution. We ain't got no time to piddle-paddle, so chop-chop! How did you die, ya shovel-nosed bank robbin' sidewinder!"

268

"I WISH YOU WOULD DIE!" the Drageist snarled. "I TRIED TO KILL YOU TWICE NOW! BUT YOUR WILL WAS TOO STRONG FOR MY GAZE AND YOUR HEART CARRIED TOO MUCH TRUTH. YOU HAVE A STRONG, STUBBORN, THICK HEADED SPIRIT THAT WOULD NOT DISLODGE ITSELF FROM YOUR FRAIL BODY!"

Will puffed out smoke from his nose. "You want me dead," Will said, drawing his machete and pistol in the blink of an eye. "You do it the hard way, freak!"

The creature's mouth opened and grew so large that he could see nothing but its teeth. In that same instant, he realized that it was because the beast had moved in so quick, that it only appeared to grow. There was a loud *chomp* and he found himself in darkness.

He backed away and found himself slipping and falling onto the icy floor. As his back hit the solid surface, he looked up to see the head of the Drageist just inches from his own.

"WERE I NOT A SPIRIT," the monster hissed, "I WOULD HAVE BITTEN YOU IN TWO JUST NOW. YOU HAVE THE WILL AND TRUTHFUL HEART OF A DRAGONQUELLER, BOY. BUT YOU LACK THE DANGEROSITY. YOU ARE LUCKY I AM JUST A GHOST."

Will looked about and sat up. The chill of the ice beneath him stung his hand. "Where's yer corpse then? Drug off by whoever killed ya?"

The Drageist snorted and withdrew. "MOST LIKELY."

Will grinned and met the monster's gaze. "Yeah, that's how I got this dust coat. I killed a Kasucot, a big ugly snake like you."

The Drageist roared. "DO NOT COMPARE ME TO SUCH ANIMALS!"

Will smirked. "Fair enough. So, tell me more. You might as well, since we can't kill each other. You'd make an ugly coat anyway."

The beast fumed. "VERY WELL. WHERE WAS I?"

"Stolen money plates."

"AH, YES. IT WAS I WHO STOLE THE PLATES AND HID THEM IN THIS CAVE. THE ONE NOTE, FIVE, TEN, FIFTY, ONE HUNDRED, AND FIVE HUNDRED DOLLAR PLATES WERE MINE. I

WAS CONVINCED THAT WOULD FORCE THE MORTALS TO TURN THEIR GOLD BACK INTO COINS, SO THAT I COULD ONE DAY RECLAIM THEM."

Will nodded as he thought. He reached in his pocket and pulled out a handful of square grotz coins. "Well, it looks like you got half yer job done. Ain't no place in Doflend uses paper money notes. Heck, I never even knew they ever did! An' that was all yer doin', huh? Wow, I'm impressed!"

"IT'S ABOUT TIME YOU WERE!" the beast muttered. It tried to take a relaxing breath, but then remembered that it was dead. "IT IS A RELIEF TO KNOW THAT MY WORK CHANGED SOMETHING. WHEN MY SPIRIT MOVES ON AND I AM REBORN, I WILL BE SURE TO RETURN TO THIS COUNTRY TO START UP A PROPER HORDE. BUT WORRY NOT, THAT WON'T BE FOR ANOTHER...WELL...FOR A WHILE."

"What do you mean reborn?" Will asked.

"IT IS OF NO CONSEQUENCE TO YOU, TENDIKEYE. BESIDES, YOU DO NOT HAVE THE BEARING OF A QUICK STUDY, NOR THE TIME TO LEARN ALL MY SECRETS. WE MUST FOCUS ON ME GETTING OUT OF HERE, NOT THE DISTANT PAST OR FUTURE. NOW, PLEASE, HELP ME REMEMBER HOW I DIED."

Will regarded the Drageist for a long moment. "Yeah, well, I'm real glad that yer bein' so cooperative on breakin' yer own curse. Not many ghosts can attest to that. But first things first: you gotta help me get that hangin' couple down outta that invisible tree."

The Drageist nodded in approval. "IT SOUNDS SIMPLE ENOUGH. I FEEL THAT IF I FOLLOW YOU AND STAY CLOSE TO YOUR LIVING MIND, I COULD AT LEAST GET TO LEAVE THIS PLACE TEMPORARILY."

Will grasped his chin. "Well, there's problem, though. I was hopin' fer a fire breathin' dragon ghost that could *burn* through the rope. Yer winterfire can't do that."

The Drageist blinked several times before saying "I CAN STILL BITE THROUGH THE ROPE, YOU IDIOT!"

"So, it just agreed to help you?" Ivy asked for the third time since Will had returned.

"Near as I can tell," Will answered with a shrug and took a big bite out of his sandwich.

They sat across from each other at a small table in *The Country Kitchen Dinner*. Will told her everything over plates of pumpkin bread sandwiches and goat milk.

Ivy picked at her food. "And it burrowed under the ground and promised to follow you all the way to the hanged lovers?"

Will chewed what he could and swallowed hard. "Yes an' no. Judgin' by its shovel-snout, it was probably a burrower in life. But since it's a ghost, it just slid into the ground without even leavin' a mark. Soon as we get done here, I'm gonna take you home an' set up camp by the hangin' site."

"Can I go?" she asked, her eyes lighting with the prospect.

Will took a drink of milk and shook his head. "Nope. If you meet the dragon's stare, you could die of fright. It's an evil thing. Worst kinda evil, too. It's a hero in its own mind." There was an annoyed rumble from under the floorboards. Will looked down and stomped his large foot. "Quiet down you! I ain't asked fer you yet. You jus' sit tight an' let me continue my chat with the lady."

"Do you trust it?" she asked, looking down with worry.

"Little bit," he replied. "It wants free from that cave an' it believes I can help it. Fer some odd reason, it's able to leave the cave by tagging along with me."

Ivy shook her head and whispered. "Don't you know the story of Tram-Law the deceiver? Dragons can never be trusted! They are master bluffs and creative liars!" She looked around at the mostly empty diner before adding "Besides, freeing it might do more harm than good. I've read that dragon souls don't shatter and dissipate like ours. They actually stay intact after death and are eventually reborn somewhere else. Who's to say this dragon isn't some incarnation of Tram-Law himself? Will..." she placed a hand on his. Her touch was soft and strong. "Will, maybe the entire reason for the Geohex is to keep this monster imprisoned."

A thin spike of doubt shot through Will's heart and mind.

271

"The lady's got a point," he thought. He reached for his glass of milk and found that it was now frozen solid.

He and he alone heard the Drageist whisper "I CAN DO THE SAME THING TO HER IF SHE DOESN'T WATCH HER MOUTH."

Will swallowed and looked at Ivy. He turned the glass over to show her what had happened. "I think we'd better head out." he said. "I need a cigarette."

◈

Will took Ivy back home, ever wary of the slithering presence beneath his feet. It haunted his every step as he made his way to the site of the hanged lovers. Dusk approached, and the twilight of evening painted everything a sickly shade of orange. The air in the woods was still and cold, as if the wind and breeze had frozen in place. Will tread slowly, keeping his ears open. For many minutes, he listened and stepped. Then he stopped and drew his weapons. "You can come out now!"

The Drageist poked its head out of the ground and muttered "I WILL COME OUT WHEN I AM GOOD AND READY, MORTAL."

Will did not even look down. His focus was aimed elsewhere. "I wasn't talkin' to you."

There came a loud bang, and a bullet whizzed past Will's shoulder.

The tendikeye moved like lightning to his left side and ran up the branches of a tall elm. Another shot came, demolishing a branch he had just sprung off of. *"Hunting rifle,"* he thought. It was his last thought before instinct took over.

He reflexively took note of the paths of the last two shots and determined the exact direction they had come from using triangular firearm theory. The junction area of the bullets' paths pointed him to right where the rifle was located.

Leaping to another tree, he fired two shots at a large bush some eighty feet away. By the time he landed on the branch, he heard a man screaming in agony.

"Throw out yer rifle!" Will called out.

No answer or rifle came out. The scream began making gurgling sounds.

"Too good," Will muttered. He ran and leapt his way to the bush, keeping his pistol trained on it the whole time.

When he got there, he found the quivering form of Jarami, the Trotting Swan whose face he had smashed. His rifle lay by this side. There was a bloody hole in his left ribs.

Will kept his gun on him. "A smashed face wudn't good enough fer ya, ya lousy brush popper? If I wanted you dead, I'd'a shot yer head an' not yer bike wheel. Did you really think this was worth dyin' over?"

The Trotting Swan shook his head and coughed. "Not...because...of that! You...you went into the Drageist's cave and came out...alive. I volunteered to be the one..." He wheezed and coughed louder until his eyes rolled back. Then the man was perfectly silent and still.

Will shook his head in confusion. "What'd he mean by all that?" he whispered.

Out of the ground came the head of the Drageist followed by ten feet of neck. "I REMEMBER NOW!" it exclaimed with a happy grin.

"Remember what?" Will asked, annoyed by the monster's cheerfulness.

"HOW I DIED! IT WAS AN AMBUSH! A GROUP OF MERCENARIES WHEELED IN A CANNON AND SHOT ME CLEAN THROUGH THE HEART. IT WAS A WELL TAKEN SHOT, I DARE ATTEST. BUT THAT WAS HOW IT HAPPENED. AND I BELIEVE THAT AFFILIATES OF THIS MAN WERE THE MERCS WHO DID IT."

Will nodded. "You don't say," he said, checking the ammunition in the rifle. There were three shots left.

"I *DO* SAY!" declared the Drageist. "THEY WERE ALL DRESSED LIKE THIS DRAKERI. I THOUGHT IT STRANGE, WEARING CLOTHING THE SAME COLOR OF ONE'S OWN SKIN. OF COURSE, I'VE ALWAYS THOUGHT CLOTHES WERE STRANGE. I REMEMBER THEIR BELT BUCKLES BARING THE STANDARD OF A LARGE FOWL."

273

Will arched a quilled eyebrow. "Trotting Swan's killed you? With a cannon? Was this man one of them?"

The Drageist tilted its head and squinted. "I AM NOT SURE. HIS FACE IS RATHER MANGLED. I DON'T KNOW. MAYBE. PROBABLY."

Will shook his head and sighed. "Okay then. I'll jus' bear that in mind fer now." He sheathed his blade and picked up the dead man's rifle. It was of shoddy make compared to his *Falcona*.

"TAKE HIS MONEY, TOO!" the Drageist said excitedly. "MAKE IT LOOK LIKE A ROBBER DID IT."

Will shrugged a shoulder and smirked. "Such a thing would dishonor the dead, wouldn't it?" He then knelt down to empty the man's pockets. The Drageist laughed.

"HOW MUCH IS ON HIM?"

Will counted out a small handful of coins to himself. "Not enough fer him to miss."

The Drageist laughed again even harder. "YOU AMUSE ME, YOUNG TENDIKEYE! HERE, I BID YOU STEP ASIDE. I'VE A TRICK TO SHOW YOU."

Will backed off several paces, watching the monster's ugly head hover over the corpse. Its horrific mouth opened, releasing a large gout of white flame that engulfed the body for a long moment.

As soon as the beast was done, it turned to Will and urged "SHOOT IT NOW! BEFORE IT THAWS! DO IT!"

Will took aim with the newly acquired rifle and, with reluctance, fired. The body exploded, clothing and all, into millions of tiny grains of frosty tissue. It looked like a scattered pile of reddish purple sand. Will took one look at it and barfed up his pumpkin bread sandwich before he could even lurch forward.

"GOOD IDEA!" laughed the Drageist as it watched Will retch. "IT WILL HELP ATTRACT MORE ANIMALS FOR WHEN THIS MESS THAWS OUT."

Will wiped his mouth and grimaced in disgust and anger. "That's sick! That's unnatural! That's...that's..."

"PRACTICAL? COLD-BLOODED?" the monster asked, baring its fangs in a sly grin. "NATURE SHALL *ABSORB* THESE REMAINS IN A MATTER OF DAYS. EVEN LESS IF IT RAINS. I DID

274

YOU A FAVOR, YOUNG TENDIKEYE. NOW, LET US SEE ABOUT SETTING THOSE DOOMED LOVERS FREE, YES?"

They waited in the clearing until Will's watch hit 7:50. The witching hour had come.

The air filled with necrofear, but it did not bother Will as bad as the last time. Having a gargantuan dragon ghost coiled by his side probably helped him cope.

When the two lovers and the gang that murdered them appeared, Will converted any fear he felt into a calm cold rage. It was rage for the fact that ghosts even existed. Death was supposed to mean the end of suffering, not the prolonging of it.

He sat silently against an old oak watching the Drageist as the murder scene unfolded. The monster observed with studious curiosity as the men bound the lover's wrists.

"THESE MEN...THEY ARE NOT GHOSTS," the Drageist explained to Will in a deep whisper. "THEY ARE MERELY PROJECTIONS OF THE LOVERS' FEARFUL MEMORIES."

Will crossed his arms and grimaced. "Ya think that maybe you could bite the rope *before* them two are hanged?"

The Drageist grunted in the negative. "I WISH TO SEE HOW THIS PLAYS OUT."

The hangman tightened the noose around the lover's necks and glared at the woman bitterly. "You're a sick woman, Maise, for mingling blood with this round ear. You think it's decent to bring children into the world, knowing full well that you are going to *out-live them*?" He slapped her across the face. "Human blood is a disease, Maise. You know that. You know that, and you didn't even care. You don't deserve to be a mother." He looked at his friends, ignoring the woman's cries. "Let's get this over with!"

The Drageist laughed as the gang of men hoisted the lovers up. "FOOLISH MORTALS! HUMANS LIVE A HUNDRED, DRAKERI LIVE A THOUSAND, HALFBREEDS LIVE FIVE HUNDRED. BUT ALL SUCH LIFETIMES ARE STILL MERE BLINKS IN TIME. WHAT

275

DOES THE SHORTENED LIFE OF A CHILD MATTER WHEN NOTHING EVER REALLY CHANGES? EVEN IF IT LIVED ONLY TO BE A TODDLER, WOULD IT BE SUCH A WASTED LIFE IF IT WAS AT LEAST HAPPY WHILE IT LIVED?"

Will gave no answer as the lovers were pulled up, kicking and choking. But the Drageist's words would live with him until his dying day.

When the gang of murderers disappeared, he got up and walked over to the spot where the woman had tried to talk to him. "Maise?" he said to the corpse-ghost as it hung still. "Maise, it's me from the yesternight. I brought help this time."

The woman did not respond.

"Maise, please wake up, girl," he told her.

The woman's eyes shifted once more to tendikeye.

"Cut'em down," he told the Drageist.

The beast complied by gently nipping the knot of the noose. As slow as paint runs down a wall, the lovers descended to the ground.

The man stepped and turned so that he could meet the eyes of his beloved. With sad, tired eyes he kissed her gently on the temple.

She smiled softly and kissed his mouth before whispering "It's okay," into his ear. She looked once more at Will and nodded.

In a slow, dreamy voice she said, "Brice Norred. Claytonn Morre, and his brother Entwan. Iry Dwas. And Rusty Feldurhau. These are the men that killed us. The caven trees saw fit to keep us as ghosts, so that one day a hero would witness our demise and offer us justice."

"I'll do it," Will told her, placing a large hand on his chest. "Where are those cowards hidin'? I'll make sure they regret this."

The ghost woman frowned. "They are all hiding beneath the ground. In graves. It was so, so long ago."

Will shook his head. "So, how am I s'posed to avenge you an' free you both?"

The woman looked around as if listening to several voices. "The caven trees are appalled to have their roots in the same soil as those men. You must find their graves, extract their bones, and burn them. You must then plant in each emptied grave a single

276

caven nut."

Will took a deep breath. "That sure is a lot to ask, miss."

"It is," she agreed. "The graves can all be found in and around Pevulanium. Please, Will Foundling. You have come further than any other. Complete this task and necrofear will ever conquer you again."

Will looked up to see the Drageist smiling at him. "I WILL GLADLY ASSIST YOU. MY SPIRITUAL LIBERATION CAN WAIT."

Will sighed through his hawk-like nose. He did not trust this monster. He looked back to the ghosts and swore, "I'll get it taken care of. You got my word on that."

Will looked back at the ghost lovers. They gazed at him with sad, tired, but hopeful eyes. He scratched the back of his neck and looked at the woman's swollen belly. "Even if I do this, the way you were wronged won't ever be set right. Those men got to live out their lives, while you both...I mean you *three* hung here cursed."

The lovers began to fade away as the woman replied, "Those men were cursed as well. You will find that their remains will not be so cooperative when you extract and burn them. We thank you, Will Foundling. And good luck!"

With that, the lovers were gone.

Will hunkered down and sat cross-legged, thinking about the magnitude of his day. It had been full of death and cold. He was hungry, but felt too sick to eat.

The Drageist regarded him and sighed. "GET SOME SLEEP, YOUNG TENDIKEYE. I WILL MEET YOU AT MY CAVE IN THE MORNING. WE HAVE GRAVES TO ROB." It then sunk and slithered into the ground without making a sound or disturbing a single leaf.

Since childhood Will had been a terrible liar. His mind lacked the creativity and imagination required to forge a good falsehood and tell it like one actually believed it. When it came to combat, deception came easy. But in social situations, the truth was all he could ever rely on. And as he grew, he found that he hated lies

277

and secrets as much as anything, for his entire life had been composed of them. And so, when he returned to the home of Daiv Tchanly and his daughter, Ivy, he left nothing out on what had transpired on their property.

"Are ye sure no one will find the body of that Trotting Swan?" Daiv questioned while sipping coffee in his favorite chair. The old tendikeye sat hunched and troubled.

Will nodded to the old man's question. "The hunveins ain't visible tonight. Clouds overhead. The comin' rain'll wash it all away."

Daiv set his cup down on the table next to the shoddy rifle taken from the dead man. He closed his eyes and cradled his head in thought.

Ivy, who sat on the couch swing nearby asked, "So, if he didn't try to kill you for shooting his bike...? Did he really say it was because you entered and left the Drageist's cave?"

"Yep. His last words," Will answered. "I'm sorry this had to happen on yer land."

Daiv let out a nervous laugh. "Was there no one else with him? This area is full of eyes and ears."

"He was alone," Will assured him. "But him bein' missin', his friends'll figure him fer dead soon enough. I reckon I got a lot of dung to dig through 'fore I find out more. The Drageist said that Trotting Swan's killed him sometime after the Omni-War over two thousand years back. They hold the secret to why the dragon became an' stayed a ghost fer so long."

"How ye figure?" Daiv asked.

"Because they think I uncovered some clue from the cave. And I did, a little bit. Me an' the Drageist are gonna figure the rest out."

"You shouldn't trust that thing," Daiv warned, his mouth tight and face reddening.

"I trust that it wants to be free," Will countered. "Way I see it, me an' that monster got the same goal an' the same enemy: endin' the Geohex an' the Trottin' Swans."

"You can't take on the entire gang, boy. There are at least a dozen in this town alone."

Will shrugged. "My pistol happens to hold a dozen bullets. Mind if I smoke, or have I worn out my welcome here?"

Daiv opened his mouth in anger, but his rage soon melted into weariness. "I need a drink. A real one. This coffee ain't helpin' me the way I need it to. Who else wants one?"

Will and Ivy raised a hand as the old man made his way to the liquor cabinet.

Ivy looked at Will for a moment. She got up from the couch and stretched out her arms and wings with a long yawn. "It's late. I'm tired. I'm going with you to find those graves tomorrow."

Will shook his head. "The Drageist don't like you, Ivy. It threatened to freeze you solid at the diner."

"Why would it do that?"

"It didn't like how you were talkin' about it. It could freeze you with its breath or kill you with its sight."

Ivy sneered and put her fists on her hips. "Then tell it I'll stop talking about it in a bad way. I'm tagging along whether you like it or not. This is my town, not yours. I'll go where I please. Besides, if the Swans want trouble, they got trouble coming!"

Before Will could argue, Daiv returned with the drinks. More pepperwine.

"Daiv," Will pleaded. "Tell yer daughter that it'll be too dangerous fer her to tag along."

Daiv laughed and handed him a cup. "Me tell *her* what to do? Heh! That's a good'n. In case yer eyes've failed you: she's a grown woman."

Ivy smiled smugly, took her drink, and downed it in one pull. "I'm takin' this with me when we go." She picked up the rifle on the table.

"What are you gonna do with that?" Daiv asked. "The second a Swan recognizes it, they might start trouble."

"Let'em," she answered back. "I've killed men before. Remember those nut thieves I got back when I was fourteen?" She looked at Will before her father could respond. "There was two of 'em, right? Stealing our caven nuts! They already had several sacks full when Daddy confronted them. I hid in some nearby brush, waiting quietly with Daddy's deer rifle. As soon as they saw and heard him coming, they began pulling their guns. I didn't wait. BANG! BANG! Done, just like that. We reported to Sheriff Poge, and she and her deputies hauled off the mess. And that was that."

Will searched her pretty eyes for self-doubt and found none.

279

"Fair enough then, Ivy. We'll head out at daybreak. But you follow my lead."

She smiled with a sly determination that gave Will a warm tingle.

"*She may not be from the homecell,*" he thought. "*but she's still one hot little biscuit!*"

Daiv sat down his chair with a strained groan. He downed his cup and let out an uneasy sigh. "Would that I were younger, or at least more spry. I'd accompany you both."

Will shook his head and smiled. "No need, sir. Yer needed to hold down the fort in case them rottin' Swans come lookin' fer their buddy."

The old tendikeye chuckled. "A rottin' Swan is better'n a Trottin' Swan."

Will grinned. "Well put, old timer. Well put."

Will and Ivy embarked in the morning when the hunveins above were too bright to be distinguished from one another. At Will's behest, they took the long way around Pevulaneum, running through every patch of woods they could thread themselves through.

Ivy did her best to keep up with the young man. It was not a question of endurance, but raw speed. Were they on an open plain, she would use her wings to lighten her steps and propel her inertia. But in the thick, winding woods her wings only got in the way. While Will, wingless and accustomed to brush running, seemed to slither through the brambles and thickets without slowing down. Her wool clothes would get snagged on thistles and branches, while his smooth scaled dust coat went through the underbrush undisturbing and undisturbed.

A sharp bur went into her mouth. She spat it out and asked in a growling whisper, "Why can't we just run branches?"

"Can't risk bein' spotted. We gotta get to the Drageist first before we enter town."

"Why?"

Will sighed through his nose. "I hate to admit it, but the dang thing just might come in handy."

As they neared the location of the cave, Will stopped. Ivy, caught unaware, ran into him, sending them both face-first onto the ground. Before she could even open her mouth, she felt his hard, rough hand clasp over her lips. She turned her head so her eyes could meet his.

His face was grim as he mouthed the word, "Quiet."

She nodded and he slowly removed his hand, brushing her lip. She made no sign of liking the feeling, but she did.

Will pointed to what he had spotted just in time. Through the tangling jumble of stunted trees, clinging vines, and slow wrestling plants, a small patch of purple could be seen. And beyond that patch was the hill that led up to the Drageist's cave.

With the utmost care, the two tendikeye inched their way toward the purple patch until Will made the gesture to stop. Ivy could see him now, a Trotting Swan facing out of the brush with his rifle facing toward the warning sign at the hill's base. The drakeri man made a grunt of discomfort as he shifted from resting on one knee to the other. His back was perfectly exposed.

Ivy tapped Will on the shoulder and raised her rifle in silent question. Will shook his head and mouthed the words, "Stay here."

She nodded in reply and watched as Will stalked his way toward the kneeling Swan. Her heart began to race when she saw that Will's hands were empty. *"What is he doing?"* she thought.

It happened in an instant. Will's cautious steps turned into a burst of silent speed. Like a constrictor snake on an unsuspecting mouse, Will had a hold of the rifleman, his right arm coiled tightly around the man's neck, while his left arm had him locked in a half-nelson. The man twitched and jerked for a few seconds, but Will showed no sign of budging. The only sound that was made was the man's legs kicking the soft dirt. Will whispered something to the man, and the man went still. Will's right arm loosened just a little and the man let out a gagging whisper. An exchange of whispers followed between the two men for about a minute until Will once more tightened his arm.

The Trotting Swan kicked and struggled for several sickening seconds until he at last went limp. Without looking back, Will made a gesture for Ivy to proceed.

281

"Is he dead?" she asked as she drew near.

"No," Will replied as he emptied the man's rifle. "Just out cold. Should be fer a while." He then reached down and grabbed the unconscious man by the wrist and forearm. With a fast, jerking twist, he caused the limb to pop until the hand dangled limply from the wrist.

Ivy felt like vomiting at the sight and sound of such a gruesome deed. "You broke his wrist!"

"Nope," Will said with a grin. "I *dislocated* it. This fella was very helpful in answerin' my questions an' concerns. So, rather than kill him, I'm just cripplin' him a bit." He then reached down and repeated the same motion on the other wrist.

"I think I'm gonna throw up," Ivy sighed as she covered her eyes.

Will laughed softly. "No need, Miss Ivy. Once this fella comes to, he'll be in enough pain to empty his own guts."

Ivy shook her head and covered her mouth. "You don't understand," she said with a nauseous burp. "I feel it wanting to come up."

"Okay, then," Will sighed with a shrug. He took her shoulder and guided her over to the unconscious Swan. "Puke on *him* then! I dare ya! Go ahead, let her rip!"

Ivy's eyes grew wide as her face jerked in Will's direction. "What?!" she cried.

Will grinned. "Just make sure you aim fer the body. Pukin' in his face might wake him up...or worse yet, drown him."

Ivy looked at him in disgust. "I am not doing that!"

"Why not? He could do with a little more non-lethal misery when he wakes up. Just think about it: fer the rest o' his natural life he'll tell people *'Don't mess with tendikeye! They'll dislocate your wrists and puke on ya when yer sleepin'!'*" He ended his words with a dopey expression that caused Ivy to erupt with laughter.

"You are such a dork!" she laughed.

Will arched an eyebrow. "Looks like yer feelin' better now."

"Yes. Yes, thank you. What did he tell you before you choked him out?"

Will pointed to the southeast. "He informed me about his buddy's whereabouts, just on the other side o' the path that leads to the Drageist's hill. I need you to stay here an' stand guard while I

282

give that other guy the same treatment. If you hear gunshots, it means he heard me comin', and I had to kill him. Either way, I'll be back in a jiffy."

She gasped in astonishment. "Gee-manetnee! The Swans were actually waiting for us to come here. They really don't want you making contact with the Drageist. But why?"

Will pointed down at the defeated Swan. "This guy didn't know. I don't think the next one will either. Daddy Long Legs gave 'em the order to whack me." He turned to leave. "Be right back." He felt her hand tug at his sleeve.

"Not just yet," she whispered softly, pulling him toward her.

Will went along with her pull and found himself pressed against her. Their eyes met for a few seconds, and then their lips met for a few seconds more. It was not a kiss of new found love, nor was it completely an act of lust. It was mostly just a celebration of the moment. And when Ivy opened her eyes, Will was gone.

❖

Will returned a few minutes later.

Ivy had heard no gunshots while he was away. "Did the second one tell you anything different?" she asked.

Will shrugged. "Said his name was Greg, he had a wife and three little girls. He didn't want to die. Just followin' orders, yak yak yak."

"Did you knock him out and *dislocate* his wrists, too?"

"Dern tootin'," he answered. "He seemed like the good family man type fer bein' a cold-blooded backshooter. C'mon."

They went to the foot of the haunted hill. Ivy waited by the old warning sign as Will made his way back up to the cave entrance.

When he got there, he found the Drageist's head facing out from the shadows. The monster's face no longer disturbed him. But the fact that the beast knew he was coming made his soul itch.

The Drageist spoke. "YOU HAVE ARRIVED. GOOD. I FOUND SOMETHING. COME INSIDE."

Without pause, the beast curved its great neck, pointing its head inward, and slithered back into the cave.

283

Will followed, resenting being told what to do. Before stepping fully into the shadow of the entrance, he turned and shouted down to Ivy "Hold on! I'll be right back."

As he turned to continue his way in, to his shock and surprise, the Drageist's massive face was mere inches from his own. "YOU BROUGHT YOUR FEMALE WITH YOU?" the monster growled accusingly.

Will spat on the side of the rocky entrance. "Yeah, an' you'd better get used to it," he answered with chilled breath. "Like you, I'm *lettin'* her come along on *my* investigation. An' jus' like yesternight, yer gonna keep in the dirt, unseen an' heard only by my ears. You hear me, dragon?"

The Drageist's eyes blazed with white fire. It opened its mouth, but Will cut it off by adding, "And if you decide to slither outta line an' do somethin' to throw off my aim, such as murderin' an innocent, then I'll call off figurin' out yer problem. You'll be stuck in this cave another thousand years, denied the glory o' life, bein' nothin' but a local spook in a poor town. You got ear holes on that ugly head o' yers?"

The Drageist blinked and made a disturbing rumbling sound that may have been laughter. "VERY WELL, YOUNG TENDIKEYE. THOUGH NONE OF YOU TWO-LEGGED ABOMINATIONS ARE INNOCENT, I WILL HEED YOUR WARNING AND SUBMIT TO YOUR DEMAND. YOU HAVE THE MAKINGS OF A FINE TYRANT, AND I CAN RESPECT THAT."

Will followed the beast deep into its cave. On the farmost wall the monster used its snout to point at a huge layer of ice which had formed over the rock.

"OBSERVE," the monster said. "THIS PATCH OF WALL IS DIFFERENT THAN THE REST. CAN YOUR MORTAL EYES SEE WHY?"

Will peered into the luminous section of frozen water. It was in two layers. The outermost layer was smooth, crystal clear ice. The innermost layer was full of small cracks in a pattern like a spiderweb. The cracks led up to a hole in the rock itself. The hole was almost perfectly round, about the size of Will's large fist. Will had fired hundreds of bullets in his young life, bullets which had hit all manner of targets, including solid rock. This looked like one of

284

them.

"Cannonball?" Will asked.

The monster nodded. "THE VERY SAME THAT SLEW ME ALL THOSE YEARS AGO. IT PIERCED MY HEART AND IMBEDDED ITSELF IN THE ROCK OF THIS CAVERN. I...SENSE...THAT IT HAS SOMETHING TO DO WITH MY STILL BEING HERE."

"How ya figure?"

"I AM ONE WITH THE ELEMENTS, ESPECIALLY THE SOIL, ROCK, AND MINERALS. WHATEVER IS IN THAT HOLE, IT IS NOT MADE FROM IRON. IT HAS NOT RUSTED, CORRODED, OR ERODED IN ANY WAY. AND..."

"And...?"

"AND I CANNOT GET TO IT!" the Drageist admitted bitterly. "I CANNOT EVEN MELT OR SHIFT MY OWN ICE OUT OF THE WAY, MUCH LESS THE ROCK ITSELF. I NEED YOU TO DO IT FOR ME."

Will nodded. "Okay, I will in due time. We got business to attend to."

"BUT I WANT YOU TO GET IT NOW!" the monster growled. "NOW THAT I KNOW WHAT IS KEEPING ME HERE, I NO LONGER WISH TO STAY! USE YOUR GUNS TO BLAST THE ICE AND YOUR SWORD TO PICK AND PRY IT OUT."

Will shook his head. "They ain't the right tools fer the job. 'Sides, I ain't wastin' my bullets an' keen edge fer no cannonball."

"BUT IT IS SPECIAL, I SENSE IT!"

"Well, that's all fine an' dandy, dragon. But first thing's first. Let's get to findin' them graves!"

The Drageist sighed icy fire out its snout. For the first time, it looked weary and old.

He looked at the tendikeye standing far below him. "I SHAN'T SUFFER THE LIFE OF A SLAVE, YOUNG TENDIKEYE. I WANT TO REST AND BE REBORN. IF I ASSIST YOU IN FINDING THESE GRAVES, DO I HAVE YOUR WORD, YOUR WORD OF HONOR, THAT YOU WILL TAKE OUT THAT BALL FROM THE WALL?"

Will felt sympathy for the beast. "I give you my word," he

285

swore.

The Drageist exposed a hundred fangs in a wicked grin. "SPLENDID!" it exclaimed with wicked fervor. "THEN THAT MEANS THAT SOON I WILL BE FREE OR YOU WILL BE DEAD! HARK AND MARK ME, YOUNG TENDIKEYE: IF YOU BREAK YOUR WORD, THEN MY WINTERFIRE BREATH WILL FREEZE YOU SOLID!"

Will regarded the gloating monster. "I got nuthin' to fear from you, ya freak of nature. I don't lie, cheat, or deceive when it comes to agreements. If that cannonball really is the key to yer release, then we'll be rid of each other good an' soon."

Will stepped back out into the light of day. Several feet below his boots, the Drageist slithered along in the hard ground.

Ivy waited patiently at the bottom of the hill wearing worry on her face. "I saw them head back up the road. The men you choked out and crippled," she said.

"How long?" Will asked.

"Couple minutes ago. They were moaning and crying the whole time."

"Headache and messed up wrists'll do that. I wouldn't worry. They'll go to town an' go to their homes or the closest relatives first. Word'll spread shortly after. Daddy Long Legs himself or maybe another swan might take a shot at me out in the open."

She shook her head. "What then?"

"We kill 'em. So, if you wanna turn away from this an' mind yer pappy..."

She swallowed and shook her head once more.

Will sighed. "Thank you for yer help, Miss Ivy."

She smiled. "Ha! I ain't helping you. You're helping me, me and this whole town. The swans need to go and stay gone."

"AND SO DO I!" the Drageist roared impatiently. "BY MY STOLEN BONES, YOU TWO ANNOY ME TO NO END!"

Will stomped on the ground. "Cork yer hole, dragon! You ain't got no fears o' dyin'. These swans mean business. We got to go search all throughout this town lookin' fer five specific graves while makin' sure we don't catch a bullet in our skulls."

The Drageist grumbled. "SO, YOU ARE PARANOID ABOUT THE ONES IN PURPLE? I CAN DEAL WITH THEM. JUST LET ME

SEARCH THROUGHOUT THE TOWN AND I CAN FREEZE THEM ONE BY ONE. THEY SHOULD BE EASY TO SPOT."

Will admitted to himself that the offer was tempting. But deep down he still knew that the swans were men, men with families. Perhaps they had done evil things. And he himself was not the fairest of fighters, for that matter. But to give the order to deliver so much death to so many people that he did not even know, it was simply not in him to do so.

"No thanks," he told the Drageist. "My druther is to let each of 'em pick livin' or dyin'. If I see guns in their hands, I'll put bullets in their bodies. If they pull a blade, I'll pull mine an' make 'em eat it. An' if they try to be fancy assassins like them last two boys, I'll ferget mercy an' dislocate their skulls from their spines."

"TOUGH TALK, MORTAL," the Drageist rumbled from beneath Will's boot. "ARE YOU SAYING ALL THIS TO REASSURE ME AND THE FEMALE THAT YOU CAN HANDLE IT? OR PERHAPS YOU SEEK TO REASSURE YOURSELF?"

Will gave no answer.

The two tendikeye and the monster in the ground under their feet went straight to town.

Part 3

When they reached the border of Pevulanium, six armed Trotting Swans stood in the road. Others sat on velocipedes, but they dismounted when the two tendikeye came into view. By their stances, Will could tell they meant business.

The one Swan that towered above them all, Daddy Long Legs, gently brushed the brim of his hat with his finger. The other men reluctantly followed suit. It was a salute, but every man's eyes boiled with hate.

Will inclined his head, returning the show of respect. But he knew it was just a show. He and Ivy stopped about eighty feet from the gang. He saw Daddy Long Legs' eyes shift from his own rifle to

287

the rifle in Ivy's hands.

Daddy sighed and shook his head. "Jarami was a family man," he said dryly. "He has a son of twelve years. The boy should have his father's rifle."

Will shrugged. "I suppose so," he replied, lowering his eyes. Then his gaze shot back up, cold and serious. "What'll ya give me fer it?"

Many of the Swans raised their guns in anger, but Daddy Long Legs motioned for them to stand down. "I will allow you safe passage through this town. Once. And for the lives of the two men, friends of mine, whom you maimed but granted mercy, I will grant Daiv and his daughter Ivy amnesty for your misdeeds, so long as you leave town and stay gone."

"I made friends with the Drageist," Will said with a daring grin. He watched as Daddy's eyes grew wide. "Well, not friends per se. More like allies. He told me about how you Swan's killed him with a cannon, or was that yer gran' pappies who did that? Musta been a while back, even fer you Drakeri."

The Swans looked at each other nervously. Will's ears caught someone murmur "He knows too much, Daddy!"

"Yeah, I know plenty already!" Will shouted, parting his dust coat to show his steel. "And I intend to find out the rest. And there ain't a dang thing you bike peddlin', mud-humpin', poison sellin' bastards can do about it!"

Daddy Long Legs took a long step forward, his eyes cold and longing to take life. "Then take my challenge, you little prickly headed dung-skin! I'll plant you in my garden like all the other trouble makers who've roused my hand!"

Will spat in the dirt. "You really want to kill me in a fair duel, don't ya? That's where you excel, idn't it?"

Daddy raised his chin. "That is how civilized men settle their conflicts. Can you be a gentleman just this once, savage?"

"WILL", the Drageist said below, addressing him by his name for the first time. "I SENSE THAT IF I BREATHED ON HIM, HE WOULD NOT FREEZE. HE IS HONEST."

Will sighed and crossed his arms. "Okay then, Daddy. Tell ya what. Give me three days, startin' tomorrow, to conduct my investigation on this Geohex ya'll Swans seem to want to keep on

288

the land. An' then after that, we pull steel at one another, I'll either share what I've found with my friends or take it with me in death. Sound good?"

Daddy Long Leg's hate-filled eyes changed into a look of pure bliss and relief. His smile was bright, and all pride and malice seemed to vanish without trace. Will's words made him happy. Letting out a laugh of pure elation, he strode up to the tendikeye and offered a courteous bow. "I promise you, Mr. Foundling, you will not regret this deal!"

Will smiled and returned the bow.

"Because you'll be dead!" Daddy laughed.

Will laughed along with him and raised his finger, indicating that he got the man's joke. "Either way, Daddy, you'll be rid of me."

Ivy's jaw dropped, watching these two men so tense with opposition moments before, acting like friends.

Daddy laughed again and gave Will a friendly pat on the shoulder. "You are a dead-man-walking, young sir. And it is not in my facility to hate a dead man. I consider Jarami and the others already avenged. Therefore, will you have one of your last meals at my home? Tomorrow night? My wife will make a pot roast that will curl your quills."

"Sounds good," Will agreed. "But I only eat hunted meat. My apologies to you and the Mrs."

Daddy took off his hat. "No, *my* apologies. I should have known better. But do come anyway. I'll have her fix you something else."

"You got yerself another deal, Daddy."

Daddy gave Will another pat on the shoulder and kept his hand there. "If you break your word and leave town, we'll kill the girl and the old man, and burn down their tree house. That means no more caven nut butter." He looked at Ivy and grinned.

"It won't come to that," Will assured him.

Daddy Long Legs reached into his money pouch and took out ten fifty grotz coins. He offered them to Will with the words "Take these for Jarami's rifle. It's at least four times the gun's worth. Keep these coins safe on your person until after our duel. I aim to get them back off your corpse."

Will nodded and looked over at Ivy who reluctantly gave up

289

the gun.

With the deal done, Daddy Long Legs and his men took their leave.

Will and Ivy stood in silence on the edge of town for well over a minute. Once the last Swan was out of sight, Will felt something big and heavy slam into the side of his head. By the time his shoulder hit the dirt, he realized that it had been Ivy's foot.

"You fool!" Ivy yelled, standing over him. "Daddy Long Legs never loses a gun duel! He will kill you. You may be Harker, but this won't be no game of seek and find!"

Will got up, showing no sign of injury. "Yeah, you just let me worry about that, Miss Ivy. I understand yer upset I gave yer new gun back, but—"

His words were cut short as she threw up another boot to his head.

Seeing it coming, Will dropped to a squat, spun around with his leg extended, and swept out her supporting leg. Ivy dropped solid onto the dirt.

As Will rose up out of his spin, she was already back on her feet. Growling, she grasped him by the collar and tried to pull his head down into her rising knee. But his own hands stopped the knee from coming up. Will then felt her wings bashing into the side of his head like a flurry of hook punches. More annoyed than hurt, he grasped her by the knee and pulled her down onto the ground in a complicated leg lock from which there was no escape.

"Calm down, girl!" he told her.

"Let me go!" she hollered back.

"Ivy, I promise you, if you stop kickin' my ass I'll let go o' this pretty o' leg o' yers. Now, I'm sorry about givin' him the gun back."

"This isn't about the gun, you dimwit!"

"I know! I know! I shouldn'ta promised that duel."

"He'll kill you!"

Will rolled his eyes and let her go. He took several steps away as she got back up to her feet. He tried to smile and shrugged. "It'll be okay, Ivy. You'll see."

Ivy took several deep breaths. She was too angry to speak. Turning away from him, she ran and leapt her way to the direction of her home.

290

The Drageist rumbled with laughter as its evil eyes poked out from the ground. "IT HAS BEEN TOO LONG SINCE I WITNESSED A TENDIKEYE MATING DANCE, YOUNG MORTAL! HER HARD STRIKES WERE GREAT INDICATION OF HER LIKING OF YOU. BUT I AM CURIOUS, DO YOU REALLY THINK YOU CAN BEST THAT DRAKERI IN A GUN DUEL?"

Will shrugged. "Won't matter none. Bullets can't kill me."

"OH?"

"Nope. Even if he hits me dead-on, I'll just return fire and end his reign of fear. Won't be no honor in it. But he'll cease to be a problem to folks in the future. Most I'll have to worry about is a nasty bruise from the bullet. I was cursed by some lemuertian protection maxim."

The Drageist scoffed. "YOU DIRTY CHEAT. I DO BELIEVE YOU ARE WORTHY OF MY RESPECT, AS MUCH AS I RESENT SAYING SO."

"Believe me then, monster. I resent having it, yer respect that is. Now, let's go grave huntin'."

There were two types of graveyards for Drakeri: warrior sites and family sites. But they find the notion of public grave sites abhorrent, so the locations both kinds were well-kept secrets. Will and the Drageist knew the last names of the five lynchers. It stood to reason to ask people who shared their names where the graves might be.

Will stood on the doorstep of the Morre household. He flicked his cigarette off to the side and knocked on the door. He heard the labored shuffle of footsteps and the door creaked opened. A bent, elderly drakeri woman in a white sweater stood in the doorway, her eyes so wrinkled and shriveled that the inner and outer pupils of her eyes were nearly covered..

"Yes," she greeted them in a shrilly voice. She shook as she spoke, as if she were on the verge of crumbling into a pile of purple dust on her doorstep.

"Uh, afternoon, ma'am. My name is Will Foundling. Are you a relative of Claytonn and Entwan Morre?"

"Claytonn and Entwan Morre, you say?" she asked with a high rattle. She thought for a moment. "Why, they are buried out back with my husband. They were his father's uncles, I think. Long dead before I married into the family. Never met them, but I pulled weeds out around their grave markers enough times. What do you want?"

The Drageist laughed beneath their feet.

Will tried to keep a straight, calm face. "Ma'am, I'm investigatin' the Geohex. Are you familiar with the ghosts of the hanged lovers out in the woods?"

The woman's toothless jaw dropped. She reached out and pinched Will's sleeve. "Come inside now, young man. Please. I'll not have you catch cold or attract the neighbor's attention. Come in now."

Will stepped inside and obeyed the woman when she motioned for him to sit in an old rocking chair.

She made him a cup of *hawklash* tea, then sat down in a chair facing him and met his eyes with a dire stare. "The Morre's are a good, upstanding family," she stated. "At least, they were when I married one of them. No one, and I mean *no one* outside of the family knows about what Claytonn and Entwan did that horrible night. It was a different time then. They were narrow-minded fools. It was a terrible thing to do, what they did to that poor couple."

Will took a deep breath and glanced at his tea. "Family secret, then?"

She nodded. "My husband, Tym, told me three decades after we joined together. His uncle, Filp, was told by Claytonn himself. Tell me, sir, how did you come to know of Claytonn and Entwan's involvement?"

He told her everything, gradually finishing four full cups of tea as he did. It was early evening by the time he was done.

The old woman, whose name was Egotha, said nothing as she mulled over what the tendikeye had said. "You need to dig them up and burn them then?" she asked.

"Yes, ma'am," he answered. "It's the only way to end the curse."

She looked at the floor and took a deep, troubled breath and

292

sighed through her nose. "I don't know if Tym would approve. They were his kin. I'm all that's left of the Morre's. Tym, bless him, cared not that I worked in Tanglefoot for so long. He cared not that it may have been the reason I was barren. He would not want you to disturb the resting places of his family." She looked back up at Will as she considered it. "But Tym was also an understanding man, now wasn't he? Yes. Yes, he was. Yes, he was."

She got up from her chair, took the tea cup back, and cleared her throat. "There's a shovel in the shed. It's unlocked. In the backyard, you'll find a small path leading to a copse of cypress. In a clearing, you will find them. If they are indeed cursed for their crime, I hope that you can break it."

Will stood up and gave her a respectful bow. "I'll do what I can, ma'am. Thank you."

The old woman turned and shuffled out of the room. "I'm going to bed now. I'd rather not see you again, Mr. Foundling. Goodnight."

❖

Will walked up the small path, shovel in hand. The Drageist slithered along beside him.

"WELL, THAT WAS EASY," the Drageist mused. "DO YOU SUPPOSE SHE MAY BE DYING IN HER SLEEP RIGHT NOW AS WE GO TO EXHUME THE BONES OF HER RELATIVES? PERHAPS YOU SHOULD DIG *HER* A GRAVE AS A SMALL TOKEN OF THANKS."

"Hardy har har!" Will muttered.

The monster's eyes gleamed to see Will so annoyed. "THE PREGNANT GHOST WOMAN SAID THAT THE BONES WOULD NOT BE 'COOPERATIVE' WHEN YOU EXTRACT THEM. WHAT THINK YOU THAT MEANS, YOUNG TENDIKEYE?"

Will shrugged a shoulder. "Don't know fer sure. My guess is the bones jus' might link up, become bonewalkers, an' try to do me in. That's what cursed bones do, right?"

"MORE OFTEN THAN NOT," the Drageist agreed. "THE

293

ERODED SOUL MAY WILL THE BONES TO MOVE AND RESIST BEING DESTROYED. IT IS A SHAME THAT MY REMAINS WERE REMOVED FROM MY DEATHPLACE. I COULD HAVE CONTROLLED MY BONES TO KILL YOU."

Will grinned without looking at the monster. "Ingrate. Then you'd still be in that haze o' confusion, not even knowin' yer dead."

The Drageist smiled and nodded. "YES, YES. QUITE TRUE. I SURMISE THAT YOUR INNATE STUBBORNNESS IS PSYCHICALLY CONTAGIOUS, AND THAT IS WHY YOUR PRESENCE HELPS TO PREVENT ME FROM FORGETTING."

They came upon an orderly cluster of thirteen grave markers all facing south. This was done to keep the north wind from eroding the names, dates, and epitaphs. All the same, most of the grave markers had been worn bare by the winds. It was hard telling which ones belonged to Clayton and Entwan.

"I CAN REMEDY THIS PLIGHT," the Drageist declared with no shortage of ego. Taking its time, the Drageist looked closely at each marker, concentrating in stillness and silence. After several minutes, the beast pointed out two graves with its shovel-shaped snout. "THIS ONE IS ENTWAN MORRE AND THAT ONE IS CLAYTONN MORRE."

"How ya figure?" Will asked.

"I FIGURE NOTHING. THE STONES THEMSELVES HAVE TOLD ME THE WORDS ONCE CHISELED UPON THEM."

"An' you jus' asked them like that?" Will asked, doubt in his voice.

"YES. I MENTALLY CONVERSED WITH THEM. I AM A CREATURE OF THE EARTH, YOU TWO-LEGGED DOLT. DOES IT TRULY SURPRISE YOU THAT I AM GEOPATHIC?"

Will rubbed his face in his palms. "Alright. Alright. Enough with the new words. My brain can't take it! I'll just do my part and get to diggin'."

Will jabbed the head of the old rusted tool into the soft ground dampened from the recent rain. As he levered the flat piece of steel to break loose a chunk of the dead soil, the long wood handle began vibrating. The sudden shaking startled Will into letting go for a second. But defiantly, he grasped the handle again and pried loose the clump of dirt. A feeling of terror and agony surrounded him, as if it were something the grave itself projected. Gritting his teeth, he stabbed again with the shovel and broke another chunk of dirt loose. The grave seemed to wail in pain and madness inside his head, with an intensity that stung his brain, yet he heard no sound. His breathing became labored.

The Drageist looked back and forth at Will and the grave, squinting its evil eyes. "TENDIKEYE, STOP. YOU DO NOT SENSE THINGS AS I DO. THE GRAVE SWELLS WITH AIR-OF-THE-VOID. ZEROTH ENERGY, THE BREATH OF DEATH. IF YOU KEEP DIGGING YOU WILL SURELY DIE."

Will ignored it and shoveled an even larger chunk. Then his eyes went bloodshot. He trembled and gagged. Then he dropped to one knee and retched into the small hole he had made.

The Drageist shook its head in disappointment. "TWICE NOW I'VE SEEN YOU VOMIT, MORTAL."

Will spat and shuddered. "There's gotta be a better way to get these bones out."

The Drageist looked at the mess on the ground. "WELL, OBVIOUSLY DESECRATING THE GRAVE WITH BILE WON'T WORK." It laughed to itself. "NOR WILL SIMPLE DIGGING. THESE TWO GRAVES ARE FRAUGHT WITH THE ESSENCE OF DEATH AND NOTHINGNESS. THE MORE SOIL YOU DISTURB, THE MORE DEATH-BREATH YOU RELEASE. WOULD THAT I HAD AN EARTHLY FORM ONCE MORE. I COULD SHOVEL THIS GRAVE IN SECONDS AND WITHSTAND THE POWER OF IT."

Will stood and shrugged, his face blank of expression. "Well, maybe you can still shovel the negativity out? Then I can jus' shovel the dirt?"

The Drageist glared at him in shock. "THAT IS...A RATHER STUPID SOUNDING IDEA. YET, FOR SOME REASON...OR NO REASON AT ALL...IT MAKES SENSE. I'VE WONDERED A TIME OR TWO IN MY MANY INCARNATIONS HOW ONE GHOST COULD OR WOULD INTERACT WITH ANOTHER. YOU STUMBLED ACROSS AN INTERESTING IDEA, YOUNG TENDIKEYE, IN SPITE OF YOURSELF."

295

Will scowled and gave a sarcastic nod of thanks.

The Drageist faced the grave and lowered its shovel-snout into the dirt. The monster's eyes snapped wide, and it stopped still.

"What's the matter?" Will asked.

The beast rammed its head into the dirt of the grave like a swan spearing its head for a fish.

Will backed off and drew his weapons without thinking. He could not tell what was happening, at first. But it looked like the Drageist was...feeding. Will froze in fear and fascination.

After a dozen seconds, the beast's head arose from the ground. The cat-like slits that were its pupils had widened to the eye's entire girth. "OH, WHAT A FEELING THIS IS!" the Drageist exclaimed with a shudder.

Slowly, it turned its head and gave Will a smile that sent prickling sensations over the tendikeye's skin.

"I COULD NOT BELIEVE THAT WHICH I COULD NOT FATHOM, BUT THE TRUTH IS SELF-EVIDENT." It laughed low and hoarse and mad.

Will scowled at the beast. "What did you just do?"

"PUT YOUR TOYS AWAY, YOUNG TENDIKEYE. I AM JOYED BY A NEW DISCOVERY. I FELT SOMETHING TUG AT MY SNOUT WHEN I IMMERSED IT IN THE DIRT. NATURALLY, I SNAPPED AT WHATEVER IT WAS. AND TOO MY OWN SURPRISE, IT TASTED DELICIOUS."

"It?" Will asked, his heart filling with dread at the word.

"SOUL. I TASTED SOUL. TASTED AND CONSUMED. IT FOUGHT ME A LITTLE, NOT UNLIKE A CORNERED ANIMAL. BUT I FEEL IT NOW BEING DIGESTED IN MY NOBLE SPIRIT."

"You jus' gulped down a ghost without thinkin' about it first?!"

"I HAVE NOT EATEN IN AGES," the Drageist said. "SERIOUSLY, MORTAL, YOU SHOULD BE HAPPY FOR THE BOTH OF US. I JUST EMPTIED THIS GRAVE OF ITS NEGATIVE ENERGY SO YOU CAN DIG UP THE BONES WITHOUT DYING. I FEEL I AM ENTITLED TO A REWARD."

"But what you did wudn't natural!"

"DON'T LECTURE ME ON NATURE, YOU METAL

296

TORTURING, ROCK BREAKING, SOIL RAPIST. YOU HAVEN'T THE RIGHT. NOW PUT AWAY YOUR FALSE FANGS AND START DIGGING. YOU HAVE BONES TO BURN AND NUTS TO BURY."

Will choked on his rage as he watched the monster turn away and bury its head into the grave of the second brother. He holstered his pistol and sheathed his yashinin machete. He was working beside evil, and he was powerless to stop it. Holding his tongue, he returned to digging up the bones of a murderer.

✧

Drakeri were a long-lived race. There was little reason why, other than legends of fairies and dragons in their bloodline. Whatever the case, it was probably the same reason their corpses decomposed so slowly.

Will's heavy feet had stomped the shovel until nightfall. After two millennia, the skeletons were still intact. The ancient bones of the two brothers had to be plucked from the dirt one at a time. Will worked without distraction or complaint until the job was finished, and he set the bones into two neat piles. After thinking about it, he decided to burn both skeletons together. No sense in being formal. The bones were dry and brittle and needed little more than some dead grass and a kiss from his flip top lighter. Lighting a cigarette with the same flame, he sat down and took in the heat.

"YOU STILL NEED TO BURY THE NUTS, LITTLE SQUIRREL," the Drageist teased.

"I know. I will," the tendikeye said, thinking. He took a long, soul-caressing drag off his cigarette and regarded the monster. "Can I ask you sumpthin', dragon?"

The beast's head perked up. "YOU MAY."

"You think them souls you just ate will shatter like they're s'posed to once I set yer spirit free?"

"WHAT DO YOU CARE? YOU DID NOT KNOW THEM, AND THEY WERE MURDERERS. BESIDES, ENERGY IS ENERGY. IT GROUPS TOGETHER AND BREAKS APART IN STRANGE WAYS, AS IT ALWAYS HAS. I AM A PREDATOR. THEY WERE PREY.

297

THE ONLY DIFFERENCE IS THAT WE ARE ALL GHOSTS."

"Yer a monster," Will said, blowing smoke out.

"HA! AND YOU ARE NOT? I SMELL THE BLOOD ON YOU, AND THE DEATHS YOU CAUSED. AT LEAST I EAT WHAT I KILL. EVENTUALLY."

"Every man I've killed had it comin'," Will argued.

The Drageist smiled and nodded with dark satisfaction. "AS DO WE ALL, YOUNG TENDIKEYE. AS DO WE ALL."

Will sneered and looked back at the bone pyre. His face softened, and he decided to change the subject. "Say, dragon?"

"YES?"

"Is it true that Drakeri come descended from dragons an' fairies?"

The Drageist rolled its eyes and shook its great head. "UTTER NONSENSE. THE VERY NOTION THAT MY RACE WAS THWARTED BY THE SEDUCTIONS OF INSECT-PEOPLE IS INSULTING."

Will thought and grinned. "It'd be pretty embarrasin' if it were true, wouldn't it though?"

The beast growled and bore its many rows of fangs. "I'M GOING BACK TO MY CAVE. HAVE FUN PUTTING ALL THAT DIRT BACK." The Drageist sank back into the ground, leaving the tendikeye alone.

"Hey, Dragon!"

The Drageist's head sighed as it rose back from the ground. "WHAT?"

"Are you sure you remember all the names o' the men we need to dig up?"

"OF COURSE."

"Prove it."

The Drageist groaned and sighed again. "BRICE NORRED, CLAYTON AND ENTWAN MORRE, IRY DWAS, AND RUSTY FELDERHAU. ARE YOU SATISFIED?"

"Yep." Will made it a point to memorize the names this time.

He did not have any fun shoveling the dirt back, as the Drageist had suggested he do. Long into the night, he shoveled by

298

the dying light of the burning bones. When he was nearly done, he took two caven nuts from his pocket and planted them in the empty graves of Claytonn and Entwan Morre. After patting the dirt down with the borrowed shovel, he returned the tool to the shed were he'd gotten it.

By the time he returned to Daiv and Ivy's house, he was too tired to eat, and slept on an empty stomach. And as the world faded away around him, he dreamed of the Drageist swallowing Daddy Long Legs whole; that he was able to kill them both by firing a single well-aimed shot through both of their long, menacing bodies. He did not remember the dream when he woke up.

◈

Daddy Long Leg's house was the largest in town. In fact, it was the former city hall. After years and years of collecting expensive firearms from the hands of those he had killed, the lead dealer made enough to offer the city of Pevulaneum a deal. In exchange for the deed at a reasonable price, the city could buy new building materials for a new building from some of the local, Trotting Swan-owned manufacturers at a discount rate.

The deal went sour, and many of the Swans did not adhere to it. As a result, the new city hall building ended up being half the size of the original. A few city officials, including the mayor, threatened to sue Daddy Long Legs for fraud. Because of a certain ancient town law that allowed any and all disputes to be settled by pistol duel, the matter was soon dropped. The mayor thought it best to simply lose face than lose his entire head.

As Will approached the two-story edifice of red brick and white stone, he surveyed the layout of the property. On all sides were eight ruins of foundations from houses which had been burned down deliberately. Daddy Long Legs did not like having neighbors too close. To the Southeast was a field blanketed by dead oak leaves. And within that field, a gated cemetery. Will squint his eyes to see the words in the wrought iron sign. *The Garden of Fools.*

He approached the tall double-doored entrance of the house and hammered on it with the meat of his fist.

299

The loud dull thuds were soon answered by a smiling drakeri woman in her summer years, not yet middle-aged but no longer youthful. She wore a hideously glamorous dress. Her dark indigo hair was a wadded mass of curls secured by a purple velvet ribbon, the nakedness of her face hidden behind a mask of cosmetics. But other than her decadent sense of fashion, she might have passed for beautiful.

"Mister Foundling, so nice of you to visit!" she said with a smile. Some of her teeth were so crooked, they looked like they were cowering behind each other. "I am Cymbre NcRuse, Daddy's wife."

Will's quilled eyebrow raised. "NcRuse? Is that yer maiden name?"

"It is. Do you know someone else by that name?"

"Did. Not no more though." He peered into her eyes unblinking. His face was neutral and his voice was calm. "I plan on killing your husband, Cymbre. If you are related to the NcRuse that I knew, then maybe it's fer the best that we both don't know how. I'd like a simple, no-strings-attached killin' if you follow my meanin'."

Her smile sharpened. "Won't you please come in?"

"Much obliged, ma'am."

She led him in through a hallway full of glass doors, each one a former office of some public servant. It was an elegant, if not quaint conversion. He saw through the glass that each office had been changed into a parlor of some sort complete with upholstered furniture, tea sets and doilies.

Finally, they came to a spacious room without windows. Will never would have guessed that it had been the old public court room. A grand table had been set for three. There was a basket of hot wheat rolls, a heaping bowl of red apples, and a massive pot of cheesy broccoli and potato soup. At the head of the table sat the man who wanted Will dead.

Daddy Long Legs rose from his seat, offering his hand to the tendikeye, but quickly he withdrew it, remembering that members of Will's race only shook hands with family members.

Will smiled all the same and gave a small bow, which the tall man returned. As the tendikeye's head rose back up, his eyes caught the sight of something that made him gasp in fright.

Hanging high upon the wall was a skull mounted to a placard board. It was not a yellowish, white skull composed of

300

calcium, but a silvery, white skull composed of scandium. The skull was long and came in two sections split down the middle with a single eye socket and nostril on each half. The sections came together in a vicious union of fangs that curved inward like a pair of clasped hands. There was no lower or upper jaw. The entire skull was evolved to open and close like some monstrous two-eyed pincer claw, and was just as wide and twice as long as an ox skull.

Will stood beneath it, frozen in dread and wonder. "Where did you get that?" Will asked his host, his voice lowered in disgust. "Where did *you* of all people get a Lemuertian skull?"

Daddy Long Legs grinned and admired his horrid decoration. "Beautiful, isn't it? His name was Scrape. You can thank him for the Geohex. Well, he is partially to blame, fact be known. *They both* had their own reasons for laying it on the land. Would you like to sit down?"

Will's blue-gray eyes snapped to the tall drakeri. "No. I want answers. Who were *they*? How did this all happen?" His jaw tightened. "Tell me."

Daddy scoffed. "I plan to, little seed. I plan to. Have a seat. Eat your fill. Your mystery of the Geohex is about to become a quest. And once you know everything, you will know that your efforts here are wasted. Then you will die by my hand."

Will glanced at Cymbre. "First things first," he said. Ever so courteously, he pulled out her chair for her.

The lady of the house gave a nod and slight curtsy before sitting.

As soon as her chair was scooted in beneath her, Will grasped the fine china bowl at his sitting place, used it to scoop up a helping of the chunky soup, slurped it down like pint of beer, placed the slop-covered bowl down upon the table cloth, and then sat down. All the while he kept his eyes locked on Daddy's. "That was delicious. I'm full now. Talk."

The tall man smiled and lit up his pipe. Will joined him by lighting up one of his cigarettes. After a few long puffs, Daddy Long Legs sat back and regarded the skull upon the wall. Clearing his throat, he began his tale.

"The Gray Dust Poppy used to grow only in Ses Lemuert. But roving Lemuertians, such as Scrape up there, knew that it could also grow on the graves of the accursed. The corpses of those who

301

committed great evil, or had great evil done to them, bleed out a negative energy that fertilizes the soil in such a way to allow the flower to grow from it. Such energy is easy for a Lemuertian to control. They feed off of the misery of the living and the dead. Scrape wanted to prolong the misery of the dead in our county so he could feed off it while living here in secret. In the guise of a Drakeri man, he approached our ancestors with the proposition of creating the land-curse for the purpose of growing the flower for easy profit. The apple barons in those days left little wealth sharing with the common folk. Many a desperate man formed a brotherhood dedicated to overthrowing the orchard-owning tyrants.

"So a deal was struck amongst the incognito Lemuertian and the founders of the Trotting Swans. Among those men was my great grandfather, Nathud. More on him later. Certain...markers were put in place throughout the land. Markers that would irrigate the negative energy throughout the county. As the centuries passed and bad things happened, hauntings and ghosts emerged, as did the poppy that would fetch a high price outside our borders and feed many families. Scrape grew strong off the torment and misery of the dead. He also grew careless. The Trotting Swans eventually found out that they had a monster in their midst. My great grandfather had a gun fashioned from *vaughn* that a necrotheurge made."

Daddy pulled out the blue metal pistol from his holster and set it on the table.

Will's eyes widened as he looked at the gun as if for the first time.

Daddy continued, "My great grandfather Nathud used this very gun to slay the monster, put three bullets in its black heart. This necrotheurgic gun bestows the mineral properties of *Cobalt* on its ammunition by the power of death. Goes through their hides without stopping like regular lead. With Scrape dead and the markers in place, my little club has reaped the benefits of those little flowers for thousands of years. Through the power of death, my county and my people can live and prosper. And with the markers in their proper places, hidden, some hidden in plain sight, the curse can *never* be lifted."

Will felt the sweat of fear emerge from beneath his clothes. His eyes never left the big blue pistol on the table. *"If this gun can turn lead bullets into cobalt then that means it can actually kill me!"*

he thought as dread boiled in his guts. His eyes shifted back to his host. With a dry throat he asked, "What are these markers yer talkin' about? How do they work?"

Daddy Long Legs emptied his pipe and sighed. "All I'm willing to say beyond what I've already told is this: the markers are made of a special iron ore. It conducts negative ghost energy like copper used to conduct lightning in the Age of Lightning and Oil. We fashion this metal into conduits that keeps the energy circulating throughout the land. From time to time, when we come by more of this ore, we make a new conduit and connect it with the ground. We have them planted throughout the county. You'll never find them all."

Will thought of the Headsman's Axe back in Drowsy Nook. "Is the ore hematite? I hear tell it's awfully rare in Doflend."

Daddy Long Legs did not answer, but his eyes met briefly with those of his wife.

Will regarded the basket of apples on the table. "I take it these are imported?"

"Yes, sir," Daddy answered. "Apples haven't grown here since the hex was put in place."

Will sniffed and cocked his head. "You really think the folks o' this county are better off with you an' yer so-called-brotherhood runnin' drugs outta it?"

Daddy shrugged and looked around at his handsome home. "Works for me."

Will gritted his teeth. "What about all the souls that can't move on? Channelin' an' irrigatin' all this death theurgy is keepin' people tied to this place. It ain't natural, and it ain't right."

Daddy Long Legs leaned forward, his head looming high above the table and Will. With a menacing glare he answered, "But it works for me!" He slammed his fist onto the table, rattling every dish and glass on it. "It works to *my* and every other Swan's advantage. All we care about, all we can afford to care about, is ourselves and our families. To waste with all those who failed to be born one of us! We cultivate death and use it to fertilize our soil. Then we take what it yields and sell it. Death is the one true power. And I gladly put my own life on the line in order to feed it, as I will with you when we duel."

The tall man raised one of his long arms and pointed. "Let

303

me show you my monument to death. Follow me, little seed. Let me show you my Garden of Fools!"

❁

The two enemies made their way across the vast field toward the gated graveyard. Will noticed very few blades of grass stabbing out from the many layers of dead leaves on the ground. It was Autumn's gown, but it lacked luster. The leave's colors were not vibrant as with other trees in that country that time of year. No bright oranges, yellows, or reds, only dull mockeries of such shades. Two rickety old posts stood in the middle of the field. Will recognized them as *turn posts,* markers used to measure out a pistol duel.

When they reached the gates, Daddy Long Legs produced a large key and gave Will a hateful grin. "Here, honored guest, let me show you where you'll be staying." He unlocked the gates and both men entered.

Each and every gravestone was identical, one hundred total, ten rows of ten. Each was filled with dirt and decay save one. Daddy Long Legs lit his pipe and smiled.

"It has long been my deal that anyone who could beat me in pulling steel would win all my land and possessions. But it wasn't just my wealth that drew challengers, it was my skill. The speed of my hand is measured in hundredths of a second. I can shoot the wings off a house fly. I can empty my chambers in the blink of an eye. I can even do all these things in cold weather with cold hands. Many people here were willing to duel me for greed, others for pride of skill. The third reason, my favorite fact be known, was revenge. Many of those I killed had family that thought their passion for vengeance would speed their draw and guide their aim. Fools! All of them, fools planted in the ground. Hence the name of my garden.

"But you, Will Foundling, you are the biggest fool of them all. You don't care about my wealth, being better than me, or avenging anyone. You want to be a big fat hero so that apples can grow here again." The drakeri's eyes widened. "And for the first time ever, I am defending not only my life and land, but the way of my life and land. You are unique amongst all these rotting idiots beneath our feet. But you will still get the same deal as them. Kill me, you get my house, my land, my money, and my trophy wife if you so wish."

Will did not care much for being called a fool. And he felt an insult burn inside of his own mind and shoot out of his mouth. "You call that a trophy wife? Puh! More like a third place trophy!"

Will felt the tall man's fist strike his cheekbone. It did not hurt but it jarred him. He stumbled back a pace and steadied himself.

Daddy Long Legs stared in shock at his own fist. Will's words had made him react without thinking. He looked at the tendikeye and growled with anger.

Will only smiled and put up is large hands, taking a fighting stance. He watched the tall man stiffen as if he was so not sure what to do. Perfect. Will threw a devastating kick at the inside of Daddy's shin. The tall man never saw it coming.

As boot hit bone, the Drakeri yelped in pain. His guard lowered and balance compromised, Will rushed in close, grabbing Daddy's wrist and elbow, and rotated them in directions never intended by nature. Daddy felt betrayed by his own arm as its mangled state drove him hard into the ground. Will was just about to stomp his throat before he saw Daddy's hand flash.

"Stop!" Daddy Long Legs demanded, still laying prone at Will's feet. His long barreled *vaughn* pistol was in his hand, pointing it up at the tendikeye.

Fear and outrage flooded out of Will's mouth. "You rump-stuffin' sister boy! You threw the first insult *and* the first punch!"

"And I'll throw the first bullet, too, prick!" Daddy slowly got up, wincing in pain. "You got some tricky moves, I'll give you that. But I've got the one move that counts. Soon, you will be my one hundredth kill. I will complete my Garden of Fools and retire. Your soul will feed the dirt that grows my poppies. Go on, look at them! I personalized each headstone with an epitaph that shames the dead beneath it. Doing so traps the soul. Each one of them I dueled in that field we just crossed. Then I personally tossed their miserable corpses in the holes I readied for them. And as the dirt gets piled on, the soul stays behind to rot and feed the Geohex. It's my little

305

contribution to the grand design."

Will's glare shifted to the headstones. They were not monuments to the dead as much as mockeries. One by one he beheld the inscriptions. Four of which, he would remember until the end of his days.

RANSELL WAHTAG
DIED 2802 A.T.
THE TEARS OF HIS MOTHER,
WETTED HIS FACE,
HER PRIDE AND JOY,
BECAME HER DISGRACE.

OMARR CIPHTEN
DIED 2750 A.T.
DESPERATE FOR MONEY,
THIS FATHER-TO-BE,
TRIED AND FAILED,
FOR ALL TO SEE.

MAYLA OEKLEE
DIED 2789 A.T.
SMUG AND PROUD,
OUTSPOKEN AND LOUD,
THOUGHT SHE WAS SKILLED,
BUT GOT HERSELF KILLED.

But out of all them, the one inscription that boiled his heart was this:

JESSE HOWARD
DIED 2734 A.T.
A TENDIKEYE.

It was not so much that Daddy Long Legs had killed a fellow tendikeye. Will had never known the man. It was the fact that a tendikeye had been *buried*. In the dirt. To bury a tendikeye in the ground was a grave insult. Will looked around and saw five more graves just like it. His people, buried, their imprisoned souls left to rot.

"Oh yes!" he heard Daddy's voice brag. "I *dared* to bury those big-footed, spikey-headed monsters. No need to give them an epitaph. No need for you either." He began to laugh. "Hell, I just might leave yours blank!"

Will fought every urge to look at Daddy. If he did, he knew he would die trying to kill him. Balling up his fists, he spoke in a soft, clear voice, "I'm going to take it all away from you, Long Legs. I'm going to erase what all you've done. And when you are through, I'm gonna fill every Trottin' Swan that gets in my way with regret and bullets."

Before Daddy could respond, Will leapt high into the air, flipping backward, over the cemetery fence and landed with only the sound of dead leaves crackling.

As the tendikeye turned to walk away he heard Daddy Long Legs say, "Those words may comfort you when you say them, boy, but you're just as dead the other fools. I'm too fast! You *will* fail! Remember, Will Foundling: you dug a hole for yourself, and there's no way out!!!"

The Swan's words sank deep into Will like a set of poisonous fangs. Because the truth hurt.

Part 4

The following morning, Will knocked upon the door of the Norred household.

A kind-faced drakeri man answered, his wife and their daughter behind him. The man's eyes widened as he beheld the visitor on his doorstep. "Will...Foundling, is it?"

"Yessir," the tendikeye replied with a smile and a nod. He was carrying a shovel that Daiv had lent him.

The man peered at him. "You...ended the Headsman's curse in Drowsy Nook, right?"

"Yessir, I did. Me an' my friends." Will smiled wide, pleased to hear the news had spread.

307

The man swallowed. "And...soon you'll be facing off against Daddy Long Legs, too?"

"Yessir," Will replied, displeased to hear that news had spread, as well.

The man looked to his wife. "Excuse us, dear." He stepped out and closed the door behind him. Eying the shovel, he asked "What is the meaning of your visit, Mr. Foundling?"

About twenty minutes passed as Will told him everything. Since Will was asking to dig up the bones of one of his dead relatives, Will thought it fair to let the man in on the full truth. Needless to say, the man, whose name was Meil Norred, had his doubts.

"This all sounds so crazy," he said with a troubled brow.

Will nodded and shrugged. "If I was crazy, I might've not bothered bein' up front with you." He pulled out two cigarettes and offered Mr. Norred one.

The stranger took it. As the two men lit up, he regarded his visitor. "Is the...Drageist with you now? I mean...beneath us?"

"No," Will told him. "I didn't bother gettin' him today. I don't want him eatin' no more souls, evil or not. Besides, I got me a plan on how to go about it without getting' necro-sick from diggin'."

Meil Norred scratched his double-pointed ear. "By Retaeh's breath. Are you sure that one of my ancestors did that so long ago? Lynched an expecting couple? I mean, I know there was a time when people were intolerant, but—"

Will interrupted. "Would you let yer daughter inside marry a human? Knowin' that you'd outlive all of yer grandbabies? You may say yes, but there still must be a part of you that wouldn't like the idea."

The man frowned and took a moment to think about it. "Well, I guess I should probably lend you a hand then. I'll grab my shovel and meet you around back."

The Norred family plots were quite extensive, and a large portion of them were overgrown and cluttered with living and dead vegetation.

Meil Norred expressed embarrassment. "I don't know which I should be ashamed of more: digging up Brice's grave or letting it become overrun with brush."

Will surveyed the natural mess in the way. "The only one who should feel shame here is Brice. His ghost anyway." Will's

308

yashinin machete hissed as he drew it from its sheath. He walked into the brush in a steady gait, slashing and cutting his way through with casual ease.

"Your sword makes for a good brush cutter," Meil Norred remarked as he followed behind.

"It's meant to be," Will explained. "It's a *tuntrum* blade. The tendikeye of yore had little iron to come by. Pretty rare in my homecell. So, whenever sumthin' was made from it, it usually had to serve the two most important purposes o' survival; combat an' occupation. Yashinin machetes were made to cut paths fer hunters an' guides. But they were also meant fer openin' necks an cleavin' skulls. Take my shovel an' yer shovel, fer instance. Yers was made jus' to dig. But see the iron butt on the end of my handle? That's a counter balance fer when I'm jabbin' the spade end at some feller's face. Also, my spade-head's a bit narrower so it can sink in like a spear. *Tuntrum.* Useful things never go outta style."

Meil Norred half smiled as he stepped over a freshly severed tree branch. "You people are good farmers, I hear."

"The best," Will said.

They passed by several old headstones until they reached the grave of Brice Norred. Old vines had covered most of the name, but it was indeed him.

"How are we going to dig his bones out if digging will kill us?" Meil Norred asked.

"We're gonna dig just off to the side of the burial dirt. That's the part that's infected. Then I'll dig sideways to the bones once we're six feet deep. Sound good?"

Meil Norred shook his head. "None of this sounds good, to be perfectly honest. I...I want to help and all. But if this grave is really haunted, then I'm putting myself at risk."

"Think of it like purging a puss-filled wound," Will told him.

"Oh, I understand that it would be helpful to the forest and the hanged lovers. It's just, I am putting myself at risk, I know it!" He laughed nervously. "I...I really hate to ask you this, but is there any reward for helping you? I have a family to feed."

Will smiled. "You want money? Is that all? Hell, whatchu do fer a livin'?"

"I'm a shoemaker. And my wife makes the best wool socks in town."

Will laughed and his grin widened. "Well, ain't that a sweet fit! Tell ya what: in return fer yer permission an' assistance in diggin' up yer relative an' burnin' his cursed bones, I will reimburse you with three hun'erd grotz, provided yer dear wife hooks me up with a dozen pair of size twenty-three socks. It's a hard size to come by outside o' Cloiherune."

Meil Norred took a deep breath. "Three hundred and fifty?"

"Deal!"

Meil Norred smiled and offered his hand for a shake. Will bent to custom and took it and the deal was good and done.

The two men began digging just off to the side of the grave. Neither detected anything like what Will had felt with the Moore brothers. All the same, Will was nervous. He hid it well, but felt it all the same. The thought of dueling Daddy Long Legs had never left his mind since leaving the Swan's big house.

"I won't be fast enough," he thought. *"I seen his hand move. Or rather, I didn't. Ninety-Nine dead challengers an' he's still alive. An' that gun o' his! If it could kill a full grown Lemuertian it'll tear though my hide just as easy.*

"Dang it! Why'd I agree to that duel? 'Cause my head turned out to be thicker than my skin, that's why! An' if I hoof it, Ivy an' Daiv get whacked. I could always kill Daddy while he sleeps, nice and easy. But then I might hafta whack his friends, too. It'd make the others look bad, too. Rev would be mad as a hell. Of course, if I do manage to kill Daddy fair an' four right angles, then I'll be famous throughout the county. Then Uncle Brem will be sure to hear of me...if he ever happens to pass through..."

Will considered these things for a while as he dug.

Their hole had reached nearly six feet deep when Meil Norred's voice interrupted his thoughts. "Mr. Foundling?"

"Yeah?"

"I very much doubt that you'll be able to beat Daddy Long Legs. Rumor has it that you're a dangerous man. But I've watched most of Daddy's duels. You really should just leave town. All that money just isn't worth it."

"I know," Will said as he stabbed up another clump of dirt.

Meil Norred frowned. "Look. It's good of you and your fellow Excursionists to try to undo the Geohex. It's kept the county poor for generations. But the Trotting Swans keep thriving because

310

of it with all these horrible blossoms that sprout up. Even if you can combat the ghosts, there's still the Swans to contend with."

Will shrugged and showed no sign of worry. "If that's the way it's gotta be. And even if Daddy kills me, I can still dig all these bones up an' end the lover's curse."

Meil Norred let out a sad sigh. "He *is* going to kill you."

Will stabbed his shovel deep into the dirt. "What kind of hero would I be if I didn't put myself at risk?" He managed to give the man a cocky grin.

Meil Norred met his eyes and replied. "The dead kind?"

Something sprang out from the lower part of the dirt wall beside them. A dirt covered limb curled around Meil Norred's ankle and snapped it like a twig. The man screamed as he fell. His mangled leg was being pulled into the dirt wall.

Will reacted by swinging the *tuntrum* shovel and jabbing at the limb. It resembled an arm made of rock and dirt. With a well-aimed thrust, Will rammed the spade head into the arm's shoulder. Using the tool's leverage, he popped the arm clean off, freeing Meil Norred.

As the wounded drakeri scooted behind Will into a safer corner of the hole, a loud rumble came from the dirt wall. A shape emerged from the soil. It was like a drakeri, only made up of earth and stone. Its right arm was at its feet, twitching.

Will spotted the faintest bit of bone protruding from its shoulder. *"The skeleton is inside that thing!"* Will thought.

"Traitorous ingrate!!!" the gravething bellowed, looking down at Meil Norred. "Betrayed by my own blood!"

Will wanted to swing the shovel, but the hole they were in was too narrow. He tried for another thrust, but the gravething rushed past it. With a telling slam, the gravething's stone fist bashed into Will's nose with the force of a bileer's kick. It was enough to stun the tendikeye long enough for the monster's jaws to open up hideously wide.

Will screamed as the nerves around his collarbone felt the cold flint teeth of the angry thing. Its jaws clamped down hard, but Will's bone wouldn't break. The gravething latched on as the tendikeye dropped the shovel and drew his blade. Swiftly the curve of his yashinin made a deep gash in the monster's midsection. The gravething did not even notice.

311

"It ain't got no guts, stupid!" Will thought. Bringing up his blade, he pushed it hard against the dull inside edge, pushing the sharp side into the monster's neck.

The blade bit halfway through before the monster's teeth let go and the monster took a half step back. Will saw it raise its arm for another bash to his head. He had to drop his machete to catch the flailing limb and lock it into a grapple. The monster roared and rebelled against the arm lock. The twisted arm broke clean off in Will's hands as the monster closed in for another bite.

Will raised his forearm for protection as the monster bit it like a rabid wolf. Will yelled with pain and fury then took the dangling arm still in his right hand and swung it hard into the monster's half-cleaved neck. The head broke off in a cloud of clay dust as its body fell limp to the ground. Gritting his teeth, he bashed the head still biting his arm onto his rising knee, breaking the skull to pieces.

"Get me out of here!" he heard Meil Norred scream. The man was cringing in the corner, having the worst day of his life.

Will knelt down to check the man's ankle. It was broken, but the break was clean and the bone had not torn through the skin. "Lemme get you inside. You'll live." As he picked the man up and leapt out of the hole, Will asked "So, uh, ya think that three hun'erd an' fifty I owe ya will cover the doctor's bill?"

"No!" Meil Norred answered indignantly.

Will sighed. "Well, tell ya what: if I manage to kill Daddy Long Legs, you can have his house. Sound good?"

Meil Norred laughed and winced in pain. "You'd better win then! Oh, how will I explain this to my wife?"

Later that day, on the doorstep of another household.

"The answer is *no*, and that's final!" declared Jamsun Dwas, the great great grandson of Iry Dwas. "I don't care if he was a murderer. He needs to rest in peace."

"But he ain't!" Will argued. "His bones an' all the dirt around 'em are possessed by his cursed ghost. A ghost kept together

312

by ancient evil and all other kinds o' real bad witchworks. It is the will of the shrunken caven trees that I extract them bones, burn 'em, an' plant a caven nut in the grave. I've done it once already today, an' I assure you that this will help toward the undoin' of the Geohex."

Jansun Dwas crossed his arms. "Yeah. I heard about Meil and his broken leg. Word travels fast in a small town, stranger."

"You don't hafta help me dig if you don't want to. Just stay in the house, an' I'll take care of it. If you want, I can pay you like I did Mr. Norred."

The man huffed in offense. "I am not some desperate shoemaker. I don't need your money. I just don't believe it's right to disturb and desecrate bodies."

"But it's already disturbed! You can burn the bones yerself an' keep the ashes in an urn."

The man rolled his eyes. "I do not own an urn."

"Then use a sugar jar!"

"You're crazy! Get off my property!"

Will groaned, turned, and stomped off the man's front steps, carrying the shovel Daiv had lent him. Just as he was about to step into the road, he turned back and shouted, pointing with a big finger, "I hope you can sleep comfortably knowin' that there's a friggin' *ghost* in yer back yard! An' if it ever manages to get loose an' suck yer soul out in yer sleep, don't blame me! 'Cause I done tried to help yer sorry ass!"

A small spike of paranoia subtly wedged itself in Jansun Dwas' mind. He felt his stomach churn and his purple skin rise with goosebumps. He looked to the tendikeye and yelled, "Wait! Come back!"

Will turned to face him. "Tell ya what," he started, sensing the man's sudden uneasiness. "You can watch me dig from a safe distance. An' if the bones don't get up an' try to kill me, then I'll leave 'em be. But if I gotta contend with another dirt an' stone covered bonewalker, I'm gonna bust it up like I did the last one. Sound good to you?"

Jansun Dwas blinked several times as he nodded in agreement.

Will dug up the grave of Iry Dwas in the same manner as he had Brice Norred's. And sure enough, the earthclad remains of the long dead drakeri animated and tried to kill him.

313

Will was ready this time, and leapt out of the hole, shovel still in hand. After a few well-timed downward swings and jabs, he managed to beat the horrific creature to pieces.

After witnessing this efficient act of heroism, Jansun Dwas' attitude toward Will changed to one of gushing admiration. He helped build a fire for the bones, offered planting tips for the caven nut, fixed Will a hearty lunch, and even offered the tendikeye a full body massage. Recognizing the eagerness in the man's eyes, Will politely refused the last favor and took his leave.

He went to the road, tired, sore, and dirty. "One more grave," he said to himself.

He had been asking around town for the home dwelling of the Feldurhau family earlier that day. At first, he thought people were lying when they said that no such home existed in Pevulaneum. But the entire town knew of Will now. They all knew he'd stirred up trouble with Daddy Long Legs and his gang, and had caused Jarami the brush popper to go missing. They also knew that he had entered the cave of the Dragon's Ghost and returned alive. And they knew that he was an investigator, part of an independent group of Excursionists whose goal was to end the Geohex. Knowing all this, the common folk of Pevulaneum treated Will with polite paranoia. They sensed he meant well, but he also meant trouble. He was stirring the pot while rocking the boat.

He went door to door asking if anyone knew of a grave in town bore the name Felderhau. The oldest Drakeri in town, a 1,267 year old house painter named Wulfum Grad knew of such a family that had died out some seven hundred years ago. He told Will the address of the property they had once owned. A family by the name of Htims lived there now.

"*Good,*" Will thought. "*If they ain't kin to Rusty Feldurhau, an' his grave is on their property, then they're less likely to protest me diggin' him up.*" He walked with assurance from this thought as he made his way across town. The light from the Huncell walls grew dim as evening came.

◊

314

Will came to a wide house with a rusted tin roof. The remains of an old wagon sat decaying in the front yard. The lawn had not been cut in years. Saplings poked up here and there throughout the tall grass. Wind chimes and other dangling décor filled the full-sized trees in the yard. The front porch was lit by a single lantern that hung upon a rusty nail, as a hearth fire flickered in the front window.

Stepping onto the property, Will got a sick feeling in his stomach. At first, he wrote it off as jitters from the impending introduction of himself to strangers, but soon he realized it was actually dread. He rapped on the door with two knuckles, stepped back, and reminded himself to breathe as he waited.

From inside, he heard a woman say, "No, you still need to rest. I'll answer it." Light barefooted steps on hardwoord floor approached the door, then it opened. A drakeri woman in a beige house dress stood in the doorway, a look of shock expanding her eyes. Her mouth gaped and her balance seemed to falter as she beheld the tendikeye on her front porch.

"Uh, evenin', ma'am...er...miss," Will started, nervous and humble. "My name is Will Foundling. I'm conductin' an investigation on the Geohex, an—"

"Can you wait right here?" she interrupted.

"Uh...yeah. Sure thing."

She turned and disappeared briskly back into her home. Not nine seconds later she returned, leveling a very big musket at Will's chest. As Will's surprised eyes took in the sight of the massive firearm, he heard her scream, "You son of a bitch!" followed by a loud boom.

The scatter shot hit him dead on in the chest. Will flew back off the porch and into the grass. He tried to breathe, but couldn't. His writhing body kept him from getting up as his chest felt like it had been slapped by a colossal whip. His chest bones screamed in torment, and from the way they shifted inside, he knew several of them were cracked. He wheezed and coughed, fighting for one thin breath. He was able to lift his head.

Standing above him was the woman, her face filled with equal parts fear and hatred. Raising the musket like a club she bellowed, "Die!"

Will was too stunned to do anything about it. Although the

315

scatter shot had not dealt a fatal wound, it was enough to render him helpless for the time being. Over and over, he felt the hard steel of the musket come down on his face and raised arms. The hits stung, but he was able to stay coherent.

"Stop," he managed to croak. He took another painful breath. "Stop it! I'm not...here to...hurt nobody!"

"Well, I am!" she cried, her eyes flooding with tears of rage.

Just then, a man came out followed by two frightened children. He wore all purple, and both of his wrists were covered in bandages and splints. Will recognized him as one of the men who had tried to ambush him outside the Drageist's cave.

"Marna, stop this at once!" he ordered.

The wife ignored him and kept beating, growling, and crying. The husband stepped between her and the prone tendikeye. "I said stop it, woman!"

"Why should I, Eldon?!" she yelled. "Because Daddy Long Legs is going to kill him anyways? Is that why? He *hurt* you! Why should that tall spider get the satisfaction that is due me?"

Calm and stern, the man said. "Marna. Thank you. I love you. Now, get back in the house and take the kids with you. Please. Put my musket back and don't touch it again until I say otherwise. If you don't, then I swear I'm going to slap some sense into you, I don't care *how* shunted up my wrists are! Now get!"

The woman's expression became one of confusion and remorse.

"Please," her husband said one more time.

Marna started crying and nodded her head. She took the musket and her children back inside, leaving the two men alone in the front yard.

The Trotting Swan known as Eldon Htims looked down at Will, his face a mixture of puzzlement and disdain. He saw that the tendikeye's shirt had been shot to shreds. There was blood on his chest but not much. The fact that Will still *had* a chest amazed him. "That gun should have killed you."

"Yeah," Will agreed, struggling and failing to sit up.

Eldon took a deep breath. "I should have killed you, too. Back there at the cave. I was planning on it."

Will's pride became bolstered by the pain. "Yeah, an' look what it got you."

The Swan laughed. "Look what it got us both! How is it you survived that blast, stranger?"

Will sat up this time and winced. "Even if I knew fer sure, it still wouldn't be none o' yer business."

"You got into our business first."

Will scoffed and sat cross-legged. He reached for a cigarette in the pocket of his dust coat. "The dead need to rest an' dissipate. It ain't right or natural to keep all them souls from shatterin'".

"Cry me a river," Eldon scoffed.

Will scoffed back. "How 'bout you go *bleed* me one, buttpit?" He put the cigarette in his grinning mouth, pulled out another one and offered it to the Trotting Swan.

Eldon smiled at the sight of the tobacco, then lifted his wrists. "Much obliged. You mind helping me out? I can't light it like this."

Will got up, slowly, one knee and foot at a time. He put the cigarette in his enemy's mouth, lit it, then lit his own. They both took a few drags in silence before Eldon gingerly used two of fingers to clasp it.

"You let me live after I tried to ambush you. That's why I kept her from finishing you off. Just so you know."

"She had a right to be pissed," Will replied. He looked up at the darkening huncell dome. The hunveins were coming out. "Y'know, Eldon, you honorable criminals got lots in common. You put on this show of courtesy an' politeness an' fairness. Daddy Long Legs does it to give himself an air o' high dignity. But I get the feelin' that most o' y'all do it to make yourselves feel less guilty, more justified. Y'all are keepin' spirits from movin' on an' poisonin' yer fellow drakeri with that death blossom."

"You can't judge me," Eldon protested. "You haven't lived my life or struggled my struggle. You think it's easy smuggling and selling these flowers? Every year when me and my friends run them, we run the risk of getting caught by cops or attacked by rival runners. We Trotting Swans have lost many a good man who only wanted to keep his family fed."

Will scratched his nose. "Why not just be done with this Geohex an' grow somethin' else? Embrenil ain't too far from here. You could sell yer goods at the city market."

Eldon shook his head. "This is the only life I know. Same as

317

my father and grandfather. It's in my blood. Can you understand that?"

Will lowered his eyes. "No, sir. I'm sad to say I can't. I ain't got no father now. Never really did, fact be known."

Eldon raised his arm and gently placed his hand on Will's shoulder. "I am truly sorry for that."

Will nodded and raised his eyes. "Well, can't be helped. Anyway, I came here to dig up the grave of Rusty Felderhau. It's cursed somethin' fierce. He on yer property?"

Eldon raised an eyebrow. "Yes. In the woods behind the house."

Will explained why he needed to dig up the grave.

Eldon had his doubts. "Well, such a thing would be counterproductive, me letting you end a curse. But..."

"But what?" Will asked.

"But, fact be known, I have always felt bad for those cursed lovers and their unborn child. I guess because I have kids of my own. Also, I am still a bit grateful to you for snapping my wrists and not my neck. And I feel a bit guilty about my wife shooting you. It didn't kill you, but I could tell that it hurt. So, I'll tell you what; if you let me kick you in the balls, just once, then I'll allow you to dig up that grave. Deal?"

"Are you serious?" Will asked.

Eldon nodded.

Will sighed and rolled his eyes. "Fine, fine." He stepped directly in front of the man with his feet apart. "Go on. Go 'head."

Will was tough, supernaturally tough. But not tough enough to shrug off a vengeful kick to the tenderest part of his body. Eldon's boot struck hard and true with a loud smack of leather to denim. Will felt a violent sickness flood his lower abdomen and the air shot out of his lungs once more. He collapsed to the grassy ground, coughing and groaning.

"We are even, tendikeye." Eldon's face was one of cruel satisfaction.

"Good to know," Will coughed.

Eldon knelt down so to meet Will's eyes. "I give you permission to dig up that grave...but only *after* you duel Daddy. Now, good night to you." The home's owner got up and went back inside.

Will gritted his teeth and got up, again. Picking up the shovel, he limped back toward the home of Daiv and Ivy to call it a night.

When he arrived at Daiv and Ivy's *frezje*, he saw that the lights were still on. Slowly and with strained effort, he leapt up to the front door.

"I'm back," he announced, loud enough for those inside to hear.

"Just a minute then," Daiv answered from within.

Will then had to wait for Daiv to disarm the ward that protected his house from Will's curse.

"Okay, it's safe," the old man said. "Come on in. An' don't ferget to wipe yer boots this time."

Will stepped inside to find Daiv and Ivy sitting in the den smoking pipes and drinking coffee. A plate full of meat, bread, and broccoli sat on the table by the empty chair that Will had been using.

"That looks good. Smells good, too," Will exhaled as he wiped his boots on the doormat.

Daiv and Ivy did not respond. They only stared into space as they smoked.

Will frowned as he took his boots off. He set the *tuntrum* shovel in the corner of the room by the coat rack. Sitting in the empty chair, he waited for one of his two hosts to break the silence. He maintained his patience uncomfortably until Daiv finally spoke.

"Day after tomorrow then?"

"I'm sorry?" Will replied, trying to understand the question.

"The day after tomorrow. That's when you duel Daddy Long Legs?"

"Oh. Yessir."

Daiv winced. The wince turned into a grimace and he shook his head. "Ye were stupid to take that challenge. Daddy is over six hundred years old. Not only is he a natural at speed, but he is trained. He draws, fires, and holsters all in one snap. Fastest thing I've ever seen. Faster than a blink, ye understand?"

"I understand," Will answered.

"An' his bullets go right through a train rail. His father killed a malruka with that gun o' his. You'll die by that gun, mute foot. It's a pure shame."

319

Will took a bite of his bread and shrugged. "There's this trick I know, a Harker trick. Whenever a gun gets pointed at me, I spot how the barrel is angled. Judgin' off that angle, I can dodge the bullet. That way, I can dodge his first shot and return two o' my own."

Daiv scoffed. "Yeah, I've heard of Harkers doin' that. But ye won't get a chance to spot that angle, not with Daddy. I'm real sorry, Will. But ye've dug yerself a hole ye can't get out of."

Will's ears perked at the old man's words. He glanced over at the shovel in the corner. His eyes narrowed as a thought came to him. As he dug into his food, the thought wormed around inside his brain. His tongue barely tasted his dinner as he ate. The thought grew into an idea, and he immediately wondered if it was a good one.

"Hey, Daiv," he started. "This'll be a standard pistol duel, right? Nothin' odd or fancy?"

The old tendikeye nodded. "Ye'll both stand back to back, then a judge gives the signal. Then ye both run to yer turnposts. Once you reach'em, ye are then allowed to turn an' draw an' shoot. But don't be reckonin' that ye'll be able to reach yer turn post 'fore he does. Them long legs o' his allow him to move as fast as we can." Daiv lowered his head an' laughed bitterly. "Funny thing is, on occasions when he's able to reach his post before his opponent does, he still allows 'em time to turn an' pull their piece. I don't think it's fairness that makes him do that. I think he just likes to see the disappointment in their face when he pops a round through their body. Sick shunter."

Will chewed a piece of broccoli and nodded as he pondered Daiv's words.

Ivy let out a frustrated sigh. "Ah, to a hell with it all!"

The two men turned to face her.

"Enough o' this waste! Papa, let's just leave this place, this town and county. I'm all grown, and sooner or later I'm going to have to start looking after you. If we disappear, that means Will can disappear. He only agreed to the duel for our safety anyway."

A flash of anger lit Will's eyes. "You ain't leavin'. You shouldn't hafta be bullied or banished from yer own home. This is yer land an' place o' raisin', Ivy."

Ivy shrugged. "You're a homeless wanderer, and you seem

320

to be doin' all right."

Will clenched his eyes shut and bared his teeth. "But I ain't, Ivy. I ain't doin' all right. This life I lead, well, it don't feel like I'm in the lead of anythin'."

She shook her head. "But you get to go on adventures an' solve problems. Be a hero."

"I wander because I ain't got no home or family, Ivy. You still have both. An' the problems I solve are never my own. Each day is a gamble fer me. No bet I make is ever a safe one. So, I bet big every single time. An' even when I win I still get nuthin'."

"Then why play the game?" she asked.

Will shrugged. "Because this game is all I got."

The following morning did not start well for Will. His chest screamed in pain as he sat up in his cot, his muscles reminding him that he had dug up two graves and battled the post-mort monsters within them.. From his collarbone to his sternum, he was covered in an ugly purple bruise and hundreds of tiny red scabs.

"Dang musket," he cursed. He saw that Ivy was in the room with him, sitting in her nightgown and drinking coffee. The robust smell and the sudden desire for it made him blink out of doziness. "Mornin', Ivy. Can I get me some of that?"

She grinned at him mischievously as she finished her cup. "You want some of this?" she asked dangling the cup handle on her fingertip. "Or do you want some of *this*?"

In a flash of motion, she stood up and threw off her gown, exposing a strong athletic form covered in smooth, mocha skin. Like most tendikeye women, her breasts were small and firm, perfect for running. But her hips and thighs were a luscious mass of curved muscle.

Will froze as she stood there naked, not four feet from him. In a stunned panic, he looked about the house. "Ivy, yer dad-"

"He's out chopping wood," she said taking a slow step toward him.

"But I thought you were mad at me?"

321

"Oh, I still am," she answered. Before he knew it she was on top of him, and the cot beneath them collapsed.

Will groaned as his sore chest muscles sent hateful messages to his brain. "Agh! Go easy on me girl!"

She did not go easy. Not at all. After a long while working through intense pain for even more intense pleasure, Will Foundling nearly passed out. The two tendikeye lay down in a sweet embrace on a hard wood floor, sweating and panting and enjoying the release.

Will rolled himself a cigarette, which he shared with her.

"I'm not usually so forward," she told him. "It's just..."

"I might die tomorrow," he said.

Her face began to contort as tears welled in her eyes. "You're stupid. You're just so stupid."

"I know, Ivy. I know."

She sighed and rubbed her eyes, stopping the tears before they fell. "I don't usually cry this easy either." She let out a small laugh. "It's funny. I knew you weren't going to be here long. Fact be known, I sure could use an autumn fling. Oh, well. I guess I'll go get your coffee now."

Just as she was about to get up, Will grabbed her arm and pulled her back down with him. There he held her a long while, touching her and caressing her into blissful relaxation. Sharing the heat of their bodies, they kissed and nuzzled each other without shame or care. Love was not necessary for the affection they both so desperately needed.

When they finally got up and dressed, Will gave her one more tender kiss on her forehead before asking, "So, was that worth a sandwich, at least?"

She rolled her eyes and playfully squeezed his lips together. "Yeah, yeah, I guess. You got points for the snuggle time."

Will grinned and gave a nod of thanks.

Just then, Daiv came in carrying an arm load of chopped wood.

"Good mornin', Daiv," Will said with a smile. "Need me to go down an' grab another load?"

"Naw, it's fine," the old man returned as he placed the wood by the stove. "So, what's yer plan today, mute foot? Yer date with death is tomorrow, ye know. What does today entail?"

322

Will smirked as Ivy handed him a cup of coffee. "Well, Daiv. I reckon I'm gonna head back up to the Drageist's cave an' set its spirit free. Then later on tonight..." He stopped to take a sip of the morning beverage. It was hot, bitter, and delicious. "Then later there's somethin' I gotta go do."

"Do what?" Ivy asked as she cut two slices from a loaf of wheat bread.

"Somethin' hush hush. A secret Harker type mission. But you can come along fer when I get rid of the Drageist, if you are so inclined, Miss Ivy." He gave her a cocky grin.

She smiled back sweetly as she built up his sandwich thick and high. "Oh, I am very inclined, Mister Will."

Daiv glanced back and forth at the two of them. Then he shook his head and let out a sigh that only tired old men can produce. "Okay then. I'm going to take a nap now. Have fun riddin' the town of the dragon, kids. Let me know how it goes."

They ran together through the town, Ivy by leaps and bounds with help from her wings; Will by the shear velocity of his legs. Side by side, they tore through the dirt streets, the wind hissing through their quills and past their ears. They passed a bar called Qlary's Mug House. From it came a man's shout.

"Hey! Tendikeye!"

Will and Ivy stopped and turned.

A stout looking drakeri man with thick forearms and a balding head emerged from the rickety building flanked by two other men. Soon the entire bar had emptied, and a small crowd formed behind him. The man and his two friends, Will noticed, were not wearing the purple colors of the Trotting Swans, nor were they armed. But the hostility in their faces and walks was strongly apparent.

Will met the stout man's angry eyes and called out, "If you want trouble, Mister, yer in it!"

"Jarami was my brother-in-law," the man growled. "They say you smashed up his face, killed him, and then hid his body. My

323

sister has been real messed up over it. Personally, I think she was a fool for ever marrying the sot. He was an abusive drunk, and I could care less about him dying. But my sister...she loved him anyway. And so I'm going to beat the piss out of you. Drop those fancy weapons if you got the stones for a fair fight."

Will sighed and nodded in compliance as he unbuckled his belt. "Fine with me, bud. But you might know I'm due to duel Daddy Long Legs tomorrow. If you kill or cripple me, he might take offense to it."

"I won't," the man swore. "I'll just make you wish you were dead!"

Will grinned as he handed Ivy his weapons and dust coat. "You can try, bud!" He stepped toward the man and sized him up. He was easily a foot shorter than Will, with thick limbs that would compromise his speed and reach. *"Gotta be careful,"* Will thought. He took a fighting stance, fists up, and waited.

The stocky man did not hesitate or bother to circle him first. He charged right in, ignoring the punch that landed from Will's fist, and tackled the tendikeye to the ground.

Will put his arms up to block the man's fists, but they came down too hard and too fast. Punch after punch nailed him solid in the face. And with each strike, the tendikeye became more and more slow, until finally his eyes closed and he went limp in the dirt.

Realizing his victory, the stout man stood up and spat on Will's chest. He then turned to a cheering crowd who hoisted him up on their shoulders.

"Har-old! Har-old!" they chanted. They carried him back inside the bar where they bought him food and drinks for the rest of the day.

Ivy rushed by Will's side, kneeling down a cradling his head. "Will! Talk to me! Wake up!"

"Are they all gone yet?" Will asked, still keeping his eyes closed.

Ivy arched an eyebrow. "Yes? Are you going to be okay?"

He opened his eyes and smiled. With little effort he got back up to his feet, not seeming dazed or stunned in the slightest.

Ivy gave him back his things and cocked her head to the side. "You let him win," she said.

"Of course." He put his gun and blade belt on.

324

Ivy crossed her arms, looking confused and suspicious. "And none of those punches hurt you, did they? Because of your curse."

Will shrugged. "Well, the ones on the nose stung a bit. But yeah. Did it look convincin'?"

She nodded. "Very. Do you do this often? I mean, lose fights and pretend to get hurt?"

Will threw on his dust coat and considered the question. "I hate to lose, unless I don't really feel like winnin'. Like jus' now. That feller had more of a reason to fight than I did. So, I let him win. He was gamblin' with his family's honor. He'd already lost honor by havin' his sister's husband get killed. An' he was willin' to risk more to fight me. He took a big chance. I respect that."

Ivy looked down at his shirt in disgust. "But you still have his spit on you."

Will looked down at the glob of saliva. "Well, at least it ain't his blood. Spit's easier to clean off."

Ivy waited at the base of the hill as Will entered the Drageist's cave.

Carrying the *tuntrum* shovel, he called out into the darkness. "Dragon! It's me, Will. It's time to set you free." There was no answer, but Will could hear the beast stirring deep within. Stepping down into the cavern, he came upon the massive ghost coiled high in its icy den.

"WHERE WERE YOU YESTERDAY AND YESTERNIGHT?" it asked in a deep angry rumble. "I THOUGHT WE WERE GOING TO DIG UP MORE GRAVES."

Will shook his head. "I took care of it without yer help."

"I KNOW," replied the monster. "I FOLLOWED YOU THE WHOLE TIME. I WAS…AM VERY DISAPPOINTED. I WOULD HAVE LIKED TO EAT MORE SOULS. I COULD HAVE, YOU KNOW. BUT I PREFERRED TO WATCH THOSE SKELETONS GIVE YOU TROUBLE."

Will shook his head. "No more. No more of you. I'm here to

325

free yer spirit. That's it." He walked over to the iced covered crack in the wall and raised the shovel.

"WAIT! HEED MY WORDS!" the Drageist pleaded. "YOU STILL HAVE THE SOUL OF RUSTY FELDURHAU IN THAT TROTTING SWAN'S BACK YARD. AND THEN THERE ARE THE NINTY-NINE SOULS TRAPPED IN DADDY LONG LEGS' GARDEN OF FOOLS. IF YOU LET ME GO OUT AND EAT THEM, ALL OF THEM, THEN YOU'D BE PUTTING THEM OUT OF THEIR MISERY. THEN…THEN YOU CAN FREE MY SPIRIT. THINK ABOUT IT. IF YOU FREE ME NOW, AND THEN DIE TOMORROW BY DADDY LONG LEGS' GUN, THEN ALL OF THOSE SOULS WILL BE STUCK IN THE GROUND TO SUFFER AND SUFFER FOREVER AND EVER. IT IS HEROIC TO GAMBLE WITH YOUR OWN LIFE, WILL FOUNDLING. BUT IT IS NOT HEROIC TO GAMBLE WITH SO MANY SOULS! THEY WILL SHATTER AND SCATTER ANYWAY ONCE THEY ARE FREED. BUT IN ME THEY CAN REMAIN INTACT FOREVER."

Will lowered the shovel and his head, absorbing the Drageist's words. "They make you stronger, don't they? The souls."

"YESSSSS. THEY DO. AND WHEN I AM REBORN FROM THE DEPTHS OF THE GROUND I WILL BE GREATER IN STRENGTH AND MAJESTY. AND YOU SHALL ACHIEVE IMMORTALITY BY TAKING YOUR RIGHTFUL PLACE IN MY ETERNAL MEMORY. YOU, MY LIBERATOR, MY SAVIOR. YOUR NAME WILL NEVER BE FORGOTTEN. WHAT SAY YOU?"

Will peered up at him. "I say…fer a creature without lips, you sure know how to kiss ass!" He then struck at the icy wall with all his might.

"NO!" the Drageist protested. "I WILL NOT BE DENIED!"

Will ignored he monster's cries and pleas. With each solid jab of the spear-like shovel, the wall of ice lost a large chunk. "Hey, Dragon!" Will yelled as he worked. "Remember when you said all these frozen people around us would thaw out an' come back to life as soon as you were freed?"

The Drageist growled and bared its teeth. "I ONLY SAID THAT SO YOU WOULD FREE ME. BUT THAT WAS BEFORE I

TASTED THOSE SOULS."

Will shook his head. "Figured." He stabbed at the ice again, hard, revealing the hole in the stone wall. He reached into the hole and felt something round and smooth and metal.

"I WILL FIND YOU, WILL FOUNDLING!" the Drageist roared. "I WILL HASTEN MY GROWTH TO REINCARNATE SOONER. I WILL SEEK YOU OUT WHEN I AGAIN DRAW BREATH. AND IF YOU ELUDE ME, THEN I WILL KILL EVERY TENDIKEYE I FIND!"

Will tried to pull on the metal ball, but it was hard to get a grip, and his fingertips slipped off of it.

"I WILL SLAY EVERY TENDIKEYE IN THE CLUSTER! HOW DARE YOU DENY MY WANT, YOU, A WEAK AND FRAIL MORTAL! I WILL NEVER FORGET THE INSULT OF HAVING TO RELY ON YOU TO FREE ME FROM THIS PRISON! I OWE YOU NOTHING, YOU FREAK!"

Will grabbed the ball again. Instead of pulling, he tried to twist it, first clockwise, then counter clockwise. Twisting with all his might and concentration, the ancient cannonball once used to slay a dragon came loose in his hand. The roar of the Drageist stopped. Out of the corner of his eye, Will saw the Drageist sink into the ground like a limp, dead snake sinking into a murky pond.

The once cold air of the cavern grew warm, and Will could hear the trickling of water all around him. The icy covered walls melted away and the stale water it made quickly evaporated. Dozens of dead bodies fell to the cave floor. And from the preserved corpses came the souls of the dead. The spirits stood around the tendikeye, filling the cave with their ghostly glow.

Many of them, including a little boy, were smiling at him.

"Thank you," the boy said. "The Drageist kept us all prisoner and fed off us. Thank you, sir, for breaking our terrible curse."

Everything in Will's logic told him that he should be terrified. But he wasn't. At that moment, ghosts no longer scared him. All around him he could feel the gratitude of the spirits.

"Happy to help!" he called out with a grin. "Now, go! Forget this life an' start new ones. Keep the cycle goin' like it should. Go clean and in peace!"

The spirits of the dead exploded into millions of pieces and scattered in all directions, free from memory and remorse. Will admired the smooth dark polish of the cannonball in his hand. *"Yep,"* he thought. *"It's just like the Headsman's Axe, alright. I can't wait to show the others when we meet back up. Rev'll be impressed, I just know it!"*

Will left the cave and descended the hill, finding Ivy waiting for him. He showed her the cannonball. It was a perfectly round orb, polished smooth and reflective like dark silver. Hematite. Giving it to her, he said, "Take it an' hide it, jus' in case I die tomorrow. This thing is once piece of a greater puzzle that keeps the Geohex active. No matter what happens, the Trottin' Swans must never get it back."

Ivy nodded and placed the orb in her carrying bag. "What now?" she asked.

Will looked back up at the cave. "Now, we go back to town an' tell anyone an' everyone that the Drageist is done for. And that there're about two dozen corpses that need to be tended to."

Ivy took a doubtful breath. "Good luck convincing people that it's safe to go in there again. After that?"

"After that we wait fer the hunwalls to dim an' night to fall. I wanna sneak onto a certain man's property an' do some diggin'. An' I need you to be my look out."

"Are you digging another grave?" she asked.

Will looked away and lit up a cigarette. He seemed bothered by the question. "Maybe. Prob'ly."

Part 5

The big day had arrived whether it wanted to or not. All the townsfolk of Pevulanium gathered to witness what was expected to be Daddy Long Legs' one hundredth victory. Throughout the decades and centuries, few previous duels had drawn such a turnout. Once in a great while, a bold, would-be hero with some measure of fame would cause people to at least make meager wagers on the duel, but no one ever truly believed that Daddy Long Legs could be beaten.

Either way, many people were glad that this would be Daddy's final duel before retiring. They were sick of seeing people die for nothing. After years and years it had ceased to be a sporting spectacle. To them, Daddy was a crafty spider who could trap his prey by way of pride and greed. No one really liked him, but most feared him enough to pretend they did.

Will Foundling stood close by one of the turn posts, the one furthest from Daddy's mansion, fact be known. Taking off his green scaly dust coat, he hung it on the post and turned to face the crowd. With expert eyes, he singled out everyone he had met in his short time there. He then glanced over at the Garden of Fools and shuddered. He was afraid, unsure if his strategy would work. He was no lead dealer, no fancy pistoleer duelist. He was an ambusher, a bushwhacker, and a specialist in woodland skirmishes. Standing on that leaf covered field, he felt naked and almost helpless. Almost.

"I hope this works," he thought as he raised his hand to the crowd, grabbing their attention.

The crowd quieted down purely out of respect for the tendikeye's last words.

"Townsfolk of Pevulanium. My name is Will Foundling. I want you all to be aware that my reason fer fightin' today ain't fer greed. I an' my compatriots of Four Winds – One Storm are tryin' to end the Geohex in yer county one curse at a time. The Trottin' Swan's stand in opposition to this, which ain't no big secret. An' so, hopefully, me an' my team can solve our differences with the Swans by havin' a fair an' square duel to the death."

"You're an idiot, and you talk funny!" someone shouted from the crowd.

Will ignored it and continued. "An' jus' so y'all know that I ain't motivated by greed like those that came before me, I am goin' to make each and every one of you a promise. I hear that Daddy Long Leg's wealth is around four hun'erd thousand grotz. If I win, then every one of you will get an equal share of that money. This I swear before you all!"

The townsfolk reacted to the promise with curious amusement. It was indeed a nice gesture and idea. And such a generous gift would do wonders for the poor town's economy. But still, most dismissed the idea as a vain hope.

"Good luck, Will Foundling!" a single, unseen stranger cried out.

It was all Will needed to hear. He grinned in spite of his fear.

Just then, the front door of Daddy Long Legs' mansion opened, and out he came, followed by his wife, Cymbre, and twelve other Trotting Swans. All of them, even Cymbre, were armed with pistols or shotguns.

Will recognized two Swans as the men whose wrists he dislocated. He avoided eye contact with every one of them save Daddy. The tall drakeri's eyes were cold, calm, and confident. His wiry, looming stature shifted smoothly as his imposing gait brought him across the field. The sound of his and his entourage's footsteps on the dead leaves was all Will could hear through the soft autumn wind.

"It's a good day to die," Will said as Daddy reached the opposing post.

"It's an even better day to kill," Daddy replied. He removed his hat and placed it on the post. "I've decided what to inscribe on your gravemarker. '*Here festers Will Foundling. A double-bastard, unwanted by both parents.*'" The tall man grinned. "What think you of that?"

Will shook his head in disgust and pity. "I think it's a shame that you won't live to feel the pain of defeat, Daddy Long Legs."

Daddy gave Will a slight nod. "Fair enough. Let my name be your last words, tendikeye. Death awaits you."

The two enemies met in the middle of the two posts, where a bent, yet dignified old woman approached them.

"Good morning, gentlemen. I am Sheriff Maviel Poge, and I have been elected by the town council to ensure that this duel is done lawfully and with civility on both sides. The rules are simple. You will start by standing back-to-back, feet together, and knees straight. I will give the signal word, which on this day shall be "apple." Upon hearing this word, you will both be allowed to turn and run to your respective posts. Once you have run past your respective post, you will then be allowed to turn, draw, and fire your weapon until the other man is dead. If you cheat, you are a murderer, and will be executed on the spot. Are there any questions?"

Will looked over at the woman and raised a hand. "I jus'

330

gotta make it past that post, right?"

"That is correct, young sir."

Will swallowed. "An' I can dodge his shots, too, right? That okay? Once I get there?"

The old woman frowned in thought.

Will heard Daddy scoff behind him. "You won't be able to dodge me."

Maviel raised her chin. "Yes, it is legal to dodge and duck...provided that you make it past the post." She paused and added "But you are not allowed to use your post as cover, if that was your strategy, young sir."

Daddy laughed out loud.

Will grinned. "No, ma'am. It wudn't."

The old woman and everyone nearby backed away a good, safe distance. "Are you ready, sirs?" Maviel asked loud enough for all of Pevulaneum to hear.

The two gunmen nodded.

"*APPLE!!!*"

Each man had fifty feet of ground to cover. Will covered his with eight swift steps and a desperate diving leap that took him the rest of the way.

Daddy cleared his distance in a matter of seconds using his long steps and insect-like speed. Both men reached the turning point at the exact same time.

Daddy Long Legs heard the sound of many sticks breaking and leaves crumbling as he turned and drew his pistol. His long spindly finger began to squeeze the trigger as his eyes faced forward to see his final opponent. But Will Foundling was nowhere to be seen! In that split instant of confusion, Daddy saw a gaping black hole in the ground just past the tendikeye's post. The faint sight of quills and the twin barrels of Will's Mark Twain Special poked out of the hole, just long enough to fire two rounds of hot lead in Daddy's direction.

The tall Drakeri, unaware the terrain of his old familiar battle ground had been secretly altered by the implantation of a foxhole disguised by leaves and sticks, caught both of Will's bullets in his throat and forehead. The angle and momentum of the shot caused his lifeless body to flip backward like a discarded ragdoll, falling and landing violently onto the bloody remnants of his head

331

and neck. For several seconds, the body twitched and pumped blood onto the ground before curling up into a ball.

Every onlooker gasped and winced at the sight of the fearsome giant brought low. All faces were frozen, stunned, and shocked. No tongue stirred.

No one even breathed until old Daiv Tchanly uttered the astonished words, "He really *is* a Harker!"

Will Foundling stood up from the belly-deep hole in the ground, still holding his pistol. He passed a dire glance over the dumbfounded Trotting Swans before turning his attention to Sheriff Poge.

"What say you, Sheriff? Is this duel concluded?"

Before the old drakeress could find the words to reply, Cymbre NcRuse raised her voice in a blood curdling shout. "Cheater!" she yelled, stepping forward and pulling at her sidearm.

The other Swans began to follow suit and readied their guns.

Will instantly ducked back down into his foxhole. He was ready for this.

"Wait!" The sheriff demanded with outstretched arms. "I am the judge of this duel, Cymbre, not you!"

The newly made widow gave the old woman a nasty sneer. "Back down, old buzzard! This tendikeye cheated! Back down, or learn your place the hard way."

The old woman huffed and fumed with indignation. Balling her wrinkled hands into fists, she stepped boldly between the Swans and Will. "Hear me, tendikeye! I have lived a good and worthwhile 957 years. I never thought I'd live to see Daddy defeated. You followed the rules, and I hereby declare you the winner! And if these parasitical cowards wish to shred my body with bullets, I say let them! And I wish you the best of luck, for that is what your kind revere most, in avenging me and this town for the poison and pain they've brought."

She focused her stern gaze at Cymbre. "You have one hour to collect your tacky dresses from that mansion, Cymbre. It is now the property of Mr. Foundling, as are all the money and valuables located within. Take only what you alone can carry. I declare this matter concluded."

The crowds cheers came loud and clear, a jovial release from fear and oppression. It was no longer about Daddy Long Legs versus a foreign stranger. It was about the Trotting Swans versus the townsfolk of Pevulanium. And the townsfolk that day had won! Will's victory was their victory. It was the beginning of the defiance of a subtle tyranny that had plagued the town for far too long. Many cried, for their relatives had been killed by Daddy. Many were just happy to get money to feed their children.

Meil Norred cried out for joy as he steadied himself on his crutches. "I got a new house! I got a new house! Oh, thank you, Will Foundling!"

Will heard the man and yelled back, "Happy to help, Mr. Norred! Just bear in mind that the place is full of stairs!"

Meil looked down at his broken ankle and frowned. Then he shrugged and went back to rejoicing. His ankle would heal in time, as would the whole town of Pevulanium.

Eldon Htims of the dislocated wrists left the company of his Trotting Swan brethren and whispered something into Will's ear, "A deal is a deal, buttpit. Make sure you dig that grave late at night when everyone is asleep. And don't you dare tell anyone about our deal."

"You got it. Thank you." Will returned.

Eldon shook his head, looking dissatisfied. "Bear in mind that this is not over. Other Swans will come for you and your people. I'll be staying home to heal my wrists. You'll have no more trouble from me. But the others..." The man said no more and walked away.

Will passed a glance at the remaining Swans and the widow Cymbre NcRuse. They were all walking away, talking and planning. Will tried to listen or read their lips, but the crowd of cheering townsfolk surrounded him.

It was a day of celebration. The property of Daddy Long Legs was emptied. Everyone got a fair share of money in their pocket and a souvenir or two. In the end, every person got about a month's pay. But it would do the local economy good.

Will Foundling kept only two things for himself: the *Vaughn* pistol and the two hundred grotz that Daddy had given him. He and some of the enthusiastic local youths took sledge hammers and busted the cursed headstones of *The Garden Of Fools* into rubble.

The corpse of Daddy Long Legs was thrown into the grave

that had been meant for his one hundredth kill. The children of Pevulanium, many of whom had grown up afraid of Daddy, took great delight in chucking the pieces of the busted gravemarkers into the hole where Daddy was tossed. The plot was full of broken rock in a matter of minutes.

Many relieved families dug up their kin in the garden, in efforts to move their remains to family plots. At the humble request of Will, the bones of all the tendikeye buried there were exhumed and burned in separate brush piles.

"These ain't the only dead that need tendin'," he told the large group of townsfolk who were eager to help.

He led them to the cave of the Drageist. Using the *Vaughn* pistol, he shot down the warning sign at the base of the hill. A single bullet shattered the thick wood post.

At first, most of the townsfolk were too scared to follow him up. But eventually, they saw that the cave had no dragon ghost haunting its interior. They emptied the cave of the Drageist victims and carried them respectfully down the hill.

Will took one last look around inside the former lair of the monster. As if by chance, he found a single bluish white scale the size of a turtle shell. He studied it for a moment before shrugging and tossing it back on the ground. *"Better to let a local kid find it,"* he thought with a smirk.

He stepped out of the cave, greeted by the enthralled townspeople. They cheered and chanted his name. "Will Foundling. Pistol Duel Champion. Drageist Slayer. Liberator of the Dead." Throughout the whole day, he was treated like their hero. Men offered him drinks. Women offered themselves. But through it all, Will managed to stay clothed and sober.

Later that night, he escaped the crowd for one last deed. He came to the grave of Rusty Feldurhau behind the home of Eldon Htims. Sitting lazily against the headstone was a skeleton caked in dirt. The skeleton had dug itself out of its own grave.

"'Bout time you showed up," the skeleton muttered.

"Rusty Feldurhau?" Will asked, crossing him arms.

The skeleton picked off an earthworm from its rib cage and nodded before tossing it into the grass. "Do I not frighten you, hero?"

Will shook his head. "I've seen worse."

The skeleton laughed and looked at him. "So, I've heard. The caven trees speak very highly of you. They tell me that you have but me to destroy for your task to be complete."

"Yeah."

The skeleton hung its head and sighed. "Would that you had been born sooner, hero. Or that I had never been born at all. I led that posse. I put the noose around those lover's necks. I killed them and their unborn child. For thousands of years, I have been cursed for it. All around me I have watched the town I grew up in fall to ruin. The trees, hero. The trees! The trees were what made this town grand! I had to watch my own family line dwindle and wither in that house. We were nut farmers, you see. My crime made us destitute. I am ready to die, soul and all. And I am sorry that I lived, for the way I lived. Please, make an end of it now."

Will took out his canteen of pepperwine and dumped the entire contents onto the skeleton. He lit the sulking bones with his lighter and watched them burn to black dust. Taking a caven nut out of his pocket, he dropped it in the hole the skeleton had crawled out of.

No sooner had he covered up the hole than Will's ears caught something loud and weird. He had never heard a sound like that before, yet it seemed familiar. It came from the woods on the outskirts of town.

"Ivy! Daiv!" he gasped as fear took hold of his heart. Through the festive town he ran, over tin rooftops, over bonfires in backyard parties, through the dusty streets, and past numerous startled townsfolk. Onward he made his way to Daiv and Ivy's tree house.

The lights were on. The front door was wide open. "Daiv! Ivy!" he yelled inside. But there came no answer.

Behind him, he heard the sound of mixed laughter of two voices. Without pause, he turned and made his way deeper into the woods. He did not have to go far. High, high, high up in the tallest caven tree Will had ever seen were Daiv and his daughter Ivy. They were standing on a limb, picking caven nuts the size of rugby balls.

Ivy looked down, her face in a wild grin, to see Will's astonished look of puzzlement. "Will! They grew! The caven trees shot up and grew!"

"It a miracle!" Daiv laughed, as he held up one of the huge

nuts. "I can make four jars of the finest butter with just this! There must be thousands like this one! I'm going to be a rich man!"

"We can hire helpers from town! Dozens or maybe even a hundred!" Ivy declared. "Will, you did it! The caven nuts will bring this town back to the way it once was!"

Will looked all around him in the dark woods. Reaching high into the night were countless caven trees that dwarfed every oak and maple. The forest itself had changed. Everything seemed fresher, healthier. No more curses remained in Pevulaneum.

In the days that followed, Will witnessed the complete resurrection of a small town's spirit. With Daddy Long Legs dead, the Drageist gone, and the caven trees restored to their former glory, the once poor and downtrodden townsfolk were renewed by hope for a brighter future. Will Foundling was a mere mortal tendikeye. But there, in the hearts and minds of those people, his name and memory became immortal.

Just before he left town for good, he laid down with pretty Ivy Tchanly one last time. For hours, she listened as he told her his life story as far as he understood it. There were too many deeds in his past left undone, too many scores to settle, too many questions left unanswered. She understood that he had to leave, but that did not make it any easier on her seeing him go.

When Will Foundling, the Liberator of the Dead, left town, he took the main road in broad daylight. A part of him had hoped that the remainder of the Trotting Swans would attempt an ambush. They never did. They were too busy planning something worse.

The morning he left it had rained and rained throughout the previous night. Will opted to take the main road back to Drowsy Nook, not wanting to get his boots soggy in the fields and forests. They were a sturdy pair of boots, meant to endure the elements, but Will saw no need for unnecessary wear and tear. Finding a cobbler skilled enough to make new boots for a tendikeye was rare in Doflend.

The rain died down to a mere drizzle. With every dozen

336

steps he ran, Will could feel the day getting warmer. The yellow daylight stabbed through an ominous cloud slowly passing over most of Wraith County.

Will smirked as he ran. *"Should I tell 'em all about it, or should I just let the locals tell 'em once word spreads?"* he thought.

On either side of the gray gravel road, there were gray fields and gray trees. Fallen autumn leaves had soaked up the cold rain and lost their lush vibrant shades. All was dull and devoid of beauty found in more healthy lands. All but the tiny speck of red that approached from further down the road.

Will squint his eyes. It was a Drakeri female wearing a blood red hood and cloak. *"Z'at Polly?"* the tendikeye thought, hoping. *"Must be!"* He quickened his pace to a dead-out sprint.

At first, he was excited to be meeting with his teammate. But the closer they got, the more uneasy he became. By the time he was within shouting distance, he stopped. His stomach felt queasy. Something wasn't right.

"Polly?" he called out. "Hey, Pol. Z'at you?"

He was answered with laughter. He had only heard Polly laugh once in the short time he knew her. But being a Harker, that was enough to know the difference.

As the woman approached, he saw that her body was similar, her walk was nearly the same, and her face almost identical to his friend's.

He drew his Mark Twain Pistol and yashinin blade.

The woman's laughter intensified. Her wicked expression, her eyes. They were the same eyes he felt himself making: eyes filled with killing intent.

"You are Will Foundling, praised as a savior in Embrenil! Where is she?" the woman called out in furious demand. "Where is my daughter, de one you call Polly Gone?"

Will knew that only suicidal tendikeye traded words with malicious theurges. He answered her with two bullets. His Mark Twain Special roared its stutter-shot report. *KA-KRAK!*

He watched the woman's head and chest explode in splashes of blood. But just as soon as the liquid spread out it went back, reforming into the shape of an unharmed woman. As he watched her entire body ripple like the surface of a pond, Will Foundling tasted despair.

"I am Veluora," she said, taking a step forward. "De Red Witch of Chume!"

Will took a step back, his heart pounding in his ears.

Veluora smiled, opening her perfectly shaped mouth and said, *"Blood for Blood."*

In the deepest pit of his chest, Will felt his heart being squeezed. Warm thick blood flooded out his eyes, ears, nose, and mouth. His body stiffened and shook violently. His weapons fell out of his hands. Somehow, he maintained his balance. "

Back away!" he told himself. He bent his knees, dug his heels into the gravel, and launched himself backward high into the air. He landed poorly and collapsed onto his back. By pure instinct, he got up and leapt backward again. In mid-leap, the tremors in his body subsided. He landed in a deep squat, rubbed the blood from his eyes, and saw Veluora charging him. She spread out her arms and long, spike-covered veins slithered out of her wrists like writhing tentacles.

"Gotta keep my distance!" he thought. *"That maxim dang near did me in!"*

Veluora moved with liquid grace, matching Will's speed with ease. Even from thirty feet away, her jagged veins could reach him.

Will dodged and ducked the incoming lashes with desperate abandon. He had trained to evade fists, feet, elbows, knees, blades, clubs, and even bullets. But avoiding ten yard long whips covered with ten inch spikes he'd have to learn on the fly.

There was no time to pull his rifle, Falcona, from her case. Will doubted the weapon would even matter in this fight. He considered turning to run but judged the theurgess' speed to rival his own. Her spiked vein-whips cracked and whooshed all around him.

There came an all-too-brief instant where Will thought he was getting a grasp of her attack patterns, her timing, and her methods of assault. But then she leapt high into the air and raised her shapely leg in a grand kick, and more veins shot out of her ankles!

"How!?!" Will thought in amazement and terror.

Veluora dashed and leapt, flailing her arms and legs like a barbarous ballerina, each limb sending forth and snapping multiple jagged tendrils with uncanny momentum and merciless velocity.

The tendikeye became caught up in the snapping barrage like a confused mouse between many alert cats. For what seemed like minutes on end, the veins whipped him around like a rag doll, feeling like daggers on iron chains. He cursed his supernatural durability. It was only prolonging the inevitable. If not for his "curse" and his snake scale dust coat, he'd have been torn to bits. Death was coming though, eventually.

"But not today!" Will thought, gritting his teeth. *"Not by her!"*

He found his footing and focused on his target. Like a dervish he charged at her, spinning hard and fast with each step. The spikes of her veins glanced off the stern scales of his coat. He reached for and pulled out his canteen flask from his inside pocket. Still spinning and closing in fast, he unscrewed the flask's top and splashed its contents directly into the face of the grinning witch.

Veluora let out a scream that cracked into an ear-piercing squeal. She drew her veins back into her arms and fell to the ground, covering her face in agony.

Without compassion or mercy, Will dumped the rest of the pepperwine onto her yelping head until even her long silky hair was drenched with the stuff. Pepperwine was not only one of the spiciest substances known, but it was also one hundred and eighty proof alcohol.

Will stomped on her stomach with his size twenty-three boot, knocking the wind out of her. He then whipped out his flip-top lighter, ignited it, and tossed it at her face.

Veluora fought to breathe again as her entire head burst into flames. She inhaled to scream, but her lungs filled only with fire.

Will put his boot on her chest to keep her from rolling around. "Burn, witch!" he screamed at her.

She threw up her arms and shot out her veins, but they came out like weak little worms. In less than a minute, Veluora's head was nothing more than a charred black skull. Her body lay still in the wet gray pasture.

Will looked down at the corpse and shook his head. He had just killed Polly's mother. He did not know what disturbed him more: that he brutally killed his teammate's kin or that his

339

teammate would be happy to hear about it.

He turned and made his way back to the road. His face, chest, and hands stung with numerous cuts. Blood and sweat mingled before dripping off his chin. He saw his pistol and sword lying in the gravel getting wet. He let out a bothered sigh at the thought of them getting rusty.

"You are quite adorable," came a voice very close behind him. Will turned with a jolt.

As he did, Veluora tackled him to the ground. She was completely healed, even her clothes looked unscorched. But she was smaller now, diminished to the height of child. Her jagged veins slithered out of her wrists and ankles, coiling around Will's arms and legs.

Will knew countless ways to out-wrestle stronger opponents and escape numerous locks and holds. But theurgically controlled veins were too strange, too alien for him to contend with. Veluora had him pinned and helpless on the ground.

Her cruel and beautiful face gazed down at him. She tilted her smiling head this way and that as Will struggled uselessly beneath her.

"Oh, the things I could do to you right now!" she laughed. "Such a handsome face. Such a lean body." She grinded him in a shameless straddle. "Mmm. And such creamy, sweet blood." She lowered her ample chest against his and slowly licked his blood-soaked cheek, moaning in ecstasy as she did so.

Will shook his head and squeezed his eyes shut. "You sick witch!" He held still in terror and restrained rage as she licked his face clean.

When she stopped, he opened his eyes just in time to watch her eyes flash red. "How... interesting..." she said with curious bemusement. "You... you really aren't so bad, Will Foundling. You've killed many for a boy your age. Your father would be proud."

Will bared his teeth. "What do you know, you mystic freak?"

"I know more dan you do about you, Will... 'Foundling' is a bit reductive considering your natural parentage."

Will gazed up at her in sudden realization. "You did that blood trick on me, like Polly can do. You read my memories in my blood, didn't ya?"

Veluora cleared her throat as if offended. "I did more dan

dat, young man. I saw your entire life. I followed your bloodline back to even before your father's seed stabbed into your mother's egg. I know deir names, Will. I know why you were left on de doorstep of de Cottersba household. And I know of a way to end your protection curse. There's no shame in wanting to be vulnerable. Especially when it would allow you to return home and take vengeance on Pang. What he did to your family...oh...how unforgiving he was! De unforgiving are unforgivable, yes? Such a sweet irony." She cackled madly as she watched him take in her words.

Will stared up in amazement. "You found out...all that by drinking...?

"Yes, yes!" she interrupted, rolling her eyes. "And I will swear on my philocreed dat I will relay to you all dat your blood has told me."

Will nodded in understanding and furrowed his brow. "An' all I hafta do in return is let you take Polly back to Chume."

"*Help* me take her back," Veluora corrected. "I need you to distract or kill de other two when I reclaim her. Do dis, and I will reward you wit' de truth of your bloodline. Deny me, I will command your blood to fill de one appendage I have not constricted around... yet... and shunt you hard and fast as I torture you long and slow until you die *Die DIE*!!!"

Will took a deep breath and let it out. Out of the corners of his eyes, he watched the spiky veins coiled around his arms, holding them down straight and spread-eagled. He then noticed that the veins were only wrapped around the sleeves of his thick coat, and not his naked wrists.

"*Oh,*" he thought, surprised that he did see the opportunity sooner.

In one smooth motion, he sat up, letting his arms slip out of his coat. He looked Veluora dead in the eyes, his nose touching hers.

Startled, the witch's head snapped back.

Then without word or warning, Will grasped her jaw and hair and broke her neck in a fast clean snap.

Veluora and her horrid veins went limp.

Not wasting any time, Will threw her off and rolled away on the cold wet grass. He let out a shriek of disgust as he untangled her slippery sharp veins from his ankles. He got up and dashed for his

341

sword and pistol. He jumped, dived, grasped them both, rolled, and then stood up facing her in a kneeling fighting stance.

But Veluora lay still, perfectly still as death. For several of the scariest moments in Will's life, neither of them moved. The colossal gray cloud had moved on, taking its gray cold drizzle with it.

Will did more than watch as he waited for the body to stir, he listened. His quill-covered ears harked for the sound of grass rustling beneath her, for some hiss of breath in the air. Nothing.

Taking careful aim, he fired a single bullet into her small, child-sized head.

Then her body collapsed, clothing and all, into a shapeless puddle of blood. Faster than what seemed possible, it soaked into the ground leaving no trace of the woman called Veluora.

Gone.

Chapter 6
Army of the Dammed

Part 1

It moved stealthily between the thin trees on the creek bank, its spindly form nearly disappearing behind every tree it moved passed. It was nearly as tall as a man, not as intelligent, but far more cunning. Its serpentine neck sat like an angry cobra atop its avian body. Nearby, the unsupecting prey was slurping up the brown water, unaware of what was coming. The predator moved in, one in color with the gray and blue weather, seen but unseen. The spindly body and snake-like neck arched and twitched, and in a flash the gopher was in the Great Cobalt Heron's beak. The struggling critter fought to no avail as the furtive bird's spear-like beak pinched its neck flat. After a couple of deft shakes the gopher's neck broke, and the Heron swallowed it whole. After washing the furry food down with a few gulps of water, the Heron took to the air. When it was no longer in his sight, Hindin Revetz resumed his walk down the shady road.

This was the third time he had spotted a Great Cobalt Heron by the water. Upon each sighting of the bird Hindin felt the chi in his chest stir, alerting him that this was of important significance. Rarely did he receive a divination in front of his eyes. Such omens were usually viewed behind them during his lengthy meditational katas. It seemed that either Nature was trying to tell him something or that he may have inadvertently peeked over Nature's shoulder to see what it was working on.

"Interpreting outer omens like these are difficult," Hindin thought as he walked. *"It requires an open mind, without the strictness of logic and without the misleading whims of creativity.*

343

Somewhere between logic and creativity is the answer. I dare not entertain present speculations just yet, lest I become entrapped by the wrong notion. If only Will were with me. He could have told me more about that bird, what sex it was, how old, primary diet, etc. Such knowledge might be useful. Then again, the omen was for me, not him"

Before departing Drowsy Nook, Hindin had learned that the small village of Victor's Grove was haunted by the ghost of a necrowitch who had lived and died there long ago.

He personally despised the term witch as it was a slur against theurges, and even the most reviled theurges did not seem deserving of the unsavory term. Still, Hindin accepted that he was in a rural part of Doflend, and such forms of prejudice often had to be tolerated.

"It is a sad thing that ignorance must sometimes be ignored," he thought as he briskly made his way up and down the country road. To his right were rocky woodlands rising and falling like frozen ocean waves covered in half-dead trees. To his left was a muddy creek called the Joachim, which in old drakeri means "muddy creek."

Following the muddy Joachim creek, he came to the tiny village of Victor's Grove. The creek had been dammed, causing the water level to rise and form a lake in a nearby valley. The other side of the dam sloped down like a ramp, with a box-like enclosure the size of a small house near the bottom of the creek bed. From beneath this enclosure, going through the dam itself, came a small but steady current of water which allowed the creek to continue. This reservoir dam was also the bridge that Hindin had to cross in order to get to town.

"It is a rather majestic dam for such a rural community," he noted to himself. *"And the lake is vast and splendid in the dayshine. Unlike other rural dams, the stones of this dam/bridge are not merely a mass of mismatched, uncut rocks that are crudely mortared together, but stones cleanly cut and perfectly even albino granite. Such stone must have been imported."*

Upon crossing the dam and bridge, he saw that the village was the husk of a once quaint community. An elevated railway cut between the outside edge of town and the water. The ancient rails were pitted lines of rust and the wood of the track was petrified

344

from age. The first house on the other side of the track was a big green house with white trim about the high arches of the roof. It was the only two-story building in town from what he could see. Hindin heard the excited screeches of playing children.

Just as he crossed the tracks on the main village road, *they* came into view. Ten humanlings and their dog poured onto the street, shouting, laughing, arguing, and whining. They were six boys and four girls dressed poor but proper. All were of a look, with the same dark hair and stern eyebrows. When they beheld the tall malruka standing not twenty feet from them, they all went still and quiet, just as rabbits do when they sense a larger beast.

"Good day, children," Hindin said with a cheerful nod. "Are your parents nearby?"

"It's the Man-Squisher!" a boy exclaimed in a choked whisper.

"What?" Hindin asked, unfamiliar the term.

"Edifice Man-Squisher from Drowsy Nook!" another boy shouted, pointing his finger. "He's here to squish us!"

Most of the girls and two toddler boys began to scream and cry. Hindin was at a loss for words as the other kids picked up rocks.

"Leave us alone, Man-Squisher!" shouted the eldest, a boy of around fourteen. He chucked a stone that pinged off Hindin's steel cheek. "Go back to Drowsy Nook!"

"No-No," Hindin stammered. "Children, you are mistaken. I am but a -"

More rocks came, rocks and words that struck just as harshly.

"We don't want you here!"

"We won't let you squish us!"

"Hey, duzn't he have a cannon-gun? Where'z his cannon gun?"

"Go away you big metal monster!"

"He's ugly!"

"BARK BARK BARK!" barked their dog.

All the kids threw stones from the road and nearby train tracks, pelting the giant stranger from all sides.

Any cool Hindin had when he walked into town was lost as he shouted "Unruly brats! You dare throw *ROCKS* at me? What if I threw the bones of your ancestors at you? For shame!"

345

All he could do was stand there and dodge the barrage of stones and insults. Then, over the shouting, came the loud slamming of a house door followed by the commanding roar of an irate mother.

The short-but-stern humaness emerged from the large green house armed with a greasy spatula. "I will not tolerate racism from my own flesh and blood!" she declared in a reedy shriek. One by one she smote the bottoms of the rock-chucking children. None were spared the justice of her spatula, not even the dog.

Once punished, the humanlings fled as their mother cried out, "That isn't Edifice Teige, you nitwits! You'd better stay gone 'til bedtime!" Turning her face to Hindin, he could now see where the kids had inherited their stern eyebrows.

"Sir," she began. "I sincerely apologize for my wicked children's behavior. Are you all right?"

Hindin nodded, relieved to hear the lady was well-spoken. "I am, madam. I surmise that Edifice Teige has a less-than perfect reputation throughout the rest of this county?"

The woman nodded. "He's a bit of a boogie-monster with his history of squishing men into puddles. That, and he rarely lets anyone passing through Drowsy Nook leave this county. Reasons he gave for that were often mendacious."

Hindin raised his chin. "I see. Then... you should be informed that his blocking and squishing days are over. He is dead."

The woman raised her chin, as well. "I was already informed, sir. Word traveled faster than you did. I take it you are a member of the Excursionist group that did him in?"

"Four Winds – One Storm," he said with a courteous bow. "I am the Chimancer, Hindin Revetz."

The lady smiled and returned the gesture. "Pleased to meet you, Hindin. I am Näncine Strother, Zoonomist and keeper of the Laid Back Hotel."

"You are a theurgess of animals?"

"No no, only a disciple of the philocreed. It's given me the strength and peace of mind to weather the pangs of motherhood and cope with the charm of my husband. Would you like to have a seat on my patio?"

"I would, Näncine. Thank you."

"I would invite you into my house for supper, but..."

346

"I understand. I have no need for your food, and your wooden floors have no need for my weight. Thank you all the same."

The big green house was L-shaped. Nestled in the corner of that L was a cracked and pitted patio. At its center was a raised fire pit full of dying embers that leaked withering fingers of smoke into the air. Around the pit a half dozen trunk-sized logs were arranged for seating. Hindin took the largest.

Näncine sat the one next to him. Tossing her spatula down and letting out a tired laugh, the middle-aged woman remarked, "Of all the beasts I've studied, none are as wild as Fevärian children."

Hindin smiled and set down his duffel bag of books. "Speaking of beasts, many chimancers such as I study the defense and hunting methods of certain beasts to better our martial capacity."

Näncine arched an eyebrow and crossed her arms, a knowing smile forming on her lips. "There's more to animals than fighting, Mr. Revetz. All animals, not just certain ones, have value. Animals are beings with simpler minds, but clearer purpose than people. They know their roles in nature and reality, unlike us. There is much to learn from each of them, more than just violence. Each beast carries lessons to teach and virtues to instill in all facets of life."

Hindin tilted his shiny head and pondered. "What do you know of Great Cobalt Herons? I encountered one three times on my way here."

Näncine inhaled through her nostrils. "That was the King of the Creek you saw. Well, that's what *I* call him. He's a flighty king, elusive, aloof, and evasive. Those are his virtues."

Hindin nodded, enjoying what he was learning. "I see. Are there other zoonomists here? Have you a theurge who might know more?"

She shook her head. "Just me. And perhaps my children, someday, should they choose the path. We have no theurge here, only a white temple where I and two other ladies give sermons and teach the sciences of our respective philocreeds. We are a lay coven, if that makes any sense."

Hindin arched a steel brow. "You are the wise women of the village then?"

Näncine let out a big laugh. "Well now, don't give us too

347

much credit. We're just doing our part to keep our community literate and decent."

"**I'M NAKED! Hee hee hee hee! I'M NAKED!**" shrieked a skeleton as it ran through a nearby yard. It was man-sized with bleached bones and arms flailing wildly as it ran. And sure enough, it wore no clothes.

Hindin stood at once to face the post-mort intruder.

But Näncine rose too and touched his arm. "Sit down. Just ignore him," she whispered sharply.

"But...!"

"Ignore him. It's only Mortimur. Pay him no mind, and he'll go away."

Hindin shook his head in confusion. "What?"

"Sit down!" she demanded.

But it was too late. Hindin saw the face of the boney interloper turn at them with mischief in its fleshless visage. "**I'M NAAAAKEEEED!!!!**" it yelled before running at them.

Näncine rolled her eyes as she sat back down. "Too late," she muttered. "Sit down, Mr, Revetz, and please be quiet. He'll leave in a few minutes."

"I can destroy it," Hindin said, shifting into a stance. Without wasted time or effort, he moved in and struck the thing square in the chest with his palm. The mad collection of bones exploded into dust and debris. Appeased, Hindin bowed at the sight of the explosion. But just as he leaned forward the pieces flew back together, reforming the dancing skeleton without or crack or mark on its animated bones.

"You cannot rescind that one, sir," Näncine told him. "Pound him to powder, and he will still reform."

"**I'M NAKED! LOOKIT Mah DO-DADS! HEE HEE HEE!!!!**" the skeleton laughed as it hopped atop the untaken sitting stumps. Back and forth the bones of Mortimur the Daring hopped and skipped and danced and flipped.

Sensing no danger and taking Näncine's cue, Hindin reluctantly sat back down and did his best to ignore the unwelcome guest.

For several minutes, the bonewalker pranced around them cackling and screeching, until finally, by some mad whim, it took its

348

leave of them and frolicked away.

"Who in Slate's name was that?" Hindin asked in a careful whisper.

Näncine leaned in. "Mortimur the Daring, the Shrieking Streaker of Wraith County. He was a benevolent necrotheurge who tried to break the Geohex long ago. He failed and ended up like that."

"Most disturbing," the malruka said, pinching his chin. "Tell me, how else does the land curse manifest, particularly here in this village? I have heard tales of a female ghost, a necrotheurgess."

The humaness made a ponderous hum and nodded. "Prudence Bavus is her name. The Beaver Queen, they called her. She built that very dam you crossed to get here. To know her history, you must first know the history of the village."

"I am eager to know," said Hindin, his posture becoming impeccable.

Näncine threw a few sticks in the fire pit. "It all began with Victor Bavus, the man who felled the first tree and founded the village way back about three thousand years ago. Now, because Victor's family was so large, he was able to stake a claim substantial enough to cover this entire valley. He and his wife had many children, you see. But after the government acknowledged his claim, it was soon discovered that the thick woods of the densely forested valley contained thousands of ancient tombstones. The valley was in fact a graveyard from a more ancient time. Most likely these were the graves made for the fallen soldiers of the fabled *Battle of the Sorrowful Harvest.* Such an archeological find caused the government to withdraw the claim, but Victor Bavus held tight to it and would not part with his new land for any price. He cleared the valley of its trees and built his village. And he gathered up every tombstone and stacked them into a gargantuan pyramid for children to play on.

"Years passed and the village prospered. His children grew and his wife took ill. After her death, he remarried to a woman named Prudence Lough, a young and striking drakeress of strong bearing and strange humor. The two were married for thirty-four years, not long at all by Drakeri standards, before Victor passed away, leaving Prudence his entire estate. In the years that followed, rumors spread of her being a witch and the cause of many

349

unexplained occurrences.

"Prudence supposedly asked a family to see their newborn baby. Apparently, she was quite fond of them. The family refused and she cursed the child. The child, a girl, eventually died of an illness at the age of nine, but the illness was never determined. The town doctor reported that she had a boil on her neck that, when lanced, produced not puss, but a gooey hairball. The child's death occurred about a month after the lancing.

"In another occurrence, Prudence once offered to buy a cow from a woman, but was refused. She cursed the cow, making it jump the fence and run away. It took the owner three days to find and retrieve it. But from then on the poor beast would only produce bloody milk.

"It was also rumored that Prudence could be trapped in a chair if one stuck a knife's point in one of the chair's legs. Apparently it was a way to trap witches. A little boy tried this once while she was visiting his parent's house. He crawled stealthily behind her chair, took an awl from his trouser pocket, and shoved it into a chair leg. Prudence turned her head, gave the boy the evil eye, and then stood up from the chair laughing. But from that day forth she always had a slight limp in her step.

"A man named Arlan Brunt claimed that Prudence Bavus had transformed him into a bileer and then rode him all night to some Witch's Ball deep in the forest. He said he awoke the next morning tied to a tree, naked and out in the middle of the wood.

"Another man, a hunter named Wilton Brikx, claimed that his rifle had been cursed by the widow Bavus. He said that all of his bullets would miss whenever he shot at game. To break the curse, he forged a silver bullet, loaded it into his afflicted firearm, and shot a photograph of Prudence Bavus at point blank range. Thus was the curse broken.

"These are the most prominent legends, of course," Näncine said, resting her hands on her knees. "And I can assure you that her spirit still dwells here, causing mischief and grief to us all from time to time."

After hearing Näncine's account, Hindin frowned skeptically. "With all due respect, it seems to me that Prudence Bavus was not a theurge at all, but a woman who was blamed for every misfortune or malady that had befallen the town."

350

Näncine smiled at this. "Oh?" she said, seeming to already know what Hindin was getting at.

"Here was my reasoning," Hindin began. "The dying little girl and the cow both suggest that disease was a part of her philocreed path. If so, then necrotherugy could not have been responsible. Disease is one form of life overcoming another form. Even if death results, life would still prevail, if only for a short time. Necrotheurgy is simply about death. Thus, it is more likely that the diseases were acquired naturally, this being an unsanitary pioneer settlement at the time.

"The story of the chair, while amusing, is utter nonsense. Stabbing an inanimate object someone is sitting in could not possibly affect them, even by theurgical means. I've never read or heard of such an occurrence.

"The man who claimed that she transmogrified him into a steed was most likely a liar trying to get out of trouble. Only a master zoonomist can change someone into an animal against their will, as you may well know.

"As for the cursed gun of the hunter, more nonsense. A gun is a weapon and weapons bring death. They are sacred to necrotheurges and their disciples. To hinder or destroy a weapon goes against Necrotheurgic doctrine, particularly in Bone Ladder sects. The man was most likely a poor shot to begin with.

"And as I listened to your rumors I separated the facts. Here they are: Prudence Bavus was a female land owner. This made her a prime candidate to be suspect of malign theurgy. She owned more land than anyone in the village, worse yet, she acquired it through inheritance. Such a woman would not be welcomed as a standard member of a trailblazing community. She was obviously an unwanted outsider and treated as such."

Näncine nodded, impressed. "You make a good argument about the facts, Mr. Revetz. But I have not told you all of them yet. There is still Prudence Bavus' greatest cursed contribution to the town: the dam and bridge that form the lake from Joachim Creek, the very same ones you crossed just now." She pointed to the dam.

"Victor's Grove was founded just before the Omni-War, at a time when lightning could still be tamed and made to power machines and light houses. The village was too remote, and even its neighbor town, Copse dur Crakktun up the road, lacked the resources to send enough lightning to power Victor's Grove. Prudence hatched a plan to use the thousands of tombstones that her husband had cleared to build a great dam which could use the creek's muddy current to generate lightning for the town.

"At first, the villagers were wary, because the resulting dam would create a lake that would flood and fill the great valley where the ancient *Sorrowful Harvest Battle* had been held. But Prudence, being a persuasive woman, managed to convince the majority that the soldiers in the soil were long since made dust and that their souls had all shattered and moved long before the town was founded.

"And so, the Tombstone Dam of Victor's Grove was built, and for three short years, the village prospered. Then came the Omni-War, and soon after Slate's Proclamation that ended it." Näncine leaned forward, giving Hindin a dubious look. "And I don't need to tell you about *that*, now do I, Mr. Revetz?"

Hindin shook his head.

Näncine nodded and continued "And when Slate cast his maxim throughout the Cluster, the lightning powered machines stopped working. And the Tombstone Dam was no exception. It was after this that the Gloam Period came, where peoples all over the eight huncells had to adjust to simpler means of survival. Victor's Grove did not fare well in that time or any time since, I dare say. The villagers had put all their funds into building the dam. Even though Prudence was clearly not to blame for this misfortune, the townspeople grew to resent her. They thought she had looked into the future and knew what would befall them. For that, they drowned her in the lake. And it is in that lake her spirit resides along with her army of the dammed. Tell me, Mr. Revetz, are you familiar with the Battle of the Sorrowful Harvest?"

Hindin felt his crown chakra stir as he searched his memory. Although his brain was of gold and granite, he had a sedimentary mind, each layer an orderly collection of information and lore. It took mere seconds to delve the layer he had sought. His emerald eyes shifted behind steel lids, settling ponderously on the burning sticks in the fire pit. Reading from his mind's eye, he recited by memory the poem on a page he had once read.

Clear those patches - Clear those rows,

352

Clear the field of all that grows,
Now we harvest - Now we reap,
Prematurely as we weep,
Summer's still young - Crops half grown,
Tears and Blood will soon be sewn,
The generals made us cut it down,
To have their final battleground,
A level place to fight and die,
As we farmers starve and cry,
Bound by honor the armies agreed,
To lay aside cruel strategies,
Face to face and head to head,
The soldiers charged to join the dead,
No clear winner by battle's end,
Both causes lost - Wounds too big to mend,
Clear those bodies - Dig those graves,
Farmers made gravedigger slaves,
Cover those bones - Set up stones,
No more crops will e'er be sewn.

"My, but aren't you well-versed!" Näncine exclaimed with a slap of her knee.

Hindin shrugged and raised his chin. "If it was worth someone's time to write something, it should be worth my time to read it. It is a historical poem by Mazil Whortshellean, inscribed in one of these books." He gave his bulky duffel bag a friendly pat.

"How is it you kept in mind something so obscure?"

"Chimancy," Hindin said. "I recall everything I read, see, and hear. Just as I have trained my body to react properly to any physical challenge, so too have I trained my mind. My chi and chakras are nearly in perfect balance."

"And what exactly are *chakras* and *chi,* for that matter? I'm curious."

"Chi is the blood of the Soul. The seven chakras are the organs of the soul, each one corresponding, to the major organs of the body. Chimancy stimulates the proper flow of chi and instills the proper alignment of the chakras. When all is working as it should, the mind and body become faster, stronger, and more efficient."

Näncine's eyes widened. "And... can you fight as well as you

353

can think?"

Hindin only smiled. "We digress. Tell me, please, of this army of the damned."

The woman inclined her head in agreement as she stood up with a strained sigh. "Very well. Walk with me, my back is getting stiff."

As he was shown around the massive green home Hindin remarked, "This seems a fitting enclosure for raising ten children. Did you not say that this was a hotel, as well as your home?"

"Indeed. This is the *Laidback Hotel,* the oldest building and business in Victor's Grove. Sadly, the train hasn't stopped here in two thousand years. Still, I keep a few rooms open for those who happen by."

Hindin smiled warmly at the ancient wooden structure. "I am sure the interior is quite nice."

The backyard was shaded by an enormous sycamore nigh as tall as the house. High up the tree's trunk was a band of rusted steel, evidence that the tree had been split by wild lightning and then shackled back together in an age past. Beyond the sycamore was a view of Tombstone Lake framed by wild brush and rusted railroad. Though he had crossed the lake only minutes before, Hindin Revetz felt as if he was beholding it the first time. It seemed a heaping bowl of mud soup with one side of that bowl being a high wall of white marble.

"A bridge...a dam made of tombstones," Hindin said, marveling at the gargantuan structure. "Stones of remembrance. Too eroded to bear the names of ancient warriors, but still smooth enough to build with."

He heard Näncine speak behind him. "They're in the water, all those legendary soldiers. When the people of this village drowned Prudence in that lake, her unshattered soul gained dominion over it. The lake is full of two things: overgrown creek fish and bonewalkers armed with spears. These post-morts never venture far from the banks. But they make sure that no one comes near it, not even to fish. They guard it, protect it, and have for almost three millennia. And anyone who dares challenge them soon finds themselves at the ends of dozens, sometimes hundreds, of spear points.

"I can't tell you how many times I've had to keep my nitwit

children away from it. The soldiers of the Sorrowful Harvest truly had been disturbed and offended when their grave markers were taken, and they still hold a grudge to this day. All that water, all that energy that is supposed to be flowing, the dam stifles that natural flow, causing a build-up of death energy. That energy keeps all those thousands of bones moving. That's how I think it works, at least."

Hindin looked down and regarded the now stoic woman. "I am inclined not to dismiss your theory, Näncine. Naturally flowing water has been documented to break up necrotheurgic powers. Lakes, ponds, and other static liquid masses tend to cultivate the zeroth energy, or death energy as you call it. That is why haunted lakes are far more prevalent than haunted rivers. And this is also why many post-morts, including laiches, have trouble crossing rivers without help.

"Furthermore, the reason these ancient bonewalkers have not rotted away is on account of the zeroth energy preserving them. The same goes for why their spears have not rusted. Weapons are sacred to death philocreeds." Hindin shrugged as if the solution seemed stupidly obvious. "Why not simply destroy the dam? The natural flow would be restored."

"Many have tried," the woman sighed. "But the bonewalkers kill anyone who attempts to damage it. They allow people to cross it, but that's all they tolerate."

Hindin crossed his lithe arms and frowned, his eyes settling on the lake once more, and thought about the Great Cobalt Heron.

"*The King of the Creek*," Hindin thought. "*Thrice he came to warn me.*"

Granite muscles slid silently beneath steel skin. Flesh-shaped stone and metal moved like silk in a strong, steady breeze. It was early morning on the patio of the *Laidback*. The village still slept and dreamed, but Hindin was wide awake as he flowed from one posture to the next, from one speculation to the next. The kata he performed was called *Heron Cools Its Wings*, a rehearsed library of defensive movements inspired by the noble bird. As he moved, he pondered.

"*One movement can mean many things, but an omen can only mean one,*" his mother had told him long ago. The kata was much more than martial practice. It was meditation in motion. He knew each movement literally by heart, as it employed the energy generated from his heart and lung's chakra. He felt confident with every move in the form save one. *Hopping Heron* it was called, a retreating jump off the left foot followed by a landing on the right. The left leg remained bent and lifted, acting as a low shield from toe to knee as the arms and hands spread outward. When done correctly no attack could land squarely, if at all. It was the perfect defense, and Hindin Revetz had yet to perfect it.

It was the landing on one foot that vexed him. Although his posture seemed perfect, his movements fluid, his foot still made the slightest of sounds when it touched the ground. Sound meant that the landing was not controlled. It meant that somewhere in the execution his balance was off and that he was not yet ready to use the technique in combat. Never mind the fact that he weighed 920 pounds, and had practiced the move on uneven concrete.

"*There is still something lacking,*" he thought.

Näncine Strother emerged from the side door as the dayshine lit the morning. "It's one o'clock," she announced with a mug of coffee in her hand. "May your first hour be a blessed one, sir."

"As with you, Näncine. Thank you once more for letting me stay the night on your patio. Are you sure you will take no payment for giving me refuge?"

The woman raised her chin. "You already paid me with an afternoon and evening of enriching conversation. To a mother raising ten children, that is worth more than money. But you really should get shelter soon. My back feels a hard rain coming. I suggest that when you go to visit the other villagers, you proposition a drakeri man named Irl Parques. The floor of his home is solid, he has the space, and he needs the coin."

Hindin bowed. "Thank you for the suggestion, Mrs. Strother. But before I go, may I have your leave to investigate the town without being harassed by your gang of ruffians?" He smiled.

The humaness tilted her head back to let out a cackle. "You do, sir. You do. My brats will do you no harm or disservice. You are

356

free to sleuth about. Good luck to you."

◈

The village was smaller than it looked, composed of four blocks divided by a dirt crossroads and peppered with old houses in varying states of disrepair. Most of the homes were abandoned, long left to rot and be swallowed by the surrounding forest. Having learned what he needed from Näncine about her family and her knowledge of the ghost, Hindin proceeded to the property next door.

It was a ramshakle saltbox house. No one answered the door after he knocked, but the clack of an axe splitting wood could be heard around the back. He followed his steel ears to a sight his emerald eyes weren't ready for. In the shaddy backyard, a woman chopped wood with an axe while another woman chopped rabbits with a cleaver. It was the quickness with which these women reacted to his presense that surprised him, for they both turned his way with blades poised for combat. But, just as soon, the ladies lowered their weapons and exhaled sighs of relief.

"Oh, sorry, sir!" said the lady with the axe. "We thought you were Yar the Hunter come to give us grief again."

"I am not. I am only Hindin Revetz. My apologies for startling you both."

"How can we help you?" asked the woman butchering bunnies. "We got meat and pelts for sale. My wife, Ydeeth, here makes glassware."

The wood chopper smiled pridefully. "I can make glassbowls, glass cups, glass jewelry, glass pipes - - "

"No, thank you," Hindin said, bowing slightly and raising his hands. "I am a geotarion, with no taste for meat, and while I will eat glass if starving, I prefer unrefined sand. I am investigating the witch-ghost, Prudence Bavus. Have either of you ever had an encounter with her?"

Yudeeth stretched her back and let out a tired sigh. "I have. I could even tell you about it. But I'm not good at talking while chopping wood."

357

Hindin grinned. "Well, it is fortunate that I can listen while chopping wood."

The three people laughed, and with the subtle agreement made, Hindin took the axe and split logs while Yudeeth talked. She took her time in sharing her account, but Hindin worked with near mechanical efficiency. By the time he was done he merely learned that the ghost would sometimes freeze their rabbits to death at any given time of the year.

As he prepared to leave, Yudeeth remarked "Shame we couldn't do business with you."

The words found Hindin't heart, and he regarded the glass red earrings the woman wore. "Are your earrings for sale? I have a friend who might like them, and if she does not I could just eat them."

Yudeeth gave him a queer look, but a deal was made and both were satisfied.

❁

Hindin happened by the town temple. The second largest structure in the village next to the *Laidback Hotel,* it was a typical rural Doflend temple, resembling little more than a barn with a steeple nailed to the top. The front door was closed and it had no windows whatsoever. The entire structure had been painted white, identifying it as a *free temple* where any philocreed could be taught.

Turning right at the corner of Victor's Lane and Gryne Road, he came to what looked like a small house or a large shack built into the branches of a weeping willow tree. "*Were it not Autumn I am sure the leaves would have hid that from sight,*" he thought as he approached the tree house.

"Hello?" he called out as he stepped toward it. "Does anyone live here?"

He was answered with an arrow that flew from one of the shadowy windows. It hissed through the air before sinking into the ground before the malruka's feet. Hindin stopped.

"You are on the property of Yar the Hunter!" a voice called out from the window in a tendikeye accent. "What business do you got with me, ruke? I don't like walking statues in my yard! I don't like walking statues at all, fact be known!"

"Do you like ghosts better?" Hindin asked.

358

The voice laughed. "Ha! Both are unnatural! Both ain't really alive! Pieces of theurgy trash, if you ask me!"

Hindin frowned. *He still carries the ignorance of his culture. Unlike Will.* He called up. "I am here to ask you only about Prudence Bavus. Would you please come down and tell me what you know? Or...," he paused, "if you know nothing I can be on my way."

Yar the Hunter leapt through the window, a blur of quilled wings and rawhide leather. The tendikeye landed not twenty feet from Hindin, his short bow notched with another arrow. On his hip was a quiver full of them. He was very tall and thin for his race, with dark eyes and darker quills. Hindin guessed he was in his forties, surmising from the bits of gray in his wings.

"Know nothin'?" Yar growled. "I know the surroundin' forests better'n any round ear or drak in the ville. I provide everyone with good, wild meat and edible vegetation. I ain't like them bunny-killin' slags down the road, filthy clam traders. Gaining an animal's trust as you would a pet before killing it is immoral and wrong!"

Hindin spread his hands. "As a *geotarian,* I am in no position to argue that."

The tendikeye sneered. "You ain't in any position to argue nothin', ruke! You even *move* wrong an' yer eyes are toast."

Hindin looked up at the tree house. "You live alone, yes? Most immigrant tendikeye such as you associate only with others of their kind. Yet you seem to live a life of quasi-hermithood here."

"Why I choose to live in Victor's Grove is beyond yer askin', ruke," Yar said firmly.

Hindin tilted his head. "Were you a criminal of some kind, perhaps in your misspent youth?"

Yar shot the arrow.

Hindin slapped the shaft out of the air. As the malruka took a fighting stance, the tendikeye had already drawn and notched another arrow.

"Would you prefer to discuss the local hauntings instead?" Hindin asked, deepening his stance.

Yar stood aghast, his eyes wide, his spine stiff. "No ruke is that fast."

Hindin's emerald eyes glinted. "It has more to do with

359

timing than speed."

Yar cleared his throat, lowered his bow, and put the arrow back in its quiver. "If I had had a gun..." he started. Then he closed his eyes and shook his head. "The Beaver Queen ghost. On rare nights, she reveals herself to me while I hunt fer deer in the woods. The situation is always the same. I stalk my prey, notch my arrow, take aim...and then without warnin' she appears between me and my intended kill, yelling and cackling like mad. The deer or whatever I been huntin' gets startled off, and then she laughs at me. I usually run from her. I fear no living man or woman. But ghosts put out foul, unnatural *necrofear*. It's too overwhelmin', I tell ya."

He opened his eyes and licked his lips "But one night I found the stones to loose an arrow at her. It was a direct hit to her chest and the arrow *bounced* off of her. Quite strange fer a disembodied soul..." He looked at Hindin and sneered again, but not as harshly as the last time. "Yer faster than the average ruke, I'll give ya that. But *she* won't care, nor that army she commands. They'll drag you down to the murky depths, and you'll slowly rust to death. Good riddance, I'll say!"

Hindin regarded the splintered arrow on the ground near his feet. Then he looked up at the shabby treehouse the hunter lived in. Reaching into his pocket he pulled out a gold one hundred grotz piece. The square coin made a loud *PING* as he flipped it to the tendikeye.

Yar the Hunter caught it in one hand, suspicious confusion in his eyes.

"For the arrow," Hindin said before walking away.

Continuing on, he came to a crossroads whereby a quaint bungalow stood. "*A bungalow has no basement or cellar,*" he thought. He approached the door and rapped upon it with the knuckle of his index finger.

A lean and lanky drakeri man answered. He looked tired and unkept. His goatee was on verge of becoming a full beard. His eyes widened a bit as he took in the sight of the seven foot malruka at his doorstep. But just as soon his features sank and settled. "What?" he muttered.

Hindin smiled brightly, showing off his marble teeth. "How do you do, sir? I am Hindin Angladar Revetz, Chimancer of the Excursionist team Four Winds – One Storm. We are permitted investigators in the middle of solving and undoing the haunted curses of the Geohex. I am here to collect information on your local ghosts, and, if it is within my power, break the curse and send the unruly spirits on their way to dissipation."

The man's lazy eyebrow almost raised. "Uh huh. And if it isn't in your power?"

"Then I will return here with my teammates, and we will do it just as gallantly as we did in Drowsy Nook."

The man rubbed the back of his neck and winced. "Yeah, heard about that. So, the Headman's Axe is loosed?"

"And resting on the shoulder of my friend, Sir Röger Yamus of the Black Vest."

The man managed a nod and offered his hand "Irl Parques, I am. Pleased to meet you." He sounded more cranky than pleased.

Still, Hindin gladly shook his hand. "Likewise," Hindin returned. At first, Hindin felt the warmth of the man's hand. Then he felt something...off. *"His chi is not flowing as smoothly as it should. Is he drunk or disturbed?"*

The drakeri's bleary eyes squinted. "And what would you have of me?"

"Information and shelter," Hindin answered. "In return, I offer fifty grotz per night to a maximum of one week."

Irl blinked. "This isn't an inn, sir."

"I can pay more."

Irl raised both hands and shook his head. "No, no. That's not what I mean. I mean there's no needing to pay me so much. You offer me what inns charge for room, board, and other odd services they may supply. My bungalow isn't worth fifty grotz a night."

"Do you need the money?" Hindin asked.

"Well, yes."

"I need the shelter," Hindin reasoned. "Not food or a bed or any odd service, only protection from the rain." He paused and frowned. "Unless your home is full, of course. I would not wish to impose."

The man scoffed, as if offended. "No, no. It's just me here now. The wife left and took the kids last year. Come on in. I'll tell

361

you why she left. It's all the witch ghost's fault."

Hindin learned Irl's trade the second he entered the man's home: leatherworking. Hung in array upon the walls of the main room were raccoon-skin hats, beaver pelt hauberks, wolf tail scarves, buck skin jackets, doe skin vests, stag skin coats, black bear fur chaps, cow hide pants, bull hide breeches, badger pelt gloves, opossum skin cowls, copperhead skin belts, and boots made from snapping turtle hide.

"Nothing will fit you, I'm afraid," Irl muttered as he took a seat in a chair covered in hide and fur. "Have a seat, Mr. Revetz. I'll tell you about that witch ghost."

There was other skin-covered furniture in the room, but Hindin dared not risk crushing it. He sat on the floor cross-legged, yet still at eye level with his host. "If you please," he said with an encouraging nod.

Irl let out a sigh and half-stared, half-glared at his inquisitive visitor. "One night last year, she appeared running, dancing, and laughing around the house. My family and I all sat huddled in this room, shivering from fear and cold. The longer she danced, the colder it got. Late into the night, she sucked out our heat and put her supernatural necrofear into us until morning came, then she ran back into her cursed lake." Irl looked away, sat back in his chair, and rubbed his brow. "My wife miscarried that night. The stress and fear was too much for her."

Upon hearing this, Hindin silently named the ghost of Tombstone Lake Enemy. "I will avenge your loss, Mister Parques," the Chimancer swore.

Irl scoffed bitterly and stood up. He reached into his pocket, pulled out a key, and tossed it to Hindin. "Come and go as you please. I'm going to take a nap. Leave the money on the table."

❖

The next home, a dilapidated barndominium surrounded by the hollowed-out carapaces of at least a dozen scarab beetles all larger than a carriage. A human named Byränus dwelled there with his two teenaged sons, Jäng and Bürent. They were the thatchers and carpenters of Victor's Grove. They hunted the huge insects every Summer and converted the carapaces into one-bileer carts to sell to the local farmers.

"Is it dangerous work?" Hindin inquired.

Byränus answered by showing him his long barreled musket rifle.

Hindin gave the weapon a glance before changing the subject. "Have any of you ever seen or made contact with any of the soldier bonewalkers in the lake?"

Byränus nodded, pulling up his sleeve to show a mangled scar on his shoulder. "When I was young and stupid, I went down to the bank on a dare to impress the other kids. The second I touched the water, a bonewalker rose out with a spear and stabbed me. Took forever to heal."

His son Jang had a worse injury. "One day, while we were thatching a roof, I was carrying bundles up the ladder. Then the ghost of Prudence Bavus appeared, all naked and see-through. She ran up and pushed the ladder out from under me. Fell and broke my leg in two places. Winter fever nearly killed me as I mended."

It was at this point that Hindin's own personal logic got the better of him and he asked, "Why do people still bother living here in Victor's Grove?"

Byränus scoffed. "Nearly everyone who lives here is descended from settlers. This patch of land has been in my family for twenty seven centuries. Besides, we're too poor to move, like everyone else here. Since Victor's Grove lost its town status, the Doflend government no longer sends us aid of any kind. There's no taxes, no civil structure, and no law enforcement. People here simply survive or die. My two sons are the only ones of my four to survive past childhood." The man frowned and swallowed hard. "We buried my wife not more than ten years ago."

"I am sorry," Hindin said.

"Yeah, me, too."

❁

Next, in a derelict conch house, Hindin met Clayton NcRill and his wife Lirotta. Both were elderly farmers and followed herbonomy as their philocreed.

"You are part of Näncine's lay coven, are you not?" Hindin asked Lirotta.

363

The old woman nodded. "Devout study of its teachings have enabled me to grow enough food to feed all of Victor's Grove year after year." Her eyes glinted with pride.

They were a very old couple, humans of some Drakeri descent, their heritage barely noticeable. Still, it was enough for their families to be cast out of Karsely during the schism in Fevär yestercentury. They were very kind to their visitor, answering questions liberally.

"I feel that my friend Will would enjoy meeting such fervent farmers," Hindin thought as he conversed with the couple. "Perhaps after we end the Geohex, I could bring him by for a visit. I would relish a chance to see Will's reactions to the ideals of theurgic agriculture."

"What is your take on the local curse," he asked after learning all he cared to about turnips.

Lirotta frowned. "Once every few years, for no reason other than being wicked, the ghost of Prudence Bavus emerges from Tombstone Lake and causes a premature frost to kill a portion of our crops. I've seen the mad wench appear as a nude hussy, mostly-transparent as she runs through our fields, laughing madly and freezing everything she touches."

"Like the rabbits," Hindin thought.

The next house was the home of Arsa and Plede Huchiss, cloth makers. The couple grew cotton, kept sheep for wool, and owned two cows to produce their chamber lye. They knitted, tailored, weaved, and mended as the seasons permitted. They had four children—two sons and two daughters.

This home too was sometimes plagued by the mischievous Prudence ghost. From time to time she would sneak onto the property where the newly woven textiles soaked in big closed pots of chamber lye. She would cause the lye to freeze, thus bursting the clay pots and hindering the bleaching process. This seemed almost absurd to Hindin.

"Why is she so bent on tormenting this village?"

The last home was of Mairlisha Venprutten and her husband Bharibis. They were very courteous and excited by meeting a man of stone and steel for they were devout practitioners of geonomy, the dominant philocreed of Hindin's people. They made their living as potters and sold their earthen wares out of the back of their carriage each week at the Copse dur Crakktun marketplace. While not true theurges they knew many different theurgic recipes for making theurgic pottery. They were even able to cleanse the necrotheurgic curse energy from soil and clay they collected and run it through a sacred filtration process before turning it into pots and potting soil. This allowed them to grow many tiny apple trees, each bonzaied by removing the taproot.

"If only a few dozen Geotheurge Masters could be called to cleanse this humble county in such a way!" Hindin thought.

Mairlisha was the third member of Näncine Strother's coven and also taught at the white temple. Zoonomy, Herbonomy, and Geonomy...Animal, Plant, and Ground.

"*A fine trinity,*" Hindin mused. "*Yet, lacking in the power needed to vanquish their enemy.*"

It was now the end of the day, and Hindin Revetz had met the entire populace of Victor's Grove. He enjoyed meeting everyone, despite the few attitudes of hostility and indifference. But the enjoyment left him uneasy. He wondered if he missed some subtle social clue that his teammates would have better picked up on.

As the Hunveins above dimmed with the gloam hour, he looked again upon the outstretched surface of the vast, unnatural lake. It now seemed to him a bloated mass, a festering boil in need of lancing. He felt disgusted by its contents and awed by its malign ingenuity. "*How horrible it is,*" he thought. "*This structural monstrosity chokes off more than a creek's flow, but also the growth of a community.*"

Part 2

365

During their excursion into the county, Hindin had taught himself the rudiments of pyroglyphics, the written language of Fire. He learned that fire itself speaks through its own language by taking the shapes of the symbolic characters. He tried reading candles, but their flickerings were too fast and subtle for him to understand. Candles and other small flames conveyed to him only confusing hints and metaphysical metaphors when he asked them questions. But the *Book of the Sacred Flame* from which he had been reading stated that advanced masters could read entire bonfires to divine numerous details on a person, place, or thing. *"I've no doubt that Lurcree Katlemay of Embrenil was such a master,"* Hindin thought.

It was an overcast night, but the first drop of rain had yet to fall. Hindin took advantage of the privacy of Irl's backyard while all of Victor's Grove slept. For the fortieth time that night, he raised his hand and attempted to cast the mystical maxim, *A burnt child fears the fire*. However, Hindin could not cast it to save his life. For an hour he had strained to analyze the words and their meaning in order to manifest a small flaming ball that he could direct with his will, something to vanquish enemies from a distance. But his efforts were in vain, as no such flame resulted.

To relieve his frustrations, he performed another moving heron meditation, and the answer to his hindrance came clear to his mind. *"I have never been a burnt child, nor have I ever been truly afraid of fire. So it stands to reason that while I may have understood the maxim on an academic level, I do not, and perhaps cannot, understand it on a theurgic level."*

Upon more reading and study, he learned that fire reveals the nature of all things by how those things *burn*. The revelation of the nature of the thing brings destruction to the thing itself. This new found wisdom made him feel uneasy. *"It is little wonder why pyrotheurgy resonates within so many corrupt individuals. I must be careful how I study this path."*

His stomach felt more and more strange as he strained to learn. *"Hunger,"* he realized. *"Why am I so hungry?"* His abdomen had been growing warmer since leaving Embrenil. He sat in the backyard grass, searching his pyrotheurgy book for answers. On his nose rested a pair of spectacles crafted by a pyrotheurge he had helped kill not too long ago. The lenses were theurgically enhanced, he was sure of it. But no matter how much he read and reread the passages of the books, the spectacles did not lead him to any helpful revelations.

He took them off as his stomach cramped with hunger. Taking out the red glass earrings he intended to give to Polly, he frowned as guilt engulfed his heart and lung chakra and hot hunger engulfed his navel chakra. He popped the ear rings in his mouth and chewed. *"Perhaps I can buy some more glass from Yudeeth Eruta tomorrow."*

He then eyed what he was holding. The lenses of the eyeware were round and smooth. To Hindin, they were like cookies, unattended and inviting. *"They are mine, after all,"* he thought. It was his last thought before popping the lenses out of the wire frames and munching on them like a thieving child. When the last of the shards were ground to sand and swallowed, the guilt hit him.

"No! What have I done? Why couldn't I resist? Oh, they were so delicious! If only I had more!" Then he looked down to see his hooded jacket smoking from within.

Without wasting time, he removed his jacket, stripping naked to the waist. The six muscles of his abdomen glowed red with heat. Flames jetted out of his navel in bright orange. To his astonishment, the flames took the shape of a face that looked up at him.

"Hindin!" the flame roared "I am your *dan tien*, your navel chakra, your hunger, and your passion. The glass you have eaten has allowed me to manifest thus, and to speak to you more directly. There is little time, so you must listen!"

"I am listening," Hindin said, for he was so frozen in awe and wonder and could do nothing else.

"For what do you hunger?" asked the flame.

Hindin paused before answering. "Justice and well-being for all beings."

The flame frowned. "Stop acting like such a saint. Good or Evil, your desire would stay the same."

"I want... I want to know everything, to learn all there is to learn. Doing right by others... it sets me at ease, makes me glad."

"But only knowledge gratifies you and makes you truly happy."

"Yes," Hindin said, nodding. "I admit that, to my shame."

367

"And it is that same shame that stifles me, stifles you. Fire is passion, and you do not feed it."

"But I do!" Hindin argued. "I read whatever I can, wherever I can."

"You read. You absorb to stimulate and *feed* your crown chakra but you do not *consume*. Fire consumes. You must feed me, us. You must eat the right minerals to refine yourself from within. You must learn... proper nutrition!"

Hindin's eyes widened. "If I do this, will I then be able to defeat the Prudence ghost?"

The flame's frown widened. "How the shunt should I know? I'm just your belly growling at you!" Then it disappeared.

Back within the rustic den of his host, Hindin alternated between meditating and sleeping throughout the night as he pondered what the soulfire had said. When he heard Irl's door open, followed by the sound of boots, he knew it to be morning.

Hindin opened his steel lids to see his new landlord dressed in a heavy leather coat. Reaching for a hat and walking stick by the door, Irl said, "I'm going out for the day. Be sure to keep the house locked up."

"Where are you bound?" Hindin asked, getting to his feet.

Irl put his hat on. "Copse dur Crakktun. Paying my children a visit."

Hindin smiled. "Wonderful! But before you embark, would you first accompany me to the Tombstone Dam-Bridge?"

Irl frowned at the idea, but then nodded. "I suppose."

It was not a far walk, perhaps no more than a hundred steps, before they reached the gargantuan structure. How foreboding it now seemed to Hindin as he stood upon the thousands of grave markers. To his right was the vast lake full of skeletal soldiers, the men once honored by those very stones. And far below to his left, beyond the sloping dam wall was a rocky creek bed choked off to little more than a stream.

He regarded Irl, who did not seem the least bit bothered by

the place. "Does being here not scare you?"

Irl shrugged with his hands in his coat pockets, his eyes squinting in the cold wind. "They only come if you get too close. If you lean over the edge to see your reflection, they come to say hullo. Good luck being able to face them for long. The necrofear overcomes you."

Taking the man's suggestion, Hindin leaned over for a look. His height allowed him to see his entire head and shoulders on the still surface. In less than a minute's time, he saw a Drakeri skull float up from under his peaceful visage. The skull was soon joined by two others on either side. They wore archaic helmets of a design Hindin was unfamiliar with. At that moment, he detected the necrofear. Detected, not felt.

As the odd sensation went through him, he explained to Irl: "Malruka do not feel fear the same way as flesh and bone beings do. When organic beings see a ghost or animated corpse, it reminds them on a subconscious level that they will someday die, causing them in turn to tremble and quake. When Malruka encounter such creatures, we are simply appalled by how unnatural they are. Unlike other races, we malruka are ever certain of how and when our natural death will come. I have dealt with bonewalkers before. Such creatures are mostly mindless and often follow routines they had in life. If someone distracts or interrupts them from their routine, they become agitated and violent. Unless a necrotheurge is controlling them, they are little more than a nuisance. Still, I must admit, the notion of an entire army of them following the routine of killing in an orderly fashion is a daunting thought. Daunting and Haunting..."

Never taking his gaze off the boney faces just below the murky surface, Hindin addressed the bonewalkers. "If you are indeed the remnants of soldiers fallen, bear my words to your master. But if you are but mindless puppets, let your master hear and heed me through you. I am Hindin Angladar Revetz, Chimancer of the Lotus of the Eight Thorns and Eight Petals, 108th successor. In the name of all that is right and natural, I command you to abandon this post, let this dam yield to the current, and move on in spiritual dissipation. Do this, Prudence Bavus, or I will destroy everything you cling to, from your existence to the twisted faith that maintains it."

He waited for reply, but the skulls gave no sign. And so

frowning, he thought, "*What a fool am I. They are under water and have no ears. How could they have heard me?*" Gathering his determination, Hindin lifted his closed fist and pounded it into his open palm, producing a horrible ring, after which he pointed down at the bone walkers with clear and exaggerated malice in his steel face.

Three fifteen foot long poles shot out from the lake's surface, each tipped with iron spikes speeding for Hindin's face. He righted his posture just in time to avoid them.

"*Pikes! Not spears!*" he thought as took a step back.

He heard Irl scream. Out of the corner of his eye, he saw his landlord run halfway to his home before turning to watch.

Three skeletons clad in battered bits of armor sprang from the lake like grasshoppers, pikes in hand. Two landed to block Hindin's way off the bridge. The third landed behind him. Their jaws open in silent battle cries, the bonewalkers sent many jabs and stabs at Hindin's head.

Dodging and swatting away the incoming points of iron, Hindin ducked and weaved through the attacks. Each time a point came close his third eye, his chakra would alert him, giving him just enough time to evade. To his own surprise, Hindin found himself using Heron-Style to improve his defense. Using great circular blocks to bat away their weapons, Hindin closed in on the two bonewalkers, blocking them from entry into the town.

Before he could reach them, the two armor-clad skeletons leapt back into the lake, followed soon after by the third.

In long, fleet strides Hindin made it to Irl Parques' side before turning back. The bridge was empty, the lake calm, and Irl was pale and shivering.

Hindin rested a hand on his hip. "They are trained in fighting malruka," he said.

"Wh-What?" asked the terrified drakeri beside him.

Hindin used two fingers to point at his emerald eyes. "Destroy our eyes, and we are blind and useless. They didn't bother with the rest of my body. They knew my most vulnerable part, my race's weakness." Hindin narrowed his gaze at the site of the skirmish. "For many warriors nowadays, this is a common tactic. However, the Battle of the Sorrowful Harvest occurred thousands of years before the advent of my race. Even this dam-bridge was built

370

in a time when very few malruka existed. So, it stands to reason that these bonewalkers are not, in fact, soldiers of that ancient battle, but soldiers of a latter period who were in life accustomed to battling malruka."

He paused and shrugged. "Or these bonewalkers are indeed soldiers of the Sorrowful Harvest, and they are being controlled by a necrotheurge who is familiar with fighting malruka. Or it is some combination of these theories. I must admit, I find it odd that only three bonewalkers came out to fight me when the lake supposedly contains thousands. Was I being measured? Tested? I certainly felt like a rook between three pawns. What do you think, Irl?" He looked down and to the side to see that Irl was now missing.

Turning around, Hindin saw the man stomping away. "Irl? Are you alright?"

Irl did not look back to answer. "I don't have time for this crap!"

As Hindin watched him make for the road to Copse dur Crakktun, he considered his landlord's words. Speaking low, he said, "You may not have time for this, Irl. But I do." The Malrukan Chimancer made his way back to the dam-bridge.

This time, five armed-and-ready bonewalkers leapt out to meet him.

More ready than before, Hindin engaged them in melee, leaping into their pikes as harmlessly as a Heron lands amongst river reeds, dodging and slapping the incoming points. Catching a thrusting shaft in one hand, he pulled its wielder close to be demolished by the devastation of his steel palm. Once armed, Hindin used the pike like a staff, dashing the heads off of two more armored skeletons before blocking and bobbing past the thrusts of the remaining two. Closing in, he dropped the captured pike and vanquished the last of them with a kick and a chop of his hand, sending armor and bone flying. Picking up a skull, a helmet, and a pike, he then marched back up toward Irl's cottage.

Halfway there, Hindin spied the ten Strother brats spying on him from within a shrubbery. The children's mouths were agape, their eyes wide.

Smiling, Hindin raised the captured weapon above his head, saying "Behold, children! I just caught a pike from the lake!"

None laughed at the joke. They only kept staring.

371

Hindin frowned and grumbled. "Uneducated brats! Have you no appreciation for homonym humor?"

"What's a hominy humor?" a boy asked, still slack-jawed and bug-eyed.

Hindin winced and moaned before making his way back to the cottage.

He emptied the contents of his duffel bag, dumping books in a pile on the den floor. Sifting and searching, he found a few tomes of Doflend histories he thought he needed. He had already read and memorized every book in his possession. But he kept them all for the comfort of certainty. After reading the passages he sought and then reflecting on his recent combat, he took out his journal and put to written word his thoughts on the day.

As for what I learned from the fight. The attack methods and patterns of the bonewalkers were identical, and once properly analyzed, predictable. There was no difference in their techniques or skill levels. They were essentially all the same fighter. Even in highly trained and disciplined military regiments, there are subtle differences in offensive proficiency. This leads me to almost conclude that the bonewalkers are being controlled by one being. Who, I know not. It very well may be someone who resides here in Victor's Grove. Everyone is a suspect at this point.

As for the pike, skull, and helmet, I consulted several of my books on the subjects of anatomy and archaic weaponry and armor. The skull is indeed that of a fully grown Drakeri male. However, the pike and armor are not of the same historical period. The pike is of the same design of those used during the Battle of the Sorrowful Harvest, but the lightweight helmet comes from a much later period when Drakeri began to utilize firearms in their battles. However, judging by the crude way the helm appears to be assembled, I would assume that it might be a replica not more than three thousand years old. Due to its shoddy construction, I highly doubt it would pass as accepted gear for any self-respecting military regime.

372

This evidence leads me to believe that the bonewalkers in Tombstone Lake are not *the cursed remains of long dead soldiers, but mere necrotheurgic puppets dressed up to make everyone believe they are. The construction of the Tombstone dam-bridge did not disturb the resting remains of those soldiers of legend. If anything, the actual remains of the real soldiers were absorbed into the soil ages ago, armor, bone, and all. Whoever is behind the Geohex, I surmise, is also behind this deception. Something tells me that the supposed ghost of Prudence Bavus will yield yet more information.*

I suspect that the bonewalkers are guarding something in that lake. Why else would a powerful necrotheurge go to the elaborate trouble of posting them there?

Enough writing for now. I must practice my Heron-Style if I am to destroy them all.

Hindin stood and shook his arms and legs loose of any tension from sitting so long.

Just has he was about to commence his practice, Irl entered through the front door. As the door opened and closed, Hindin saw the gloam of evening outside. Irl, who seemed to pay him no mind, made way straight for his bedroom door. In his hand, he carried a bottle of some brown fluid.

Hindin greeted him with a warm smile and much enthusiasm. "Irl, you are back! I gave gleaned much from my encounters with bonewalkers! Would you care to listen..."

But by then it was too late. Irl, wordless, went into his bedroom, slamming the door behind him.

"What a selfish fool I am," Hindin thought, suddenly ashamed. *"I should have first asked how his visitation went."*

Another night passed. No sound stirred within Irl's room as Hindin stepped out into the chill morning air. Before walking to his destination, Hindin stopped by the unhaunted, unflooded side of the dam-bridge. Atop the small house-sized brick box at the bottom of the dam's slope, he saw a Great Cobalt Heron perching and grooming itself. It then flew to the creek water flowing out from under the dam, caught a massive silvery catfish and then flew away. This omen Hindin pondered as he made his way to the White Temple.

The front door to the barn-like structure was ajar. When he ducked his head to enter, he saw that everyone in the village was there (save his landlord Irl). All wore the best of their clothes and were seated on benches.

Näncine Strother rose to greet him. Taking his hand, she said, "Thank you for coming to share your truths with us, Mr. Revetz."

The Chimancer bowed and smiled. "It is my honor to be allowed to share them here. Thank you for inviting me."

All were silent as Hindin took his place before the assembly. Hindin was somewhat surprised to see Yar the Hunter in attendance, seeing as how tendikeye hold no regard for mystical philocreeds. Still, he gave the matter little thought. Turning to the assembly, he began his sermon of Chimancy.

"We are not our minds. We are not our bodies. We are the people we have known. We are the places we have been. We are the things we have touched, created, and destroyed. We are events, events which interact with each other, creating one event in total. We are not permanent beings. We are the sum of what our bodies and minds have done with their time. We are our actions. We are our ideas, our concepts. We will end when the results of our actions cease to matter to all persons, places, and things. We are what we cause to happen. We are the arts we practice. Our minds and bodies are not *us*! They are merely our tools. We are CHI! We are simply energy running its course, ever changing and reshaping with other energies we interact with in a cycle perceived as Life and Death.

"We are, quite simply, impermanent spirits residing in impermanent minds and bodies, lightning in fragile jars. Therefore, friends, do not perform actions with your body nor make decisions with your minds. Use your spirits to direct your fates and your mind and body will follow. Flow like the wind and the rivers, be still like the air and the pond. Be, yet do not be. Exist, but forget that you do!

"Let your chi flow freely. Chi is the natural life energy that connects our minds to our bodies. It is the blood of our spirits. When the barriers that hinder communication between our minds

374

and bodies are removed, then all reality will be clear to you. You will be able to make the right decisions without doubt or fear.

"And do not bother with fear. Fear hinders the flow of our spirits. Death and pain are not the end. Though our bodies die and our minds cease to function, though the very stuff of our souls is rent asunder into countless fragments when these mortal forms give out, do not let the Power of Death and Necrotheurgy suspend you in a life of terror or, worse yet, an afterlife as a ghost held intact by misery and hate. I do not denounce all Necrotheurgy. To each their own path. But when one person's path hinders another person's path there is a problem. And one such problem I have vowed to solve here in Victor's Grove. I will demonstrate what chi can do. Energy will exist as it wishes to, free and flowing, not trapped and stagnant.

"Thank you, everyone."

The assembly seemed bemused by his sermon, but most seemed to recognize that Hindin meant well. Hindin was no stranger to such reactions from those so unfamiliar with his philocreed.

As he took his seat on a stone bench he thought, *"It seems that while I can preach the truth, I have yet to learn to teach the truth."*

It was then Näncine Strother's turn to give a sermon of her own, comparing aspects of sentient life to animals and their place on the Food Web. One thing she said in particular Hindin felt was well worth remembering: *The beast is more savage than man when he is possessed of power equal to his rage.* He liked that.

Then Lirotta NcRill, the old farmer's wife gave a sermon of beautiful metaphors comparing life lessons to plants and how they grow.

Lastly, Mairlisha the Potter gave a sermon on the importance of solid foundations, both literal and figurative.

Upon hearing these philocreed sermons, Hindin realized just how different Chimancy was from more common philocreeds. Animals, Plants, and Ground were aspects of reality that could be perceived on the outside of the body with all five senses. The perception of Chi took an inner-sensory perception that most could not fathom without instruction. At this he considered, *"Perhaps in my pursuits of understanding Pryrotheurgy I have been focusing too much on the outer workings of the theurgy and not the inner workings...”*

After the sermons, Hindin spent most of the day conversing with everyone and answering questions about Chimancy. He even went as far as giving a lesson in joint rotation for increased flexibility. After that he showed of a few fancy techniques to entertain the Strother children and other children of the town. And they, the future of Victor's Grove, apologized for throwing rocks at him.

And all the while throughout the day Hindin tried to sense if any of the adults were offended by his denouncement of Necrotheurgy in his sermon. None appeared to be. But that did not mean that a hidden disciple of Death could not have been amongst them all.

“Someone or something is commanding those bonewalkers in the lake. Could it be one of you?”

◈

Later in the afternoon, Hindin made his way back to Irl's cottage. With each step he drew nearer to the home, the colder he felt. Dread seized him as he approached the front door and opened it.

In the den, Irl hung by his neck from a rawhide strap suspended from a beam. A small stool lay prone beneath his feet.

As quickly as Hindin could, he lifted Irl up and snapped the strap loose from beam with a hard tug. He laid the man down and found that he was not breathing and his pulse was weak.

“His chi flow is almost non-existent,” Hindin thought. *“Without the adequate flow I can only put so much cleansing chi into his internal circulation. His heart/lung chakra is fading fast.”*

Irl did not respond to touch or sight. But fortune had it that the last sense to leave a dying body was hearing. Irl Paques was yet able to hear Hindin's *koan* before his heart stopped.

Thus Hindin spoke*: “Breathe in through the whole body, Breathe out through the whole body. You must always return to the breath! Be mindful of the Gateless Barrier!”*

376

No sooner than Hindin spoke the *koan* of revival that he saw Irl's mouth, nostrils, and every pore on his body open wide to inhale and exhale all the precious air they could.

In a less than a minute, Irl awoke taking deep, steady breaths (although he had not recovered to full wakefulness). Hindin saw in the man's grimace that Irl was quite drunk and upset.

Irl's quivering lips opened and spoke. "Let me die, you stupid rock monster! My... my children don't need me...wife don't need me..."

Hindin frowned like a disappointed aunt. "I need you, Irl, to relax, breath, and keep silent."

"Shunt you, rock monster!" Irl shouted before vomiting all over his own face.

Hindin shook his head. "Reason is not on your side right now, Irl." Fast and sudden, he rapped Irl's jaw and ribs with his steel knuckles, striking precise points of pressure.

Irl Parques lost all consciousness.

With the utmost care Hindin cleaned off his landlord and put him to bed. Staying by his his side for the rest of the day and night, Hindin resolved, "When he wakes, I will give him the help he needs."

When Irl awoke early the following morning, after much coffee and convincing, he told Hindin why he'd tried to end his life. "My wife Corina divorced me and moved to Copse dur Crakktun with our children. She quickly remarried a man named Dugless Peersin, the yard manager of the Copse dur Crakktun Rail Car Repair Station. He's also a Trotting Swan, so nobody messes with him. He's the nephew of Copse dur Crakktun Judge Wrenk. On top of this, Dugless Peerson's boss and owner of the Repair Station is none other than the Count of Apple County, a man named Slanidrac Norton. Because of that son of a sow Corina was able to get full custody of our children. I'm allowed visitation rights, but I'm ashamed of my poverty. And whenever I go there, Dugless Peersin does all he can to exploit that shame and dishonor me in front of my children."

He gave Hindin a look, venomous and bitter. "The day after you first paid me for board I walked all the way to Copse dur Crakktun and spent the money on presents for my kids. I arrived at the Peersin household with a sack of gifts. My children were surprised and overjoyed at first. But then Dugless Peersin went out and bought them all lambs to play with." Irl ground his teeth. "My kids dropped the toys I gave them to play with the animals. I didn't blame them. The lambs were better gifts. So, I left, bought a bottle of whiskey, went home, got drunk and tried to hang myself."

Tears welled in his eyes as his face trembled with anger and grief. "I'll not forgive or thank you for stopping me. But I'm too sick to try to get back at you and too poor to kick you out!" He then wept for a long while, all through the morning. Still quite weak, Irl stayed in his bed nearly the whole time.

During that time Hindin took the liberty of finding all of his landlord's liquor stash and poured it out the window. And it was then that Hindin first saw *her*.

The ghost of Prudence Bavus stood out in the front yard in broad daylight. Hindin was at first puzzled that he was able to see her, for he was no necrotheurge and his Malrukan physiology was not adequate to facilitate necrosight by any other known means.

Prudence was semi-transparent and nude. Her hair was a tangled mess, and her crystalline face held no trace of goodwill.

"I've been working on him for a while now," the visage said, glaring at Hindin. "He almost became one of us yesternight. Another ghost story for Victor's Grove."

"And how would that suit your needs?" Hindin asked from the window.

"The dead are without need, Chimancer."

"But not without want and desire," Hindin replied. "Your spirit lives on by your hate, Enemy. You cannot hope to achieve metaphysical fission if you do not accept that permanency is a lie."

"My spirit will *never* shatter and scatter to the winds!" she shouted. "This town accused me of witchcraft and drowned me in yonder lake."

She pointed behind her. "The whole town! Everyone remembers the imagined crimes I committed, but it was not passed on to their children that I was stripped naked and held down in that murky abyss! I was no witch, no necrotheurge. But I became a ghost and gained such powers in death. It is *I* who command the army of the lake! I could command it to slaughter this town and half the county if I wanted to!"

To this Hindin nodded and replied, "You say *army* and not *armies*. So, I am correct in deducing that those bonewalkers are not soldiers of the Sorrowful Harvest Battle. Who did this to you, Prudence? Who let all of your goodness whither and preserved your hate within this horrific state you are in? What necrotheurge was powerful enough to create a ghost that can continue to think and learn, and not just be trapped in reaction to memories? Who is the maker of this Geohex?"

At this the she-ghost grew troubled. "Leave this town," she growled. "Leave this town and never come back, or I will kill every living thing in it."

Hindin raised his chin. "If you kill the descendants of your murderers, Enemy, then will not your hatred die with the town? How can you continue to hate if there is no one left *to* hate? And if you cannot hate, how then can you continue to be?"

Prudence had no answer for that. And Hindin did not wait for her to formulate one. He dived out the window, shoulder-rolled on the ground, and ran toward her. She screamed in rage and charged him with her hands up like claws.

Darting to her left as she closed in, Hindin chopped at her arms, breaking them off that the elbows. In an instant, he followed up with a round kick to her core. His steel and stone shin smashed through her small body without slowing down, and it was then that Hindin realized that the she-ghost was made of solid ice. *"That is why I can see her!"*

Without a second wasted, Hindin stomped on the rest of her until only shattered bits of ice remained. Then Hindin heard her voice cackling all around him. The cackling died off somewhere down the road by the lake. He grew unnerved, for confusion was a rare sensation for Hindin. *"How can a ghost be made of ice?"*

He spoke more with Irl after the encounter and told him what Prudence had said about Irl becoming another ghost in Victor's Grove. At first, the landlord did not believe it. Then Hindin showed him the ice in his yard. They went back into the cottage where they talked until late in the evening, mostly with Hindin listening.

"We had no money to move out of Victor's Grove. So, my wife left with the children and moved in with her school boyfriend, whom she promptly married after divorcing me." Irl made a bitter scowl. "I still love her, against my better judgment. Copse dur Crakktun is her town of birth. When she agreed to be mine, it was I who convinced her to move here. It was my fault our unborn was murdered. I was too proud to move." The man's face hardened with icy resolve as he looked at Hindin. "Well, I'm not too proud for anything now. As soon as you're gone, I will more than likely try to commit suicide again. Then I hopefully *will* become a ghost, so I can forever torment the witch who tormented me and mine."

Hindin leaned down to meet the man's glare. "If I destroy the ghost of Prudence and end the Geohex, would your wife possibly return to you?"

Irl's glare softened at the thought. "I am...uncertain."

Hindin smiled. "There is always hope in uncertainty."

Irl scoffed at is words and spat on the floor.

So Hindin knocked him unconscious again and tucked the man into his bed. "I will not have you kill yourself while I am out investigating," Hindin said as he turned up the covers.

Hindin was on his way back to the Tombstone bridge-dam when he was intercepted by another icy form of Prudence Bavus' ghost. Like a spiteful cat, she went right for his eyes with her claws. Hindin evaded to one side and used a series of cutting knuckle strikes to burst her torso apart.

Leaving the pieces, he continued toward the bridge.

In a matter of seconds, she appeared again and came at him from the direction of the lake. There on the road in front of the

Laidback Hotel, Hindin employed his most devastating and lethal strikes on his foe.

With an open fingered swipe, he slashed off the top of her head from her eye sockets up. A quick, circular kick to her spleen area finished the rest.

By that time, Näncine Strother and her entire family had come out to see what all the commotion was about.

Hindin attempted to explain the piles of ice on her street, when low and behold another Prudence she-ghost came running at him from the lake.

The family was, at first, terrified at the sight of her. But once Hindin bashed the icy apparition to bits with his elbows, there was too little of Prudence left to be scared of.

Ignoring Näncine and her husband's sudden eruption of questions, Hindin proceeded closer to the lake and dam-bridge. Not thirty steps closer, and he saw Prudence emerging from the lake itself screaming and shouting all manner of archaic profanity.

This time, Hindin used the wing-like strikes and kicks of the Heron to break her apart, which was a true joy for him since it is a chain attack sequence of all lethal strikes and he was able to use each and every one.

And so it went on for about an hour. Hindin would try to get close to the bridge and a new Prudence Ice Ghost would emerge from the lake just by the dam-bridge to get smashed by him again.

Hindin took into account that fighting both her *and* the pike-wielding bonewalkers might not be as easy as fighting them separately, for her frozen forms required his full strength and attention to break. He decided to be cautious and did not venture any closer to the bridge.

After smashing the 216th Prudence, he turned for a retreat and they ceased to emerge. By then the entire town had already gathered a safe distance behind Hindin to watch his spectacle of combative ice breaking.

Altogether the villagers of Victor's Grove bombarded Hindin with words of praise mingled with questions.

"Mr. Revetz, what does it mean?" asked Lirotta NcRill.

"Why was she made of ice?" asked Clayton NcRill.

"What did you do to provoke her?" asked Yar the Hunter.

"What if your chimancy isn't enough to stop her?" asked

Yudeeth the glass maker.

Hindin almost seemed to hunch over, his eyes lost in some haze of thought. "I have no answers," he told them. "Please, excuse me." He then went back to Irl's cottage to contemplate his long night of fighting the same ice ghost again and again.

"*What does it mean?*" he wrote in his journal. "*I feel like a lost amateur. A novice! I used every strike I knew and nothing could stop her from coming back again and again!*

Chi is a bad match for Ice. Perhaps I can find an answer in one of my pryotheurgy books."

Part 3

After reading and meditating long into the night, Hindin returned to his journal to record his thoughts.

I may have found an answer. It is now 7:86 at night, and I have done much research and meditation. Ghosts are cold because they are made of death, which is made of nothingness. They are immaterial spirits locked in a void (but not like the nirvanic void of chimancy). The Enemy has somehow managed to utilize this aspect of death, this coldness, to form bodies of ice around her spirit, encasing her cursed soul and providing it with a vehicle with which to make physical mischief. She is able to do this countless times if she has enough calm, still and possibly necrotheurgically-charged water to freeze. Each time I smashed her, her invisible spirit would go back to the lake to form a new body.

This fills me with unease, for she fought with me for over an hour. She might have picked up on some subtle weakness in my combat style. Because she controls the bonewalkers, I have little doubt that she will utilize them better when directing them to combat me. I must stop fiddling around and destroy that dam.

But first I must destroy Enemy Prudence Bavus once and for all. My mother taught me nothing of combating ghosts, and, as

382

far as I know, ghosts are without chi for their chakras. The organs of her soul are eroded. The townsfolk thought me impressive, but I am now painfully aware that a Chimancer is not the hero they need. But they may need a pyrotheurge...

I have only been aware of my spiritual receptiveness to fire and heat since the investigation in Embrenil. I am intrigued by this potentiality, but without a proper teacher, I feel dismally lost on how to proceed. I have read many maxims of the Sacred Flame. Here are some examples that appeal to me.

"The mind is not a vessel to be filled but a fire to be kindled."
"Fire is never a gentle master."
"Just as fire is hidden by smoke, so is wisdom hidden by selfish desire."
"Yesterday is ashes. Tomorrow is wood. Only today does fire shine brightly."
"The teachings we find in books is like fire. We fetch it from our neighbors, kindle it at home, communicate it to others, and it becomes the property of all."

The last one above is my favorite, of course. But it is a very powerful maxim that is, according to the book, one of the most difficult fire maxims to cast, especially in combat. It has also been known to burn the caster alive if misused. But at this point I cannot seem to cast any. Not without a target anyway...

◈

Irl Parques woke up enraged, when he realized Hindin had dumped out all of his alcohol.

"Get out of me home and my life!" Irl ordered, when he saw the empty glass bottle, which also had chunks bitten out of it.

Hindin shook his head. "I refuse, Your well-being is now my responsibility, since you have given that responsibility up."

Irl's purple face went black with rage. "You meddlesome boulder! You self-righteous dirt baby!" He grabbed a sweeping broom and swung it at Hindin's head. It broke against the steel man's blocking arm.

Responding naturally, Hindin knocked Irl out again. He then let out a sigh of frustration as he hefted up the unconscious landlord.

After putting Irl in bed, Hindin was just about to make breakfast when there came a knock at the front door. He answered, and it was Mairlisha the Potter.

"I need to speak to you!" she said. She was scared, joyful, and excited all at once.

"Do come in," Hindin offered. "I have coffee brewed."

The frantic woman raised her hands in refusal. "I need you to come with me, Mr. Revetz. It's a miracle! A wonder of nature! Please! My granite boulder wants to talk to you!"

Hindin's eyes narrowed. "You're boulder...is talking?"

"Yes! Yes! Come On!"

Hindin had his doubts about her sincerity and sanity. But he locked up the cottage and accompanied her to her adobe. True enough, when they arrived at her home, Hindin saw that the big, pink, decorative boulder's surface had formed an animate pair of eyes and a mouth.

"Greetings, grandson of the Pedos!" the boulder said when he approached. "Mairlisha's faith in us allows me to talk. Little time, so you listen! I am your Witness, if you wake up."

"Who are you? Why do you address me as Grandson?" Hindin asked.

"I am Asthenos, Mother of Lithos who is Mother of Pedos, from which you were taken and shaped. Bios is very sick around here because Pedos is stabbed by sick blood iron. I come from far below where this granite rock comes from. Hydros is fat and heavy, and she causes a crack to grow and form far below. Will you wake up? Say yes."

Hindin was unsure of what the rock was telling him. "Are you claiming to be a ground spirit?"

The boulder winced. "I am no spirit. Stupid concept! We *are* the Ground. I am Asthenos, First Lady of the plates. Lithos is Second Lady. Pedos is Third Lady. Bios is Fourth Lady. After her is Atmos, who touches and shapes Pedos and Bios and Hydros. Bios is sick because Pedos is injured and her wounds are infected."

384

Hindin squint his eyes. "Are you referring to the Geohex, by chance?"

"Yes!" Asthenos answered. "It is an itch we cannot scratch without your awakening, Hindin Revetz. But the scratch will only do so much good. Not cure sickness all around, but help."

"What must be done?"

"Break the water-wall. Let Hydros flow once again."

"Destroy the dam? How?" Hindin asked.

The boulder's eyes widened. "Wake up! Wake up and we will be your witnesses. There is too much heavy water above us, too much water! Weighs down upon us, floods deep cracks making new cracks and widening old. Pressure of big still Hydros lets water between platter/dishes. But our dishes will not move unless you remove the blood iron thorn of infection."

"Blood iron?" Hindin asked. "Is this *blood iron thorn* hematite?

"Yes! It is making us sick."

"Where was it hidden, Asthenos? Were is the thorn located?"

"Inside the water-wall, said the boulder. "You cannot hope to go in and pluck it out. Too deep inside amongst the stones of memory. You must sit above the thorn on top of the water-wall, in the middle. Sense it with your feet. Feel its pull. Sit and wake!"

"Sit on the bridge? For how long?"

"Until you wake up!"

"But I *am* awake!"

"Only a little bit, Grandson. Like these soft children of Bios, you walk in a dream. Become one with us, if only briefly, to cleanse this wound and cure this sickness. I, Asthenos, am the rock far below. I am soft because I am hot. Let your Sacred Flame soften your igneous parts so that your soulblood can flow like lava, gentle but destructive. Wake up and we will be your witnesses."

"But how can I just sit and meditate on that bridge with the ghost and bonewalkers attacking me?"

Asthenos looked at me blankly. "How the shunt should I know? I am merely this huncell's *dan tien*! Farewell, Grandson Hindin. And remember that the Ground supports you... always!"

The face on the boulder disappeared.

Mairlisha and Hindin stared at each other for a long

385

moment as they tried to make sense of the sentient omen. They then agreed to enter the woman's abode and consult every geology, geography, and geonomy book she had.

Her personal library was far more extensive on the subject of ground than anything Hindin possessed in his duffel bag. For a long while, they discussed layers of Huncell crusts, ley lines, fault lines, ingenious rocks, sedimentary rocks, various minerals and their spiritual applications, worked and hewn rock, Malrukan relations to the Ground, georganic theory, and many other things to help them derive meaning from what Asthenos had told them. Together, they came up with a multitude of theories of what Asthenos was, and what she meant.

As he took his leave of Mairlisha's home, Hindin encountered The Great Cobalt Heron once again. It was standing calm and still atop the very same granite boulder Asthenos had spoken through. For a thoughtless moment, the malruka and bird regarded each other. Then Mairlisha came out wielding a broom. She tried to shoo the large bird away. Then something happened that struck Hindin with the awesomeness of Truth. The Heron hopped silently onto one foot and snapped the incoming broom in two with its wing. Then it flew away. The movement was fast, but Hindin had witnessed the bird's technique in clear detail.

He gave the woman a quick bow. "I must go. Thank you, Mairlisha."

"Well parted," she said with a smile.

He soon found a secluded place behind an old barn and practiced what he had witnessed. It only took a few tries, but Hindin could now finally land on one foot without making a sound. Deep within he felt his chakras stir and whirl with new found freedom and grace.

"My Heron-Style is now complete!"

❖

Irl was doing much better now. Still suffering from alcohol withdrawal, he put forth the effort to eat and rest. He also agreed to let Hindin stay for the remainder of his investigation. Both Hindin and Irl had a long discussion about his situation in which the Chimancer shared with the broken-hearted landlord many zenical modes of thought. For Hindin, by giving others encouragement he also encouraged himself.

"You are trapped in an illusion of unfulfillable desires disguised as needs," he explained to the broken-hearted landlord. "But I have hope that you can one day find your way out of it. If your thoughts do you wrong, you must dismiss them and seek new ones."

Hindin asked around the village wondering if anyone had known that Prudence Bavus had been drowned in the lake by the past village folk. It seemed that part of history did not survive into their current stories and legends. He then went down by the lake to confront Prudence again.

Sure enough, the icy she-ghost emerged from the same part of the lake she had many times before. She ran at him, screaming and cursing in her icy form, no differently than their previous encounters.

Hindin held his steel hand up and stated clear and bold "Enemy Prudence, two questions, please."

She stopped and growled with a hateful grimace. "I'm not answering anything for you, Chimancer!"

"First question," he began. "Were you drowned during the Winter?"

Her face revealed slight confusion. "No. Why?"

"Second question then. That spot by the lake's shoreline that you keep emerging from, is that where the village folk held you down beneath the water? Is that the exact place where you died?"

Her hollow eyes blazed with suspicion.

He continued talking. "The reason I ask is because it seems an ideal place to drown someone. It is not too deep. A group of strong men could still wade and hold a person down until they drowned. Is that where it happened, Enemy Prudence? Were you murdered in the same spot where you freeze the water? The water, that spot. It was your coffin, yes? The focal point of your transition to becoming a ghost. You are more than merely holding on to your anger, you are quite literally frozen in it."

She screamed and ran at him.

Hindin smashed her with a single Heron strike and turned back to the village. With each step, everything became more clear him. He could not put it into words. But when he had confirmed that Prudence could only form her ice bodies in *that* spot, he *knew* what had to be done *and* how to do it.

When a theurge learns something new it is because their spirit had figured it out. Hindin's spirit was informing his mind and his mind was commanding his body. All three parts of his being had joined as one for one purpose. A pryotheurgic maxim appeared in Hindin's mind as he approached the adobe home of Mairlisha the Potter. With all his strength, he picked up the granite boulder that Asthenos had spoken through. And with all of his soul, he cast the Fire Maxim!

"Latching on to anger is like grasping a hot coal with the intent of hurting another, you are the one who gets burnt!"

Deep within his abdomen, he felt his navel chakra ignite. The granite that made up his core grew to a volcanic temperature. The heat traveled upward through him, split apart up his raised arms and expelled out of his hands and into the boulder. He felt little pain, for it happened so fast. The destructive heat, every bit of it, moved through and into the boulder, making it glow like a hot coal. With it, Hindin ran to the lake, toward the very spot where Prudence Bavus became a ghost. But before he could get close enough, the icy form of the she-ghost stood in his path. His arms and legs were hindered by the weight of the boulder to defend himself. She ran at him, charging with mad purpose, her claw-like hands ready to tear out his wide emerald eyes.

Then the Strother brats charged out of the Laidback Hotel. Just as they had greeted Hindin when he had first arrived in their village, they pelted Prudence with many rocks and sticks. While none of the projectiles caused her dense form any damage, one stick in particular landed just right between her ankles. The she-ghost tripped in mid-charge and shattered face-first in the street.

With the way now clear, Hindin ran to the edge of the lake and tossed the hot boulder in, creating a loud splash. A hissing cloud of steam erupted from where Prudence Bavus had died. It rose into the air as big as a three story house. The surface of the water rippled and boiled in an enormous circle. Dead fish floated up fully cooked. And all around him Hindin heard the ghost of the Enemy scream in raging protest.

He pointed at the vigorously boiling section of the lake and exclaimed, "Try making a new body in that!" He could not resist the verbal jab. Deep down he blamed his friend Will for influencing him in that instance.

Approaching the bridge, he heard Prudence scream, "Stop him! Stab out his eyes! Knock him off the bridge! Drag him down and hold him until he rusts away!"

Just then, hundreds of pike-wielding bonewalkers leapt out of the lake and onto the dam-bridge. Hundreds of iron points fixed onto Hindin's location.

"Praise to the Great Cobalt Heron of Joachim Creek for showing me the Way of the Wing," Hindin thought as he engaged the massive host on the narrow platform.

Just as he had prior witnessed the noble bird evade and snap the broom of Mairlisha the Potter, so too did Hindin dodge and sunder the pikes of the post-mort horde. Never before, in battle or practice, had Hindin ever known such exhilaration and serenity.

One by one (and sometimes two by two) the bonewalkers shattered, littering the bridge with their broken, wet bones and armor.

By the time Hindin made it to the half way point of the bridge, he shouted, "If you wish to see them all destroyed, Enemy Prudence, then by all means keep sending them!"

"Stop!" the voice of the invisible ghost yelled.

The remaining bonewalkers froze in perfect stillness. Then at least a hundred more leapt out of the water, replacing the ones he had destroyed. He was at the center of the bridge, and now blocked on both sides.

"I can still destroy them all," Hindin called out.

For a long moment, all he could hear was the water near the shore still boiling. Not a bone about him moved.

Then Prudence spoke. "What is your plan?" she asked, her tone mocking.

He answered the voice. "I am going to sit here and meditate on this dam-bridge until I find the way to destroy it."

"Ha! Impossible! I personally oversaw the construction of this dam. It was built to last forever! That is why they called me the

Beaver Queen! That stupid rock will not stay hot forever, Chimancer! And not even you with your fancy chops are powerful enough to split this dam in twain!"

Hindin shook his head and felt pity for his Enemy. "You have dammed more than this creek, Enemy Prudence. You have dammed yourself. You are beyond my redeeming."

He heard her cackle in defiance. "You are indeed a fool! Why, you are not even a real person! Malruka exist only to be war-slaves! That was your original purpose, to kill for your masters! And what a noble purpose it was. Now, you have no reason to live and every reason to be broken down for scrap! So, go ahead! Be my guest. Sit and ponder uselessly. You are nothing more than a weapon, sharp but aimless. Go on! Sit and find failure. My soldiers will make no more moves against you until dusk. By then, your rock will have cooled, and I can return to keeping the village as I always have."

Hindin heard her words but did not believe them. Nor did he fear her. He felt the stone walkway with his feet as Asthenos had so told him. There was a slight pull on his left heel, a sort of invisible force pulling downward. He sat directly upon it, crossed his legs, and closed his eyes.

Immediately, Enemy Prudence commanded her minions to beat their pikes against the bridge in an effort to distract him.

Hindin ignored them. From that point, the day wore on long and slow.

During that time, Prudence told him her life and death story in an effort to steer his point-of-view toward her own.

He ignored her.

She boasted about all the wickedness she had caused over the millennia. Childrens's deaths. Starvation. Seeds of hate between neighbors and loved ones. It was an effort to anger him.

He ignored her.

She offered him knowledge of the ages and distant past. She promised him boundless information if he would only give up his endeavor.

This was her cleverest attempt to stop he who loved knowledge so much. But he was too focused on his present goal to care.

Finally, after hours of resisting her, she asked Hindin Revetz this: "Who are *you* to do this? What right have you to dethrone me, to destroy what I have built? Who or what makes you the one to free these people from the fear of Death and Suffering? Who were you to show them a new way of thinking at the white temple? Who is there to see you champion this cause? The villagers are all hiding in their homes, shivering with dread. I have an army to stand with me! Who do you have, Hindin Revetz? Who will bear witness for you?"

To this, he said nothing. But with an epiphany knew the answer. He answered her only by reaching down and gently touching the stone on which he sat. At that moment, Hindin fully realized that the stone was connected to other stones that reached far down to touch the Ground. Pedos, Lithos, Athenos--they were the Ground and his Geological Grandmothers. He felt their wills rise up to meet his fingertips and then descend back down to the elemental depths far, far below. The truth was revealed to him that all things were connected.

Then the Ground shook.

The once mighty Tombstone Dam of Victor's Grove buckled as the inner surface of the Huncell shifted. The weight of Tombstone Lake pressed against the weakened structure. Jets of water sprung out from between freshly made cracks on the dry side of the wall. The stagnant spirit of Prudence Bavus screamed out in anguish and faded as the dam collapsed with Hindin and hundreds of bonewalkers atop it.

Hindin fell amidst a colossal rushing wave of water, stone, and bones. He felt the current take hold of him and not let up as the Tombstone Lake bled out onto the old course of Joachim Creek. All around him was darkness and rushing water. Loosened marble tombstones bashed into him as he was carried far, far away from Victor's Grove.

Hindin lost consciousness, feeling that his moment had arrived, that moment of a hero's death.

◈

Between life and death he dreamed. Never do malruka dream unless it is by some theurgic happenstance. Whether it was prophecy or merely some tidbit of cosmic information invading his psyche, Hindin did not know.

He heard Asthenos tell him, "Well done, grandson. Now, you must seek out the Hejna Stone."

"Where is it?" Hindin asked. "What is it?"

"Go to the Wilds of Chume. The stone is many things to many beings. You destroyed the dam. Soon, you must destroy the dame!"

Then the dream ended and was, like most dreams, forgotten. Hindin would not recall it for a long while after.

◈

He awoke the next morning several miles down the newly replenished creek, buried face down half way deep in soft, cold mud. He got up and found himself on a bank near a town he did not recognize. Other than his steel skin itching from the onset of rust, Hindin was fine and surprised to be so. The Morning was calm and chilly. Reluctantly, he used the creek water to wash away the mud on his face and clothes. His leather hooded jacket was torn to tatters.

As he started to wash his back, he found something hard and slender clinging to his steel skin. He pulled it off with some effort, and found that it was a solid bar of polished hematite about two inches thick and four feet long. It held an uncanny magnetic charge that stimulated his chi flow slightly, suggesting that it was theurgically enhanced in some way. It reminded him of the hematite axe of the Headsman back in Drowsy Nook.

"*It must have been the implement used in the bridge-dam's construction to help pin the curse to the land. It must have broken free from the crumbling tombstones and stuck to my skin during the flood.*" He looked about his surroundings. "*Are there other hematite implements embedded in earthly structures throughout the county that are all causing the Geohex?*"

He entered the nearby town. He placed the bar back behind his right shoulder where it clung to him once more. There it stayed like a sword in a sheath.

He saw a sign that read: *Welcome to Copse dur Crakktun -*

392

Named in honor of the Fevärian explorer Fernando Copse dur Crakktun. First Town Founded in Apple County.

At first viewing, he saw the town was built on a series of rolling hills with all the houses and streets constructed in close proximity. At the foot of those densely inhabited hills, a series of railroad lines converged into a station complex with a repair yard for train cars. The very first building Hindin came to was a large mansion atop a small hill with a stately sign that read: *Arlingtun Manor.*

"*A marvelous edifice,*" he thought as he made his way up the hill, up the marble front steps, and onto the grand porch that wrapped around the bottom of the house like skirt. "*Perhaps they may know of a place where I might acquire some oil and sandpaper. I feel rusty already.*" He tugged the rope of the doorbell and waited.

A small, old, heavy-lidded drakeri man answered the door. He was bundled up in a thick sheep skin coat with a matching hat and mittens. About his shoulders was a wool blanket. "Can I help you?" the man asked, his voice soft and his eyes blinking.

Hindin smiled and bowed. "Please, forgive my disheveled appearance, sir. I am Hindin Revetz of the Excursionist team Four Winds – One Storm. I am invest---"

"---investigating the Geohex?" the old man finished, his mouth managing a groggy smile.

"Why, yes," Hindin said with a bright smile. "Word of our endeavors has made it your way?"

The old man nodded. "I read the paper." He blinked a few times before giving a lazy shrug. "Are you here to see our ghost?"

Hindin arched a perplexed eyebrow. "I...came here initially to see about oil and sand paper."

The small man chuckled. "Well, we have that, too. Come on in. I'm Phill the House Sitter." He turned and went inside.

Hindin followed after the man. "My thanks and well met, Phill. It is by strange fortune that I am here, for I did not come on my general business. So, then this house is truly haunted?" At once, Hindin sensed that something was not right. His damp canvas pants stiffened nearly solid. He looked down to see them now coated with frost. "What?"

Phill the House Sitter turned with a grin. "Cold enough for

393

you? That's part of the curse here."

Hindin saw the man's smokey breath, and he felt his own warm navel chakra stir in reproach. "It is freezing in this mansion. Outdoors it is but an Autumn chill. But here it is like winter. How?"

Phill smiled languidly. "Let's adjourn to the den, and I'll fill you in. You like legends?"

Hindin nodded.

"Good. You're now part of one."

The two men sat down close to a raging fire in a hearth that barely kept the room warm. With a large mug of steaming coffee in his hand and a tray of chocolates on a table by his chair, Phill the House Sitter told Hindin the legend of the mansion's ghost.

"Well, let's see. The mansion's first owner was a guy named Skelt Arlingtun. It all happened two thousand five hundred years ago, back in my grandfather's time. Mr. Arlingtun's daughter Spricca was kidnapped and held for ransom, or so he thought. He delivered the ransom money to the kidnappers somewhere on the outskirts of town, hoping to get her back. His daughter was indeed there safe and sound. But when he gave the kidnappers the money, it was soon revealed to him that his own daughter was in league with the kidnappers and in love with one of them. She and the kidnappers rode away with the money never to be seen again.

"Weeks later, Skelt Arlingtun received word that his daughter's body had been found in Joachim Creek. She was still wearing the same dress that she had fled in. It became clear then that the men she was in league with had killed her shortly after they ran away with the money. Skelt Arlingtun was inconsolable and he hung himself."

Phill took a sip of his coffee and laughed. "Since then, Mr. Arlingtun's ghost has haunted this mansion, keeping it cold all year round. But that's not such a bad thing. The current owners, Wendy and Marchil Seerzbothum, come here during the summer as a convenient way to escape the heat. The rest of the time you'll find me here watching after the place."

Hindin looked about the stately den. "Do you ever get scared here?"

The old man shrugged. "Occasionally. But Mr. Arlingtun isn't a bad ghost so much as a sad ghost. He doesn't put out *necrofear* so much as...I dunno...*necrogrief*. Fact be known, I've lived here my entire life, and I think he sees me as family. So, I'm safe."

Hindin removed the hematite bar from his back and presented it for the old man to see. "Are there, by chance, any pieces of hematite in the building that have been here since the time of Mr. Arlingtun's passing?"

Phill's mouth frowned in confusion, but he soon nodded as the answer to the malruka's question occurred to him. With popping knees, he arose from his chair. "Come with me."

❖

In the lowest part of the mansion, which was also the coldest part, was a magnificently carved marble pedestal standing about five feet tall. Upon that pedestal was a bust of a pretty drakeress. A brass plate below it read: *Spricca Arlingtun.*

"Skelt Arlingtun had it commissioned and cast shortly before committing suicide," Phill said. The old man seemed bothered, and would not look directly at the memorial piece. "Ever since I was a little boy that thing gives me the shivers."

Hindin examined the bust, and it did indeed hold the dark, gleaming, luster of hematite. When he touched it, feeling its magnetic pull, he was sure it was a cursed item. "*It feels exactly like the necrotheurgic bar on my back. What metallurgist would use hematite to create a bust? This is too queer to be coincidence.*"

He looked to Phill and most humbly asked, "Might I be allowed to remove the bust from the mansion to see if it will break the household's curse?"

The old man tittered. "The owner would love that, fact be known. But you aren't the first to have that idea. The marble pedestal and bust itself can't be moved, even by a malruka. It's frozen in place by the ghost, I think."

Hindin decided to test this theory and try to push over, lift, or otherwise move the pedestal and bust. It seemed just as stubborn to budge as the Headsman's axe had been. He then had a hunch about something. He ran his steel hands up and down the pedestal and felt a magnetic pull coming from inside it.

"Ah!" he declared. "There is more hematite running through the pedestal, and I've little doubt that it is attached to the bust from beneath it!" He tapped the marble with a finger. "If this solid piece of hematite, being comprised of the bust and the bar that runs through the pedestal, is pinned to the marble floor beneath it, and this hematite is just as indestructible as the Headsman's, then this explains why it cannot be moved."

Phill the House Sitter tilted his head. "Huh. That...that makes sense. I'm sure that if I had steel hands, I could have felt what you did and figured it out, too."

"Without a doubt," Hindin replied, inclining his head. He walked around the pedestal three times while pinching his chin. He then looked again at the House Sitter. "May I have your permission to destroy the pedestal?"

At first, Phill was reluctant because it was not technically his property. But he figured since he was on good enough terms with the current owners, that they would pardon him for allowing its destruction.

After several well placed kicks, including inverted sidekicks and low round houses, Hindin was able to break the pedestal apart. But the newly exposed hematite bar and bust remained unbent and still imbedded in the floor.

Hindin tried to pull it out. He tried to kick it loose. He even tried stomping the floor it was transfixed to break loose from the floor's hold on it. Nothing worked. It remained undamaged by his hardest strikes.

Then something happened.

He turned his back to the bust and bar, trying to attempt a rear heel mule kick. The bar from the Tombstone Dam flew off his back and magnetically attached to the bar beneath the bust of the pretty girl. The gleaming bust animated as if it were alive and released a horrific female scream that echoed throughout the household. Hindin found it quite unnerving, but it was all too much for poor old Phill.

The elderly drakeri fainted then and there.

The pretty face of the bust contorted and wailed with the sound of ultimate suffering. Shock and betrayal were in her cries. In terror and misery, the bust head cried the words, "No! No! I love you! Why?" But the words were soon cut off by choking and gurgling sounds.

"*She is re-experiencing her drowning!*" Hindin thought. "Spricca! Spricca! Wake up! You are home now! You are home!"

Not knowing what else to do, he placed the gold circle of his palm atop her head. Chi met chi, spirit met spirit. And for a moment, his mind welded to that of the ghost. Thought to thought, the Chimancer and the ghost of the murdered daughter communed.

"*What's happening?*" Spricca asked.

"*It is called a mind weld. I am Hindin, you're friend and guide through this. Tell me Spricca, what do you remember last?*"

An eerie serenity brought on by Hindin's chi kept the ghost calm and alert. "*I...we had the money...Razba, Margel, and me. We rode off leaving Daddy broke and fooled. After a while, we stopped by the creek to water our bileers. Then...then...Margel grabbed me. At first, I let him. I thought he was going to kiss me. But then he started to drag me to the water...I was so frightened...so afraid. He grabbed my neck and forced my head into the cold water. I fought back, pleading and asking why. Then he held me under, squeezing my throat. Some of the time, I loosened his grasp, but there was only water to breath. I...don't know if I died by drowning or strangling....it was both. The man I loved murdered me. He used me to get my father's money...then he murdered me. I...I stayed there for a long time, in the creek. Even after my body floated down stream. I stayed there under the water choking and gasping and crying. But no one could hear me...see me...*"

"Your father died shortly after you did," Hindin told her. "His spirit still haunts this house."

"*I was in the creek. How did I get back here?*" she asked.

"*I am not certain. Perhaps...*" Hindin paused. Then it came to him. "*I think I carried you here...on my back. I had this necromagnetic rod attached to me. It must have absorbed your stranded spirit when I washed down the stream.*"

"*I don't understand,*" she said.

"*It is not important. All that matters is that you are back*

397

home with your father.”

“But we’re both dead.”

“True. And you have both suffered for too long in your ghost-like states. It is time to let go of your heartbreak, both of you. I am going to break the mind weld now. When I do I want you beseech your father aloud for forgiveness.”

“I...I...am so ashamed.”

“That is for him to hear, dear Spricca. Not I.” He raised his hand off the hematite bust and the mind weld ended.

Slow and timid the eyes of Spricca's visage opened.

Hindin met her gaze with a soft smile. “Tell him now,” he whispered.

The final words of Spricca Arlingtun were thus: *“Papa? Papa, I don’t know if you can hear me. But I’m sorry, Papa! I’m so...so sorry... I was stupid for thinking that Margel loved me. I’m sorry I made you do it. I love you, Papa, and I know that I did wrong.”* Her eyes closed, and the gleaming bust went still.

As this happened the entire mansion grew warmer, the chill dying with so much sorrow.

Phill the House Sitter woke from his faint, sat up, and looked around. “How'd it get so muggy in here?”

Hindin gave no answer, only a smile and a helping hand up. Once more, he tried again to pull the rod and bust free from the floor. It came out with ease. He then attached it to his back along with the bar from the Tombstone Dam. After a long exchange of gratitude with Phill the House Sitter, Hindin took his leave of the old man and the mansion.

❖

His next destination would have been back to Victor’s Grove. Hindin was eager to see how the villagers were fairing after the destruction of the dam-bridge. He did not need to go so far.

Just as he made his way to the road out of town, the villagers of Victor’s Grove, every last one of them, had arrived together at Copse dur Crakktun.

Surrounding their hero, the villagers told him what had

398

happened after he was swept away.

After the dam collapsed and the lake drained away in a massive flood, the ghost of Prudence Bavus and her bonewalker army ceased to be. When the waters lowered, for about a mile down stream the banks and shallow creek bed became littered with broken tombstones, scattered bones, hundreds of pike, and huge fish—cat fish, bluegill, carp, pikes, gar, and walleye--all the fish that had resided in the lake before it drained away.

Irl Parques had the brilliant idea to string the fish on the long pikes left behind by the bonewalkers. Soon, it became an entire village effort with everyone involved, even the children. They collected thousands of fish and strung them on the pikes through the mouth and gill. They then loaded the fish into the Scarab Carts that belonged to Byränus the thatcher and they hauled the fish to Copse dur Crakktun to sell.

They were all delighted and surprised to see that Hindin had survived. He, too, was overjoyed to see them all together, working as a solid community to support each other.

He commended Irl for his initiative in gathering up the fish.

Irl returned with kind words of Hindin saving both him and his village.

The Chimancer was all too happy to help them haul the cart loads of fish to the Copse dur Crakktun market place. There the entire town of Copse dur Crakktun came to buy fish and to hear the story of how the Tombstone bridge was destroyed. Nearly everyone in the two communities were impressed by what Hindin had accomplished. When called to give an impromptu victory speech Hindin addressed the crowd.

"I can say without pride or ego that no one other than myself could have broken the curses of these two towns. Not because of what I can do, but by who I strive to be. It was devotion to my path of truth that gave me success, for my path led me here. The true praise and credit belongs to Nature itself: the Heron, the Boulder, the Ground, and even the water Hydros for guiding me through my investigation and trials. To them I give eternal thanks. I will always strive to listen to the truth within and outside, and I encourage you all to do the same."

All the villagers of Victor's Grove came back that night with a tidy profit that would help them start new lives in a community now cleansed of fear and death. As he spent his last night in Victor's Grove before returning to Drowsy Nook, Hindin hoped that his friends and teammates had fared well in their own investigations. With great anticipation he looked forward to seeing them again and sharing what all they had learned.

✵

The following morning as Hindin made his way down the rural road he could not help but strut. The source of his pride was not his victory or new found wisdom, but the new garment he wore. As a token of appreciation, Irl the leathercrafter had made him a new hooded jacket to replace his torn one, sewn from the skins and scales of tremendous catfish and blue gill. Although it had been thrown together in a hurry and still carried the slight odor of fish, it was a handsome jacket both regal and functional.

"I cannot wait for Will to see it," he thought. *"With his coat of serpent scales and mine of fish we are sure to make an awesome pair."*

Clinging to his back were the two hematite rods he had claimed as evidence and trophies. Over his right shoulder peeked the still face of Spricca Arlington. They were more than just necromagnetic, he had deduced. He had channeled his chi through each of them to break the very curses they had transfixed to the land. *"Perhaps I can find further use for them later."*

As he made his way around a curving piece of road that hugged around a steep hillside, he abruptly encountered a familiar face approaching from the opposite direction. It was a face he had never beheld before, yet he knew one just like it. The drakeress resembled Polly in every way save her long wild hair streaked with red. Her boots and gown were of the deepest crimson and her eyes shown as red coals glowing in a forge.

Hindin stopped walking at the sight of her. After three more steps, she too stopped, and she smiled. Not more than twenty feet apart, they shared a moment of greeting without word or gesture.

Calmly, Hindin removed the bars from his back and the new jacket from his torso. After placing them gently on the ground, he regarded the woman before him and bowed. "Veluora, Red

400

Theurgess of Chume. Even before I met your daughter I had heard tales and read stories about your theurgic atrocities. You would force Polly down a path she does not wish to go. You would have her become a murderess and torturer within the bounds of a philocreed that serves no good. I would offer to redeem you as I will her someday, but your crimes and guiltless mindset prohibit me from even trying. It saddens me that I must name you Enemy. Your end is but moments away."

To this she merely shook her head and said, *"One cannot get blood from a stone."* As the maxim left her lips, her skin broke out in scab-like patches that sparkled like rubies. Like pools of crystalline blood the patches grew over the entire surface of her lithe form until she resembled a glittering statue of gorgeous gore. Cackling, she said, "I will flense the steel from your body and turn your eyes into ear rings!"

They both charged at once.

In shape and size, Veluora was little different than the ice ghost he had fought. But the comparison ended there. With grace preternatural, she leapt and spun like a top in mid-air. At the last instant, she extended a leg, ending her spin with her heel clanging against Hindin's neck.

He answered with a kick of his own to her belly before she could land. But her blow had ruined his balance, rendering his kick ineffectual.

Regaining their footing, the two foes fought with swiping chops, spinning kicks, and other lethal flourishes. Hindin fought like a Heron, majestic and flowing. Veluora fought like a spiraling fiend, erratic and bounding. Neither combatant could land more than glancing blows, their movements being so fluid and deceptive.

"Her skin is too hard," Hindin thought. *"And her strikes are so fast!"* Putting his longer reach to use, he went on the defensive to better study her movements for patterns.

Veluora seemed to sense his strategy. "Ha! You're lucky dat I can't use my veins in dis form! You cannot hope to penetrate my ruby armor!"

"I broke a bridge with but a touch," Hindin thought. Realizing that Heron-Style was too similar to Veluora's twisting acrobatics, he shifted to Puma-Style. *"Puma hunts the Heron,"* he thought. His stance deepened as his open hands bent at the second

401

knuckles, wings becoming paws.

The Blood Theurgess was too busy spinning to notice his change in posture, much less his attitude.

Twice he hit her in rapid succession, halting her aggressive rotation and knocking her from the air. As she landed stunned but unhurt upon the ground, Hindin closed in for the kill.

Veluroa was too quick for him. Up in an instant, she stepped sideways, narrowly avoiding his pouncing charge. Hindin's paw-fists hit dirt. Veluora's foot stomped solid into his rib area.

Still on all fours, Hindin swept out his leg and caught her ankle. As she fell, Hindin rolled toward her until he found himself atop his enemy, pinning her to the ground. The struggle was short, for although she was supernaturally strong, Hindin was larger, heavier, and had the upper hand. Grasping both her wrists in one hand and pinning them to her chest, Hindin raised his steel fist, knuckles aimed at her sneering face.

"You are no stone," he told her. His fist came down, cracking her sparkling head like an egg. As a flood of blood welled out from the cracks in her face, her scab-covered skin cleared. Watching the light of life fade from her now crooked eyes, Hindin stood.

Solemnly, he bowed once more to what he thought was a fresh corpse. "I took no pleasure in killing you," he said.

Veluora's eyes blinked and met his own. "Then you miss the whole point of killing, Chimancer."

Too startled to react, Hindin could only watch as the body turned into blood and sunk traceless into the ground. As Hindin backed away, looking this way and that, he felt confusion turn to dread.

Chapter 7
Count Slanidrac Norton

Back in Copse dur Crakktun the slender, lean frame of Mr. Thrush Raisinbread stood just outside the County Hall, the place where the Count both resided and governed. Thrush wore a brown flannel shirt and worn-out blue jeans. His deep, dark, purple hair was long and tied behind his head in a plump braid that went down past his shoulder blades. Although he was the deep indigo shade of most Drakeri, his squared jaw suggested a distant Human heritage. His thick muttonchops framed a wide frowning mouth that always looked like it was holding something bitter. Stern eyebrows hovered over harsh eyes.

His nose sniffed at the air. "*The whole town still stinks of fish,*" he thought.

It was the first time Thrush had ever laid eyes on the huge orange brick building. Even though he had resided in nearby Barnhart these past forty-two years, he had never felt the urge to visit Copse dur Crakktun. He preferred to lay low. In the back pocket of his tattered blue jeans was a letter he'd received the day before. It read:

To Mr. Thrush Raisinbread,

Your presence is requested at my office in the Copse dur Crakktun County Hall. I would like to offer you a very lucrative position of employment. It is my understanding that you are the strongest man in Barnhart, so strong that you even beat Fulton Gladish in an arm wrestling match. I have need of a man like you. Please, come to my office tomorrow and hear me out.

403

Sincerely,
Slanidrac Norton, Count of Apple County
P.S.
Those who can be forced do not know how to die.

Thrush rolled his eyes as he surmised what kind of job the Count would offer. *"He no doubt wants me to work at his railroad car repair station. I've heard that place has a high turnover rate due to on the job injuries. And that he's always looking new strong backs. He takes full advantage of these desperate folk. I'll hear the man out and politely refuse. Copse dur Crakktun is far too crowded a place and the roads too busy for hunting."* He grit his teeth. *"Why did I even bother coming anyway? Why did I not simply send a letter of refusal? Since when do I grant requests?"*

He walked into the building, loathing each step he took. He was soon greeted by a pretty woman in a lovely dress.

"Hullo," she said. "Are you Mr. Raisinbread?"

He nodded and winced, hating that someone he did not know would know him.

The lady smiled and offered her hand. "Welcome to County Hall, sir. The Count is expecting you downstairs. May I get you anything?"

He took her hand. It felt smooth and warm, and it pulsed with life. "No. No, thank you, I mean."

"Are you sure?" she asked, not letting go. "We have coffee, tea, fresh milk..."

"I'm fine."

The woman's smile widened. "But you must be thirsty from your walk here. Barnhart is nearly twenty-two miles away." She squeezed his hand, not letting go.

He could feel her blood coursing through her fingers and palm. Her perky, serene smile filled his mind with dark, perverse thoughts. "I am not thirsty right now. I'll be fine. Please." It took all his will to stay polite and mild.

The lady let go and turned around with a smug curve on her lips. "Right this way then, Mr. Raisinbread."

She led him down a series of hallways and stairs. When they reached the Count's empty office, she showed Thrush in and bade him to sit in the empty chair across from the Count's large

404

mahogany desk. "Count Slanidrac will be with you shortly, Mr. Raisinbread."

Thrush looked up to her from the chair. "How shortly?"

She smiled and gave his shoulder a playful pinch. "Soon."

Thrush grimaced as he watched her exit and close the door behind her. *"Cheeky little sheath,"* he thought. *"You wouldn't be so bold knowing you were in the presence of a laich!"*

"Ah, but she does know," came a man's voice from across the desk.

Thrush's turned his head and he was nearly startled out of his seat. He looked in puzzled shock as he beheld the Count of Apple County, better known as Wraith County, sitting across from him. The Count wore a delicately tailored suit of gray velvet and black corduroy. In spite of being a Drakeri, his hair, even his eyebrows, were a dull yellowish color like dead grass. On his wrists he wore ornate hematite bracelets.

"How did you get in here?" Thrush demanded.

"Through the floor," the Count answered casually. "Tell me, did my assistant offer you refreshment?"

"Yes," Thrush answered, bewildered. "And I politely refused her, as I will you."

The Count laughed and waved the man's words away. Reaching under his desk, he produced a small covered platter and set it before the laich. "Try to refuse this, my friend!" He removed the lid, revealing a pile of fist-sized hearts. "Fish hearts! For you, my honored guest! You would not believe how easy they were to come by!"

The smell of the heaping mass was both reviling and intoxicating to Thrush's senses. He froze in his chair, not knowing what to say or do.

"Eat," the Count said with a grin. "I'm sorry, they are but animal hearts, but planning so many murders just wasn't feasible on such short notice. I do have a county to run, after all. I'm sure you can understand."

Thrush still had no words. Slowly, he picked up the top-most heart and stuffed it into his mouth. After only a few chews, he swallowed it with little effort.

The Count smiled. "I'll get to the point with you, Thrush, for I can tell you are agitated. I am a Necrotheurge accomplished in

405

both goal and method. I am the Wraith of Wraith County, the beginner of eternal end. Recently, four Excursionists have been undoing my work and, in doing so, are learning my methods. The Geohex of this county is of my own design. Over the millennia, I have manipulated countless desperate souls, both embodied and disembodied, to aid me in affixing a curse to this land, a curse that still needs tending from time to time. I am enlisting your help as of today. Hemogoblins are few and far between in Doflend. As a bloodsucking fiend you will be of much use to me."

Thrush squirmed in his chair. "Why are you telling me all this? How do you know about me?"

The Count seemed puzzled by the questions. "I've known about you the moment since you crossed the borders of this county. This land attracts death-blessed folk like you. That and its relative lawlessness keeps thirsty men like yourself from being bothered. You really do have an amazing method of hunting, Thrush. I and the Trotting Swans have known about your hunts all these forty-two years. You run alongside cargo trains as they enter the county. You hop on and climb them until you find a nice juicy hobo. You then drain the hobo and eat his heart before leaping off. And usually the train conductors don't notice the body until the train is hundreds of miles away from here.

"I know every death that happens in this county, Thrush. I know the names of who dies and who or what kills them every time. I know when someone is close to death, or beyond it like you, dear friend." He smiled with monstrous conceit.

At this point Thrush might've considered running away. But the Count seemed so casual and open he found it hard not to be intrigued. "I used to rob trains for money...back when I was alive. I don't really need money anymore, just blood and hearts to maintain my own." The laich leaned back in his chair and crossed his arms. "All right. I'm impressed, but not yet convinced why I should help you. What could a theurge of your power need with me?"

The Count blinked his eyes and said "The band of Excursionists called Four Winds – One Storm. They are shunting everything up."

Thrush nodded and chuckled. "Word is spreading of their deeds throughout the county. I myself witnessed Lady Gone end the pistol duel curse in Barnhart. A sweet young thing, that one. They

406

say she also cleansed the coal mine of ghosts, too. Not to mention what the team of them did in Drowsy Nook."

The Count let out a scoffing hiss. "Which brings me to why I summoned you here, Mr. Raisinbread. I want you to be the new Sheriff of Drowsy Nook."

Thrush laughed. "Me? But I have no experience in law enforcement."

"But you do have experience in combating and avoiding it. You see, I *know* who you really are, Hemogoblin. Your mind is an open book to me. Before relocating to my county a half century ago, you saw a thrush pecking at raisin bread on a window sill. Before that you were the notorious laich outlaw known as Gurn the Stave, train robber and master of the steel quarterstaff. So, tell me, Gurn or Thrush; why a staff and not a sword or a gun?"

Thrush's eyes narrowed. "I don't want my prey to bleed so much before I drain them. Now, if you don't mind, Count Slanidrac, I have some questions for you. Firstly, why choose me for Sheriff of Drowsy Nook?"

The Count steepled his fingers and tilted his head with a wry smile. "Strategic reasons. Drowsy Nook is the closest town under my influence to the city of Embrenil. And Embrenil is the closest city to Apple County. For anyone in this county to get to Embrenil, they must first go through Drowsy Nook. The Trotting Swans have all long viewed the city as the ideal place to sell their Gray Dust Poppies, more people to sell to means more profit. Unfortunately, the city's law enforcement there were all too aware of where the drug was coming from. Too much was getting to be too much.

"I tried to tell the Swans to cut back on their trips there, but they were always too desperate or greedy to take heed. So, I secretly hired a man named Farnuff to be the town Sheriff and keep them from traveling through town. It worked for a long while until a large group of Swans got fed up with him. Through a necrotheurgic divination, I learned what would soon occur. The band of Swans would ride into town, kill Farnuff, get stupid, and hold the town hostage. So, I hired a malruka who was down on his luck, a man named Edifice Teige. I let the Swans go in and kill Farnuff without warning him of the impending attack I had predicted. Then I made Edifice wait three days before going in to kill the Swans and become the town's hero."

407

"Why make him wait the three days?" Thrush asked. "Why let the town suffer in fear? Enjoyment?"

The Count shrugged. "Well, that and I did not want it all to seem too convenient a salvation. Anyway, Teige became the new sheriff and the Trotting Swans never again dared to smuggle drugs through Drowsy Nook. Unfortunately, the whelp ghost there took it upon himself to try to execute Teige for passive-aggressive murder. The attempt at punishment left a nasty notch on his neck."

"I know what happened after that," Thrush interrupted. "The entire county knows. Four Winds – One Storm came into town and broke the Headsman's curse and killed Teige, when he murdered a deputy instead of surrendering to answer questions about his notched neck. It's a shunted-up situation with many loose ends, as far as the public is concerned."

The Count leaned forward. "And I need you to tie up those loose ends, tie them up and drain them dry. Four Winds – One Storm must be stopped. I need you to help me kill them so that I can repair the damage they have done. And I need a tough, reliable Sheriff for Drowsy Nook to keep my Swans in check."

Thrush arched an eyebrow. "Do you really think those Excursionists will find out *everything* you've just told me?"

The count made a dismissing gesture. "They need not know every detail of the Geohex in order to undo it. They have already disconnected five of the necrotheurgic hematite conduits that I use to keep the county cursed. They are on the right track for undoing everything I've accomplished. A bomber need not know how a building was constructed to bring it down. A viper need not know how to fly or build a nest in order to steal a mother bird's eggs. And a tomb-thief need not know how to mine and make a treasure in order to dig it up and pilfer it.

These four thorns in my side are no different. I want and need them dead, Thrush. And after we kill them and reclaim the hematite implements they have stolen, I will make their spirits into ghosts to haunt the towns they once saved. Think about it, a team of heroes go into a haunted county to lift its curses and purge its ghosts, but end up becoming a part of the very ghost legends they sought to investigate. Such an event would solidify the infamy of this land. Wraith County, a place where even the ghosts of *heroes* dwell in cursed misery!"

408

Thrush nodded again in complete acceptance and understanding. Then another question arose in his mind. "It's strange, Count Slanidrac. Everything you've told me, everything I've heard from you... Why am I so...not bothered by it? Yes, it is true I may be a monster. But I also love my independence, or at least I did. Why is it I am not freaked out by the meaning of all this? Why do I feel so inclined to trust and serve you?"

The Counted grinned darkly. "Because you have no will of your own, Hemogoblin. You are driven by hunger and desire, not willpower, as all laiches are. I owned you the second you read my letter."

Thrush frowned in confusion. He pulled the letter from his back pocket and unfolded it. His puzzled eyes scanned over the text. "I don't understand," he said in a worried whisper.

The Count, still grinning, glanced down at the letter. "Go ahead and read the last line, the post script. Go on. Do it."

Thrush looked down at the shaking paper in his purple hands and read aloud. "Those who can be forced do not know how to die."

"Exactly!" exclaimed the Count with a snap of his fingers. "I cast the maxim on you through the paper made from a dead cypress tree. You are a post-mort. You are dead, yet not dead. Therefore you do not know how die. And because of that you can be forced...by me."

Thrush shook his head as he tried to make sense of what the Count was saying. "But...this maxim. I do not reckon it means what you reckon it means."

The Count laughed deep and loud. "Oh my poor dear Thrush! You are no theurge! When it comes to maxims it is all about context! Come now! I will let you in on the plan!"

Chapter 8
The Legal Battle

Polly returned to Drowsy Nook after a cold rain left it damp and muddy. She saw her team's covered wagon out in front of the local inn. The vehicle had been fully repaired and the words: *Four Winds-One Storm* were painted on the canvas cover in fancy red letters. This made her smile.

As she drew closer atop Waltre, she saw Will walking out from the wagon's other side. He carried a bucket of red paint and a paint brush. He did not seem to notice her as he looked up at the big wet letters.

"I like de color!" Polly called out.

"Figured you would," he answered, not bothering to turn around. "Red was the cheapest anyhow."

Polly got off her bileer, trying not to splash too much in the muddy road. "Are de others back yet?"

"Yep." He turned around. "An' we got a whole lot o' cussin' an' discussin' to do." His eyes were grave and his face was full of long scratches and bruises.

Polly looked down and noticed his large hands looked the same. "What happened to you?" she asked. "Did swords do dat? A ghost? Were you out-numbered?"

Will took a deep breath and looked over at her bileer. He walked to the animal and sighed through his nose as he unbuckled its saddle. "A lot's gone on, Polly. Rev says it'd be best if we all jus' sat around a table an' shared what all we did." He looked at her, worry and relief in his eyes. "I sure am glad yer okay, Pol. This county is more dangerous than we first thought it'd be. More'n jus' spooks an' curses."

Polly crossed her arms and looked down. "De Trotting Swans," she whispered.

Will frowned as he pulled the saddle off. "More'n that, too," he whispered back.

◎

"Polly-pop!" Röger shouted when he saw her and Will enter the inn's lobby restaurant. The burly human stood up so fast from the table where he and Hindin sat that his chair tipped over. He rushed over and picked her up in a big bear hug.

Polly tried to act annoyed but reluctantly smiled and laid her head on his shoulder. "I missed you, too, Röger," she said, laughing. "Though I am loathe to admit it."

"Hand her over, Sir Röger!" Hindin demanded, taking Polly from Röger as if she were a small child.

Polly smiled excitedly as she wrapped her arms around the Malrukan's neck. "Hindin! I can't wait to tell you what I – OW!" Her cheek bumped hard against the side of his steel face.

Röger looked at something Will was holding. It was wrapped in a blanket. "What is that, a crossbow?"

Will shrugged. "That's what I thought at first. It's sumthin' Polly brought with her."

Polly hopped down from her hug with Hindin and rubbed her cheek. "It's a miner's pick. De head is made of hematite just like de execution axe."

The three men exchanged glances.

Hindin cleared his throat. "Well, it seems we all have something to bring to the table."

"Show and tell time!" Röger exclaimed with a loud clap of his hands. "Here, I'll go get my axe." He turned as if to go upstairs to his room, but stopped suddenly. "Oh wait!" he said as he gave Polly a wry grin. He held out his hand in the direction of the stairway. Polly noticed a hematite ring on Röger's middle finger.

Her pointed ears perked as she heard a loud thud and a rumbling, dragging sound along the upstair floor. She then heard a man scream and a door slam shut. In seconds, she saw the

412

Headman's Axe float down the stairway and whiz over into Röger's grasping hand.

"Sir Röger!" Hindin bellowed. "I have already explained why you should not do that! The good people of this town do not need to see that weapon floating around on its own! Think! They might perceive it as he local ghost returning for vengeful justice."

"Or justified vengeance," the Röger shot back.

"How did you do dat?" Polly asked, more intrigued than impressed.

Röger spun the huge axe like a baton in his fingers. "I just have a magnetic personality, baby."

Hindin groaned. "He is only half right, Polly. Allow me to explain. Magnetism *is* the key to the Geohex, *necromagnetism* to be precise. You see, all magnets have four poles, or energy transmitters. Non-theurges are only able to perceive the North and South poles of a magnet. These mundane poles transmit small amounts of gravitational force. Then there are the East and West poles that only those like you and I can detect. These poles transmit theurgic spiritual energy.

"Hematite, particularly this grade we've discovered, is able to transmit necrotheurgic energy underground from magnet-to-magnet, creating a web-like circuit of death power that perpetuates and maintains the Geohex." He let out an astonished laugh. "Who knew it would be something so simple!"

Polly nodded. She understood what he said just fine, but did not agree with the simple part. She took the pick from Will and unwrapped it, revealing the dark, gleaming metal it was composed of. "Dis was embedded in a rock wall in a coal mine."

Will reached into the inside of his dust coat and pulled out a perfectly round and smooth hematite cannon ball. He held it up to Polly's eye level. "This was stuck in a rock wall inside a cave."

Röger held up the axe. "This was in a petrified tree stump." He then held up his ring. "And this was banded and secured around a petrified wooden pole."

Hindin reached behind the table and produced the two hematite bars, one capped with the bust of a drakeri maiden. "And these were both embedded in marble man-crafted structures that were connected with the Ground, a bridge and pedestal to be exact. They, like Sir Röger's ring and axe, seem to have an attracting bond

413

with each other."

The Four stood silently for a moment, and without exchanging words, placed all the hematite objects into a pile on the round wooden table. They each took a seat and regarded the pile with mixed expressions.

Will let out a dissatisfied, "Humph," and called out to the waitress. "Hey there, Bwavan! We're all gonna order lunch now. After that keep the drinks comin' til supper time. Then we'll want supper. After that keep the drinks comin' til closin' time."

The waitress' eyes grew wary as her mouth gaped open. "You all plan on being here the rest of the day and evening?"

"Yes, ma'am. We got a lot o' catchin' up to do. An' speakin' o' ketchup, get me an' Röger each our own bottle. He an' I had a tiff yesternight sumthin' fierce 'cause there wudn't enough fer our deer brisket."

Röger laughed, causing his shoulders to bounce up and down, then whispered to Polly, "It was a really dry deer brisket."

The waitress rubbed her forehead and eyes with her free hand. "All right, all right," she said with a sigh. "But I'm just letting you know that we are almost out of wild deer meat, Mr. Foundling."

"Not fer long then," the tendikeye replied with a cocky grin. "I'll hunt you up another before too long. An' you can call me 'sweetheart' around my friends. I don't mind!"

Both Polly and the waitress rolled their eyes and shook their heads.

Throughout the course of the afternoon and evening, they each took turns telling what they had been through. They compared the facts of each investigation, asked questions, and pondered the meaning of their findings. There were times when someone would whisper about a particular part of their story, and the others would have to lean in to listen. With pen in hand, Hindin compiled a list of all the ghosts and post-mort creatures they had encountered:

-The Apple Baron on Coach Road P
-The Headsman's Son
-Jerf Bendre's thieving hand
-The Coal Miners and their Ox.
-Hundreds of Canaries
-The Pistol Dueling Skeletons

-The Two Hanged Lovers
-The Drageist
-The 5 Haunted Lyncher Graves
-The fat sucking Muerchi
-Papa G. T.'s Smokehouse Delicious Creations
-The Apple Baron NcKoons
-The Streaking Skeleton
-Prudence Bavus
-Hundreds of Bonwalkers with Pikes
-Skelt Arlingtun and his daughter, Spricca.

Hindin reasoned a next course of action. "Considering we all barely succeeded in and survived our investigations I feel it best to keep our company intact. Extra eyes and minds will improve our chances of success."

Will lit his eighteenth cigarette of the day. "An' I doubt the Trottin' Swans'll attack us if we're all together. They're a buncha cowards."

"What if you're wrong?" Polly asked the tendikeye.

Will sat back in his seat. "Then they're a buncha fools, too! Besides, the general public is with us in what we're getting' done. We got official permission to investigate any bad goin's-on thanks to good ol' Chief Taly back in Embrenil. We're officiated an' bona fide heroes doin' what needs doin'."

Röger shook his head. "But so are the Swans. They're technically the local militia. They kill the occasional monster and pretend to keep order. They rely on the Geohex to grow and sell their drug flowers. And, as bad as it sounds, the people need them to keep the economy afloat. Who knows how much power they really hold here? Or how many there are? We're all pretty tough, but we're only four and the Swans are many."

Hindin spoke up. "From what we have learned, they have nearly replaced the true law enforcement. Taxes pay for such support, and the majority of the populace is too poor to be taxed. Because of this, local government is equally sparse. There are few public officials and many seem to hold no real power. There is no Chief Justice to preside over the sheriffs. There is no Grandmaster Theurge to unify the philocreeds of the people. There is only a Count, a man named Slanidac Norton.

415

"If we, as official investigators and legally sanctioned criminal combatants were to openly condemn and move against the Swans for running the drugs throughout Doflend and perpetuating this Geohex, then I have little doubt that the Swans would retaliate and try to murder us under the guise of defending their territory from foreigners who would disturb their way of life. If anyone would or should have the executive powers to decide which group is legally in the right it is the Count of Apple County. I believe that we should go to Copse dur Crakktun to the County Hall and petition the Count. I believe this is what we should have done from the beginning. Unfortunately, our scope then was too small. Now the bigger picture has presented itself, and I see no better alternative."

Everyone at the table was quiet as they considered Hindin's words.

Then Will shattered the silence. "Brown Gut Snake, Rev!" The tendikeye stood and slapped the tabletop. "Even if we get the go ahead from some fat cat behind a desk, them bike-peddling rump-stuffers won't give a shunt! You need to get yer eyes polished and yer head in the right place. I say we don't waste no time. We go to the rest o' the towns as a team an' yank out any piece o' hematite we find. If we run into trouble, then we knock it outta the way, be it spook or Swan!"

Röger stood up to face Will. "What about our other problem? The one that messed up your face?"

A sick feeling invaded Polly's stomach. "What *other* problem?" she asked. "And just what did happen to your face, Will? I asked you before. And you made no mention of it in your investigation story. How did it happen?"

Will frowned angrily. He could not look her in the eyes. "I ran into yer momma, Pol. We each did on our way back to town. Strange thing is we all fought an' killed her."

"That is not how I see it," Hindin argued. "I saw her body turn into blood and sink into the ground. It was some theurgy beyond my understanding."

Polly sat utterly still in her chair, her face devoid of any emotion. Her eyes sought Röger.

Röger's eyes reflected something rising inside of her: fear. "We...we all thought we'd killed her for you...until we put together that we fought her in three different places all around the same

416

time."

Polly looked away and started to tremble. Her jaw and eyes clenched shut as her chest rose and fell with hard, unsteady breaths. "You...all of you...you choose *now* to tell me dis?"

Hindin crossed his arms, sensing her distress. "Polly, we are sorry, but—"

"*Shut up!*" she screamed, startling the malruka. Her lavender complexion darkened to purple as her fear flipped into anger. "You all waited until dis late hour to tell me? Why are we still here? Why aren't we running away?" Her eyes filled with tears as her throat mangled her voice. "She will kill you all! She will take me back and make me like her!"

"So, she is not dead." Hindin said calmly. He got up and placed his hands on Polly's shoulders, keeping her still. With a grave face and stern voice, he said, "Polly, we are not going anywhere until we understand the situation. How was it that she was in three different places at once? You know her and share her theurgy. How did she do it? Did she clone herself or....what exactly? Please, get a hold of yourself and help us understand."

Polly looked up at her friend and broke into a sob. "We have to run away, Hindin. We've...we've done enough in dis county already. We can just go. Please."

Will crushed his cigarette in his bare fist. He hated seeing a woman cry, especially one who was usually so strong. "Maybe it'd be best, Rev. Polly knows her better'n we do."

Röger spoke up. "We don't now what else she capable of. I could feel her power, Hindin. See it in her eyes. She's an ancient hemotheurge master. I think we should follow Polly's advice."

Hindin looked at his teammates one by one. "Will, you are a fool. Röger, you are a coward. Polly, you are being a bad friend."

"How?" she asked, blinking.

He took his hands off her shoulders. "Because you have more faith in your enemy than your friends. It is not befitting of a theurge of any philocreed." He regarded all his teammates. "Why choose to run? And yes, I did say *choose*. As if there was not a choice! I am ashamed that after hearing your individual tales of bravery and astuteness that you would not greet this new challenge with the same intelligence and willpower. Do you think that performing a heroic act yesterday makes you a hero today? It does not. That was

417

then, this is now! Heroism is a thing to constantly strive for. Veluora the Red is a villain of unfathomable cruelty. To let her run free and run away is the action of foolish cowards that lack faith in themselves and their comrades!"

No one said anything for a long moment. Then Polly wiped away her tears and sniffled deep and loud. She sat back down in her chair. The others did, too.

After clearing her throat and taking a breath, she spoke. "Dere is a Red River maxim dat allows a crimson theurge to split demselves. I dare not utter it because I am underdeveloped and it might kill me. De living divisions are called *fractites*. Dey are not clones of de theurge, but equally divided parts of dem.

"My mother is capable of dividing herself by four. She must have used de maxim to cover more area to try to find me. De fact dat she tried to kill you all when she encountered you means she's studied up on us. She must have heard all about us in Embrenil."

Polly's eyes widened in shock. "She was in Embrenil!" she gasped. "She knew where I'd go! By my blood, de bitch knew where I'd go!" Fresh tears began to pour down her cheeks. She looked at her teammates as she cried.

"I don't know why I did not tell you all dis. It...was not your business den. I came to Embrenil for two reasons. De first was de temple orphanage she kidnapped me from when I was little. But Chief Taly told me dat it was closed down. She had murdered de entire staff and all de children when she took me. De second reason...de second reason...."

"It is all right, Polly. Continue," Hindin said.

Polly closed her eyes and let her secret out. "I wanted to meet my *father*. He is a barber named Dale Yonoman. Veluora told me she chose him because an omen told her dat his blood was just right, dat his seed would produce the perfect offspring. She seduced him and disappeared. He never knew about me. But she told me about him. When I ran away from her, I went to Embrenil to, I don't know, meet him and see if he might accept me. I went to his shop. I met him. He...he even gave me a free haircut. But I was too afraid and too stupid to tell him who I was. I met you all shortly after dat." She pinched her seven-sided tattoo and labored through her grief. "De thought of her visiting him to try to find me...it is not a thought I had until now. Why didn't I tink about dat? How can I know she

418

didn't kill him just like de people in dat orphanage?"

"Polly," Will said, his quill brow furrowing. "If me, Rög, an' Rev were each able to beat a quarter-strong piece o' yer momma, a fractite as you call it, then the four of us together could beat her when she's whole, don'tcha think? We could put a stop to her fer good." He looked over at Hindin and exchanged nods with him.

Polly shook her head. "I don't know. I would say dat I am at least a quarter her strength now. But she is de one who trained me. She knows how I fight. And now she knows how you three fight."

"But we also know how *she* fights," Hindin argued. "And bear in mind that no amount of strength, be it physical or theurgical, can match against a well-planned strategy. We need only out-think her."

Röger pushed his beer mug away. "Veluora has the wisdom of ages. After hearing her talk, I could tell she was one of the smartest people I've ever met. And with all those generations of memories she claimed to have, it's like she as all that experience, too."

Hindin arched a steel eyebrow. "Sir Röger, you have lived for one hundred sixty-one years, yet you still display the look and attitude of a human in his late twenties."

"So? What's your point?"

Will grinned and answered for Hindin. "I think he means age don't mean brown gut snake." He looked over at Polly and his grin melted away. She sat hunched in her chair with her eyes lowered. "Polly?" he said softly.

She did not respond.

"Polly?" Will repeated.

She turned her face to him. "What?" she said coldly, her eyes harsh and mean.

"If she did kill him, yer dad, then I'll make it my personal mission to put her down an' avenge him fer you."

Polly scoffed. "You? A tendikeye who is weak against theurgy? She'll probably kill you first when de time comes!"

"Good!" Will shouted at her.

"Why is dat good?"

"Because I don't want to live in a world where *you* suffer so needlessly!"

Polly's head snapped back with the shock of his reply. She

419

looked at the tendikeye. Beneath his stern, cool gaze she saw her own pain, hate, fear, and sorrow reflected. She wanted to reach out and embrace him, to drown his negativity with her own. But instead she got up from the table and ran upstairs.

The three men looked at each other, all unsure of what to say or do. Röger picked up his beer and drank it all in one pull. Hindin stared blankly down at the hematite objects on the table. Will put out his cigarette.

About a minute later, Polly Gone came walking back down the stairs. Her face was clear and calm. Her posture straight and relaxed. "I just realized two tings," she said to the men at the table. "De first ting is I don't want to suffer needlessly either. Not anymore."

"And the second thing you realized?" Hindin asked.

Polly let out an embarrassed laugh. "I realized dat I haven't checked into a room here yet. I ran upstairs wit' no place to go."

Röger erupted into a belly laugh. "You dummy!"

Polly laughed out loud and slapped her palm against her forehead. "I know!"

❁

The following morning the Four met again for breakfast. The inn served them cornbread with chives and bacon baked inside it.

"So," Röger started. "Where do we go from here?"

"It hasn't been decided yet," Hindin replied, glancing at Will and Polly.

Will picked the bacon bits out of his cornbread and set them on a coffee coaster. Not looking up from what he was doing, he said, "I stand firm on what I said yesternight. Go to the rest o' the towns an' pull up hematite. Kill Swans if need be."

Hindin rolled his eyes and regarded Polly. "Polly, what would you like to do?"

Polly sat rocking in her seat, nibbling a piece of cornbread in both hands. "I tink we need to go somewhere private and spar together. I'll try to show you every maxim and trick my mother

420

showed me. We need to train as a team anyway, I tink."

Röger grinned and nodded with excitement. "Good thinking, Polly. I've had this one idea where I use my axe, Headlauncher, to cut a guy's head off and then Will jumps up really high and kicks the head into another guy's head." He clapped his hands together. "Just think! Chop! Whizzzzz! KICK! SMACK! We'll call it *The Severed Headbutt!!!*"

Will chuckled. "That'd take a lot o' practice, my friend."

Röger spread out his hands. "All we need are pumpkins and fence posts. Once we get our coordination down, we'll be a terror on the battlefield."

Will shook his head. "I don't do battles. I'm a Dasaru Harker. I do skirmishes."

Röger shook his head mockingly. "Same difference, you picky baby. There's nothing worse than a finicky fighter." He mimicked Will's accent. "Oh, there ain't enough trees 'round here fer me to prance around in! Whatever shall I do?"

Will laughed. "At least I didn't come back to town ridin' no dead ox! Brown Gut Snake, I swear! It won't be easy hitchin' that thing up with the other animals. They're spooked enough as it is sharin' a stable with the danged thing."

Röger dismissed it with his hand. "I love my new mount. I'll never have to feed or water it. It won't stink or leave dung all over the place. I personally think we should sell the bileers and have Papa G. D. make us three more."

"You can't be serious," Hindin said with a frown.

"I am. I like my mounts like I like my women: low maintenance and easy to ride."

Right then, five people entered the establishment. Two of the five they recognized as Deputy Drume Arteen and old Deputy Kellyr. The other three were a grim-faced drakeri man with a solid steel walking-stick, a pretty drakeress with a mole near her nose, and a rather shrunken old drakeri man carrying a wooden gavel that looked way too big for him. The five approached the table of the Four without saying a word.

The Four rose from their chairs.

"Peace and good morning," the pretty drakeress said with a polite smile. She was dressed in a fancy leather traveling dress with a wavy wide-brimmed hat and carried a briefcase. "I am Elin Hoit,

421

Prosecuting Barrister of Apple County." She gestured to the man with the walking stick. "This is Thrush Raisinbread, the new sheriff of Drowsy Nook."

"And I am the Honorable Judge Wrenk," the old man added.

"Wait," Polly said, confused. "I thought Deputy Arteen was going to be de new sheriff." She gave the deputy a worried look.

Deputy Arteen wore a sour expression. His eyes reluctantly met hers.

The fancy lady tilted her head, bowing slightly in Polly's direction. "Deputy Arteen was considered for the position, but Count Slanidrac deemed Mr. Raisinbread more fit for the job." She then raised her chin and addressed all at the table. "Would the four of you please come with us to the town courthouse?"

"Why?" Röger asked.

"To hold court, of course," the old judge answered.

"For what, may we ask?" Hindin questioned with a furrowed brow. "For a trial?"

The old judge let out a laughing sigh. "No, my boy. Only a hearing. Given the delicacy of this matter, lawful procedure is key. You are not being arrested, nor are charges being brought against you."

"Yet," Sheriff Thrush added flatly.

Everyone at the table gave the Sheriff wary look, except Will. The tendikeye grinned at him darkly. Thrush took immediate offense to this, but kept his mouth shut.

Barister Hoit cleared her throat. "We are here to make sure that your... activities...in our humble county have been conducted in a legal manner. The former Sheriff, Edifice Tiege, sent us a letter upon your initial arrival to this town. While the letter stated that you were legally sanctioned investigators, he neglected to copy your official permit word for word. I ask to see this document so that it can be determined whether you four are in fact criminals or heroes."

Hindin raised his palm, his emerald eyes wary but peaceful. "I bear the document on my person, Madam Barrister."

"Excellent," she replied. "Shall we go then?"

◎

Judge Wrenk was the oldest and most powerful justice of the peace in the county. At the request of Count Slanidrac, the old judge came all the way down from his home in Copse dur Crakktun to hold court in Drowsy Nook. With the child ghost of the Headsman gone, a justice of the peace was now required to settle important matters again.

The spry, elderly drakeri led the way to the courthouse as the others followed, his jowls held high.

"Your honor," Deputy Arteen said, stepping alongside the judge. "We haven't actually used the courtroom for, well, longer than I've been alive."

"What is your point, Deputy?" the judge huffed. "And why aren't you telling this to your new sheriff. There is a chain of command we all must adhere to."

Deputy Arteen straightened his posture. "I'm sorry, Your Honor. I just wanted you to be aware that we haven't had a chance to get in and clean it yet."

"A little dust won't kill us, young man," the judge laughed with a shake of his big gavel.

They all went up the courthouse steps single file where the young deputy unlocked the entry doors. The small crowd piled into a cramped lobby as the deputy fought to unlock the doors to the courtroom.

After trying several keys, he looked at the sheriff and judge, embarrassed. "Sorry. I was sure I had the key."

"I probably have it," said Deputy Kellyr as he squeezed to the front. The older deputy tried every key he had with no luck.

"Move!" Sheriff Raisinbread ordered gruffly. He raised his steel staff. "I'll break it in!"

"Wait, please!" Polly requested, stepping in front of the sheriff. Reaching down with her right arm, she grasped the door's old brass handle. Without anyone seeing past her long, wide sleeve, she made one of her veins slither out of her inner wrist and burrow into the keyhole like a searching snake. After a few seconds of squirming, the lock popped and she pulled open the door. The vein returned to her wrist without anyone seeing it.

The judge tilted his head. "What theurgy did you use to do

that? There are rumors, my dear, that you are a Blood Theurge."

Polly smiled politely. "I used no theurgy, Your Honor. It was just a trick. Sleight of hand."

The old judge frowned and scoffed. "Hmm. I'm sure that's not the only trick you know."

Polly pretended to be deeply offended. "Sir! Are you accusing me of being a whore? How dare you?!"

The judge blinked several times and stuttered. "N- N-No! I-I-I-I did not mean to insinuate *that*. I only meant that you are probably a woman of many secret talents!" He looked over at the other faces in the lobby. "Honest!" he shrieked. He looked back at Polly. She was sneering with her arms crossed and shaking her head.

She shook her head. "After you," she said, stepping out of the way.

The judge hugged his gavel close to him and let out a flustered "Hrrmph!" He stepped into the courtroom. Not three steps in, he yelled at everyone behind him. "Hold! All of you, keep back!"

Everyone did as ordered, but Hindin, Röger, Will, Polly, Sheriff Raisinbread, the two Deputies, and the Barrister huddled close to the door to see what was going on.

The judge stood just inside the large courtroom that was covered in thick layers of spiderwebs. At least six arachnids with bodies the size of bowling balls and mandibles like curved jagged knives were crawling on the webs, making their way to the frail old man in the black robe.

"Out of the way, Judge!" Will shouted. "Let me shoot 'em."

The judge answered in a loud clear voice. "Order! This is *my* court, Mr. Foundling. I decide how things proceed!"

Underneath bushy eyebrows, the old judge's eyes focused on the advancing giant bugs. He squared his hunched stance and addressed the monstrous creatures. "I find you all guilty of trespassing on government property, threatening a justice of the peace, and desecrating this sacred room of Law. I sentence you all to death!"

With a mighty swing, he pounded his gavel against the old wood floorboards. Each spider let out a shrieking hiss and rolled onto its back. The Four Winds watched in astonished horror as the creatures' hairy legs bent inward as they died.

The judge spoke again. "I now hereby order the condemned to clean this court of their mess. Take your webs and go to the nearest forest. Once there, be still and rot."

At the second sound of the judge's gavel, the dead spiders animated and rolled over to stand and crawl. In a fast, orderly fashion the post-mort arachnids tore down the countless strands of web into bundles that resembled gray masses of cotton candy. In a matter of minutes, the courtroom was clear of webs. The animated spider corpses pulled the bundles of web along the ground as if they were huge egg sacks. Out the entry door they went.

Everyone scurried out of their way without needing to be asked. When the bugs were gone, the judge called out, "You may all enter now."

Everyone filed in and took a seat save Hindin. He did not like the frail look of the ancient wooden chairs. His emerald eyes shifted to the judge as the old man took the bench. "I have never heard of a necrotheurge as a practicing judge," the Malrukan remarked loud enough for all to hear.

The judge settled into his elevated seat and shook his jiggling jowls. "I am no necrotheurge, Mr. Revetz. Only my gavel is blessed with such powers. It has been passed down from judge to judge in Copse dur Crakktun for generations."

"It is an interesting weapon," Hindin said.

The judge grimaced and growled. "This sacred instrument of Law is no mere weapon, Mr. Revetz. It dispenses karmic justice through the power of death. Upon a fair sentencing within the bounds of any courtroom, it shrivels transgressing appendages, blinds unlawful eyes, deafens criminal ears, and stops murderous hearts. And though it is a terrifying instrument, it is fair and incorruptible. It only harms those who deserve it."

"How can you be sure, Your Honor?" Hindin questioned.

"Because those who are wrongly found guilty remain unaffected by the theurgic sentencing. It has happened on occasions where the accused was wrongly sentenced. They remain unharmed. But such happenings are rare." The old judge smiled darkly with a mouth full of broken, black teeth. "You see, Mr. Revetz, just as Drowsy Nook has had no need for a judge, so too has Copse dur Crakktun had no need for an executioner." He slammed the gavel

425

down, scaring everyone in the room but the Lady Barrister. "This court is now in session!"

The entryway doors slammed shut and the windowless courtroom filled with an eerie glow.

"Mr. Revetz, if you'll please be seated," ordered the judge.

Hindin spread his hands. "Pardon me, Your Honor. But my weight will break the chair."

The judge pointed at the Barrister with his gavel.

"Barrister Hoit, do you have something in your briefcase for Mr. Revetz to sit on?"

"Yes, Your Honor. I have just the thing." She placed her briefcase on her table and popped it open. From it she produced a cleverly folded bundle of paper. Getting up from her seat she walked over to Hindin. "Do you know what this is?" she asked.

"An origami stool," he said with a thankful nod.

"Correct," she replied. She pulled the paper bundle at both ends and it unfolded into the shape of a tall stool. She placed it in front of the malruka.

"My thanks, Madam Barrister," Hindin said as he was about to sit down.

"Wait," she said, stopping him. "May I please see your certificate of Investigation?"

Hindin glanced at his friends. None of them seemed to approve. Reluctantly, he reached into his jacket pocket and handed the document to the woman. He then sat down as she went back to her chair and table.

"Psst!" Polly whispered to Hindin. "Hindin. Why is it dat malruka can't damage paper? How can dat ting support your weight?"

"I will tell you later," the malruka whispered back. "It has to do with how the malruka were first crea—"

"Order in the court!" the judge called out with a bang of his gavel. There was utter silence and the judge commenced the hearing.

"This is a private hearing between officials representing Apple County and the four Excursionists known as Four Winds – One Storm. The purpose of this hearing is to determine whether or not the exploits of these persons were conducted legally. If the documentation they have provided does not sanction their

426

investigations and disturbances throughout our county, we will immediately determine what crimes they may have committed and try them accordingly. Are there any questions?"

"This is Brown Gut Snake!" Will spat, standing up from his chair.

The Judge banged his gavel, and all the strength went out of the tendikeye's knees. Will fell back into his seat, a look of shock on his face. *"What'd he do to my legs?"* he thought.

"That was not a question, Mr. Foundling," the Judge admonished. "And watch your mouth in my court or I'll paralyze your hypoglossal and laryngeal nerves for the duration of this hearing!"

Röger looked over to see Will growing frightened. He raised up his hand politely.

The Judge smiled and said, "Yes, Mr. Yamus?"

Röger turned his gaze at the judge and shrugged in his seat. "So. Is this whole court thing just a ruse to trap us? I mean, I get that upsetting the status quo in this county is making us enemies."

The Judge frowned. "I am not your enemy and this hearing is not a ruse, Mr. Yamus. But this court has it on high authority that *you four* played a role in the killings of every militia man in Tanglefoot. Justifying such bloodshed shan't be simple."

The burly human crossed his thick, tattooed arms. "You want to know if I killed all those Trotting Swans in Tanglefoot? Well, I did. And I acted alone and out of self defense. On top of that, those buttpits were getting in the way of my investigation. But if you want to construe that into murder then you'd better bang your fancy mallet while you still have a chance." Röger leaned forward in his seat, his brown eyes grim inside his helm. "I've survived death maxims before. And if the Law fails to do what's right, then there is going to be chaos. And I'm a master of chaos, buddy."

The Judge did his best to not show fear, but his jowls trembled. "None can master chaos, young man," he stated with a faltering squeak. "Nor can a man defy death forever."

"Try me, buttpit," Röger dared darkly.

The old man's eyes widened in rage. He raised his gavel and opened his mouth to speak.

Röger's hand reached behind his back to grasp his axe.

"Wait!" shouted Barrister Hoit. She sprang up from her

427

chair with her hand raised in a halting gesture. No one in the court moved or made a sound. She held the Investigation Permit in her other hand. "Your Honor, the prosecution moves to dismiss all possible impending charges. They have done no wrong in our county."

"What?!" the Judge cried, his face contorted with confusion and disappointment. "Madam Barrister, are you mad?"

The Barrister wet her lips, her eyes cool and cautious. "This document sanctions their actions, Your Honor."

The Judge glanced back and forth at Röger and the Barrister. "Let me read it aloud before this court." He held his hand out.

The lady Barrister sighed as she approached the bench. "You won't be able to read all of it, Your Honor."

"I've brought my spectacles, Barrister!" the Judge huffed.

"That's not what I meant."

"Oh, shut your face and hand it over!"

The Barrister gave up the large piece of parchment and fought not to roll her eyes. She went back to her seat as the Judge put on his thick eye glasses. The words were scribed on smooth hempen paper. The letters were blue ink. Enclosing the text were several drawings of snowflakes. The judge huffed and began to read aloud:

"By the Power of Authority invested in me by the Free People of The Confederated Capitalist Democracy of Doflend, I, Waltre Taly, Chief Justice of Embrenil and Master of the Frigorific Path, bestow full rights of Criminal Detection, Apprehension, and Use of Necessary Lethal Force equal to Civic Detective Rank to the individuals known collectively as 'Four Winds-One Storm.' These individuals, Polly Gone, Hindin Revetz, Will Foundling, and Röger Yamus, will carry these rights with them throughout any of Doflend's Seven City-States. Local Law enforcement is expected to allow, but not necessarily assist, them in any investigation they wish to conduct. Only a Chief Justice can order these individuals to cease an investigation."

"This order is my last order as Chief Justice and it cannot be undone, not even by my self.

"-Chief Justice Waltre Taly the Frigorifist of Embrenil."

The Judge snorted and spat. "This says they can only investigate in cities, not rural areas like ours. That is my interpretation of this document. Therefore, their actions are illegal!"

The Barrister shook her head. "I am afraid you are wrong. Even I as prosecutor would interpret it that way. But it does mean anywhere in Doflend, and it cannot be interpreted in the prosecution's favor."

The Judge shook his jowls. "How can you be so sure, Barrister?"

The lady glanced down at the parchment he held. "Read the rest of it, Your Honor."

The Judge frowned in confusion. He looked back down at the permit, checking both sides for additional text. "I did read all of it!" he shouted, annoyed.

The Barrister did her best to remain calm. "Please, Your Honor. Let me show you." She gingerly took the parchment back and held it up for everyone to see. "I ask the court to examine and recognize these snowflake shapes around the border edge of the permit."

"Yes. What of them?" the Judge asked.

"These are no mere decorations, Your Honor. These are *cryoglyphics*, Cold theurgical writing. They issue further stipulation that I doubt even Four Winds – One Storm were aware of." She looked at the four Excursionists. "Am I correct?"

The Four looked just as puzzled and intrigued as the Judge.

Polly spoke up. "Are you saying dat Chief Justice Taly put secret text into de permit?"

"Yes, Ms. Gone. And fortunately I am able to read several theurgic written languages, this being one. These snowflakes are actually complex characters that convey and carry the theurgic will of the Frigorifist who wrote them."

"What does it say?" Hindin asked, growing excited.

The barrister cleared her throat. "It says: *'And should these four individuals ever fall into corruption within the boundaries of Doflend, and they commit a cold-blooded act of unscrupulous self-interest such as murder purely for personal gain, then their cold blood shall freeze inside their veins and their hearts will shatter inside their chests.'"*

429

The lady Barrister let out a humble, yet defeated sigh. "You see, Your Honor. If these Four Excursionist *had* committed actions that would violate the stipulations of this permit, then the theurgy that these *cryoglyphics* contain would have killed them. It would have froze them to death from the inside."

"That sly old fox," Will thought.

Polly shivered with the thought, *"It's a good ting I did not murder Austen Belnap. Den again, Polly Gone is not my real name."*

The old judge began to blink hard and erratic. "Wait, wait, wait! Madam Barrister, are you saying that the Permit does include rural areas because that piece of paper did not kill them?"

"Yes, Your Honor. It would seem that the will of Chief Justice Taly includes rural areas."

The judge rested his cheek on his fist as he let out a feeble growl of frustration. He thought for a moment before pointing a spindly finger at the Permit. "How can we know for sure that is not a forgery, or that it is truly theurgical?"

The Barrister addressed the court. "Does anyone here have a match?"

Hindin nudged Will with his elbow. Will looked up at him grumpily.

"Give her your lighter," Hindin told him.

"But I don't want to!" Will protested in a hoarse whisper. "I don't trust her with any o' this!"

"Trust me, my friend," the malruka replied.

Will sighed and reached into his inside pocket. "Here ya go, Ma'am!" he called out to the Barrister, tossing her his flip top lighter.

At first she fumbled to catch it, not expecting it to be tossed to her. The lighter bounced off her palms several times as she struggled to trap it in her grasp.

Then the nimble hand of Sheriff Thrush Raisinbread snatched it out of the air. Everyone's head snapped back in shock at the sudden sight of him standing next to her. No one had seen him get out of his chair and move the ten or so feet to get to where he now was. It was as if he simply appeared there.

The new sheriff handed the lady the lighter, a smug grin on his lips.

She took it and glared at him. "No showing off," she said told him. "It's not becoming of an authority figure."

A muffled laugh sounded from behind the closed lips of the sheriff. He backed away to his chair and sat, laying his steel staff across his knees.

The Barrister woke the flame in the flip top lighter. "Behold!" she exclaimed, placing the flame under the permit.

Röger, Will, and Polly shot up from their seats. Hindin held them back with his great long arms. "Wait!" he cautioned them.

Everyone watched for several seconds and then close to a minute as the small fire waved along the bottom edge of the parchment. The paper did not so much as smolder or scorch, but remained intact and unburned. The Barrister flipped the lighter shut and addressed the court. "As you all can see, these four Excursionists have the blessing of a powerful theurge and Chief Justice. Because they have not violated this permit they have not violated the law." She let out a defeated sigh. "It seems that they are every bit the heroes the people say they are." She tossed Will his lighter and gave Hindin back the permit.

"Preposterous!" wailed the judge.

The Barrister clenched her teeth and addressed him. "I am sorry, Your Honor. But we of the Law cannot touch them."

"Preposterous! Mystic bunkum! Theurge malarkey!" the Judge raved in his seat. "I did not travel here all the way from Copse dur Crakkton to let these degenerate vigilantes escape what is due them! They murdered our militia men and stole historical relics! They are stirring up the dark energies and ghosts of our humble towns, putting our people at risk!" He raised his gavel high. "I hereby *dismiss* that permit as viable evidence! This is *my* county! And I will not have some big city snowflake theurge place limits on my judgments!"

The Barrister's eyes widened in fear. "Your Honor, no!" she cried, raising her arms. "You cannot hope to overrule this!"

"Shut up!" roared the Judge. "The Permit is hereby void and revoked and that is final!" He brought the gavel down, smacking it hard onto the top of the bench.

The courtroom flashed with a blue dazzling light. A violent gust of cold wind nearly blew everyone out of their seats. The entry doors of the courtroom slammed open.

431

When the light faded, everyone saw the Judge sitting perfectly still, a thick layer of ice coated over every inch of his body. His mouth was open as if letting out an angry scream. But all that came out was a whimpering moan that seemed to say "Help meee...."

A burst of laughter came from the seats. To everyone's astonishment, it was coming from Sheriff Raisinbread. "Well!" he laughed as he stood up and approached the bench. "So much for *that* plan!"

He grasped his steel staff and reached toward the Judge with it. After a series of controlled taps, the ice shell encasing the Judge crumbled. The Judge let out a shivering screech as the ice came off of him.

The old man looked down at The Four with trembling eyes. "Th-Th-Th-There is no need for a trial. H-H-Hearing dismissed. Th-Th-Th-This court is adjourned." He then very, very gently tapped his gavel.

Sheriff Raisinbread laughed all the more as the Judge got up and speedily left the courtroom.

Polly could not help but observe the man. *"Dere is something strange about dis one,"* she thought. Her attention went to her teammates who had begun conversing.

"That was outright amazing!" Hindin exclaimed to Will and Röger.

Will lit a much-needed cigarette. "You kiddin' me, Rev?" he asked as a cloud of frost escaped his lips. "That old coot Taly put us under a hex without lettin' us know."

"At least it was reasonable," Hindin argued.

Röger let out a heavy scoff that took the form of frosty vapor wafting from his helm. "Reasonable, my ass! He laid a trap for us in that permit. What if there comes a time when one of us needs to kill but because of the circumstances, Waltre Taly would have considered it murder? I mean, his will is in that paper."

Hindin raised his palm. "Considering what we have already got away with it would seem that the Permit offers plenty of leeway. I am not worried."

"Well, me an' Röger are!" Will fired back. "We don't want to stay under the sway of some retired theurge's power. Besides, you ain't got nothin' to fear anyways! You ain't got blood or a heart

432

subject to freezin'!"

Polly watched as the frost cloud of Will's breath mixed with the smoke of his cigarette. She then looked back at Sheriff Raisinbread. The man was conversing with Deputies Arteen and Kellyr about reopening the entire courthouse and electing a new judge for Drowsy Nook. There seemed nothing special about their conversation.

Then she noticed it.

When then Deputies talked, frosty breath escaped their mouths. But the only thing escaping Raisinbread's mouth were questions and orders.

"*He's not breathing!*" Polly realized with dread.

She focused on all the blood surrounding and feeding into her eyes. The world went dark around her. Through an inky blackness, she saw only the cardiovascular systems and blood of everyone in the court, like glowing beings made of red and blue cords and a heart pumping blood throughout everything. She looked at Raisinbread and found the answer she was looking for.

Right where his stomach was located was a mass of blood. From that mass came a tube called a *legosial trunk* that pumped the blood directly into his heart just under the *right ventricle*. To Polly's knowledge, there was only one kind of creature that possessed a *legosial trunk* as part of their anatomy. "*A Hemogoblin laich!*" she thought with silent terror. She undid her theurgical sight.

As her vision returned to normal, she saw that the Sheriff was glaring at her.

"Can I help you with something, young lady? It's rude to stare."

She shook her head timidly. She wanted to scream what she had found out to everyone in the room. But then she remembered some words of wisdom that her mother taught her. *A patient killer is an effective killer.* All her fear washed away, and she gave the Sheriff a demure, sweet smile.

Thrush returned a look a bemusement and then resumed his cocky swagger. "*Tasty little thing. Oh, and cherry-ripe, too!*" he thought. "*She must fancy me, being a big man of the law. Oh, I'll give her what she wants and more, to be sure, to be sure.*"

Polly looked over at her teammates. They were still arguing over whether or not they should still rely on the Permit. "*When and

433

how do I tell dem dat dere is a laich in our midst?" she thought.

Before she could say anything, the Four were approached by the Lady Barrister. The three men stopped arguing, their attention stolen by her strong presence.

"So much for keeping the peace," she said bitterly.

Hindin stood, towering above her. "We have no intention of stirring up trouble, Barrister Hoit." He folded the oragami stool and handed it to her.

"That's not what I mean, Mr. Revetz. I know full well of your altruistic intentions to end the Geohex. I meant that you and your comrades are causing more trouble than you are quelling. As an agent of the law, I only tried to subdue your efforts. Had you been found guilty of investigating illegally, I would have requested to have the four of you kicked out of the county for your own good, as well as the good of the populace."

Hindin furrowed his brow. "Explain."

"The law has only so much power in Apple County. I'm loathe to admit it, but the Trotting Swans run things here."

"And what of the Count?"

She smiled sadly. "Count Slanidrac is only one man. He hasn't the funding to afford a real police force. He had no choice but to designate the Swans as Militia. There are simply too many of them to brand as criminals. Now, I tried, I honestly tried just now to get you booted out of the county for the good of everyone. Now, I am asking all of you: please go."

"No," the Four replied as one.

The Barrister nodded and swallowed hard. "You cannot hope to kill or arrest all of them."

"Ma'am, the Swans ain't our concern," Will said. "We're jus' gonna purge yer land and leave. Jus' you be a dear an' spread the word that me an' my friends got a right to be heroin' about, and we shouldn't be havin' no problems."

The Lady Barrister smiled at the tendikeye. "A splendid idea, Mr. Foundling. Which brings me to plan B. You see, in the event that I and Judge Wrenk could not oust you from the county, I was to deliver to you this." She handed them an envelope, which Hindin took. "This is from the Count himself," she said confidently. "He told me that if you cannot be beaten, then you must be joined."

Will arched a quilled eyebrow. "How's that exactly?"

434

"Plan B is to publicly honor you as heroes at the County Fair. You are already gaining favor with the people. Once the Count talks you up, then it will be foolish for the Trotting Swans to continue hindering you." She leaned forward. "But make no mistake, The Count's motives are purely political. If he cannot get rid of you, then he will use you. He will secure your reputation as heroes to secure his public image."

Röger nodded as he sneered. "All because he can't get rid of us legally."

"Exactly," the barrister replied with cold eyes.

As the rest of the team considered her words, Will crossed his arms and let out a wary sigh. "An' let me guess, once we're all together at the fair, the Trottin' Swans're gonna blast us to waste. This is a trap, plain an' simple."

The barrister shook her head. "Mr. Foundling, do you honestly believe the Swans would attack you so openly, in front of everyone in the county? Bear in mind that the Swans are a shrewd brood. They are drug runners first and assassins last. While every Swan in the county will undoubtedly be there, they would be utterly stupid to disturb the peace at the County Fair by murdering public heroes. If they do try to kill you, it will be with as few witnesses as possible. My guess would be they will attack you all sometime when you resume your investigation."

Will took out another cigarette and put it in is lips. "Y'know, honey, you got a cute lil' rear on you an' you can talk *real* good." He lit his cigarette as he eye-balled her up and down. "But jus' 'cause a viper has a pleasin' curve when it moves, don't mean it won't sting ya when y'ain't lookin'."

The Barrister tilted her head and smiled placidly. "Such eloquent and wise words. It is a great mystery why tendikeye lack the articulate wisdom it takes to work theurgy."

"It ain't no mystery, ma'am. While every other race has *wisdom,* we tendikeye have *common sense.* Which is why you ain't foolin' me none one bit."

The Barrister stepped toward the tendikeye, her eyes discerning, her lips smiling. "You are an ex-cop," she said plainly.

Will was startled by the remark. He took a step back.

The Barrister continued. "No, *cop* is not the right word for your kind. I'm willing to bet you were a *Bonewarden* in your

435

homecell. You are young yet, but the mark of such office still clings to you."

"What is a *Bonewarden* ?" Polly asked, raising her face up to Will.

"It's like a town sheriff," the Barrister answered, not taking her eyes off of the tendikeye. "They are elected in pairs to share the town. They are the protectors, judges, and executioners of their communities. And they are usually elected young because the term of office is ten years. Once elected, only the most serious of offenses can get them ousted. And almost always death or banishment follows ousting. So, Will Foundling, just what did you do to get kicked out of your homecell? You could not have served a full term. I pray you tell me, for I might be able to use that same reason to get you kicked out of this county."

Will's eyes blazed with hate. Polly, for a brief instant, felt more afraid of him than any ghost or monster she had encountered. Will spoke. "Lady. Yer lucky yer a woman."

The Barrister laughed in his face. "Only fools trust luck, tendikeye!" With that, she grasped the handle of her briefcase and turned to leave out the courtroom.

As subtle as a viper, Polly expelled a slithering vein from her wrist. It snaked its way beneath a chair and hooked around the Barrister's ankle as she was strutting. With a loud thump, the woman fell teats-first onto the floor. Hindin rushed to help her up.

"Thank you," the Barrister grumbled harshly. She turned once more to look at the Four. "One more thing: The Fair's main attraction is a bileer show contest. I have heard that your animals are quite impressive. You may wish to consider entering them. Good day, Four Winds – One Storm." She turned on her spiked heel and left.

Polly looked up at Will. "Will, how right was she? Were you really one of dese *Bonewardens*?"

Will nodded.

"And what did you do to get...?"

Will took a deep drag of his cigarette. "My curse," he replied in a puff of smoke. "Once the people in town figured out I was bewitched, they freaked out. Fact that I was adopted didn't help. People I knew and loved and grew up around my whole life kicked me out outta fear."

Polly placed a hand on his shoulder. "How did dey find out?"

Will swallowed hard. "I saved someone. An' in doin' so, revealed my secret. An' that someone ratted me out. I saved their life and then they ruined mine! An' when I get this curse offa me I'm going go back an' make them pay!" He brushed her hand away and exited the courthouse.

Polly watched with concern as he left. She then looked up at Hindin. The malruka had the same look.

"He has told me everything about his past," confessed Hindin. "He honestly does wish to be a hero to bring his mentor out of hiding. But his life goal is to avenge a wrong done to himself rather than prevent wrongs done to others. I have tried and failed to show him that the life of a hero is more honorable than that of an avenger. But he just does not see it that way."

"So, he has a score to settle," Röger remarked.

Hindin's perfect posture broke as his shoulders slumped and his head hung low. He looked to be on the verge of tears. "He is a reckless fool. Because of his 'curse,' his death has been avoided several times. If only he could see that it is a gift."

Polly felt a finger tapping on her shoulder. "*De laich!*" she thought. "*Just stay calm, Polly!*"

She turned cautiously and found that it was only Deputy Arteen. He was smiling, delighted to see her. "Welcome back, Polly," he said with a slight bow.

"Oh! Hullo," she returned shyly, brushing her short hair behind her pointed ears. "Tank you."

"I heard about what you did in Barnhart, the dueling skeletons and the coal mine. I am quite impressed."

"Tank you," she said again, shrinking a little and smiling brighter than she meant to.

The deputy stepped closer, his voice lowering. "So, um, since you and your friends are going to the county fair, would it be safe to presume that our date is still on?"

Polly's eyes widened. "Our date? Oh! Yes, our date. Well, we all haven't decided if we are going yet. We still may have to investigate other towns." She looked over at Röger and Hindin.

The two large men shrugged. "*I'd* like to go," said Röger.

Hindin let out a weary sigh. "I do not know yet. Perhaps.

437

Come, Sir Röger. Let us go keep Will out of trouble." The two men left the courtroom.

Polly looked back up at the handsome, kind face of the deputy. "If you see me dere," she told him.

The deputy laughed. "That's what you said last time."

Polly giggled. She could not help it.

"Deputy!" Sheriff Raisinbread called out from across the courtroom. "Please be kind enough to show me my new office."

"Yes, Sheriff," Deputy Arteen answered.

Just as he was about to step away, Polly grasped him by the collar and pulled his head down to her face. After placing a kiss on his cheek, she whispered in his ear. "Don't trust him."

Arteen gave no sign that he had heard her. He merely smiled and told her, "Go catch up with your friends. I'll see you later."

As Polly ran out and down the courthouse steps, she realized something that made her cringe with dread. *"Oh no! I also promised Izzyk dat I would be his date at de fair! What am I going to do? How am I going to kill dat laich? What am I going to wear? And how am I to avoid my mother when my friends are being such moody imbeciles?"*

Chapter 9
Divining Rods

Miles outside of Drowsy Nook the two tallest members of Four Winds – One Storm trudged their way through a sparse glen of cedars. Magnetically attached to Hindin's back were the two hematite rods he'd claimed from Victor's Grove and Copse Dur Crakktun. In his hands was a self-drawn map of Wraith County.

"Please," Röger groaned. "Please, just try to explain to me again what we're doing out here."

As Hindin walked, he alternated looking at the map and their surroundings. "Some would call it a rite, others an experiment. I choose to simply call it eavesdropping. Although we have gleaned much, there is still much to be learned, particularly who is maintaining this Geohex. Such a great and ancient scheme must have a great and ancient schemer. I intend to find out all I can about this elusive wraith on this day by using his theurgy against him. Tell me, Sir Röger, are you familiar with voodoo?"

Röger spread his hands. "A variation of necrotheurgy. The theurge puts pins in a doll to hurt enemies from far away."

Hindin smiled. "And acupuncture? Are you aware of that?"

The silver helm atop the human's shoulders nodded. "Chimancer healing practice. They use needles and pins to make people healthy. Can you do that stuff?"

Hindin stopped and looked around as he folded his map. "I am somewhat proficient in the practice." He pocketed the paper and removed the bars from his back. "Sir Röger, voodoo and acupuncture are related theurgical techniques. Mirror opposites, in fact. Voodoo is used to harm. Acupuncture heals. Think of this cursed land as the voodoo doll. These hematite implements are the needles used to harm it. By my calibrative calculations, the spot on

439

which I stand is the half-way point between Drowsy Nook and Barnhart. Beneath us is a *ley line*, a sort of messaging path made by the axe you now carry and the pick in Polly's possession. Although these implements are now removed from their designated connection points, the necrotheurgic flow of energy still faintly exists.

"By performing what the ancients called a *wire tap* I will connect myself to this flow and thus 'tap' into the mind of the one from aforth it springs. You see, I cannot heal this land through acupuncture. I lack the power. But I can diagnose the problem. By learning about our enemy and his intentions, we can better overthrow him."

Röger's brown eyes narrowed inside his helm. "Uh huh. And why do you need me? To help you drive those bars into the ground?"

Hindin spun the bars in his fingers like batons. "Not at all. I need your nose."

"My nose?"

Hindin knelt and stabbed both bars into the dirt. Using his palms he hammered them deeper until only a foot poked out from the surface. From the pocket of his jacket, he pulled a ball of twine and some dried plants. "This is sage," he said as he tied the plants to the bars. "It is the plant of wisdom. Its aroma must be smelt during this kind of divination. I have no sense of smell. So, I require your presence to smell the sage, so that I can tap into our foe's subconscious mind."

Röger shook his head. "That's stupid. Why does it have to be smelled?"

Hindin sat cross-legged before the bars before looking up at his friend. "Sir Röger, How can a smell exist if no one is there to smell it?"

Röger had no answer for that. Deciding to remain silent, he sat down across from his friend and watched him go to work.

Once the sage bundles were tightly secured around the rods Hindin placed his hands upon them. Closing his eyes and straightening his posture, he spoke deep and clear. *"Yesterday is ashes. Tomorrow is wood. Only today does fire shine brightly."*

Röger watched as little flames crept out from between Hindin's fingers as the bundles he grasped began to smoke. The

440

smell was pungent, yet relaxing.

A low rumble came from Hindin as he started to hum. A single undying note rang from within him for well over a minute.

"He doesn't need to breath," Röger thought. *"He can just keep humming without stopping."*

The droning note continued, never wavering in pitch or volume. Hindin's brows came together as he concentrated. Röger continued to inhale the upward twisting sage smoke. Rippling air surrounded Hindin as if he were a campfire, yet Röger felt no heat save from the Malruka's hands.

As for Hindin, he felt his own inner heat and chi weave together by aid of his vibrating throat chakra. Like delving vipers, he sent his two energies spiraling down along the hematite rods to enter the stream of profane energy. In his mind, a wooden door appeared shaped like the lid of a casket. Hindin kicked it down and passed the threshold, ducking so as to not hit his head.

When he stepped through the portal, he ceased to be Hindin Revetz the Malruka. His name was Jülo, a boy, a youth, a man, a corpse, a ghost, a wraith. He was all these things in the timeless ocean of memory. With the boy's eyes, he saw the lights of the city go out and the cars falling from the atmosphere. With the boy's heart, he felt the terror and confusion of leaving the Huncell of Humanity, the proud and noble Fevär, for the rustic heartlands of Doflend, where the Drakeri there resented him and his family.

Jülo felt the branches of the apple tree on his bare feet of bone and skin as he picked the apples alongside his family. He heard his father pleading with the Apple Baron NcKoons.

"Please, sir. One more blanket is all I ask."

"What's wrong with the one I gave you?"

"Nothing, sir. But my son and daughter are growing. And it's not big enough for us all to share."

"Ha! Like you round ears know anything about sharing! As far as I'm concerned, it's your fault the electric heater in your shack doesn't work! It's your fault my trucks won't run and my computers won't turn on. Slate would not have existed if you short-lives weren't such warmongers!"

His father's voice lowered. "Please, sir. That was the Regime's doing, not mine. Please. Winter approaches."

"Apples and shelter was all I promised you, and it's more

441

than you deserve. Now get back to work!"

The boy then sensed winter all around him. The crunch of snow between his toes. The ruthless cold on his face and body. The coldness in his heart as he and his sister followed the men who bore away their mother's body. Father was still sick in the shack, and would follow his wife soon enough. When finally orphaned, the boy felt the contained warmth he shared with his sister. There was enough blanket to get them both through the frosty season.

Summer came, as did a group of men. Uninvited, they broke into the children's shack. All eyes went to his sibling. He tried to defend her, but the men blackened his eye and stole her away. When he went to the Apple Baron for help, the old fat drakeri blackened his other eye. She never came back. The shack and the blanket were all his.

Years passed. The boy became a youth. While picking apples a branch broke under his weight, and he fell to the ground. He felt the bone in his shin snap and tear through flesh and skin. The Apple Baron was more concerned with the broken branch than his broken limb.

"This is more than you deserve!" the Apple Baron said as the physicians tied him down to a table. The youth felt the teeth of the handsaw biting through his wounded leg. He heard only his own screams for the next three days.

The youth, crippled and unemployed, wandered the county, his rags and a crutch his only possessions. He felt the gravel hit his face as he tripped and fell on a lonely crossroads. The night was cold and the next town was miles away. Even if he got there soon enough, there was no guarantee of food or shelter. He was a homeless, orphaned, crippled, round-eared foreigner. Unwanted. He no longer even wanted himself, so he laid there and waited for Death to come. He waited six minutes until it became Midnight.

A tall man appeared. Scrape, he called himself. He helped the youth up, holding both his hands. "Walk," he told the youth.

"But I need my crutch."

"Walk," the man called Scrape said again.

The youth then felt both his feet upon the gravel. But when he looked down he saw that his leg was still severed.

Scrape let go of the Jülo's hands, and the youth did not fall. "You stand upon your *phantom limb*, Jülo, the ghost of your dead

442

leg. It is part of your spirit, a spirit that finds power and truth in Death. My soul is as yours. We are both necrotheurges."

"Why?" the youth asked.

"You long for it, do you not? To die and become numb to the pain and misery of life? To transcend the pangs of love and hope? You want to die, or at least, you want to die just enough to not be bothered with the necessities of living. Peace in death."

"Peace in Death?" the youth repeated. He walked around on his two legs and considered their differences. His living leg was cold and sore, covered with cuts and blisters. His ghost leg felt nothing, yet sensed *everything*. He looked to the tall man. "Yes. Give me this peace."

The tall man laughed. "I cannot give you it. I can only show you the way to it, my apprentice. Now behold my true form!"

The tall man grew taller and ceased to be a man. Fact be known, the creature did not grow so much as unfold. Its limbs were jointed like fingers, the legs with two knees, the arms with two elbows, But its fingers were very unfinger-like. Gleaming talons sprouted from its hands like limp wet locks of maiden hair. Its dark blue skin was not quite reptilian, not quite insectoid. But its head was like no animal Jülo had even heard of. A vertical maw split the entire face down the middle. On either side was a nostril and an alien eye brimming with cruel joy and congenial malice. The maw opened, showing sharp teeth.

As the creature spoke its face opened and closed like double doors edged with fangs. "In all of Apple County, all of Doflend, and indeed all of the Burtlbip Huncell, there is no one as miserable as you. Others may have suffered more. But the exact pains you have endured have cured your spirit to perfection. Hold to your misery, and I will be your loyal friend. Hold to your righteous hatred, and it will give you power. Your blackened soul has drawn me from afar. How happy it makes me to find you at last."

The eyes of the youth widened. "What if I don't want to stay miserable?"

The Lemuertian laughed. "It has been a part of you for too long. You'll never get over the loss of your loves. Besides, I like your misery and misery likes company. Fear not, apprentice, for in the Philocreed of Necrotheurgy we are brothers. I will teach you my secrets and include you in my designs. Power to rule over this land

443

will be ours, and none will dare hurt you again."

The youth marveled at his new found ally. "I want justice," he said. "I want justice for the death of my parents and theft of my sister. I want NcKoons to pay. I want justice for all the wrongs the Apple Barons have committed on my people!"

"Now, now," said the Lemuertian as he placed a friendly claw on the youth's shoulder. "Justice is impossible for such scum. Paradoxically, there can be no justice for murder but by murder itself. So, justice will not fit what is fitting. However, there is always room for revenge."

Jülo crossed his arms. "What's in it for you? What design do you speak of?"

The freakish eyes of the looming terror glowed with delight. "Do you know why we Lemuertians are so bad to weaker races such as yours?"

"Because you're evil. That's what mother said."

Scrape chortled. "It is not so simple. All of my race posses a latent psychic ability called *antiempathy*. We feel the opposite of what other creatures feel. Your misery is my joy, which is why I treasure you so. And since I am a necrotheurge I can also feel the misery and suffering of ghosts. And believe you me, boy, the anguish of a ghost brings pure bliss to my heart. My goal is simple: to create as many restless cursed spirits in this county as possible. My design, however, is quite complex. It will require centuries of subtle scheming, deft manipulations, and the forging of powerful instruments to transmit our energies from point to point."

Jülo shook his head in confusion. "But I'm only human. I don't have centuries."

Scrape gestured in dismissal. "A small hurdle. All you need do is---"

The memory melted away, as did the boy, the crossroads, and the monster. Hindin Revetz found himself in a black void. There was no up, no down, and the dreadful feeling of no escape.

"All he had to do was what?" he asked aloud, searching for a way to renew the memory.

A voice answered. Soft and stern it said, "All I had to do was will myself to die."

"Who is there?" Hindin demanded. "Show yourself!"

The voice laughed in a booming cackle, making the malruka

feel small and vulnerable. "Why, who else could it be. It is I, Jülo! Though I haven't used that name in so long. Did you really think this experiment would work? Did you really think there is difference between a subconscious and conscious mind when it comes to a wraith? I've been aware of you this whole time, Mr. Revetz!"

Hindin chided himself. "Oh, what a fool I am!"

"Now, now. Do not be so hard on yourself. I am still very impressed by this effort, you poor, misguided child of the ground. But it seems that your divination has now become a revelation."

"What do you mean?"

The form of a man-corpse appeared before him. The Wraith was so skeletal and mummified that its race was no longer discernible. From the knee down, one of its legs was replaced with a peg of gleaming hematite.

"Behold my parlor trick!" said the Wraith, grinning.

Over the bones and tattered clothes and even the metal peg leg a new image formed around the Wraith. He now appeared as a living human, young and strong. Then his skin changed to purple, and he changed into drakeri man, fat and short. He then transformed into a tendikeye woman, middle aged and pregnant. He took on the appearance of several people in fast succession before finally reverting back to that of a grinning one-legged corpse.

"I can be anyone," said the Wraith. "I have been many different individuals throughout this county's history. And with great care I have guided several to ghosthood."

"You are an illusionist, as well?" Hindin said, astounded.

The Wraith put up his hands. "I am no illusionist. As you beheld, when my necrotheurgic powers began to manifest, I found that I could walk smoothly on my phantom leg. But I still wore this peg to disguise my talent. People marveled when they saw me walking on my peg without the slightest limp because my phantom limb was invisible to their eyes! But not to the eyes of Scrape or those with *necrosight*.

"You see, Hindin, I am a pure necrotheurge. I *wear* my spirit on the outside of my body. I can manifest it, meaning I can make it become visible to mundane eyes, as any person I want. It's a knack I've developed over the millennia. With disciplined concentration, my soul can absorb and bend light, giving me any visage I desire others to see. Were I to end my manifestation and

445

return to the invisible state of a common ghost, then all would then be able to see my peg-leg and the rest of my true body as you see me now which, I must admit, is not the prettiest thing to behold. It is a trick of both physics *and* metaphysics, if you can wrap your head around that."

"I understand," Hindin said grudgingly.

The Wraith smirked and continued. "Thanks to this trick I have cultivated the Geohex since starting it. I maintain anonymity by changing identities every generation or so. Anyway, I'm getting off track. Allow me to boast about my hematite peg-leg! Because of how I lost my leg, no other necrotheurge could have laid a curse such as the one I laid. Hatred and purpose in even proportion is all a theurge needs to lay a curse.

"Now, usually when you lay a curse you must sacrifice something dear to you to make it work. But every thing dear to me had already been lost, everything but my own life. I stuck this peg-leg of mine into the ground and gave my own life force so that every stinking apple tree in this county would never again bear fruit! That may seem silly, but I am a master necrothreurge with a vendetta against apples. I kept my soul from shattering when I died. I became part ghost-part post mort.

"When I was alive, my body kept my spirit intact. But now that I am dead, my spirit keeps my body intact. And night after night, I stick my peg-leg into the ground and repeat the maxim that keeps this land cursed: *Death is a better, milder fate that than tyranny.* And when this nightly rite is performed, the energy I emit and emote is directed and redirected to and through other necrotheurgically-charged hematite conduits which I have placed throughout the county in every town! And thanks to this influx of necrotheurgic energy, ghosts and cursed spirits and unresolved everlasting tragedies can live on through death!" The smirk on the Wraith's face drooped. He hunched forward and began to float around Hindin like a hovering vulture. "At least that is how it has been for the last 2,800 years...until *you* came. You and your team of meddling misfits!"

"Are you yourself not a tyrant?" Hindin shouted. "You enslave souls and starve the innocent! You are no better than the Apple Baron who hurt you!"

"Wrong!" the Wraith growled, pointing a finger at him. "His

446

motivation was greed and bigotry. Mine is enlightenment. I exist to remind all living things that death is the one true power, that happiness is a fleeting lie, that the very act of living calls for punishment."

"It will all end," Hindin said, feeling his fears bleeding out. "We will find the rest of your hematite, and we will find you."

The Wraith scoffed. "How do you propose to find a needle in a haystack?"

Hindin stared at the Wraith and laughed. It started with a titter that turned into a belly laugh. "Why, with a *magnet*, you stupid spirit! And you've already supplied us with several!" Hindin stopped laughing. His emerald eyes glittered wickedly up at his enemy. "I was able to find your mind with my new rods. I bet I could devise a way to locate your body, as well. What do you think?"

The mostly-skull head of the Wraith tilted, the empty sockets blazing with cold hate. "I think it best to debate you spiritually, you smartass robot!" The Wraith raised its arms and said, "*Death is most unfortunate in prosperity!*"

One hundred smokey skeletons emerged from the Wraith's body and flew toward Hindin, their mouths and hands open and hungry.

Hindin raised his open palm, facing the descending host. "*If you want one year of prosperity, grow grain.*"

The smokey skeletons halted, their hollow eyes filling with confusion.

Hindin continued. "*If you want ten years of prosperity, grow trees.*"

The skeletons looked at one another, as if searching for meaning in the strange words.

"*And if you want one hundred years of prosperity, grow people!*"

The skeleton's empty skulls filled with wonder and burst in dying wisps of smoke, their bodies fading to nothingness.

"*Death will hear of no excuse!*" the Wraith cried.

The floating man-corpse grew in size, larger than any tree, taller than any mountain. It opened its immense jaws and knelt down to bite and swallow the malruka whole.

Hindin's eyes widened from the impending danger. Placing his palms together, he closed his eyes and shouted, "*Blame yourself as you would blame others; excuse others as you would excuse yourself!"*

When he opened his steel lids, he was back in the sparse glen of cedar trees sitting across from Röger. "What happened?" asked his helmed friend.

Hindin blinked several times before he could answer. "I...I excused myself."

Chapter **10**

A Dance of Kicks

On that same morning, the Hunveins above and beyond the little county began growing brighter with the light of day, Polly Gone slept comfortably in her bed at the inn, blissfully dreamless under a wool blanket and cotton sheets. A pillow full of wild turkey feathers supported her pretty, drooling head.

Three loud knocks on her door startled her out of peaceful oblivion. "Hey, Pol! Polly? You up, girl?"

"I am now," she answered, sitting up on her elbow and rubbing her face. She coughed harshly and sniffled. The room felt cold as guilt.

"Can I come in?" Will asked.

Polly looked at her pillow and let out a grunt of disappointment. She wanted so badly to sleep again. "Just a minute." She got up, keeping her blanket tight around her, and took little shuffling steps toward the door. Unlocking it, she opened her door just a crack and looked the tendikeye face-to-face. "What is it?"

"I need to talk to you about some things," Will said. He was fully dressed and smelled like coffee.

"About what happened yesterday?"

"Nah. About what's gonna happen real soon."

Polly's eyes narrowed. "What did you have in mind?"

Will formed a sullen grin. "I need you to get dressed. I found a clearin' in a nearby copse. We can train there." He paused and swallowed. "I need you to show me how to kill yer momma."

Polly took a deep breath and swallowed. "Shouldn't we train as a group? Wait for de others?"

"I learn better one-on-one," Will said. "Always been that way."

Polly nodded. "I'll get ready and meet you out front."

449

The tendikeye and the drakeress made their way to the secluded clearing. The light of morning was slowly gaining strength.

"Take off yer boots," Will told her. He turned to face her, flicking the cigarette away as he did so.

Polly raised her chin, not liking how the tendikeye was standing--like he was ready to pounce. "Why?" she asked.

"Yer momma had long spiky veins that came out her wrists jus' like you. I'm willin' to bet you can do the same outta yer ankles just like she did. She whipped the tar outta me with 'em."

Polly knelt down and began to unlace her boots. "Dat was de *Ballet de Lash,* de whip dance. It is de supreme fighting style of all hemotheurges. It takes decades to master." She slipped her boots off, revealing her two-toed feet. She arose with a pout on her lips. "And I am terrible at it. I ran away before my training could be completed, remember?"

Will took a few steps back and crossed his arms. "Well, jus' show me what you know."

Polly swallowed and raised her arms in a dancer's pose. Then she slowly raised her leg and exhaled as the jagged, tendril-like veins sprouted from her wrists and ankles.

Will noted they were about half as long and menacing as Veluora's had been.

"Can you get 'em any longer?" the tendikeye asked.

"Shh! No. I am concentrating," was the only reply he got.

He watched in wonder, disgust, and even with a hint of carnal interest as she moved. Polly's veins whipped like blue ribbons flowing around her as she danced. She was not the most graceful creature. The reluctance in her face reflected in her stiff movements. The entire routine was so basic that it barely resembled the devastating fighting method of her mother. Nonetheless, Will saw beauty hidden in the movements and the girl making them.

When she was done, Polly turned to him, out of breath. "I have not done dat in a while."

Will half-smiled and paced around her. "You seem to be better at grippin' than whippin' with them veins. Grapplin' an'

450

snatchin', that is."

Polly nodded as sweat formed on her brow. "I lack de grace for whips. I prefer to wrestle victims, I mean *enemies,* wit' my veins. De barbs on dem are more jagged and hook-shaped, perfect for snatching and tearing flesh. While my mother's veins are straight like spikes."

Will flared his lips in morbid curiosity. "Why is that?"

Polly shrugged. "Genetics, a difference in personality, or a combination of the two."

Will took a few steps closer to her until he was about eight feet away, just out of range of her veins. "Throw a few whip-kicks my way. I wanna see how they work from a safe distance."

Polly threw a few front snap kicks with her toes pointed out. Channeling the proper momentum, she was able make her ankle veins crack like a whip from six feet away.

Will cringed to see those jagged veins cracking barely two feet away from his crotch. "'Kay. Now switch legs."

Polly groaned and changed up her stance. After trying and failing three times, she accidentally whipped herself in the face. A few drops of blood fell from her lacerated cheek before her eyes glowed red and the wound closed up. "I lack de finesse," she grumbled. "I don't want to do dis anymore. My power is too low."

Will shook his head. "Keep tryin' It's a real useful way of attackin'. You need to figure it out, an' I need to figure out howda fend against it."

"You're putting pressure on me," she bitched.

Will rolled his eyes and removed his dust coat. As he unbuckled his weapon belt, he said, "Yer kicks jus' need work. Lemme show you how *I* kick."

"I kick just fine," she protested. She drew her veins back into her limbs.

Will scoffed. "Let's see it then, girl." He took a relaxed fighting stance and grinned playfully.

Polly smiled darkly and moved in on him. Knowing he could withstand the punishment of bullets and blades, she took fearsome delight in not holding back. She cut loose with a fast roundhouse aimed for his jaw. The kick was perfectly timed, or so she thought. Will's huge hand grasped her ankle just inches from his face, his thick, long fingers trapping her leg. Polly growled. She jumped from

451

her supporting leg, swinging her free foot hard and high. Will ducked, thinking the kick was meant for his head. He was wrong. Polly's kick landed hard and solid on the wrist of his grasping hand on her other ankle. It did not hurt him, but it made him let go. Polly landed roughly on both feet.

"Nice trick," Will said, still crouching low from ducking. Without warning, he planted his hands on the ground and swung one of his big-booted legs in a fast sweep kick.

Polly had no time to evade or jump. With resounding force, the tendikeye's shin caught her just below the knees. For an instant, Polly found herself sideways in the air. Then she crashed face first into the dewy grass.

Pushing herself up, she turned her dew and sod-covered face to Will. "You are lucky I don't use my theurgy," she hissed.

Will shrugged. "Yer lucky I don't use my gun an' blade. Get up."

They sparred for several minutes more. Polly's kicks and punches were well-timed and carried a respectable amount of force for a person her size and age. But in the end, Will's complex hand grapples and acrobatic kicks proved too deceptive and advanced for her. Polly was an expert in the basics of hand-to-hand combat. But Will Foundling's strange methods confused and out-witted her every attempt to best him.

"What style are you using?" she asked, throwing a left hook at his head.

Will spun with the strike, letting it glance off his skull. "It ain't a style. It's a combat method." He used the momentum of the spin to boot Polly's backside.

Polly gritted her teeth. "What is it called?"

Will caught her by the wrist and twisted it, making her yelp and lose balance. In an instant, he had her on the ground, limb-locked and pinned.

"Give up?" he asked, his face neutral.

"Not until you tell me how you learned to fight like dis!"

Will grinned. "Fair enough." He let her go and got off her. Helping her up, he said, "It's a tree-part method."

"Did your mentor teach you?" she asked.

"Two parts," he replied. "Uncle Brem taught me Hammercock an' Hay-bale."

452

"What's a hammercock?" Polly asked, almost afraid of the answer.

"A hammercock is a specially bred rooster from my homecell. Y'see, we tendikeye love cock-fightin', but we hate killin' domesticated animals. They trust us, y'know? So, we bred our chickens to have big heavy feet jus' like us. Once we had roosters with feet big enough, we trimmed the spurs an' talons off of 'em an' made "em fight. An' instead of tearin' each other to shreds they jus' club each other silly. Worse thing that happens is a rooster gets knocked out. Well, anyways. We tendikeye got to studyin' how them roosters swung their heavy legs around. Over time, the Hammercock Method o' kickin' became a respectable way o' settlin' disputes on-the-fly. It's nothin' special though, pretty common."

Polly nodded. "And what is 'hay-bale'? Your grappling method?"

"Yep. We take hay bales as big an' heavy as a man. Then we stick wooden poles through 'em 'bout as thick as an arm. Then we wrestle'em."

"You wrestle an inanimate object?"

"Yep."

Polly crossed her arms. "How does dat work?"

Will shrugged. "If I had some poles and a hay bale, I could show ya."

Polly nodded. "And what of de third part of your style...er...combat method?"

Will grinned as he went over and picked up his scale hide dust coat. Putting it on, he explained, "Rev an' I's first Excursion together was huntin' down a kasucot in Gurtangorr. A kasucot is a flyin' snake about fifty feet long with a hun'erd foot wingspan. Real nasty. Some folk call 'em skyvipers. It's the one monster that krilps have trouble killin'. Krilps are fast an' strong an' fearless, but they can't fly or use projectile weapons to save their lives.

"Now, kasucots are real nasty, like I said. Their fangs can pierce krilp hide, they're venomous, they can swoop an' crash like hawks, an' they got this natural defense that makes 'em near unkillable."

With sudden swiftness, Will spun around in a blur of motion like a dervish tornado. He stopped just as suddenly with a grin on his lips. "Whenever threatened they spin around *real fast*, like that.

453

Arrows, bullets, spears, even Rev's fancy slaps an' kicks--they spin around so fast that everythin' jus' glances off their scales. Rev said the thing had somethin' in its brain called *pre-cog-nishin* that helped it spin at jus' the right instant. Anyway, me an' Rev had the hardest time huntin' an' fightin' that thing. But I figured out a way to kill it.

"My bullets an' the scythe o' my rifle are pokey-piercers, but my yashinin machete is a slashy-cutter. While Rev was distractin' the thing, I chopped its neck at a solid square angle. The dumb sumbitch tried to spin outta the hit, but the friction of its own spinnin' made it saw its own head off against the edge of my blade. After that, I had its hide made into this handy dust coat and I've learned to copy the kasucot's dervish defense."

Polly smiled as she stretched her lower back. "I am impressed, Will, I must admit. I like de way you tell stories. I would hear more about your past excursions should you feel inclined to tell."

Will returned the smile. "They ain't all that excitin', but sure, after we end this Geohex."

Polly stepped closer to him, fidgeting. "Will?" she asked softly.

Will felt his cheeks grow warm. "Uh, yeah? What?"

"Could you teach me some of your hammercock and hay bale moves? Sometime when we have time?"

Will sighed. "No. Can't. You ain't a tendikeye."

Polly's face contorted with anger. "Racist!"

Will shook his head. "It ain't that, Pol. You need the heavy feet and big hands of a tendikeye to pull off them kicks an' grapples. Without heavy feet you can't get the right momentum to pull off the spins an' turns. An' without big hands you won't be able to grab and seize, right. Sorry."

Polly huffed in resentment. "Fine."

A cold morning breeze swept through the clearing, and Polly was aware that her feet felt cold. As she slipped her boots back on, she recalled what she had discovered about Sheriff Raisinbread. Nonchalantly, she asked, "Will? Have you ever combated a laich?"

The tendikeye shook his head. "Naw. Rev has before he met me. Röger has lotsa times. Why? Have you?"

She nodded as she tugged up on her laces.

Will let out a dissatisfied laugh. "It ain't fair. How did you manage to encounter one?"

Polly looked up, recalling the memory. "It was two years ago, sometime after my sixteenth birthday. A hemogoblin was hunting in my mother's forest. We found wild animals drained of blood with deir hearts torn out. De carcasses were miles away from our chateau, but all were found encircling it in every directions."

"The laich was scoutin' yer home," Will said plainly.

Polly nodded as she got her other boot on. "As far as de monster knew, two defenseless females lived alone in dat big house. My mother could have hunted it down easily. But she wanted to have fun with it and train me at de same time. She taught me all about Hemogoblins, like how dey drink blood to breathe."

Will's quilled eyebrows scrunched together. "They drink blood to *breathe?* How's that work?"

"Well, it isn't technically breathing. One of de reasons dey drink de blood of de living is to stay oxygenated so dey don't rot and fall apart over time."

"Ox-uh-jin-ated?" Will asked with bothered confusion.

"Yes. You know, like how de oxygen in de air we breathe goes into our blood to keep us alive and healthy?"

Will crossed his arms and shook his head. "There ain't no air in blood. Otherwise it'd come out all fizzy when I cut it outta people."

Polly blinked several times before she could talk. "*Please* tell me you are joking."

Will only looked at her like she was crazy.

Polly placed her hands on her face and rubbed it hard. "Never mind. Just. Never mind. Dere's no point."

"What?" Will asked, taking offense.

Polly waved the question away. "Don't worry about it. Let's go back to de inn. I'm hungry."

"Wait," Will protested. "How'd you kill the hemogoblin? Finish yer story."

Polly ran her fingers through her hair and sighed. "I had to be alone, to lure de bloodsucker. Hemogoblins can sense...virginity in females. Please, don't ask me how. But dey find virgins irresistible. Anyway, my mother instructed me in a strategy and den sent me out in de woods in de middle of de night wit' nothing but a dagger, a basket, and a nightgown. I made it look like I was gathering mushrooms. It was dark, but I can see circulatory systems in de dark when I want to. I could see de laich drawing near out of de corner of my eye. I was terrified, but I regulated my pulse to stay calm. Hemogoblins are as fast and strong as jungle cats, but dey only have two legs like de rest of us.

"Wit' out it noticing, I drew out a long vein from my ankle and created a tripwire wit' it between two nearby trees. De Hemogoblin charged, tripped, and fell face first right at my feet. He looked just like a Chumish man, but only on de outside. I plunged my dagger into his back, through his heart, out his chest, and into de ground."

"Long dagger," Will remarked.

Polly shrugged a shoulder. "It was more like a short sword, but with a bodkin-shaped blade. It was very nice. I miss it sometimes. Anyway, it didn't kill de Hemogoblin, only paralyzed it. De heart is de center of its cardiovascular system, and thus its weak point. I had to drag it by de heels all de way back to de chateau. My mother was waiting on de front porch wit a hatchet and a bucket of water. I had to cut out de monster's heart wit' de hatchet wit' out removing de dagger right dere in de front yard. It took forever, and I did not feel clean for a week after. But I can say dat I have successfully killed a Hemogoblin." Polly then thought to herself, "*I'll kill Raisinbread by myself. I need a murder-sacrifice anyway. He'll do. But I need to make de kill alone. If de others know dat he's a laich den dey might slay him before I can get a chance.*"

Will gave her a queer but impressed look as he buckled his weapons belt. Then he remembered why he'd drawn Polly out into the clearing in the first place. "So, you know me well enough, Polly. You get the gist of what I can do. I managed to kill a weaker version of yer momma by overloadin' her with damage. Can the same be done when we meet the real her?"

Polly regarded his guns and blade. "My mother can turn to blood instantly, and she can heal instantly. Sharp weapons and solid bullets do little to hinder her. You need a musket or shotgun. De scattershot will shred her thin and separate large portions of her. Poison, venom, toxins, disease--her system can clear all dat out. But a powerful acid or fire will hurt her de worst. She can also die by freezing, but can withstand cold weather for a long time."

456

Will rested his hands on his hips and spat into the grass. "Gonna hafta make a war blanket then." Before Polly could ask, he explained, "A war blanket is a big patch o' cloth that's sticky on one side, but flammable all the way through. You throw it on whatever yer tryin' to kill. It tangles 'em up, then you set fire to it. There's lottsa cheap ways to fashion one. The trick is to make sure the flammable substance dudn't neutralize the sticky substance."

Polly cringed. "Dat might work. Come on. Let's go."

As the two walked back to the inn for breakfast, Polly spotted the combined courthouse and police station down the muddy street. The thought that a bloodsucking laich made its home and office there in the building's basement made her guts crawl. She pinched the septegram tattoo on her right arm and thought, *"I'm going to murder you, Sheriff Raisinbread. I'm going to cut out your heart and when what's left of your soul shatters it will make my own anima stronger. Your final death will make me stronger."*

Just down the street under that same courthouse, Sheriff Raisinbread sat lazily behind his desk. He slowly spun his solid steel quarterstaff in his nimble fingers as he fantasied about how sweet Polly Gone's heart would taste.

In his small bachelor home, Deputy Drume Arteen was cleaning house and thinking about the young woman in red who had bewitched him.

And in a humble tailor's shop in the town of Barnhart, a young man named Izzyk Spinser was getting himself fitted for a new shirt and pair of slacks. In his heart was the faint hope that he would see Polly at the Fair.

Outside of the town of Tanglefoot, Papa G.D. and his closest family and friends were ritualistically slaughtering dozens of pigs, bovines, sheep, and goats. The crowd at the impending Fair would have to eat, after all.

In the forest surrounding the town of Pevulaneum, Daiv Tchanly and his daughter Ivy (along with a slew of new employees) gathered caven nuts to sell at the Fair. They had already made enough cavenbutter to fill every jar they owned.

In the village of Victor's Grove, everyone was eating fish again for breakfast.

And finally, in the County Hall in Copse dur Crakktun, Count Slanidrac the Wraith bided his time. *"All my pieces are in*

457

place," he thought. "*First, I will kill them. Then I will make them my servants. In time, they will learn to enjoy their amortality.*"

Chapter 11

The Heapsboro Bileer Show
and
County Fair

Part 1

In the farm town of Heapsboro, a flock of hawks flew through the cool morning air. Nowhere else in all of Doflend did such communal raptors exist. They seemed no different than other hawks indigenous to these lands. Yet only in this town did they fly together in tight formation, hunt like a pack of winged-wolves, and sleep together in the tall pines dotting the farmscape. As their ominous shadows passed over a huge barn, another 'flock of predatory birds' gathered inside the red-hued structure.

The barn was crammed with nearly every Trotting Swan in Wraith County. In the middle of the crowd stood a loose circle of men in a summit meeting of sorts. Some of the men were old and carried a measurable degree of wisdom. Some carried a strong bearing and intense personalities. Some were richer than others, and held economical sway over various parts of the county. These were the leaders of the Trotting Swans, the commanders of Count Slanidrac's militia. They were discussing the Count's dreadful plan to kill the meddlesome Excursionists who dared to upset the way things were run in their homeland and their way of life. But not all of the leaders were present for this sacred, secret meeting.

"Where's Fulton Gladish and his crew?" one leader asked impatiently. "Barnhart isn't that far!"

"The Count sent him a letter just as he did us," another leader added.

A third leader shook his head. "It just doesn't make sense

that *he* of all men would be late!"

"Well, never mind him then!" the first leader bellowed. "We can fill him and his crew in later. Are we all aware of the plan?"

"Yes!" every man answered.

"Good! Now remember, it is imperative that we appear as simple keepers of the peace, because that's what we are, after all. Especially around Four Winds-One Storm. We need their deaths to look like accidents. If it looks like we deliberately shoot them, the common folk might turn on us!"

A young Swan raised his hand. "But I heard that at least three of them are bulletproof!"

The leader waved his hand in dismissal. "The bullets will serve as a distraction to the real threat. The Count has sworn on his *philocreed* to employ his every resource to make sure they are all dead by morning. I have faith in him, as should we all. For it is he who provides us with the flower that keeps our families fed. We owe him our trust and, on occasions such as this, our service. I have faith in his power."

The leader cast a discerning eye over the compacted crowd of gun-toting men. "And to any who are not brave enough for the task ahead, you are free to return home. But know that you leave in shame and will be treated like a fugitive beginning tomorrow morning at this same time. You must take your family and possessions and flee this county never to return. Deserters of this sacred brotherhood will endure and behold every horror we can think of for them and their kin. Understood?"

"Yes!" every Swan answered exuberantly.

"Who is with me?!"

"I am!" every man returned.

The Trotting Swans spewed out of the barn's entrance and made their way to the Heapsboro Fairgrounds. The morning glow of the Huncell shined upon the citizens of Apple County waiting to get inside. The Swans mingled with the men, women, teenagers, children and elders as the gates of the Fair opened to let everyone in.

❖

The Fairgrounds consisted of three parts.

First, there was the wagon park, which was a long patch of ground that sloped up to the Fairground fence and gate. There, the patrons parked their wagons, carts, carriages, coaches, and steeds. Men and a few boys armed with crude muskets and spears patrolled the area to prevent theft. None of them were Trotting Swans.

Secondly, there was the Fairground itself. Surrounded by a tall wire fence, the huge flat lot equaled the size of four rugby fields. Its floor was completely comprised of white gravel with only the occasional weed or blade of grass poking up. The area was filled with festive tents, booths, and steam-powered carnival rides including a carousel and a fifty foot tall *Ferrous Wheel* that hissed jets of steam up into the air. The air was thick with the smells of food, and every tenth step brought a new aroma to the nostrils.

Huge tents full of wooden folding chairs and crude platforms allowed local musicians to play for the enjoyment of those who enjoyed listening or dancing along. Children ran and screamed with excitement. Lovers of all ages wandered hand-in-hand. Old folks gathered and talked about current events. And purple-clad men drakeri armed with pistols and shotguns wandered the paths of the festivities keeping the peace. Every one of them were Trotting Swans.

On the other side of the Fairgrounds lay the bowl-shaped outdoor *alcedrome,* filled with long benches and stone steps with a huge fenced in dirt floor at the bottom. The floor was circular and about forty meters in diameter, perfect for showing off bileers. At the far end of the floor was a vast stable where many a creature was penned. The oddly pleasant smell of herbivore dung filled the surrounding air.

And it was there that Four Winds – One Storm drove their wagon in through a rear entrance. After paying a fee for stable space, they parked their vehicle within the confines of the massive complex. As they unhitched their animals one by one, the three bileers bugled with relief and immediately trotted to a corner of the stable in a nervous huddle. The post-mort ox, who had been pulling the wagon with them, let out a dull, uncaring *moo* as Will undid its straps.

The tendikeye grimaced at the monstrosity with disgusted

461

disapproval. "We need to burn this danged thing an' buy us a new bileer," he barked.

Röger laughed and playfully punched Will's arm, making him stumble. "No. What we *should* do is sell these bileers and get three more oxen just like Oxy here."

Hindin frowned at the idea. "You cannot be serious!"

Röger shrugged. "You're right. I can't." He let out another hardy laugh.

Polly jumped out of the wagon's back. Her stiff knees popped as she landed on the mushy clay floor. She let out a coughing, raspy hiss. "I hate you all for bringing me here dis early."

Will spread his hands. "Well, yer free to sleep in the wagon until yer ready to get out an' about."

Polly hugged herself and let out a long straining yawn. "I'm cold and it stinks in here."

Will chuckled and rested his hands in his hips. "Smells like a normal stable to me, princess."

Hindin stepped between the two of them. "Come now! Let us go forth and behold the festivities. This is a harvest fair and there's sure to be many an interesting activity."

Röger pulled some grooming brushes out of the wagon. "You guys go on ahead. I'm going to get the bileers registered and ready for the show later. I looked at some of the other bileers competing tonight and I think ours have a shot at winning."

Hindin shook his head. "Sir Röger, all you think of is money, food, women, and competition."

Röger shook his head back at Hindin, mockingly. "That's because they're all related, big guy. Now, go have fun! I'll catch up with you all later."

Hindin, Will, and Polly left the stable complex, leaving Röger alone with the animals.

"Look at that thing! It's huge!" Will exclaimed as he beheld the colossal *Ferrous Wheel*. "I ain't never been up in one before! The metal it's made of is mish-mash of a whole buncha metals. That why they call it such an' why it holds up so strong."

462

Polly arched an eyebrow as they reached the main part of the Fairgrounds. "Do dey detest steam machines in Cloiherune as well as theurgy?" she asked.

Will shook his head, not taking his eyes off the ride. "Nah, we jus' don't use 'em fer fun is all. Iron is rare in my homecell, always has been. That's why whenever we make sumpthin' outta steel it has to serve a dual purpose. *Tuntrum*—it means both weapon an' tool. We make steam-powered vehicles called *worthwerks* that function as tractors an' tanks. We had us a little one in my hometown that the whole town shared. Rusty piece o' junk if you ask me." Will gazed at the giant wheel with child-like awe. "I wanna go up in it! Who's comin'?"

Hindin shook his head. "I do not trust my weight with that contraption."

Polly shrugged. "Maybe later. Right now I'm hungry."

"We should also keep together and not be too distracted," Hindin added. His emerald eyes shifted left to right. "Let us not forget that we are surrounded by potential enemies."

Will grinned deviously and leaned in toward his friend. "Rev, yer fergittin' I'm the scout here. I'm goin' up to get a look-see at the layout o' this place. Terrain matters, bud." He let out a low chuckle. "Course, I will be enjoyin' myself in the process!"

Hindin let out a frustrated sigh. "Just remember, the count will be honoring us at five o' Clock."

Will patted his friend's arm. "Don't you worry none. Neither o' you. I'll be able to hark any call you shout out an' with my speed I'll never be too far away!" He placed his large hand on Polly's head and playfully messed up her hair before running off. A trail of gravel dust and nasally laughter followed him.

"Bastard!" Polly hissed through clenched teeth.

◊

Polly and Hindin wandered the gravel pathways of the festivities. They both followed her nose to a pastry stand being run by a drakeri family.

"Oooh! Conchas!" Polly gushed as she beheld the mountainous display of frosted bread on the stand counter. "I love conchas!" As she approached the stand and opened her money purse, someone called out her name.

"Polly! Over here!"

She turned toward the sound and saw a familiar young man not thirty feet away. "Izzyk!" she answered. She unconsciously ran her finger's through her short hair.

The young man approached her nervously. He exchanged friendly nods with Hindin before offering his hand to the enormous steel-skinned man. "Hullo. You must be Hindin Revetz. I heard about what you did in Victor's Grove. All of Barnhart has, I think. I've only read about heroes such as you in Dangerosity Guides!"

Hindin shook the young man's hand, saying "Thank you, sir. Izzyk is your name? I do not think Polly mentioned you before." He shifted his eyes to her.

"I didn't," Polly answered. "I only told you boys about de ghosts I encountered, de real one's anyway." She managed to give Izzyk a knowing grin.

Hindin glanced at the two of them. "I see. Well. Perhaps I should...depart. You two may have catching up to do?" He looked at Polly, unsure what to discern from the situation.

Polly let out a small laugh. "It's fine, Hindin. I just promised Izzyk dat I would be his date if I came here."

Hindin straightened and crossed his arms, his face full of uncertainty. "I see. Well, that is fine with me. How long will it take?"

Polly looked at Izzyk and shrugged. She had no answer.

Hindin frowned and nodded. "Very well. Please, be careful. Have fun. Be safe. Enjoy your time here and stay aware of your surroundings. If you would."

Polly gave the bumbling malruka a reassuring hug. "Don't worry, my friend. I just have a few private matters to attend to and we'll all be together again. Stop worrying."

Hindin managed to uncross his arms and nod in compliance. He watched as the young Izzyk bought Polly a concha before the two young people walked off together. As he watched Polly get further and further away, she turned once more and gave him a reassuring wave.

Hindin sighed sadly, swallowing his parental worry, and

464

waved back.

◇

Will buzzed with gleeful excitement as he sat down in one of the swinging steel compartments of the *Ferrous Wheel.*

The ride usher told him politely "Sir, could you please scoot over? The line is getting long, and we need to squeeze as many people on as possible."

"Oh, sure!" Will responded without thinking. He moved over as two human women squeezed into the compartment. One was middle-aged and rather plump. The other was a pretty redhead in her twenties or thirties.

"Hi," the redhead said with a friendly smile. She showed no hint of shyness as she pressed her hip against the tendikeye's.

"Howdy, ma'am," Will replied. "This yer first time goin' up in one o' these?"

The redhead shook her head. "I come here every year. You?"

Will nodded. "First time."

"Are you nervous?" she asked, her smile becoming wry and flirtatious.

Will couldn't help but grin. "Yeah, but in a good way."

A safety bar was pulled across their laps. They rose up slowly as other compartments were being filled with people. Will felt the cool morning wind blow through his quills as he surveyed the expanse of the Fairgrounds.

As the colossal wheel began picking up speed, he committed to memory the placement of every tent, every ride, every odd attraction. The circular sensation of repeatedly defying gravity filled him with a strange sense of wonder as he fell in love with the machine. A seed of inspiration sprouted in him as he studied the steam-powered engine that propelled the ride. He'd never much cared for the invention before because such things only existed for work or war. But as the idea of a steam-powered toy that he could ride around in blossomed in his mind, he made a decision right then and there.

"*Someday,*" he thought "*I'm gonna get me a steam car. No!*

465

A steam truck! An' I'm gonna learn how to build 'em an' fix 'em and work on 'em! I'm gonna drive anywhere I please an' show it off to the world!"

"You look like you're having fun," said the pretty redhead.

He nodded without looking at her.

The woman noticed the weapons poking out from his dust coat. "Say, are you by chance one of the Excursionists from Four Winds – One Storm?"

The ride ended as Will turned his attention to her. "Yes, ma'am," he said with pride. "We're here to scare yer ghosts away. I'm Will Foundling. Feel free to spread the word."

As they got out of the compartment and stepped back onto the solid ground the woman said, "I'm pleased to meet you, Mr. Foundling. Please, tell your comrade, Sir Röger Yamus, that Rose Quartz sends her regards."

Will bowed respectfully. "Will do, Miss Rose."

The pretty redhead smiled and grabbed his collar with both hands. Pulling him close, she said softly, "And I give him this for me." She placed a lingering kiss on the tip of his large nose.

Will felt hot blood rushing to his face.

Her soft, plump lips left his nose and curved into a smug smile. "Bye now," she said.

Will watched dumbfounded as she and her companion walked away. He shook his head to clear his pleasantly foggy mind and looked back up at the *Ferrous Wheel.* *"Someday,"* he thought.

"So, how are your mom and dad?" Polly asked as she took a small bite of her concha.

Izzyk sighed and stared straight on at nothing. "They're doing better. Dad still hasn't fully forgiven her."

Polly swallowed her bite and shrugged. "She might not ever fully forgive herself."

Izzyk glanced at her sharply. "Could we talk about something else?"

Polly shrunk a little, regretting her words. "Okay. Like

what?"

He regarded her as they walked. "What everyone in the county is talking about: you and your team. I've heard of theurges and heroes doing amazing things in far off places, but never in Wraith County. They say that most of the Cluster isn't as civilized as Doflend."

Polly recalled a myriad of images from her past. "It isn't," she said. "I was raised in de Wilds of Chume. Dat's why I speak dis way. Over dere, de lands, de forests cannot be tamed or reasoned wit'. Nothing makes sense and every living ting is insane in some way. Borders between domains shift constantly. Here in Doflend, I am strong. But amongst some of de Chume Fey dere, I am an insect. I sometimes wonder how I escaped into dis country."

"I'm glad you did," he said with a cheerful smile. "I mean, a lot of people are."

Polly smiled sweetly at the young man and playfully bumped shoulders with him. He took her hand in his, and they walked in contented silence, eating their conchas, with no place to go. It was a pleasant feeling they shared for far too short a time.

"Polly!" a man's voice cried out from a distance.

Polly recognized the caller's voice and let go of Izzyk's hand. Through a crowd of fair-goers, she spotted Deputy Drume Arteen in the not-so-far distance. The man rushed to them with cheer on his ruggedly handsome face.

"You came after all!" he said with a manly, yet adorable smile.

"Yes," Polly said, giving Izzyk a nervous glance before turning her attention to the deputy. He was clean shaven and looking quite debonair in his uniform. "Hullo!" she said with a nervous, guilty laugh. She unconsciously backed away from both men.

"You were supposed to let me take you here on my horse," the deputy said as he spread out his hands.

The man looked so glad to see her it made her wince with shame. "I came wit' my team," she blurted. "Sorry...!"

"That's okay!" said the deputy . "I'm just glad you came." He took a step closer to her and noticed Izzyk. "Hullo," he said to the young man.

Izzyk looked back and forth at Polly and the deputy before

467

uttering "Polly...?" His eyebrow furrowed in concern and confusion.

Polly felt guilt and embarrassment as she held out her hands, urging both men to keep back. She felt the cold sweat of shame beneath her scarlet clothes. *"Mother would be so proud,"* she thought.

"Wait, wait!" she told the men. "I'm sorry. I'm sorry. I'm a stupid girl. I am so, so sorry!" She covered her face and began to explain. "I did not tink dat I would ever have to go to dis silly fair. But my idiot friends dragged me along. Izzyk, Drume, I promised you both at different times, in different towns, dat I would be your date *if* I came here, but I never thought dat I actually *would*. I am so sorry."

At that moment she should have stopped talking to let her words sink in. But the *crazy door* in Polly's mind became unhinged, and all manner of words spewed out of her mouth. Words formed from improperly digested thoughts and a rancid cocktail of mismatched emotions. Polly laughed with frightening giddiness as she continued to speak.

"Dis goes against everyting I've been taught, everyting my wicked mother tried to make me believe. She would have wanted me to lead you both on, hurt your feelings, and den kill you both. I've done two-out-of-three so far wit'out even meaning to! *Men are useful,* she would tell me! Dey always take de bait! Agh! I'm such a...a...a witch! What if I don't want to kill de men dat I like? What den?"

Izzyk and Drume shared glances of concerned perplexity.

Polly ranted on. "She never let me have a boyfriend! Well, unless I eventually murdered him, de evil bitch. But when I finally met somebody, what happened? What happened?" Polly frowned in hyper disappointment. "It turned out dat *he* wanted a boyfriend, too!" She let out crying laugh. "And now I meet two very nice men far away from Chume, and I have to end up hurting dem both. Drume. Izzyk. I'm sorry." She giggled madly as tears peeked out the corners of her eyes.

At that moment, the two men should have walked away, *run* away. But they could not help but feel drawn to her. She seemed to them vulnerable and dangerous at once. Relaxing and exciting. Polly's charismatic madness, the hidden power of the hemotheurge, had tricked them into thinking with their hearts.

"It's okay, Polly," Drume said with soft concern. "You aren't a bad person. If anything, you are just too kind."

Polly wiped her eyes and shook her head. "You lie to me and yourself, Drume ."

Izzyk stepped forward and took her hand. "You've nothing to apologize for, Polly. It was an easy mistake."

Polly drew her hand away. "Or an easy deceit," she muttered.

Drume clapped his hands loud and hard. "Well hey! I have an idea! A solution, more like. He'll get you for the first half of the day, and I can have you the latter half." He looked at Izzyk. "Sound good to you, kid?"

Izzyk resented being called a kid. But before he could say no, Polly interjected.

"I refuse," she said harshly. "I will *not* be passed around! I'll do as I please!"

Drume frowned and spread his hands. "Well, then, what will please you, Polly?"

Polly's face went blank. She had no answer.

"A contest!" they heard a voice shout at them.

Their heads turned to behold Sheriff Thrush Raisinbread, leaning coolly against his solid steel quarterstaff, his eyes grim, his smile wry. "Why not have her choose one of these childish carnival games? The winner gets her company for the rest of the day." He lowered his eyes, his closed smile curving tighter. "And if I may be so bold, I too should wish to compete."

Izzyk and Drume sneered in wary revulsion. Then, to their shock, they saw Polly grinning dark and pretty at the Sheriff. "Dat's a wonderful idea, Sheriff."

✧

"Ye back-stabbin' butcherin' betrayin' round-eared son of a whoore! Git yer abominations away from my stand, or by my hands, I'll knock the red outta yer eyes!"

"You spikey-headed gray-winged treehopping nut-hugger! You'd best mind your tongue and your manners lest I barbeque

469

those shriveled wings of yours! Oh yes, I can smell them cooking already!"

It always hurt Hindin to see two old men fighting. All wisdom had been set aside to make room for their growing pride. The fight had been escalating the last few minutes but they had not yet come to blows. It was between an old dark-skinned human and an elderly tendikeye.

The human's barbeque stand was set up directly opposite from the tendikeye's caven nut stand. The human had a full grown post-mort sow that was butchered, barbequed, and animated to walk around near his stand. Fair goers were encouraged to cut pieces of meat from the sow as free samples of the human's food. The old tendikeye didn't like it one iota. The combination of a murdered domesticated animal and necrotheurgy were too much for him to bear.

Hindin immediately recognized the men as Papa G. D. and Daiv Tchanly from the stories he had heard from Will and Röger.

As the screamed insults got louder and meaner, Hindin fretted for both men's safety. He saw a pair of drakeri men standing nearby. They were dressed all in purple and holding shotguns.

He went to them, waving for their attention. "Pardon me, sirs. Are you not Trotting Swans charged with keeping the day's peace?"

"What of it?" one of them asked with a look of disdain.

Hindin pointed at the two men arguing. "Well, it is plain to see that these food venders are at odds. It is an unfortunate clash of cultures. Perhaps you both could break it up and arrange for one of them to move their stand to another location. I would be glad to help transport their wares."

The Swan scoffed and shook his head. "The Fair is full. There's no place else to move. Besides, what care we about two worn-out shortlives fighting? If they're not harming drakeri why should we be concerned?" The two men turned their back to him and walked away

Hindin frowned, seeing that there was no reasoning with the peacekeepers. He looked back at the arguers and marched toward them like a parent about to separate two warring toddlers. "Now, see here!" he bellowed over their insults.

Papa G. D. and Daiv saw the huge steel-skinned man and

470

instantly got quiet. They both took a step back from each other.

Hindin spoke loud and clear enough for everyone in the vicinity to hear. "Sirs! Sirs! I am a malruka. As a geotarian, I dine on neither flora nor fauna. Therefore, I am partial to neither caven nuts nor barbequed meat. But today is a day of peace and festivity. Can we find a solution so that it may remain so?" Daiv pointed at the human, poison dripping from his every word, "This man betrays the trust o' the animals he keeps! He raises 'em and kills 'em and profits off their meat! He lacks the honor of a hunter!"

"This is not Cloiherune, sir. Tendikeye laws have no hold in Doflend," Hindin reminded him.

Daiv sneered and continued "But he's usin' death energy to make his carcasses walk around!"

"There's no law about animating animal corpses!" Papa G. D. argued. He looked up at Hindin. "I was quite literally minding my own business when this bent old buzzard started hounding me with insults! He needs to get over himself before I knuckle-out the rest of his teeth!"

"That will not happen while I am here," Hindin said firmly. "The two of you will return to your stands and continue to provide festive nourishment for these gathered masses."

Daiv huffed. "An' just who are *ye* to tell us what to do?"

"I am Hindin Angladar Revetz, friend and comrade to Will Foundling and Sir Röger Yamus. And for their sakes, I beg that you both employ tolerance toward each other on this day."

Papa G. T.'s face grew solemn, and he nodded. "You must be the Bridge-Breaker of Victor's Grove," he said reverently. "I do not pretend to understand your *philocreed*, Chimancer. But I still respect a man who perfects his path." He then looked warily at the old tendikeye. "And I am willing to purchase eight caven nuts from this man as a sign that I mean him no ill will."

Daiv raised his chin and regarded the human. "I would be obliged to halve the price o' them nuts, if ye only keep yer creepy dead pig on yer side an' away from my stand."

"Done," the old human agreed. He extended his hand for a shake.

The tendikeye made no move. "We tendikeye only shake hands with family. I'll just git yer nuts, an' you go git my money, an' we can call it quits on this dispute."

471

"Fine by me."

The two old men exchanged tough-faced nods before going back to their stands. Hindin helped carry the rugby ball-sized nuts from Daiv's stand to Papa G. D.'s. In the end, the two men thanked Hindin for settling their fight.

Just before he left them, Hindin remembered words once uttered by Näncine Strother, and shared them with the two men. "The beast is more savage than man when he is possessed of power equal to his rage."

"What's that s'posed to mean?" Daiv asked, arching a silver quilled eyebrow.

Hindin spread his hands and shrugged. "Some words of wisdom are meant to be devoured by a mind. And some are merely meant to be chewed upon for a time before the mind spits them out again. I leave it, to you, sir, to decide how your mind receives them. I bid you good day."

Two Trotting Swans were passing through the stable complex. All around them the stalls teemed with bileers and their owners. Coats were being brushed and hammers chimed as steel shoes were nailed onto upturned hooves. Curved antlers gleamed as buffing cloths rubbed fresh coats of horn polish onto their surfaces. The domesticated elks fed on oats laced with bits of acorn, caven nut, and walnut as they were being pampered and prepared for the show. There were all kinds of bileers there, each kind bred for a different purpose, whether it be for farming, travel, war, or some other odd labor. They came in all shades usually found with mammals, such as brown, black, tan, white, or (in the case of Röger Yamus) a beautiful shade of golden auburn. But, as beautiful as they were, the two Trotting Swans weren't there to survey the beasts. They had their eyes on the big human grooming them.

"He killed all our brothers in Tanglefoot?" the chinless swan asked the other in a safe whisper.

"At least half of them, I heard. The rest were back shot by those Slipknot Harlots. The slags even took their guns and bikes

472

before hightailing out of the county."

"Traitorous whores!" the other spat. "We give them security and they repay us with lead!" He regarded the tall tattooed human brushing his bileer's coat. "How did he take so many of us? All I see is a big sword and the Headsman's Axe."

The Swan shook his head. "Dunno. It was outside the NcKoons property. He cut them all to pieces. He must've ambushed them, the coward."

The chinless Swan swallowed hard. "Maybe he's a theurge, like the malruka and girl. Those tattoos on his arms, they might be theurgic runes that protect him somehow. He might be a ...what do you call those battle theurges?"

"An edgeweaver?"

"No. I think they're called bladereavers. Or is it bladebraiders? Or razorraider or... I don't know for sure."

The two men narrowly avoided a steaming pile of bileer droppings as they walked by.

"I highly doubt he's a battle theurge. He's a boastful brute, I've heard. He'd've made it known. Say, do you know if Fulton Gladish and his boys have gotten here yet?"

The chinless Swan frowned and shook his head. "Not yet. I hope we'll have enough guns when the diversion comes. Do you know when the diversion's supposed to be?"

"Right after the Count's speech."

"I knew that. I just forgot when *that* would be."

"5:50 o'clock. Right after the bileer show." The Swan regarded his chinless partner and formed a thin smile. "And when the time comes to repay those four outsiders back for crippling our way of life, we're going to witness the Count's full power at work. To be honest, I've been dreaming of a day like this since I was a boy. The Count, Our Master in Death, working his miracles to defend us. I wish the Count would have ghosted my dad or grandad so they could be here today. To see and participate, you know?"

The chinless Swan smiled and slung an arm over his friend's shoulder. "I know, brother. I know."

An uncanny **MOOOOOOOOOOOOOOOOOOO** blared throughout the vast interior of the stable complex. Pigeons emptied their bowels and flapped frantically in the high rafters above. Bileers bucked and called out in sudden fits of dread. And the hearts

473

of nearly every groomer there stalled from the faint wave of *necrofear*.

"For the last time, *no!*" Röger shouted at his post-mort ox. "No, you cannot be in the show! You are not a bileer! Now, shut up and stop begging for attention!" He let out a hardy laugh and glanced around at his many competitors. "I named him Oxy Moron! He's too dumb to know he's dead! And he's an *Ox*! *Ha*!!!!"

❖

Polly had never played carnival games before, much less seen them played. She had to choose carefully if she wanted to get Sheriff Raisinbread alone with her.

"*What would a laich be good at?*" she wondered as she inspected the game booths. Her three prospective dates were never far behind her. She looked for games that tested brute strength. Surely the laich would win at that. But all she found were games of skill mingled with chance. In the end, she narrowed it down to three.

The Hoop Toss cost one grotz piece to play. The player received three tin hoops to toss at a small forest of painted sticks that were hammered into the ground. The red sticks were four feet high, the blue sticks were three feet, the green sticks were two feet, and the yellow sticks were only one foot high. The sticks were arranged in a random cluster. The object of the game was to toss a hoop onto two matching colored sticks. To win the game would mean a prize of a live chicken that could be redeemed at the end of the day.

Next was Candle Ball. A wide bucket full of water was set next to a ten foot tall ladder. Around the bucket's rim were set eight lit candles. The player paid one grotz piece for a small pumpkin. They had to climb the ladder, stand on the designated rung, and either drop or throw the pumpkin into the bucket. If it splashed just right and put out all eight candles, the player would win a live kitten that could be redeemed at the end of the day.

The last game was The Cheating Husband. It consisted of a wooden wall depicting a life sized man standing with his pants down around his ankles. A four inch hole was cut right were the heart would be located. The player paid one grotz for a sweeping broom. The broom had to be tossed javelin style through the hole in the depiction's chest. One square coin bought one throw, one chance. Winners received a dove in a small wicker cage that could be redeemed at the end of the day.

Polly eyed the games thoroughly before turning to the three men. "I want a dove," she said demurely.

"Okay!" Izzyk was the first to proclaim. Confident and determined, the teenager reached into his pocket and bought a chance at the booth.

The booth operator, a happy-faced portly man, handed him a broom with words of luck and encouragement.

Polly knew he would miss before he even threw it. His stance was too narrow and his form was awkward and unpracticed.

"*I'm sorry, Izzyk,*" she thought with a heavy heart. "*None of dis is fair to you.*"

The young man sent the broom flying. It turned sideways in mid air and slapped across the depiction of the Cheating Husband's waist.

Izzyk hung his head and stepped aside.

"Cheer up, kid," Deputy Arteen told him as he handed the booth man a grotz. "We might all miss and you'll get a second try." He took the broom in hand and focused on the hole in the wall. As he took aim, he resembled a great warrior or hunter about to chuck a spear into a certain kill. With deadly force, he launched the broom.

An ear-piercing crack echoed out from the booth as the point of the broom handle thudded into the throat of the Cheating Husband. The broom made little noise in comparison as it fell to the ground.

Sheriff Raisinbread let out an amused laugh. "Well done, Deputy! It's nice to know you're still lethal even if you miss!" He paid the booth man as Arteen took his place next to Izzyk.

Polly could see the certainty in the laich's eyes as he winked at her.

Without hesitation or doubt, the new sheriff of Drowsy Nook threw the broom. The throw was perfect. The broom handle passed through the hole's center in a straight line. The bristles crunched together in a tight bundle as they lodged into the Cheating

Husband's chest.

"You win a dove!" announced the booth operator.

"No, she did," Raisinbread corrected as he pointed to Polly. "I won her!"

The booth operator turned to the pretty young woman. "Would you like your dove now or later, miss?"

"Later," she said with a smug grin. As she took the Sheriff's arm, she regarded Izzyk and the deputy with a sympathetic frown. "Sorry, boys. But it's his turn wit' me." It sickened her to say the words. "Enjoy de rest of de fair."

The Sheriff gave the two men a dubious grin before he lead the girl away from them.

"Well," Deputy Arteen said with a flabbergasted sigh. "I could use a beer. How about you, kid?" he said to Izzyk.

"I'm not old enough to drink," the young man answered flatly.

The deputy pointed to his badge. "Trust me, kid. You won't get into trouble. We both need a drink, and more to follow. I'm buying. Let's go."

❖

The day wore on, but it did not wear down. The walls of the Huncell dimmed as half the crowd funneled into the rustic *alcedrome* for the bileer show. It was a drawn out spectacle, but a time-honored tradition all the locals took great delight in. Every person who owned a bileer got a chance to ride around the dirt floor. Some performed tricks. Some showed off their speed and jumped hurdles. And some rode purely for display.

Will and Hindin sat together, squeezed in with two thousand other spectators. When the bileer show finally concluded and the winners were announced, both men stood and cheered as Sir Röger Yamus was called out to the stage so that the bileer called Tidsla could receive the second place ribbon.

"That's *my* bileer!" Will hollered jubilantly as he clutched a bag of popcorn like a wineglass.

The tendikeye and malruka beamed with pride as Röger charged out of the stable complex astride the magnificent steed, its

476

antlers perfectly symmetrical, its auburn coat gleaming with the light of dusk, and its mighty hooves thumping the dirt floor. After doing a victory lap for the cheering crowd, Röger steered the mount to the wooden platform stage. There a festively-dressed old woman tied a red strip of satin around the bileer's huge antler.

"Well, how'd'ya like that, Rev?" Will nudged his friend with an elbow. "Too bad only braggin' rights go along with that ribbon."

"Why is that so bad?" Hindin asked.

"'Cause we prob'ly won't be around these parts long enough to brag to everyone."

"You truly believe we can end the Geohex that quickly?"

"Why not? We only got a few more towns left. We jus' gotta yank more hematite, and it'll be over, right?" He took a handful of popcorn and stuffed it in his mouth.

Hindin had no answer. Instead, he scanned over the crowd, his bottom lip pouting. "I have not seen Polly since she left with that boy. I hope she is all right. The day is fading, and she did not take a jacket with her."

Just as the last of the ribbons were awarded, the alcedrome's master of ceremony addressed the crowd. "Friends and neighbors of Apple County! This concludes the our annual Bileer Show!" The crowd responded with cheers and claps before the man continued. "And now it is my esteemed privilege to introduce our beloved Count, the captain of our land, Slanidrac Norton!"

The spectators stood respectfully and applauded as the well-dressed Count took the stage. He waved and smiled with a relaxed grace and good-natured bearing. He wore a black suit trimmed with deep dark purple velvet with big square copper buttons. His hematite bracelets glistened as he waved. His straw-colored hair did not blow as a strong breeze passed through the alcedrome. That was the first odd thing Will noticed about him.

"A warm welcome is always appreciated on a chilly day," the Count said with a swaggering grin. Chuckles and giggles went throughout the crowd. "But what a beautiful day it has been! Surely, the evening holds as much promise. As we gather here, friends, families, and neighbors, after another hard-earned harvest season, I am reminded that brotherhood is the soul of community. We of this humble county may be poor compared to other counties and city states in Doflend. But we are rich in Spirit. And that spirit is Death.

This spirit, this shadow of Death on our land has been our bane and our challenge these past three millenniums. We are defined by our suffering, and the Geohex has provided us with much definition.

"But soon I feel this suffering will end. Little by little the deeds of strangers are...cleansing our homeland. Four strangers known as Four Winds – One Storm."

The crowd erupted in cheers. The Count smiled and gestured to quiet down. "It is my deepest wish to meet and honor these four Excursionists here and now. So that all here will know and remember their names. And so those names are never forgotten...so that these heroes will always remain with us. In spirit, anyway. So, please, would Four Winds – One Storm join me on the stage?"

"Showtime," Will said, stuffing the last of his popcorn in his mouth. As he and Hindin descended the alcedrome steps, he spotted Röger walking out of the stable complex. After hopping the fence to the dirt floor, Will looked this way and that for Polly. "Where's that girl at, Rev?"

Hindin stepped over the fence and grimaced as he looked up at the bowl-shaped crowd. "I...I do not see her."

Röger gave his two friends a nod and a thumbs up greeting as they all drew nearer to the stage. But soon he, too, realized that Polly was nowhere to be seen.

Gone.

"You seem to be one short," the Count remarked to the three men as they ascended the platform steps.

None of them knew what to say. Troubled were their faces, but none more so than Will's.

"The Count looks weird," the tendikeye thought as he regarded the well-dressed man. *"Is he...is he glowin' or sumthin'? He doesn't look real...kinda like a portrait paintin' or sumthin'."* He winced and shook his head. *"Nah, my eyes're jus' adjustin' to the night is all."* He sneezed.

As the three men lined up, the Count made a gesture to a man holding an artfully carved wooden box. The man stepped forward and opened it, revealing four gold medallions on silk necklaces.

The Count proudly addressed the crowd. "It would seem that not all of them are available at the moment. It is my utmost

478

pleasure to bestow upon these brave individuals these precious medals of heroism and honor, so that wherever they go, others will know how precious these heroes are. Engraved on each medal are the words *The Valiant Taste Death But Once*, in reverence and reference to them not letting their courage or wits die as they disabled the curses in our communities." He smiled at the three men. "Sirs, if you would please step forward to receive your honor."

One by one they stepped forward, bowing their heads as the Count hung the medallions around their necks.

"This is just a stupid political maneuver," Röger thought as he went first.

"This guy looks really frickin' weird! Like he's floatin' in places," Will thought as he bowed his head. *"But not floatin'... It's like he is there, but he ain't."*

"May I address the crowd, your honor?" Hindin asked as he received his medallion, his smile warm and polite.

The Count smiled brightly. "Certainly, young man! I hear that you are a Chimancer. Please, feel free to bless us with some of your rhetoric!" The Count turned to the crowd with a grand gesture. "My friends, Mr. Hindin Revetz would like to give a speech!"

As the Count backed away to let Hindin step forward, Will's harking ears noticed something very odd. First, Hindin made very little sound as he stepped, but that was normal. What Will thought odd was that the Count's steps did not match each other. His left heel made a dull thud as his right foot made a sharp thud.

"But he's wearin' matchin' shoes," the tendikeye thought as he blinked. Suddenly, he sneezed again hard and loud. And when he opened his eyes and looked at the Count, again he saw only a rotten, thin corpse wearing the Count's fancy clothes. From the corpse's right knee down was a hematite peg leg. Will's eyes darted around at everyone else. No one seemed to notice but him. *"The allergy!"* he thought. He rested his hands on his weapons belt.

Hindin spoke, his voice strong, loud, and clear. "People of Wraith County. I will not bore you with heroic banter or idealistic sentiments. I wish only to take this opportunity to inform you all of our findings. The Geohex that your land suffers under is fixed in place by cursed pieces of hematite. Examples thus far are the Headman's Axe of Drowsy Nook, a cursed wedding ring in Tanglefoot...

479

"He's telling the public how my Geohex works!" the Count thought in utter shock.

Hindin named off all the pieces they had found and continued. "There are no doubt other pieces to be discovered. The dwellers of each town we have visited have attested that their local curses ended and broke once the hematite pieces were removed and neutralized. It is my hope that, should my teammates and I fail to pull the remaining pieces, that you the People of Wraith County can take it upon yourselves to break the rest of this curse, and that the former glory be restored to Apple County in fruitful abundance to feed your children and stimulate your economy. And that the self-cursed Wraith behind this land hex answers for his crimes." He scanned over the crowd with stern emerald eyes. "Wherever that cowardly ghostmonger may be hiding! I urge you the people to aid us in our search for these cursed objects!"

The people stood and cheered as the blossom of hope bloomed in their hearts and minds.

"He's telling them all how to...! Oh, this won't do at all! I never thought they would....!" The Count looked back at Will and Röger. The human looked back at him with a casual nod. The tendikeye was glaring at him with caged wrath in his blue-gray eyes.

"Yer a dead man," Will told him.

The Count crossed his arms and frowned with indignation. "Is that a threat?"

"No. It's a fact." Will drew steel and cleared holster in the blink of an eye, his blade and barrels less than a foot away from the Count's person. Hindin and Röger were startled and confused by the tendikeye's action, as was the entire surrounding crowd. "It's him!" Will shouted. "He's the Wraith!"

And that's when things turned ugly.

Part 2

Polly cared little for medals of honor, or honor itself for that matter. She cared only for opportunity. Her powers had waned and she needed to make a blood sacrifice. The kill had to be made by her alone. Her friends could not be involved. Had she the wicked outlook of her mother, such a sacrifice would be easy to come by. But alas, she was trying to be a good person. So, when the opportunity came to slay a hemogoblin laich she took it.

She knew that Thrush Raisinbread wanted her blood. And she also knew that he did not know that she wanted his. It would be self-defense against a monster. Stalker versus stalker. Prey versus prey. And to sacrifice such a potent creature would possibly double her own power.

She lured him behind a huge, deserted white canvas tent which had been erected for theurges to preach in. No one was nearby, and   many were at the alcedrome. Polly feigned the part of a shy virgin girl who was impressed by the Sheriff's authority and bold charm. Thrush's ego was easy to play upon. With his guard down, putting a knife in his heart would be easy.

"Kissing is as far as I go," she said with a giddy giggle. "I'm saving myself for someone special." She grinned darkly, seductively as she backed into a shadow.

The Sheriff grunted a laugh as he took off his hat and leaned his steel staff against a wooden poll. "Are you saying I'm not special, Miss Gone?"

Polly shrugged cutely.

The Sheriff smiled, his lips tight together. "Then I'll just have to prove myself by kissing you like no other man has kissed you before." He stalked toward her, only a few feet away.

Polly grinned smugly, tilting her hips and arching her back. "I bet you can't kiss me as well as Droom Arteen did." There was daring in her eyes. She put both arms behind her back and reached up her long loose sleeve, her hand finding the handle of her dagger.

"Oh, I'll take that bet." He reached out to her with hungry hands.

"*Now!*" she thought. Without a sound, she pulled her dagger free and thrust it at the left side of his chest.

Then twin gunshots rang out from the alcedrome. *Ka-Krack!*

Before her dagger could strike true, the laich turned to where the shots had come from.

"What's happen---OW!" Thrush cried. The knife had missed its mark, stabbing his arm as he turned. He looked down in shock to

481

see the sweet young girl holding the knife that had skewered his bicep.

Polly froze, her eyes reflecting fear and failure.

Sheriff Thrush Raisinbread's face went grim with rage. "You sneaky little sheath!" he growled. In an instant, his eyes turned blood red, his mouth grew three times in size, his every tooth elongated into curving scythe-like fangs, and the tips of his fingers grew into foot-long talons that were part bone, part nail.

Polly withdrew her dagger as she darted away, dodging a swipe from his gruesome claws.

"You thought to trick me, little sheath? Me?!" he hissed.

Polly was at a loss for words. The element of surprise stolen from her. "*I can't use my veins. He'll claw dem to pieces!*" she thought, as she sheathed her dagger. "*I need to escape him!*"

Thrush advanced and swiped at her again.

Polly dodged once more, barely. He was testing her, getting a feel for her movements.

"C'mon, theurge!" he dared. "People say you are a mystic of some sort. Try casting a maxim at me without a throat!" He slashed at her neck to no avail.

Polly dodged, but stumbled, falling back against the side of the tent.

"Gotcha!" the hemogoblin growled as he clawed downward with both claws.

Polly rolled out of the way just in time as the claws tore six cuts the length of her body through the tent. Unable to regain her balance, she fell through the shredded canvas and into the massive enclosure.

Fast as she could, she got up and backed away. She was inside a tent full of empty wooden folding chairs and a small platform for theurges to preach from. She hopped on it.

The laich stalked in through the slash holes. He was holding his steel quarterstaff now. "I was hoping for a pleasant evening. A little romance, something to eat. I wanted you sobbing and helpless beneath me as I split your petals apart...then I'd chew your ripe heart out of your chest! That's all I hoped for..." He took a step forward.

With her heart thumping fast, Polly raised her hand at him. "*Blood for Blood!*" she cried as her eyes flashed with red light.

Blood oozed out of the eyes, ears, nose, and gaping maw of the laich. He laughed at her. "I'm amortal, you silly sheath! Maxims have little effect on me!" He closed in faster than she thought possible. With a blur of motion, he swung his staff at her like a wood axe.

She leapt off the platform just as the steel rod shattered the small stage with a loud crunch. Turning, she raised her hand and voice again. *"It is courage, courage, courage, that raises the blood of life to crimson splendor. Live bravely and present a brave front to adversity."*

The laich laughed and shook his head, bloody spittle flinging from his fangs. "That did nothing to me!"

Polly raised her chin, her face losing all traces of fear or worry. Her heart calmed to a steady beat, and she took a fast relaxing breath. "Dat one was for me," she said. She summoned the long jagged veins from her wrists and coiled them around two wooden folding chairs. Bracing her stance, she flung the chairs at her enemy like stones from great slings.

The Sheriff blocked and shattered them all with his steel staff.

"He's not relying on his talons now!" she realized. She dashed forward, just within her veins' reach. Sending her barbed blood-cords forth like hungry snakes, she constricted them around his hands, trapping his razor-sharp claws securely around his staff. The harder he pulled or resisted the deeper the barbs dug in.

The laich wailed madly and charged at her, his huge mouth attempting to bite her face off.

With all her strength she pushed her feet against the ground and jumped, flipping over the Sheriff as he dove at her. As she landed, she turned and steadied her stance. Her veins, still attached to his hands, jerked the staff he was holding, smashing it right into his open mouth. The solid metal bar snapped his fangs like dried spaghetti noodles and dislocated his jaw.

Thrush yelped in pain and rage as his mouth flooded with his own blood. Then he felt the jagged veins coiled around his wrists tear themselves free, ripping skin and several fingers off his hands. He howled in agony, trembling as he struggled to his feet. He looked around for the girl but couldn't see her. Then he felt something hard and heavy shatter his knee joint. As he fell to the ground wailing, he

483

saw Polly running out of the tent carrying his steel staff.

In a matter of seconds, his wounds had nearly healed. He ran out of the tent with fresh new fangs and regenerated talons. Thrush sniffed the evening air, turned left, and began his hunt.

❖

"It's better to waste enemies than waste time!" Will thought as he split the Count's skull and fired two shots into the man's chest. *Ka-Krack!*

As the ancient Wraith flew backward off the platform, he looked with shock and sudden terror at the tendikeye's face. *"This is the man who stared down the Drageist!"* he thought. He felt his body thud hard onto the dirt floor of the arena, a cloud of dust rising around him. He felt no pain when the blade and bullets had torn through him, but he still sensed the steel and hot lead in his own weird way. It frightened him to be attacked so suddenly.

As the people of Wraith County gasped at seeing their beloved leader murdered, Count Slanidrac stood and backed away in a frantic hurry. In the span of a few seconds, he had been shot off the platform only to get up and back away like a terror-stricken craven.

All around him the crowd stared in shocked silence, mouths agape, eyes staring in disbelief. Women covered their mouths. Others started to scream. Small children cried and buried their faces in their mother's arms. Everyone looked at him in fear and revulsion.

"Why?" he thought. Then he saw his hands. Not the three-fingered handsome drakeri hands that he tricked everyone into seeing, but shriveled, skeletal human hands. The fear he had felt toward the tendikeye, though it had only lasted a few seconds, had ruined his concentration, shocking his disguised ghost facade back to its natural state. Everyone now saw him for what he was: a walking dead thing with a peg leg in a fancy suit.

"It's no matter," he thought. *"I'll reemerge in a decade or two with a new face and name. No one will be the wiser! And it's not like any of these curs will survive tonight anyway!"*

484

Röger and Hindin looked back and forth at Will and the Count.

"Will, how did you know?" Hindin asked.

Will hopped high through the air off the stage. "I'm allergic to ghosts an' brown gut snake!" The tendikeye hit the ground running, charging for the Count. "Hurry up, you two!"

As Röger and Hindin jumped off the stage, Will had already closed in within twenty feet of the Count. He screamed loudly as he charged, not from fury, but to make sure he could not hear any maxim the Count might say.

But the skeletal Count merely stood there grinning. "*Death is a delightful hiding place for weary men,*" the Count uttered softly.

Just as the tendikeye started to squeeze the triggers of his Mark Twain Special, the Wraith disappeared.

Will and the others stopped and went still as the surrounding crowd cried out in terror and confusion. Everyone could feel *it* growing, emanating from the spot where the Count had stood: *Necrofear*, the invisible emotional explosion that destroyed all reason and resolve.

Night fell as the people of Wraith County cried out in horror. In the hearts and minds of everyone in the alcedrome, the spirit of the Wraith spoke.

"*Four Winds – One Storm! For your sins of necrocide I damn your spirits to eternal ghosthood. You lived as heroes. You will die as heroes! Behold! THE REGIOPACALYPSE BEGINS!!!!*"

He then spoke only to the hearts and minds of the Trotting Swans. "*My Swans! Stick to the plan! I'll be sending the diversion shortly!*"

Not far from the Heapsboro Fairgrounds was a scenic patch of land where the dead rested. But they did not rest easy. Beneath the tombstones of the Heapsboro Cemetery, over one thousand stomachs growled along with over one thousand throats. All who were buried there had been embalmed secretly with a necrotheurgically-treated fluid that not only slowed the rotting

485

process, but reanimated the nerves and brain. Though the souls of those dead had long since shattered and scattered, a sort of faux spirit had infiltrated and cultivated inside their emaciated remains.

Long in agony and hunger, they had awaited a night like this, a night when they were needed. This was Count Slanidrac's secret army. In the 'barracks' of dirt and rotted wood, his soldiers had howled for countless years to be freed to feed.

The lids of their coffins splintered as they pounded and tore their way upward, through wood, through dirt, and finally through the fine trimmed sod of their graves.

Bregenites! Perhaps the simplest and most economical of laiches that a necrotheurge could create. With minds like brain damaged, terrified, raging, inconsiderate, over-caffeinated idiots, they moved like adrenalized drunks, running and stumbling, falling and crawling. Pain and hunger beyond a living person's threshold was the only thing they were allowed to feel. And the not-so-distant lights and sounds of the County Fair were all they were allowed to see and hear.

❖

The Fairgrounds had grown sparse as nearly half of the fair-goers were in the alcedrome.

"He'll be able to track me like a hound," Polly thought as she ran toward the game booth area of the Fairgrounds. She knew she had a ways to go. The maxim she had cast on herself bought her a few minutes of fearlessness. It allowed her to think efficiently enough to remember where she had been and know where she was going.

"I have to throw off my scent. But first I need to make sure he won't get his weapon back!" As she ran, she held up the steel quarterstaff as if offering it. Blood seeped through the pores of her palms as she uttered the maxim, *"As iron is eaten away by rust, so the envious are consumed by their own passion."* With sticky hands dripping with crimson, she coated the staff and let it fall to the gravel-strewn ground.

"Now to throw him off!" she thought. She came to a petting

486

zoo full of baby goats. It was nothing more than a gated pen being attended by a severely obese human man with a blonde beard.

He saw her running toward him. "I'm sorry, miss. The petting zoo is closed after dark."

Polly stopped right in front of him and placed a hand on his neck. "I'm sorry, too," she said, meaning it. Her eyes flashed red. The large man looked scared before he dropped to the ground unconscious.

"I'm wasting my power," she muttered as she opened up the gate. "I should have punched him out!" About thirty baby goats looked up at her. She raised both hands high, and with all her will, shouted at the captive goat audience, *"Blood is thicker dan water!"* Blood spurted from her wrists and fingertips, coating the horns and backs of the small animals. "Now get out of here!" she told them in a loud whisper.

She kicked and shooed the kids until they ran out of the pen in several directions. Polly hopped the other side of the fence and ran. She felt herself lagging and exhausting. *"Used too much blood...too much power...one more maxim...one more..."*

Not very far away, Thrush Raisinbread grinned with delight as he noticed his prized weapon laying on the ground. "I can smell her blood on it," he remarked as he reached down to pick it up.

Just as his clawed fingers wrapped around the staff, the steel bar crumbled into tiny bits. He looked at his palm. It was covered with jagged flakes of rust and sticky bits of blood. Clenching his hand into a fist, he roared with rage. "You bitch! I'll gnaw your veins and slurp up your arteries!"

He continued on her trail, sniffing and hissing, growling and cursing. The many gravel lanes of the Fairgrounds were now darkened by nightfall, illuminated only by lanterns and torches. The lanes had less people than earlier in the day, but there were still plenty who were out and about. Couples, children, vendors, musicians... *"Witnesses,"* Raisinbread thought. *"I need to calm down. She knows about me. She might tell others...her friends."*

He forced his teeth and talons to shrink back down. *"Can't have anyone else see me like this. I need to find her...take her by surprise..."* He suddenly caught her scent in the air. He turned his head toward the smell, a dark hungry smile on his lips. With the swiftness of a mountain cat, he dashed toward the sweet perfume that was her blood.

Out of breath, Polly finally reached her destination. "I want my dove now!" she told the game master at the The Cheating Husband game booth.

The portly old man smiled and nodded as he rubbed his hands together. "Certainly, my dear." He gestured up to the many caged doves he had hanging on display. "Is there a certain bird that strikes your fancy?"

"De younger de better," she answered flatly. "And give me one of your brooms, too. Please!"

The young woman's sense of urgency caught him off guard. Startled, he reached up and fetched a young doveling in a tiny wicker cage.

Polly snatched the little tweeting thing out of the cage before the man could even try to hand it to her. As she clutched the bird in one hand, she forced open its tiny wing with the other. With a sudden yank, she pulled out a feather as the bird chirped in pain.

The man looked down at her hands and the bird. The wing started to bleed. "What are you doing to that poor dove?!" he cried.

"I needed a fresh pin feather!" Polly hissed with cruelty in her eyes. She tossed the dove aside, sending it fluttering wounded to the ground.

The man's face twisted into a look of horror and grief for the tiny bird. "Well, why not just use a chicken?"

Polly shouldered past him, causing him to topple to the ground. She grabbed one of his brooms and stuck the bloody feather deep into its bristles. She looked down at the prone game master, her face crazed and beautiful. "Because chickens cannot fly!" She winked and her open eye flashed with red light. She held on tight as the broom pulled her high and far into the night air. Gone from sight.

As the Fairgrounds below her grew smaller and further away, Polly wrapped her legs around the broom's long handle. Steering the broom level, she rode it through the night air and fought the urge to cackle. *If Mother could behold me now!* she thought smugly. Wasting no more time, she pulled her dagger from her forearm sheath and began to whittle at the end of the broom.

Far below, Thrush Raisinbread chuckled as the smell of his prey grew stronger. *"She's close,"* he thought as a trail of drool spilled out his lips. *"Probably hiding. I'll have her soon! I'll sneak up from behind, grab her, cover that pretty mouth, drag her off somewhere dark and quiet...oh yes..."*

He inched his way toward a large stack of beer kegs. *"She's right behind those barrels! I can hear her breathing and trembling!"* Stepping without a sound, he tip-toed around the side of the barrels. *"Almost!"* Slowly, carefully, he peeked around to see her. Only, Polly was not there at all. All Thrush saw was a goat kid covered from horns to tail in female drakeri virgin blood.

His eyes widened. "NO!" he huffed and growled. His face contorted with rage and disappointment. He clenched his teeth and groaned as if in pain. "NOOOOOOO!!!!! That little sheath! I'll kill her!" He ran up and kicked the baby goat with all his might. The poor thing flew nearly two hundred feet away.

There was a pudgy boy riding a wooden bileer on the Carousel having the time of his life. It was his first time riding the ride without his mother's help. As the steam powered pipe music played, lanterns revolved and shone light through multicolored glass the pudgy boy had never felt happier. Then a baby goat flew at him, hitting him on the side of the head and knocking him off the bileer. Other than the psychological, damage the boy was unharmed. But the bloody baby goat was very, very dead.

Thrush Raisinbread stalked the Fairgrounds, kicking goats wherever he found them. Hunger and lust consumed his mind. He longed for his mark, his prey, his victim. He looked everywhere for the girl. Everywhere but up.

High above, Polly finished sharpening the end of her broom into a fine, strong point. The cool wind passed through her short, silky hair as she looked down to find her mark, her prey, her victim. "Dere he is!" she whispered to herself.

Thrush was walking, pacing, stalking, circling aimlessly. In all his centuries as a hemogoblin, he had never, *ever* lost a victim. He was almost frustrated enough to cry. "Where is she?" he whimpered. "I...I...wanted so badly just to eat her heart...chamber by sweet chamber... What am I going to do? What will I tell the Count? She got away!" He stopped pacing and hung his head, dejected and defeated. "And she only pretended to fancy me, too. That's what hurts the most..."

"Now!" Polly thought as she flew down at him like a

489

swooping silent hawk. His back was turned. He was no longer pacing around. Polly's aim was true.

Fast, hard, and unexpected, Sheriff Thrush Raisinbread felt the point of Polly's broom burst through his body, skewering his heart. Polly had tried to brace for the impact of colliding with her target or possibly finding a good way to roll out of it, but such was not her luck.

As the broom impaled the laich, she tumbled over him, landing hard, rolling and dragging on the gravel ground. The world around her spun as her head and left shoulder throbbed. Her mouth filled with blood and vomit. She wretched as she lay stunned on her side. Blood streamed into her eyes. She tried to move her left arm. It wouldn't obey. She rolled on her side and moved her right arm instead.

She saw that her forearm was shredded and felt her scalp had been split wide open. She sat up and saw that her left shoulder was dislocated and the collarbone had snapped. Every move, every breath caused her agony. *"Good ting I cast de Maxim of Courage,"* she thought. *"It's keeping me from going into shock."* Her eyes shifted to look around her.

People were gathering, pointing, asking questions.

"She flew a broom through that man!" a teenager shouted. "She's a witch!"

"She's Lady Gone! Polly the Red!" a woman added. "I recognize her from Barnhart!"

Two men stepped through the gathering crowd. They were dressed in purple and carrying shotguns. "She murdered Thrush Raisinbread, the new Sheriff of Drowsy Nook!" one of them shouted.

"Trotting Swans," Polly thought as her hopes sank. She watched helplessly as the two Swans pointed their shotguns down at her. "He is a laich! A hemogoblin!" she tried to explain.

"We should kill her now," one Swan said to the other. "She's a theurge, might hex us with a maxim."

The other Swan grinned with half a mouth full of teeth. "Agreed, brother."

Just as the two men took aim at Polly's pretty, bloody head, two quick shot's rang out. Both men stiffened and fell dead.

"Will?" Polly thought, as she watched the crowd grow

490

frightened and run away from the scene. Emerging from the darkness was Deputy Drume Arteen holding a smoking pistol.

He looked down at the impaled body of Thrush Raisinbread, his expression troubled and bemused. "A laich? So, is this why you said not to trust him?"

Polly nodded.

"And you only went on the date with him to hunt him?"

Polly winced as she tried and failed to shrug both shoulders. "On my *philocreed,*" she answered. "But it's not over yet. I still need to extract his heart."

Drume swallowed, making a sour face. "I'll help."

"No. I have to do dis alone." She slowly got to her feet and said her last maxim, using up the remainder of her theurgic energy. *"Good healing always tastes bitter."* She cried out in torment and relief as her shoulder and collarbone snapped back in place. She felt her flesh and skin begin to knit back together.

Deputy Arteen watched in awe and fear as her wounds healed almost completely.

Polly let out a sigh of disappointment as she reached to touch the gash on her scalp. "No more power left." Her face turned to the still form of Thrush Raisinbread. "Not until I sacrifice dis man." Without looking away, she told the deputy. "Tank you, Drume. I owe you my life. But you need to go now. I don't want you to see dis."

Drume started to shake his head. Then he heard people screaming outside the Fairground gates.

"Breginites!" they shouted. The word began to echo throughout the Fairgrounds. Women screamed, children cried, and men yelled as the once merry place turned into a desperate commotion of fear and confusion.

Polly turned her head to the deputy. "Go," she told him. "I'll be joining you shortly." She knelt down and grasped both sides of the broom that impaled the laich as if they were handle bars. She then began to drag him him behind a lemonade tent like a starving lioness dragging a fresh kill.

Drume reloaded his pistol and ran toward the screaming.

Behind the lemonade tent, Polly performed her sacrifice, murdering the murderer by cutting out the shredded remnants of his heart with her dagger. As the cursed soul of Thrush Raisinbread

491

shattered and scattered to the winds of existence, the pathways of Polly's mind flooded with the power of her own soul growing. The surge of spiritual energy created new pathways in her mind. Old maxims she'd been taught but could never cast now made perfect sense.

When she emerged at last from behind the tent, she saw the world through clearer eyes, heard it with keener ears. She smiled happily, bathed in the blood from her own veins and from the heart of her dead enemy, her hair clumped with gore. Her wounds were now a memory. She looked down to see the two dead Trotting Swans who had tried to blow her head off.

"Oh, Drume," she purred. "I'll have to kiss you twice as a reward. Murder is a sweeter gift dan flowers."

❁

Panic reigned in the alcedrome. Fairgoers rushed out of the bowl-shaped arena. Those without unsure footing found themselves trampled on the stone steps leading up. Friends and families became separated. Necrofear had caught like wildfire in their hearts and minds.

"He is a shunting wraith!" Röger exclaimed. "The highest form of necrobeing. Part post-mort/part ghost. I fought one once about forty years ago in Haversteen, Micca."

"Yeah? How'd that turn out?" Will asked as he looked up at the evacuating crowd.

"Everybody died but me," the Röger muttered.

Hindin shook his head. "That offers little comfort, Sir Röger."

Röger smirked, "I only comfort widows, big guy."

Will sheathed his weapons. "Well, there may be plenty yet by the ended of the night. Hey Rev, what's a...what'd the wraith say...a regiopacolypse?"

"It is an apocalypse on a regional scale. It is when a theurge of significant power destroys everyone and everything save their most devout followers."

"Over my cinders!" Will swore, spitting in the dirt. "Rög, How do we kill us a wraith?"

The human turned to his teammates. "Each wraith is different. This one? We need to destroy his peg leg." The big man pulled Head Launcher off his back.

"How ya figure?"

Röger started running toward the steps leading up to the Fairgrounds. "Come on! I'll explain on the way. We need to keep an eye on these people."

"Agreed," Hindin answered.

As the three men made their way out of the alcedrome, Röger enlightened his friends on the finer points of wraith hunting. "Firstly, Wraith's are amortal, not mortal or immortal, but amortal. Dead but not dead. He exists, but can also exist out of the reach of our perception."

"How's that?" Will asked, fighting frustrating.

"Because we can't understand *his* perception. He understands the perception of non-theurges because our perception is limited. He is able to exist beyond what we see as reality."

"So, he is enlightened and awakened within his own philocreed," Hindin said as he bounded over a fence post.

"Something like that. That's how he was able to vanish. But he's still bound to the land, to the world we know. Did you two see the way his peg leg gleamed?"

"Hematite," Will, muttered, as he leapt over the seats three rows at a time.

Hindin furrowed his steel brow. "He must use that as a.... keystone for the remaining pieces."

"Good enough," Röger shot back. "It is like a key or a theurgic wand. He channels and controls his power through it. Keeps his Geohex going. It connects him to the land, to reality itself. If we destroy his peg leg --"

"-- he will cease to exist!" Hindin finished.

"Within our scope of reality," Röger explained. "But yeah. We'll be rid of the shunter for good. But right now he's in wraith form, beyond our reach. If it is a regiopocalypse, then he's probably working a very powerful theurgy right now that will destroy us all."

"What could it be?" Hindin wondered aloud as they reached the Fairgrounds.

"BREGINITES! BREGINITES ARE COMING!" someone in the crowd shouted.

493

Röger sighed and dropped his helmed face in his open hand. "Of course. Necrotheurges *always* use Bregenites."

Will lit up a cigarette, doubting but knowing that it could be his last. "Bregs, huh? Go fer the head an' spine, right Rög?"

Röger nodded. "And protect your own. They eat brains and nerves. And their own nervous systems are highly sensitive. They feel pain but it only gives them strength. They're stupidly clumsy, making them difficult to land a solid hit on. They don't hit or kick worth a shunt, but they can grab and maul like a bear, and they do it en mass so keep your distance."

"I have little to fear," Hindin said. "For even if they overwhelm me their teeth and nails cannot maul through steel and stone."

Through the shrieking crowd, Will spotted an old man carrying a musket. His shirt was torn as if it had been savagely yanked at. His face was caked with blood and fear as he made his way through the panicked throng.

"Hey! Hey, old timer!" Will shouted as he waved the man down. He bounded to the man as the others followed. The old man halted and turned his head to the three.

Will got with in arm's reach, but still had to shout over the panicked crowd. "Old timer! Can ya tell us what happened? What'd ya see?"

The man's wrinkles jiggled as he stammered out, "I-I was guarding the wagons out front when they came up. At first I thought they were a gang of drunks coming to the Fair. But the gang turned out to be a mob! Hundreds at least! I couldn't tell what they were before it was too late. I managed to get my one shot off. Didn't see if I hit one. Most of us were fast enough to get behind the fence." His voice cracked and he started to weep. "They got my nephew, Randol! Oh, even if I live through this I still have to tell my sister!"

Will wasted no time on condolences. "Have they made it to the fence yet?"

The old man hung his head and shook it. "The wagons. Most of them still have bileers, mules, and oxen hitched to them. That's keeping most of them busy. They're feeding on them all."

Hindin covered his mouth. "Those poor beasts!"

The old man saw the gun on Will's belt. "Son, you need to get to the front! Every man with a gun is shooting through the fence.

494

Aim for their heads, boy! We must keep them back!" At that point the man took his leave of them.

Will turned to his friends. "Rev. Rög. You two get to the main gate an' tear it down."

"Are you crazy?" Röger asked.

"That fence ain't nuthin' but posts and wire. The Bregs'll have it down once the bulk of 'em reach it. We need to create a channel, a false openin' to bait 'em into. Stand just inside the entrance and kill 'em as they come. Rev, you ain't got to fear them eatin' you an' Rög's got that helmet to guard what few brains he has."

"Shunt you," Röger growled.

"Where will you be?" Hindin asked.

Will looked up at the stalled Ferrous Wheel and grinned. "Oh, Falcona an' me are gonna cozy up someplace high an' private."

"And what would you have *me* do?" came Polly's voice.

Surprised heads turned to see Polly standing amongst them. She was covered in dried blood and smiling demurely.

Hindin gasped in surprise. "Polly, where have you been? I was worried sick!"

She tilted her head and her smile sharpened. "I was being a white blood cell, battling an enemy hidden below de surface. A disease of de living blood of dese people."

"Talk normal, Pol," Will barked.

Her smile melted as she crossed her arms. "I cut de heart out of a Hemogoblin dat tried to do de same to me. It was Sheriff Raisinbread. I sacrificed him and now my power and understanding has doubled. So, Mr. Tactician, what *position* would you put me in?" She winked and grinned teasingly.

Will paused as he regarded her boldness. "Polly, blood stays hidden, unseen an' unheard, an' always on the move. Keep in the crowd an' tend to the wounded. Take out any stray Bregs that directly threaten the defenseless."

Polly's eyes narrowed as she sneered and pouted. "I would rather defend de front fence."

Will got in her face. "An' I'd rather eat a gooseberry pie, but you don't hear me complainin'!"

"I am now more dan what I was!" she argued. "You don't know what I can now do!"

Will would have none of it. "Well, save it fer later, little sister!"

He turned his attention to the crowd, surging to escape the terror at the front fence. People ran for the shelter of the tents and other temporary structures of the Fairgrounds. Others simply ran to the other side of the grounds, but dared not venture past the rear fence.

Will could sense it then, smell it even. "There's a...barrier along the fence line. It stinks o' death an' necrofear. We an' all these folk have been corralled. These bregs are only the first wave of what's to come."

Röger's eyes narrowed in his helm. "The Count meant to do this all along?"

Hindin punched his palm in anger, the impact producing a harsh chime. "The fiend! He used honor to lure us into a dishonorable snare! By the Harsh Light of Truth, I was wrong to make us come here."

Will placed a hand on Polly and Hindin's shoulder, his face grim and stern. "Boys and girls, it's high time we stopped playin' at detectives an' started bein' what we really are: Warriors."

"I loathe war," Hindin protested. "I prefer the terms confictitians or combateers."

Will could not stop his eyes from rolling. "Aw, shut up, Rev!"

❖

What started as an attack quickly turned into a battle. As the horde of stumbling corpses stormed the front fence, a line of gunmen formed just inside the wire and wooden confines. Most were Trotting Swans firing shell-clad bullets while the rest of the men used poorer arms for ball and powder. The air stank of rotting flesh, animal dung, and gunpowder. Ears filled with the choral moans and shrieks of the Bregenites and the blasting pops of guns.

The dark of night was upon them. The Bregenites were so

496

clustered and numerous that missing them was harder that hitting them. But their erratic movements made killing them difficult. For every ten bullets fired, only one would destroy a creature's central nervous system. Many of the Breginites crawled on all fours and brayed like animals, having recently feasted on the brains of burden beasts. But the hunger of the horde would not be satisfied by such simple creatures. The Bregs longed to crack skulls open to feast on crown chakra life force, to gorge on chewed memories, to munch on jumbled knowledge, to slurp up basic motor skills...

The front gate was a solid iron square of crisscrossing bars, twelve feet tall by twelve feet wide. It was attached to the fence on one side by thick hinges and by a steel chain and lock on the other. Five men stood on one side, firing bullets at the horrid faces screaming behind it.

As Hindin and Röger made their way toward it, Röger made a suggestion. "Hey, big guy, I know Will told us to open that gate but it seems a waste of effort."

Hindin's head shook in disapproval. "Are you changing the plan all of a sudden?"

"No, I'm improving it. Let's kick that thing down!"

Hindin regarded the heavy iron square and nodded. "I see your logic."

At once the two strongest members of the team charged the gate. Röger cupped his hands in front of his helm and bellowed "EVERYBODY MOVE!!!!"

The gunmen in their path had just enough time to see them coming and dodge to either side for safety.

Röger and Hindin leapt the last ten feet, a duel mass of muscle, bone, steel, and stone. Röger flew at the gate, kicking it like a jealous husband kicks a door in. Hindin dived forward with his arms at his sides. Just before he crashed headlong, he snapped his open palms forward to slam into the iron bars. Both men hit at the same time, the sound of the impact louder than any gun being fired.

The gate broke loose from the fence and flew twenty feet back into the Bregenite horde, crushing everything in its path.

The gunmen on either side of Hindin and Röger gaped in shock.

"What are you doing?" a man in a torn white shirt asked them. Through the haze of powdersmoke, they recognized him as

497

Drume Arteen.

There was no time to answer. The army of well-dressed, dirt covered corpses poured in through the opening, a rancid flood of death, decay, and dimwittedness. They spilled from the opening like blood from a fresh wound, but the wound immediately began to clot as Hindin and Röger made their stand.

Armed with Headlauncher and the strength of thirty men, Sir Röger Yamus sent heads soaring into the black of night, sometimes two or three with every swing. The heavy hematite axe showed no sign of slowing down as it sheered through necks of withered flesh and brittle bone.

The malrukan Chimancer was poetry in motion, but it was poetry too fast and strange to be understood. Even Röger had never seen him fight so oddly. Hindin's posture was hunched, his chin lowered and tucked. His legs were deeply bent but his footwork remained light, shuffling and pouncing to and fro, back and forth. And his silvery hands were neither opened nor closed, but bent at the second knuckle of each finger. And as he punched at the coming Bregenites, their wailing heads cracked and broke like rotten eggs. Whether they came at him high or low, it mattered for nothing. The fighting style was wholly aggressive, primal, and vicious, but guided by a focused mind.

"*That must be his Puma-Style,*" Röger thought as it rained heads all around him.

Together, the two men reduced the oncoming flood to a trickle. The Bregenites reacted just as Will predicted, ignoring the rest of the fence for a chance to move through the gate. The gunmen on either side of the two fighters took full advantage of the monsters distracted by the opportunity. They fired their guns with less fear and better accuracy. Indeed, it appeared that the Trotting Swans and Four Winds – One Storm were fighting on the same side.

But as the Swans watched the two tall heavy hitters, their Wraith commander spoke to them in their hearts and minds.

"*My Swan brethren! Now is the time! Our enemies are between your guns!*"

It was a simple plan. The Trotting Swans knew the Bregenites would be coming. They knew that Four Winds – One Storm would meet and battle the oncoming horde. And with a few well-placed shots, they could help the outlandish Excursionists die

498

like heroes.

Hindin was just about to punch through the screaming head of a Bregenite when an unexpected bullet pierced through the creature's temple. The malruka looked to the side to see a Trotting Swan standing twenty feet away with a smoking rifle and a smile on his lips.

"Thank you!" the Chimancer called out. "But please shoot the ones outside the fence!"

The Swan ignored him. Soon other Swans gathered around and behind Röger and Hindin in a semi-circle.

Röger saw them rushing into their new position and reloading their rifles. "No, you idiots! We can handle them! Get back to the fence!"

None of the other gunmen noticed that the seventy-three Swans had even left their sides at the fence. It all happened so fast. But even though Hindin and Röger saw what was happening, they were powerless to stop it; too busy fighting the oncoming threat.

As the Swans took aim and fired their pistols, rifles and shotguns, most of the lead blasted the invading Bregenites to bits. But Hindin and Röger felt the punishment of being in harm's way. The burly human fell as swarms of buckshot tore through the back of his right thigh and left kidney. Seven more bullets, either from the barrels of rifles or pistols, tore into his back, turning nearly every bone and organ in his torso into pulp. The new large billblade sword that he wore on his back had protected his spine, but a shot gun slug had broken the blade just near the hilt.

Röger dropped face first into the gravel, lifeless and still. Hindin had taken as much damage, but he remained on his feet. The smooth steel-skin on his back had been blasted away in crude patches, exposing the pink granite that was his flesh underneath. So great was the shocking pain that he nearly fell. Hindin stumbled and cried out as he turned his head around to see the Swans out of the corner of one eye. "We have been tricked," he uttered to himself.

"You should have gotten out of the way!" a Swan yelled at him. There was cruel mockery in his eyes.

While Röger and Hindin charged the iron gate, Will had

climbed up to the top of the stalled Ferrous Wheel with the speed and nimbleness of a squirrel. As his two friends kicked down the gate and took on the evil horde, he took *Falcona* out of her case and settled into a swaying seat compartment. With a snap of his arm, the folded firearm pieced itself together. *Ka-Klack*!

He watched his friends hack and pound the shambling Bregs as he loaded a five round magazine into the chamber. Wasting no time and taking careful aim, he fired over the fence and into the horde. A head exploded with every shot.

Whenever a Bregenite managed to get past the fury of his teammates, he sent a bullet to into its skull. No one noticed him and that suited him just fine. All seemed well until he watched all the Trotting Swans at the gate suddenly break from their positions and regroup in a half-circle behind his teammates...like a flock of birds seemingly sharing the same mind and will. His heart leapt in his throat as he realized he'd put his friends in danger. "Wait!" he shouted down at them. "Wait fer them to get outta the way!"

But no one heard and no one heeded. He watched with wide eyes as they fired at his friends and the horde alike. He saw Röger and his axe fall to the ground, and Hindin's back turn into an ugly mass of torn steel and chipped rock. Then Will saw nothing but the backs of Trotting Swans' heads.

"They shoulda waited fer me to run outta bullets up here an' join my friends down there!" he thought as and icy rage cooled his nerves. He squeezed *Falcona's* trigger. BANG! BANG! BANG! BANG! BANG! click...

He realized the chamber was empty as five Swans fell dead in a row, blood gushing out of their broken skulls. Just when the other Swans noticed their fallen brethren, Will had already reloaded and was shooting again. They scattered like flies off a carcass, running this way and that, unsure of where the shots were coming from. The remaining gunners at the fence, some thirty in total, ran as well, unsure of what was happening. The Bregenites kept coming. All that stood in their way was Hindin who stumbled about in pain from his injuries.

"REV!!!!" Will cried out to his friend. He then heard gunfire and several bullets hit his compartment and whizzed past his ear. *"They know where I am!"* he thought as he ducked down into the dangling seat.

Far down below, Hindin fought to stay conscious as more Bregenites shambled and crawled through the gate. Out of corner of his emerald eye, he saw Röger laying face down on the gravel-strewn ground, a pool of dark blood beneath him. The human's black leather vest and back was a mangled mass of bullet holes. The holes began to quiver and twitch as the shredded muscles squirmed and popped. Pieces of lead vomited up from the wounds like little mouths spitting out bloody teeth. The wounds shut closed and striped fur sprouted over them.

❖

"Tend to de wounded!" Polly muttered bitterly as she ran into a crowded tent. The canvas structure brimmed with frightened fair-goers, nearly two hundred men, women, and children huddled together. Most were cowering and sobbing.

"*De necrofear has dem,*" she thought. "Is anyone injured?" she called out.

No one seemed to hear her over their own whimpering and blubbering. She looked around, trying to see if anyone was maimed or bleeding. No one looked too serious. "*Dese people, all of dem. Dey will be too afraid to defend demselves when de Bregenites break through.*"

She looked around at the canvas walls and the tent poles that supported them. "*All de fair-goers are in tents like dese throughout de grounds. Death is coming to claim dem all. What can I possibly do protect dem other dan fight?*" Nervous and unsure, she pinched the septagram tattoo on her right forearm.

Backing out of the tent, she thought resentfully, "*De Red River Philocreed does not teach to protect others, only one's self. Mother did not teach me....*"

She felt something brush against her leg. It made her squeal and jump. She looked down to see a little baby goat, loose from its pen. It placed its little hooves on her leg and looked up at her.

"AaAaAaAaGhhggh!" it said.

Her lips twisted into a sudden smile. "*WAIT! De threshold maxim! I can expand it!*" she realized. She drew her dagger, picked up the goat, and went back into the tent. "Listen to me! Hear my words if you value your blood!" she called out in a raspy screech.

All eyes turned to her and the goat and the sharp piece of steel in her hand.

"I am Lady Polly Gone of de Red River, apprentice-daughter of Veluora de Red Witch of Chume."

"Blood mystic!" people exclaimed in shocked whispers.

Polly continued. "Hear me! When blood flows it prevents death from coming. It prevents disease from invading. It warms the body and rids our flesh of unwanted sickness. Blood must flow, always it must flow."

She drew her blade across the goat's throat, and people gasped.

Polly's eyes glowed red as she said the words, "*Immunoglobulin-anguis! De Red River is de moat dat protects our temple!*"

The blood from the kid's throat flowed out in the shape of a single slithering snake. People watched in horrified amazement as the snake slithered onto the edge of the tent's opening. Around it went, leaving a glowing trail of red. In the space of twenty heartbeats, the snake had painted a complex pattern around the tent's entryway.

Polly raised her hand as if giving an oath. Everyone stopped shivering and whimpering to hear her. "On my *philocreed,* as long as you stay in dis tent, Death will not come to you. De blood will protect you from de Wraith's theurgy and his Bregenites. Stay here and dis nightmare will pass you by."

With that, she dashed out of the tent, tossing the dead animal on the gravel. "*Dere are more tents wit' more people,*" she thought as she ran. "*I just hope I can find enough kids to kill.*"

Part 3

In the place where Röger lay bleeding now stood the Werekrilp. All that remained of the human was his helmed head sitting atop a mountain of muscle, fur, rage and the golden medal of heroism around its thick shaggy neck. In a massive claw, it held

Headlauncher as if it were a tomahawk. The matching hematite ring had grown along with the middle clawed finger which bore it. Though his wounds had healed with his transformation, the pain of the hot lead still burned in his mind.

This was not the first time Trotting Swans had shot him in the back. With his free claw, he tried to draw his newly fashioned billblade from behind his shoulder. A low rumble rolled inside the beast as only the hilt and handle came free. His virgin blade was broken. The resulting rage liberated a fury in him that no rhyme or reason could rein in. Roaring louder than a lion, he threw himself into the Bregenite horde.

Past the gate and fence and deep into their midst, he cut and clawed and chopped and tore twitching heads from jerking shoulders. Each walking corpse had the strength of five men, but the Werekrilp had the power of ten lions. Indeed, he was a lion amongst sheep. But even one lion could not keep one thousand sheep from grazing for long. There were so many, so many...

Hindin could not think, only react. Though the wounds in his back were not fatal, they still debilitated him. The Bregenites kept coming. With fists and elbows of stone and steel, he silenced forever any gibbering horror that came his way. But his feet were firmly planted as he fought just as hard to stand.

For every head he cracked open, three more would get past him and into the Fairgrounds. He heard several cracks and snaps and saw the front fence come down. Fence posts uprooted and wire went slack as the horde stumbled and pushed their way through. Losing ground and losing strength, he realized, "*We are breached! The gunmen are scattered and the people are helpless in the tents. Even if we prevail against this horde it will take too long to quell them before all is lost.*"

Out of the corner of his emerald eye, he spotted and recognized Deputy Kellyr from Drowsy Nook. The old deputy was surrounded by walking horrors. Armed only with his pistol, Kellyr turned and fired at the shrieking faces around him. One by one the horrid visages exploded until the hammer of his gun fell on empty chambers. Not wasting time, he grasped the smoking barrel with his bare hand and used the butt end like a small club. After bashing the heads of three Bregenites, the old drakeri's eyebrows raised as he realized that the gun barrel was *hot*. Screaming, he threw down his gun and grasped his burnt hand. Then the swarm of hungry dead closed in and engulfed him, biting, chewing, tearing, and searching frantically for nerves to feast on. The old drakeri's screams were cut short by chomping teeth.

◇

Will lay in the swinging seat of the Ferrous Wheel like a baby in a rocking crib. From far below him came the threatening taunts of Trotting Swans. How many, he could not tell.

"Come on down, pretty boy! We're going to pay you back for Daddy Long Legs!"

"You can't roost up there forever, you big-footed pricker!"

"You're going to be a *ghost* before night's end! You and all your friends, tendikeye!"

Slowly, Will folded out the scythe bayonet mounted beneath his rifle's barrel until it clicked in place. *Falcona's Beak,* he sometimes called it. He pressed another five round magazine into the chamber and considered his options. *"I can't straight shoot down on 'em from this sittin' box. It teeters too much. I can't climb or hop down without gettin' hit with bullets an' risk fallin'. The bullets an' fall won't kill me, but they'll mess me up bad enough."* He closed his eyes and tried to remember the layout of the Fairgrounds from below the colossal ride. *"Where would they all be?"*

Will felt a sudden jerk and the compartment started to rock. *"The ride is movin'!"* he realized. *"They're tryin' to bring me down to 'em."*

Shots rang out from below. Will heard bullets strike the outside of the dangling compartment seat.

As the *Ferrous Wheel* turned, slowly, steadily lowering him down, he thought, *"If I jump out midway they'll be in scattered positions when they shoot at me. I can't dodge bullets as I fall, but I can roll out of a twenty-five foot drop. But if I stay in here all the way to the bottom, they'll hafta stop the ride an' gather close to fire in this seat before I can get out of it. O' course, they prob'ly have enough men down there fer both."* He let out a laughing sigh and

504

shook his head. *"Screw this strategy gut snake! Brem never taught me how to fight on no Ferrous Wheel. It's time I learn how the hard way!"*

He had taken too long to think. It was only a ten foot drop. As he leapt out, bullets pelted Will from all directions like stones from slings. He was surrounded by many. He hit the gravel ground running, holding his weapon low as he dashed to his first visible target. In two dashing steps, he covered twenty feet to a fumbling Swan trying to reload his shotgun. Will held the scythe-rifle at such an angle that the thin blade disappeared from sight. And all the Swan saw was a rifle being swung at him like a club.

In an instant, the tendikeye sped past him and the drakeri man thought he had avoided the swing. Then blood spilled out of his side as a mouth-shaped wound opened up from naval to spine.

"A swath cannot be swathed!" Will thought with a wicked grin.

He felt more bullets pelt his back as he swung Falcona at another Swan holding a rifle. The Swan managed to back away as the blade made a swipe at his belly. But Will pulled the trigger in mid-swing, sending a bullet through the man's innards and spine.

More bullets pelted him. He felt welts rising all over his back, butt, shoulders, belly, chest, and thighs. Still, he ran. He could not tell how many were shooting at him. *"Twenty or thirty,"* he guessed as he fired a round through the skull of another Swan blocking his path. Pain stung from every corner of his body as he ran to escape. *"Need to get outta this leadstorm!"* he thought.

Outnumbered and outgunned, Will outran the Swans with ease... but not their bullets. Three more bullets pelted him in the right calf, left tricep, and square between the shoulder blades. Running and limping, he dodged desperately behind a large canvas tent. Throbbing from head to foot, he collapsed to his knees. He felt tears run down his face, but then saw that it was blood. He watched it drip onto the golden medal of heroism he still wore about his neck. He'd been shot in the cheek bone and the side of his head just over his left ear. Parts of him felt numb, other parts pounded in agony.

He could hear the Swans coming after him. Wincing and grunting, he stood and backed against the corner of the tent wall. Fast and smooth, he turned and fired in the direction from which he had come. Some fifty yards away, a Trotting Swan's neck exploded

505

beneath his head. There looked to be two dozen more behind that one.

Will turned back, slid the bolt to eject the shell, turned to aim around the corner and fired again. The bullet tore a quarter of another Swan's head off. The man dropped limp, but the gang was closing in.

Will ejected the empty shell and slid the bolt back into place. He could hear them getting closer. *"One shot left,"* he thought.

"He can't kill all of us!" he heard a man yell.

"He's wounded! I hit him myself, I know it!"

"Let's finish him off!"

Then Will heard a female yell, *"Blood for Blood!"*

"Polly!" Will realized. He turned the corner, ready to fire again and saw the gang of Swans rolling on the ground before him. They had dropped their weapons. Their eyes, ears, and noses were leaking blood, all the little trails flowing directly into their gaping, gasping, choking mouths. They flailed about uselessly, their terrified faces contorted into muted screams.

Polly stood on the other side of the writhing heap of men. In one hand, she clutched her dagger. In the other arm she carried a baby goat. Her glowing eyes looked down coldly at the Swans.

"Pol, what are ya doin' to 'em?" the tendikeye asked.

She put the point of her dagger to her lips as if to say *"Shhh. Don't interrupt me."*

Will watched in sickened curiosity as the Swan's purple skin went pale, and they all went still forever.

The light of Polly's eyes dimmed and she said, "I drowned dem in de Red River. Dey were fools to try to swim it."

Will swallowed, disgusted. "Whatchu doin' with that kid?"

She looked up at him, stern-faced and annoyed. "Never you mind dat, Will. I'm busy and you look like waste. Do you need healing?"

"No," he answered stubbornly.

"Liar." She stomped over the top of the corpses toward him and said, *"Good healing always tasted bitter."* Then she kissed him warmly on the cheek. As her lips lingered there, all of his welts and wounds disappeared. She pulled away and shouldered past him roughly. "Now, if you'll excuse me I have people to protect, and you have enemies to kill."

506

Will touched his cheek where she had kissed him. "Pol... why didn't you just heal me with yer hand... like always?" His eyes betrayed confusion and bashfulness.

Polly turned back to meet his gaze. She let out a laugh and shook her head in condescending disappointment. "Because my hands are full, you dumb ass!"

❁

Hindin fought to stand. He fought to move and moved to fight. He saw countless gaunt, gibbering faces and struck at them ruthlessly. His golden medal of heroism clanked against his steel chest as he moved.

The Bregenite's arms grabbed at his own, but he moved his limbs like snakes to avoid capture. The Werekrilp was far and deep in the horde, hacking and roaring. Men screamed as Bregenites tore them apart. He heard shots fired from all around, near and far. Some bullets hit Bregenites. But others hit him, as well. Countless Bregs walked past Trotting Swans as if they were invisible. He felt helpless and betrayed.

"*Die, Chimancer!*" he heard the Wraith say in his mind. "*Die a hero! Die hating the very people you tried to protect!*"

"The Swans are misguided fools!" Hindin argued. "Though they are my enemies, I will not hate them!"

The Wraith laughed. "*They knew all this would happen. They forbade their families from coming to this fair. They understand that some of the populace must die, that would-be-heroes must meet tragic ends. I will build hematite monuments for you all so that your memory and souls and my Geohex never fades!*"

All at once, every nearby Bregenite reached for him, hundreds of hands coming high and low from every direction. They had moved in unison, all compelled by one singular will. Hindin's fury and grace was brought to a halt a like suffocated flame. His arms and legs were pinned down or held immobile. He was pulled prone, buried beneath a massive heap of writhing corpse-flesh and tattered cloth.

507

"These vanguard puppets will not be the death of you, malruka. My main force approaches presently to crush you and that Werekrilp. You have lost, Chimancer. And your soul will join with my Geohex, making it stronger than ever! Die! Die hating me and hating yourself for losing!"

As Hindin struggled uselessly beneath the heap, something burned deep inside him. At first, he thought it was the very hatred the Wraith Count commanded him to feel. But as the feeling grew and heated his core, he realized that it was the truth manifesting itself as a fire within. The epiphany became a thought and the thought became words. "I cannot deal with the dead as I do with the living, dealing blows with fist and foot. There is only one correct way to lay these dead to rest. I must give them a funeral."

The Wraith laughed inside his mind. *"They've already had funerals. No grave can hold them!"*

Hindin struggled to shake his head. "Not a funeral of earth and stone. But a funeral of heat and flame. A funeral pyre!"

As the heat churned within him, he released the answer as he spoke the maxim, *"The mind is not a vessel to be filled but a fire to be kindled!"*

Hindin Revetz felt a new power blossom within him. And with it came a new agony.

Waist deep in hungry dead things, the Werekrilp threw its axe like skipping a stone. Deep into the Bregenite horde it spun, its blade launching heads upward and its haft bashed through skulls. As corpses dropped lifeless in its whirling path, the hematite ring tugging at his clawed finger. When the axe stopped spinning, it flew back in the direction it was thrown. The hulking brute caught the weapon and let it fly again where the land was thick with hungry dead. Slaying another three dozen before the axe returned to its grasp, the beast roared in early triumph.

The Bregenite onslaught had thinned greatly since he took the battle to them. There were still many to slay, but the odds no longer seemed over whelming. Breathing heavily through his silver helm, he turned his gaze to check on Hindin. Where the malruka had stood was now a tall mound of clawing and screaming Bregenites.

"No," he whispered in a deep rumble. "I shouldn't have left his side!" Fearful and enraged, the Werekrilp began to run toward the pile. Then he stopped, as if by instinct, and sniffed the air.

His eyes grew wide as the mound of restless death began to smolder and smoke. Fire spouted from between their bodies and the mound began to glow from within. Ancient flesh and bone and hair made dry by the centuries burst aflame. Slow-witted heads began to scream as flames danced atop their craniums.

As the high piled crowd began to disperse, the Werekrilp witnessed the flames on their heads spread down the lengths of their spines. Old musty burial clothes caught fire, and soon the Breginites were running, and falling and screaming and dying.

Rising from a pile of ash that had once been the shambling dead, the familiar shape of Hindin Revetz stood. His steel skin was cherry red and glowed in the night like a half-forged sword. As waves of heat wafted from him in all directions, he began running with terrifying speed and to chase down stray Bregenites that had not yet been burned. With strikes fast and smooth, the malrukan Chimancer chopped and palm struck the walking horrors. With each hit, the Bregenites exploded into charred bones and cinders.

The Werekrilp could only watch and laugh in amazement at the awesome sight. "We'll have this bloody battle won in no time!"

Then the ground trembled behind him as something drew near.

The Werekrilp turned back around, slowly looked upward, and knew the chill grasp of dread. "*So big...*" he thought.

"Dang it, Polly, I ain't about to watch you kill another kid!" Will stabbed the point of his scythe-rifle through the temple of an approaching Bregenite before leaping into the air and stomping the brittle skull of another.

"Den turn your back!" the crimson theurgess answered coldly. She had another baby goat in her arms.

The tendikeye followed her grudgingly as she approached another tent full of frightened fair-goers.

"Dere are too many of dese post morts. I will protect dese people de best way I know how."

Will bared his teeth. "You can't just---"

Polly looked back at him with blazing eyes. "Do not stand between a blood theurge and her sacrifice. Go make yourself useful instead."

"I *have* been! I've been killing Swans and Bregenites like crazy while following you around on yer crazy goat hunts. I've been *defending* you as you've been goin' from tent to tent spoutin' yer theurge malarkey."

Polly pouted her lower lip and feigned sympathy. "Poor baby. I thought you only followed me because you missed me. I don't really need your help, though it is appreciated. Dis is de last tent. One more ritual, den I'll let you lead dis dance again." She drew her blade and went into the tent.

Will heard it before he saw it. A pack of some thirty odd Bregenites came into view as they turned corner around an empty kissing booth. They were followed by ten young Trotting Swans armed with hachets, swords and clubs.

Hooting and laughing the Swans bashed and hacked into the pack, chopping heads and cracking skulls with ease. The Bregenites put up no fight, no resistance at all. Indeed, it was as if the stumbling corpses were oblivious to the men that were killing them.

Will's face became a grim mask. *"The Wraith is commandin' the Bregs to kill everyone but the Swans. What better way to make 'em look like heroic survivors."* He waited until they killed the last of the dead before stepping out to make his presence known.

"Hey!" he hollered, getting their attention. "You drug-runnin', soil-whorin', tough teat bitin', rump-stuffin', back-shootin', threurge-kneelers!" He raised *Falcona* and fired his last round. The bullet tore through the nearest man's pelvis, obliterating the bottom parts of his reproductive and digestive systems.

As the Swan fell dying and crying, another Swan cursed and

yelled at his companions, "We ran out of bullets!"

Will tossed *Falcona* to the ground and spread his large, empty hands. "Yeah! Well, I ran outta patience, boy!"

The nine Swans charged with weapons raised, their mouths vomiting curses and racial slurs.

Will dashed to meet the nearest man. Leaping like an angry rooster, he kicked the hatchet out of the Swan's hand and stomped at the man's face with his other boot, feeling the front of the man's nose and eye sockets crunch under his heel. Will landed in their midst and immediately dropped low, spinning like a top. His heavy footed leg extended as his hunkering body turned.

With two loud cracks, two more Swan's dropped to the ground with shattered ankles. As Will rose, a large club was about to come down on his head. He caught the man by the wrists, stepped around him while keeping hold, shoved his knee in the back of the other man's knee, and caught him in a belly-up choking neck lock as he fell back. Pushing off one foot to avoid a sword swipe to his neck, Will executed a sideways flip while twisting the belly-up man's head completely around.

Will landed lightly and let the Swan drop lifeless as he roundhouse kicked the swordsman's temple with the toe of his boot. The man dropped his sword and fell twitching on the ground. Another man with a hatchet dealt Will a glancing blow to his shoulder blade. The tendikeye stumbled forward as another broke a club over his forehead. He was stunned, but not hurt. Jumping out of the remaining crowd to avoid staying surrounded, he gave his head a shake as soon he landed.

Five Swans remained alive and uninjured. They turned clumsily to get at him. Flipping forward, he crashed his heel into a Swan's collarbone. The majestic axe kick sent the man crumbling into a screaming heap. Another Swan closed in.

Will spun and extended his leg, knocking the man's short sword from his grasp. Keeping the momentum, Will grasped the man's lapel and twisted, pulling the man off his feet and crashing him neck and head first into the gravel. Skull, soul and vertebrae shattered on the impact.

The next man came at him with a two-handed wood axe. Will did not wait for him to swing. He reached out, grasping the man's weapon and twisting it free. Stepping to the man's side, he pivoted his feet and spun, letting the back of the heavy axe bash into the side of the Swan's head. Brain and skull spat across the gravel. One Swan remained standing, the one with the broken club.

Will met his dumbfounded stare and dropped the bloody axe on the ground. "You can't outrun me," he told the hesitating Swan. He moved the front of his duster aside, revealing his Mark Twain Special. "You can't outrun bullets either. You have til the count of four to come at me with a new weapon. Wait too long, I'll gut shoot you." He saw fear bloom in the drakeri man's eyes. "One..." Will began.

The Swan shook his head, trembling.

"Two..."

The Swan's fear turned into desperation. He looked down for a new weapon, dropping his broken one.

"Three..." the tendikeye said.

The Swan's desperation turned into rage as he picked up a hatchet. Running and screaming, he came at Will wielding the blade for a downward chop to the tendikeye's skull.

Just as the hatchet came down, Will stepped into the swing, pivoting on his lead foot, ducking and spinning as he trapped the man's arm in a twisting arm lock. The Swan was bent forward, his arm held tight and twisted. The hatchet fell from trembling fingers. Maintaining his vice-like hold on the Swan's wrist, Will jumped, kicking both his feet forward. As his boots collided into the Swans ribs and head, Will pulled the trapped arm until his own body was straight and level with the ground.

"ROOSTER PULLS WORM!!!!" the tendikeye shouted as the man's ribs and jaw shattered and the arm popped loose at the shoulder socket. The tendikeye felt his back smack the gravel. In an instant, he was back on his feet, victorious. Pacing around his fallen foes, he stomped the heads and necks of the survivors, all but three.

Will spat, looking down at the three still living. "Usin' the soil to grow that poison drug flower. That's like forcin' yer own mother to be a whore fer yer own luxury. If you nancies had farmer's muscles, you mighta beat me."

"Please," one Swan with a snapped ankle wept. He looked scarcely older than fifteen. "Please. You win. Please, don't kill us."

Will tilted his head and noticed the young Swan wore a lavender silk scarf around his neck. It had gold thread sewn in it. He

512

knelt down without even looking the Swan in the eye and removed it. "This is purdy, fine quality, too. How'd ya pay fer it? Where'd ya get it?" He looked sternly at the Swan's face, waiting for an answer.

"Y-You can keep it!"

Will slapped the tears off of him. "Where'd ya get it? How'd' ya pay fer it? Some fancy city shop while makin' one 'o yer drug runs?"

The young Swan nodded, terrified.

Will nodded also, his mouth a relaxed frown. "Okay then."

He grasped the Swan by the hair and dragged him sobbing and pissing closer to the other Swan with the broken ankle. He placed the scarf over his shoulders and dragged the man with the shattered collarbone closer to the other two.

The three men begged and bawled as he knelt over them.

Ignoring their cries, he went to work dislocating wrists, elbows, and shoulders. Will was casual about it, as if he were merely breaking twigs for a campfire.

He had finished by the time Polly stepped out of the tent. Will stood over the three Swans with his arms crossed and a cigarette in his mouth. The Swans were laying on their sides belly to back.

Polly saw their right arms and almost laughed and threw up at the same time. "You... braided deir arms together," she said, seeing the lavender scarf around their limp wrists tied into a fluffy bow.

Will pinched the cigarette out of his lips. "I used to braid my sister's quills when I was a boy."

Polly stared wide-eyed at the three Swans. The one in the middle was dying of shock. The other two had passed out. "You'll have to braid my hair sometime. When it grows back out." It was all she could think of to say.

Will grinned. "Sure thing. Now, let's go hunt us a wraith!" He picked up *Falcona,* folded her up, and slid her into his rawhide carrying case. "Sorry, girl," he whispered to his rifle. "I'm all outta bullets. But as soon as this is over, I promise to give you a good cleanin'."

Together, the tendikeye and the drakeress ran through the Fairgrounds toward the front gate (or what was left of it).

On the way there, they came upon a pack of Bregenites.

513

Their rotten faces growled, scowled, yowled, and howled stupid and fierce.

Will was just about to draw his machete and pistol when Polly raised her hand. "No need," she told him.

"All their blood is dried up Polly," Will contended. "Yer maxims won't work on 'em."

Polly shrugged. "Dere is more to reality dan words of wisdom. Dere are also actions of wisdom." She raised her hands, unleashing her snake-like veins from her wrists. The slithering tendrils were smooth save for a clawed barb at the end of each vein. The veins seemed to attack with their own primal instinct. Like burrowing vipers they stabbed into the eye sockets of the Bregenites, twisting and pulling inside their skulls, rending and shredding brain.

"Just like picking locks!" she laughed as they dropped in twos and threes not ten feet from her.

Will lost count of all the Bregenites she slew that way on the way to their friends at the fence.

When they reached the front, they saw the tall, lithe body of Hindin glowing red, yellow, and orange in the dark of night. The malruka moved like a flickering flame amidst a dying tide of burning dead. Will and Polly watched in awe as the Chimancer chopped with blazing hands, smashing Bregenites skulls and setting their lifeless bodies ablaze. But with each successful strike, Hindin's skin seemed to grow dimmer. As they made their way closer to their friend, they caught glimpses of his face—full of pain, fear, and desperation.

"Come no further!" Hindin called out to them as he fought. "The heat...the heat is too...much. I must get rid of it...expel it all before..." And then he screamed.

Bending over and clenching his stomach, the malruka dropped to his knees and vomited lava onto the gravel-strewn ground. With every gushing heave of liquid rock, Hindin grew thinner. Finally, when a huge glowing puddle covered the ground, he stopped.

His steel skin had cooled, yet waves of heat still came off it. "I...I was not ready to cast that maxim," he said with a cough. "I could not expel all that heat out of me in time. But it was the only way." He held up his hands and gasped. "My fingers!" His sad

514

emerald eyes shifted to Will and Polly. "My fingers have fused together!

❖

Röger, the Werekrilp, did not know which to fight first--the encroaching twenty-foot tall golem made of dirt-crusted coffins and grave markers to his left or the forty-foot long, thirty feet high schoolhouse with an unnatural gait on four stumpy legs made of broken planks from its side walls crawling toward him from the right. The walking pair of horrors were at the bottom of a sloping hill littered with slain Bregenites and bullet-ridden wagons and coaches.

The casket golem's forearms, thighs, shins, and upper arms were each composed of a single casket filled with stone grave markers. Its body was a twin-sized sarcophagus depicting a man and wife at rest. Its feet and fists were massive granite headstones. And its head was an ornately carved statue of a dragon with splayed wings and a roaring head. At the base of the statue, a plaque read: *For our loving son, Juniper Beech.*

The schoolhouse beast was just a giant box of dead wood that walked. But its huge, heavy front door swung in and out like a sideways mouth opening and closing. A small box frame mounted on the roof's peak blazed with an eerie blue light like a glowing cycloptic eye. As the schoolhouse beast shambled forth, the glowing eye rang, revealing itself to be the school's summoning bell, only no little children were running to the building with books in hand. The bell's chime pierced ear and soul alike as it was a supernatural one note dirge of dread.

The Werekrilp roared back in answer, its axe held high in defiant challenge. The monster charged down the slope, leaping over wagons as it descended toward the haunted building. He heard the Wraith speak to him inside his helmet and skull. *"Come to school, Werekrilp! Come and learn that silver is not the only metal that can hurt you!"*

With each stride, the bell grew louder and flashed brighter.

515

"It's just a stupid building! Another haunted house!" the Werekrilp thought. *"I'll smash it to pieces and then fight the golem."*

As the Werekrilp drew near, the light of the clanging school bell touched his eyes inside its silver helm. An eerie chill touched the monster's chest. Through a wall of fur and muscle the chill crept. Shivering violently the monster stopped some twenty feet from the building, lifting a thick arm to shield its eyes from the harsh blue light. The sound of the bell shook the soul loose from the body. The cold that had crept in froze the soul rigid. The Werekrilp fell lifeless, shrinking back into a human corpse. Sir Röger Yamus found himself floating to the open school door.

"You are a ghost now, my friend," the Wraith said. *"The hunter has become the haunted."*

As the Wraith laughed, Röger knew only terror. He drifted through the doorway, the once frail-looking building an inescapable prison as the old gray planks of wood sucked at his spirit from all sides.

◇

The remaining Trotting Swans came running to the front. Will, Polly, and Hindin turned to face them. But it soon became obvious that the Swans were running away from something.

"Are the bregs turnin' on 'em?" Will asked, drawing his Mark Twain Special and yashinin machete.

Polly's eyes flashed red as a smile possessed her lips. She raised her hands, her thorny veins whipping free.

Hindin rose reluctantly to stand and fight. He was near as thin as a skeleton, having thrown up much of his granite and gold interior. The medal of honor had melted to his chest, the ribbon that once held it burnt away. The medal had not been gold, only plated. Now it was nothing more than a splotch of some crude form of iron. "They must not escape justice," he said, his voice weak and tired.

No sooner than Hindin spoken the words than the three of them saw that justice was already gaining on the Swan's heels. For it was not a horde of Bregenites that chased them, but common folk.

A group of dark-skinned human's led the mob. Behind them were drakeri men, women, and children, many carrying makeshift

516

clubs and sticks. They were all yelling and howling, a mix of fear and rage in their eyes as they beat their weapons against the fleeing Swans.

"Traitors!" members of the mob yelled. "Liars! Deceivers! Murderers!"

"What's happening?" Will asked his friends. He fired a shot into the air to get the crowd's attention.

Some stopped, most continued to beat, kick and surround, the thirty-odd Swans.

Suddenly, the darkness of the autumn night filled with radiant red rays. It was as if a hunvein from above had appeared among them. It was a heatless light, but red as any ember. The light penetrated everyone and everything, leaving no shadows. In that moment, all that existed was the color red. No one moved or made a sound.

"*Red means STOP,*" Polly's voice called through the redness. "Put down your crude clubs and sticks, for you deny de De Red River if you do not spill blood. Use blades to commit your murders. Blood must flow, not be trapped in a corpse's shell to thicken and rot."

A nervous laugh erupted from Will. "Don't listen to her, folks! She's only kiddin'. Hey, Pol, turn off this light show, would ya?"

The redness dimmed and all became visible again. Everyone now saw where the light had come from. Polly Gone still glowed dimly, her veins like hot red worms beneath her lavender skin.

"What is the meaning of this?" Hindin asked the crowd. "How came you all to know that the Trotting Swans were in league with the Wraith Count?

A tall, bald, dark-skinned human stepped forward. His eyes were fierce and his teeth were bared in a grim frown. He held up his hand to show that it was full of old rotten knuckle bones. "I am LëCuk the Undertaker. I took these knuckle bones from the first Bregenite I slew. Through them, I've been listening to the Wraith give the Swans telepathic orders to kill us all while still looking like heroes. You three and your monster are not the only ones who've been combating the horde.

"With my brothers and friends, I assembled this mob, ridding each of us of the necrofear. Together, we slew most of the

517

remaining walking dead." LëCuk spat and regarded the Swans huddling and cowering at his feet. "And together, we will put an end to the Trotting Swans' reign of terror and economic oppression."

"You are a necrotheurge?" Polly asked, her words dripping with acid.

LëCuk inclined his head, a smug grin revealing bright white teeth. "I am a climber of the Bone Ladder, yes. But I am no more evil than you are, blood woman."

"These men deserve a trial," Hindin protested.

"I respectfully disagree," LëCuk said. The mob behind him shouted in agreement.

Will put away his weapons and raised his empty hands. Letting out a strained sigh as he approached the lanky undertaker. "Now, see here an' hear me out, LëCuk. I've never been one fer diplomatic measures, but here goes: I commend you fer yer bravery in roundin' up these sacks o' dung. But can we hold off on killin'em all fer a bit? Wouldn't it be sweeter to make 'em all confess their crimes in front o' the whole county? That way the facts'll be known as all can be set right without a hitch."

LëCuk scoffed. "You suggest a lawful procedure of justice? The law is twisted in Wraith County, sir. The Swans saw to that."

"Not *all* the law is twisted," a man called from the darkness.

Limping slowly, the battered form of Drume Arteen emerged, covered in cuts and bruises, his left eye swollen shut. On his chest was the blood-crusted badge once worn by Thrush Raisinbread. "Lower your weapons, everyone. The battle is all but done."

He limped over to LëCuk and put a hand on his shoulder. "You've done well, undertaker. As the new Sheriff of Drowsy Nook, I am deputizing you right now. Help me bring order and law to this county once more. The Swans are defeated. Let's sort them out later. Have a few civilians stay to guard them."

He raised his voice to address the mob. "There are still more than a few Bregenites haunting the area. They won't enter the tents but they are still a danger to the county should they escape the Fairgrounds. I'm not done hunting these rotten freaks. Who is with me?"

At first, no one answered. Then LëCuk shrugged his broad shoulders. "I would be most handsome in a lawman's uniform. And my back hurts from digging too many graves. Lead the way, Sheriff."

The mob cheered in approval.

As as the two lawmen gave orders on who would watch over the Swans and who would join the hunting party, Polly approached the Sheriff with a proud grin on her lips. "I see you have an ouchy. Let momma kiss it." She stood on her tip-toes and pressed her lips against his swollen eye. In a matter of seconds, his cut and bruises faded away.

Blinking hard with both eyes, Sheriff Drume looked down adoringly at the little bloodtheurge. "Thank you," he said.

"Tank me by making a new law," she returned. "All executions in Apple County shall be administered by blood loss."

The Sheriff did not know whether to laugh or frown, so he did both. "Um..."

"This is still Wraith County," LëCuk interrupted. He pointed in the direction of the slope where the wagons were kept.

From somewhere in the distance came the eerie chiming of a bell. "Down that slope you will find Count Slanidrac and your monster friend Röger. The Count is still in wraith form in the Zeroth Dimension. But he watches and commands dead wood and dead stone and dead metal to kill you and all who remain in the tents." He looked at Polly. "Your blood markings will not serve in protecting the people from what is at the bottom of that slope. You three must descend to combat it."

Will shook his head, trying in vain to make sense of the man's words. "I can't make heads or tails outta what yer sayin'!"

LëCuk only shrugged as he turned away. "All I know is what I've said. I've been too shunting busy to get a clear divination, much less interpret it. Death is at the bottom of that hill, and it will not wait. It will come to us all unless a Storm gathers to wash it away. Make of that what you will."

They all heard a monstrous roar abruptly cut short by the bell's chime.

Both Polly and LëCuk gasped and clenched their hands to their chests. He looked at her with wide eyes and said, "You felt it, too, didn't you?"

Polly's eyes filled with tears as she began to breathe hard and heavy.

519

"Polly, what is it?" Hindin asked, placing a hand on her upper back.

"It's Röger!" she sobbed. "His heart stopped!"

Beyond the broken gate and the torn down fence, the slope was littered with ruin. The wagons and coaches which had brought the fair-goers were broken and full of bullets. The beasts that had pulled them were in the same condition, only their brains and spines had been torn out by the invading dead for sustenance. Here and there lay the corpses of men and boys who were not Trotting Swans; who had not been warned about the Regiocalypse. Most of them were headless with spines also missing. And beyond count were the remains of slain Bregenites wearing dirt and the clothes they had been buried in. In life they had been men, women, children, crones, and geezers. But death had made them monsters. Half had died by bullets, the other half by the Werekrilp's axe, Headlauncher.

But the axe and its monstrous master had also fallen. It was plain to see in the pulsing glow of the chiming schoolhouse bell at the slope's bottom. Röger lay face down, naked in the grass not twenty feet from the walking building. The huge casket golem was stomping its way toward him in a slow but steady gait.

The brightness of Polly's skin intensified, making her become a red beacon in contrast to the pale blue light of the schoolhouse bell. She was the first to scream in outrage and the first to charge down the hill.

Will matched her scream and drew his machete and pistol. As he ran and leapt down the littered slope, he fired every shot at the Casket Golem.

Hindin charged as well. And though he remained silent as he ran, his face and heart still contained the same vengeful determination of his friends.

"Stop dat ting!" Polly shouted as she leapt over a carcass. "I might be able to save him!"

"Oh, I'll get it!" Will answered. He had made it down the slope and emptied his gun in a matter of seconds while the others still made their decent. Each bullet hit the casket golem in its left leg

520

to little affect.

The Golem was getting closer to Röger's body, close enough to catch the pounding light from the bell on its lumbering form.

Will pushed his feet against the ground and launched himself through the air, his blade raised to hack at the stone dragon atop the Golem's shoulders. He could feel the *necrofear,* but ignored it. The Golem's 'head' was no *Drageist.*

Screaming fury and rage, he swung his yashinin blade in a diagonal cut, shearing through the stone statue and severing the dragon's head and one of its wings. Will's boots planted themselves on the Golem's shoulders, his legs balanced, his blade held high for another swung.

And then the bell chimed. Its eerie light flashed on the tendikeye and his heart stopped. The last thing Will heard was Polly scream. He and his weapons fell lifeless to the ground. His blue-gray eyes were wide open, staring at nothing, oblivious to the Golem raising its massive arms to crush him to pulp.

Hindin did not understand what had happened. He thought Will had merely lost his balance, fell, and was stunned. All he knew was that the Golem was about to crush his friend. He charged and leapt, a near half ton of steel-skin and granite muscle. His inner fire had weakened him, but in that instant, he was strong. He leapt ten feet up and through the air, higher than any Malruka had a right to, and slammed his palm into the sarcophagus body of the Casket Golem, right between the stone depictions of the husband and wife.

With its heavy arm raised high, the Golem tottered backwards, and fell. The bell rang once more, and both Hindin and the Golem crashed unmoving onto the ground. Hindin landed next to Will, and now shared the same still, cold, stare of death. The Golem crumbled to nothing more than broken stone and shattered wood.

Polly fell to her knees at the foot of the slope in the presence of the ringing schoolhouse bell, fearing her friends were dead. As she looked at them, tears of blood spilled from her eyes like tea from a teapot. Too shaken to scream, too grieved to move, Polly only knelt there in the grass as the wind passed through her short hair and small cape, listening to the chiming of the bell and blinking against its cold blue light. She felt many a terrible thing: fear, sorrow, loss... But she did not feel powerless.

521

She rose to her feet. "Give dem back to me. Dey are *mine*."

The voice of the Wraith spoke to her. "*This is where your philocreed path ends, red witch. Death is where all paths lead. It is the one same end, the only truth. How can an advocate for murder such as you be so willing to deny these men their ultimate fate?*"

Polly grinded her teeth. "De way you murder is unclean, unnatural," she returned. "Dey were fighters. If dey were meant to die, it should have been by loss of blood."

The Wraith laughed. "*I had hoped for that. But you killed my Hemogoblin. Cleverly done, I must admit. But not as clever as how I killed your comrades. Have you figured it out yet? Why they are dead and you still live? No? Take a minute to think about it. And while you do so, I will send some comrades of my own to play with you!*"

From the rubble of the broken Golem's chest arose the withered forms of a man and a woman. The man was dressed in a fine tailored suit. The woman wore a wedding dress of pale samite and white lace. At first, it looked as if the couple were holding hands. But after second look, Polly saw they were both holding the handle of the same knife, a broad carving blade.

"*Meet Mr. and Mrs. Obashawn. Legend has it that a jilted ex-lover poisoned their wedding cake. Together they cut the first piece and licked both sides of the blade clean, as was the custom in those days. No sooner did they finish lapping the icing off the metal than they dropped dead right there in front of their families. Thus they died and thus they were entombed, both still clutching the blade. But I will let you in on something, it was neither lover or poison that did them in. It was all my doing.*"

The Wraith's voice took on a more oratorical tone. "*Dearly Departed, I have summoned you here tonight to lay waste to my enemies. Do you Mr. and Mrs. Obashawn, solemnly swear to murder this bitch in the fashion she so respects?*"

"We do," said the post mort couple in unison. They were two bodies, but they moved as one. Light-footed and agile, they came at Polly, matching each other's steps perfectly.

The Blood Theurgess backed off for distance and summoned her veins. Without hesitation, she sent the barbed tendrils at the couple's eyes. Their reaction was lightning quick as they swiped their knife, slicing two feet of vein from a tendril.

Polly hissed at the pain and drew her veins back into her arms. *"Dese are no clumsy Bregenites,"* she thought.

As the couple closed in they tried to grasp her shoulders with their free hands while stabbing her chest with their blade. Polly planted her feet and let them try. She held out her forearm as if holding a shield and let the blade stab into it, through it, until the blade was trapped between her arm bones. Then she twisted her arm downward, ignoring the agony of the wound, and used her other hand to try to wrench the knife free from the couple's grasp. The husband and wife's fingers were as strong as steel, but their wrists were brittle as twigs. Their hands snapped off, still clinging the blade.

Polly let out a yelp of pain.

Mr. and Mrs. Obashawn went still and crumbled into piles of dust and bone, as did their severed hands.

Polly yanked the knife from her bleeding arm, grunting as she did so. Her eyes flashed red as the slit-hole in her arm healed shut.

Breathing hard, she said, "My mother and I used to knife spar all de time. She would use dat move to disarm me often. I was always too scared to try it." A smug grin appeared on her panting lips. "I figured it out, Wraith. Why my friends are dead and I am not." She held up the knife. "Dis blade is hematite. Poison did not kill dem. A cursed metal did. De metal's necromagnetic pull leached out deir souls and cursed deir bodies, yes? Deir love for each other must have activated it. Dey were ever bonded together in death through de connection of dis knife. Hematite augments your necrotheurgy, extends it. Anyway, I'm taking my friends back now. Feel free to try and stop me. I can smell your sweet disappointment in de air."

As the schoolhouse bell kept up its eerie chime and pulsing blue light, Polly made her way over to Röger. Kneeling beside him, she took the knife she held and cut the ribbon that held his medal of heroism. Polly examined the medal. Much of the gold plating had been scratched off during the battle, revealing the hematite beneath it. She went over and did the same with Will.

When she came to Hindin, she had to pry the melted metal from his chest using the knife. It wasn't easy, but with proper leverage it came loose. Polly stepped before the schoolhouse and

523

held up the three medals.

"*A very clever girl,*" the Wraith said. "*But if you want their spirits back you'll have to come inside and face the horrors within.*"

Polly took a deep breath, sighed, and closed her eyes. "No tank you. I've had enough schooling. For example: I know dat hematite is just another form of iron. And irons rusts." She dropped the knife and medals in the grass and raised her hands high, aiming them at the chiming bell. In a loud screech, she yelled, "*As iron is eaten away by rust, so the envious are consumed by their own passion.*"

Two jets of blood came out of her palms, drenching the high chiming bell. Its blue light turned red and the sound of the chiming became duller and duller with each ring, until finally the bell eroded into a dripping hunk of scrap.

Will, Röger, and Hindin sat up, alive and gasping.

Will winced as he knuckled his eyes. "Ah! My eyes dried out! They were left open too long!" He blinked hard several times to get the surface of his eyes wet again. "What just happened?"

"I do not know," answered Hindin as he got up. "We were fighting the Golem. And then suddenly we were sitting in a classroom together."

"I remember," Röger said, picking up his axe and not caring about his nakedness. "The Wraith was in there with us, telling us he was going to teach us to be obedient ghosts. He even threatened to put a dunce cap on Will for mouthing off."

"Yeah!" exclaimed the tendikeye, looking offended.

The three bewildered men gathered around Polly as she stood facing the shambling schoolhouse. Its plank legs had collapsed beneath it, making it look little more than a ruin of rotted wood. Still, they could all feel the *necrofear* emanating from it.

"He's still in dere, hiding," Polly muttered as she crossed her arms.

"It must be destroyed," Hindin said.

"I could chop it up," Röger offered, spinning his axe.

Will made a sound of disgust. "You go find some pants to cover yer shame with, tripod. I'll take care o' this haunted shack." Reaching behind his shoulder, Will pulled a slender leather tube from his rifle's carrying case. "Lucky this didn't tear," he said with a

524

half-grin. Opening the end of the tube, he pulled out a rolled up piece of cloth about two feet long. It stank like an alchemist's lab. He unrolled it, showing it to be a square sheet of cotton, and held it daintily by the corners. It was damp and one side was covered with a jelly-like substance.

Polly raised her chin in understanding. "Dat is a war blanket, yes?"

Will nodded. "I was savin' it fer yer momma. I was gonna tie it 'round her neck like a bib an' set her ablaze. But the sooner we smoke this spook out the better."

He ran up to the side of the building and swung the cloth at the dry planks. The war-blanket made a wet splat sound and stuck to the wall. Will whipped out his flip top lighter and woke the small flame. No sooner did the fire kiss the sticky rag that the entire cloth made a whoosh sound and erupted in green and yellow flames.

The schoolhouse went up like the tinderbox it was. Dry, old wood was rapidly turning into smoke, fire, and ash. And as the fires reached high into the night, Will reloaded his Mark Twain Special and Röger put on a pair of pants he'd stripped off a slain Bregenite.

"It is not yet over," Hindin uttered as he peered at the blaze.

"How ya figure?" Will asked.

Hindin's eyes grew wide. "The flames. They are are telling me so." The malruka stood as still as a gaunt statue, his once silvery skin now scorched black and pitted.

Will's face went red with anger. "Rev, I warned you. I WARNED you to not read them fire books! Look what it's done to you!"

Hindin wanted to argue. But no words came. He held his fused fingers and withered arms up to his emerald eyes, and regarded them sadly. *"What have I done to myself?"* he thought.

Then the Wraith appeared before the four of them. He did not appear as the handsome drakeri, Count Slanidrac, but as the dried up corpse of an old human with a hematite peg leg. The four friends felt an odd calm come over them.

"All the necrofear is gone," Will thought as he beheld the bent, pitiful thing standing before him.

"I admit defeat," the Wraith said in a strained, hollow voice. "On my *philocreed*, I am done. I was a restless spirit up until this point. Let this miserable county have its apples. I am done caring.

525

The great storm has come and washed away all that I have built."
He met their eyes, one by one. "But let it be known that the one who
destroys me will be forever accursed. The wraithslayer will never be
able to make children, will never find relief in a lover's touch. They
will grow old and bent before their time and know nothing but
sorrow for the rest of their days." He bared his rotten teeth and
shriveled tongue. "Who will it be? Who will be the one to finish what
the four of you have started?"

"I've lived long enough," Röger said with a shrug. "Plus, I'm
no stranger to curses." He took his axe and swung with all his might
at the gleaming peg leg. But some invisible force stopped the blow
just inches before it connected.

The Wraith grinned. "My peg and that axe are both
easterly-charged magnets. No amount of brute force can make them
touch. You are not the one to slay me, monster."

Hindin stepped up and kicked at the leg. Over and over he
tried, but it would not break.

The Wraith shook his head and laughed. "You are a
Chimancer no longer, malruka. You threw up all the precious gold
that ran throughout your body. You are a walkin ruin just like me."

Hindin backed away, looking as if he were about to weep.
"No..."

Polly looked up at her malrukan friend, trying to think of
words or actions that might comfort him. But then she looked at the
Wraith and hate replaced all her sympathy. She pointed her hand at
the peg leg and began to say *"As iron is eaten away by rust..."*

Will grabbed her wrist, gently, before she could finish the
maxim. She looked at him defiantly. The tendikeye only shook his
head at her, brought her hand to his lips, kissed her palm, and let go.
Polly frowned and stepped back.

Will regarded the Wraith, who was smiling brightly now.

"You'll do, tendikeye," the Wraith said with satisfaction.

Will let out a heavy, determined sigh and drew his Mark
Twain Special. He took careful aim at the peg leg. It would be a
perfect shot. Both bullets would shatter it to bits. Then he tilted his
head, and his brow furrowed in thought.

"Why are you hesitating?" laughed the Wraith. "Are you
finally afraid?"

Will shook his head in answer as he holstered his weapon.

"Naw, jus' had a crazy thought is all." He reached into his dust coat and pulled out another weapon. It was the large cobalt pistol he had won from his duel with Daddy Long Legs. He held it up for the Wraith to see. "Yer the one who made this, ain'tcha?"

The Wraith smiled with pride. "I am. That was the weapon that slew my master. How fitting that you'll use it to slay me!"

Will shrugged and nodded, "Yeah, about that. Well, the way I figure it, since yer the one who crafted the weapon, an' that same weapon is used to kill you, then it'd be more you killin' you than me killin' you, ya know?"

The Wraith scrunched his brow and his mouth opened. He raised a boney finger in objection. "Now, wait just a minute!"

Will did not wait. He pointed the barrel and fired. The peg snapped in the middle and the Wraith ceased to exist.

Throughout the county in fields and meadows and forests, every single gray dust blossom shriveled and died. Throughout the long dormant orchards that had once made the county famous, apple trees began to bud and flower. Beneath the surface of the soil, countless stagnant spirits exploded and their shards moved on. Every haunt became cleansed. Every ghost in every town yet unvisited came to an end. And all *necrofear* vanished from the hearts and minds of the living. The Geohex had been lifted.

The people of the fair emerged from their tents no longer afraid. They carried their children past the bodies of slain Bregenites, traitorous Swans, and fallen local heroes. And although there was no fear, there was still grief for the hundreds of fair-goers who had died that night. The grief and relief that it was now over drew tears from nearly every eye. Together, the people walked to the front of the Fairgrounds, over the broken fence, to behold the burning building at the bottom of the slope and the four heroes who stood before it.

For centuries hence, the people of Apple County would argue over who started the solemn chant.

"Four Winds-One Storm! Four Winds-One Storm!"

Before long, thousands of throats joined the chant and thousands of fists were raised in the air. The four words repeated over and over was not the cheering praise of an adoring crowd, but of the loud, solemn thanks of good, decent folk. The stink and sight of death was still all around them. Their hearts were heavy and many had questions yet unanswered about the night's terrifying events. Yet still, they chanted for the heroes who had saved them.

"Four Winds-One Storm! Four Winds-One Storm!"

And as the swollen crowd slowly began to descend the littered slope the heroes gazed up at them.

"*I am glad for this happy distraction,*" Hindin thought. "*For it seems I have walked two philocreed paths at once and crashed into myself. The wraith was right. I am lost and my chi is stifled. Yet, as I see the faces of these good people I get the sense that it was a sacrifice well made. I can only hope I feel the same in the future.*"

"*Their harvests will be plentiful, I jus' know it,*" Will thought as he beamed with esteem. "*An' not jus' the caven nuts, but the apples, too. People will work honest an' live honest again. I wish you could see this, Brem.*" Will frowned as more names and faces came to mind. "*Lili, Momma, Clawd..... I wish you could see it, too.*"

"*I'm wearing a dead man's pants,*" Röger thought, slightly sickened by it. "*Someone's going to see a headless, pantsless Bregenite and then see me, and put two and two together. Oh well. It's not as bad as people knowing I'm a lycanthrope now. Some of these people must have seen me beast out. My secret won't be safe for long. I'll have to run to a new huncell. Would the others come with me? I'll have to talk about it with them later.*"

"*I hate people,*" Polly thought as she politely smiled and waved. "*I like dem when dey are one at a time, some of de time. Dis is just like shunting Embrenil. All de silly, happy faces coming to tank us. Only now I have no where to run.*" She couldn't help but laugh at herself. "*Maybe I should grow up and learn to be more welcoming. I'm starting to tink like my - - NO!*" Her heart shook violently in her chest.

Shots rang out from the road behind them. Some of the bullets hit the burning building, others whizzed past their heads. The Four Winds turned to see twelve Trotting Swans armed with guns and blades, the steel of their weapons illuminated by the firelight. Polly recognized the biggest of them as Fulton Gladish

528

from Barnhart.

The descending crowd abruptly stopped and ran back toward the Fairgrounds.

"Get behind the building!" Will shouted.

The three others reacted accordingly, running for cover behind the blaze.

As they huddled on the safe side of the building, Will pulled out his Mark Twain Special. "There's twelve o' them, an' I got twelve bullets. You all jus' hang back an' let me cut'em down."

"Will, no! You can't! Listen to me!" Polly protested.

"They'll be blinded by the fire!" he interrupted. "I'll see them, but they won't see me so well. I can do it! I'll be fine! They won't!"

Polly shook her head. "You don't understand! My mother, she's out dere somewhere. I can sense her!"

Will was excited and determined still, but a wave of doubt passed over his expression. "Well, we'll jus' hafta worry about her after. I got Swans to kill."

Just as he was about to turn and run off, Polly grabbed the collar of his jacket. "Give me your canteen!" she told him.

"What? Why?"

"Just give it to me and go!"

Will complied without hesitation. He unhooked his round tin canteen from his belt and handed it to her. Then he was off.

Hindin and Röger watched as Polly unscrewed the canteen's lid and dumped out the water. They heard more gunshots. Most sounded like Will's gun.

Using her dagger, Polly slashed her wrist and let the blood gush into the canteen until it filled up completely. By the time she was done, Polly's lavender skin looked pale white. She raised the canteen to her lips and whispered, *"De soul cannot dwell in dust; it is carried along to dwell in blood."* The inner contents glowed red. She reached into her pocket and pulled out one of two large garnets that had been the eyes of Edifice Teige. She dropped the eye-gem into the canteen and twisted the cap back on.

"Got'em all!" they heard Will call out over the crackling flames and sudden silence.

Polly took a deep breath and handed Röger the canteen. "Keep this safe, no matter what," she told him.

The big man's silver helm nodded as he hooked it to his belt

529

loop. "Okay," he said, worriedly.

Röger, Polly, and Hindin walked out toward the gravel road where they saw Will standing amongst the freshly killed.

Polly nervously looked left and right with almost every step. "Dis has to be a trap. Where is she? Where?" But all she saw was darkness, her friends, and a dozen dead men.

The men were all lying side by side, sharing the same large pool of blood beneath them. One bullet had been spent on each man. Polly beheld the pale corpse of Fulton Gladish. Half of his neck had been blown off. *"His sons will be heartbroken,"* she thought.

"I jus' don't get it!" Will exclaimed, perplexed as he paced in front of the row of bodies. "They didn't even fan out. They stayed clustered shoulder to shoulder. An' they were the worst shots I ever saw. Not one bullet or pellet even got close enough fer my ears to pick up on." He turned around to face his friends. "It was the dangdest thing."

It all happened at once.

The blood which had drained from the dead Swans and pooled beneath them came to life. It gathered and rose into the shape of a curvacious drakeri woman. Dark liquid became skin, cloth, and hair as Veluora the Red Witch of Chume reached out and lightly brushed the side of Will's neck with her fingers.

As her eyes flashed red, the tendikeye fell unconscious. "He is far too pretty to die quickly," she said with a cruel smile. She met the shocked gaze of her daughter. "Wouldn't you agree, Polmeeshia?"

Polly screamed. She screamed in rage, defiance, fear, and helplessness. Helpless, but not hopeless.... "Mother, wait!" she shouted, holding up her hands. "Please, don't hurt dem!"

Hindin and Röger backed off by instinct, both taking fighting stances.

Veluora placed a red boot atop the back of the sleeping tendikeye at her feet, as if claiming him. "A patient killer is an effective killer!" she shouted. Quick as a cat, she ran over him and planted a solid kick to her daughter's stomach.

Polly doubled over, coughing.

"Just in case one of dem knocked you up, baby girl."

Röger came in with a swinging chop intended for the witch's neck.

Veluora ducked under it and drew a thin spike from her sleeve. Side stepping the raging brute, she jammed the spike deep and hard under his left arm.

Röger's body stiffened and his eyes widened inside his helm. "Oh," was all he uttered as he fell. Blood gushed from the wound.

"*Silver!*" Polly thought as she watched the red liquid pump out.

Hindin advanced on Veluora with a series of puma strikes and kicks. He was not as fast or strong as he once had been.

Veluora dodged him again and again as she cackled with teasing delight. "I do not need to harden my skin *dis* time," she laughed. "By my blood, I did not need to de last time either!"

A rope-thick vein slithered out of her wrist and coiled itself around Hindin's ankle. With a hard jerk, she pulled him off his feet.

As the malruka crashed back-first onto the ground, he saw Veluora point an open hand at him. "*As iron is eaten away by rust, so the envious are consumed by their own passion.*"

Hindin turned his head just as the dark liquid spewed onto it. The corrosive blood burned worse than fire as it ate away half of his face and ear. Pain immeasurable left him screaming and squirming on the ground.

"Let dem live and I will go wit' you!" Polly pleaded, getting to her feet.

Veluora turned, all poise and perfection and power. "Oh? So you can run away again someday? I tink not!"

Polly spat. "I will swear on our *philocreed* dat I will not run until I am powerful enough to kill you!"

Veluora sneered. "You've so far made a mockery of our *philocreed*, you foolish child! You heal blood dat is not ours wit' out enthralling dem! You kill to appease others and not yourself. You even twisted your own name! You are so lost and confused. Look at you, too drained to even fight back!"

Polly nodded in agreement. "My power is mostly spent, mother. You knew dat. Dat's why you only came now, no? You were too afraid to attack us when we were at full strength."

Veluora arched an eyebrow and crossed her arms. "Polmeeshia, you are doing little good to negotiate for dese men's lives. If you will but swear to end dis silly excursion and come back to me and swear to never run away again, den I will stop killing your

531

pets."

"Done," Polly answered as her eyes flashed. "I swear dat I will go wit' you and never run away again. By our *philocreed*, I swear!"

Veluora clapped her hands, satisfied. "Done den!" She placed a finger to her bottom lip and surveyed the fallen men on the ground. "Now. De tendikeye is only sleeping. De malruka should live, I tink. Your only concern is de Werekrilp. I'm afraid his heart is quite ruined from dat silver spike I gave him. In five or so minutes, his brain will die from lack of oxygen."

"I know what to do," said Polly bitterly. She turned around to walk to the road where the dead Swans lay.

Veluora raised her brows. "Yes, but *can* you do it?"

"Watch me," Polly muttered. She stepped up to the fresh corpses of the Swan's on the ground. She held out her hands to them one by one, as if feeling heat from a fire.

"Need any help?" her mother teased.

Polly ignored her to concentrate. When she stepped over the corpse of Fulton Gladish, she let out a wary sigh. "Dis one is de best match." Kneeling down, she unsheathed her dagger and cut open his shirt, then his chest. Making expert cuts she trimmed all the veins and arteries that connected the heart to the body and pulled the warm, sticky organ free.

By the time she turned around to carry the heart to Röger, she saw that her mother had already removed the ruined heart from his chest as well. Polly glared at Veluora in contempt.

"What?" Veluora asked, spreading her bloody hands. "I felt like helping. De sooner you put dat heart in de better."

Polly knelt and placed the heart inside her friend, fighting not to cry. The tears came and flowed freely down her cheeks, but she would not sob in front of *her*. Polly took a deep breath and with the last of her power she cried out the words. "*Good healing always tastes bitter!*"

She watched and hoped as the new heart attached itself to the new network of blood vessals. Just as the chest closed up, she saw the heart beginning to pump.

"Well done. He will live," her mother said, placing a hand on her shoulder. "Come, daughter. Let's leave dis nightmare."

As Polly rose, she heard Hindin calling weakly up at her.

532

"Polly...Polly, please no...Renounce your *philocreed*. It is better to lose that than your freedom." He was hard to look at. Thin and frail looking. Half of the steel skin on his head was gone, exposing the granite core beneath. One of his emerald eyes had fallen out from lack of an eyelid to hold it in place. "Do not go," he cried.

That is when she broke down. "Goodbye, Hindin," she said, quaking. "Please, tell dem I said goodbye when dey wake up. I need to go home now."

"We aren't going home," Veluora said flatly.

"What?" Polly turned to her. "We aren't going back to the chateau in Chume?" She made sure she said those words loud enough for Hindin to hear and understand.

Veluora shrugged. "We will have to make a stop dere, to be sure. But I have another destination in mind. You see, Polmeeshia, I blame myself for you running away. I cannot provide you de discipline you need. We are going to a place where you can properly learn to be de theurge you were meant to become."

Polly did her best to look and sound innocent. "Where exactly?"

Veluora laughed and glanced at Hindin on the ground. "I will tell you on de way, my sweet." She latched onto her daughter with a possessive hug and they both turned into a giant snake of liquid red. Fast out of sight, it slithered across the night-laden field, leaving no trail. Gone.

As Hindin slowly rose to his feet, the others woke up. Will yawned. Röger retched blood into the grass.

When Will saw the state of Hindin, he rushed to him. "Rev, what happened to ya, man? Are you gonna be okay? Of course you are, who'm I kiddin'? Where's Polly?"

Hindin could only look down and shake his head. "Veluora came and defeated us, Will. Polly saved our lives by surrendering to her.

"I don't feel right," Röger whimpered as he dry heaved over a puddle of bloody bile. "What happened to me?" Hindin told him and Röger managed to throw up some more.

Will was furious. He paced around aimlessly and beat his large hands against his head. "We shoulda been ready! We *knew* she was comin'! I wasted the war-blanket on that stupid schoolhouse!"

533

"It would not have helped," Hindin said.

Will pointed his finger at his friends. "We're goin' to find her. We are goin' to get Polly back. I don't care if we hafta scour through all eight huncells in the Cluster. We *will* get her back an' put her momma down!"

Hindin knelt down and picked up the large emerald which had been his right eye. He studied it with morbid curiosity and let out a sad sigh. "I see no way we can. And yet...I see no way we cannot."

Röger finally managed to straighten up, vomit and slobber dripping from his chin. "A rescue quest. I like it. I'm glad I'm a part of it. Also, all of Doflend is soon going to find out that one of the four heroes who ended this Geohex is a Werekrilp. And hero or no, I will get hunted down. So, I say we leave this county and country *tonight* and get our butts to Chume as soon as possible. It won't take much time to get the wagon ready."

Will nodded in agreement. "Let's get a move on."

As the three men began to ascend the littered slope, Röger paused, feeling an odd sensation on his hip. "What in...?" He looked down and saw that the canteen on his belt loop was shaking like a wind up alarm clock. Will and Hindin eyed it with queer looks of suspicion.

"My canteen..." Will whispered.

Hindin's emerald eye widened. "Polly emptied it and replaced the water with her own blood," he explained. "To what end, I do not know."

Röger unhooked the quivering container and slowly raised it. "She said to keep it safe."

Hindin pinched his chin. "Hmm. Keep what safe, the blood or the canteen?"

"Open it," Will said, his curiosity outweighing his fear.

Carefully, Röger unscrewed the canteen. When the cap came off, a fountain of blood bubbled out, spilling over the human's fingers and hand and onto the grass.

The puddle soon took shape: a young, lean, naked, familiar shape laying in and amongst the blades of green. When she opened her eyes, Hindin let out a cry of joy. As she sat up to see them standing around her, Will placed his scaly dust coat about her shoulders to hide her nakedness. All three men helped her to rise.

"Polly, is that really you?" Röger asked the drakeri girl who had sprung from the canteen.

At first, she said nothing, as if she were confused by the question. "Polly...," she said. "Polly Gone? Yes, dat is her name. Polly Gone is gone, Röger. *I* am *Polly Here*. She smiled bright and wicked at them all. "And you three will not be able to rescue her without me."

Epilogue

Two weeks later...

Brem Hoffin stood at the foot of the grave of Daddy Long Legs. He had heard enough versions of the story before even entering the town of Pevulanium. But he wanted to see the grave for himself.

"*Ah'll be danged,*" he thought. "*Will, Ah cain't decide whethah you are the craftiest or dumbest Harkah that's evah been instructed by me. Ah warned you that lead-dealer duels were traps, boy. But you went ahead an' dug your own trap to git out of it! Ah'll be danged!*" The old wingless tendikeye let out a hardy laugh. "Ah'll be danged!" he exclaimed

"Just *what* is danging, Mr. Hoffin?" asked the drakeri youth who stood beside him.

Brem spread his hands, huge gnarled hands that had killed many enemies. "Well, you have me there, Mr. Yonoman. My supposition is that it was an ill fate for a tendikeye to be subjected to. So ill, Ah dare suppose, that what exactly danging is or may have been is a thing best forgotten."

The youth, no older than fourteen, bit the inside of his cheek. "That sounds like, how do you phrase it? Brown Gut Snake? Nonsense?"

Brem smiled, revealing a full row of strong, slightly yellow teeth surrounded by a short beard of neatly trimmed quills. His ice blue eyes glinted. "Why Ah considah that a high compliment coming from a theurge, even a tadpole theurgling like yourself."

The boy shrugged. "The truths of our reality are subjective. The way we see things are the way things are."

"*Oh?*" Brem hooted mockingly. "Well, if you are so wise and powerful why don't you do a little divination to find where the Four Winds have blown to?"

The youth shook his head. "I'm a Subjective Theurge of the Kinetist Doctrine. It's impossible for me."

"Why is that?"

537

"Because the way I see things is the way things are."

Brem fought the urge to slap the boy. "Explain," he ordered.

The youth regarded tendikeye like an inept classmate. "I can only trust what my senses tell me. Trusting any form of sixth sense such as omens or divination or, senses forbid, enlightenment requires risky interpretation. You can lose yourself in it. The world is always changing, so the truth is always subject to change. Objectivity and Universal Truth are abstract lies. That's why I'm a Subjective Kinetist. No truth is easily obtained and objective thinking impairs growth and progress. The truth evolves as I do."

"Ah still want to slap him," Brem thought. *"Maybe Ah can at least get rid of him this time."* "Now, Jaremmy, see here. Ah admire your willingness to avenge your fathah's eyes. But you are his only child."

"That's not what the Red Witch said before she blinded him." There was an edge to the youth's voice now, though his face had hardly changed. "I need to know if Polly Gone is truly my half-sister. I *must* find out for myself."

"And if she is?"

Jaremmy Yonoman bit the inside of his cheek. "Then I may have to kill her and her mother both. They say it is bad luck to have a blood theurge in the family."

"How do you figure that?"

"All I had to do was see my father's shredded face, and I knew." The youth shrugged. "But of course that is only the current truth. I hope to be proven otherwise."

Brem scoffed. "And how do you intend to prove *yourself* to the unknown dangers that lie ahead, tadpole? You carry a big sword but your hands are as tendah as the day you were born. Heck, Ah bet that thing is older than my granddaddy's granddaddy."

Jaremmy looked down at the longsword hanging on his hip and lightly brushed the pommel. "Draw your blade, old man," he challenged.

When the youth looked up, Brem had already drawn his yashinin machete and held it up to the boy's throat. Brem did not keep it there long. In a flash, he stabbed the blade back into its sheath. "Was that unfair of me, tadpole? You'll find nothing but unfairness trekking the Wilds of Chume. Now, Ah'm sure you may have a mystic trick or two that impresses folk back in Embrenil. But

538

Ah've been through four of the eight huncells and fought dang near every kind of theurge there is. And Ah ain't nevah heard of no *subjective kinetist* before. And that leads me to think such an unknown type of theurge cain't be that impressive."

Jaremmy never moved. But his sword drew fast enough on its own. The weapon floated in the air, held by some unseen force between the drakeri youth and the old tendikeye. The razor edge touched gently against the Harker's neck. A moment passed as a strong breeze scattered the leaves on the ground.

Brem nodded, slow and careful. "I guess we'd bettah get going then. Eh, tadpole?"

The sword flipped over and went back into the boy's scabbard. Jaremmy Yoloman gave a slight bow, returning the respect and agreeing in one motion.

"**I'M NAAAAKEEEED!!!!**" shouted a bonewalker as it suddenly appeared atop the blank grave marker of the Daddy Long Legs. "**I GOTS NO CLOTHES ON! HEEE HEEE hee!!!!**"

Brem's Mark Twain Special was drawn in a flash. *Ka-Krak! Ka-Krak! Ka-Krak!* The six bullets tore through the bonwalker's largest bones, shattering them to bits. But no sooner did the bits scatter and fall than they reformed as if the bonewalker had never been damaged.

"What theurgy is this!" Brem exclaimed as he watched the bonewalker laugh and dance crude and lasciviously atop the headstone.

"**Ha ha hA Ha ha HA! Streaky-Streaky more than a PEEKY!!!!**"

Brem shook his head in confusion and disgust. "You got a foul mouth on you, dead man! Ah'm going to teah you apart with mah bear hands!"

"No need," said Jaremmy, raising his palm above his head. The gesture arrested the attention of Brem and the Bonewalker both. The young theurge gazed serenely at the animated skeleton and said, *"As a well spent day brings happy sleep, so life well used brings happy death."*

The bonewalker fell to the ground unmoving, except its jaw opening and closing with the sound of loud snoring.

Brem Hoffin regarded the sleeping skeleton and arched a

quilled eyebrow. "That was a death maxim. Ah've seen it used before. It makes people sleep forevah, even aftah they die." He turned a stern stare at Jaremmy. "How can you use a death maxim if you ain't a necrotheurge?"

The young drakeri shrugged. "I can use any maxim that makes sense to me, regardless of philocreed or theurgy."

"How z'at?"

Jaremmy grinned. "Because the truth is always subjective, Mr. Hoffin. I thought Harkers were good at listening." He saw Brem's face frown and redden in contempt. But he never saw the tendikeye's boot coming at his head. The young theurge fell to the ground, still and silent beside the snoring skeleton.

A few seconds later, Brem lit up a cigarette, leaned against a headstone, and thought about the man he now sought. "*How am Ah going to tell him once ah find him?*"

THE SAGA WILL CONTINUE IN

FOUR WINDS - ONE STORM

THE WILDS OF CHUME

<u>Glossary</u>

Alcedrome: Elk course or arena.

Algebraic Law: A philocreed based on the mathematical rules of algebra.

Anima Husk: The soul's skin or outer layer.

Animist: Also called Shamans or Blanket Mystics, theurgess specialize in communicating with souls and spirits that have no physical form.

Amortal: Neither fully living or fully dead.

Archdrake: One of three legendary dragons that once ruled over Burtilbip.

Billblade: A greatsword tipped with a large hook.

Bionomist: A chimancer who specializes in the science aspect of their theurgy, such as acupuncturists.

Birthblade: A special knife tendikeye fathers use to cut the birth cords of their newborn children. When the cut is made the father says "Your mother and I release you into this world." When the child reaches adulthood the father gives the knife to them and says the phrase once more. All adult tendikeye carry birthblades unless they are Foundlings.

Black Vest: A state employed urban monster hunter of Fevär. Given a knightly honorific to mark status.

Blind Bitch's Bane: A Fevärian expression for disapproval of the obstruction of justice.

543

Blood Theurge: A common term for Crimson Theurges /Hematologists/Hematonomists, disciples of a philocreed based on ritualistic assassination/murder, emotional manipulation, and the circulatory/cardiovascular system. They refer to their spiritual path as The Red River.

Bonewalker: An animated skeleton, a usually mindless post-mort.

Breginite: A laich that feeds on a living creature's nervous system in order to maintain their own.

Bukk: A tendikeye without wings.

Bullpie/Merde/Brown Gut Snake: Nonsense or lies compared to and named after feces.

Capon: A gelded rooster.

Chakra: One of the soul's seven organs through which chi flows.

Chi: The blood of the soul.

Chimancer: One who brings their spirit and body closer together through complex combat training and supernatural meditation. A theurge of martial arts and personal well-being.

Code of Word and Deed: The code of conduct upheld by Black Vests.

Cryotheurgy: Theurgy based on the abstract perception of Cold being a force in reality.

Dangerosity Guide: An almanac of noteworthy individuals and monsters and their exploits. A yearly publication distributed throughout the civilized parts of the Draybair Cluster.

Dan Tien: The stomach chakra.

Drakeri/Drakeress: A member of the drakeri race who originate in the country of Doflend in the Huncell of Burtlbip. Hair and skin pigmentation range in various shades of purple, violet, indigo, and lavender. Recognized by their eyes with three irises, double-pointed ears, hands consisting of one thumb and three fingers, and feet with two large toes. According to legend, they are hybrids of prehistoric dragons and fairies. However, their mundane culture offers little to support this claim. Drakeri reach adulthood at age 18 and typically live 10 to 12 centuries.

Dreamweed: A smokable herb that induces relaxation and serenity.

Druther: Choice.

Eagleton Sphere: Also called an eagle egg or handmine. A ball-shaped bomb covered and loaded with spike-like bullets. Can be used as a grenade, landmine, or short term timer bomb. Fevärian in origin.

Excursion: In ancient times this word meant vacation or holiday outing. But as the huncells grew more dangerous such trips became hazardous and unpredictable the word slowly became synonymous with adventure or heroic trial.

Excursionist: One who goes on excursions.

Ferroweaver: A theurge of melee weapons, usually swords. A warrior poet/philosopher of the highest mastery.

Fevärian: Also called humans. Indigenous to the huncell of Fevär.

Fleshbroker: A pimp.

Fleshling: A malrukan term for people made of flesh and bone.

Frigorifist: A disciple of cryotheurgy.

General Tidsla Childoon: Tendikeye bukk historical figure.

Revolutionary hero.

Geotheurgy/Geonomy: The theurgy of soil, stone and metals.

Ghost: An invisible amortal spirit. An unshattered soul. Only visible and audible under special circumstances.

Golem: A construct, usually bipedal in shape, that is animated and controlled by a piece of a theurge's soul. While some are intelligent, they have no will of their own.

Harker: A tendikeye woodland reconnaissance and bushwhacking specialist.

Hell: a place, usually a pit or low point, outside a community where garbage is burned.

Hemogoblin: A laich that consumes the cardiovascular/circulatory systems of living creatures to maintain their own.

Hemopathy: Reading or tasting blood to divine information.

Herbonomy: The Theurgy of Plants.

Huncell: A natural enclosure, part rock and part flesh, vast enough to sustain gravity, atmosphere and life. The Cells of Reality. Georganic in nature.

Hunvein: One of many vein channels that house a lava/blood-like substance called *skault* . The source of light and heat in a huncell.

Hunwalls: The walls of a huncell.

Hurklyone: A large wildcat native to Micca. Known and prized for its extremely tough hide.

Hydrotheurgy: The theurgy of Water.

Immunoglobulin-anguis: Antibody Serpent or Guardian Snake. Snakes are held sacred by blood theurges because they flow like blood when they travel.

Jubube: (pronounced jew-booby) A type of large, plump nectarine.

Krilp: A beast-like native of Gurtangorr, resembling hulking cats crowned with massive horns.

Ruan: A tendikeye guitar.

Septagram: A 7-sided star. Although, stars do not exist in this reality.

Shunt: A term for sexual intercourse.

Stonebro: Stone brother, a friendly term for malruka.

Tendikeye: The native race of Cloiherune, marked by their large hands and feet, quill-covered heads and wings, and tanned skin.

Theurge/Theurgess: A disciple of one or several forms of theurgy. They are also called mystics by some.

Theurgy: The mystical practice of defining and redefining reality as one sees it. An effort in spiritual, scientific, and artistic influence.

Tuntrum: A tendikeye word literally meaning proper or kosher. The term is used for weapons that can also be used as tools, as well as wild game that was hunted using such weapons.

Laich: A powerful amortal being that feeds on the living to sustain their potency. They come in several varieties, some with unique tastes and abilities.

Magmacock: A huge domestic male chicken enhanced by pyrotheurgy to be wreathed in flames without harming the bird. Used in Doflend penal combats. Usually slain after combat because giant flaming cocks are so hard to handle. The meat is already cooked as it is butchered and is sold to spectators.

Malruka/Malrukan: A people constructed from metal and stone. First created by tyrannical geotheurges as warrior slaves during The Omni-War, now a self-perpetuating race under rule of Slate in the huncell of Tomfeerdon. Exact life span is 200 years. Their most common philocreed is geonomy. Sexless, but most identify as male.

Maxim: A phrase of theurgical wisdom used to generate metaphysical epiphanies that alter energy in people, places, and things.

Medicine: One's personal ability to decide and steer their own fate, particularly when others oppose them.

Monster Abater: One who specializes in the removal of monsters.

Necrocide: The act of killing an amortal being, such as a ghost or post-mort.

Necrofear/Necrofright: An invisible necrotheurgic energy that instills the emotion dread.

Necromagnetism: Channeling death energy through metal, giving the metal the ability to draw and manipulate life force.

Necro-Receptive/Necroactive: Able to use necrotheurgy.

Necrosight: The ability to see ghosts.

Necrotheurge: A disciple of the theurgy of Death and/or Amortality, necrotheurgy. Notable philocreed sects include The Bone Ladder and Zerothism, enlightenment through oblivion.

Nyupe Shan Zahn: A historical drakeri Life Theurge from the Age of Technology.

Omni-War: The first and only war that included the entire Draybair Cluster.

Petraround: A geotheurgically-enhanced bullet that turns a living target into stone temporarily. Fashioned from serpent fossils.

Perceptionists: An illusionist theurge.

Philocreed: A spiritual doctrine that draws meaning from a specific aspect of reality (such as elements or other natural things) and holding that aspect in the highest regard. Most philocreeds have a related theurgy.

Pnuema: Soul, spirit.

Post-Mort: A port mortum being with a physical body.

Pyroactive: Able to use pyrotheurgy.

Pyroglyphics: The written/visual language of Fire.

Pyrotheurge: A disciple of pyrotheurgy, the philocreed of The Sacred Flame. One in a supernatural relationship with fire and heat.

Retaeh's Breath: A drakeri expression of shock, usually toward something negative.

Sizzagafiend: Also known as The Scissor Monster and The Shear Terror. There was once a Lemuertian Legba who enjoyed eating snakes, spiders and scorpions. One day, he had his cook chop up all three into a creepy critter salad. The legba consumed his meal happily, but was soon plagued with a terrible stomach ache. The ache turned to agony as an amalgam of the three consumed critters sheared its way out of the Legba's abdomen. The monster grew to become a menace to all beings throughout known history. Although it has been slain repeatedly, the Sizzagafiend always mysteriously returns.

Slate: The Pharaoh of the Malrukan race. A being composed solely of spiritual energy and living lightning. Their Father-in-Spirit.

Socionomic Revolution: When Doflend ceased to be Feudal Goldocracy once controlled by the now defunct Buresche social class of Drakeri.

Thunderjug: A chamber pot.

Underbottoms: Pelvic underwear, panties, loincloth.

Vaughn: Cobalt

Werekrilp: A human infected with a lycanthropic curse of transforming into a murderous krilp.

Witch: A slur or rural term for theurges.

Witchworks: A negating term for theurgy.

Yashinin Machete: A tendikeye tuntrum blade used to clear wild overgrowth and for skirmishing. The blade is crescent shaped, ends in two points, sharp on the outside edge, with a hole-slot on the inside edge to create a handle grip. Yashinin literally means "voting blade" in Old Tendikeye because the tendikeye show and use their weapons as a means of electing leaders.

Yestermorn: Yesterday morning.

Yesternight: Yesterday night.

Zodiologist: A disciple of zodiology, one who searches for patterns in history and sentient being behavior.

Zoonomist: A theurge of Zoonomy, the theurgy of animals.

Geography of
The Huncells of
Draybair

Draybair Cluster: the eight known huncells, first mapped out and presented by Prof. Sävva Draybair of Fevär.

Fevär: The Huncell of Humanity. Currently divided into the purely human kingdom of Karsely and the Free Republic of Meodeck.

Burtilbip: The Drake's Cradle. A huncell consisting three separate realms. **Doflend**, a confederated capitalist democracy home to the Drakeri race. The Wilds of Chume, a forest expanse populated by the Chume Fey. And Micca, home of the subterranean Miccans.

Cloiherune: The Huncell of the Tendikeye. A swordocracy composed five sovereign states; Meramac, Tarkio, Bourbeuse, Cuivre, and Wyaconda. Produces more crops than all other huncells combined.

Ses Lemuert: The Everdying. The Cancerous Huncell. Populated by various clans of Lemuertians.

Tomfeerdon: Huncell of the Malruka. Originally inhabited by the now extinct Kesslar. Ruled by the entity known as Slate.

Ocsnart: The Dead Huncell. A radioactive tundra littered with ruins. Former home of the now extinct Lonya race and former realm of the Laich Kahn Arthar.

Gurtangorr: Huncell of the Krilp Tribes and some Fevärian settlements.

Sodara: The Trembling Sea. An oceanic huncell peppered with a few sparse island states. But below its quivering waves, secret sexy things slither and swim.

551

Cities, Counties, and Towns

Embrenil: The Bone Brick City. One the seven major cities of Doflend, known for its fossil-laced architecture. Literally means "The Enduring Ember".

Vempour: The Stained Glass City. One of the seven major cities of Doflend, known for its architecture composed of natural, colored glass. Named for the Beresche goldmonger Idech Vempour.

Apple County (aka Wraith County): A once prosperous rural county famous for its abundant orchards, now a haunted land plagued by ghosts, crime and poverty.

Notable Towns in Apple/Wraith County

-Barnhart

-Drowsy Nook

-Victor's Grove

-Copse durr Crakktun

-Tanglefoot (formerly Crytus)

-Pevulaneum

-Heapsboro

About the Author

Aaron William Hollingsworth was born and raised in Jefferson County, Missouri near St. Louis. He lives in Kansas City, Missouri with his wife and two sons. He invites his readers to visit "Aaron Hollingsworth - Science Fantasy Writer" and "Four Winds - One Storm" on Facebook.